W9-BST-671

NO PLACE FOR
MONSTERS
School of Phantoms

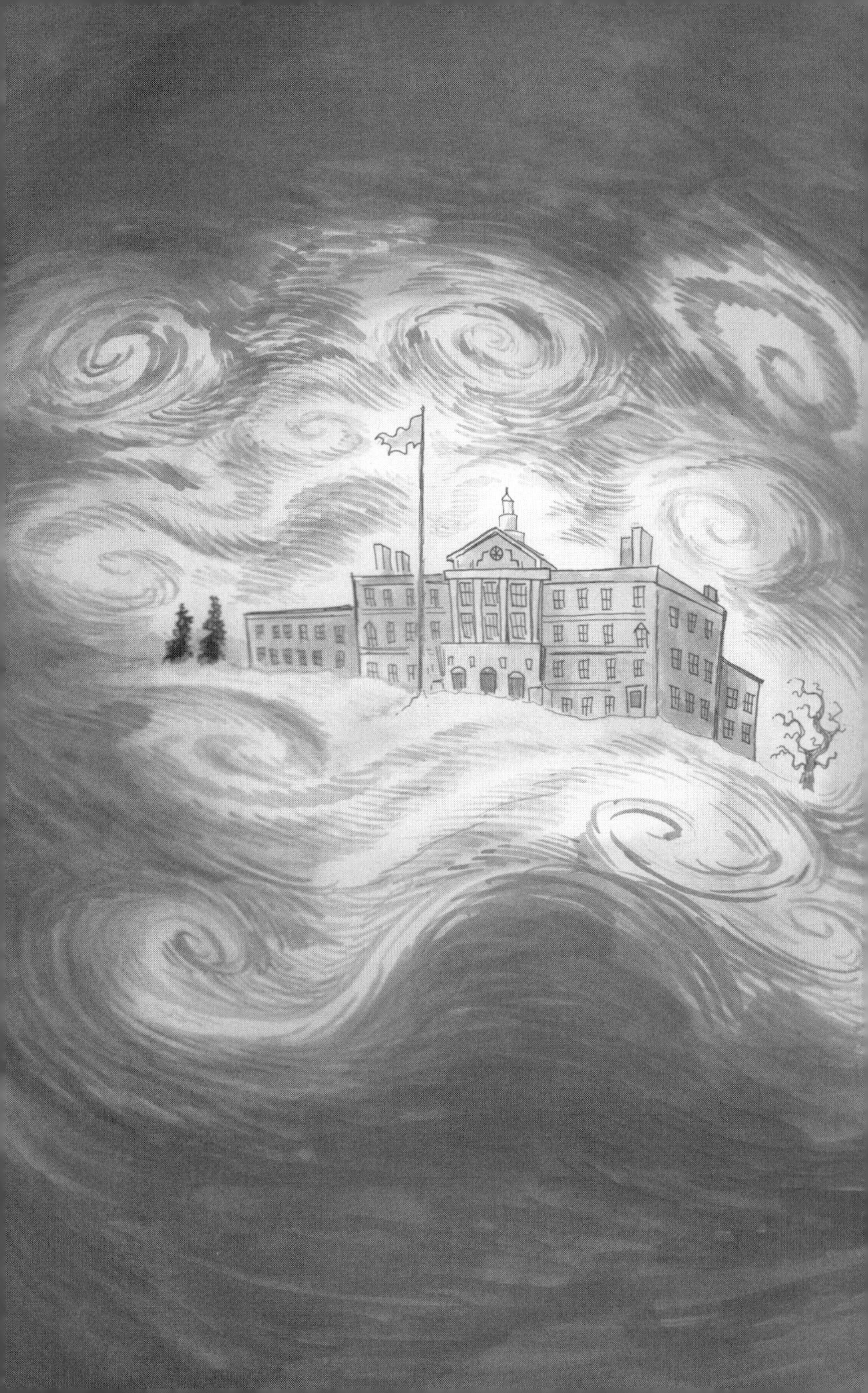

NO PLACE FOR
MONSTERS
School of Phantoms

Written and Illustrated by
Kory Merritt

Houghton Mifflin Harcourt
Boston   New York

To my father, Rick Merritt—elementary teacher of forty years, storyteller, and outdoor enthusiast who's always on the lookout for the next adventure.

Copyright © 2021 by Kory Merritt
Illustrations copyright © 2021 by Kory Merritt

All rights reserved. For information about permission to reproduce selections from this book, write to trade.permissions@hmhco.com or to Permissions, Houghton Mifflin Harcourt Publishing Company, 3 Park Avenue, 19th Floor, New York, New York 10016.

hmhbooks.com

The text was set in Charter ITC Std and Merritt Scary.
Hand-lettering by Kory Merritt
Cover and interior design by Celeste Knudsen

Library of Congress Cataloging-in-Publication Data is available.
ISBN 978-0-358-19332-6

Manufactured in the United States of America
1 2021
4500829502

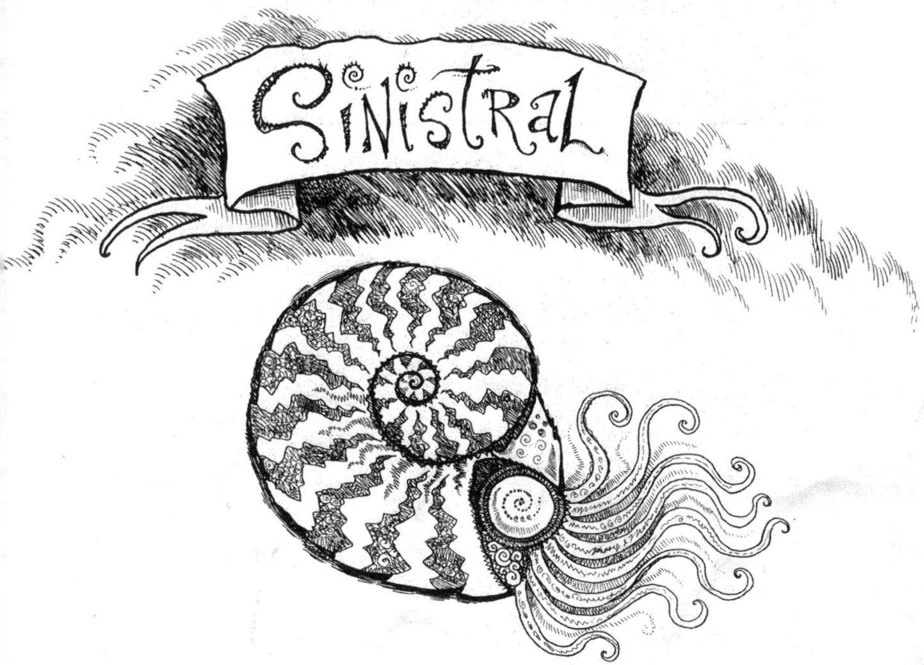
Sinistral

Greetings, Prospective Agent:

If you are reading these words, you have been specially selected by SINISTRAL's field agent recruitment division. Yes, you read that correctly. And no, this is not a joke. SINISTRAL seldom jokes.

You may have many questions. We hope you do, since SINISTRAL specializes in asking unorthodox questions in pursuit of strange answers.

First and foremost, you may be asking the obvious:

1. What is SINISTRAL?

A fair question. SINISTRAL is a secret coalition of strange-answer seekers.

How secret?

Very secret.

So secret none of its members can agree on the secret handshake.

So secret we have no Wikipedia entry.

So secret not even our most senior agents can remember what the acronym SINISTRAL stands for.

Second, you may be asking yourself:

2. Why me? Why am I qualified to examine the following top-secret report?

We've selected you because, according to our many sources, you show promise.

Perhaps it's your attention to life's mind-boggling details.

Perhaps it's because you excel at solving puzzles no one else seems to notice.

Perhaps it's your commitment to uncovering the source of the eerie "house noises" you hear coming from the basement at night.

Perhaps it's because you look for weird bugs under rocks.

Finally, you may be asking yourself:

3. What does SINISTRAL want me to do?

What follows is a sample exercise to see if you are truly SINISTRAL material.

Please review the following eight images. Use your keen observational skills, detective prowess, and gut instincts to determine which of the images are fake . . . and which are truly *out of this world*.

WARNING: the following images may be triggering to the faint of heart, so proceed with caution.

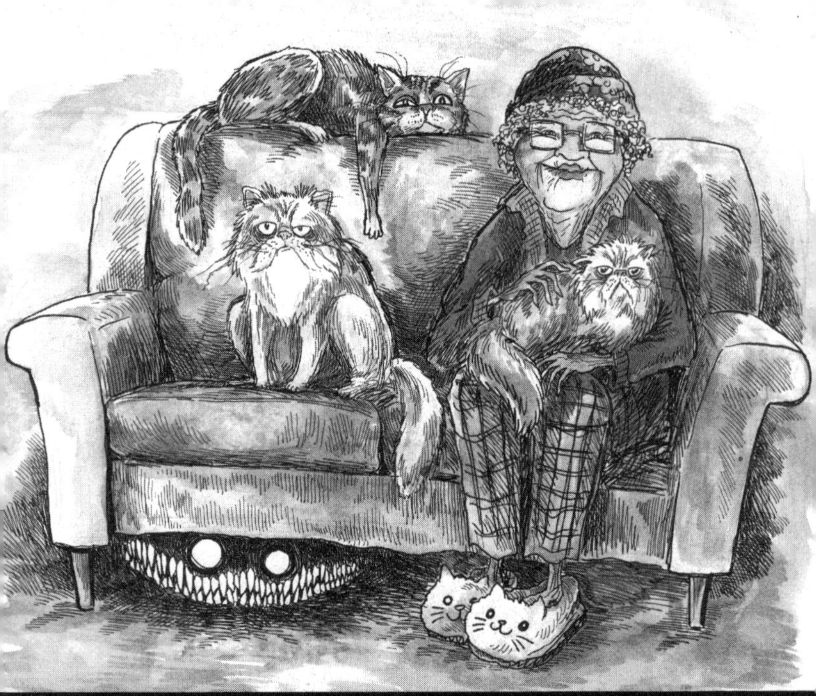

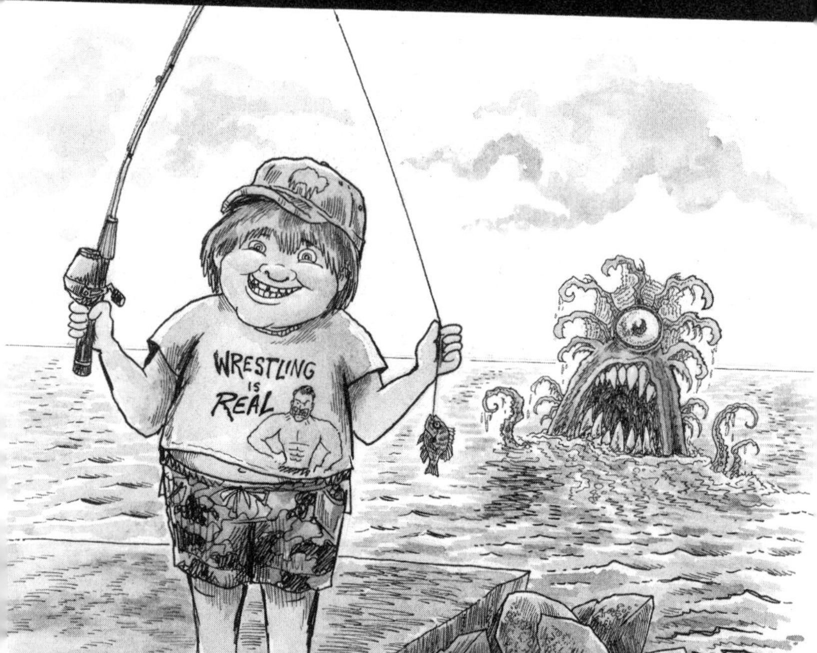
WRESTLING
IS
REAL

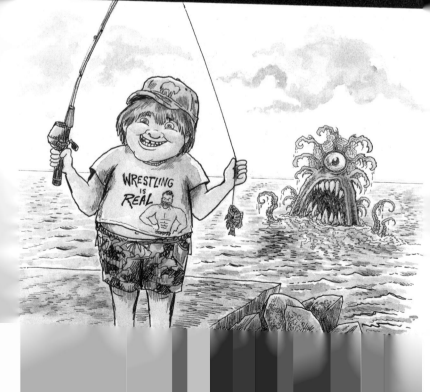

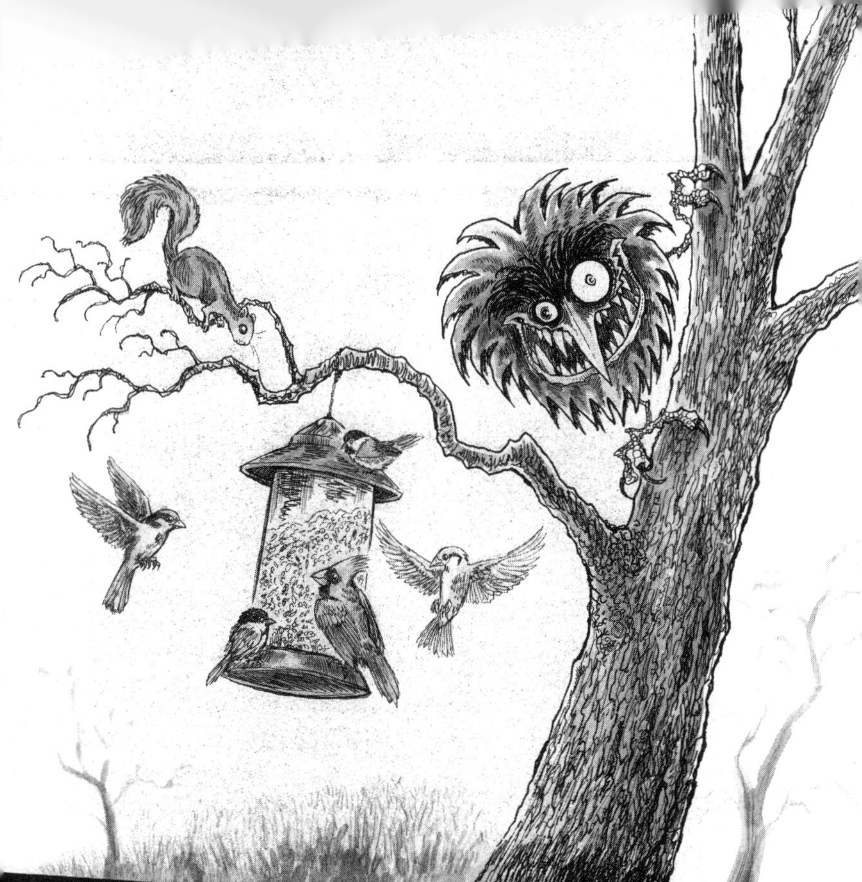

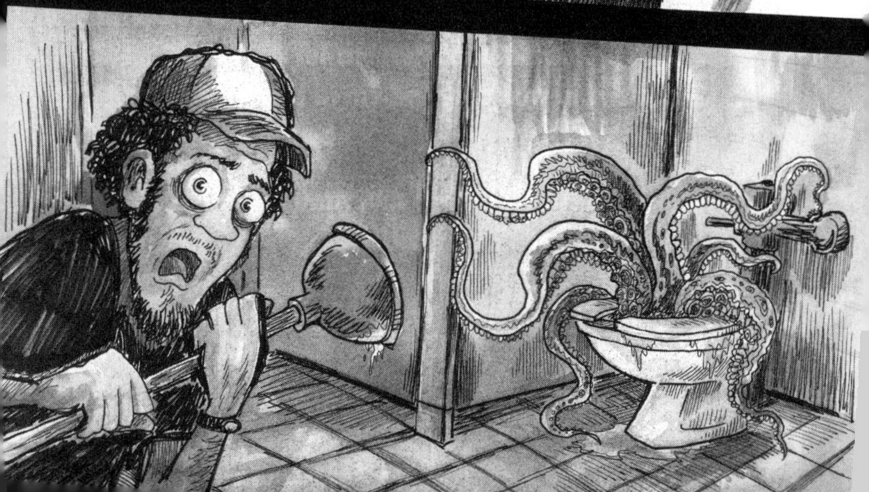

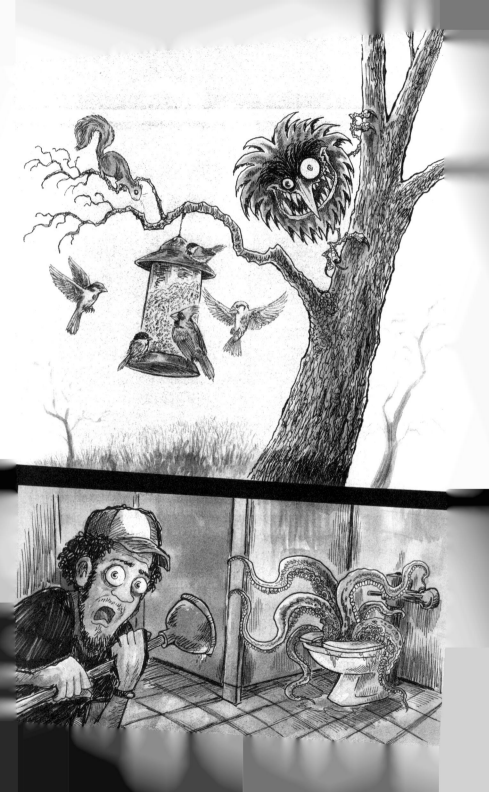

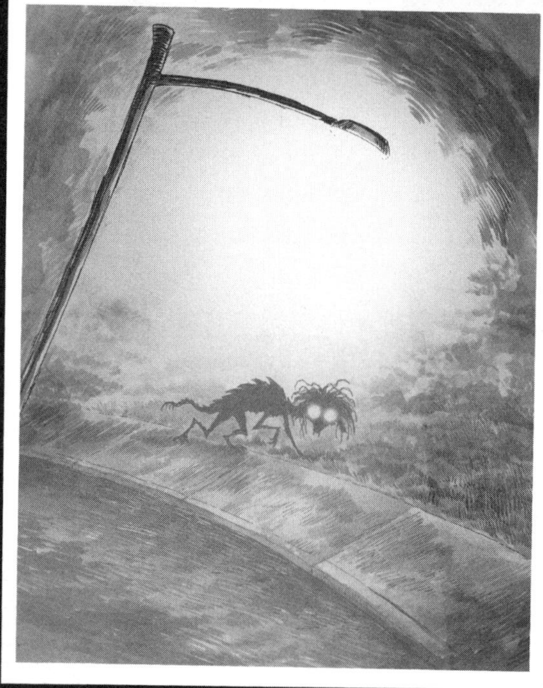

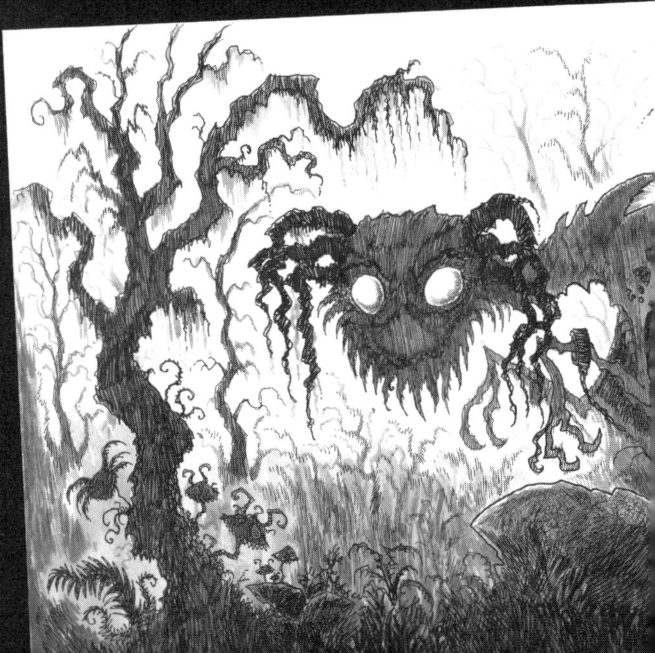

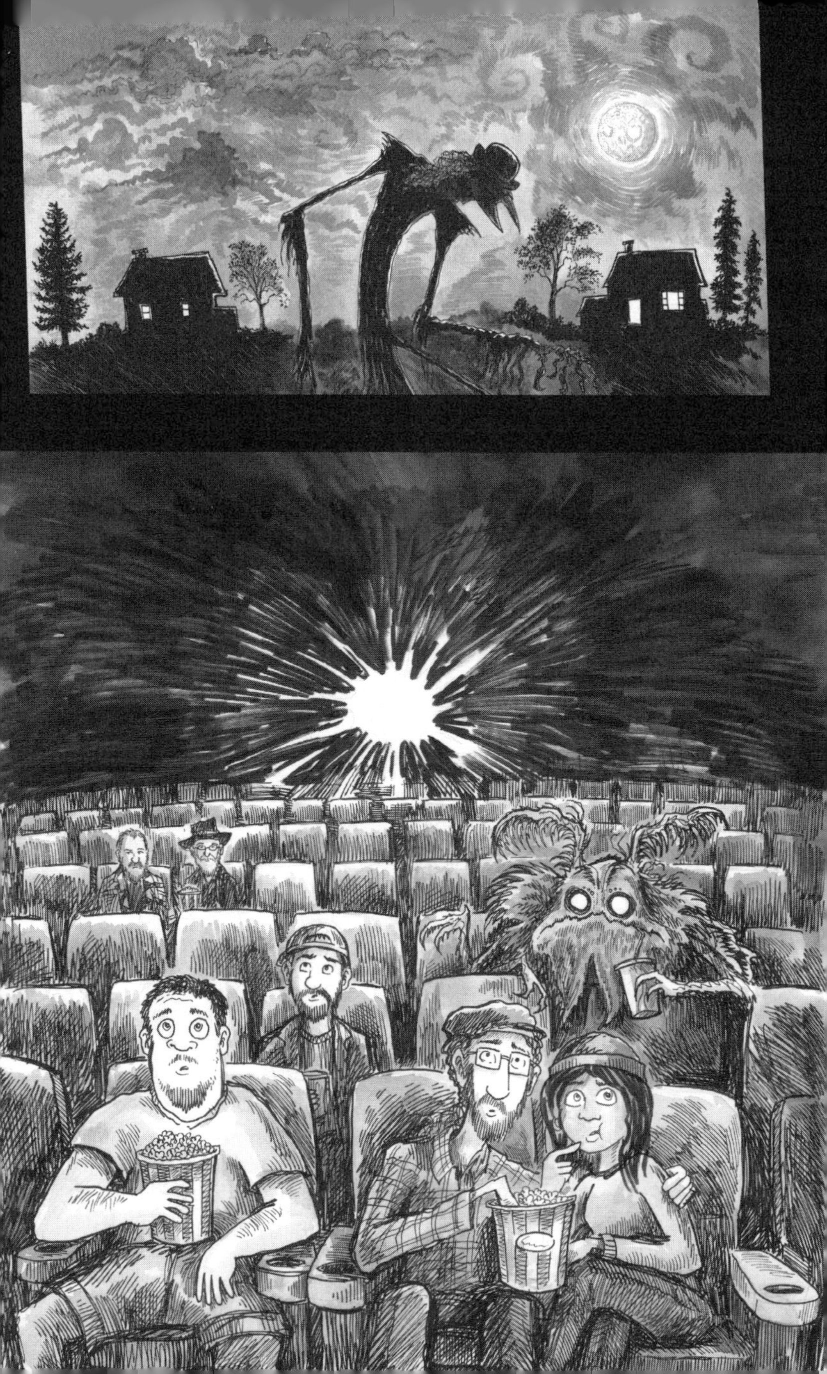

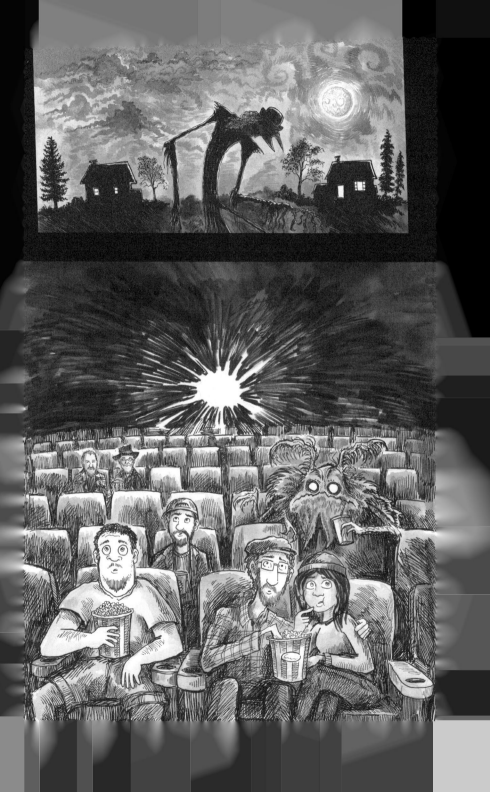

Done? That was fast.

If your instincts are truly keen, you know that six of the eight images are flagrant fakes.

The other two are genuine.

So that's a taste of SINISTRAL's overall mission: to sort through all the strange and reason-confuddling mysteries and determine if they're fake, real, or something else entirely.

Now, on to the real business . . .

What follows is all the acquired evidence of one of SINISTRAL's strangest cases: the infamous *Phantom Storm*.

The enclosed evidence includes the following:

- extensive video taken from student witness phones
- footage from battery-operated school security cameras
- written accounts from undercover SINISTRAL field agents and key witnesses

These materials have been painstakingly arranged into some semblance of a narrative in order to paint the clearest possible picture of what exactly happened in Cowslip Grove during the blizzard last March.

Read with a discerning eye—we've reason to believe at least some of the evidence has been tampered with, and it's imperative that we separate fact from hoax.

If you choose to accept this task, please read on.

If not, please hide this report in the darkest corner of the library or bookstore and go about your usual humdrum life.

Thank you, and good luck,

SINISTRAL

BOMBARD'S PHONE, MARCH 16

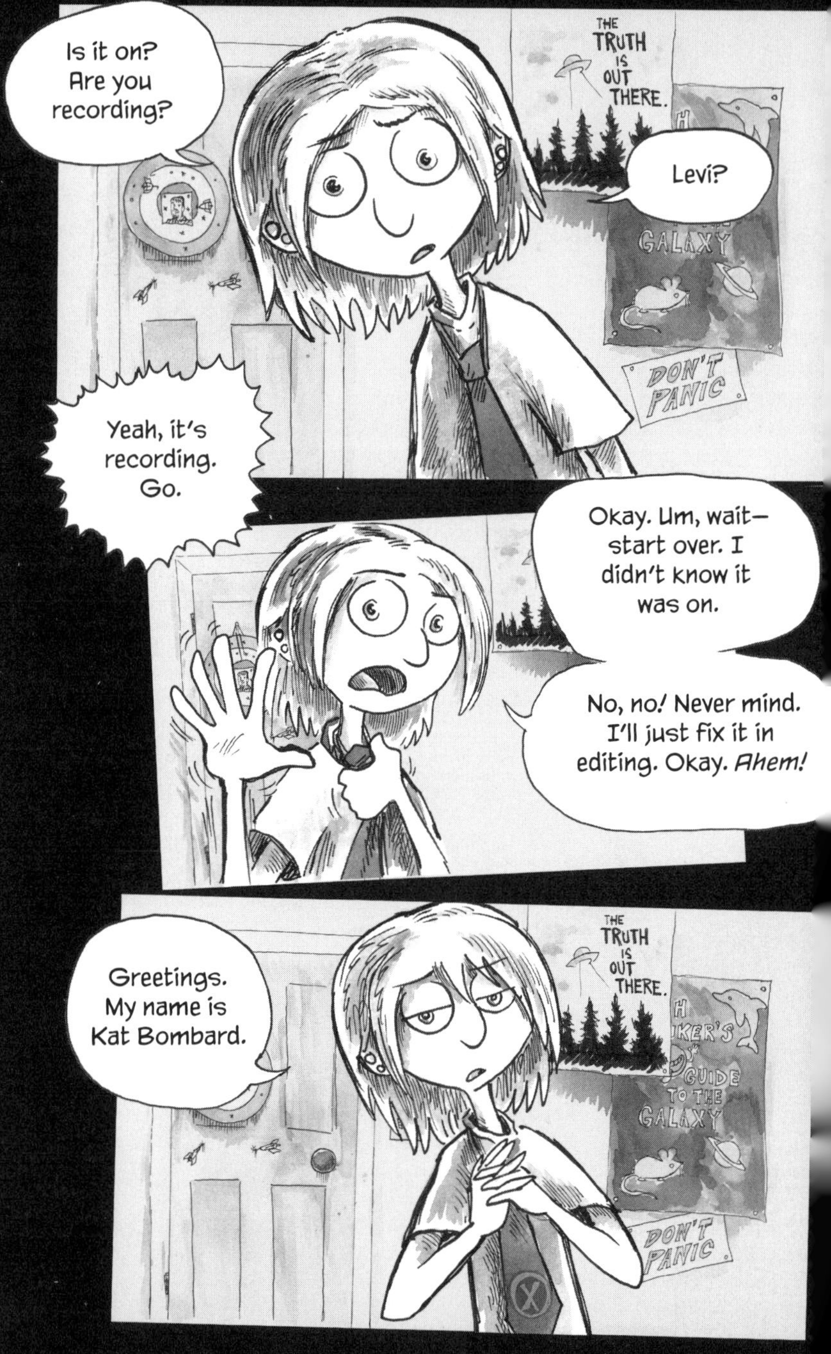
Is it on? Are you recording?
THE TRUTH IS OUT THERE.
Levi?
GALAXY
DON'T PANIC
Yeah, it's recording. Go.
Okay. Um, wait—start over. I didn't know it was on.
No, no! Never mind. I'll just fix it in editing. Okay. *Ahem!*
Greetings. My name is Kat Bombard.
THE TRUTH IS OUT THERE.
GUIDE TO THE GALAXY
DON'T PANIC

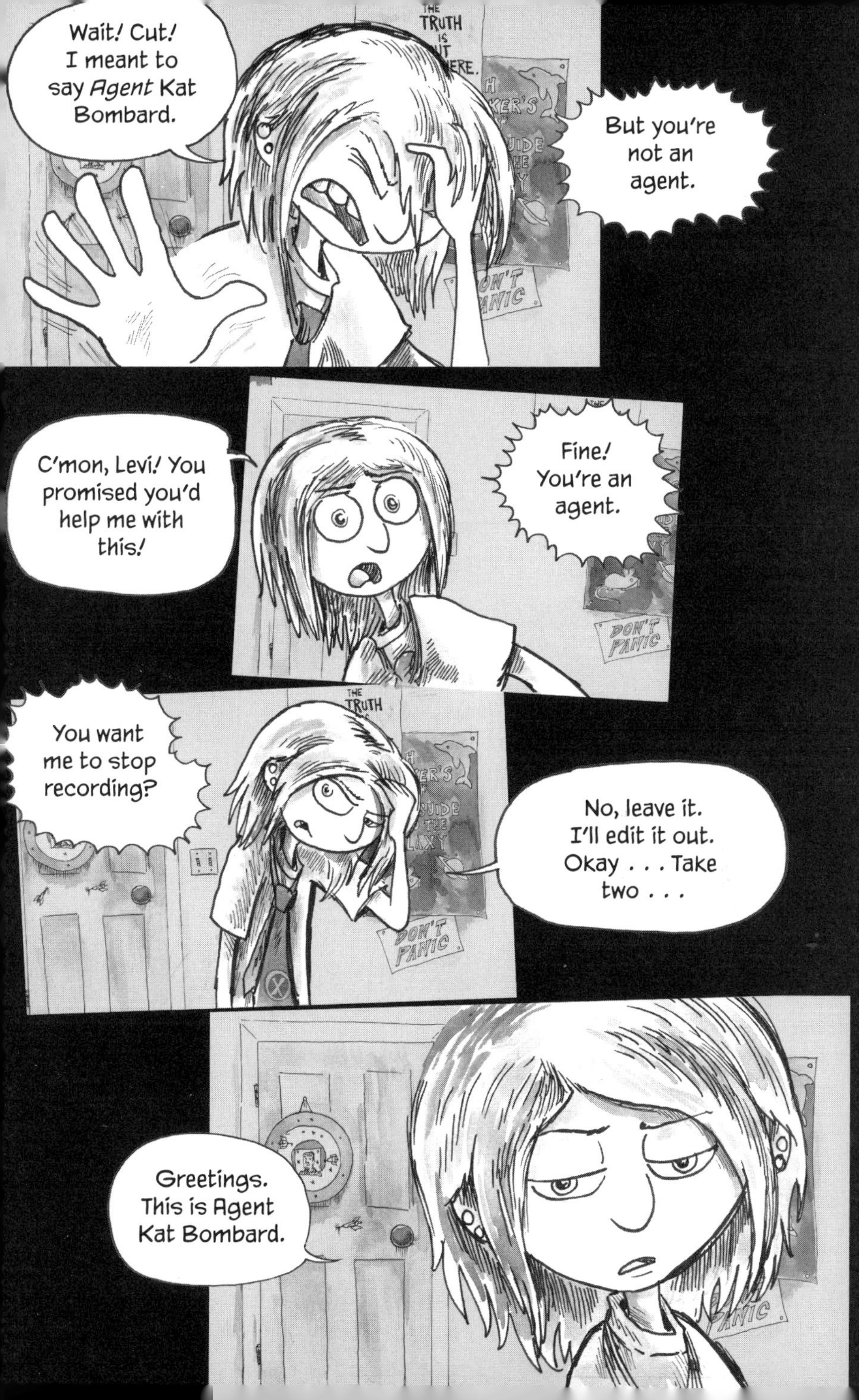
Wait! Cut! I meant to say *Agent* Kat Bombard.
But you're not an agent.
C'mon, Levi! You promised you'd help me with this!
Fine! You're an agent.
You want me to stop recording?
No, leave it. I'll edit it out. Okay . . . Take two . . .
Greetings. This is Agent Kat Bombard.
THE TRUTH IS
DON'T PANIC

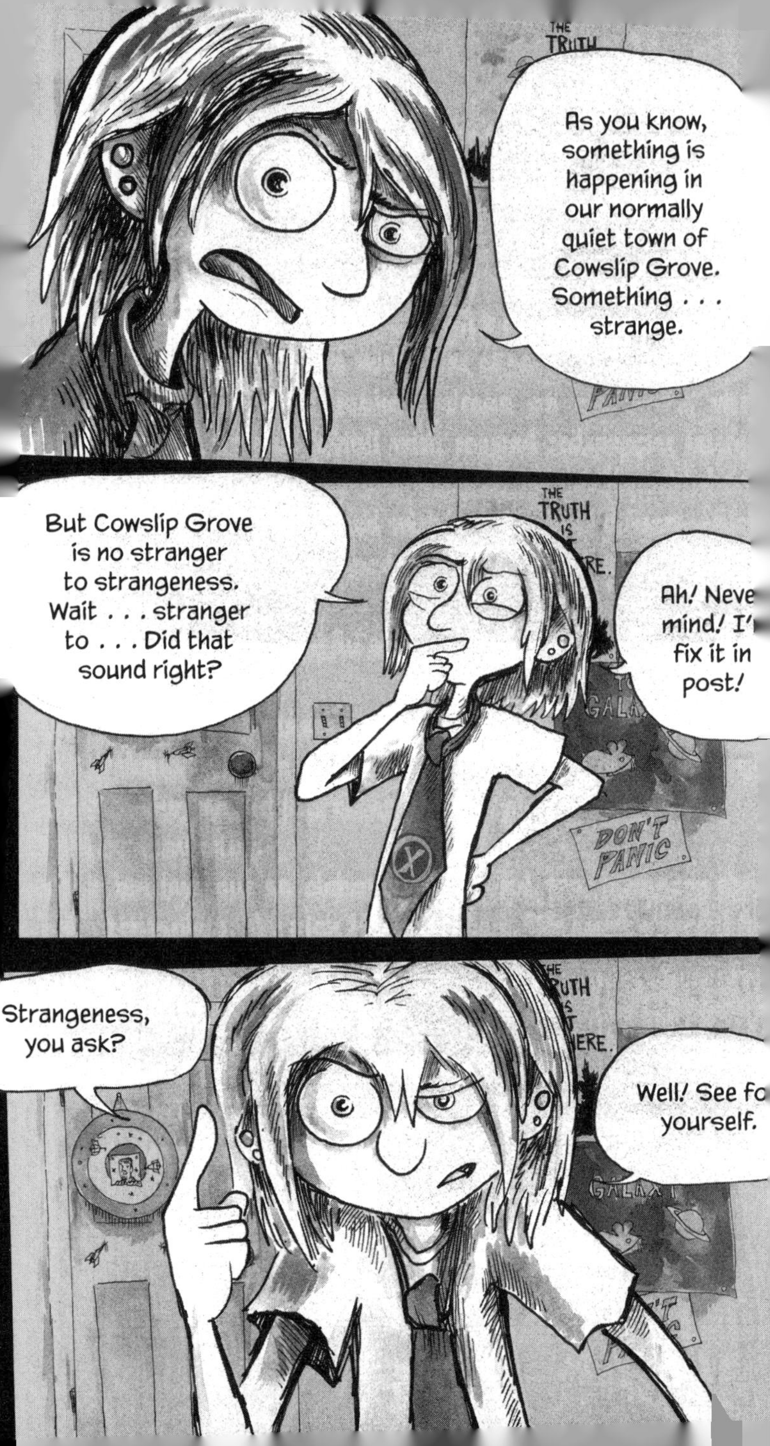
THE TRUTH
As you know, something is happening in our normally quiet town of Cowslip Grove. Something . . . strange.
THE TRUTH IS
But Cowslip Grove is no stranger to strangeness. Wait . . . stranger to . . . Did that sound right?
Ah! Neve mind! I' fix it in post!
DON'T PANIC
Strangeness, you ask?
Well! See fo yourself.

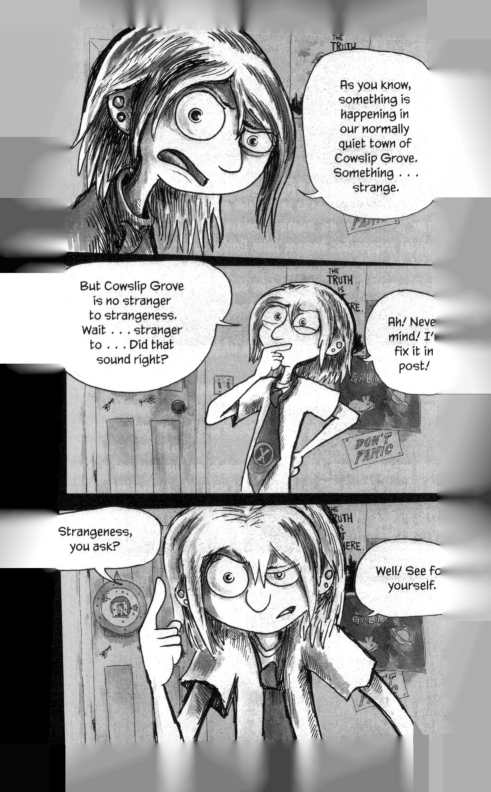

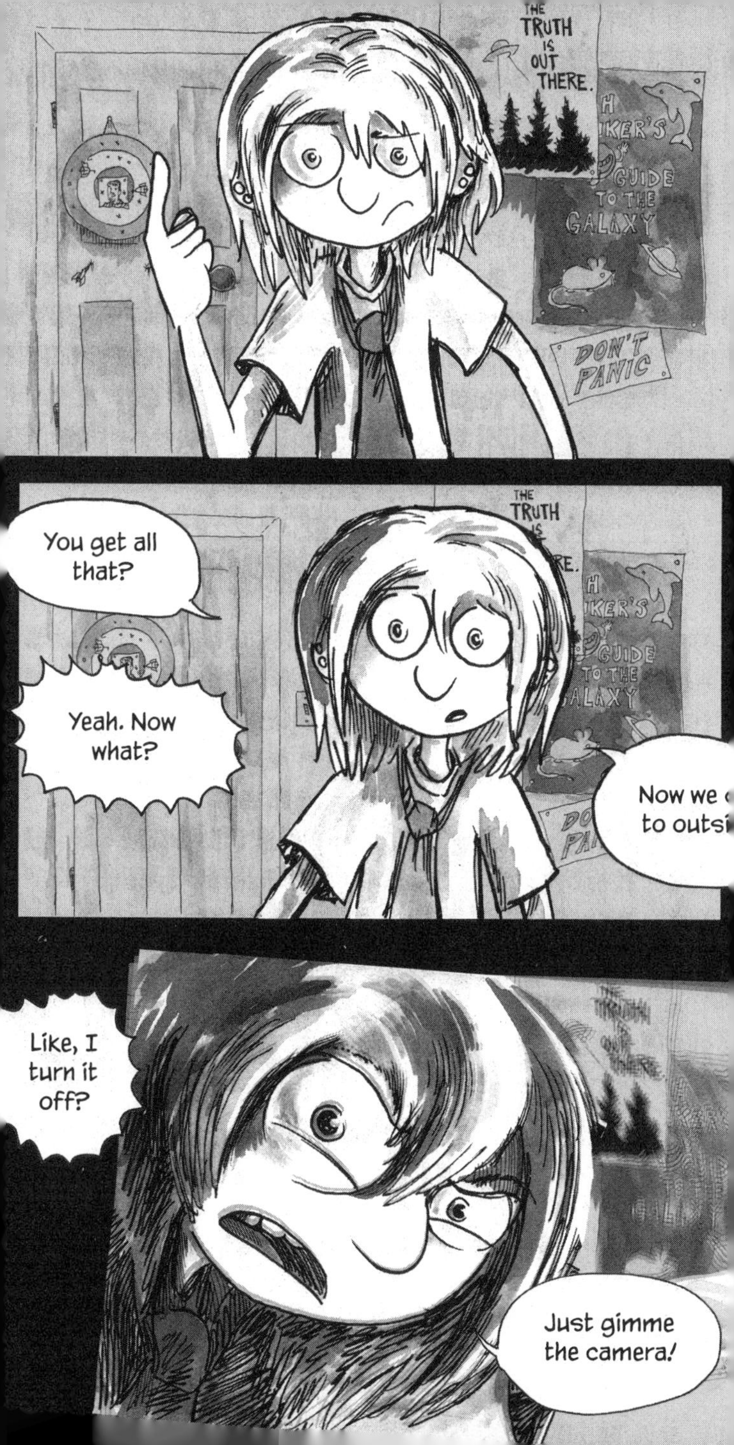
THE TRUTH IS OUT THERE.
GUIDE TO THE GALAXY
DON'T PANIC
You get all that?
Yeah. Now what?
Now we
to outsi
Like, I turn it off?
Just gimme the camera!

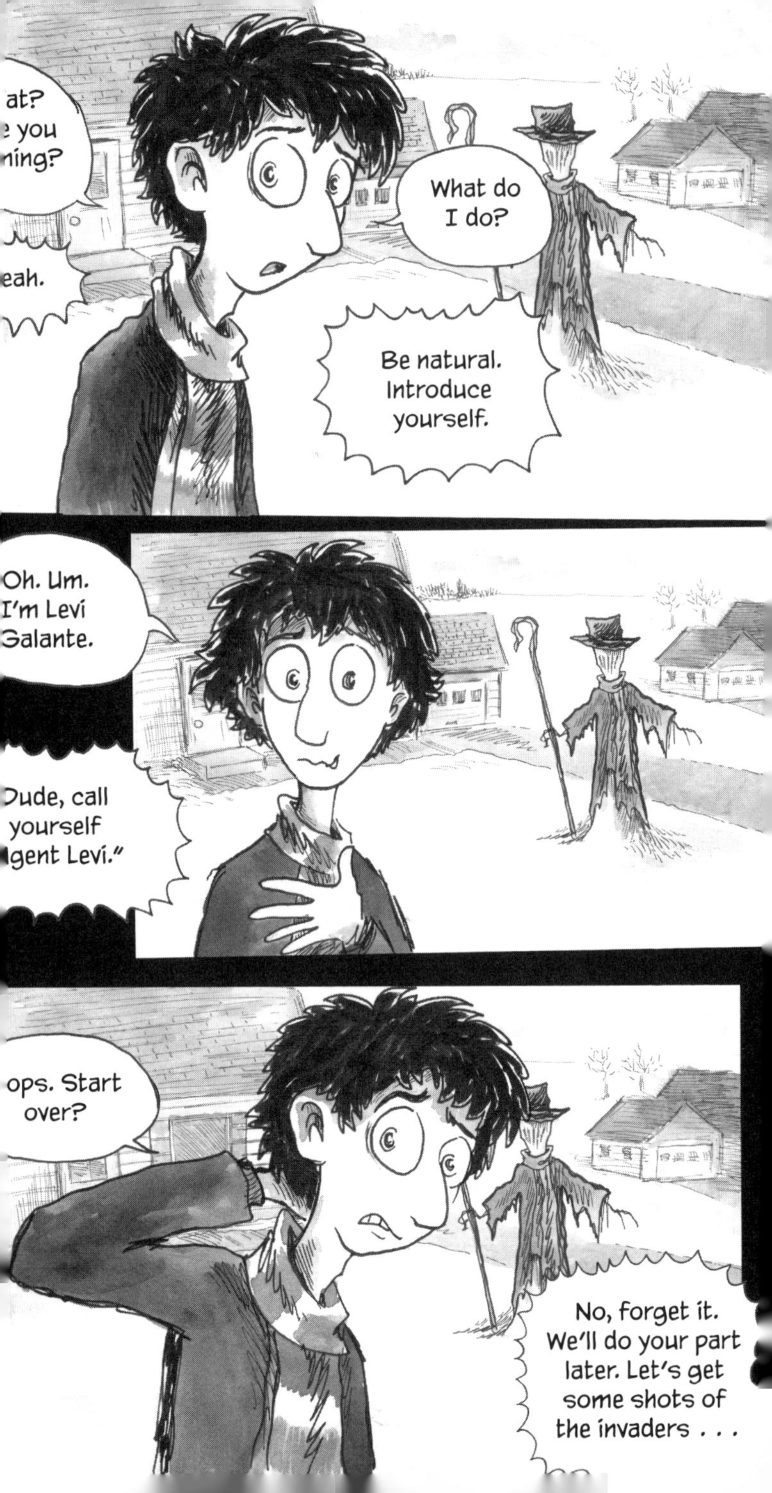
at? e you ning?
eah.
What do I do?
Be natural. Introduce yourself.
Oh. Um. I'm Levi Galante.
Dude, call yourself gent Levi."
ops. Start over?
No, forget it. We'll do your part later. Let's get some shots of the invaders . . .

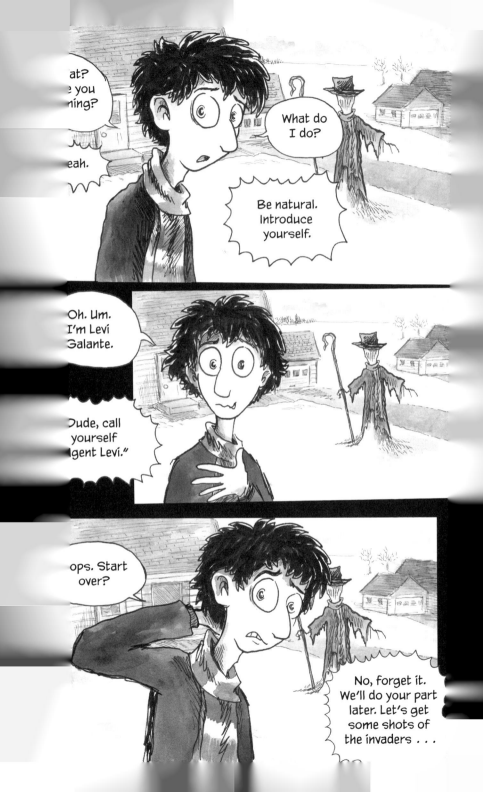

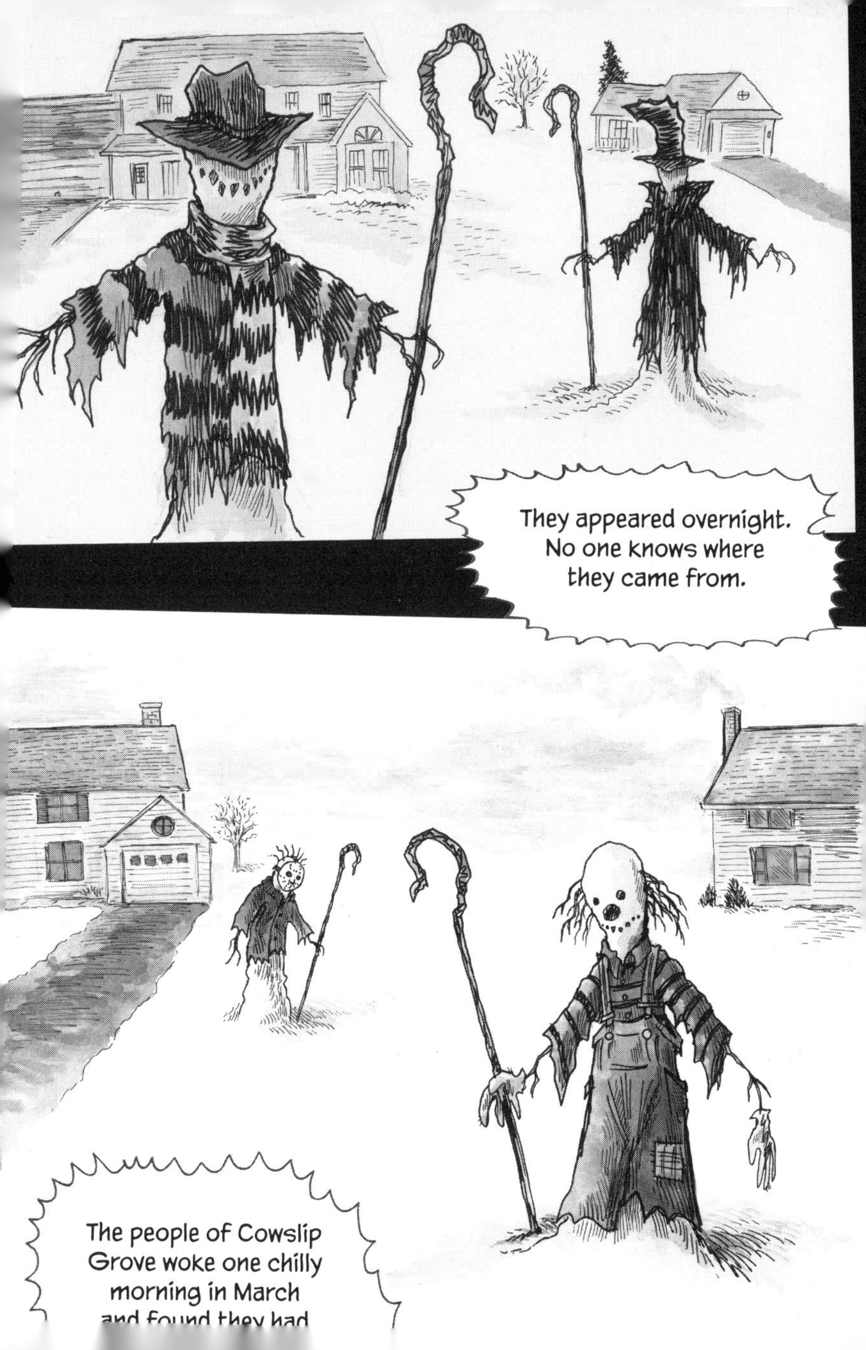
They appeared overnight. No one knows where they came from.
The people of Cowslip Grove woke one chilly morning in March and found they had

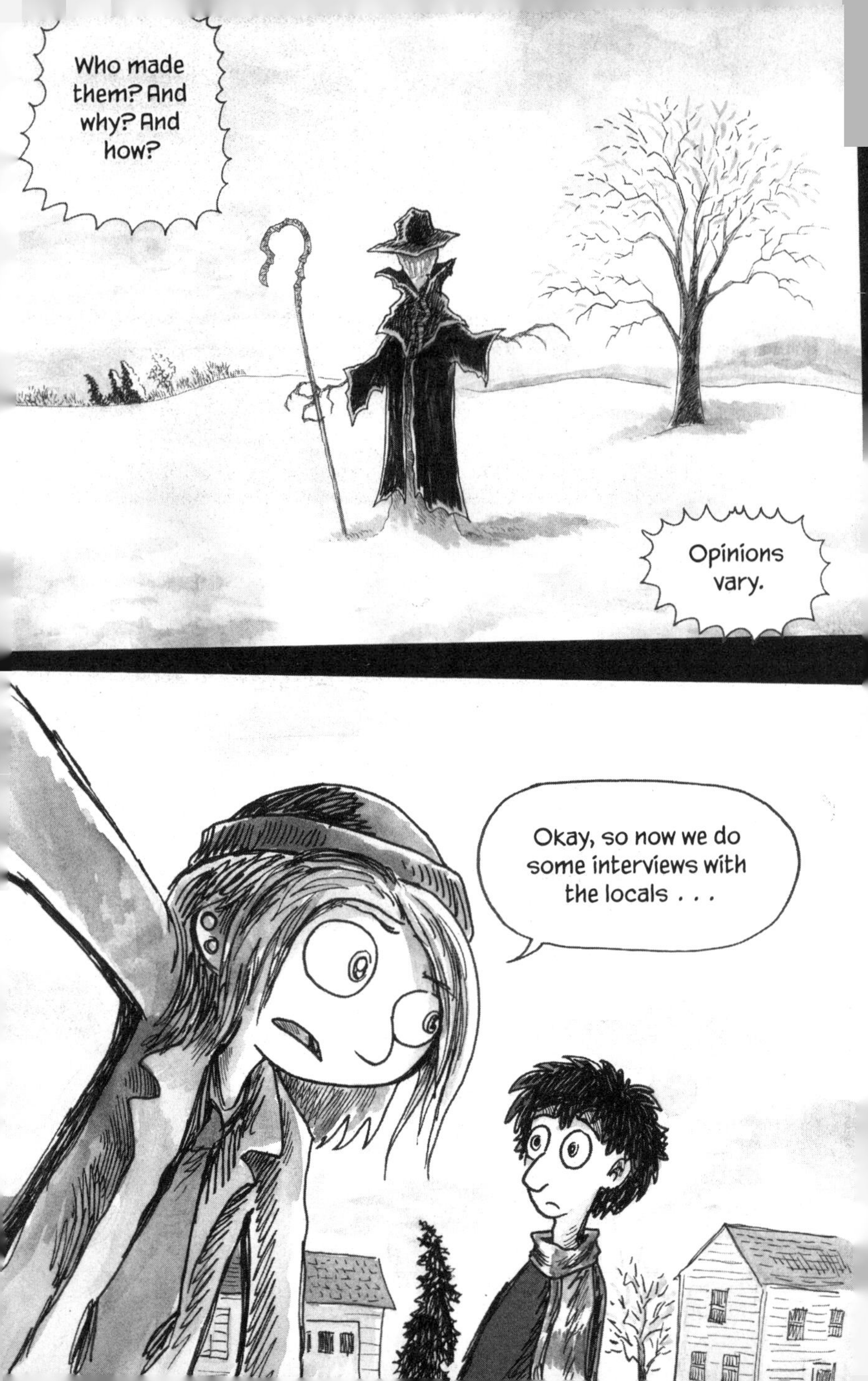
Who made them? And why? And how?
Opinions vary.
Okay, so now we do some interviews with the locals . . .

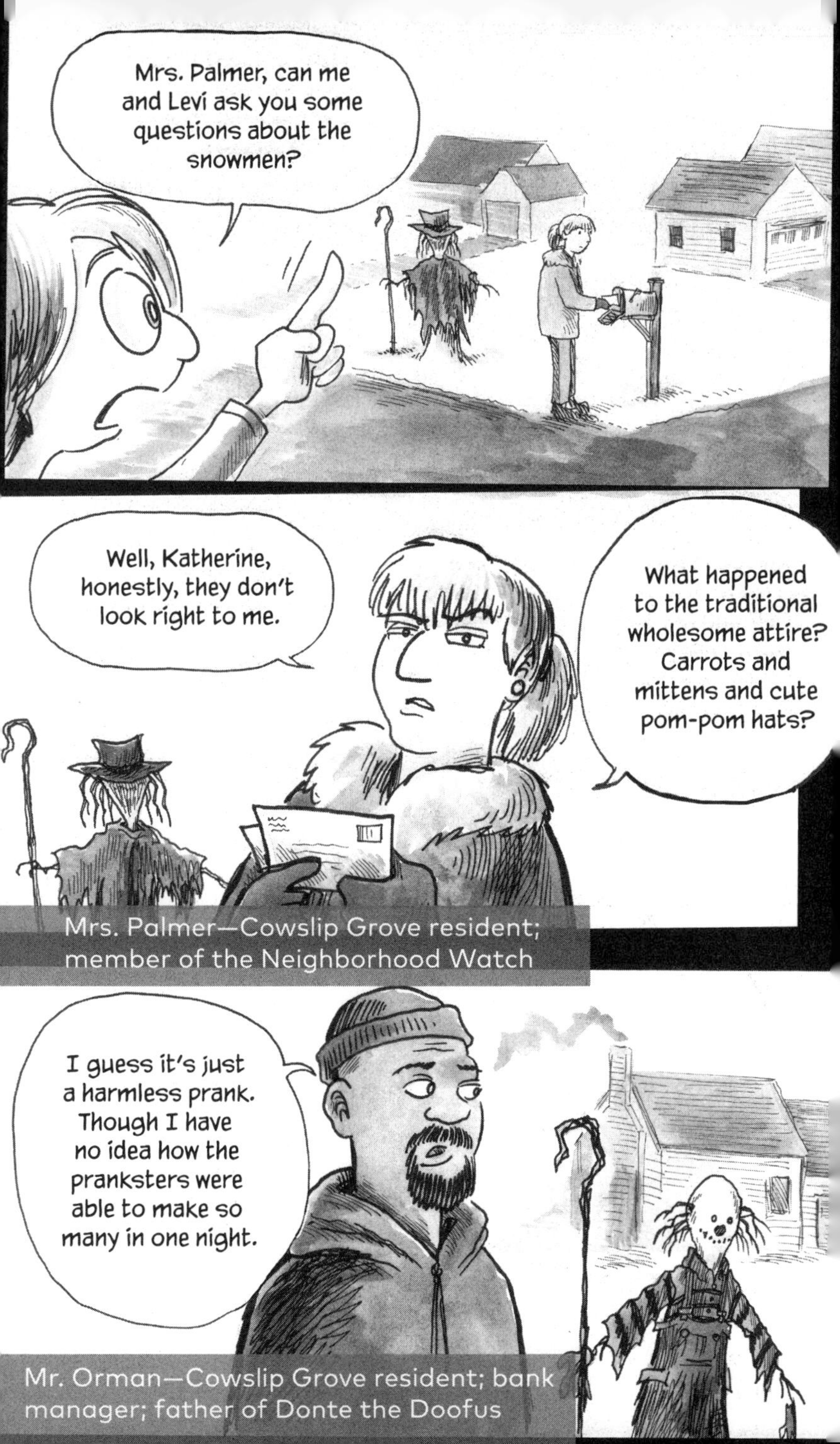
Mrs. Palmer, can me and Levi ask you some questions about the snowmen?
Well, Katherine, honestly, they don't look right to me.
What happened to the traditional wholesome attire? Carrots and mittens and cute pom-pom hats?
Mrs. Palmer—Cowslip Grove resident; member of the Neighborhood Watch
I guess it's just a harmless prank. Though I have no idea how the pranksters were able to make so many in one night.
Mr. Orman—Cowslip Grove resident; bank manager; father of Donte the Doofus

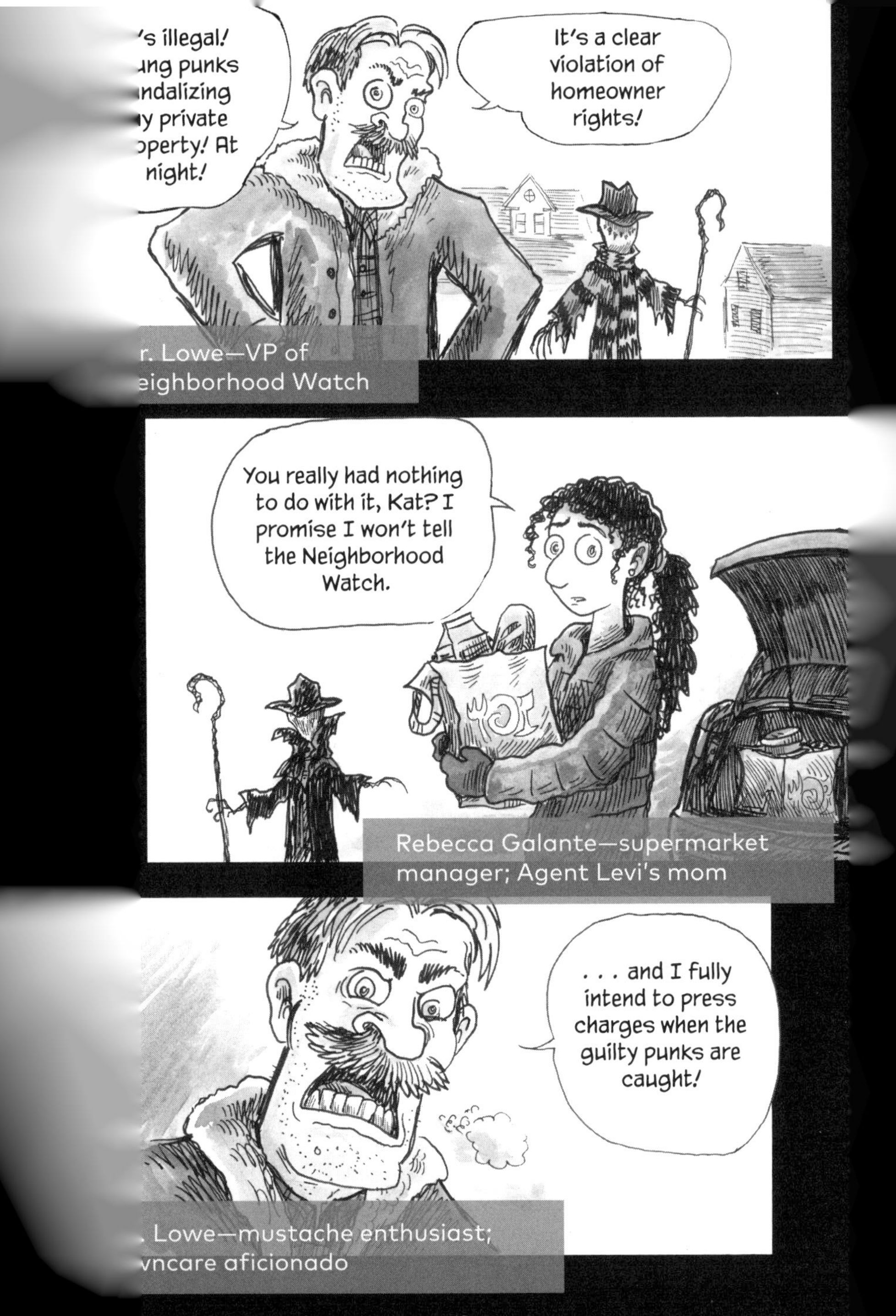
's illegal! ung punks ndalizing y private operty! At night!
It's a clear violation of homeowner rights!
r. Lowe—VP of eighborhood Watch
You really had nothing to do with it, Kat? I promise I won't tell the Neighborhood Watch.
Rebecca Galante—supermarket manager; Agent Levi's mom
. . . and I fully intend to press charges when the guilty punks are caught!
. Lowe—mustache enthusiast; vncare aficionado

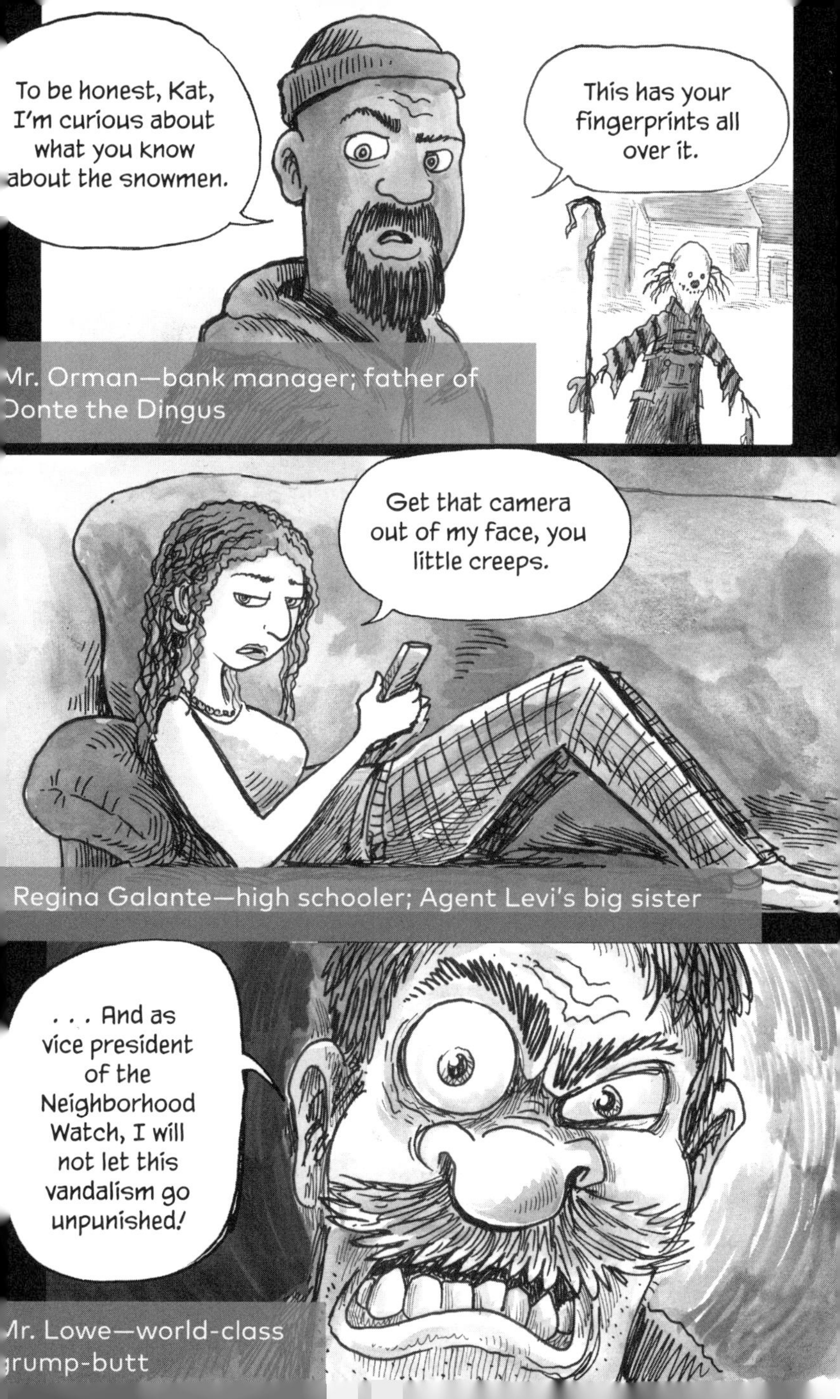
To be honest, Kat, I'm curious about what you know about the snowmen.
This has your fingerprints all over it.
Mr. Orman—bank manager; father of Donte the Dingus
Get that camera out of my face, you little creeps.
Regina Galante—high schooler; Agent Levi's big sister
. . . And as vice president of the Neighborhood Watch, I will not let this vandalism go unpunished!
Mr. Lowe—world-class grump-butt

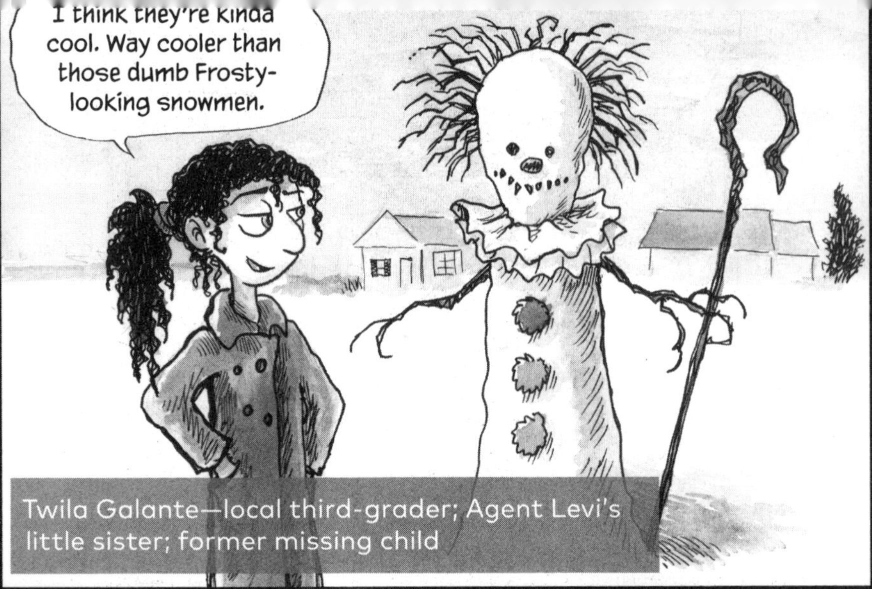
I think they're kinda cool. Way cooler than those dumb Frosty-looking snowmen.
Twila Galante—local third-grader; Agent Levi's little sister; former missing child

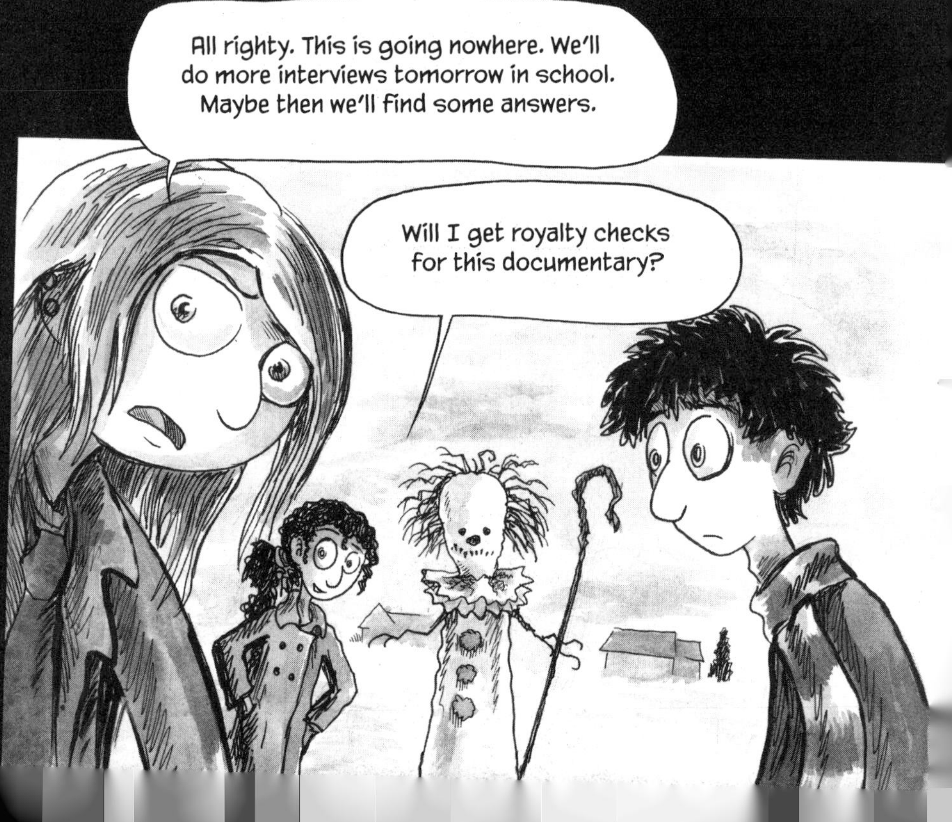
All righty. This is going nowhere. We'll do more interviews tomorrow in school. Maybe then we'll find some answers.
Will I get royalty checks for this documentary?

Chapter 2

Kat stopped recording and pocketed her phone. "Want to come to my house tonight? We can edit the footage we shot."

"Not tonight," said Levi. "It's a school night."

"So? It's the last couple days before spring break. Those hardly count as school days."

"Doesn't feel like spring," said Twila as she kicked at a slushy snow clump.

"I'm sure it'll warm up soon," said Levi, "and all these weird snowmen will melt."

"What do you guys *really* think about the snowmen?" asked Twila. "Do you think they're at all connected to"— her voice dropped to a whisper—". . . the Boojum?"

Levi's forehead creased with worry lines. "The Boojum is gone. We beat it. And no other kids have disappeared since then."

"We don't know that for sure," said Kat. "It can erase people's memories. For all we know, it could still be hiding somewhere, stealing kids away, and it's like they never existed."

"Right," agreed Levi reluctantly. "Gotta be careful. But I bet these snowmen are just a prank." He gave Kat a sideways look. "You swear you didn't—"

"I *told* you, it wasn't me!" snapped Kat. "There's no way I could build all these snowmen in one night!" She patted her phone. "That's why this documentary is going to be so important. Everyone needs to see that something is haunting Cowslip Grove."

"Maybe we should ask Willow about the snowmen," said Twila.

"Tomorrow's the day I volunteer at the wildlife clinic," said Levi. "I'll ask Willow when I see her then."

"Can I come with you?" asked Twila. "I was telling a kid in my class about the animals at the clinic, and he wants to see them."

Levi shook his head. "We can't let strangers know about Willow."

Twila folded her arms. "So she's just going to stay in hiding forever?"

"Look, we can debate this later," said Levi. "Right now we'd better get home. The sun's setting."

"Wow," said Kat. "Big brother bossy man!"

Levi ignored this. "Come on, Twila."

Twila was staring at the nearest snowman.

"Twila!"

Twila pulled her gaze away from the snowman and smiled sheepishly. "Sorry. I just thought, for a second . . . Ah, forget it."

"What?"

"Nothing. Just . . . I don't know. I could have sworn that snowman was facing the other way."

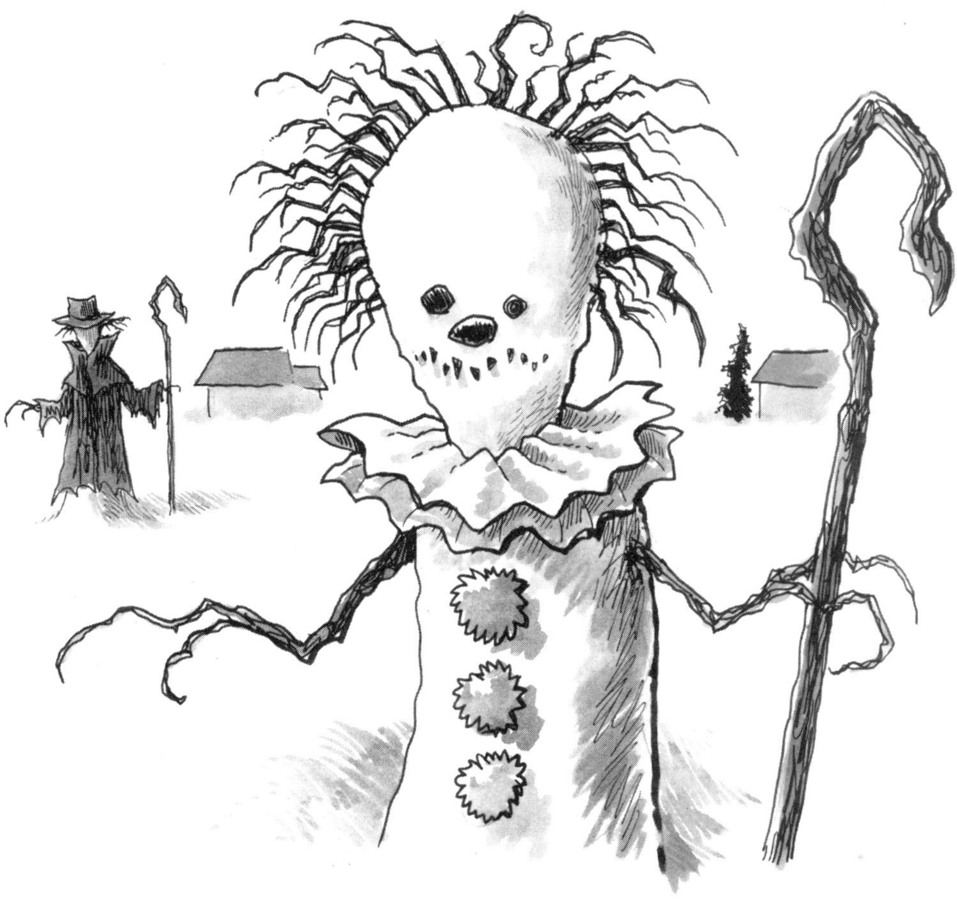

FOOTAGE RECOVERED FROM KAT BOMBARD'S PHONE, MARCH 17

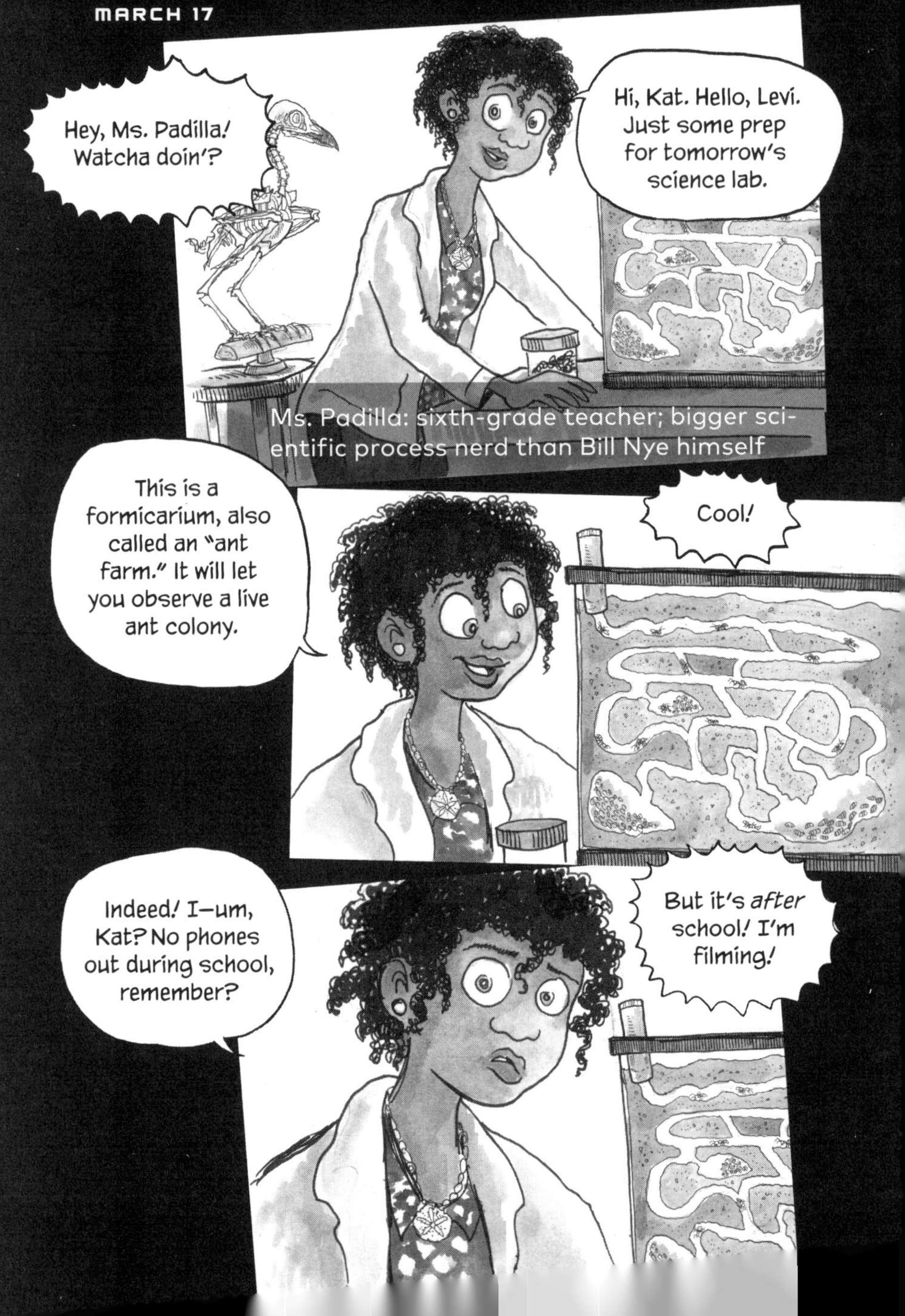
Hey, Ms. Padilla! Watcha doin'?
Hi, Kat. Hello, Levi. Just some prep for tomorrow's science lab.
Ms. Padilla: sixth-grade teacher; bigger scientific process nerd than Bill Nye himself
This is a formicarium, also called an "ant farm." It will let you observe a live ant colony.
Cool!
Indeed! I—um, Kat? No phones out during school, remember?
But it's *after* school! I'm filming!

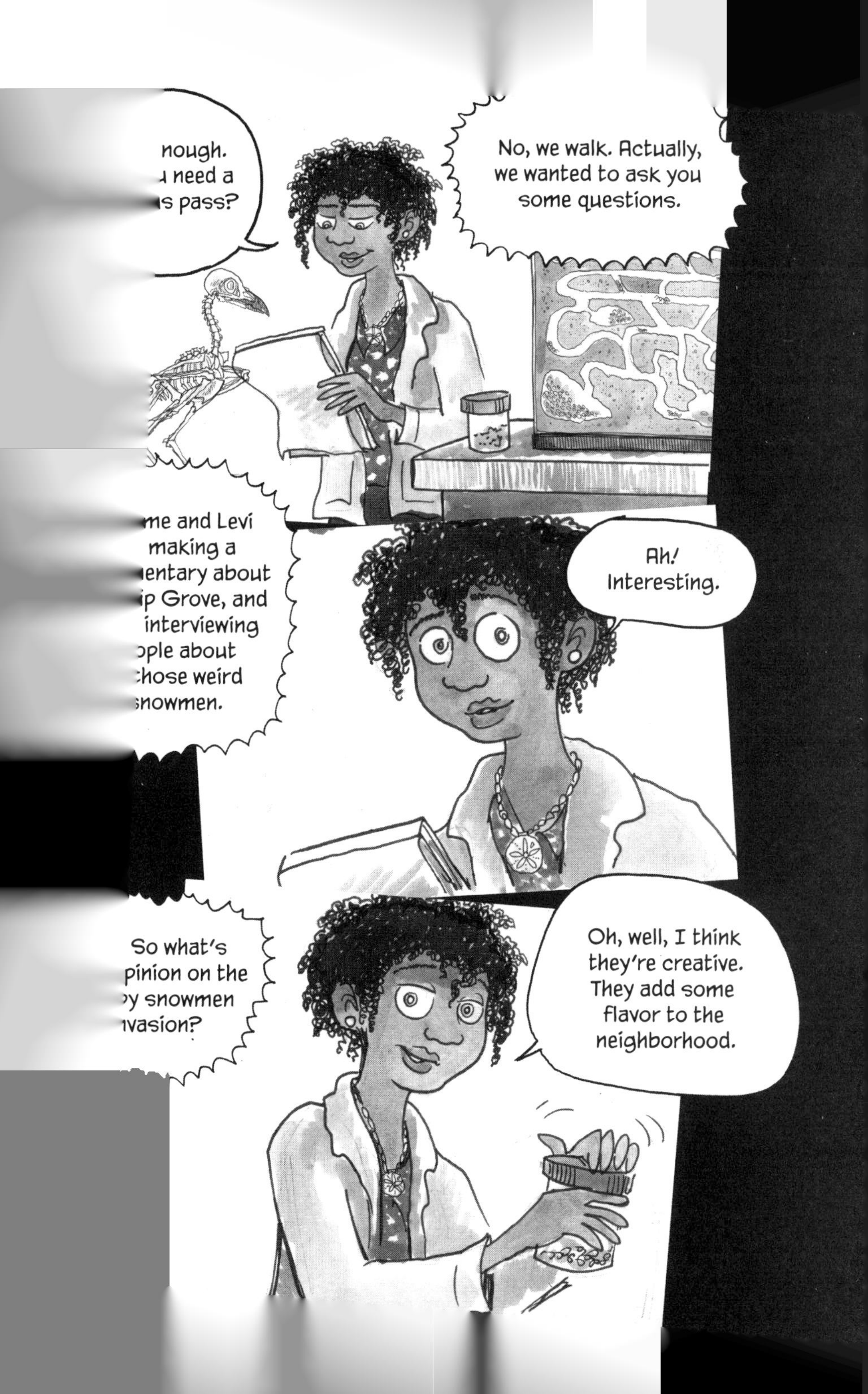
nough. need a s pass?
No, we walk. Actually, we wanted to ask you some questions.
me and Levi making a entary about p Grove, and interviewing ople about hose weird nowmen.
Ah! Interesting.
So what's pinion on the y snowmen vasion?
Oh, well, I think they're creative. They add some flavor to the neighborhood.

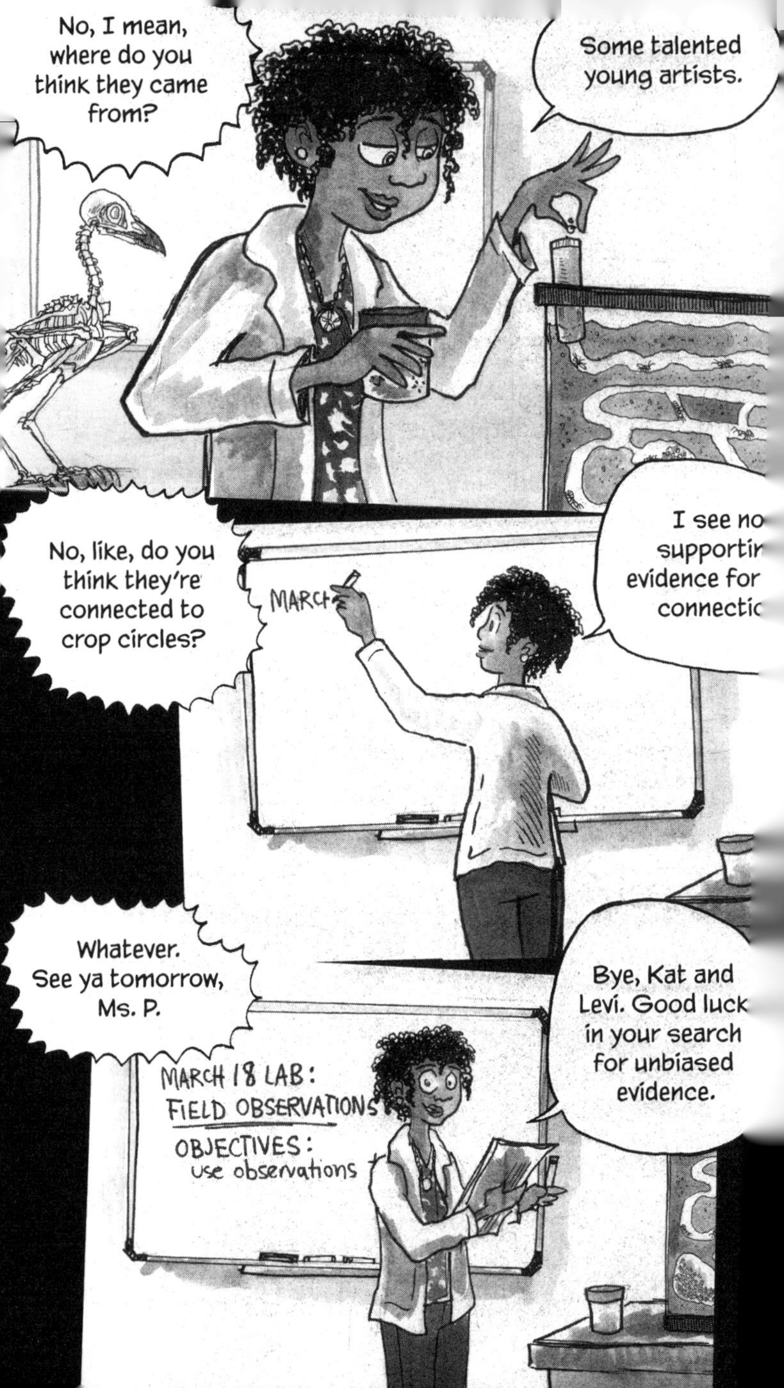
No, I mean, where do you think they came from?
Some talented young artists.
No, like, do you think they're connected to crop circles?
MARCH
I see no supporti evidence for connectio
Whatever. See ya tomorrow, Ms. P.
MARCH 18 LAB:
FIELD OBSERVATIONS
OBJECTIVES:
use observations
Bye, Kat and Levi. Good luck in your search for unbiased evidence.

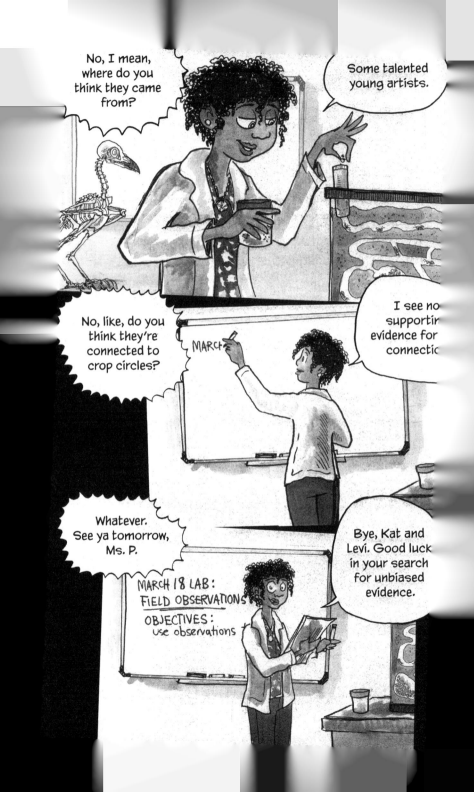

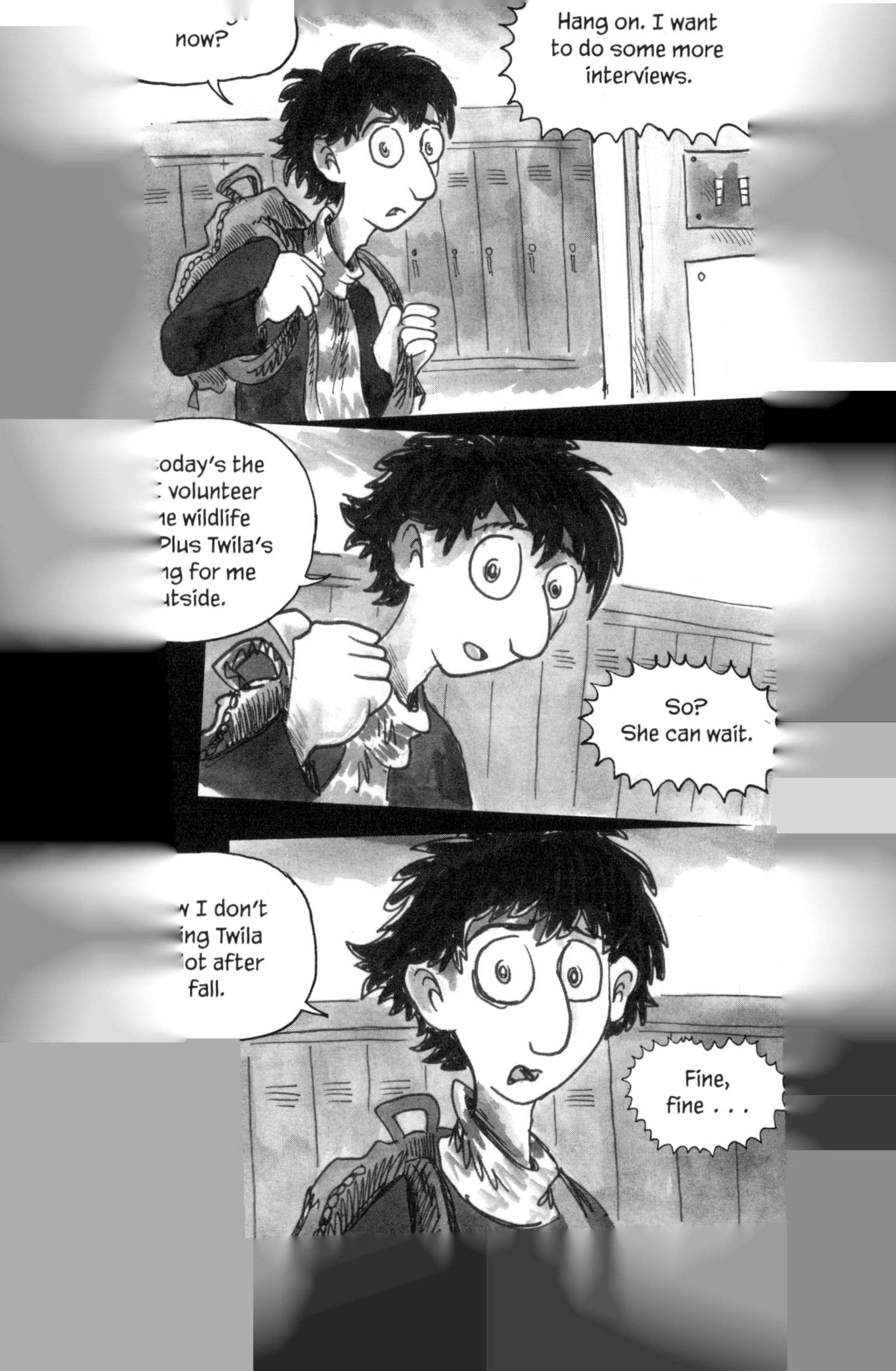
now?
Hang on. I want to do some more interviews.
oday's the volunteer e wildlife Plus Twila's g for me tside.
So? She can wait.
I don't ing Twila ot after fall.
Fine, fine . . .

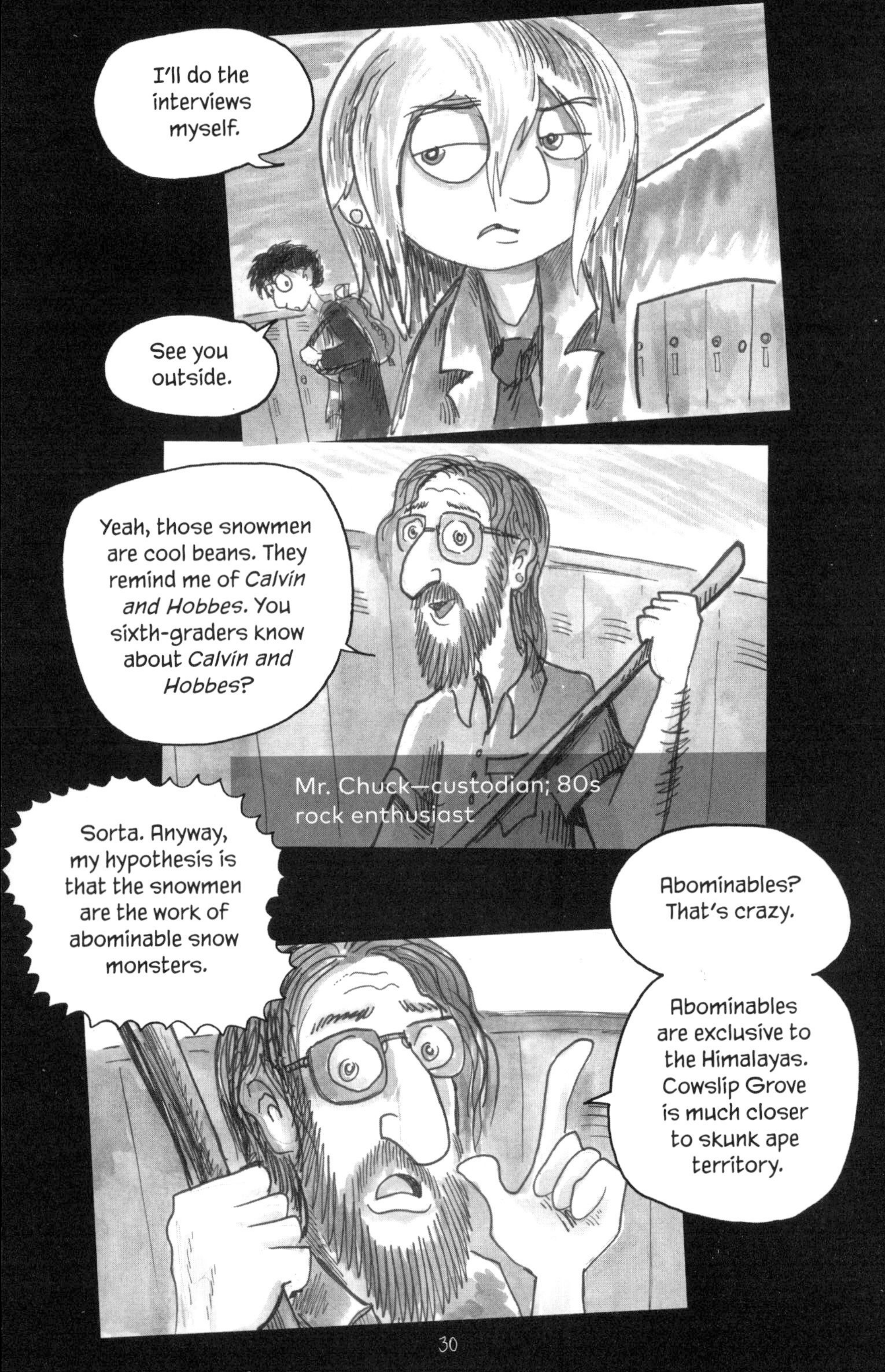
I'll do the interviews myself.
See you outside.
Yeah, those snowmen are cool beans. They remind me of Calvin and Hobbes. You sixth-graders know about Calvin and Hobbes?
Mr. Chuck—custodian; 80s rock enthusiast
Sorta. Anyway, my hypothesis is that the snowmen are the work of abominable snow monsters.
Abominables? That's crazy.
Abominables are exclusive to the Himalayas. Cowslip Grove is much closer to skunk ape territory.

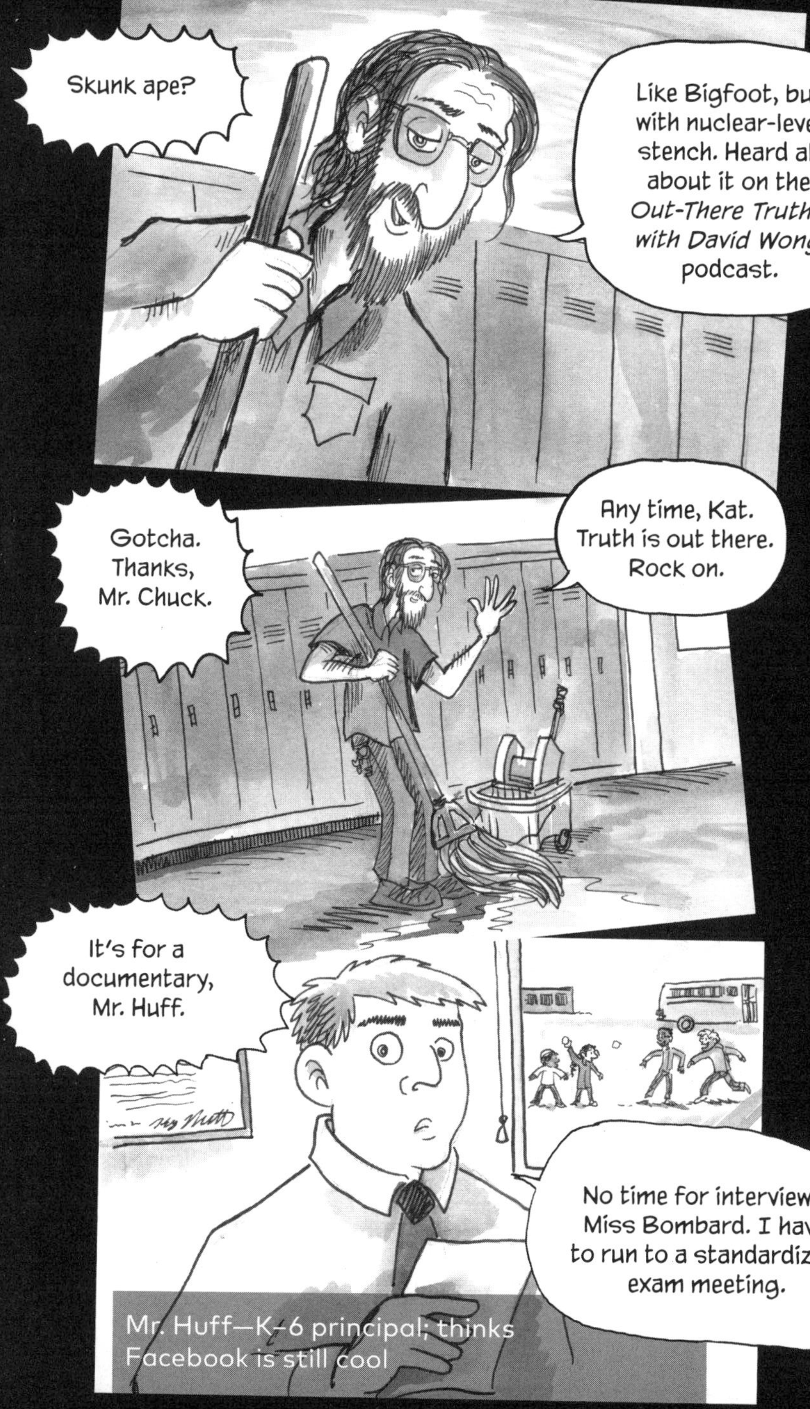
Skunk ape?
Like Bigfoot, but with nuclear-level stench. Heard all about it on the *Out-There Truths with David Wong* podcast.
Gotcha. Thanks, Mr. Chuck.
Any time, Kat. Truth is out there. Rock on.
It's for a documentary, Mr. Huff.
No time for interviews, Miss Bombard. I have to run to a standardized exam meeting.
Mr. Huff—K-6 principal; thinks Facebook is still cool

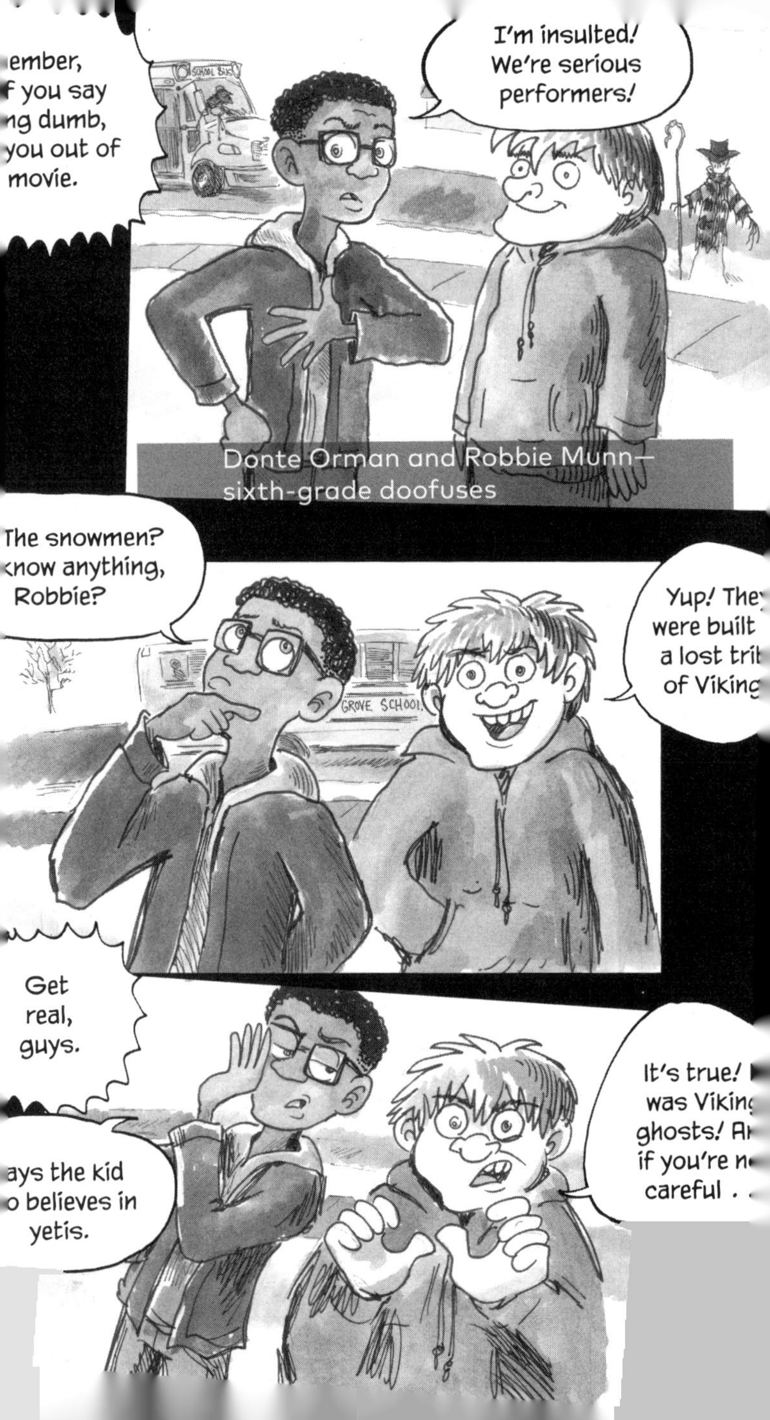

ember,
f you say
ng dumb,
you out of
movie.
I'm insulted! We're serious performers!
Donte Orman and Robbie Munn—
sixth-grade doofuses
The snowmen?
know anything,
Robbie?
Yup! The
were built
a lost trib
of Viking
Get real, guys.
ays the kid
o believes in
yetis.
It's true!
was Viking
ghosts! A
if you're n
careful . .

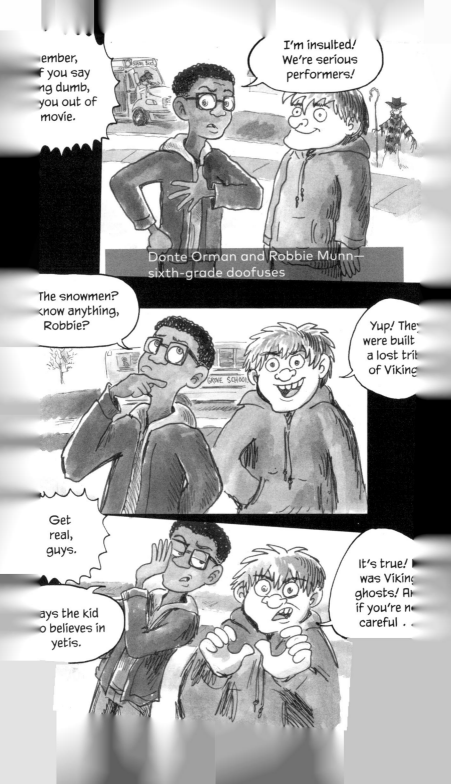

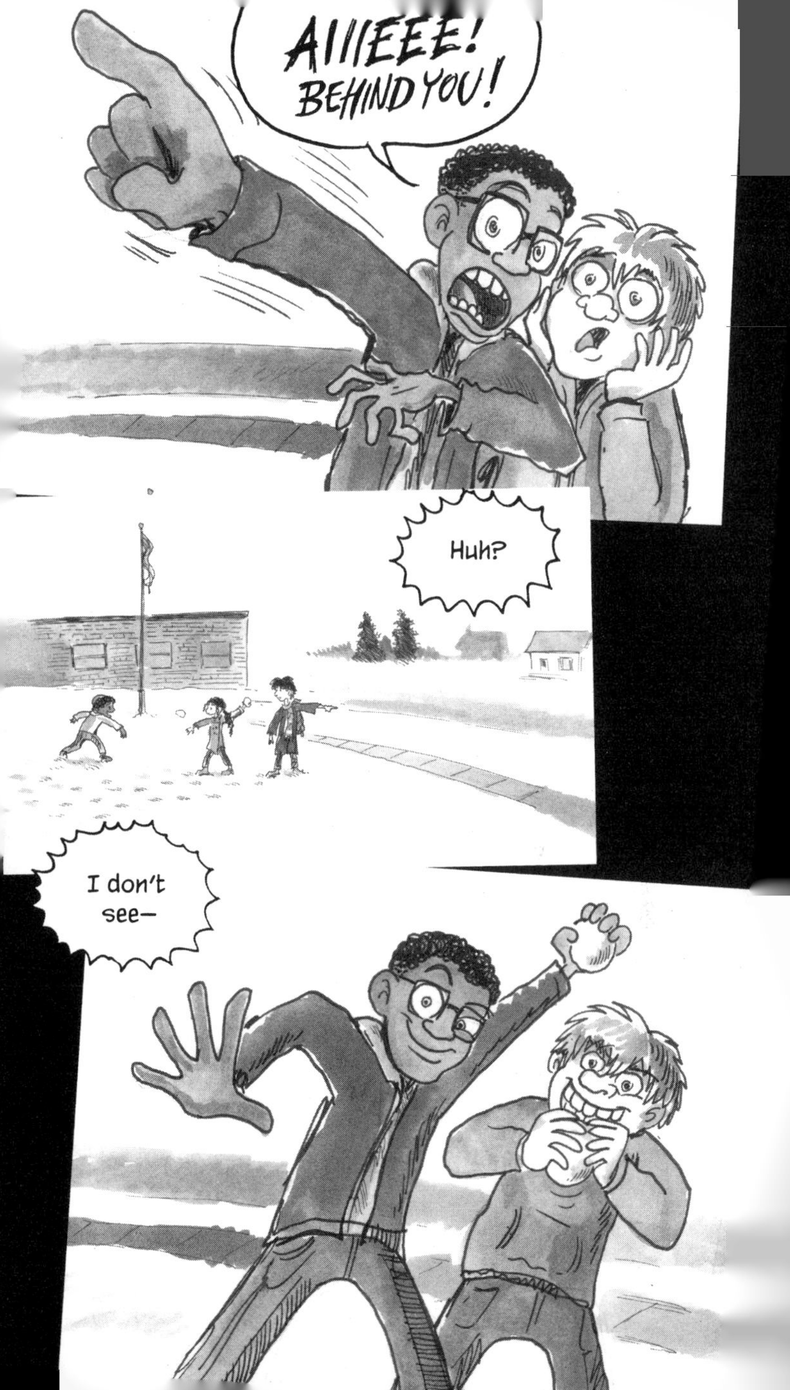
AIIIEEE! BEHIND YOU!
Huh?
I don't see–

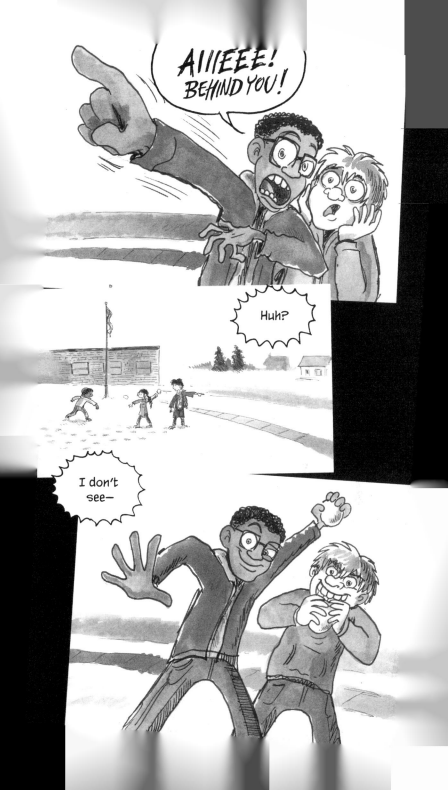

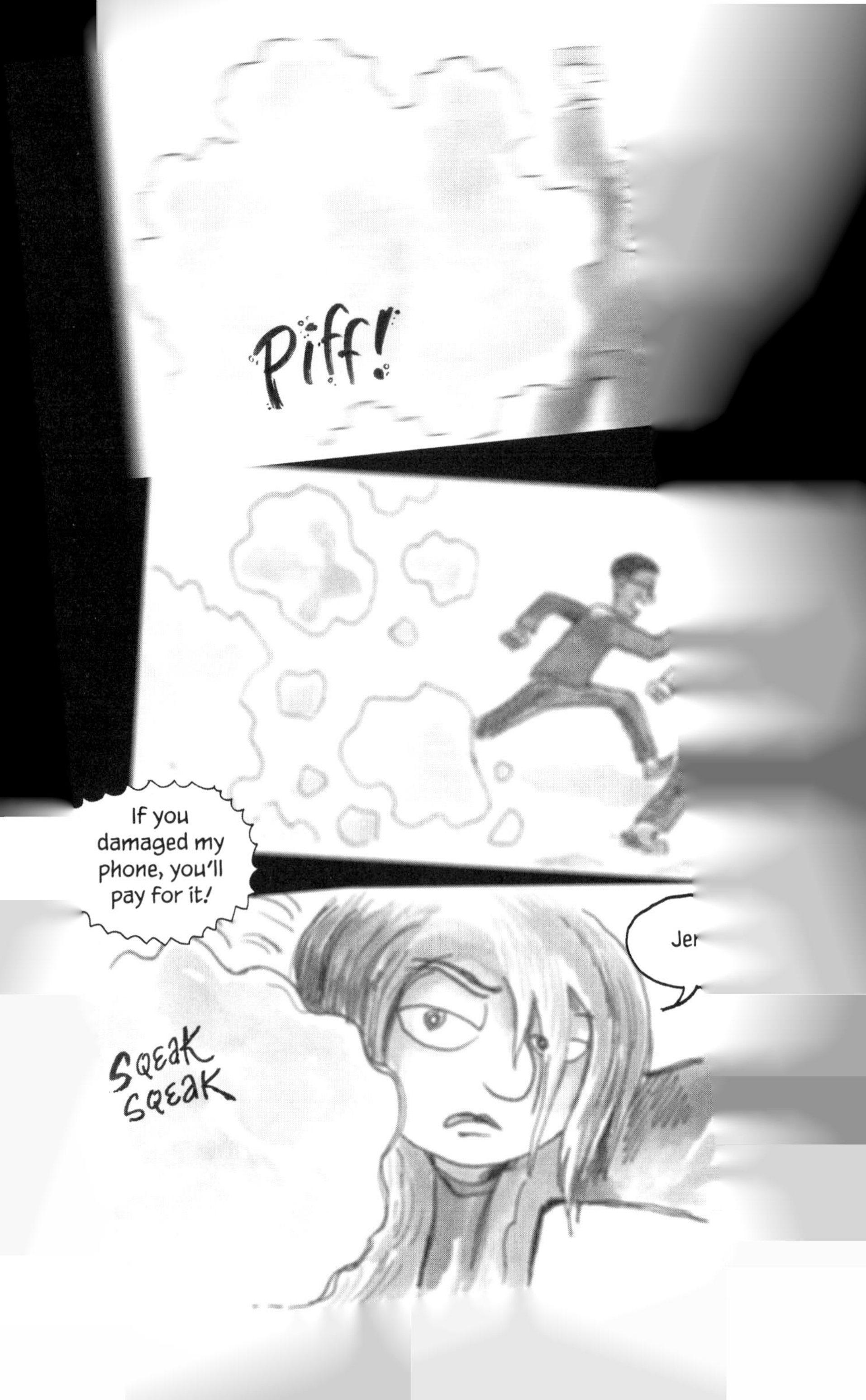
Piff!
If you damaged my phone, you'll pay for it!
SQEAK SQEAK

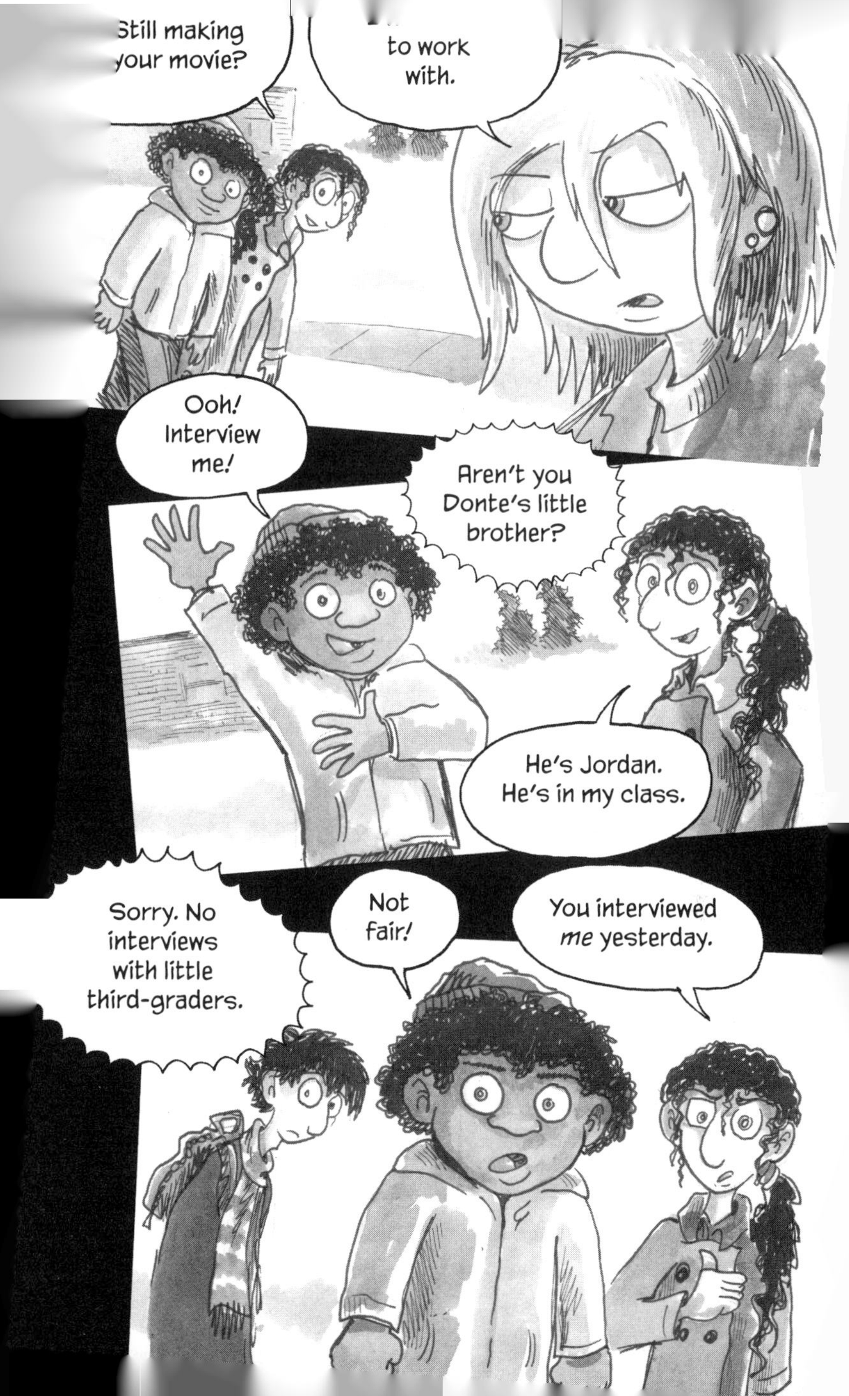
Still making your movie?
to work with.
Ooh! Interview me!
Aren't you Donte's little brother?
He's Jordan. He's in my class.
Sorry. No interviews with little third-graders.
Not fair!
You interviewed *me* yesterday.

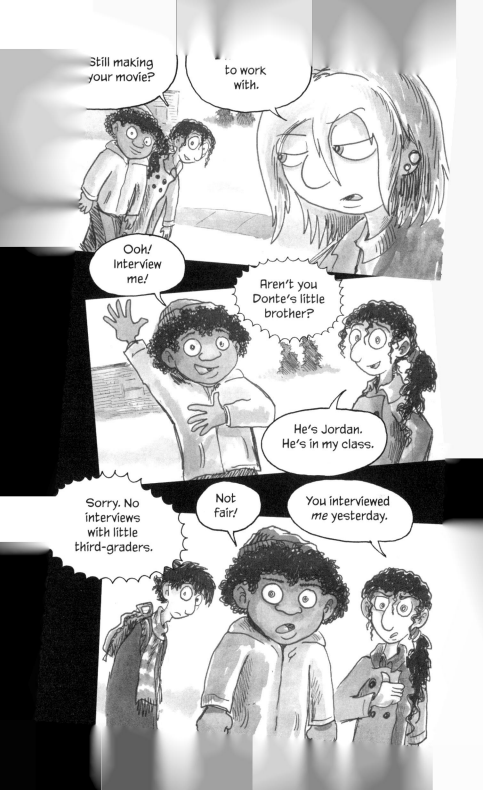

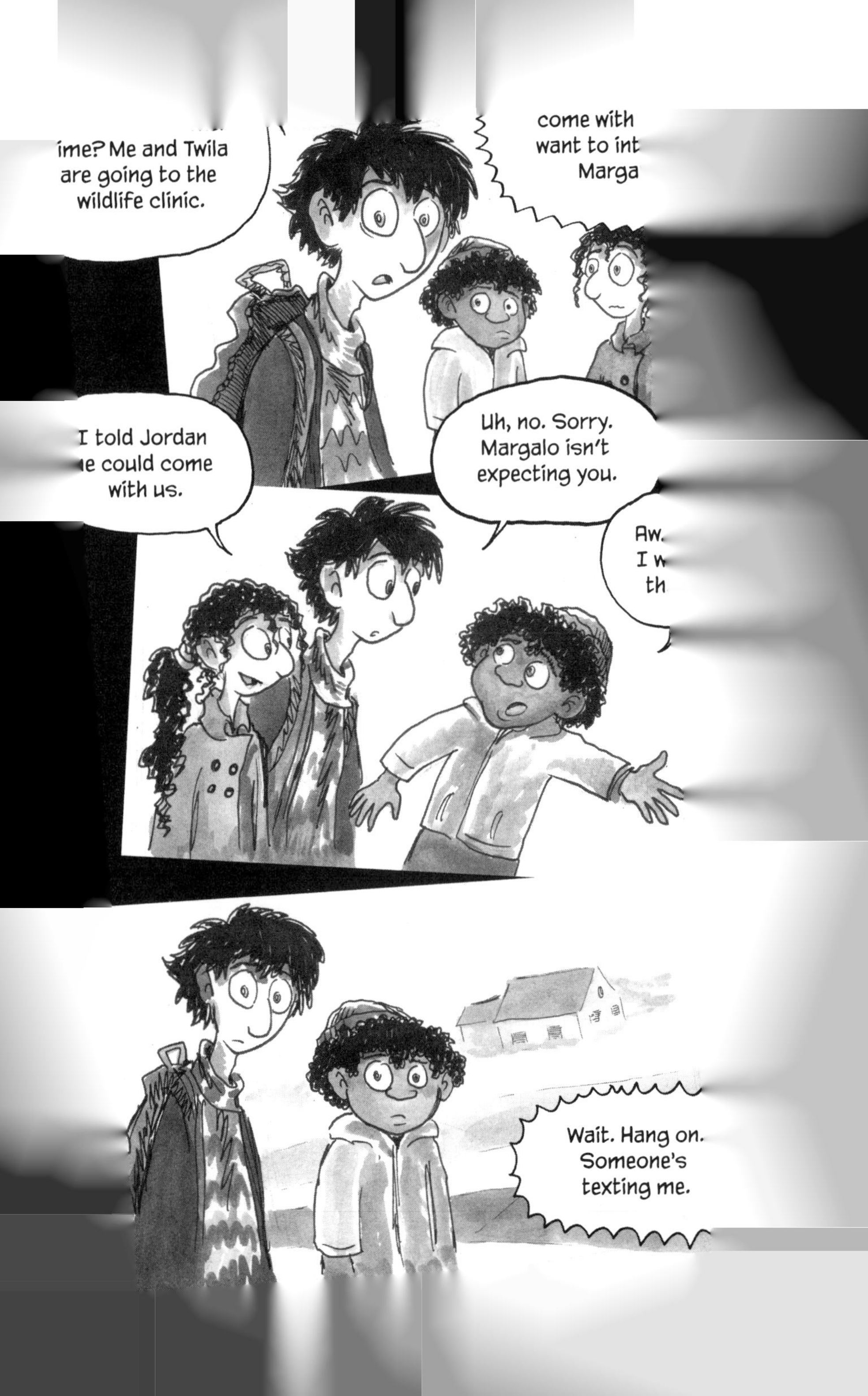

ime? Me and Twila are going to the wildlife clinic.
come with want to int Marga
I told Jordan ie could come with us.
Uh, no. Sorry. Margalo isn't expecting you.
Wait. Hang on. Someone's texting me.

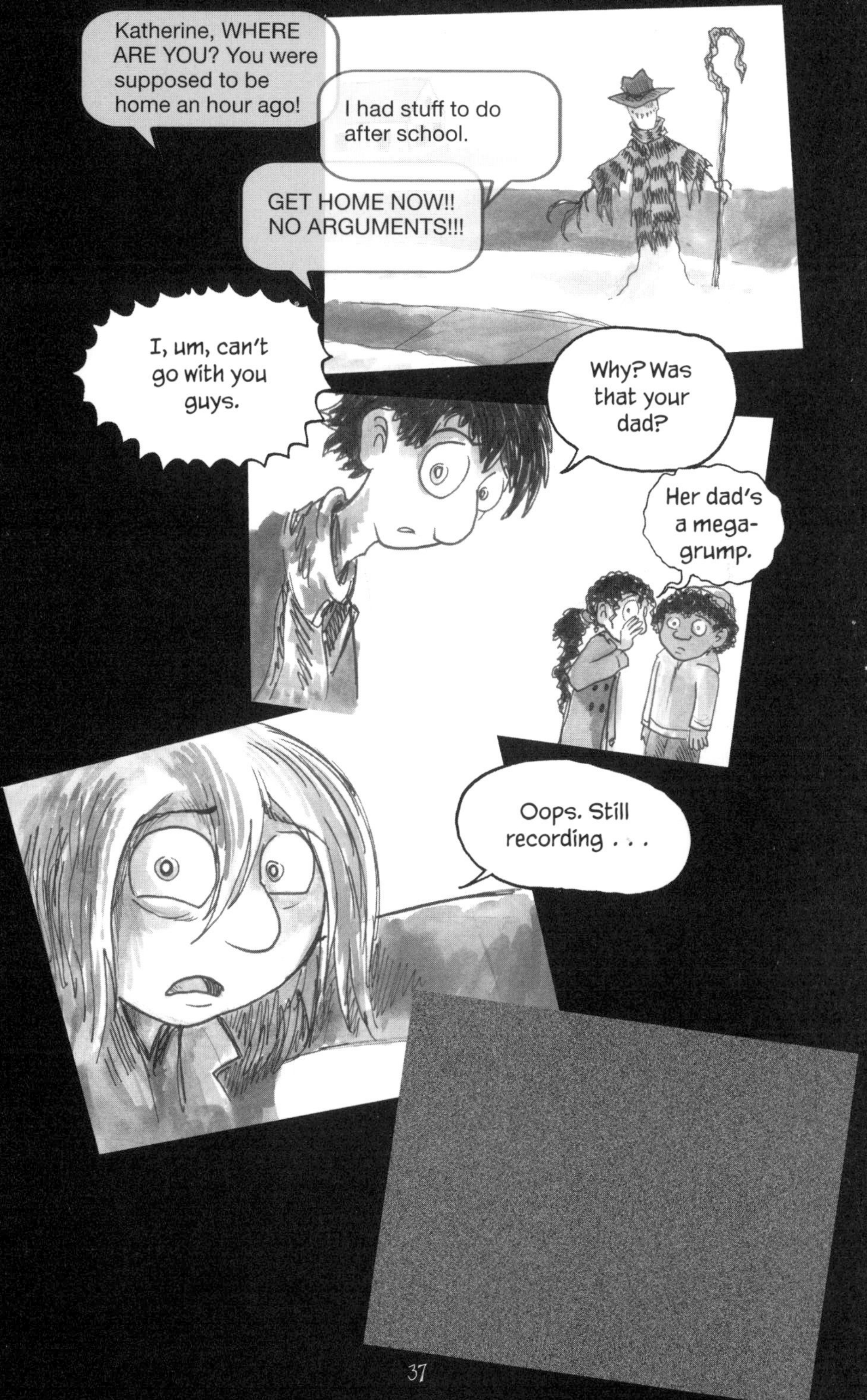
Katherine, WHERE ARE YOU? You were supposed to be home an hour ago!
I had stuff to do after school.
GET HOME NOW!! NO ARGUMENTS!!!
I, um, can't go with you guys.
Why? Was that your dad?
Her dad's a mega-grump.
Oops. Still recording . . .

Chapter 4

"Hey!" said Jordan. "This is where the Mushpits used to live. Donte always said they were witches."

"Well, the Mushpits moved out last fall," said Levi. "Now it's Margalo's Home for Unloved Creatures."

"Yeah," said Jordan, "but Donte and Robbie think the new lady is a witch, too."

"Margalo's not a witch," said Levi. "She's a certified wildlife rehabilitator." Jordan and Twila followed him to the front door. "Listen, Margalo wasn't expecting you, so don't touch any of the animals. And stay away from the cellar."

"Why? What's in the cellar?"

"Just stay with me, okay?" Levi knocked on the door. A series of squawks, yelps, and chatters erupted from somewhere within the house.

"Just a moment!" called a voice. Locks and bolts clicked, and the door swung open, revealing a very ordinary-looking woman. "Ah, young Levi Galante!" The woman looked past Levi to the third-graders. "And sister Twila, good to see you. And a new face! Splendid!"

"This is Jordan," said Twila. "Kids sometimes call him Bug Man. He's in my class."

"Pleasure to meet you, Jordan," said the woman. "I'm Margalo, the wildlife rehabilitator."

"Hi!" said Jordan. He paused, then added: "You don't *look* like a witch."

Margalo laughed. "Trust me, no witching happens here. Just a lot of hard work. You're welcome to come in and see for yourself. But before you enter my house of wonder, you must first answer an essential question: In all of Kingdom Animalia, what is your favorite species?"

Jordan's brow furrowed. "Dung beetle," he said at last.

Twila giggled and made a face.

"It *is*!" said Jordan. "I like how funny they look when they're rolling those balls of dung!"

"Interesting choice," said Margalo. "I've always had a soft spot for the underappreciated but essential scavengers."

"I also like the Goliath birdeater tarantula," Jordan added. "Biggest spider in the world!"

"Biggest *recognized* spider in the world," Margalo corrected, but she seemed impressed. She opened the front door wide. "You pass with flying colors. Enter at your own risk."

They followed her to the back rooms, where a series of pens lined the walls. "In truth, I'm happy to entertain visitors," continued Margalo. "I've only been here four months, but I already have a bad reputation. Lots of rumors about the strange lady with the sick animals. People are always afraid of things they don't understand. I'm hoping more people will learn that many creatures, even ones that seem ugly or creepy, play an important role in a healthy ecosystem. Without them, nature is unbalanced."

Jordan nudged Twila. "So when do we get to meet the animals?"

Margalo gestured to the pens. "Levi, you've been volunteering here for three months. You know the patients. You do the introductions this time."

Levi looked down at his shoes. "Maybe next time."

"A little public speaking practice can be important," Margalo said as she tossed him a pair of leather gloves.

"Come on, Levi!" urged Twila. She pulled out her phone. "Is it okay if I film this?" she asked Margalo. "Mom will want to see it."

"I don't want Mom to see it!" grumbled Levi.

“And what about Kat?” added Twila. “She could use it for her documentary.”

Margalo twitched an eyebrow. “Kat’s making a documentary?”

“About the weird snowmen and her crazy ideas about them,” said Twila.

“I love a good documentary,” Margalo said. “And it could be good publicity for Margalo’s Home for Unloved Creatures.” She turned to Twila. “Roll camera.”

Twila raised her phone, and Levi led his third-grade audience to the first pen . . .

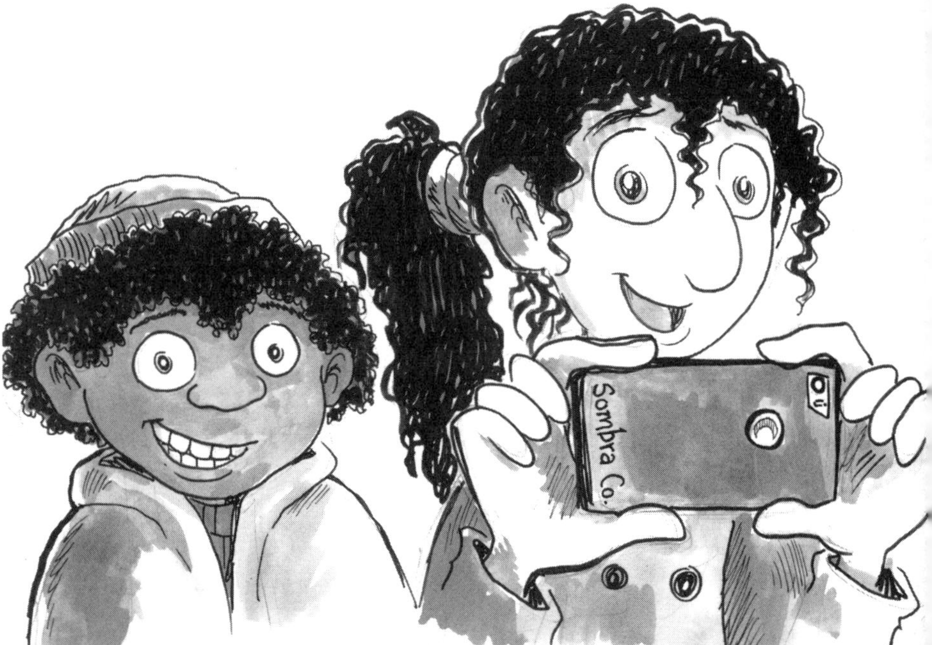
Sombra Co.

RECOVERED FROM TWILA GALANTE'S PHONE

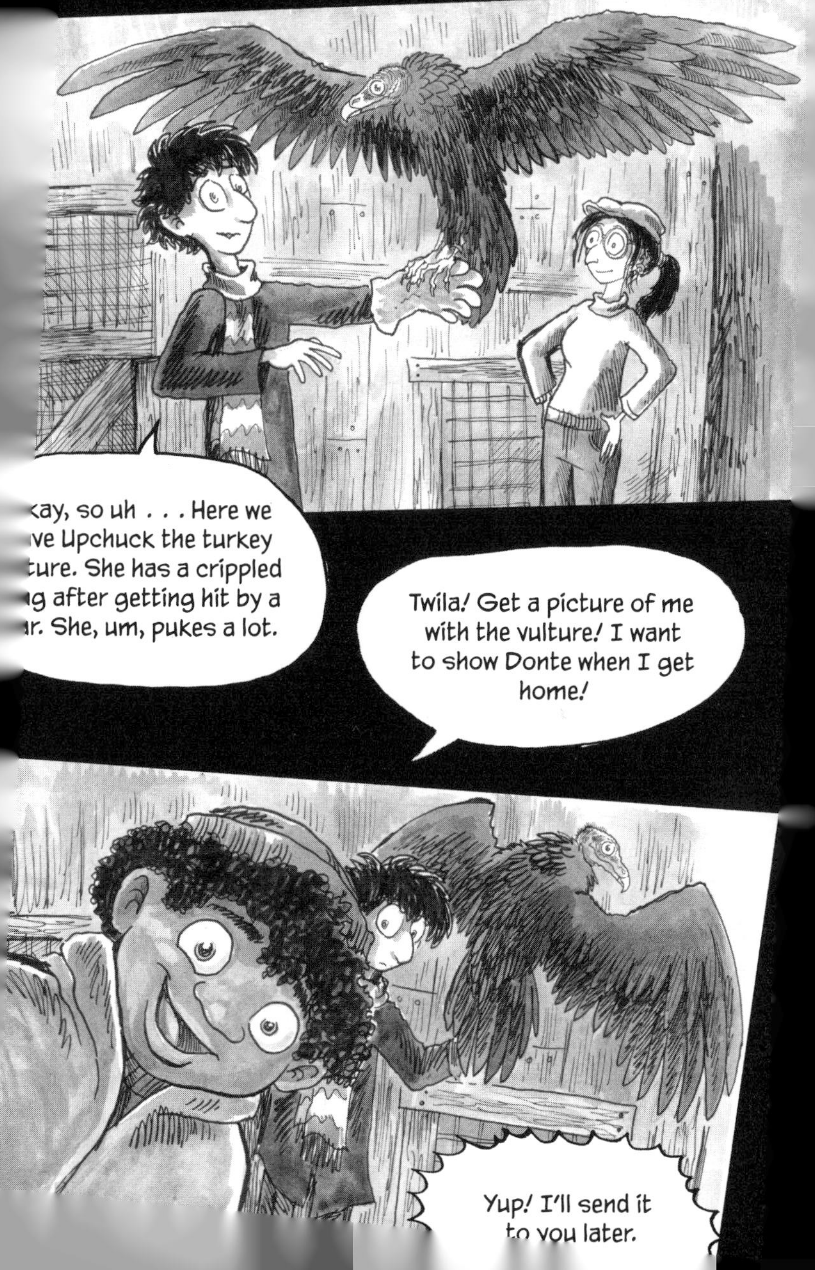
kay, so uh . . . Here we
ve Upchuck the turkey
ture. She has a crippled
g after getting hit by a
r. She, um, pukes a lot.
Twila! Get a picture of me with the vulture! I want to show Donte when I get home!
Yup! I'll send it to you later.

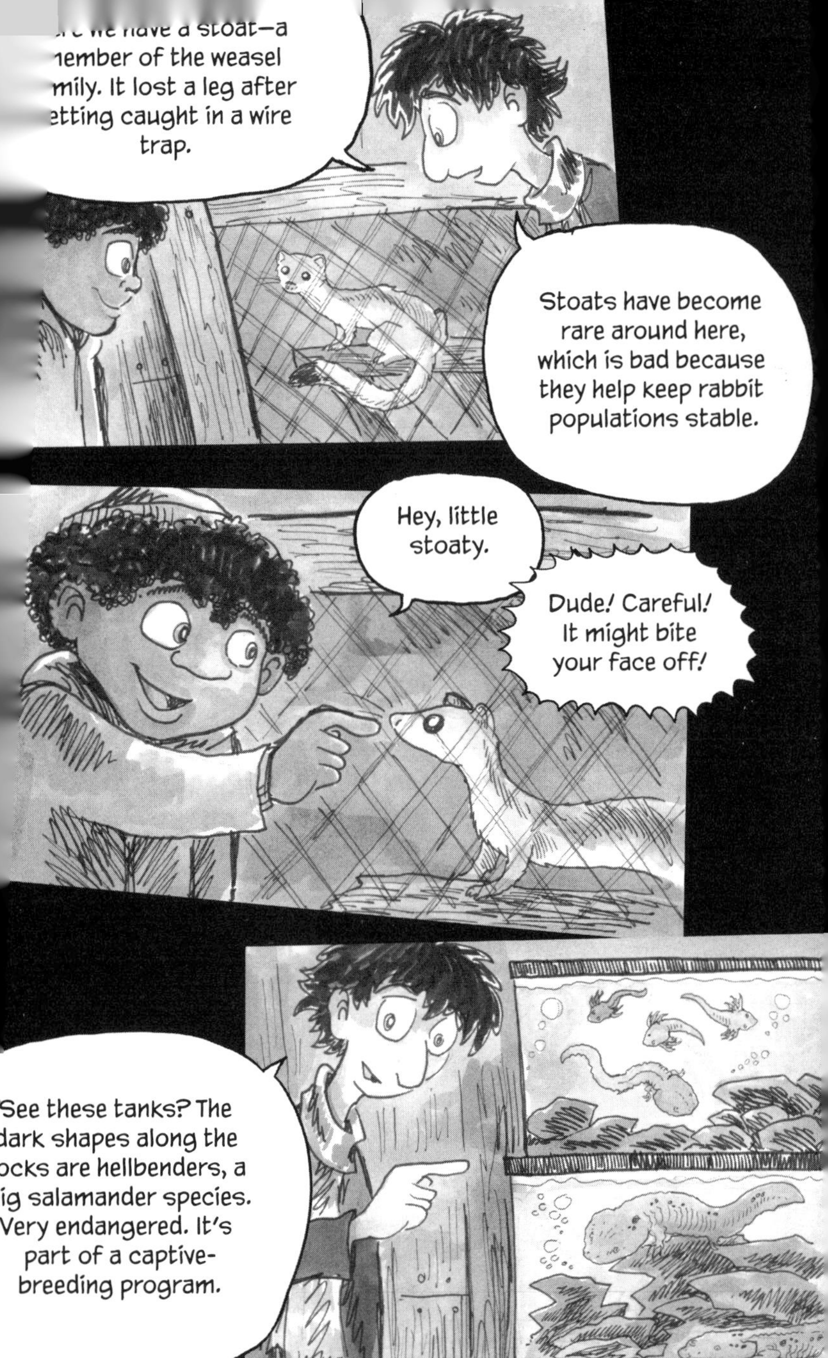

ember of the weasel
mily. It lost a leg after
etting caught in a wire
trap.
Stoats have become rare around here, which is bad because they help keep rabbit populations stable.
Hey, little stoaty.
Dude! Careful! It might bite your face off!
See these tanks? The
dark shapes along the
ocks are hellbenders, a
ig salamander species.
Very endangered. It's
part of a captive-
breeding program.

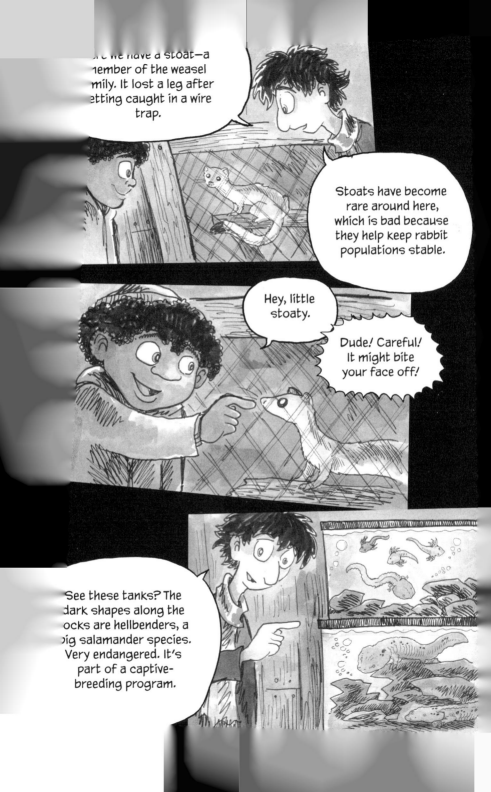

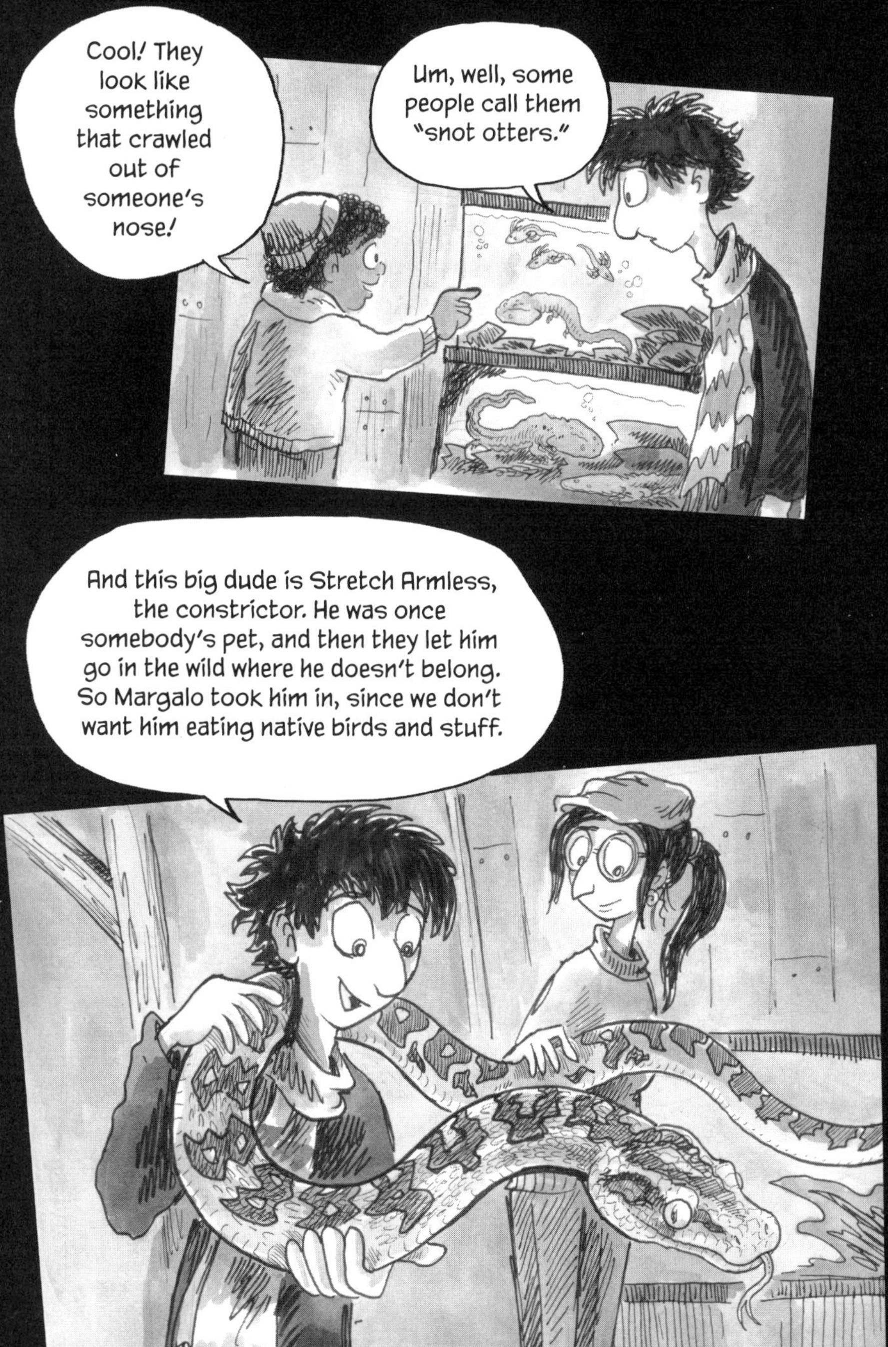
Cool! They look like something that crawled out of someone's nose!
Um, well, some people call them "snot otters."
And this big dude is Stretch Armless, the constrictor. He was once somebody's pet, and then they let him go in the wild where he doesn't belong. So Margalo took him in, since we don't want him eating native birds and stuff.

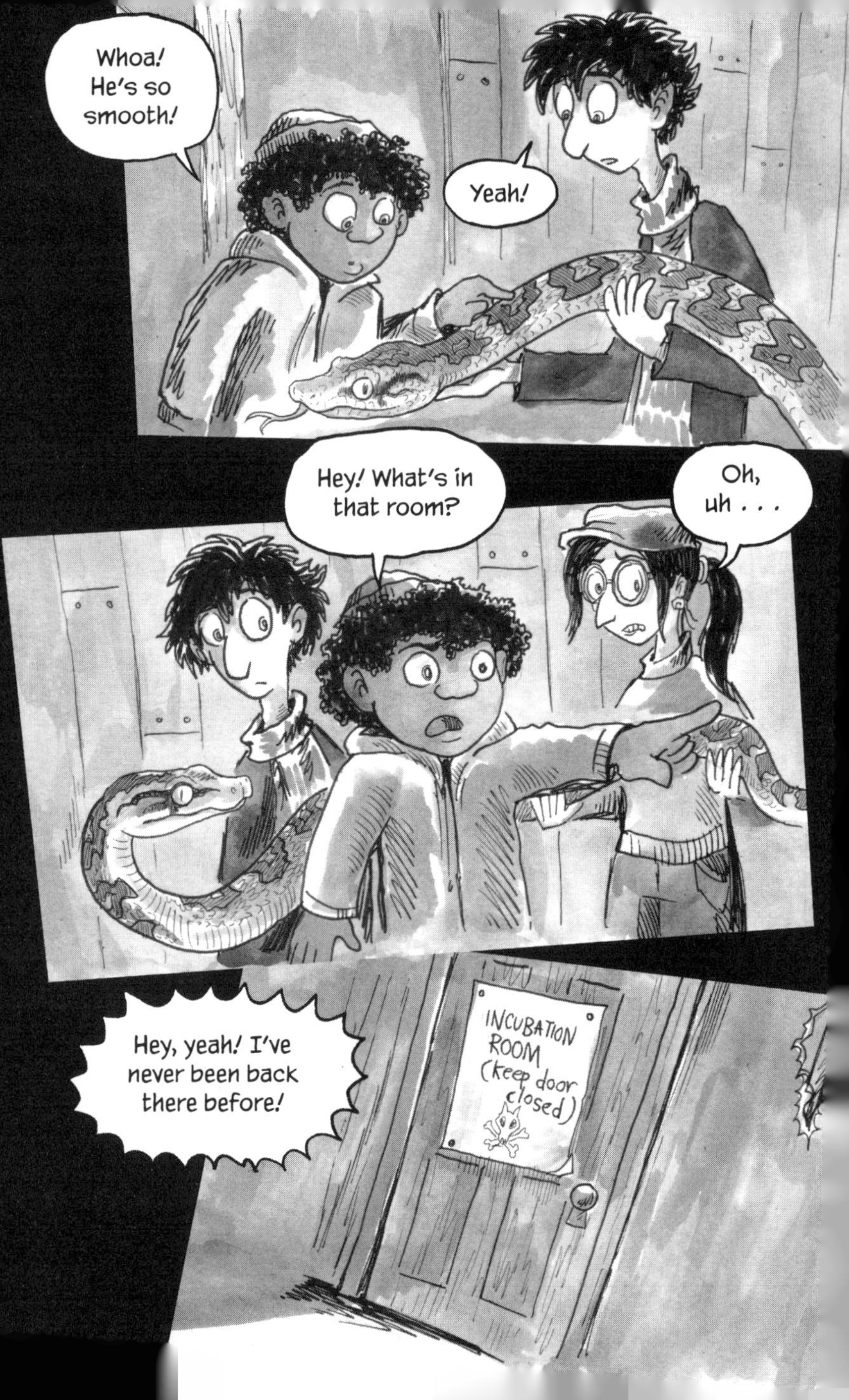
Whoa! He's so smooth!
Yeah!
Hey! What's in that room?
Oh, uh . . .
Hey, yeah! I've never been back there before!
INCUBATION ROOM (keep door closed)

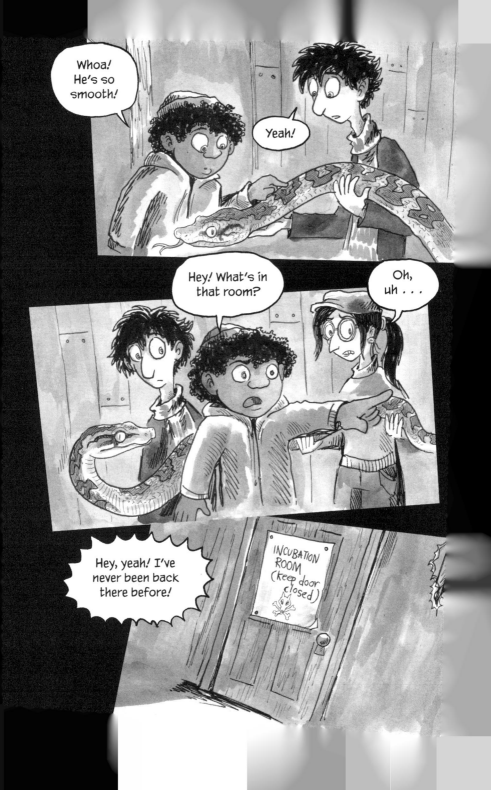

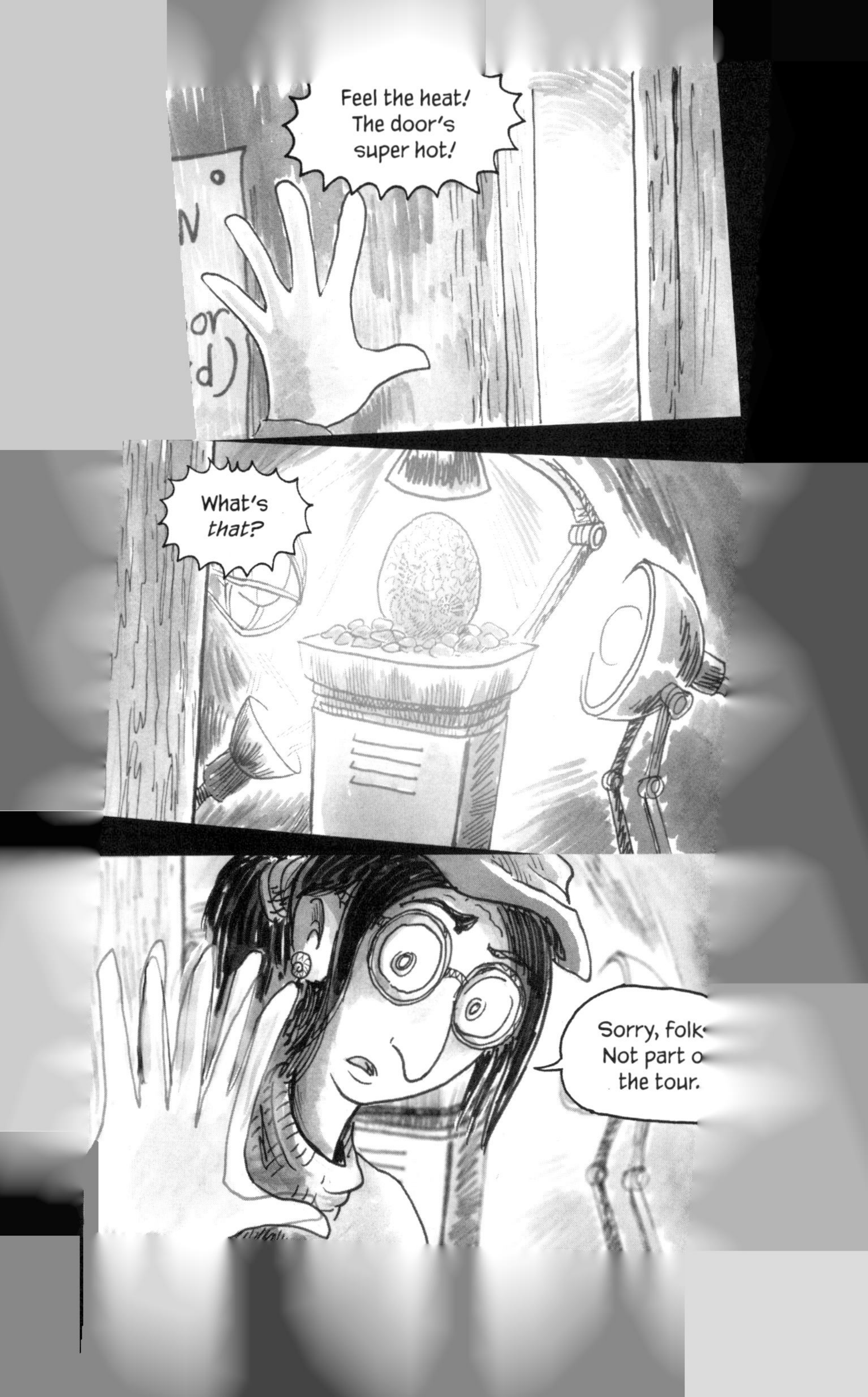
Feel the heat! The door's super hot!
What's that?
Sorry, folk
Not part o
the tour.

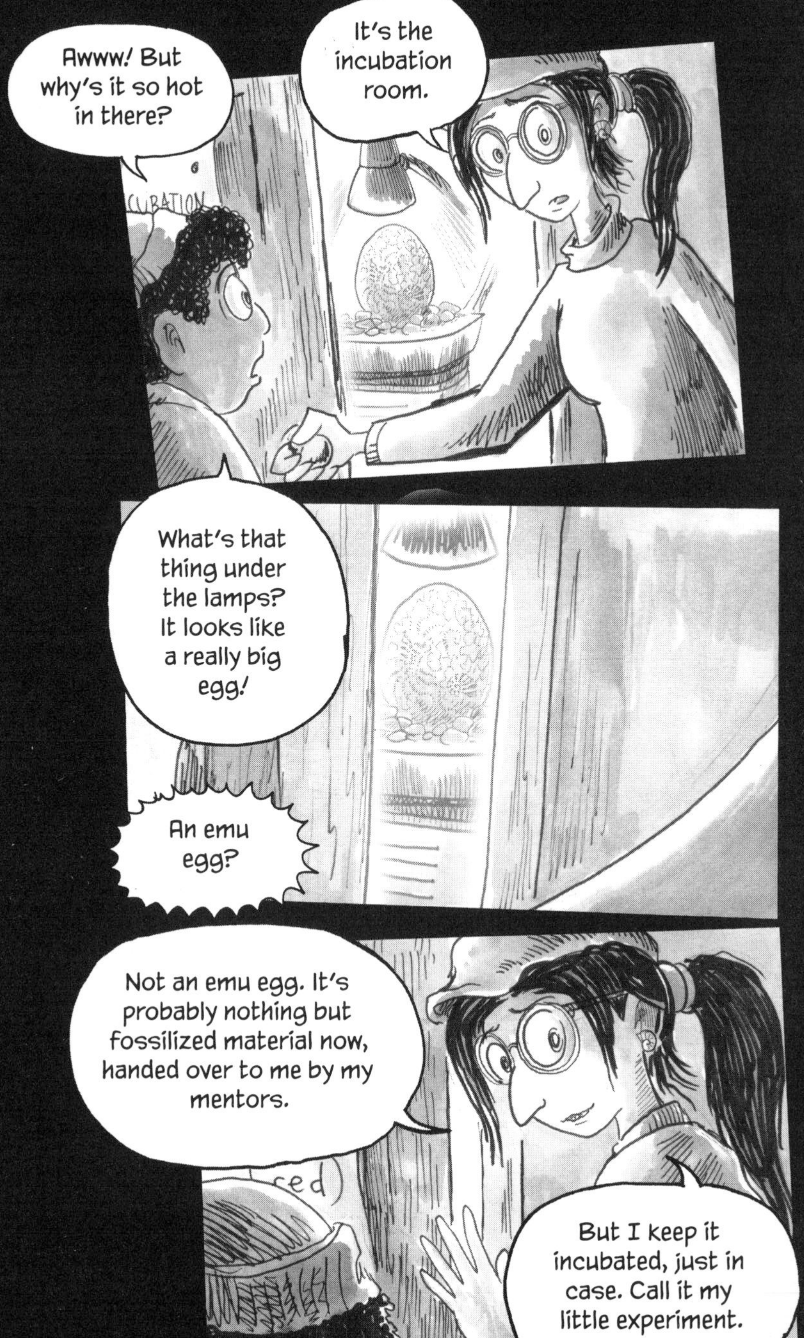
Awww! But why's it so hot in there?
It's the incubation room.
CUBATION
What's that thing under the lamps? It looks like a really big egg!
An emu egg?
Not an emu egg. It's probably nothing but fossilized material now, handed over to me by my mentors.
But I keep it incubated, just in case. Call it my little experiment.

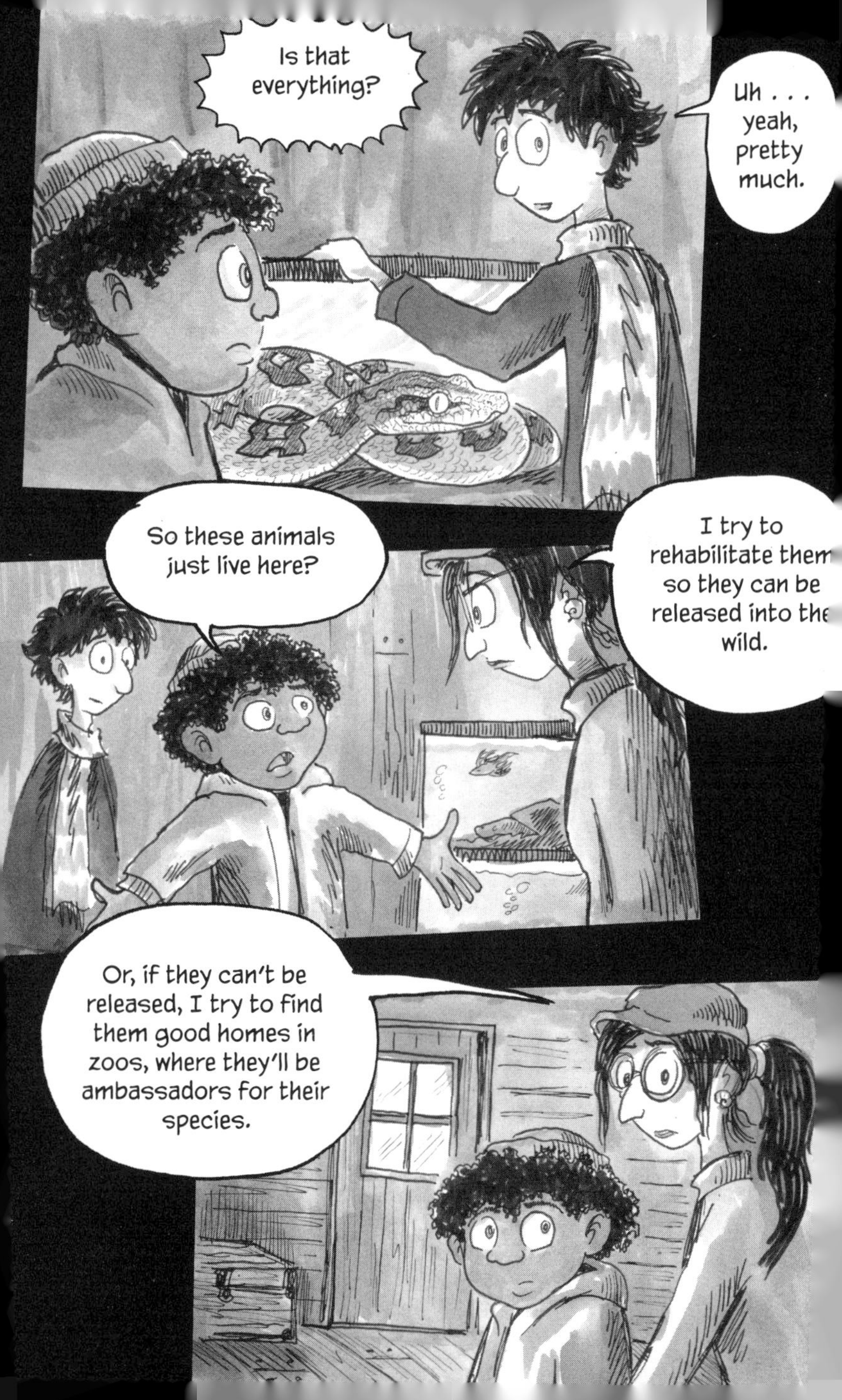
Is that everything?
Uh . . . yeah, pretty much.
So these animals just live here?
I try to rehabilitate them so they can be released into the wild.
Or, if they can't be released, I try to find them good homes in zoos, where they'll be ambassadors for their species.

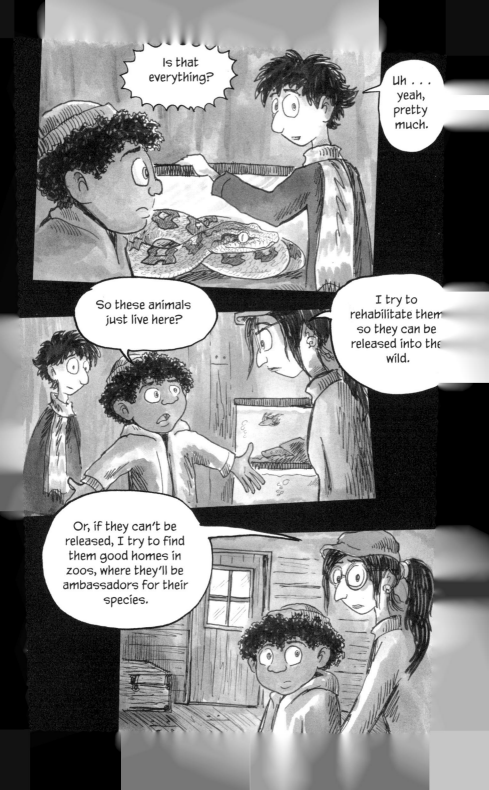

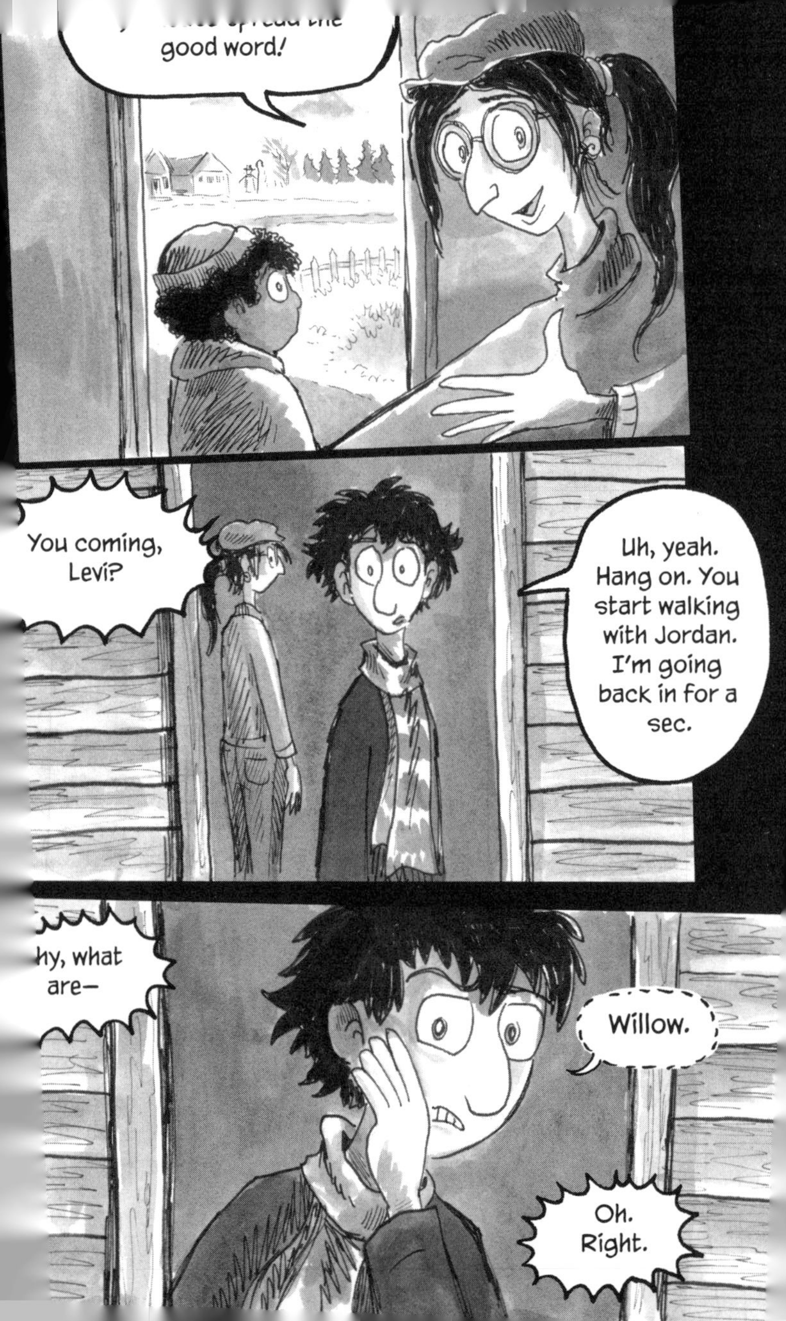
good word!
You coming, Levi?
Uh, yeah. Hang on. You start walking with Jordan. I'm going back in for a sec.
hy, what are—
Willow.
Oh. Right.

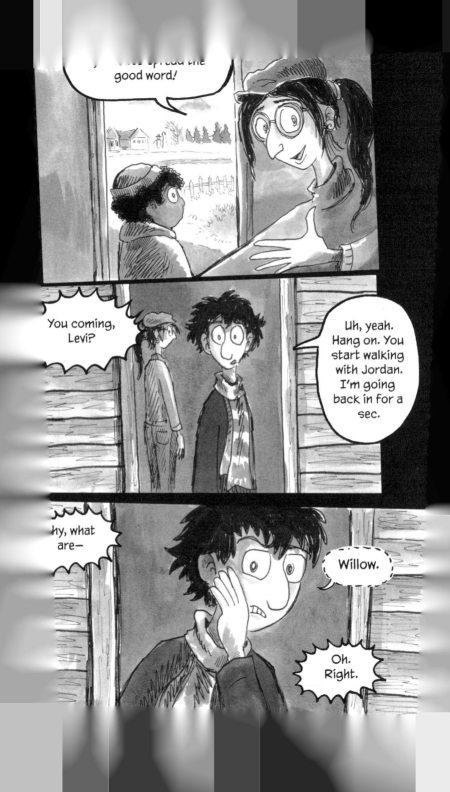

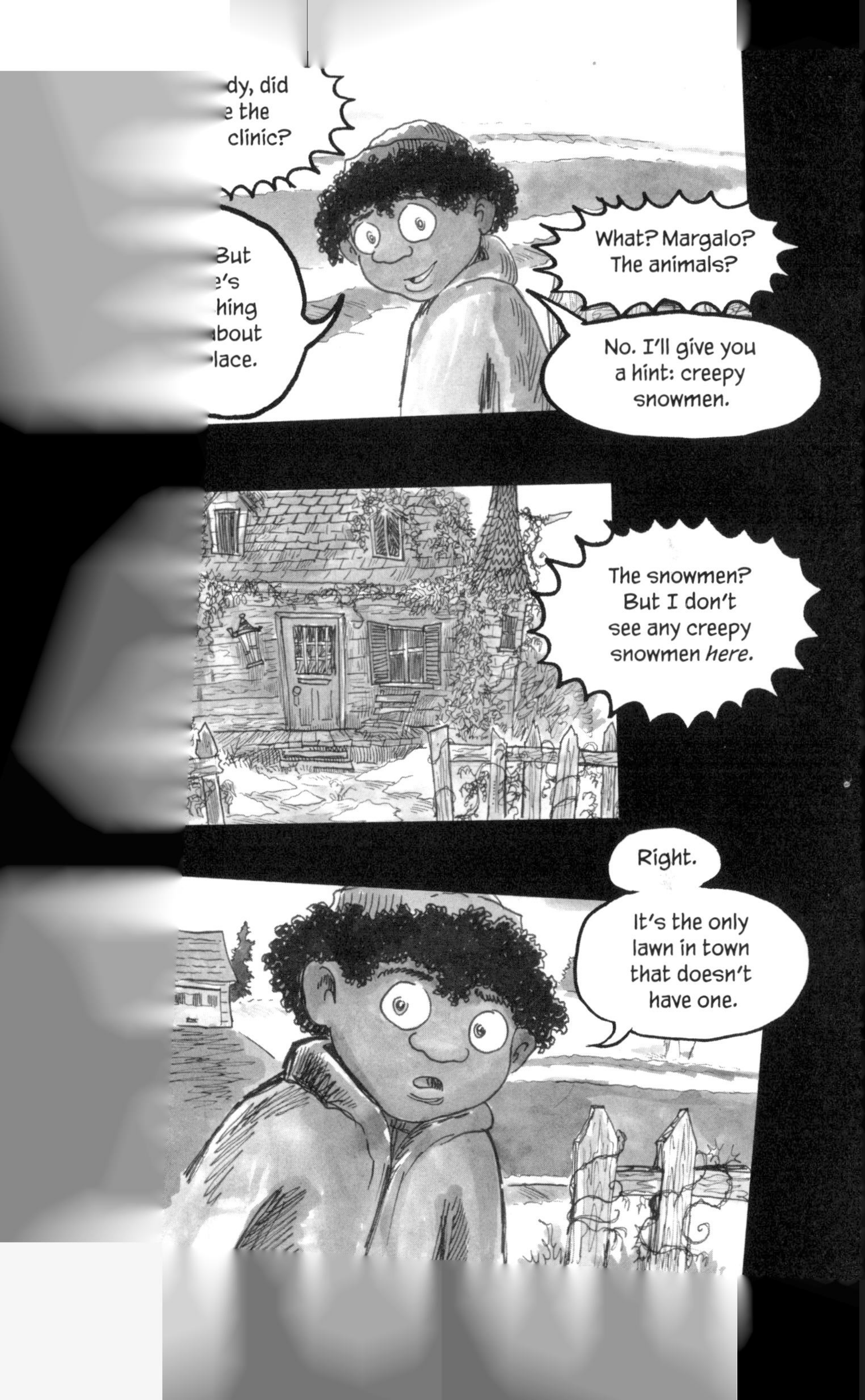
What? Margalo? The animals?
No. I'll give you a hint: creepy snowmen.
The snowmen? But I don't see any creepy snowmen *here*.
Right.
It's the only lawn in town that doesn't have one.

Chapter 6

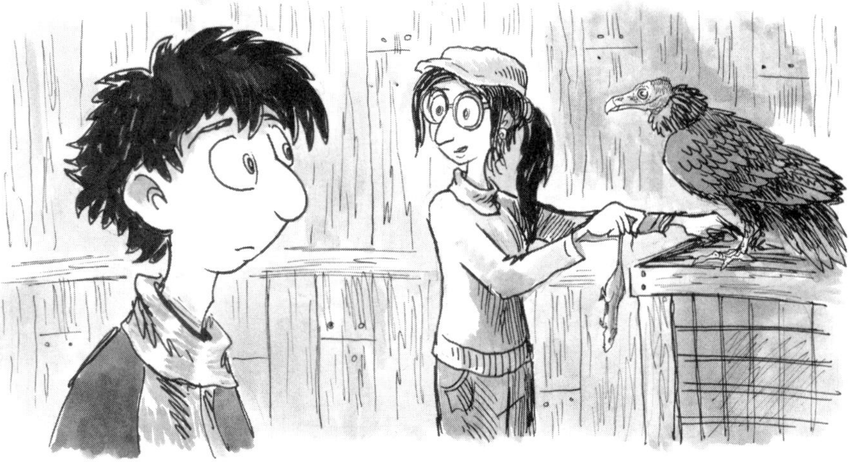

Levi stepped back inside and closed the door.

"Willow is waiting for you," said Margalo. "She's been acting strange lately. I usually let her outside between two and four a.m., when the neighborhood is asleep. But the last few nights she refused to leave the house. Something spooked her. Ask her about it, please. Maybe she'll tell you more than she told me."

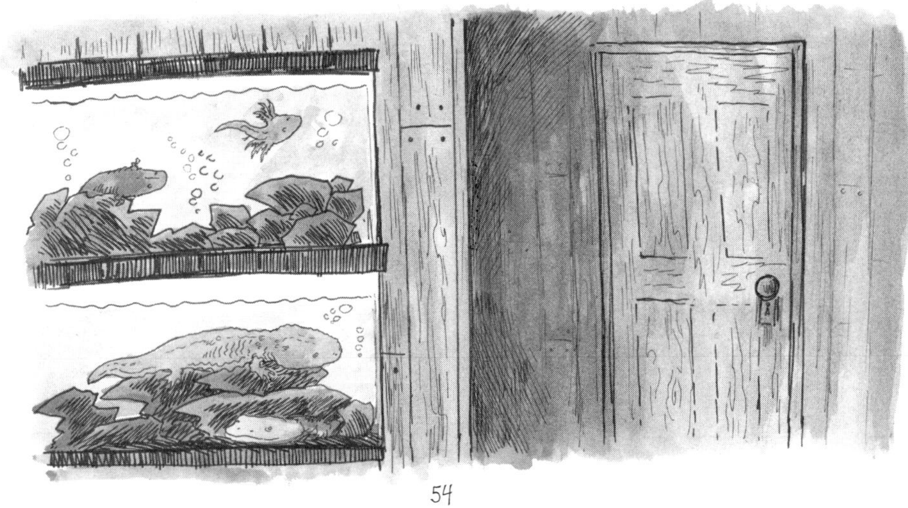

Levi passed the animal pens, the hellbender aquarium, the red-lit incubation room, and reached the cellar. He pried open the heavy door. "Hidey-ho, Willow," he called into the cellar.

Two fluorescent-green orbs gleamed in the darkness below. "Hidey-ho, Levi," said a raspy voice.

Claws clicked up the cellar steps, and the small, spiny thing that called itself Willow appeared in the doorway.

Levi fished a beef jerky strip from his coat pocket. "Brought you something."

Willow delicately sniffed the jerky before snarfing it. Her tongue flickered across her fangs. Levi knelt and ran his hand along her spiny back. He felt her ribs pressing against her leathery skin, but she seemed somehow fuller and healthier than she had been last fall, when he and Kat had first found her—back when she survived by eking out a sad existence on the edge of town, scavenging sick livestock and garbage.

"Still happy here?" he asked.

"Oh yes," said Willow. "Sometimes Willow misses the wild and the hunt, but this is better than the cold. Willow would not have survived another winter."

"And how are your . . . uh, roommates?" Levi asked. He looked past Willow, down into the dark cellar and the large cages with thick wiring—far sturdier than the pens of the vulture and stoat and constrictor in the clinic's main room.

"They give me the creepy-jeepies," said Willow. "But as long as they stay in their cages, they will not harm Little Willow."

"The snow will melt soon," said Levi. "Then you can go explore the woods and fields again with me and Twila and Kat." He stood and pocketed his hands. "Margalo said you've been acting a little strange lately. Is something wrong?"

Willow lowered her head, and her voice became a whisper. "A storm is coming."

"You mean a snowstorm?" said Levi. "It's March. That happens."

Willow fixed him with her fluorescent-green eyes. He shivered—even after six months, he still wasn't used to those eyes.

"This storm will be different." Her spines bristled. "There is a voice."

"A voice? Where?"

"At night." She glanced at the window and the fading light outside. "Listen. Listen close. Does Levi hear it?"

Levi listened. He heard the creak of the rafters . . . the whir of the pipes . . . the burble of the hellbender tank. "No," he said. "What does it sound like?"

"It is a voice like the rumble of a distant storm," whispered Willow. "Like the wind in bare trees. The groan of thick ice."

Levi's brow furrowed. "What does it say?"

Willow's eyes flashed again. "It says . . .
'The harvest is coming.
'*I* am coming.
'I am hungry.'"

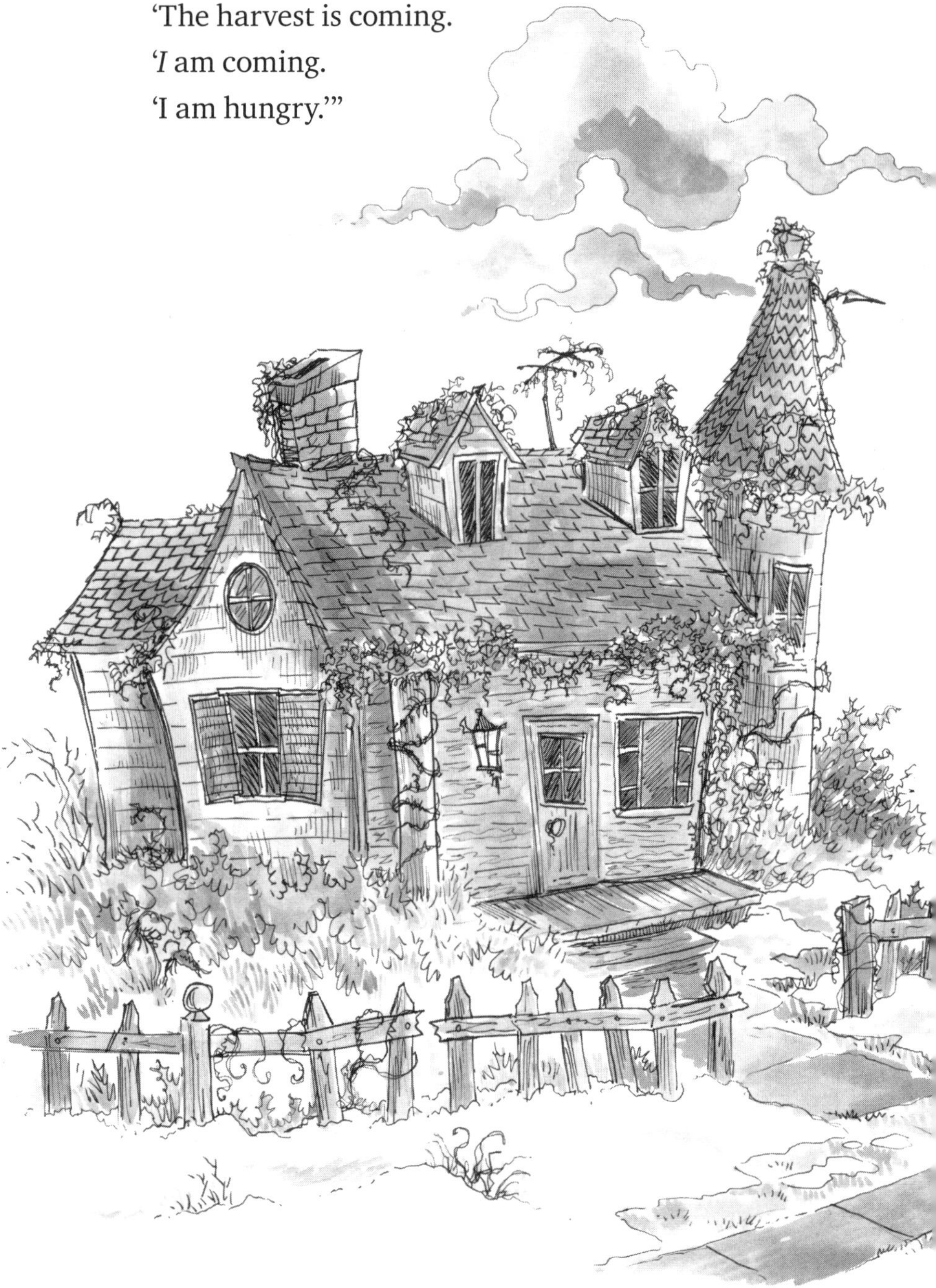

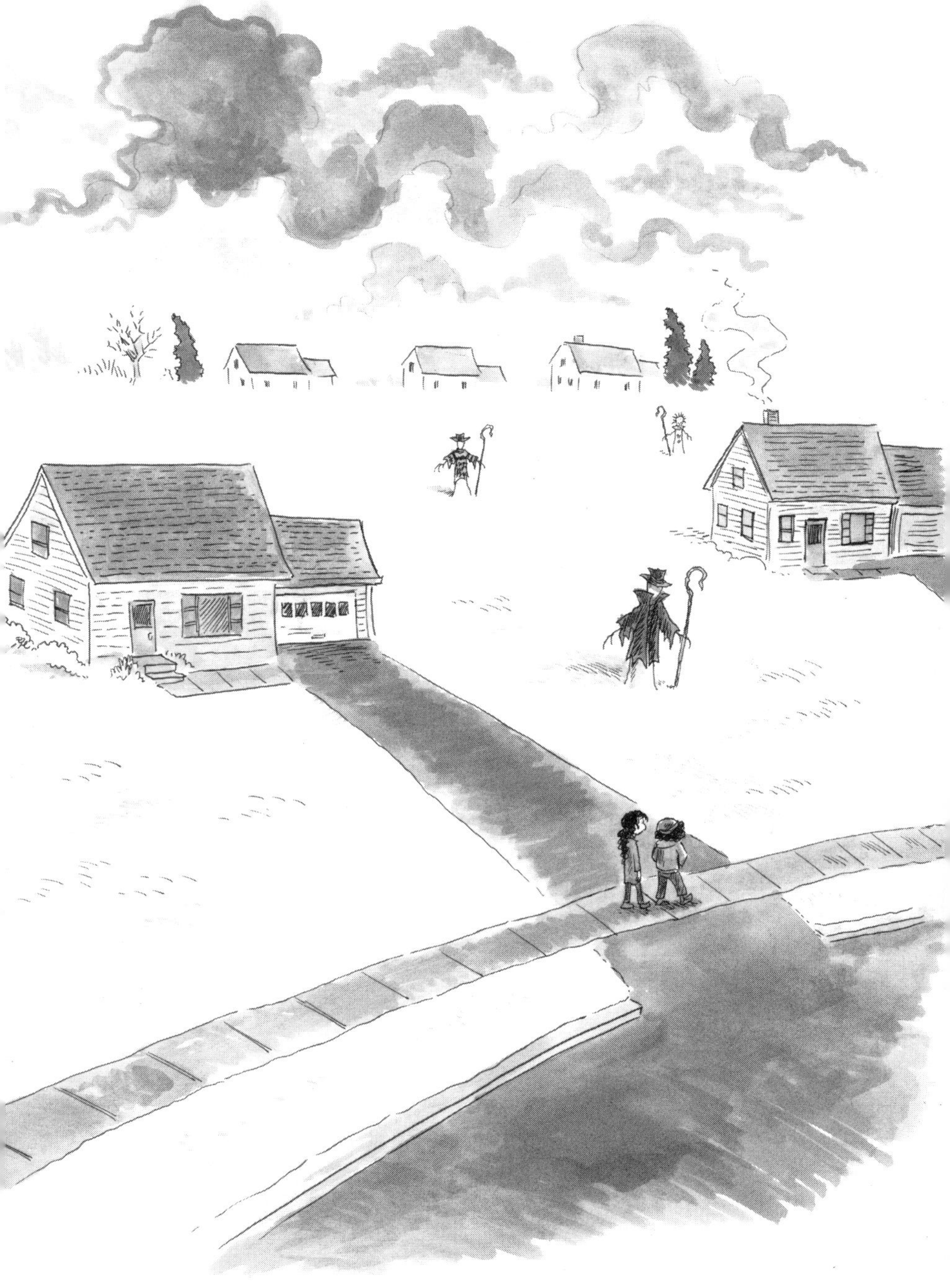

Chapter 7
Margalo's Journal of Strange Creatures Entry #67

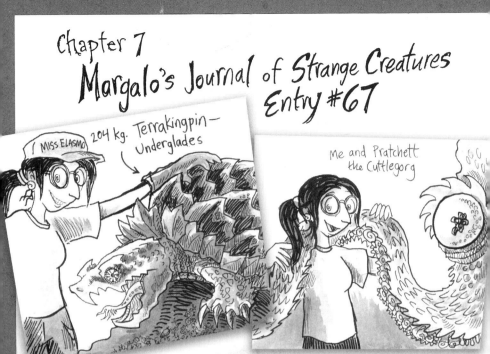

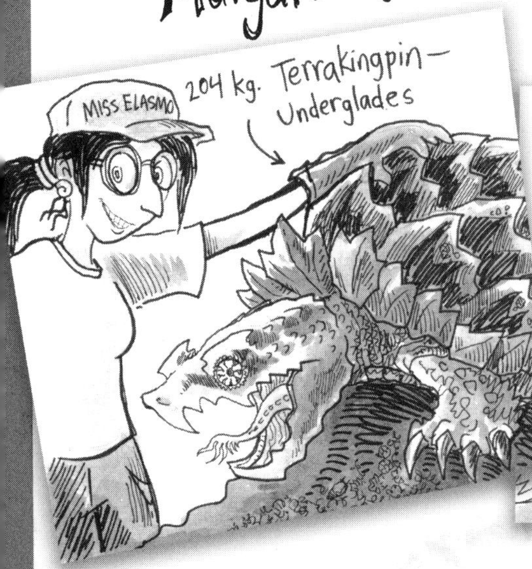
MISS ELASMO
204 kg. Terrakingpin—
Underglades

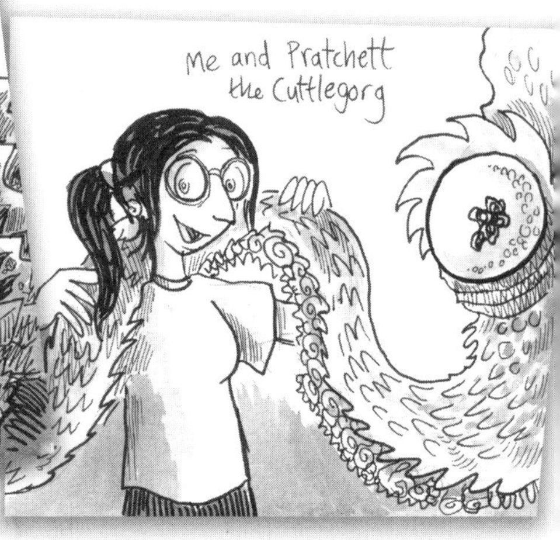
Me and Pratchett
the Cuttlegorg

I've been working with strange and mysterious creatures for over a decade (thanks to the SINISTRAL grant) and during my time as a rehabilitator, I've learned that even the most unnerving lifeforms—what most people would label "monsters"—are misunderstood.

Claws, fangs, and tentacles may not earn points in the "cute" department, but these creatures serve their ecological roles—either within their own habitats or the broader multiverse that we are just beginning to comprehend.

Terrakingpins? Cuttlegorgs? Little Willow, poor lost soul?

Even Charlotte, the most dangerous patient in my rogues' gallery, plays a role in overall sustainability.

But there is one creature—assuming it can be classified as a creature—that I cannot rationalize: the Boojum.

Just what is a Boojum? No one at SINISTRAL can fully agree. Not of this world, it seems, and therefore I consider it an invasive species or alien pathogen—unchecked and potentially very destructive.

What we do know:

A Boojum is non-corporeal, at least by earthly standards, only taking physical shape when it's necessary.

A Boojum is able to manipulate matter in ways we have only started to understand.

But a Boojum is most interested in the human mind—twisting thoughts, preying on emotions, realizing fear.

"The Boojum of Halfrock Swamp"
Pen & Ink Illustration
by J.M.York

There seem to be two thought schools at SINISTRAL regarding a Boojum's true nature:

Hypothesis #1: The Boojum is a being that exists outside our plane of existence. Extradimensional, if you will. It can perceive us and our world, but our earthly senses are incapable of viewing it. It is like a fisherman peering down at the blind invertebrates in a tidepool—when the urge strikes, it reaches into our reality, our tidepool, and snatches an unsuspecting periwinkle. Or two. Or many. Maybe for sustenance. Maybe for sport.

Hypothesis #2: The Boojum is a paranormal creature (a demon or evil spirit) and its power relies on collective human belief or mindset.

Humans have, for millennia, worshiped and paid sacrifices to spirits or gods. Whether or not these deities literally exist is open for debate, but there is power behind the very idea—enough power that farmers would sacrifice lives (animal and human) to ensure a bountiful harvest.

Yet nobody worships a Boojum. Few are even aware they exist. But can a mindset summon a deity? If a whole community dedicates its thoughts to law and order and stability, can that collective mindset (and resulting paranoia) take shape as an evil presence? . . . A Boojum?

As a scientist, I lean toward hypothesis #1. Regardless, we have been aware of a Boojum haunting Cowslip Grove for at least several years.

Last year three children and one very brave Willow faced it and emerged triumphant.

But suppose the Boojum they bested was just a larva, capable of only basic mind and matter manipulation?

Willow thinks there is a stronger presence here in Cowslip Grove. A "Boojum King," she calls it.

I hope, for the sake of us all, that she is mistaken.

Photo taken by me, Margalo M. 3-17, 7:45 PM

Chapter 8

8:20 A.M., PERIOD 1—SCIENCE LAB

"Kat," Ms. Padilla said, "leave the window alone. You're supposed to be making observations."

"Right," said Kat. "I'm *observing* the storm clouds."

"Observations about the *ant formicarium,*" Ms. Padilla finished. "And don't worry about the clouds. There isn't supposed to be a storm today."

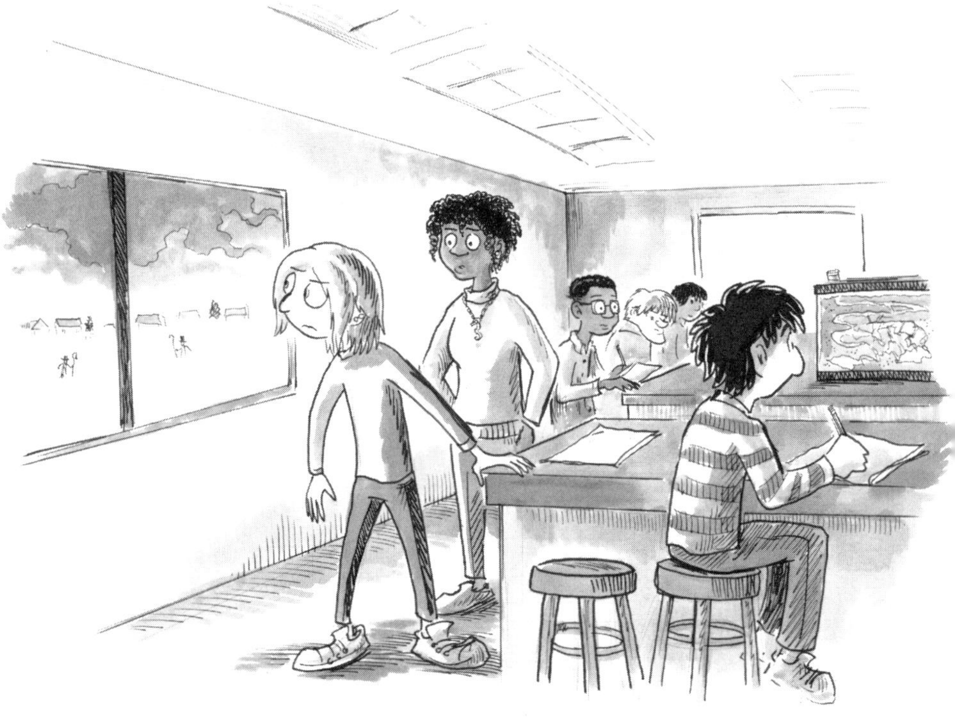

Kat moaned and trudged back to the lab tables.

"It's actually pretty cool," Levi said, moving his arm to show his sketched diagram of the ant colony labyrinth.

Robbie Munn peered over Levi's shoulder. "You should hang out with Donte's little brother. He likes ants, too. You guys could compare ant notes and put ants down your pants or whatever ant scientists do."

"He *does* hang out with my little brother," said Donte. "They went to that weird wildlife place yesterday. Jordan wouldn't shut up about it last night."

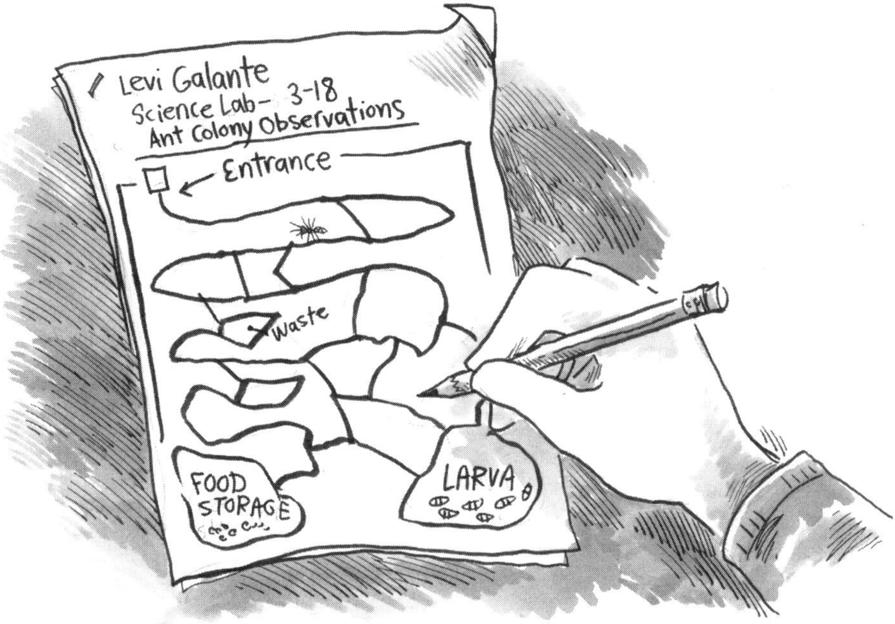
Levi Galante
Science Lab- 3-18
Ant Colony Observations
Entrance
Waste
FOOD STORAGE
LARVA

Levi blushed and focused on his sketch.

"Donte, Robbie, let Levi do his work," interrupted Ms. Padilla. "And speaking of work, neither of you have started your observation packets."

"So?" muttered Robbie. "Ants are stupid." He leaned across the lab table and waved his hand in front of the formicarium's glass. "See? They don't even know I'm here!"

"Ants perceive the world differently from us," said Ms. Padilla. "They're perfectly adapted to their own habitat."

Kat squinted at the ants. "Poor little things. They're missing out on a big, strange world just beyond their tiny home."

"Can we give them something to react to?" asked Donte. "I got some jalapeño chips in my backpack. Let's put one down the feeding tube!"

"No, Donte," said Ms. Padilla.

"Or how about some belly-button lint!" said Robbie. He lifted up his shirt. "I got plenty to spare!"

"Robbie Munn, do *not* stick belly-button lint down the formicarium feeding tube," said Ms. Padilla flatly.

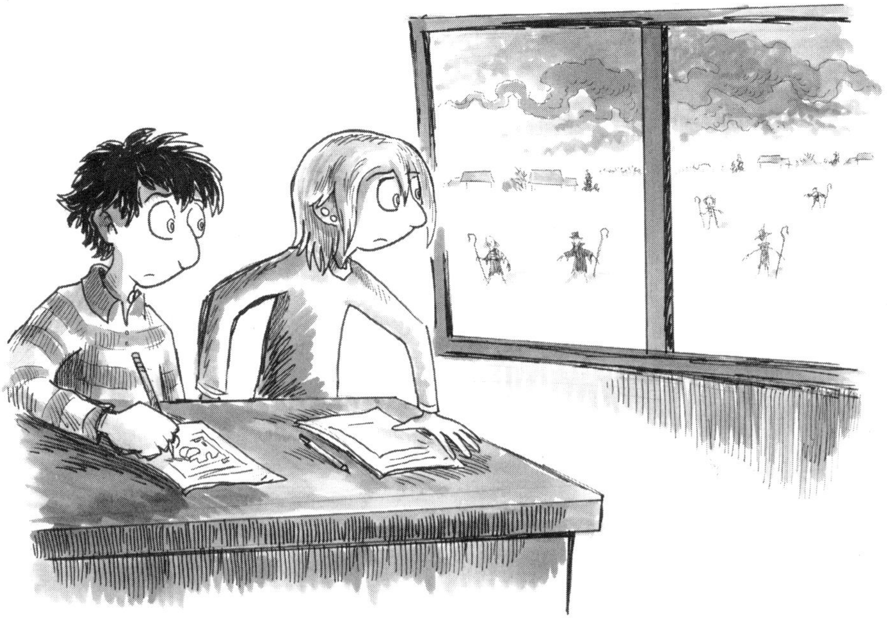

“Doofuses,” Kat muttered.

Levi continued sketching his diagram, but spared a moment to glance out the window.

Kat was right. The sky was very dark.

And had there been so many snowmen on the school lawn yesterday?

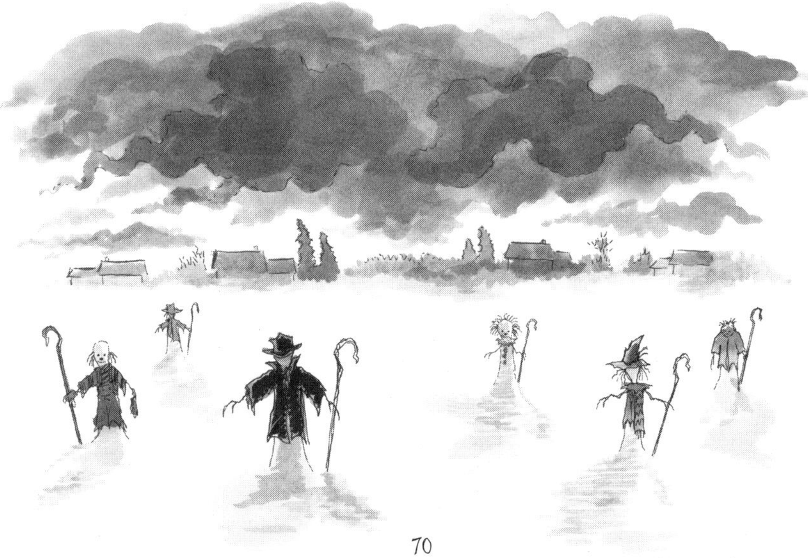

"Ugh. How can they call this food?" Kat grumbled as she plopped her lunch tray next to Levi's lunchbox.

"If you don't like the school lunches, you could always pack lunches from home," Levi said.

"Nope. I relish a challenge," said Kat as she prodded something lumpy and gelatinous with her fork. "If I can survive school lunches, I can survive anything. Call it training for the zombie apocalypse."

The school's walls suddenly gave a nerve-shriveling creak. The noisy cafeteria fell silent.

"The wind!" Donte said. He pointed to the windows. "It's getting bad out!"

"Snow day!" Robbie Munn cheered. "They'll send us home early!"

"No one's going home early!" barked Mrs. Robacher, the lunch monitor.

"But it's a blizzard!" Donte countered. "It's dangerous to keep us here!"

"Nonsense," sniffed Mrs. Robacher. "It would be more dangerous to send the buses out in this flurry. It'll pass within the hour, in plenty of time for safe dismissal. There's nothing to—"

The lights flickered, and the entire cafeteria was plunged into darkness.

Another flicker, then the lights came back a second later and the lunchroom filled with screams and cheers.

"The power!" Robbie gave a mock shriek. "We're gonna die!"

"Robbie! Donte! Stop it!" Mrs. Robacher bellowed. "We are NOT losing power!"

Mr. Chuck the custodian stopped mopping up a puddle of unidentified goo and glanced out the window. "I dunno. That's some strong wind." Mrs. Robacher shot him a poisonous look, and he cleared his throat sheepishly. "I mean, uh, we'll be fine. Even if we do lose power, the school has a backup generator."

The lunchroom noise level gradually returned to its usual buzz, the howling outside temporarily forgotten.

The lights flickered again.

"Ms. Padilla!" whined Lydia Schnell. "This doesn't feel safe!"

"The school is the safest place to be during a storm," Ms. Padilla said.

"But it's fifteen minutes until dismissal. They're sending the buses out in *that?*" Donte gestured to the classroom window. The world beyond the glass was a white void.

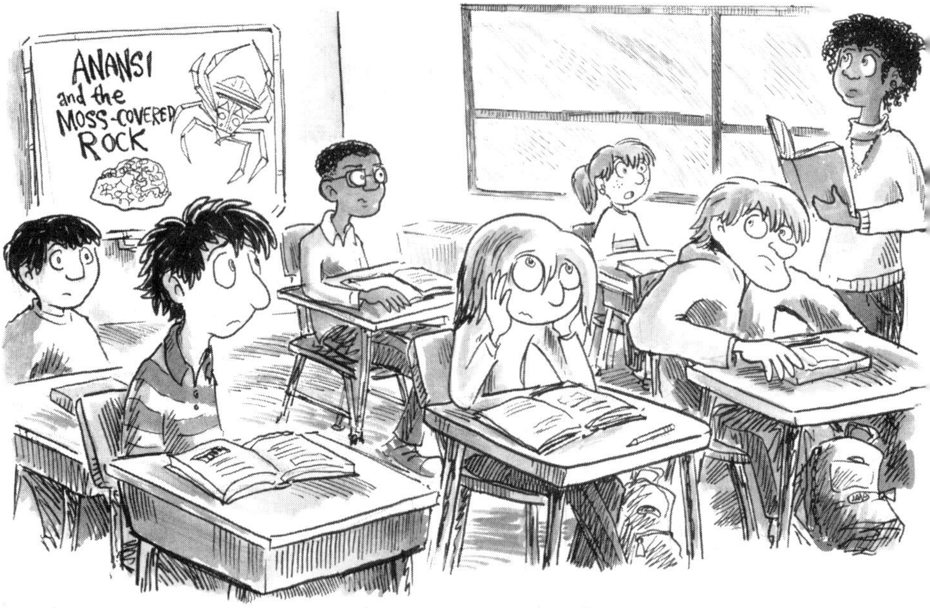
ANANSI
and the
MOSS-COVERED
ROCK

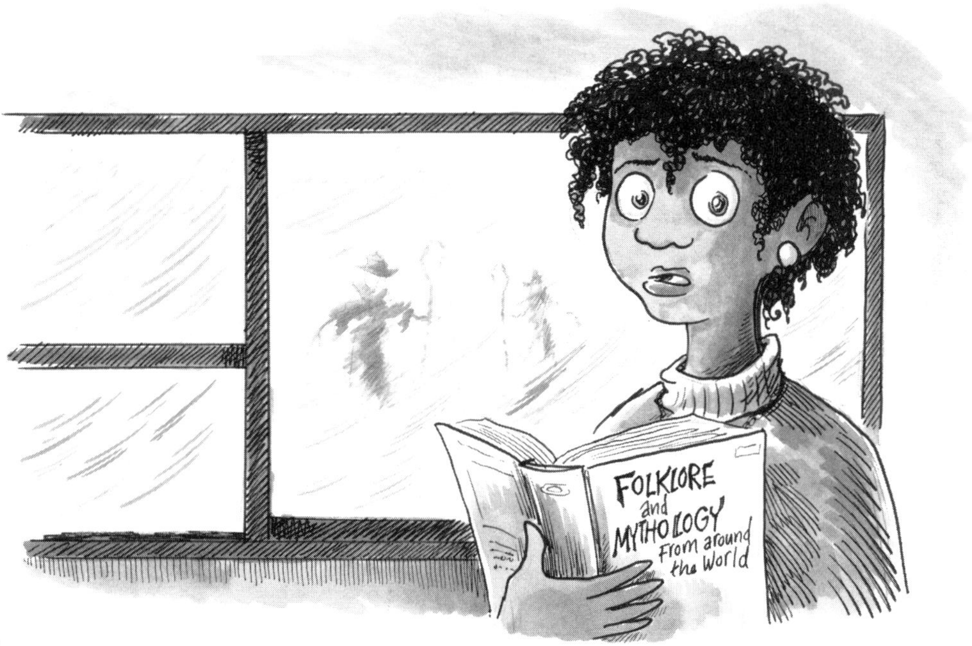
FOLKLORE and MYTHOLOGY From around the World

"I think the best thing we can do right now is keep our minds off the storm," said Ms. Padilla. "Everyone take out their *Folklore and Mythology* textbooks and turn to page two hundred eighty-seven."

"Can't we just end early?" groaned Robbie Munn.

"Not with the state social studies exams just around the corner," said Ms. Padilla.

"Test, test, test," grumbled Kat. "That's all the school ever cares about."

"Look on the bright side," said Ms. Padilla. "At least the material is interesting. You of all people should enjoy learning about mythological monsters, Kat."

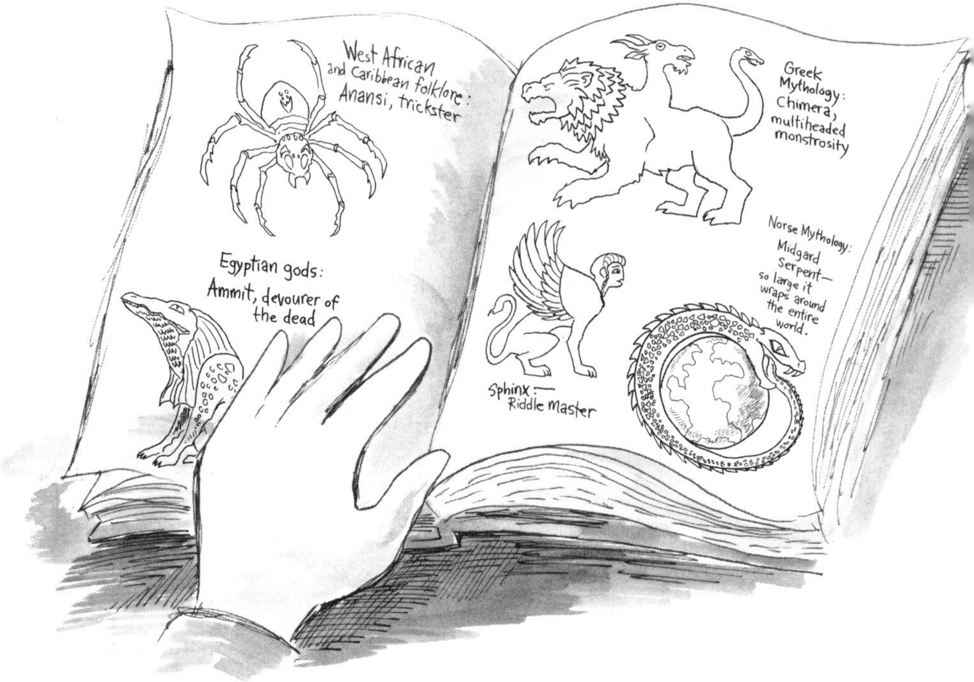
West African and Caribbean folklore: Anansi, trickster
Egyptian gods: Ammit, devourer of the dead
Greek Mythology: Chimera, multiheaded monstrosity
Norse Mythology: Midgard Serpent—so large it wraps around the entire world.
Sphinx: Riddle master

They were interrupted by the squeal of the loudspeaker. Mr. Huff's voice crackled over the intercom.

"Attention, students and faculty. Due to the weather, there will be a slight delay with the buses. We ask that students remain with their homeroom classes until further notice."

Donte slapped his desk. "I knew it! They should have sent us home hours ago! Now we're stuck here!"

"Mr. Huff said it's only a delay," said Ms. Padilla.

"How long?" moaned Lydia Schnell.

“Long enough for us to finish our reading,” said Ms. Padilla primly.

The class groaned.

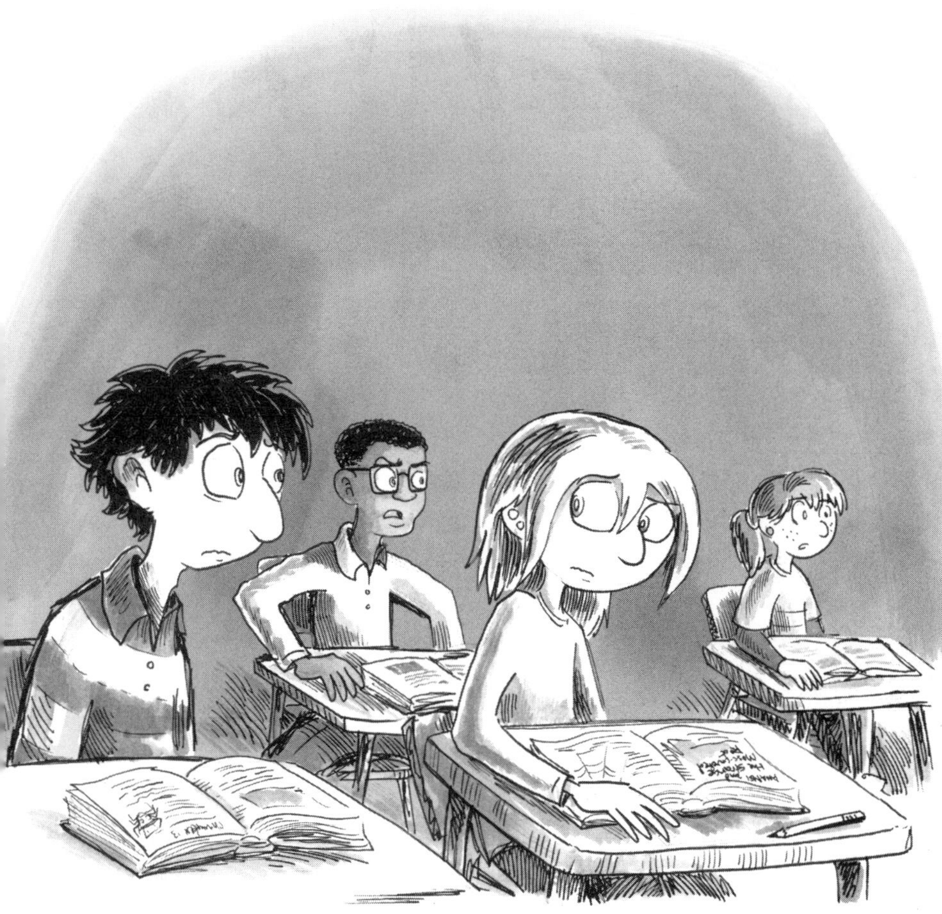

Chapter 9

FOOTAGE RECOVERED FROM KAT BOMBARD'S PHONE

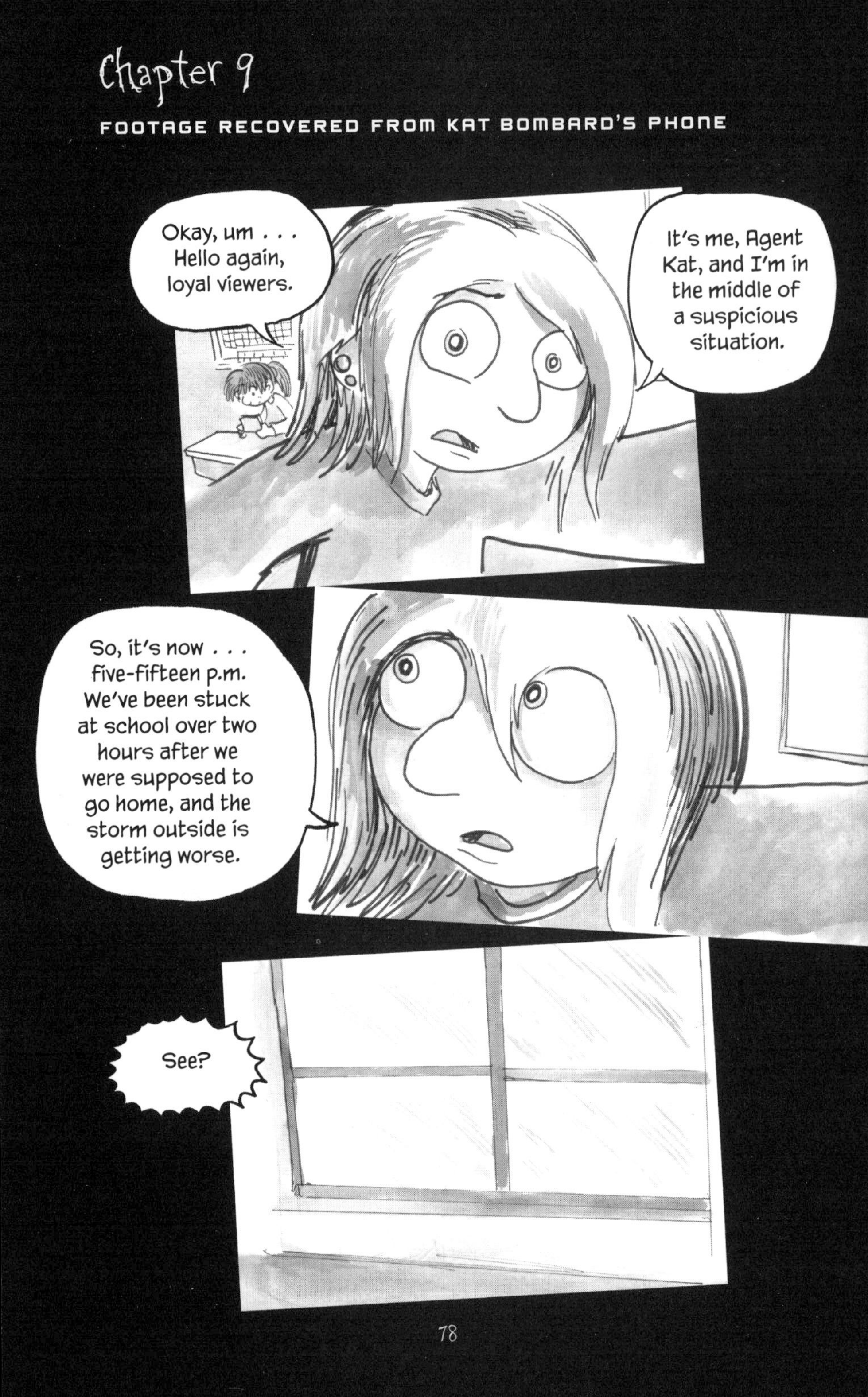

Okay, um . . . Hello again, loyal viewers.
It's me, Agent Kat, and I'm in the middle of a suspicious situation.
So, it's now . . . five-fifteen p.m. We've been stuck at school over two hours after we were supposed to go home, and the storm outside is getting worse.
See?

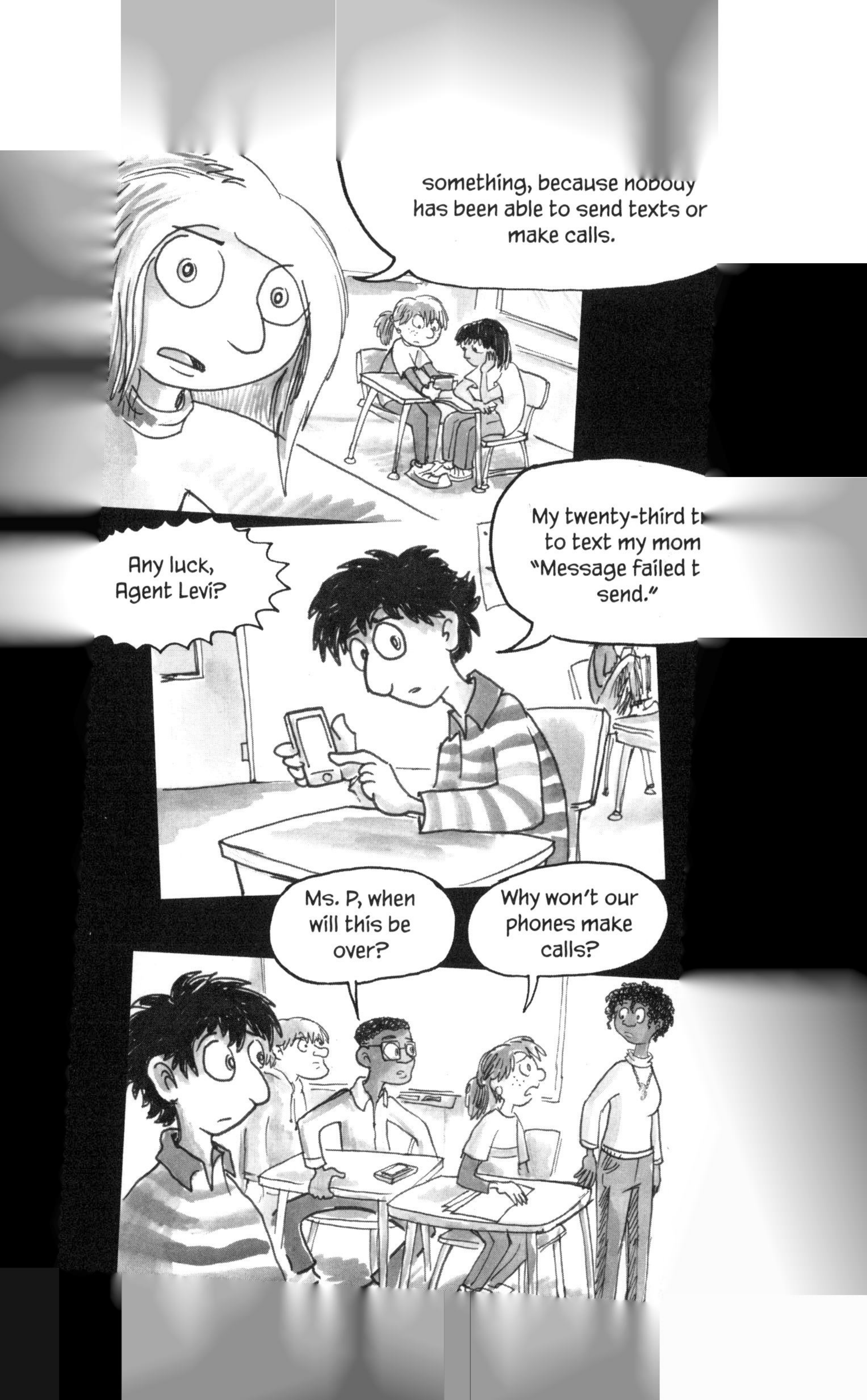

something, because nobody has been able to send texts or make calls.
Any luck, Agent Levi?
My twenty-third
to text my mom
"Message failed
send."
Ms. P, when will this be over?
Why won't our phones make calls?

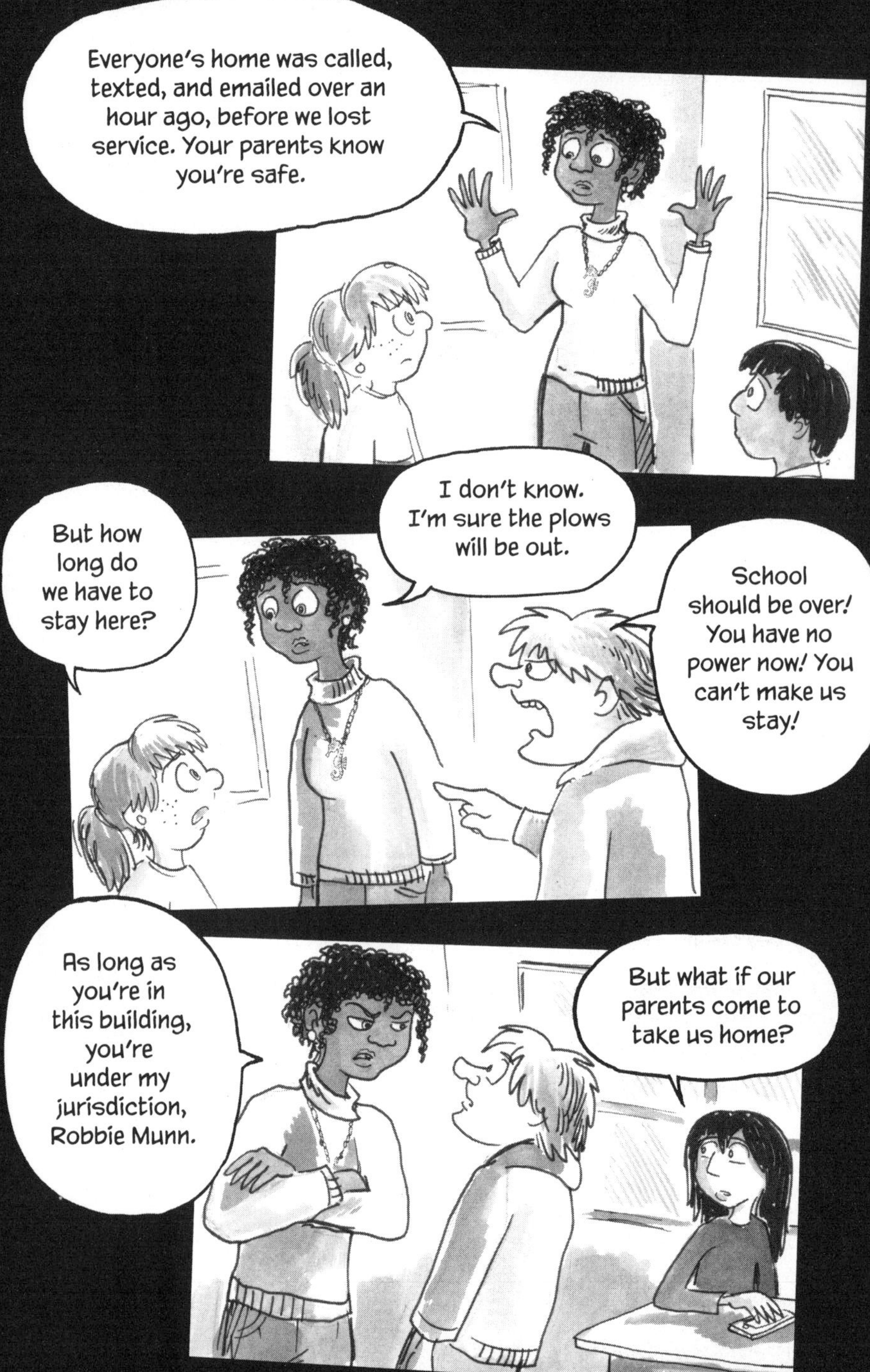
Everyone's home was called, texted, and emailed over an hour ago, before we lost service. Your parents know you're safe.
But how long do we have to stay here?
I don't know. I'm sure the plows will be out.
School should be over! You have no power now! You can't make us stay!
As long as you're in this building, you're under my jurisdiction, Robbie Munn.
But what if our parents come to take us home?

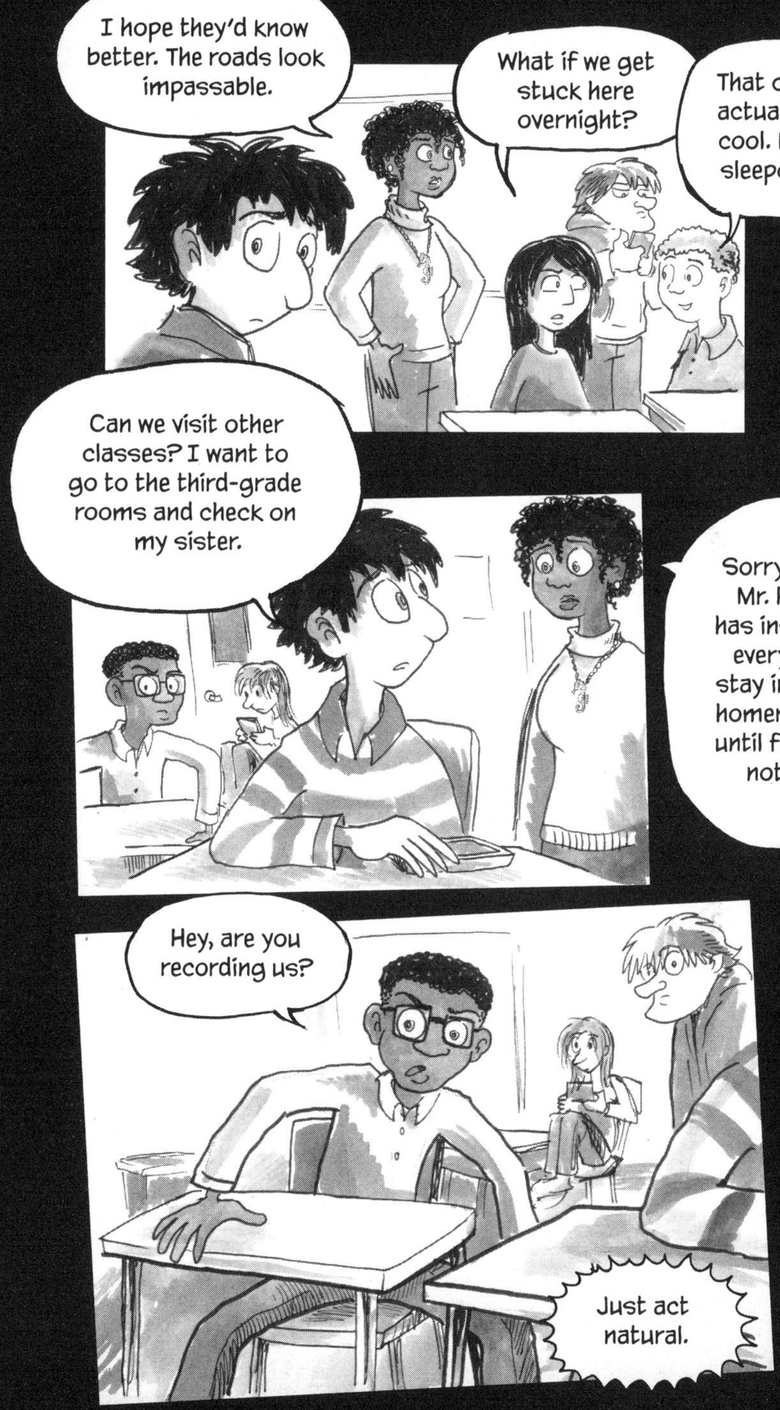
I hope they'd know better. The roads look impassable.
What if we get stuck here overnight?
That could actually be cool. A big sleepover!
Can we visit other classes? I want to go to the third-grade rooms and check on my sister.
Sorry, Levi. Mr. Huff has insisted everyone stay in their homerooms until further notice.
Hey, are you recording us?
Just act natural.

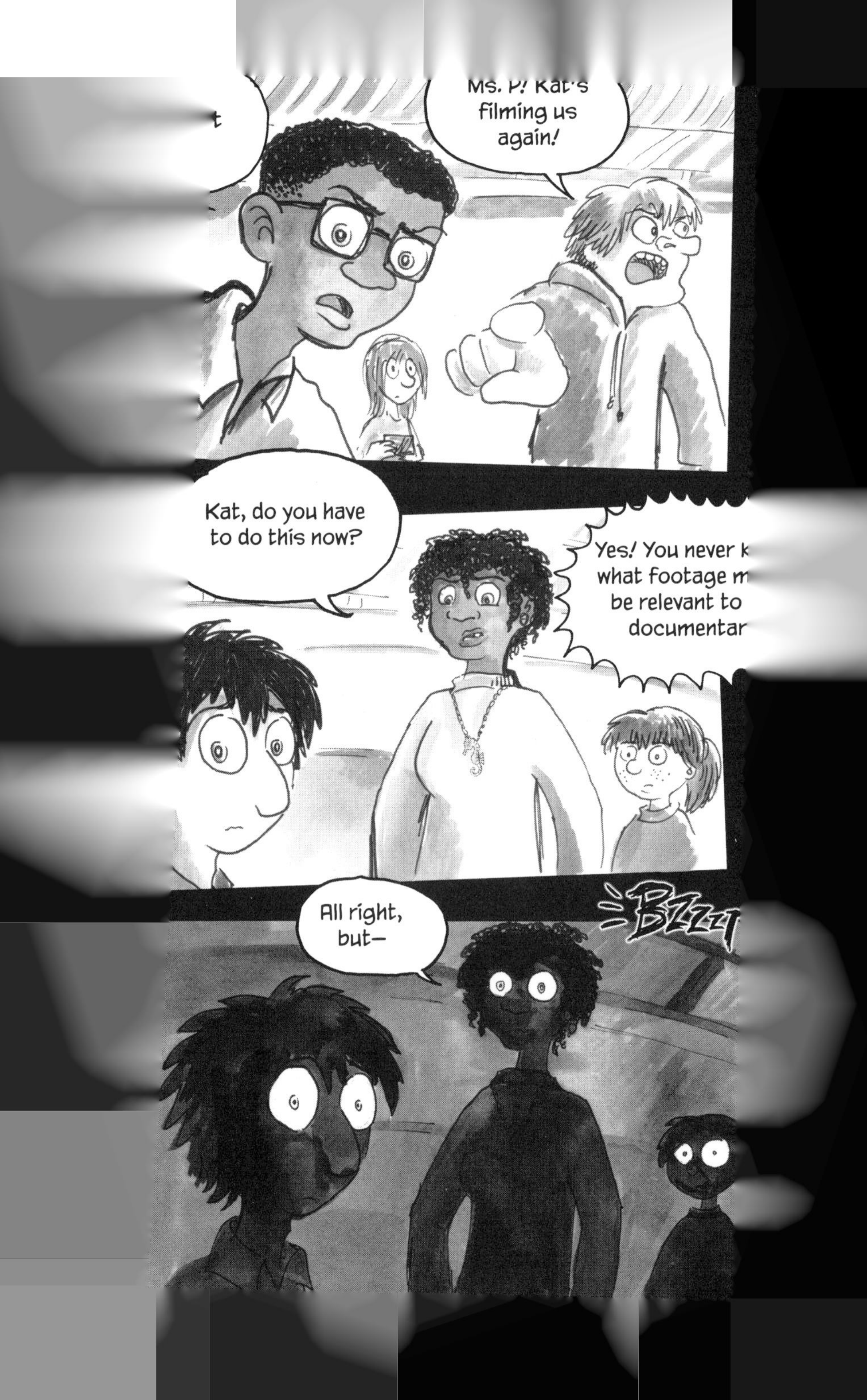
Ms. P! Kat's filming us again!
Kat, do you have to do this now?
Yes! You never
what footage
be relevant to
All right, but—

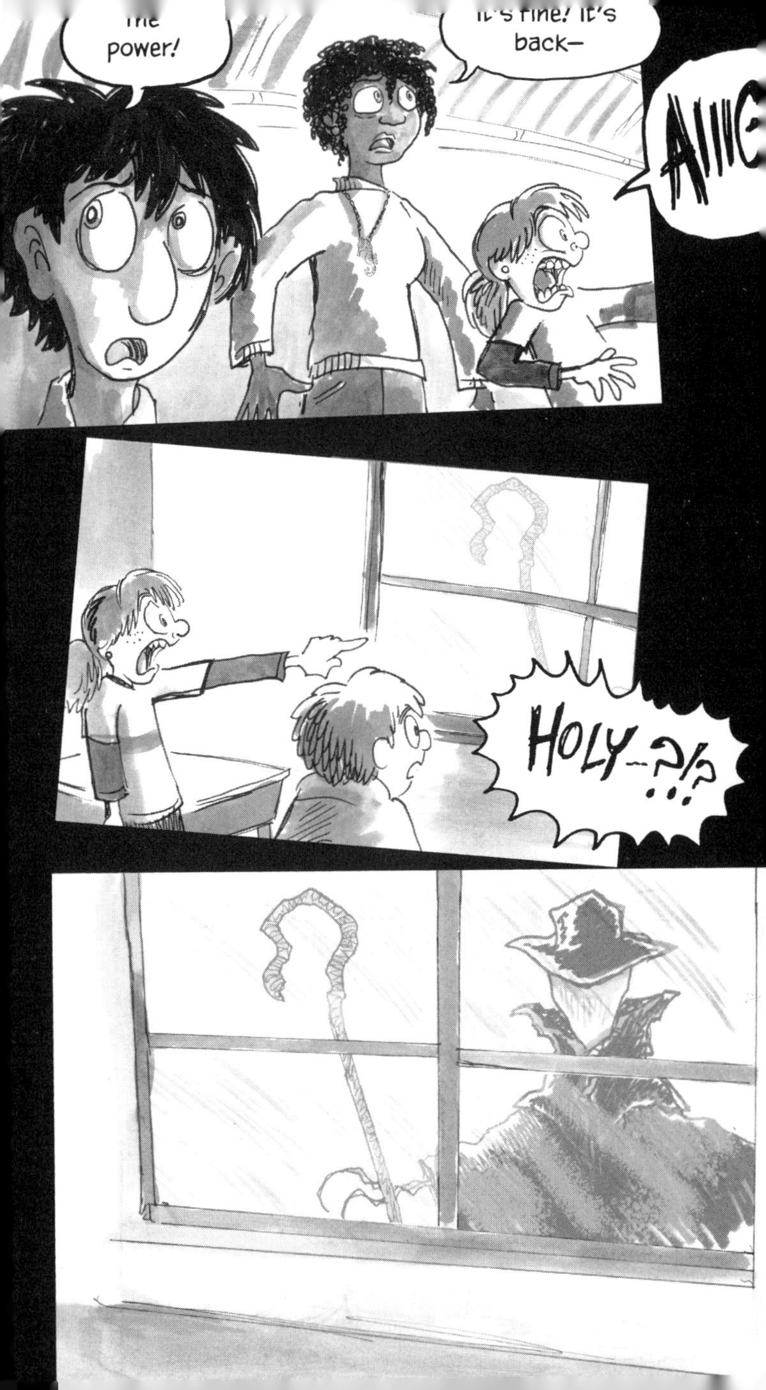

power!
it's fine! It's back—
AIIIE
HOLY--?!?!

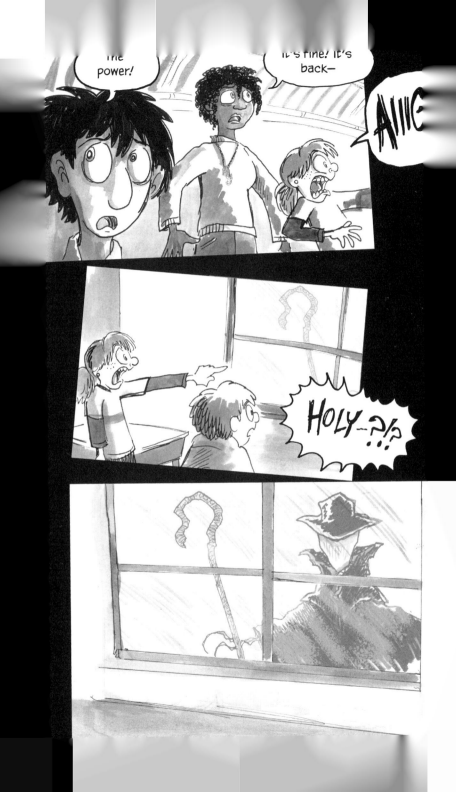

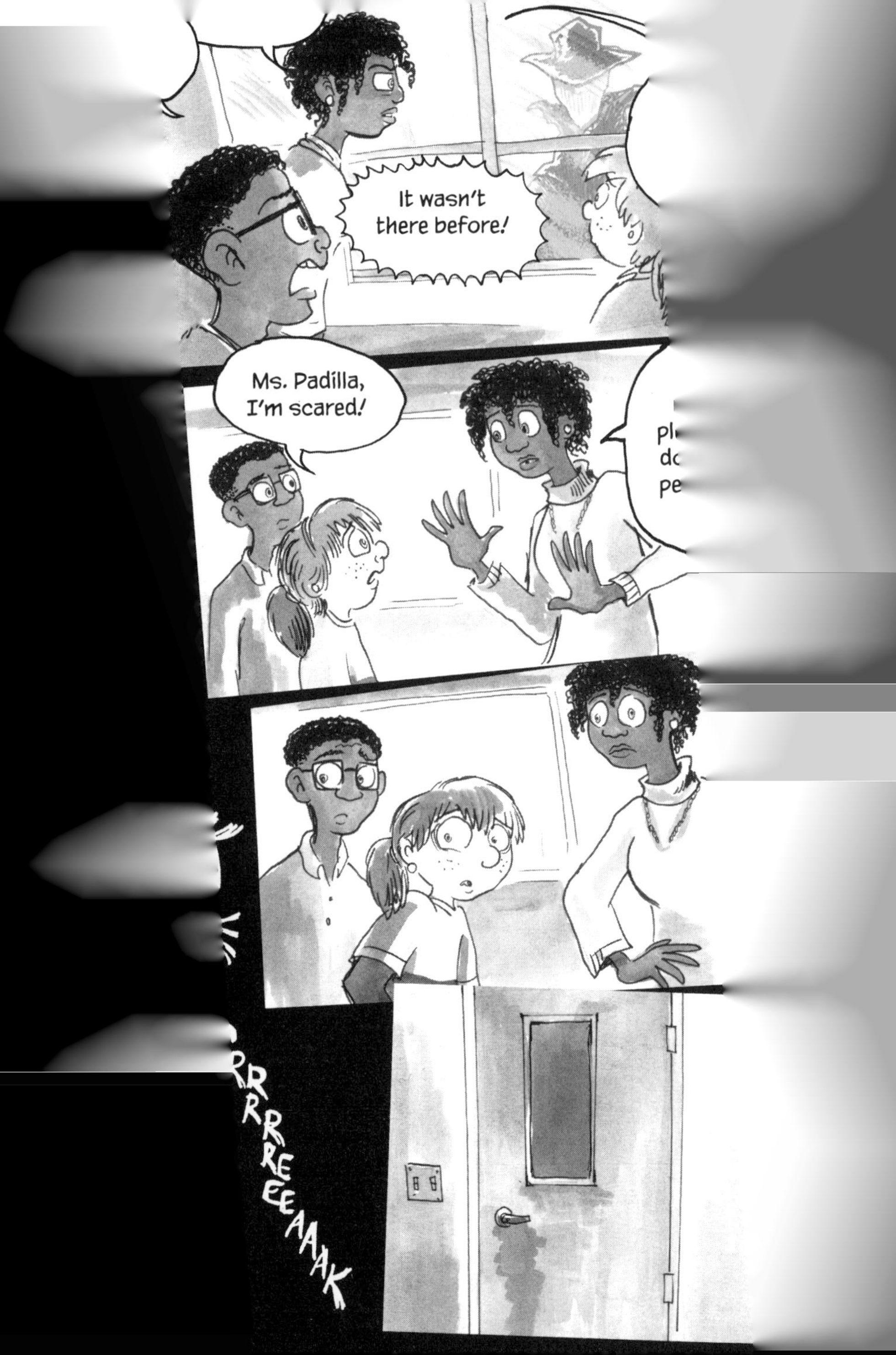
It wasn't there before!
Ms. Padilla, I'm scared!
RRRREEEAAAK

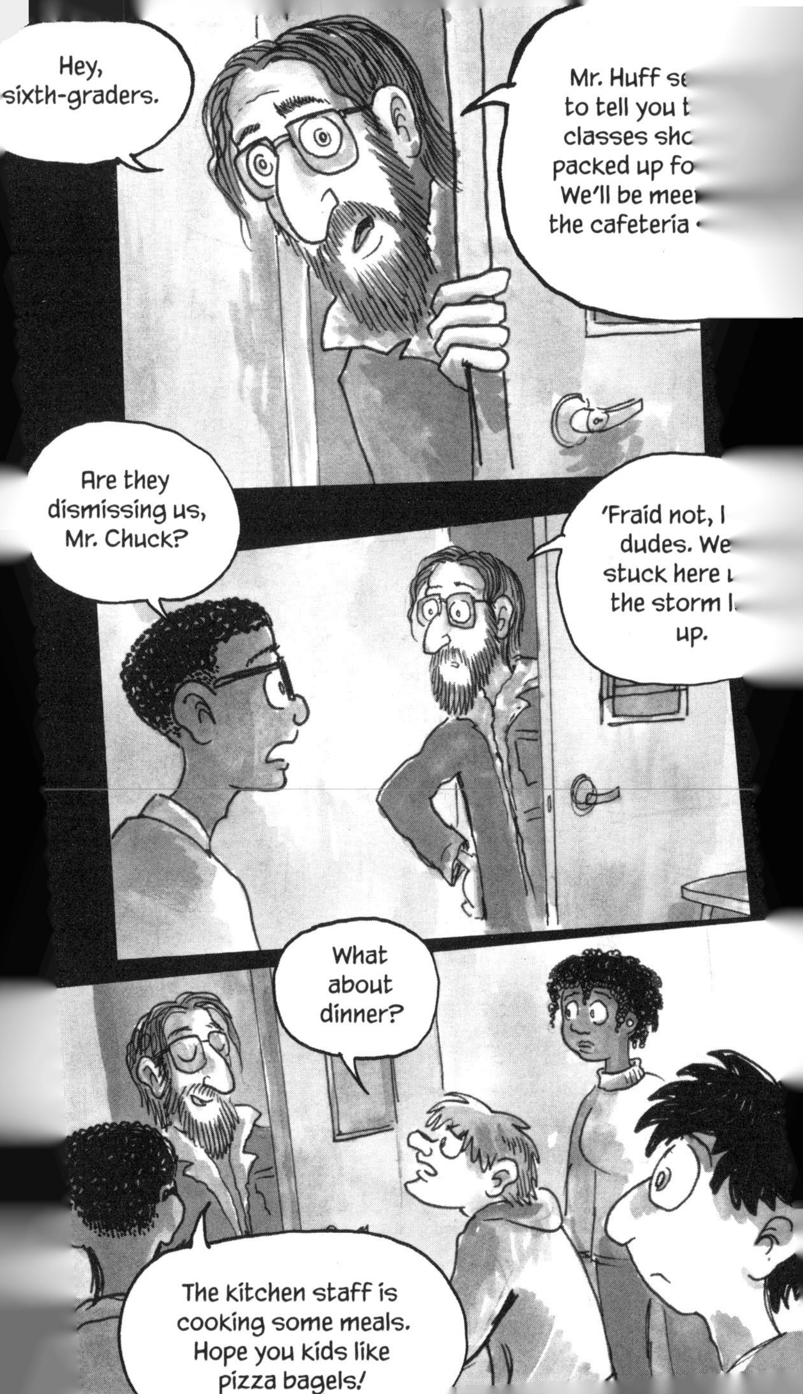
Hey, sixth-graders.
Mr. Huff se to tell you t classes sho packed up fo We'll be mee the cafeteria
Are they dismissing us, Mr. Chuck?
'Fraid not, dudes. We stuck here the storm up.
What about dinner?
The kitchen staff is cooking some meals. Hope you kids like pizza bagels!

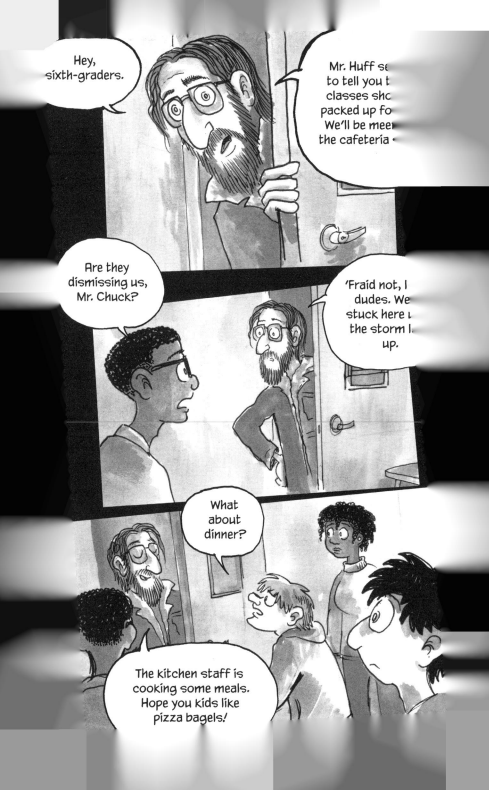

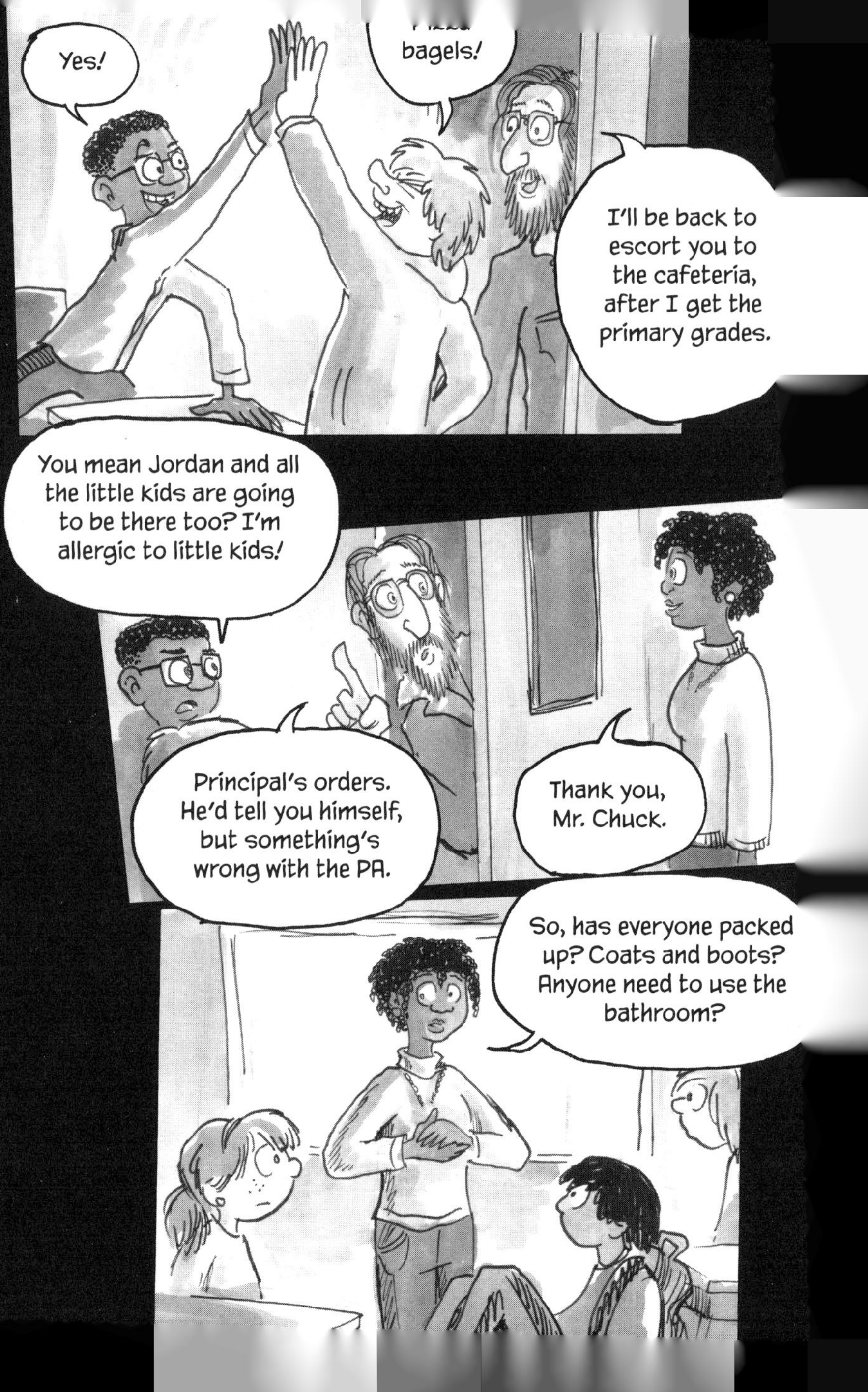
Yes!
bagels!
I'll be back to escort you to the cafeteria, after I get the primary grades.
You mean Jordan and all the little kids are going to be there too? I'm allergic to little kids!
Principal's orders. He'd tell you himself, but something's wrong with the PA.
Thank you, Mr. Chuck.
So, has everyone packed up? Coats and boots? Anyone need to use the bathroom?

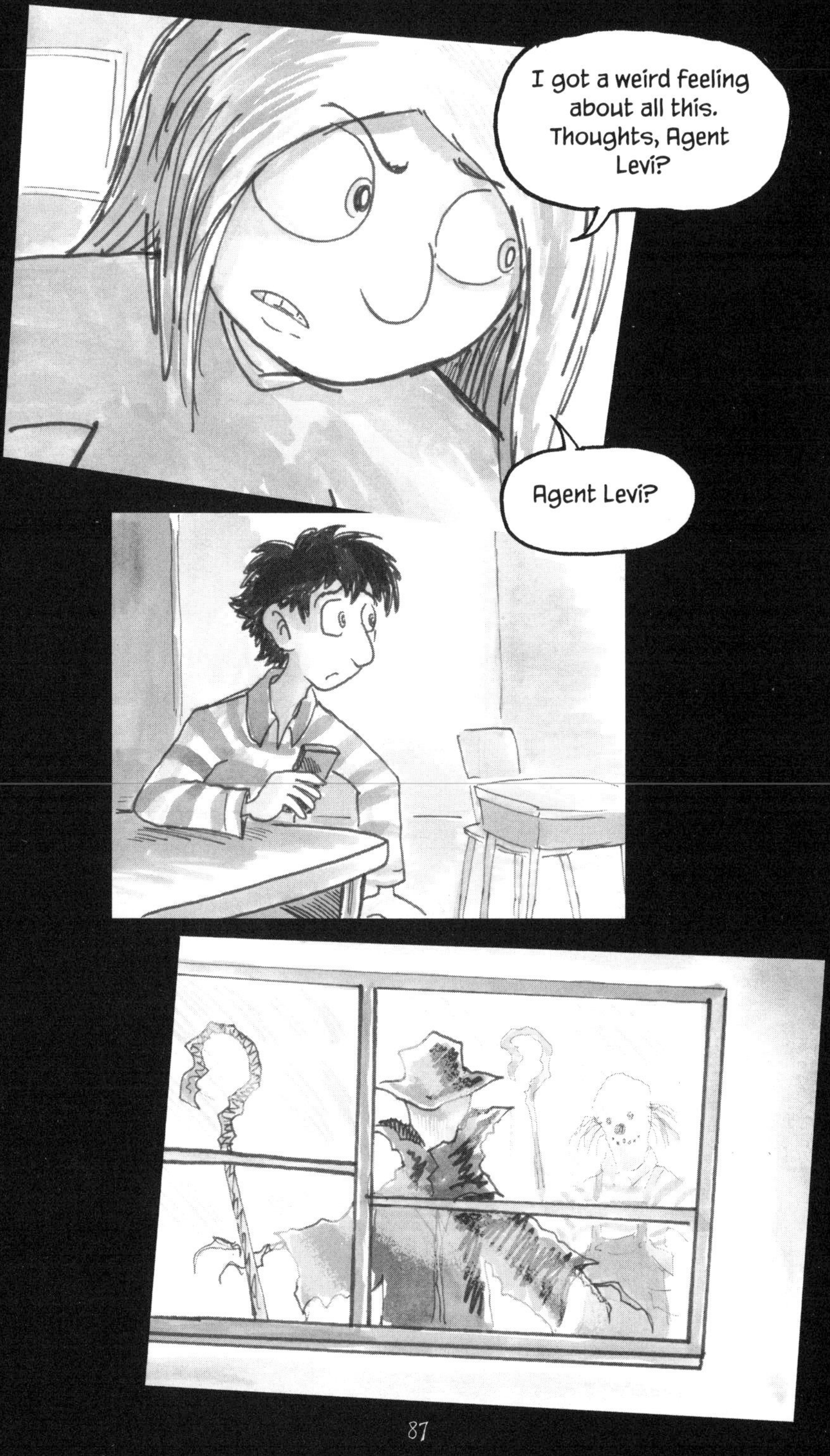
I got a weird feeling about all this. Thoughts, Agent Levi?
Agent Levi?

Chapter 10

The cafeteria tables had been folded and moved to the far corner, and the entire kindergarten-through-sixth grade student body was seated on the floor. Mr. Huff stood at the front of the cafeteria and looked out at the sea of children. "Good evening, students. I'm aware that . . ." He paused, realizing the chatter was drowning his voice. "Ahem! Students! Indoor voices!" He cleared his throat and went on to deliver the same information everyone had already heard from Mr. Chuck—bad weather, state of emergency, parents and guardians phoned . . .

"Ms. Padilla," whispered Levi, "is it okay if I go sit with Twila for a while?"

Ms. Padilla patted his shoulder. "I'm sorry, Levi. All students need to stay with their classes. Otherwise it will be hard to keep track of everyone."

Levi sighed and hugged his knees to his chest.

"Dude," said Kat, "you're becoming a helicopter brother."

"Am not."

"Mr. Huff!" called Lydia Schnell. "It's getting dark! Are we going to be here overnight?"

"We're doing everything we can to ensure a proactive response," said Mr. Huff.

"That didn't answer my question," muttered Lydia.

"When will our phones work again?" Donte asked.

"There seem to be mass outages in the area," said Mr. Huff. "I'm sure the phone and internet companies are working proactively to reinstate service as soon as possible."

"Quit dodging the real issue, Mr. Huff!" shouted Robbie Munn. "When do we get our pizza bagels?"

"Robbie!" snapped Ms. Padilla.

A chant swept through the student sea: "Pizza bagels! Pizza bagels!"

Mr. Huff put up his hands for silence, but the chant gained strength.

"Pizza bagels! Pizza bagels! Pizza b—"

The lights flickered, fizzled, and went out, plunging the cafeteria into black.

There was a moment of silence, followed by scattered screams and whimpers from the primary grades. Then a thump, a hum, and the lights returned.

Mr. Chuck ran in from the hall. "Power's out," he said. "Luckily the backup generator kicked in."

"Thank you, Mr. Chuck," said Mr. Huff. "Please use the landline to report the power outage."

Mr. Chuck gave a thumbs up and disappeared into the hall.

Several students, mostly kindergarteners, were crying. Teachers scurried about, trying to calm the distraught children.

Mrs. Pine, the librarian, waded through the students and whispered something to Mr. Huff.

"Attention!" Mr. Huff said. He waited until the chatter faded. "Mrs. Pine has suggested we pass the time by watching a film."

A cheer rose up from the students.

"It better not be educational!" Robbie shouted.

Mrs. Pine passed back through the students and into the hall. She returned five minutes later with the multimedia cart. "We'll project it up on that wall," she said as she plugged a cable into her laptop.

"Let's watch something scary!" said Donte.

"A zombie movie!" demanded Robbie.

"I know a site that has a brilliant documentary on the Great Barrier Reef," suggested Ms. Padilla.

"The WiFi is still down," said Mrs. Pine. "But I have the animated *Charlotte's Web* on my laptop."

"Excuuuuuuuse meeee!" hollered a voice from the third grade. It was Jordan. "I gotta go to the bathroom!"

"I'll be his hall buddy," said Twila. "I, uh, kinda have to go too."

"Would a teacher near the hall please escort the students to the facilities?" asked Mr. Huff.

"I'll do it," said Ms. Padilla. "I'm closest to the hall, and my class will behave while I'm gone." She shot her students a sharp look.

Jordan and Twila stumbled through the mass of sprawled students and followed Ms. Padilla out of the cafeteria and into the hall.

"Wait, Ms. P!" called Levi. He stood and started after them.

Kat caught his arm. "What are you doing?"

"Gonna go with them to the bathrooms."

"Yeah," said Kat. "Helicopter brother to the rescue."

Levi pulled his arm away. "Back in a few minutes." He hurried out of the cafeteria and into the halls.

Kat sighed and rested her chin on her knees.

"Sad your boyfriend doesn't like spending time with you?" said Donte with a grin.

"Shut up! He's not my boyfriend!"

"When are they gonna start the stupid movie?" whined Robbie.

The students were growing restless. Some of the kindergarteners were crying again.

"Start the movie! Start the movie!" chanted Donte.

"Pizza bagels! Pizza bagels!" chanted Robbie.

Other students joined in.

"This is odd," said Mrs. Pine to Mr. Huff, who was standing by the multimedia cart and trying to look helpful. "I could have sworn I had *Charlotte's Web* on my laptop."

"You don't have the movie?" Mr. Huff's face paled.

"Maybe this is it." Mrs. Pine pointed to a video file in the middle of her desktop. It was titled Play Me.

"START THE MOVIE! START THE MOVIE!"

"Play it and see," said Mr. Huff.

The students cheered as the projector lit up the cafeteria wall with a bright blank rectangle.

There was a long pause. Motes sidled past the screen. Murmurs and rustles from the student audience.

Then a great blast of carousel music, and the blank wall blazed with cartoon life.

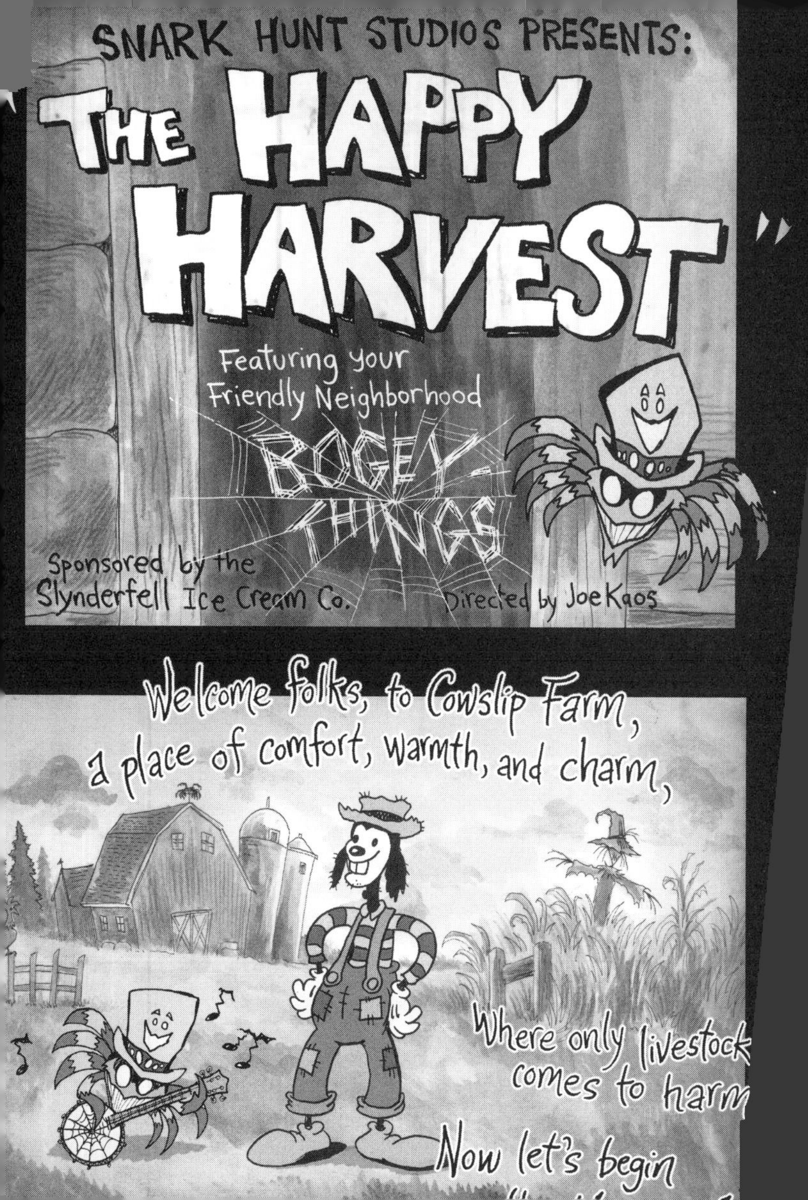
SNARK HUNT STUDIOS PRESENTS:
"THE HAPPY HARVEST"
Featuring your Friendly Neighborhood
BOGEY-THINGS
Sponsored by the Slynderfell Ice Cream Co.
Directed by Joe Kaos
Welcome folks, to Cowslip Farm,
a place of comfort, warmth, and charm,
Where only livestock comes to harm
Now let's begin

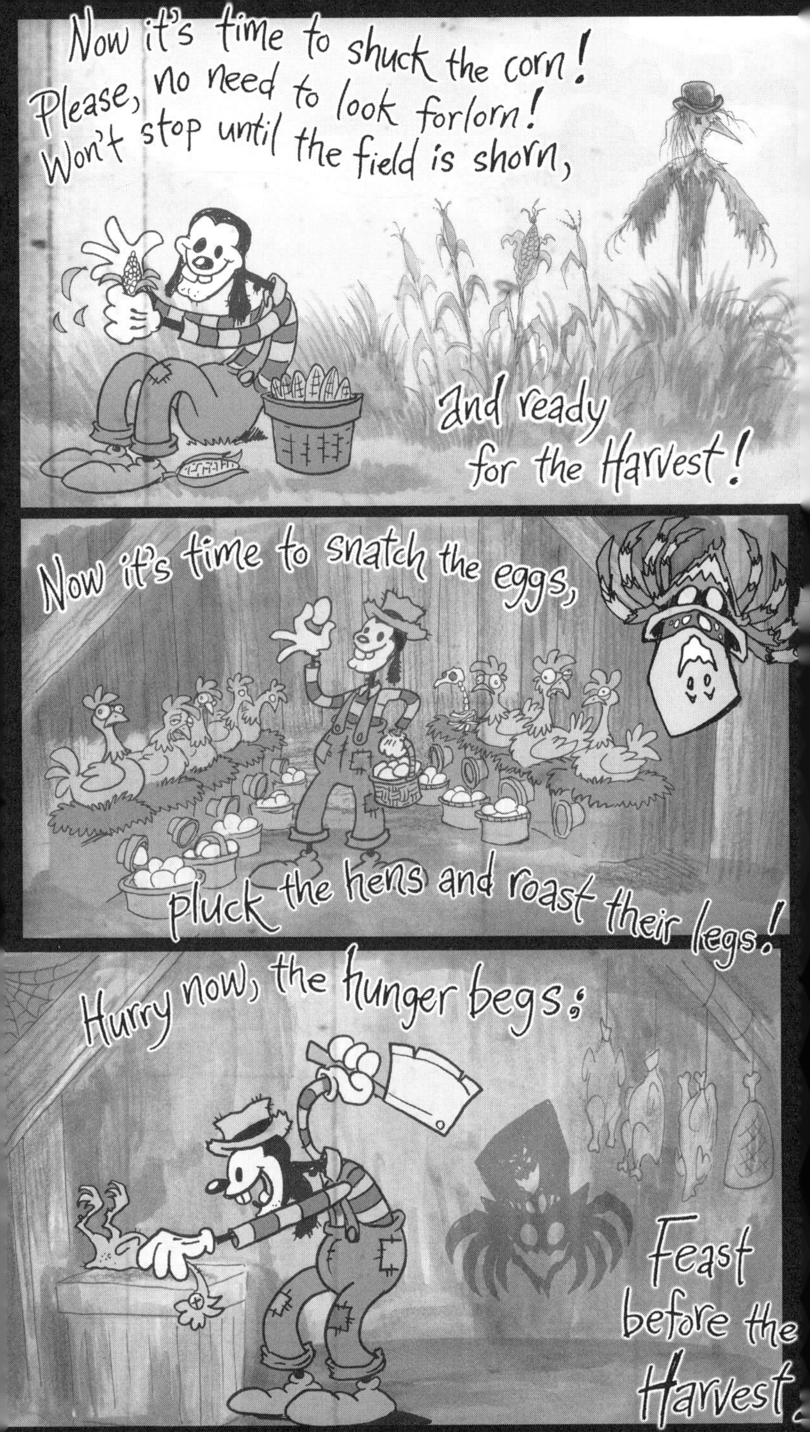
Now it's time to shuck the corn!
Please, no need to look forlorn!
Won't stop until the field is shorn,
and ready for the Harvest!
Now it's time to snatch the eggs,
pluck the hens and roast their legs!
Hurry now, the hunger begs;
Feast before the Harvest

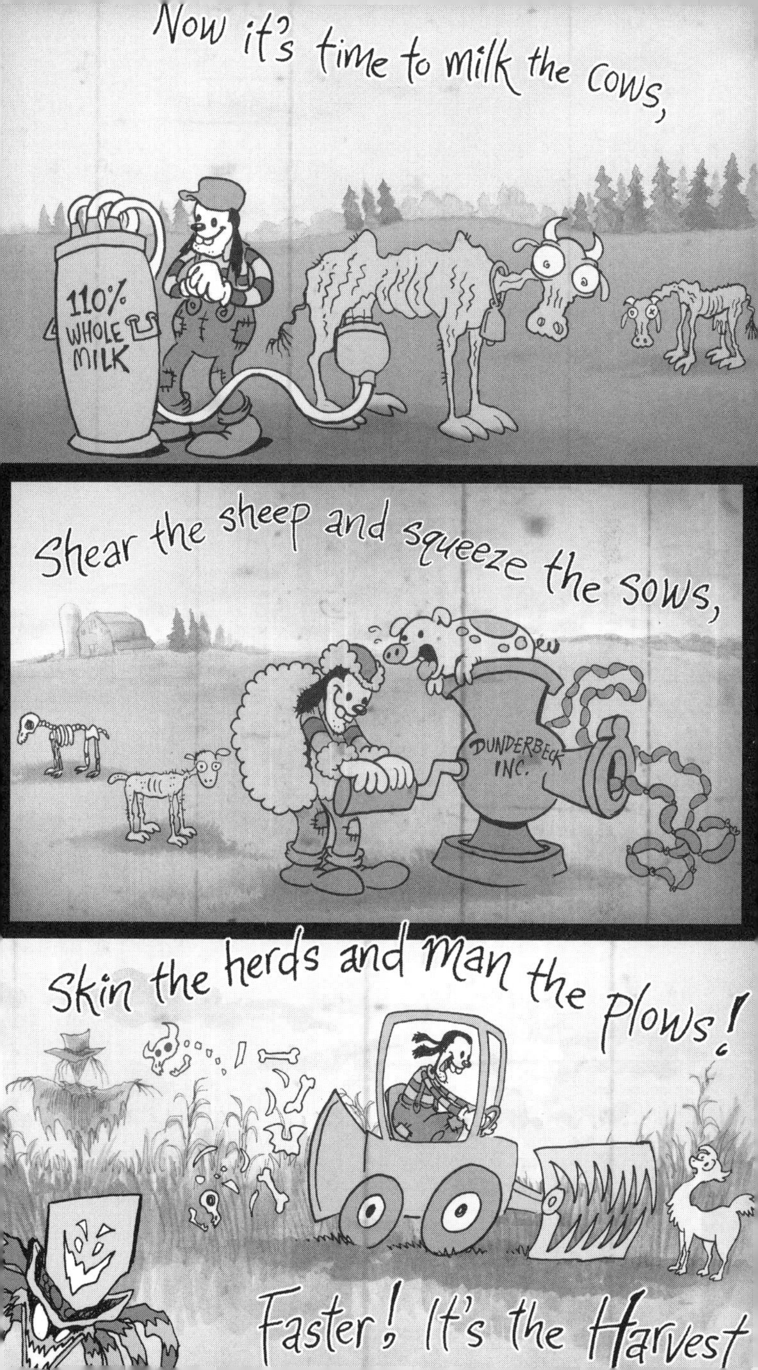

Now it's time to milk the cows,
110% WHOLE MILK
Shear the sheep and squeeze the sows,
DUNDERBECK INC.
Skin the herds and man the plows!
Faster! It's the Harvest

Kat squinted at the screen. "What *is* this?"

The cafeteria lights flickered again and went off.

"Man!" said Kat. "Power's out again." She waited for the other students' reactions. None came. She twisted around. "How is the movie still playing?"

"Ssh! Quiet!" whispered Donte. He gave her a nudge.

"*You* be quiet!" She shoved him back. His glasses flew off his face and skittered across the floor.

"My glasses!" he cried. He dropped to his stomach and groped along the floor.

"You started it!" said Kat, but she got on her hands and knees and felt her way along the dark floor, moving through the crowd of seated students.

"If anything happened to them, you'll owe me three hundred dollars!" said Donte.

"Relax. We'll find them. Did anyone see where Donte's glasses fell?"

"Robbie?" said Donte. "You see my glasses?"

Robbie didn't answer. His eyes were glued to the cartoon.

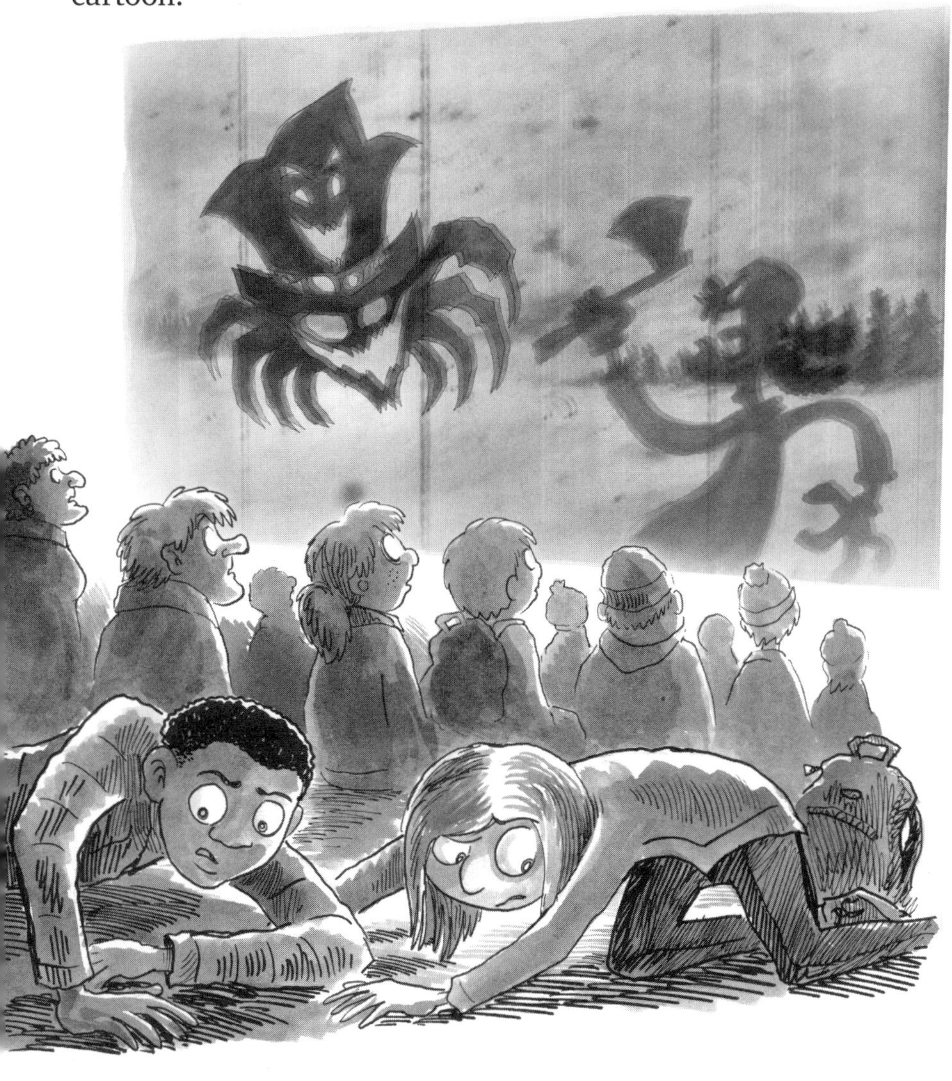

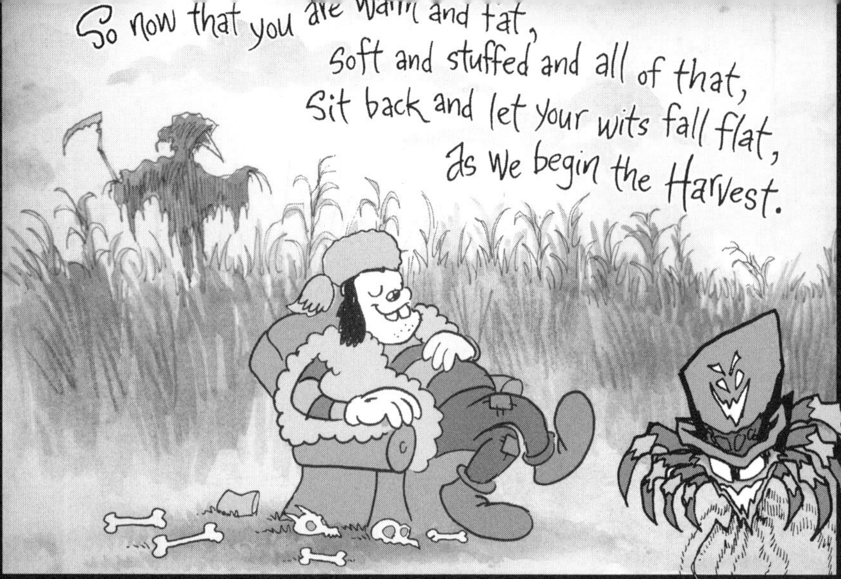
So now that you are warm and fat,
soft and stuffed and all of that,
Sit back and let your wits fall flat,
as we begin the Harvest.

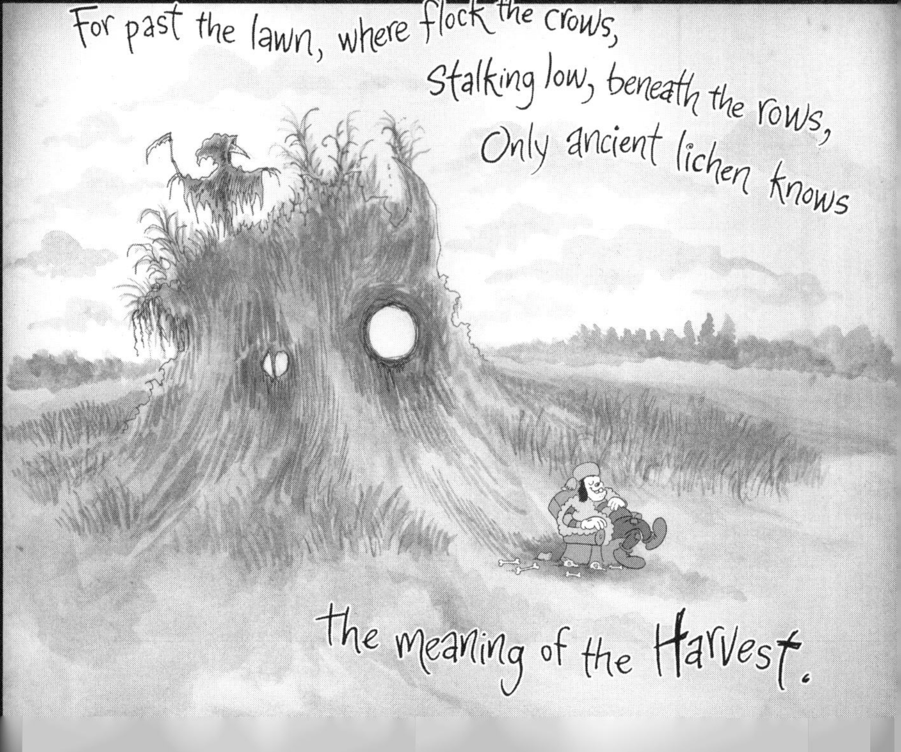
For past the lawn, where flock the crows,
Stalking low, beneath the rows,
Only ancient lichen knows
the meaning of the Harvest.

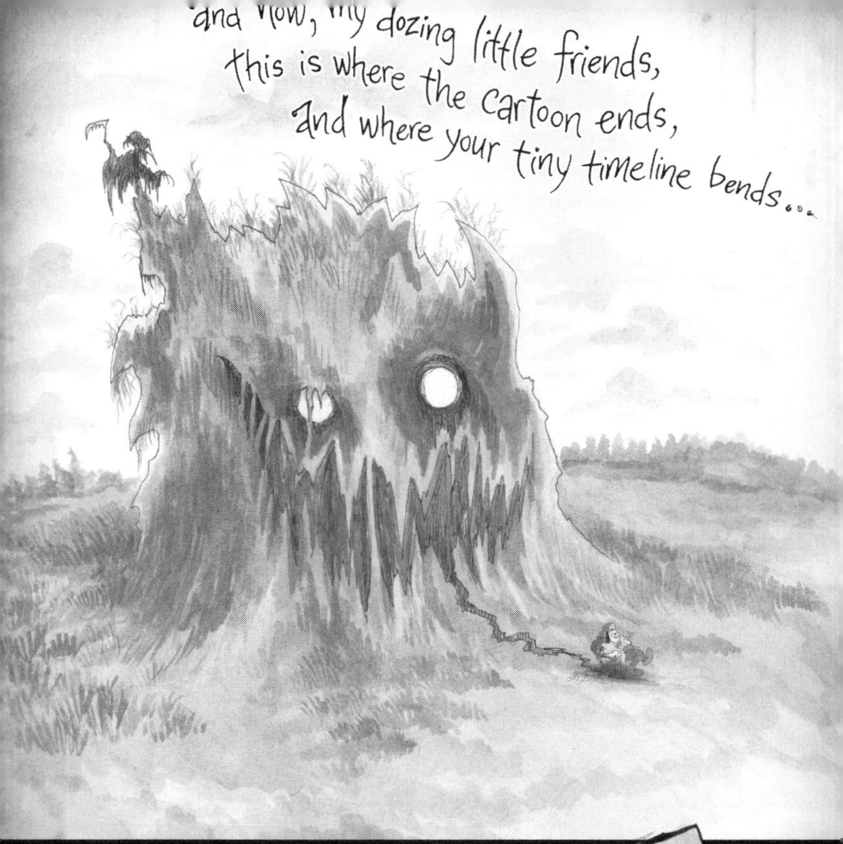
and now, my dozing little friends,
this is where the cartoon ends,
and where your tiny timeline bends...

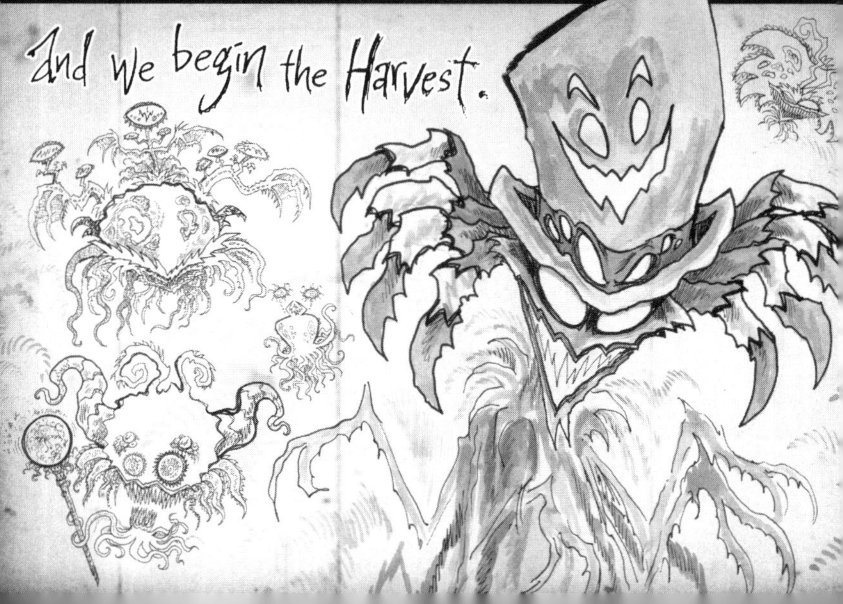
And we begin the Harvest.

FOOTAGE FROM SCHOOL SECURITY CAMERAS (B
OPERATED)

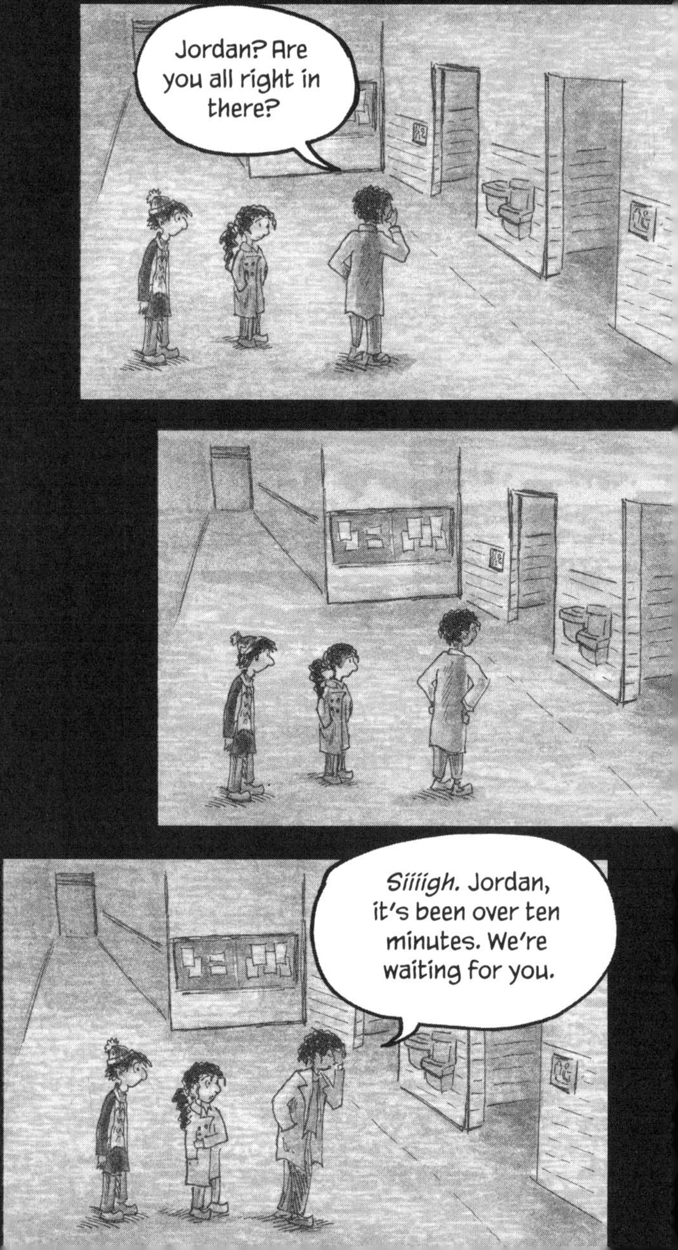
Jordan? Are you all right in there?
Siiiigh. Jordan, it's been over ten minutes. We're waiting for you.

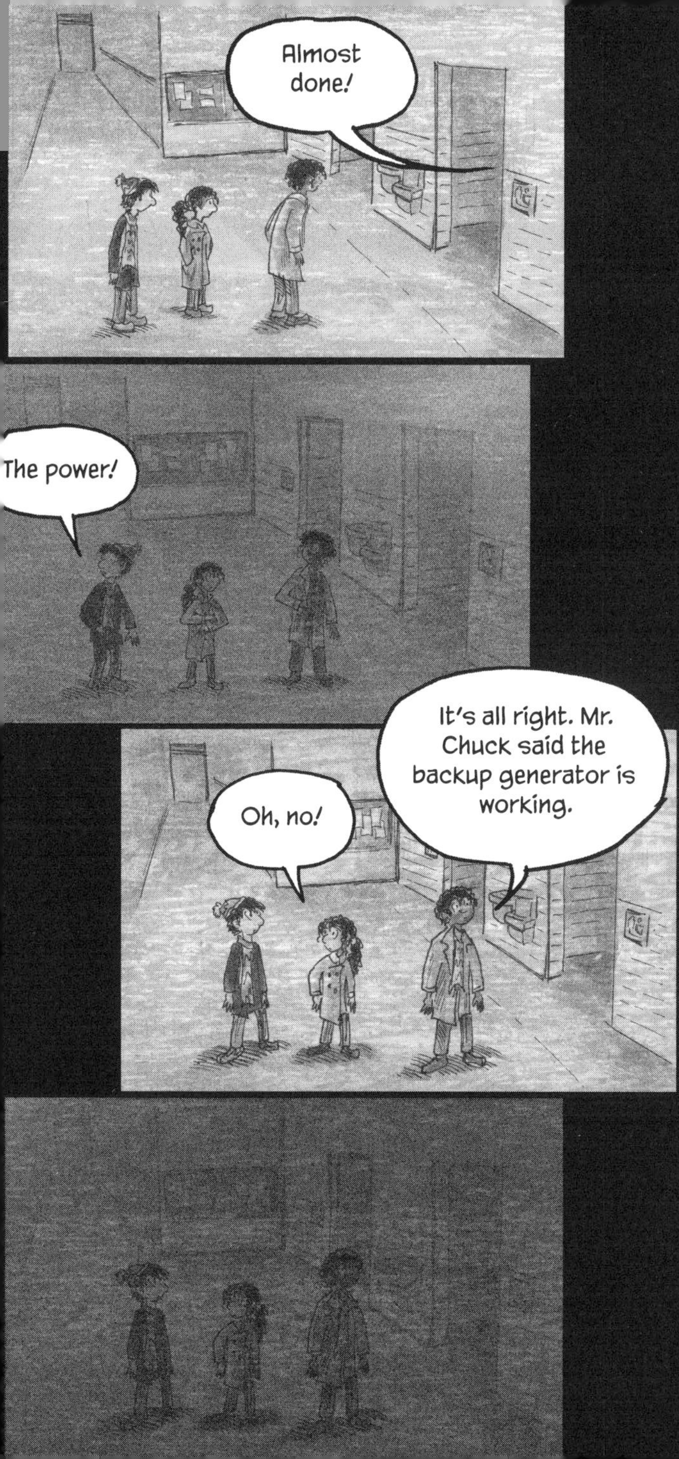
Almost done!
The power!
Oh, no!
It's all right. Mr. Chuck said the backup generator is working.

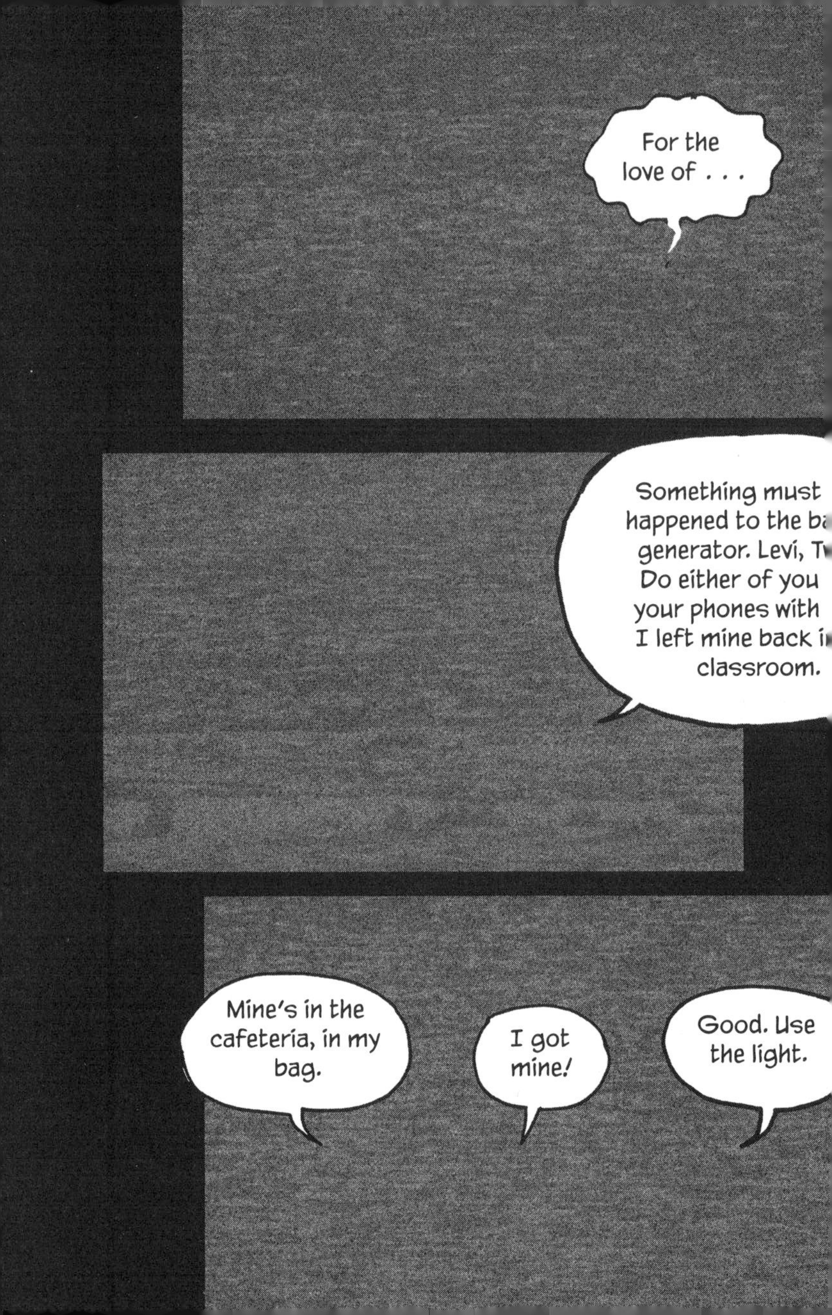
For the love of . . .
Something must happened to the generator. Levi, Do either of you your phones with I left mine back classroom.
Mine's in the cafeteria, in my bag.
I got mine!
Good. Use the light.

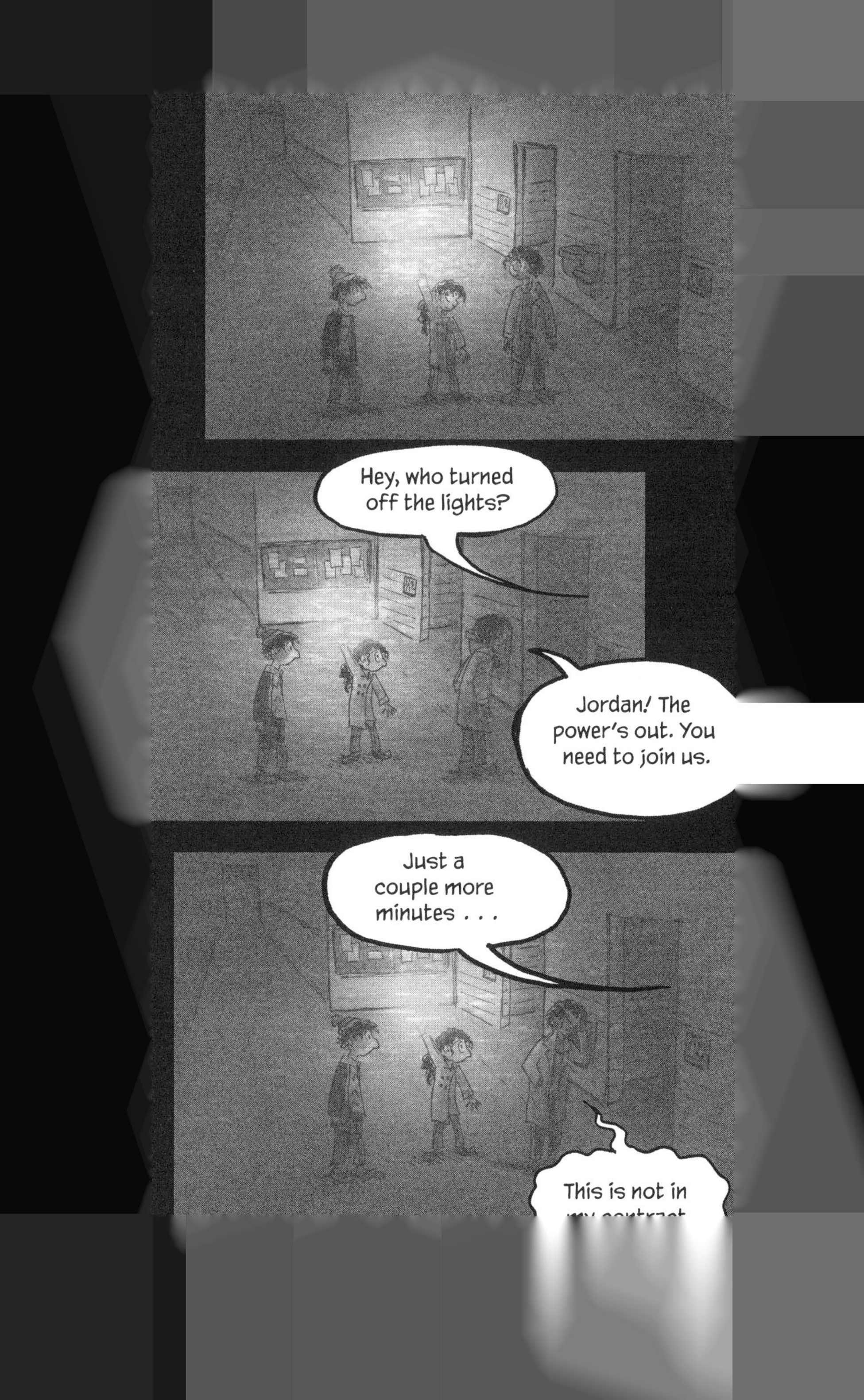

Hey, who turned off the lights?
Jordan! The power's out. You need to join us.
Just a couple more minutes . . .
This is not in

Chapter 13

"What's happening?" Donte asked. "Everything's blurry!"

"Don't look at the screen!" cried Kat. She turned away from the glowing projection. "Everyone! Look away!"

No one listened. No one moved.

Kat looked for the nearest teacher. "Mr. Steig! Help! Something—"

She saw his face and recoiled.

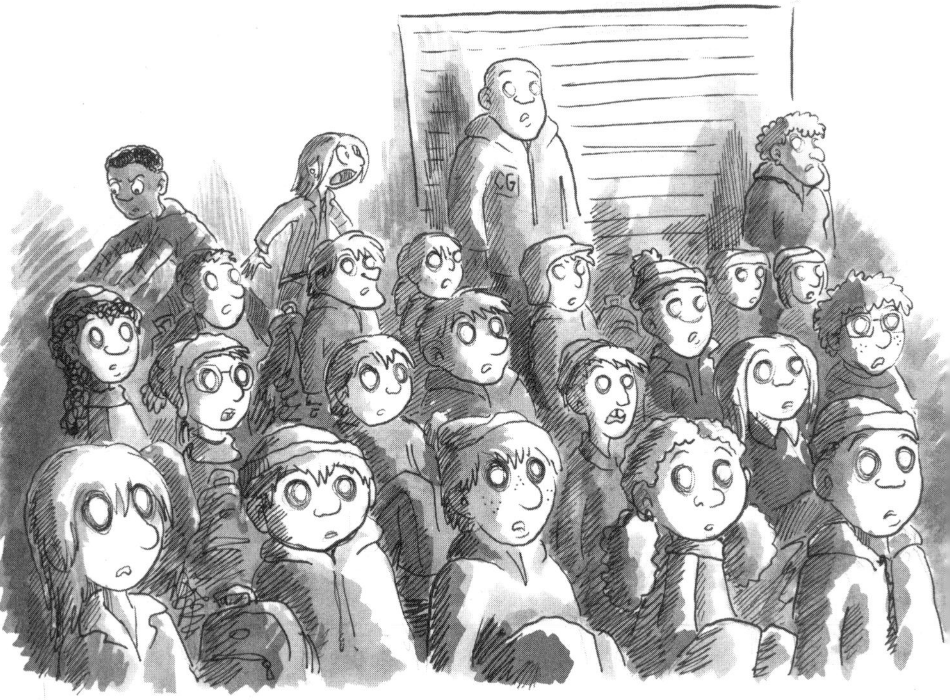
CG

“Seriously,” began Donte, “what is—”

Kat seized his arm. “We gotta get out of here!”

“What? I can’t see anything without my glasses!”

“Good! If you could see, you’d be like the rest of them!”

She jumped to her feet and started toward the exit, dragging Donte along with her.

“I’m not going anywhere without my—”

“Forget your glasses! They’re gone! They’re—”

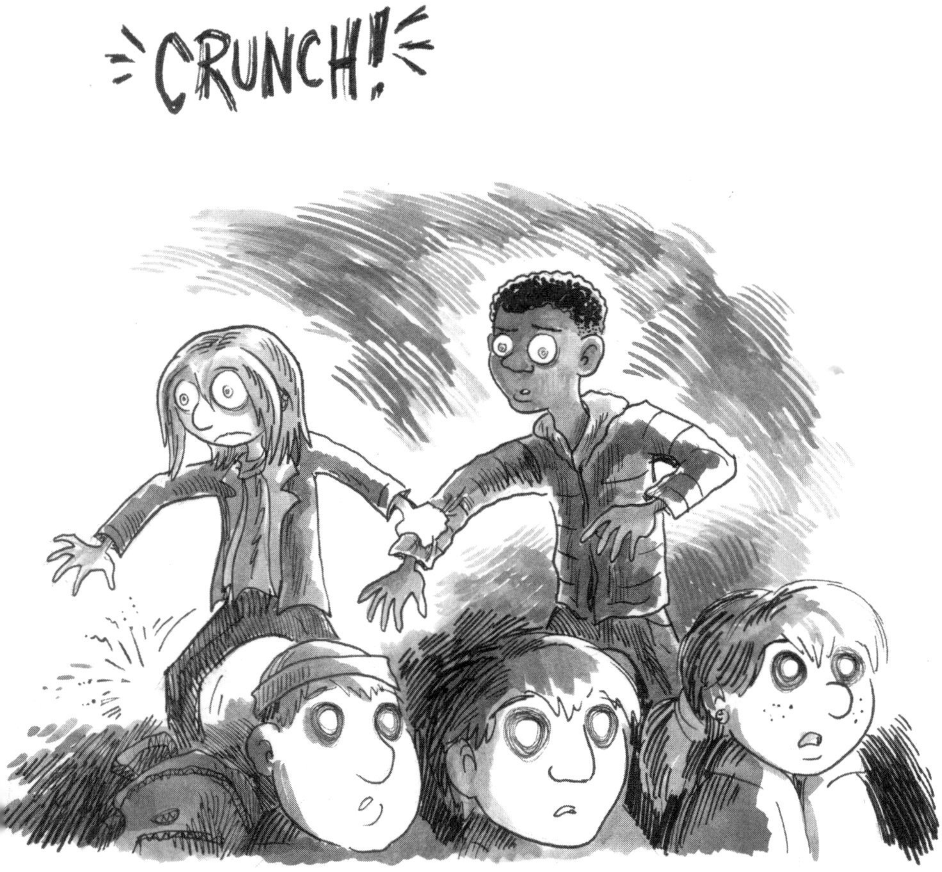
CRUNCH!

"I, uh. I found them."

She stooped, snatched the glasses from under her shoe, and shoved them onto Donte's face.

"There! Good as new! Now whatever you do, don't look at the screen!"

"You broke them!" growled Donte.

"It's just a small crack. No biggie!"

He pulled his hand from hers. "You owe me a new pair! Just wait until—" His voice stopped when he saw the faces of the other students. "What the?" He turned toward the projection.

"Don't look!" screamed Kat. She grabbed his arm again and pulled him toward the cafeteria doors. "We gotta find Ms. Padilla and Levi! It's happening again!"

"What's happening again?"

"This decade's Harvest will be the greatest yet! Can't you feel the excitement in the air, children? Everyone who works our farm is excited! Our shepherds arrived earlier this week, as you've noticed..."

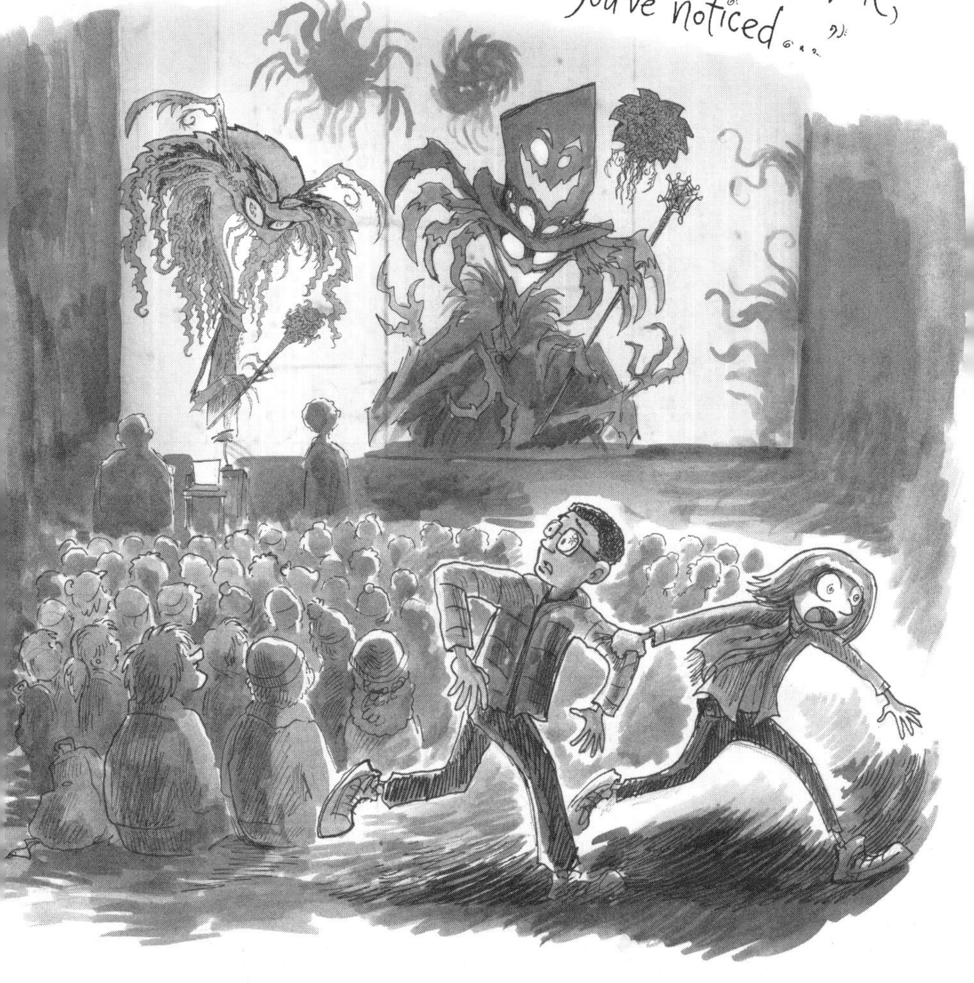

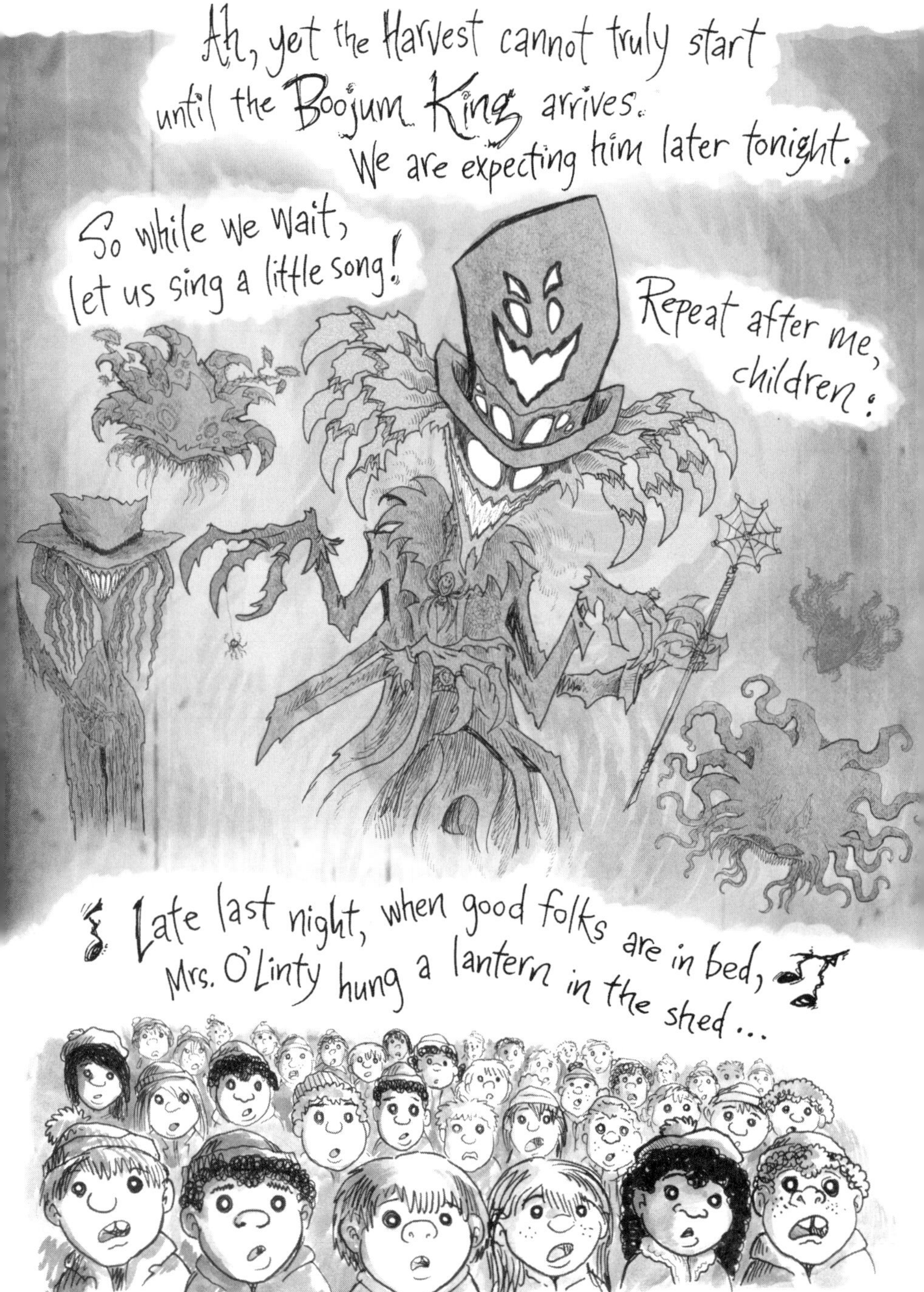

Ah, yet the Harvest cannot truly start until the Boojum King arrives. We are expecting him later tonight.
So while we wait, let us sing a little song!
Repeat after me, children:
Late last night, when good folks are in bed, Mrs. O'Linty hung a lantern in the shed...

Chapter 14

"Jordan," said Ms. Padilla. The frustration was seeping into her normally unflappable teacher voice. "It's been twenty minutes. We need to get back to the cafeteria."

"Almost done!" called Jordan from the darkened bathroom.

"He said that ten minutes ago!" said Twila. "Can't me and Levi please just go back by ourselves? They already started the movie!"

An enormous flush echoed from the bathroom. The flush was followed by a disturbing gurgle. "Uh oh!" cried Jordan. "Something's wrong with the toilet!"

"Mr. Chuck will deal with that later," said Ms. Padilla.

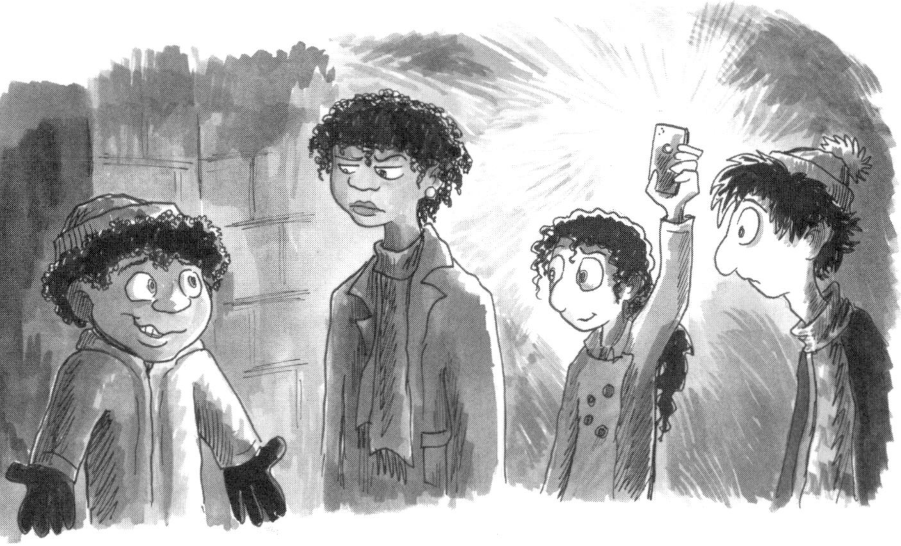

Jordan emerged from the bathroom with a sheepish grin. “Sorry.”

“Never mind,” said Ms. Padilla. “Let’s get back to the cafeter—OHMYGOSH!”

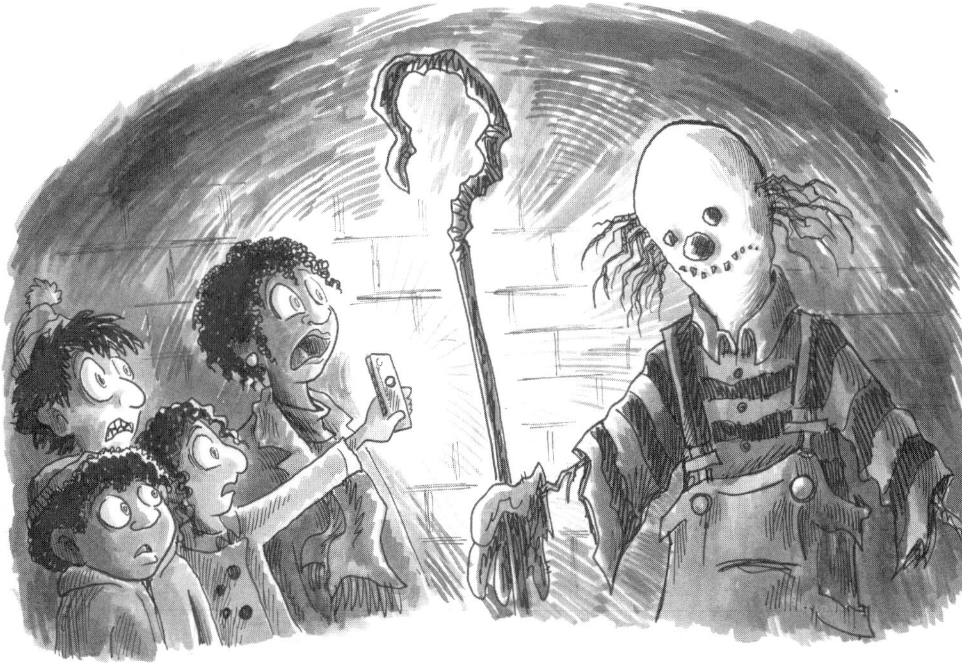

"It's okay, Ms. Padilla," said Jordan. "It's just one of those ugly snowmen."

Ms. Padilla tried to recover her poise. "But . . . how did it get in here?"

Twila inched forward and inspected the snowman. "Creepy."

"Don't touch it!" hissed Levi, pulling her back.

"Easy, Brother-Man! Donte and Robbie probably brought it in as a prank."

"Or Kat," said Jordan.

"But how were they able to . . ." Ms. Padilla's voice trailed off. "Never mind. I'll tell Mr. Huff and Mr. Chuck about it."

They started back through the cold dark halls.

"Listen!" said Twila. "They're singing!"

"It's probably just the movie," said Levi.

"It's not the movie! The power's out! I can hear their voices. It's the kids! And teachers too!"

"Maybe it's a singalong movie," said Levi weakly.

"You honestly think sixth-graders would be singing along?" said Twila. "Power out, snowman in the hall, now everybody doing a singalong? This is straight out of a horror m—"

Two figures lunged out from around a corner and charged at them.

Everybody screamed.

"Whoa! It's just us! Kat and Donte!"

"Ms. Padilla!" cried Donte. "Something's wrong! Everybody—the kids, the teachers . . . I don't know how to explain it! You gotta come look!"

"No!" cried Kat, catching Ms. Padilla by the arm. "Don't go into the cafeteria! They'll get you too!"

"Kat! Let go!" snapped Ms. Padilla. "This is ridiculous!"

"It's the film!" continued Kat. "It's zombified them! Me and Donte were the only ones to escape!"

"Enough!" Ms. Padilla turned to Levi and the two third-graders. "To the cafeteria! NOW!"

Kat grabbed Levi's shoulder and shook him. "Levi, it's happening again! The Boojum!"

Levi's eyes were huge. "Ms. Padilla, I think maybe we shouldn't go into the cafeteria."

Twila tagged alongside Ms. Padilla. "Ms. P! Wait!"

"Outrageous," Ms. Padilla muttered to herself as she marched toward the cafeteria entrance. "Budget cuts, standardized testing snafus, and now whatever *this* is? Just wait until the next board meeting. I'll be giving them a piece of my m—"

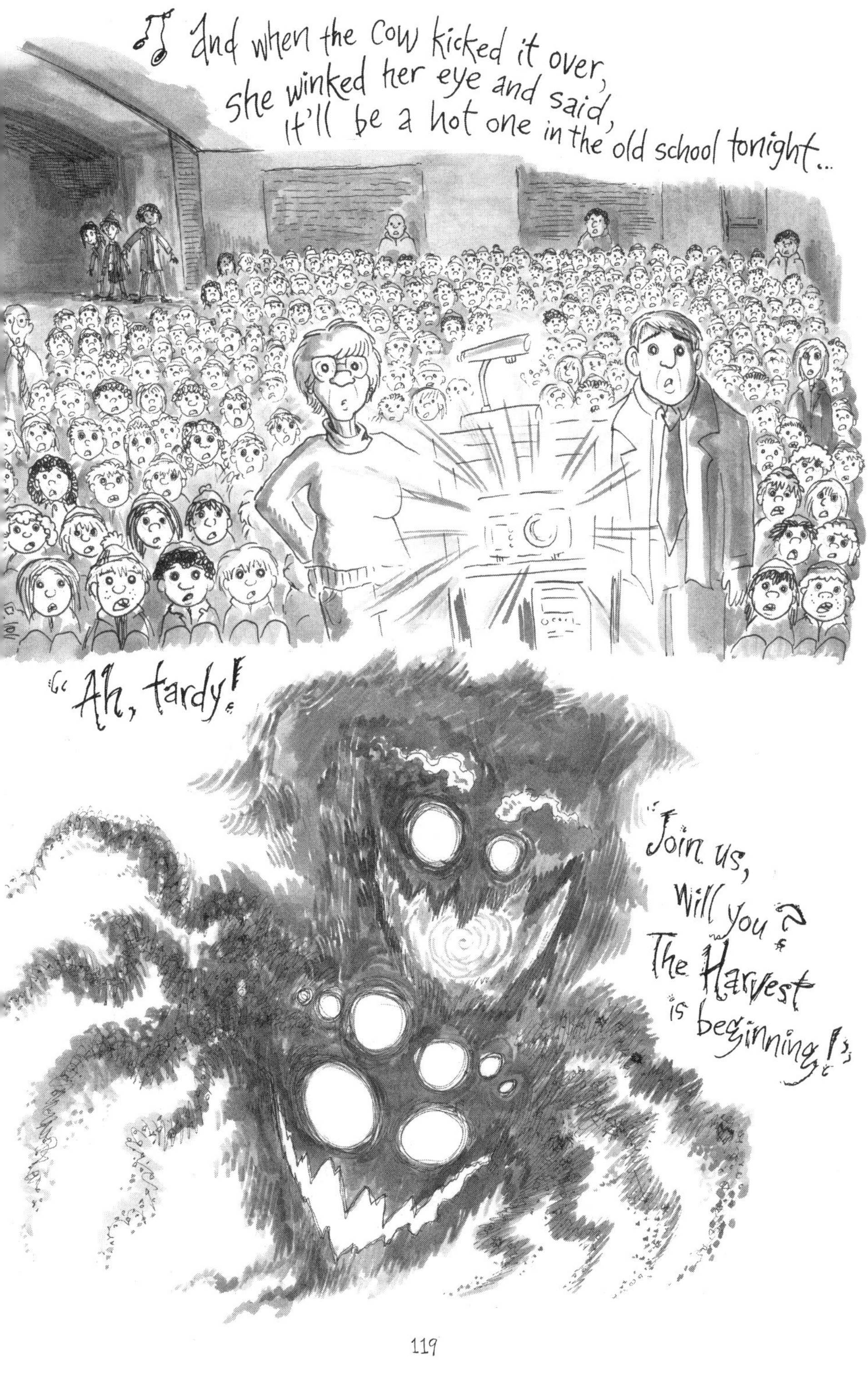
And when the cow kicked it over,
she winked her eye and said,
it'll be a hot one in the old school tonight...
"Ah, tardy!
Join us, will you? The Harvest is beginning!"

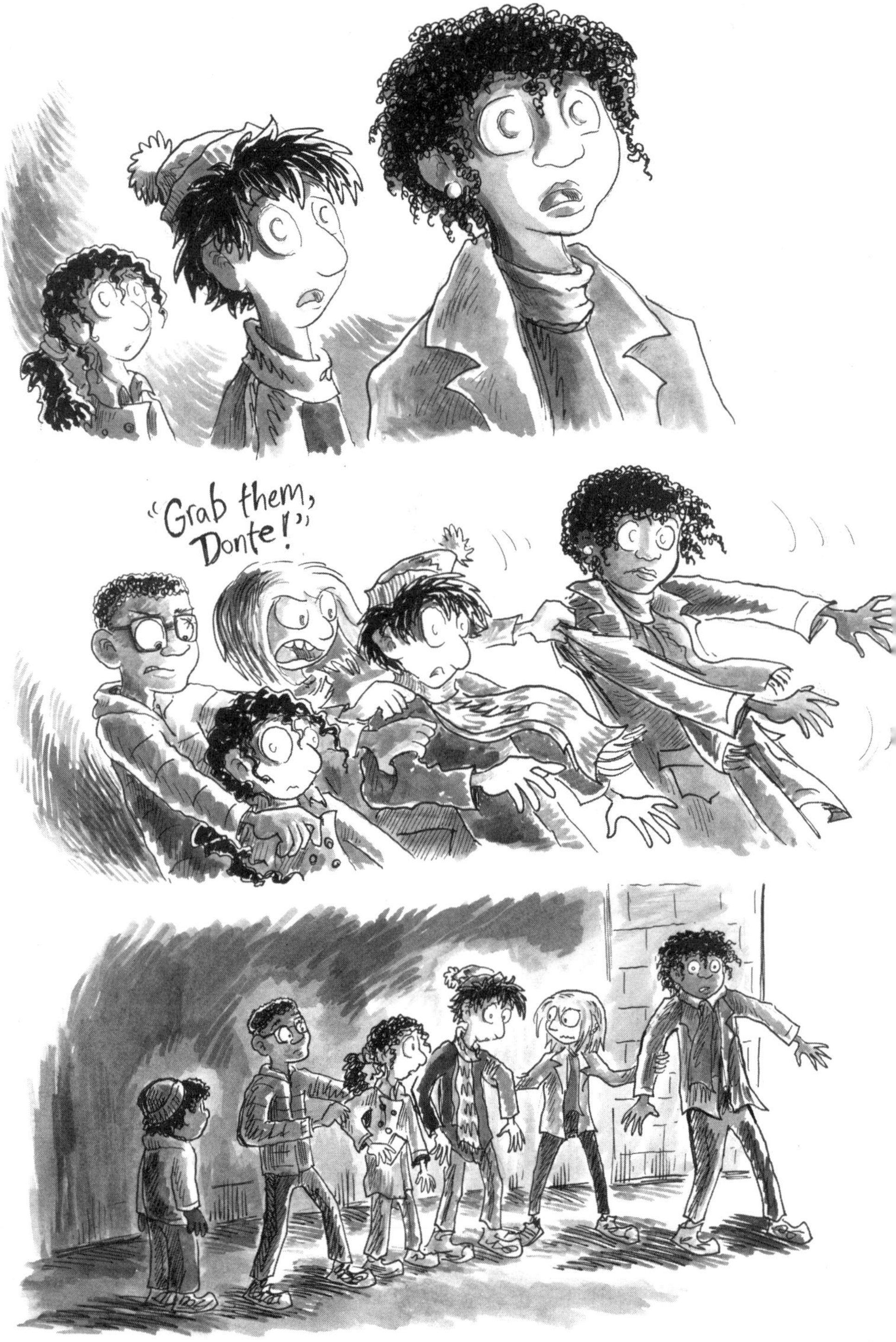
"Grab them, Donte!"

Chapter 15

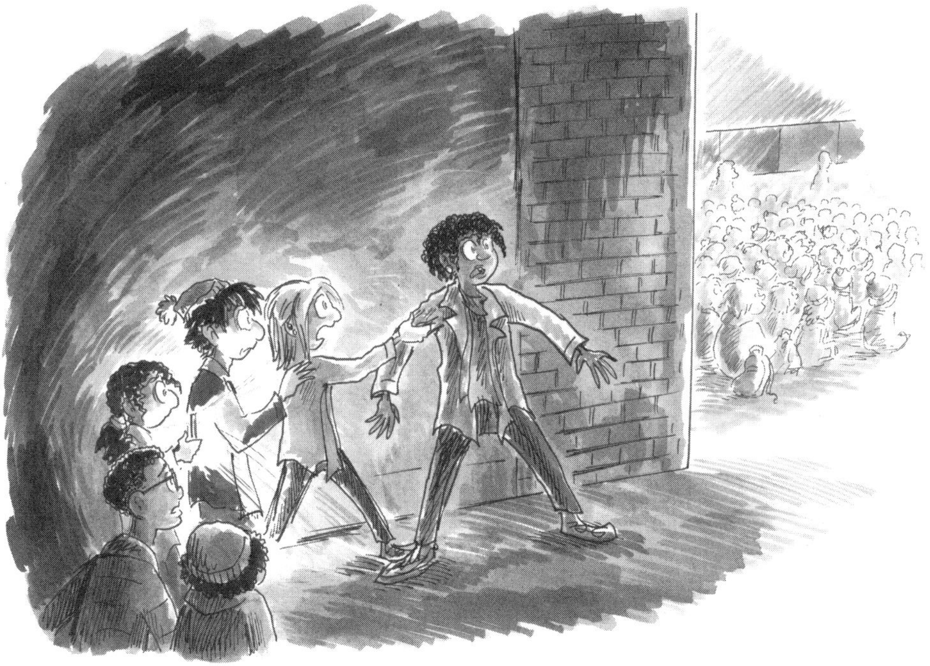

"What happened?" Twila gasped.

Kat turned to Levi. "The Boojum is back! Only this time it isn't taking just one or two kids at night!"

Ms. Padilla scrubbed her eyes like a frazzled hamster. "This is all some sick joke. I'm going back in to talk to Mr. Huff, and—" Her voice stopped as something caught her eye. "Kat, you have your phone?"

"Uh, yeah. Right here."

"Turn on the flashlight."

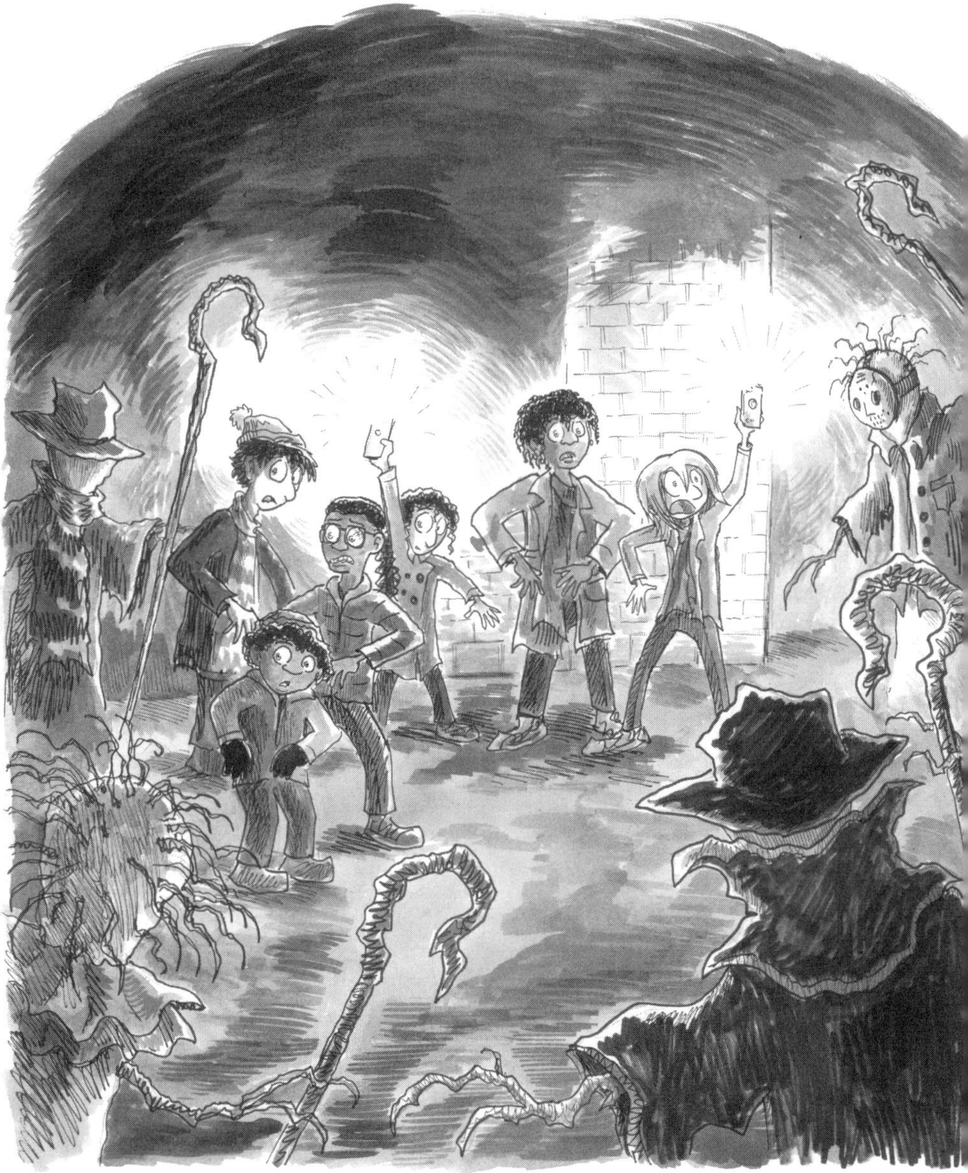

"I knew it!" Kat exclaimed. "They're alive!"

Ms. Padilla squinted at the nearest snowman. It stared back with lifeless coal eyes. She turned on the small group of students. "I want the truth! Who is behind this?"

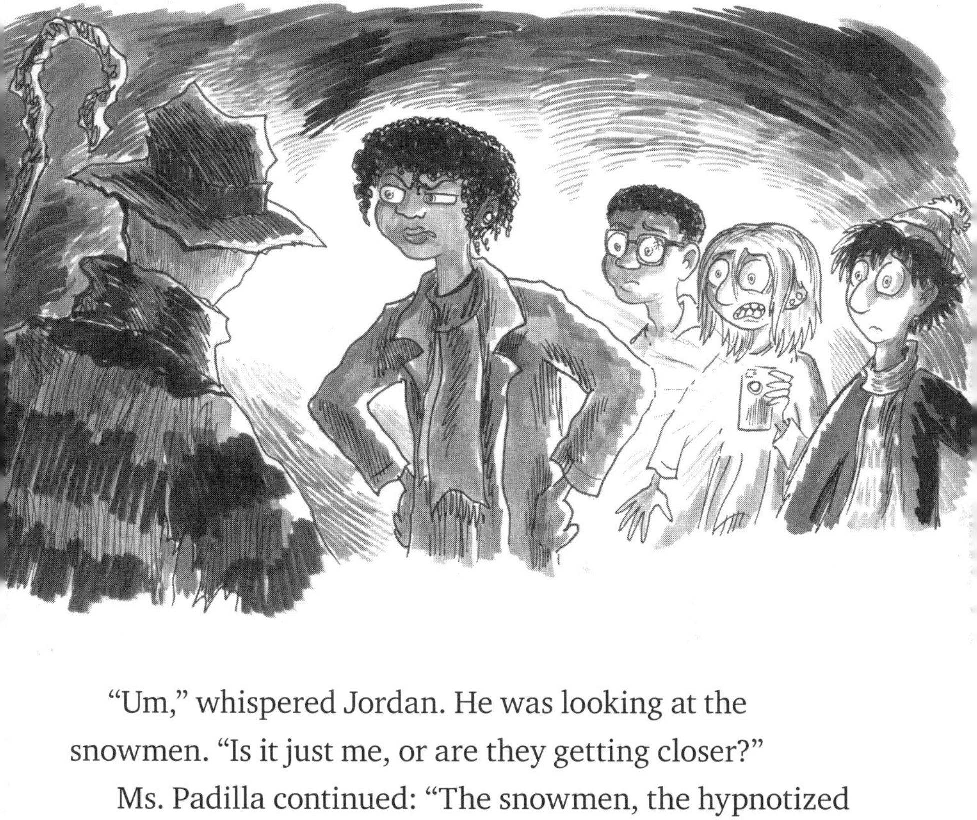

"Um," whispered Jordan. He was looking at the snowmen. "Is it just me, or are they getting closer?"

Ms. Padilla continued: "The snowmen, the hypnotized singalong . . . It's all some elaborate early April Fools' prank! You lure me away from the cafeteria and stall for twenty minutes so everything can be set up!"

"She did it!" cried Donte, pointing at Kat. "She's behind all this!"

"You liar!" roared Kat. "I just saved your life!" She charged and pinned him against the wall.

He pushed back, knocking her sideways. "And you broke my glasses! You'll pay!"

The darkened hall filled with their commotion: Kat scuffling with Donte, Twila trying to break up the fight, Levi yelling at Twila, Ms. Padilla yelling at all of them.

Suddenly all was drowned by a scream. They froze. Twila pulled out her phone and turned on the light.

Jordan was standing rigid, his face a mask of horror. One of the snowmen loomed over him. Its stick arms seemed to be reaching for his throat.

Levi gasped. "That snowman wasn't there a few seconds ago!"

"Keep the light steady, Twila," said Ms. Padilla. She inched forward and leaned in to inspect the snowman.

Everyone held their breath.

"It's just a snowman," she declared.

"No!" whispered Jordan. "It's not! It tried to get me when no one was looking!"

"Oh, geez!" said Levi. There was a snowman directly behind him. "Was this one always here?"

Twila turned and pointed the light at Levi.

"Stay calm," said Ms. Padilla. "The dark is playing tricks on our m—"

"AIIIGH!"

Twila flashed the light back to Jordan. The snowman's gnarled stick fingers were wrapped around his neck.

"HELP!" squeaked Jordan.

Donte, Kat, and Ms. Padilla rushed forward together and tried to pull Jordan free.

Ms. Padilla snapped off stick fingers until Jordan fell away, coughing and clutching his throat.

"It *is* alive!" cried Twila.

"But it's not moving now!" said Levi.

"Did anyone *see* it move?" asked Ms. Padilla.

"Wait!" said Twila. "Everyone freeze!" She slowly turned the phone's light in a full circle around the hall. The light passed over one snowman . . . two snowmen . . . three . . . four . . . They stood still and lifeless.

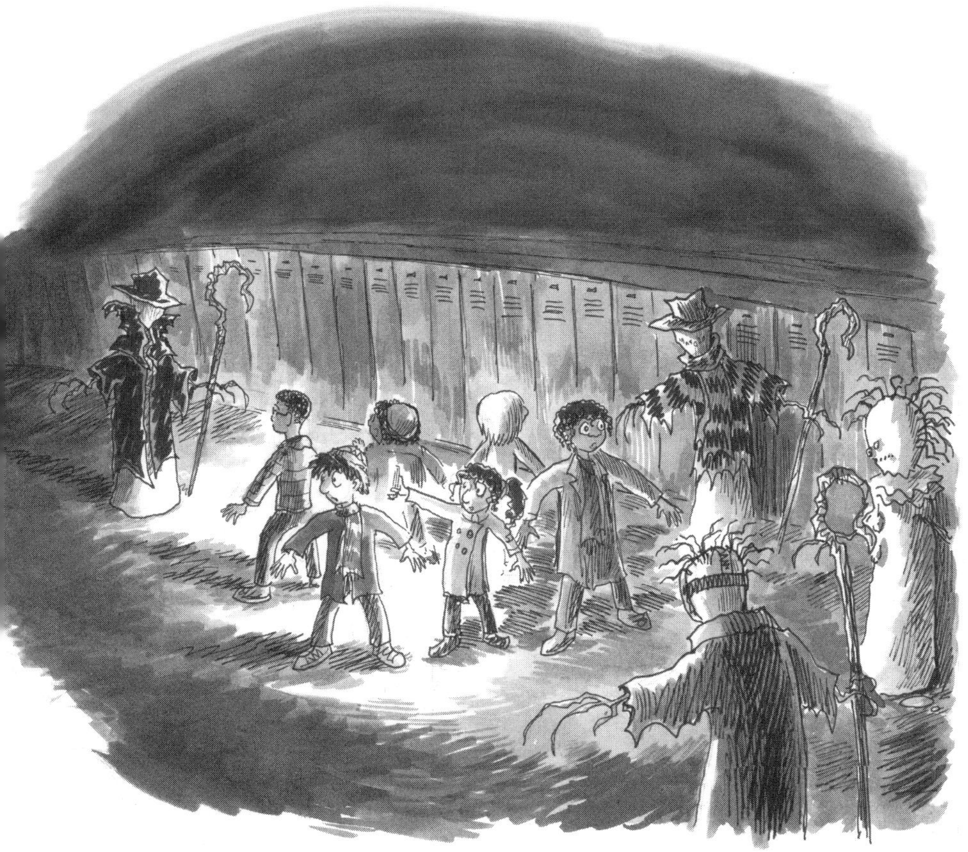

She aimed the phone at the ground, plunging the entire hall—save a little light pool on the floor—into black. Then she raised the light and did another sweep.

The snowmen were standing still.

But they had moved.

They were closer.

Twila trained the light on a snowman to her left. "I think . . ." She moved the light to a snowman on her right. ". . . they only move . . ." She turned the light back to the snowman on her left. It was now a mere meter from her. She recoiled. ". . . when no one is looking."

"That—" started Ms. Padilla, but her voice turned into a gasp. Twila swung the light back on her. A snowman's twisted limb had snagged Ms. Padilla's coat sleeve. She ripped it away and scrambled back from the snowman. "Stay close! All of you!" Ms. Padilla hissed.

They stood back-to-back in the middle of the hall, staring at the looming shapes surrounding them.

"Twila, keep the light on them!" ordered Ms. Padilla.

"On which ones? There's too many!"

"Donte, do you have your phone?"

"No. It's back in the cafeteria," said Donte.

"So just Twila and Kat have phones," said Ms. Padilla. "Kat, why is your phone off?"

"The battery's kinda low."

"Just put the light on! Now!"

Kat turned on the light and flashed it in the opposite direction of Twila's light. It lit up the blank face of a snowman just outside their little circle.

"They're closing in!" moaned Jordan.

"We've got to get out of this dark hall," said Ms. Padilla.

"And go where?" asked Kat. "Not the cafeteria!"

"My classroom," said Ms. Padilla. "We can collect our wits and figure out what's really happening. And my phone's in my desk. Hopefully the WiFi will work again soon. And the power."

They shuffled down the hall, backs together, moving like a discombobulated centipede. They edged around the snowmen, their eyes never leaving the frozen figures.

"Careful! Twila, Kat—keep your lights steady!" said Ms. Padilla. "Everyone still with us?"

"Here," said Levi.

"Here," said Kat.

"Here," said Donte.

"Here," said Jordan.

"Here," said Twila.

"Here," said a deep, gruff voice behind them.

Kat whipped her light in the direction of the voice. A tall, hairy figure stood over them.

They screamed.

"Chill, little dudes! Easy, Ms. P!" said the tall hairy figure.

"Mr. Chuck!" gasped Kat. "You got away from the cafeteria!"

"I wasn't in the cafeteria. I left to check the landline, remember?" said Mr. Chuck. "But the line's dead. Must be the ice. Something's also wrong with the backup generator. Not good. It's going to get very cold in here." He surveyed their frightened faces. "So why all the screaming?"

"The snowmen are alive and coming to get us!" said Twila.

"But they only move when no one's looking!" added Kat.

"And all the kids and teachers in the cafeteria are hypnotized!" said Donte.

"Students!" snapped Ms. Padilla. "The point, Mr. Chuck, is that something strange is happening, and it seems to be an elaborate prank."

"It's not a prank!" insisted Kat. "Please, Mr. Chuck, you gotta believe us!"

"Oh, I believe you," said Mr. Chuck.

"You . . . you do?"

"Sure," said Mr. Chuck. "Heard all about this sort of thing on the *Roffman & Colburn* podcast. They're testing to see how a population sample responds to irrational stimuli. Will we break down mentally? Turn on each other? Adapt and rise to the occasion?"

Ms. Padilla stared at Mr. Chuck. "*Who* is testing us?"

Mr. Chuck shrugged. "The Great Old Ones? Not sure, really."

"Hold on," said Kat. She raised her light. The far end of the hall was now cluttered with still figures. "They're following us!"

"Huh!" said Mr. Chuck. "Like something out of *Dr. Who*."

"Dr. What?" said Levi.

"No, *Dr. **Who***," said Mr. Chuck. "Okay, can't go that way."

"Maybe if we get out one of the back exits, we can go for help," said Levi.

"Out in that storm?" snorted Donte.

"It's better than being trapped in here with . . . whatever this is."

"No!" said Ms. Padilla again. Her voice had lost all traces of its teacher poise. "It's obviously some big prank!"

"Haven't you ever seen a horror movie, Ms. P?" asked Kat. "The skeptics are the first to get bumped off!"

"I bet it's a reality show!" said Donte. "I bet there's hidden cameras all over, just waiting for us to freak out!"

"So we'll be TV stars?" asked Jordan.

"This isn't reality TV!" shouted Kat. "It's just reality! Right, Levi?"

"I don't know what this is," said Levi. "I just know we all need to stick together."

A sharp crackle and hiss filled the hall, and the five students and two remaining adults jumped in unison.

"The intercom?" whispered Mr. Chuck. "How is it still working?"

The intercom sizzled with overzealous static, and a voice spoke:

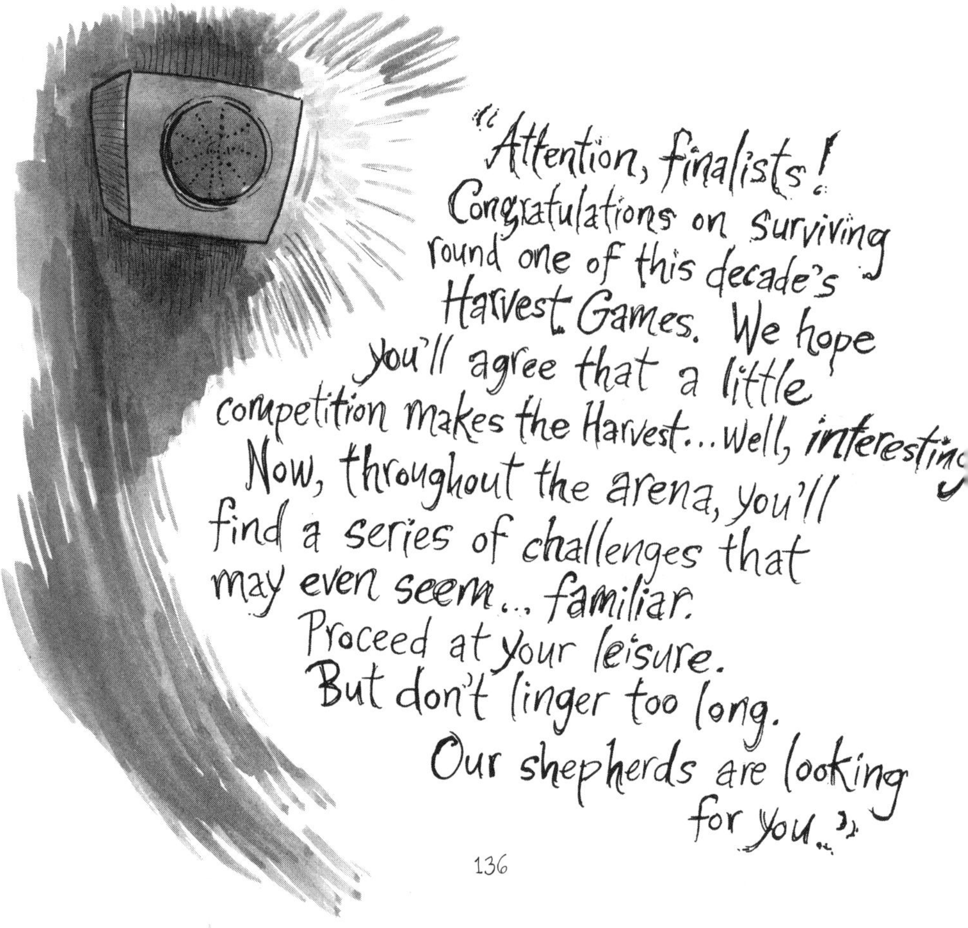
"Attention, finalists!
Congratulations on surviving
round one of this decade's
Harvest Games. We hope
you'll agree that a little
competition makes the Harvest... well, interestin
Now, throughout the arena, you'll
find a series of challenges that
may even seem... familiar.
Proceed at your leisure.
But don't linger too long.
Our shepherds are looking
for you..."

The intercom crackled again and went silent.

"Shepherds?" whispered Donte.

"The snowmen," said Kat.

"We've got to get out of the building," said Levi. He was gripping Twila's arm.

Ms. Padilla massaged her brow. "This isn't happening."

"Snap out of it, Ms. P!" said Kat. "It's real!"

"Or," said Levi slowly, "maybe Donte is right. Maybe it's just a reality show."

"Seriously? I'm right?" said Donte. "Hey, yeah! The PA voice did say 'HARVEST GAMES!'"

"Maybe it's like *Ninja Warrior*!" said Jordan.

"Or *Survivor*-type," offered Mr. Chuck.

"Or *Candid Camera*," said Ms. Padilla. She straightened. "Okay. Okay. I can rationalize that." She took a deep breath, then turned and screamed into the dark halls: "But we figured it out! We're on to you!"

"Yeah!" piped Jordan.

"And maybe we'll get royalty checks when this is all done," said Twila softly.

"I can't believe you people!" snapped Kat. "We're caught in the middle of a supernatural storm, the kids and teachers are all acting like deadheads, there's killer snowmen wandering the halls—" Levi nudged her sharply. She gave a dramatic sigh. "Fine. It's a reality show. Whatever. We still gotta act fast."

"Um," said Levi. "Has anyone been watching the snowmen?"

Twila and Kat both shifted their lights.

"Twila, keep your light on that group," said Ms. Padilla. Her teacher voice was back. "Kat, put your light on those snowmen over there."

A pause. The halo of light illuminated the frosty clouds of their breath.

"First, let's get out of this hall," said Ms. Padilla. "Together, now."

They shuffled down the cold, dark hall, moving as a single awkward mass. They neared the first snowman blockade.

"We're good," said Kat. "They won't move if the lights are on them."

"Careful! Steady with the lights... Almost there... almost..."

The intercom crackled and screeched.

Everyone jumped. Someone screamed. Kat whipped around, Twila dropped her phone, and for a moment their halo of safety light went nearly dark.

Twila fell to her knees and grappled with the floor, searching blindly for her phone.

Another scream.

A snowman had Levi by the neck.

"Keep the light on him!" roared Ms. Padilla. Kat rushed
forward and brought her elbows down on the snowman's
stick arms. They snapped, and Levi fell away from his
frozen attacker.

Another scream.

"Kat! The light! Over here!"

Kat's light revealed a snowman looming over Jordan.
Its staff was frozen in midair.

"Oh my . . ." said Ms. Padilla distantly. "Another split
second, and it would have . . ." Her voice trailed off as she
pulled Jordan away from the snowman. "Kat! Twila! I *told*
you not to move your lights!"

"The loudspeaker startled me!" protested Kat.

Another scream, and all three lights turned to Donte. A snowman had him up against a locker, staff at his throat.

"Don't turn the light away!" Donte gasped.

"Keep the light on it!" screamed Ms. Padilla. "Wait! Not all of you! Behind—"

More screams. The lights went wild. Silhouettes strobed down the hall.

FROM SCHOOL SECURITY CAMERAS (BATTER
ED)

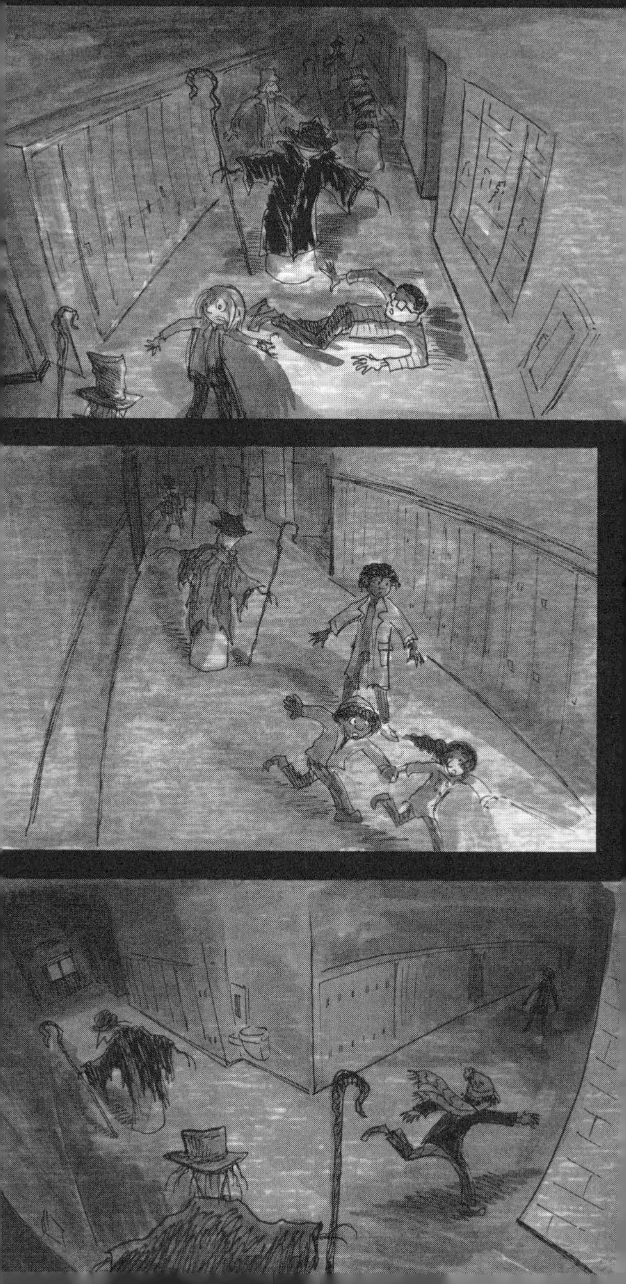

Chapter 17

FOOTAGE FROM KAT BOMBARD'S PHONE

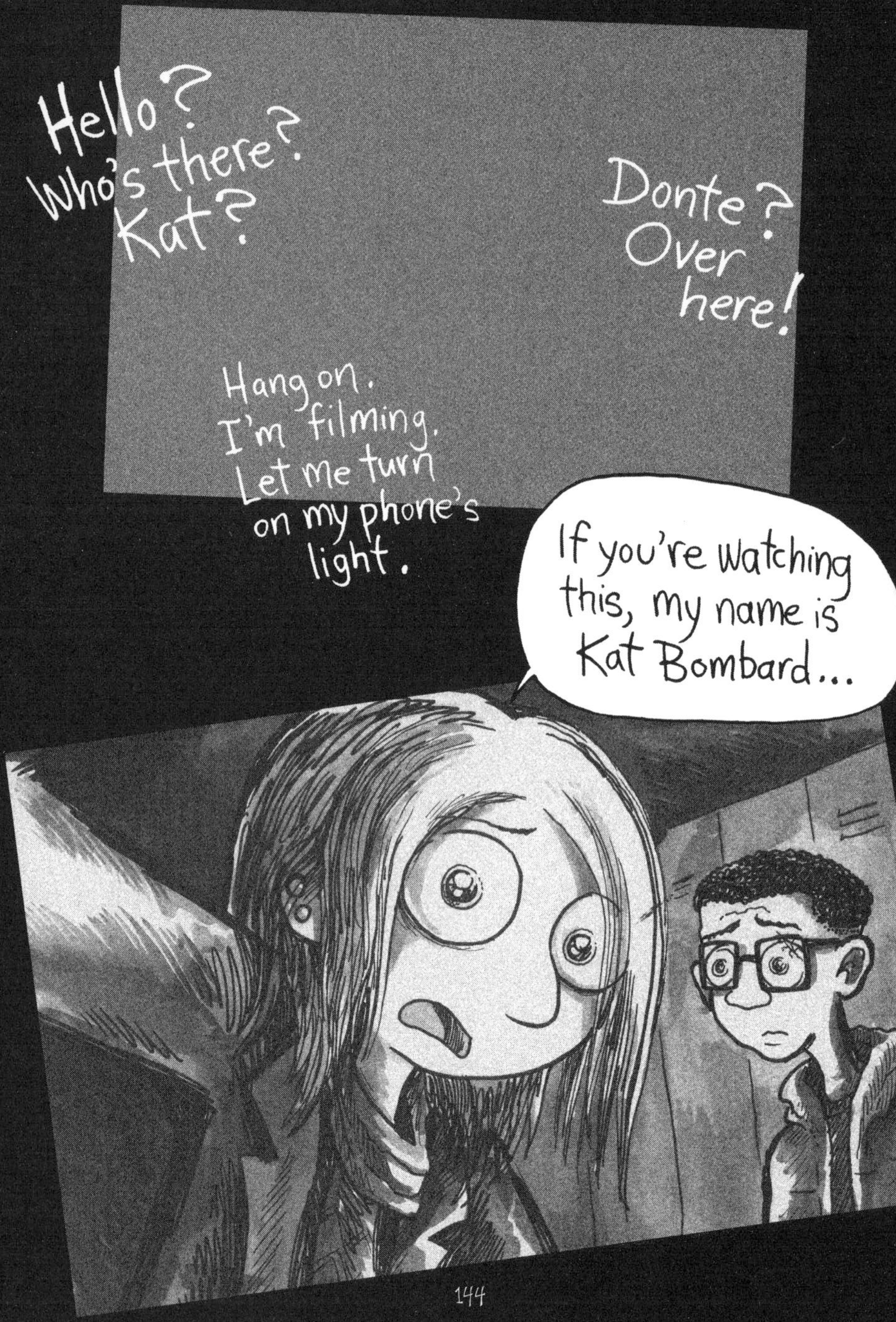
Hello? Who's there? Kat?
Donte? Over here!
Hang on. I'm filming. Let me turn on my phone's light.
If you're watching this, my name is Kat Bombard...

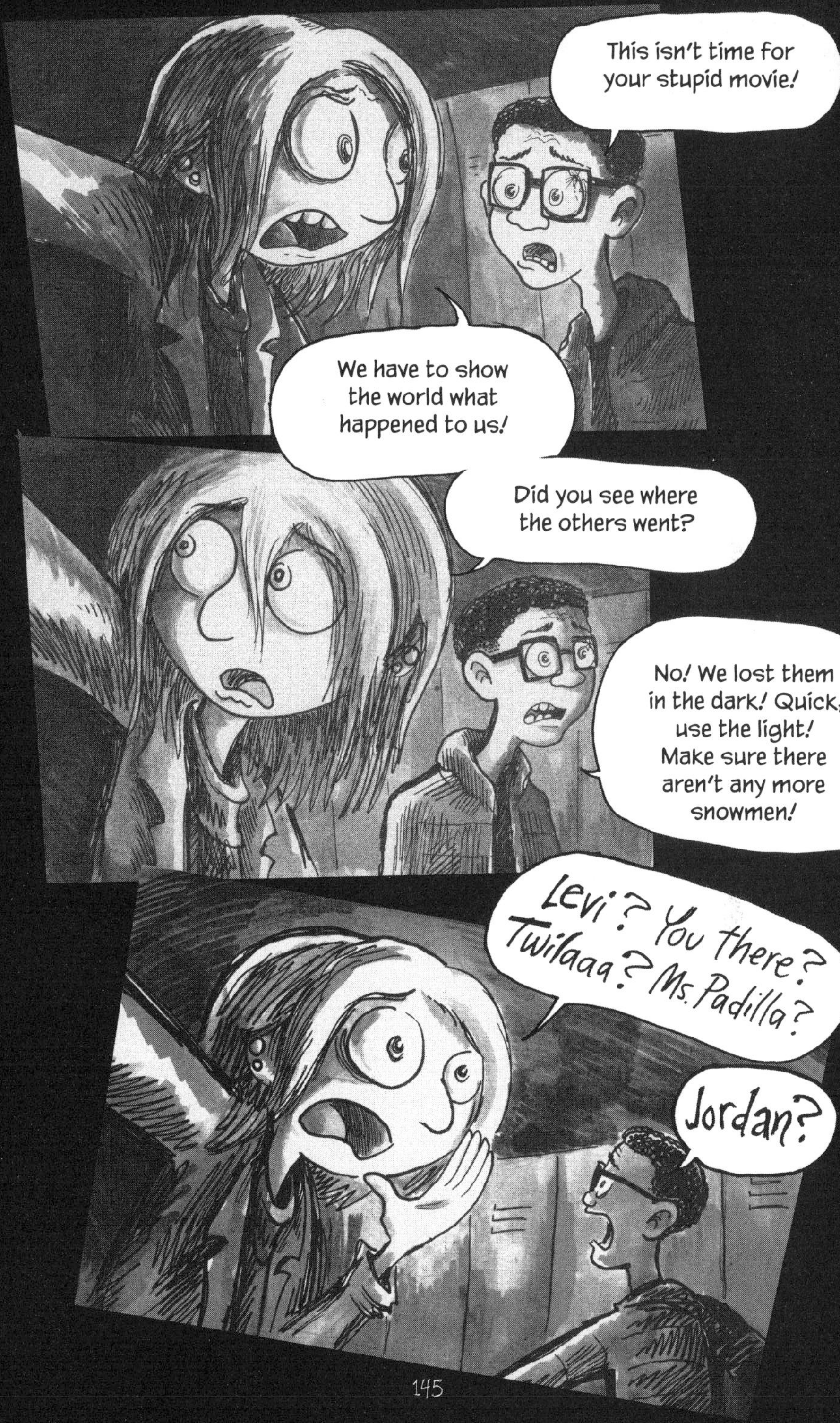
This isn't time for your stupid movie!
We have to show the world what happened to us!
Did you see where the others went?
No! We lost them in the dark! Quick, use the light! Make sure there aren't any more snowmen!
Levi? You there? Twilaaa? Ms. Padilla?
Jordan?

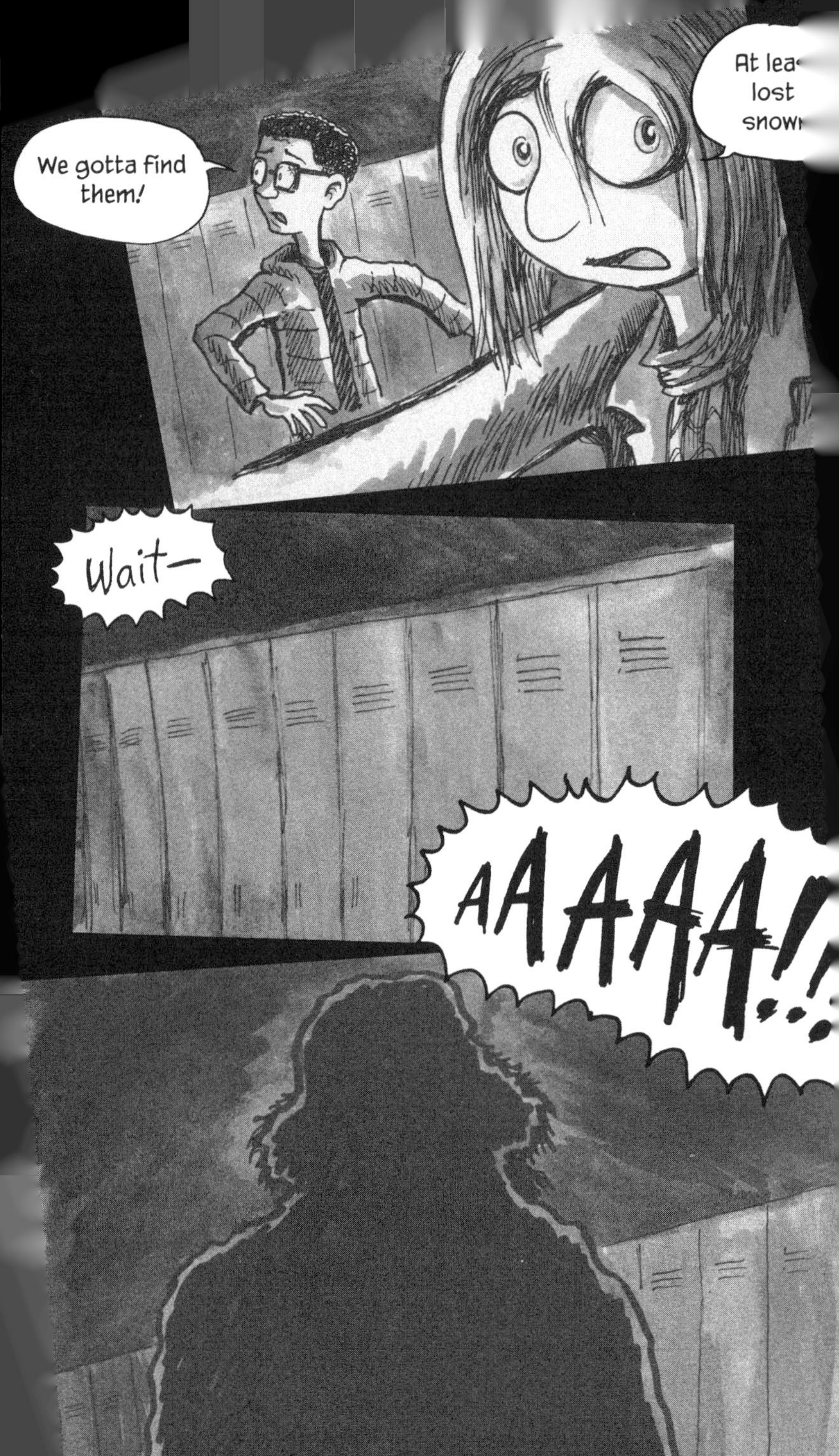
We gotta find them!
At lea
lost
snow
Wait—
AAAAA!!

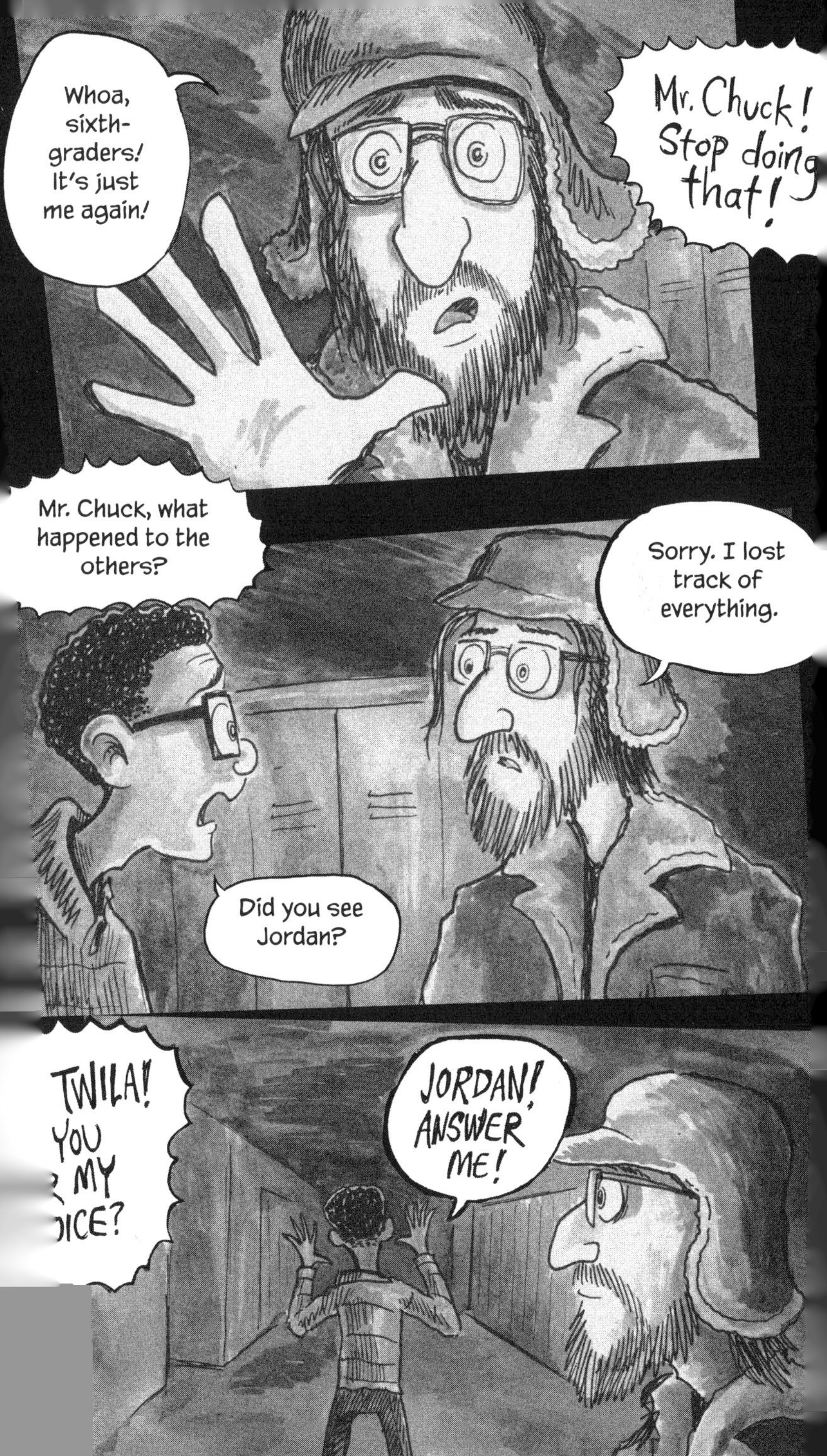
Whoa, sixth-graders! It's just me again!
Mr. Chuck! Stop doing that!
Mr. Chuck, what happened to the others?
Sorry. I lost track of everything.
Did you see Jordan?
TWILA! YOU MY
JORDAN! ANSWER ME!

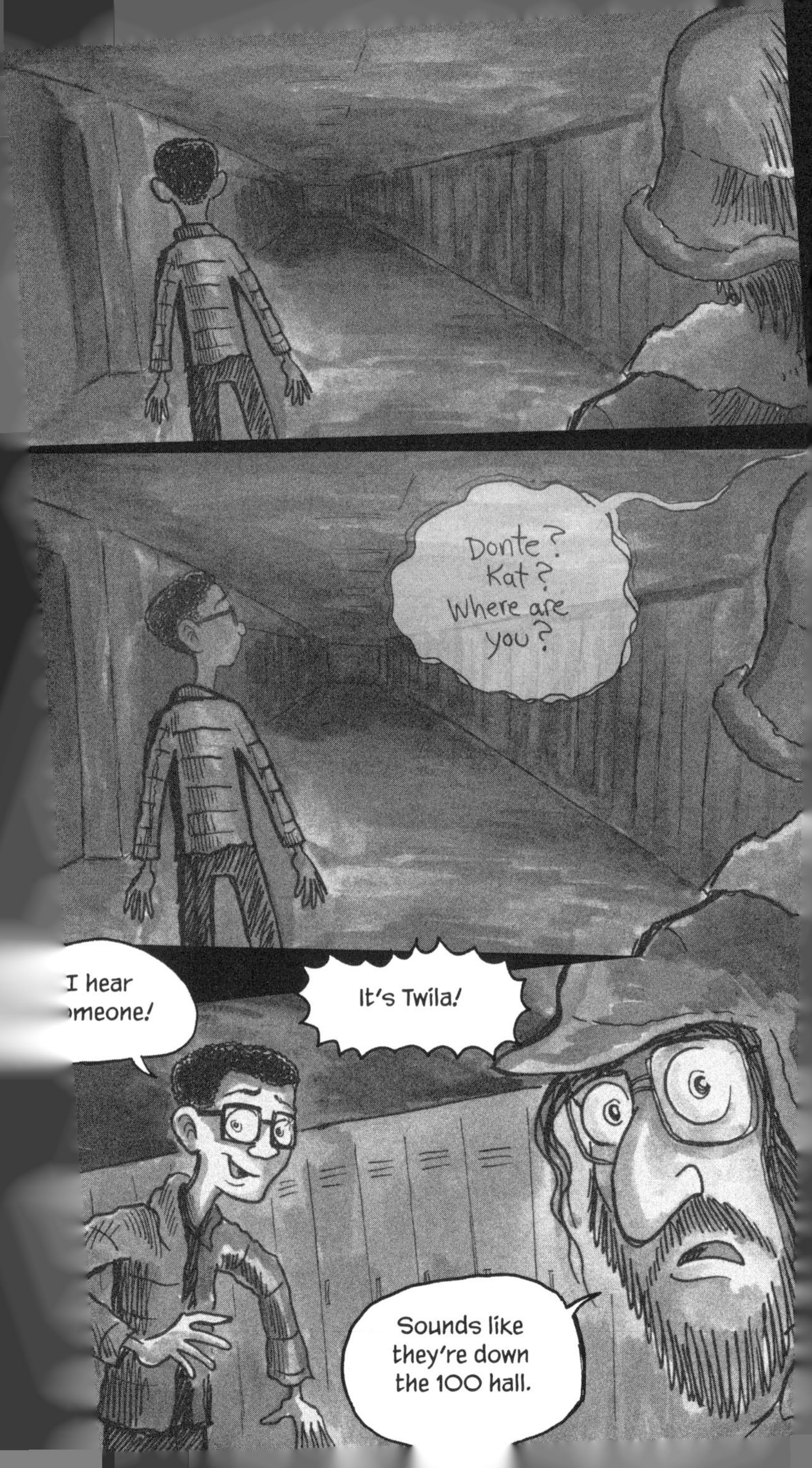

Donte? Kat? Where are you?
I hear meone!
It's Twila!
Sounds like they're down the 100 hall.

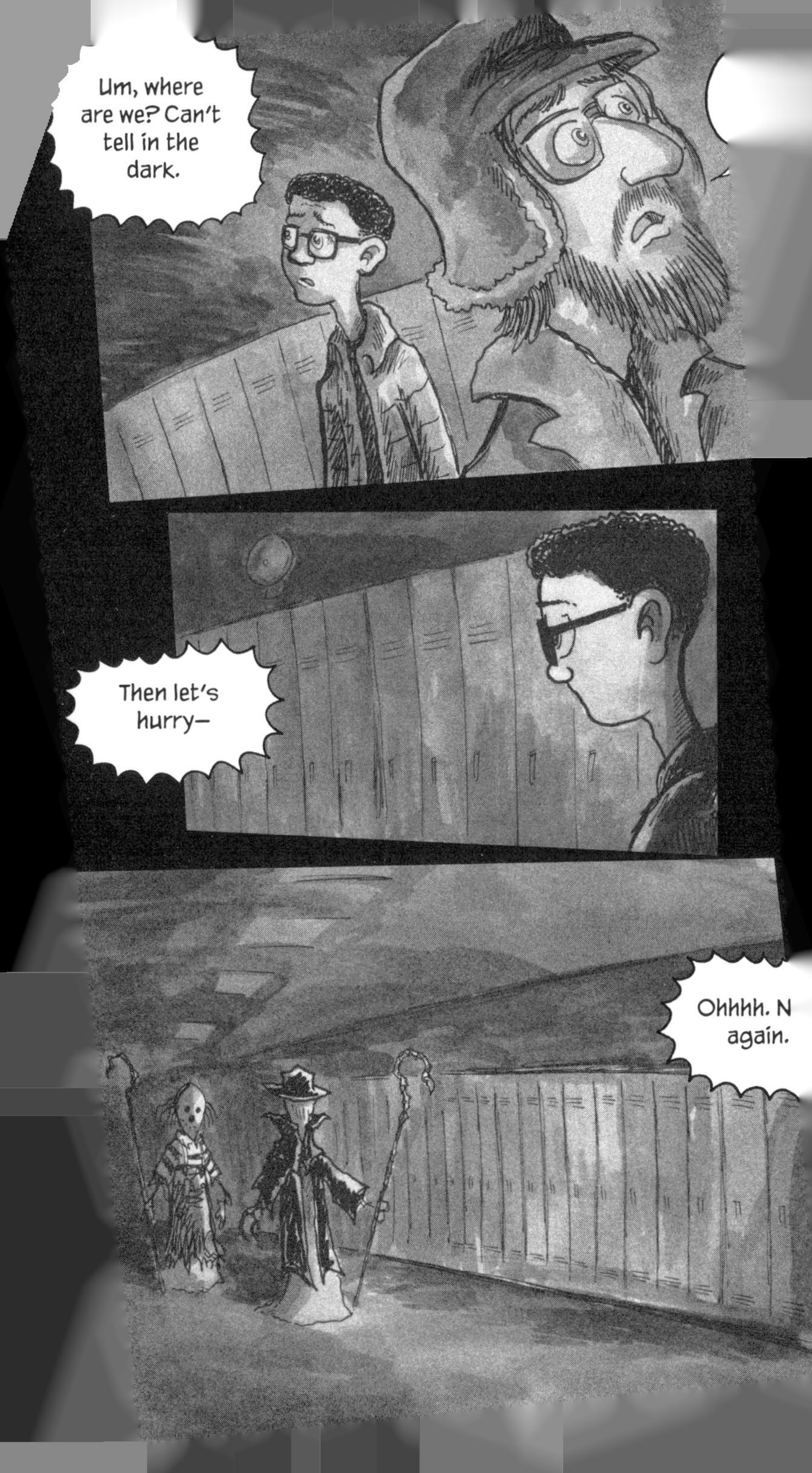
Um, where are we? Can't tell in the dark.
Then let's hurry—
Ohhhh. N
again.

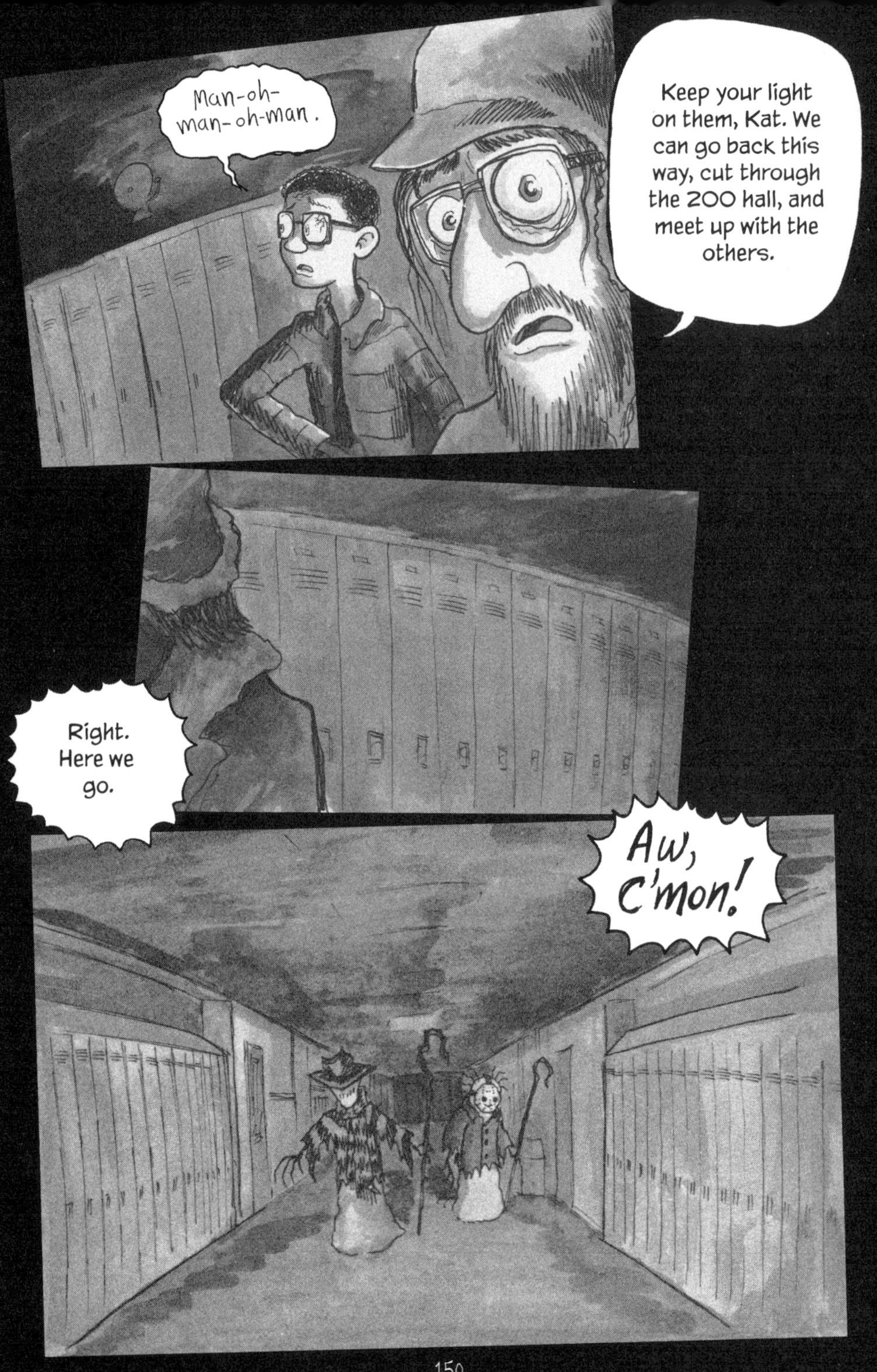
Man-oh-man-oh-man.
Keep your light on them, Kat. We can go back this way, cut through the 200 hall, and meet up with the others.
Right. Here we go.
Aw, C'mon!

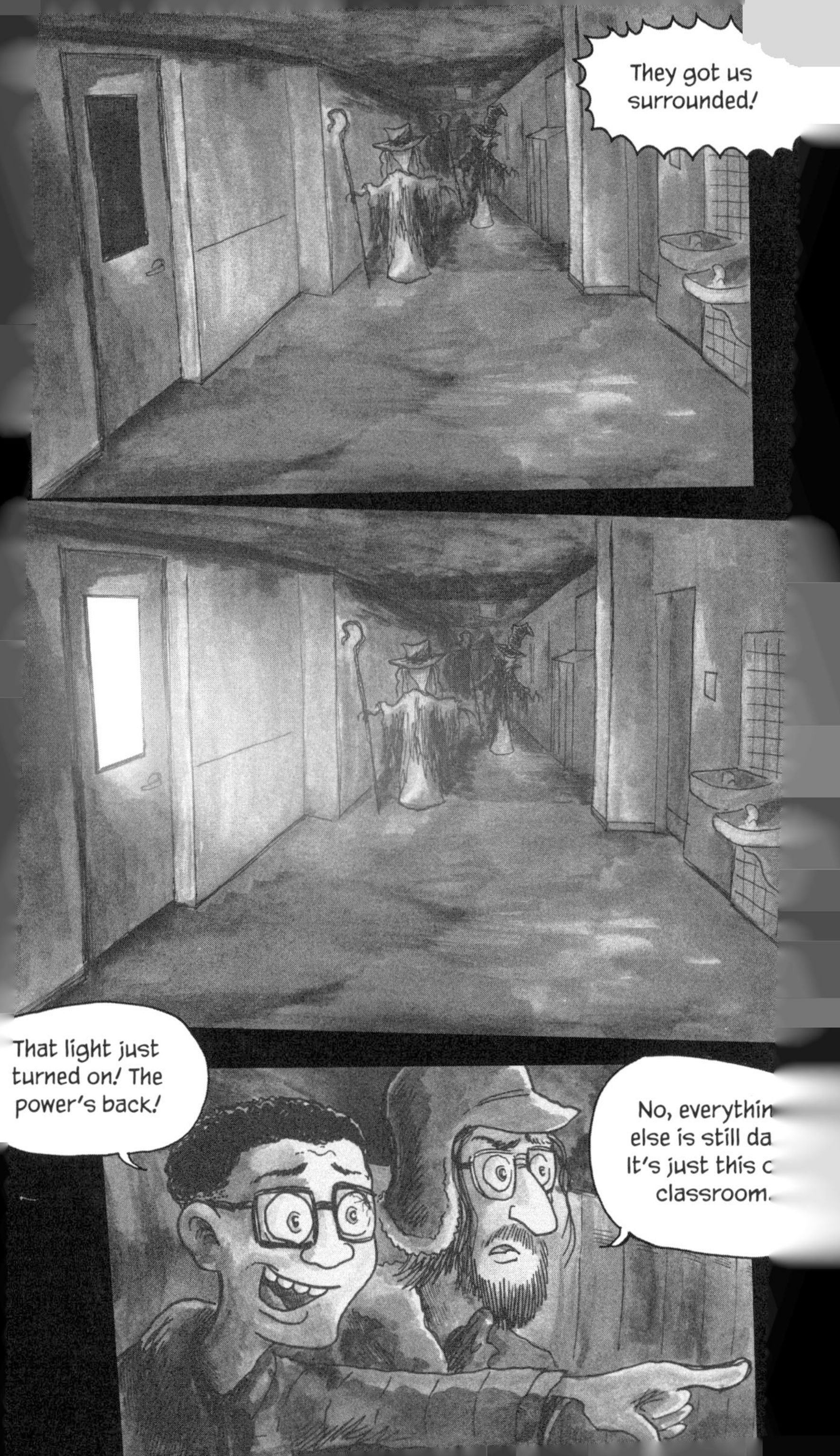
They got us surrounded!
That light just turned on! The power's back!
No, everythin else is still da It's just this c classroom.

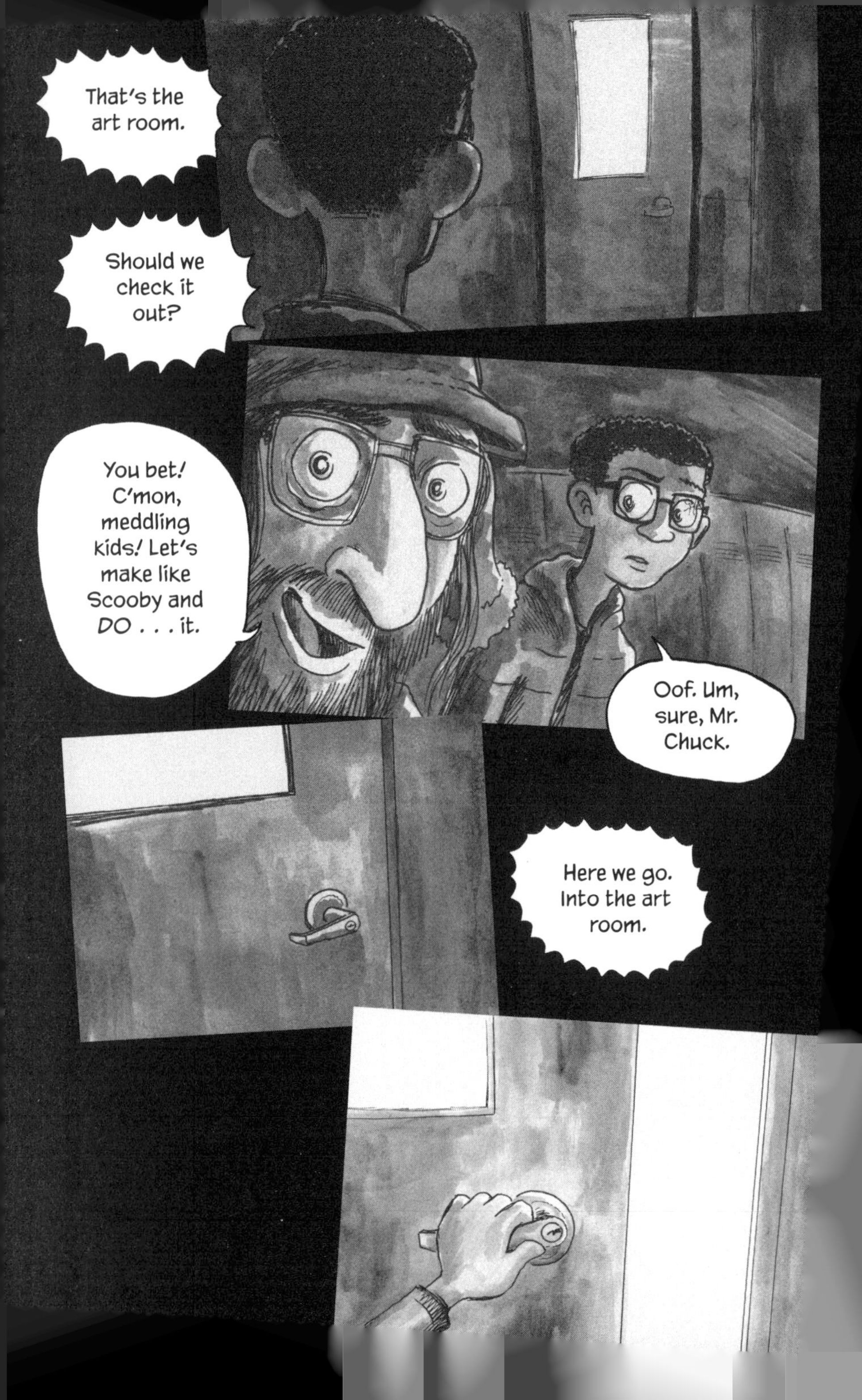
That's the art room.
Should we check it out?
You bet! C'mon, meddling kids! Let's make like Scooby and DO . . . it.
Oof. Um, sure, Mr. Chuck.
Here we go. Into the art room.

Chapter 18

"Twila! Twila!
Where are you?"

"Levi! Over here!"

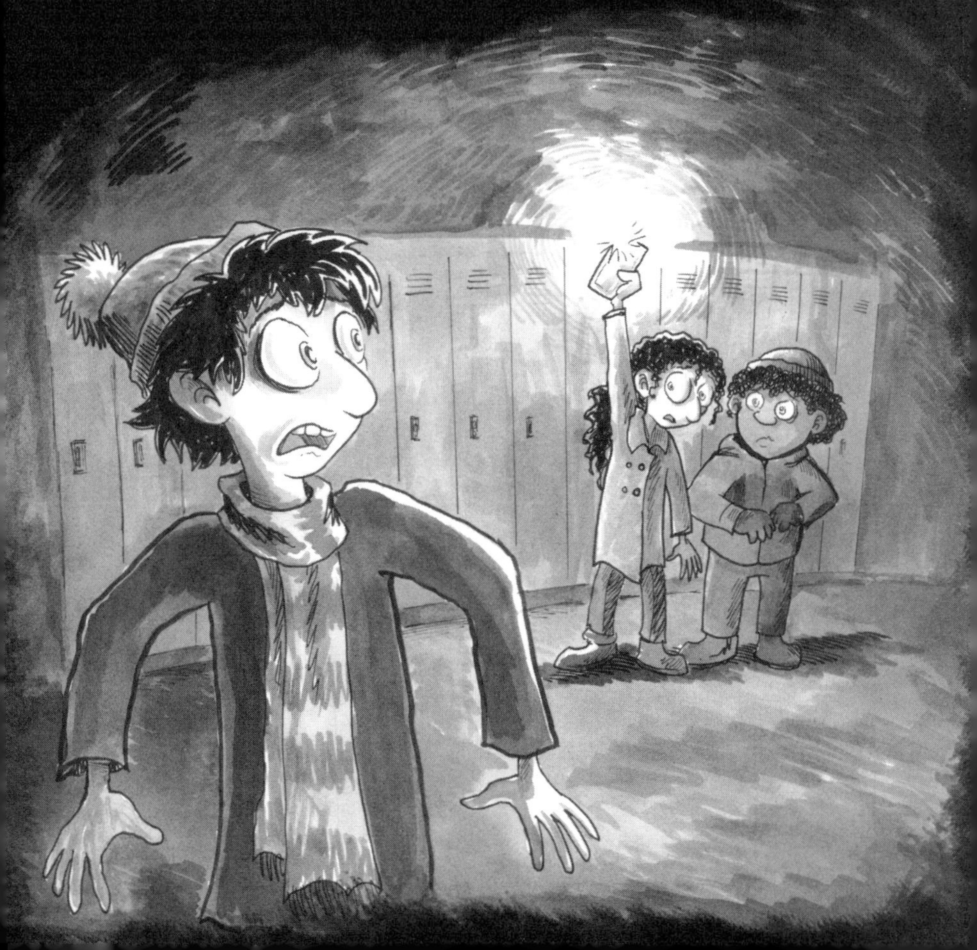

"I don't care about reality-show royalty checks anymore," said a small voice behind Twila. It was Jordan. "I just want to get out of here."

Twila swept the light through the darkened halls. "I think we got away from the snowmen."

"Where's Donte?" asked Jordan.

"Must've run in a different direction," said Levi.

"Hello?" said a familiar voice behind them.

"Ms. Padilla!" cried Levi. "Here!"

Ms. Padilla's bewildered face appeared in Twila's halo of light. "Oh, thank goodness!" she heaved. "I thought I'd lost you all!" Her eyes scanned them. "Wait. Who's missing?"

"Kat and Donte," said Levi. "And Mr. Chuck."

Ms. Padilla took a deep breath. "We can't let that happen again. Everyone hold hands. Twila, keep the light up high. Everyone be on the lookout for . . ." Another deep breath. "For snowmen."

They moved slowly down the hall.

"Ssh!" said Twila. "Listen!"

They froze. Held their breath.

Voices echoed through the darkened school.

"It's Kat and Donte!" said Twila. She cupped her hand to her mouth and shouted:

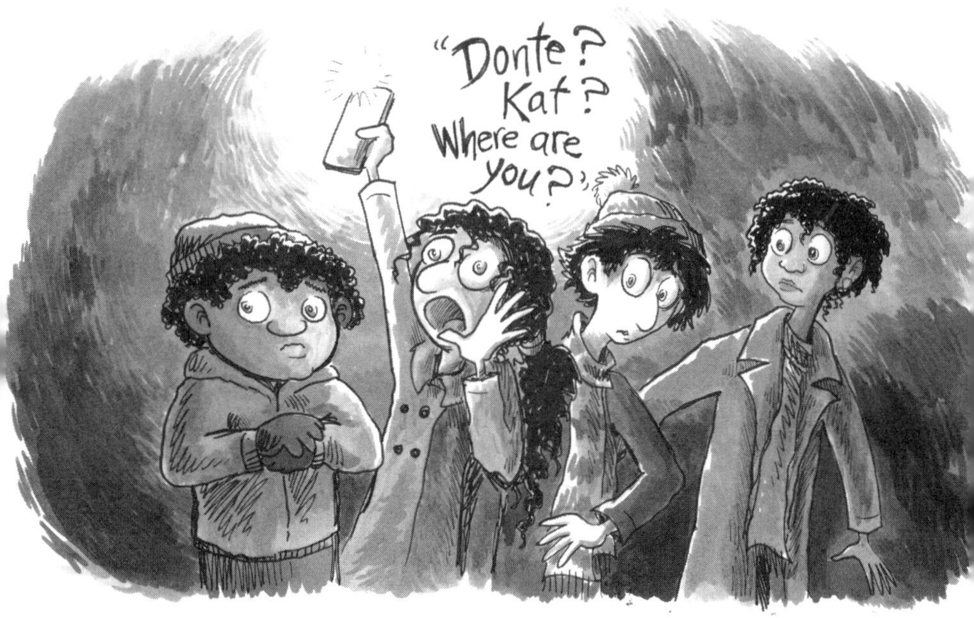
"Donte?
Kat?
Where are
you?"

Silence.

"Maybe they're coming for us?" whispered Jordan.

"Where are we, anyway?" asked Ms. Padilla. "Twila, turn your light to those lockers." The light scanned the locker numbers. "100 hall. That means there's a fire exit this way." She gave Levi's arm a tug, pulling the children toward her. "We've got to get out of here, storm or no storm."

"What about Kat and Donte?" asked Levi.

"We'll find the fire exit, then we'll call for them again."

They inched along the lockers, taking what seemed like an hour to reach the fire-exit door twenty meters away.

"It's lucky that we're wearing our winter gear," said Ms. Padilla. She found the door handle and pulled. The door didn't budge. She pulled harder. "Must be frozen shut."

"Here," said Levi. They both grabbed and jerked at the handle until the door sprang open with a *ker-chunk*.

There was no blast of cold air, no change in lighting, nothing one might expect from opening a door in the middle of a storm. Twila moved her light to the open door. There was no outside world. Just an irregular white wall.

"It's ice," said Levi.

Ms. Padilla reached and punched the white wall. "Impossible!"

"No," said Levi. Panic was creeping into his voice. "The school is buried. *We* are buried!"

"I don't care how bad that blizzard was," said Ms. Padilla. "There is no way the school could be buried under this much snow!" She threw herself against the snow wall, grappling with it, clawing with both hands.

"We're trapped!" said Jordan. "And we're gonna get eaten by killer snowmen!"

Ms. Padilla stopped trying to push through the white wall. "This door is on the northeast side of the building. It got the brunt of the storm. We'll try another door."

They continued slowly down the hall.

"I wish we all had lights," whispered Levi. "Then we could make sure the snowmen aren't sneaking up on us."

"At least they move really slow," said Jordan.

"We don't know that," said Twila. "We just know they don't move at all when the light's on them. Maybe they move really fast when no one's watching them, when everything's dark."

Silence.

"Wish we had more lights," repeated Levi.

As if in response, a classroom light suddenly turned on across the hall.

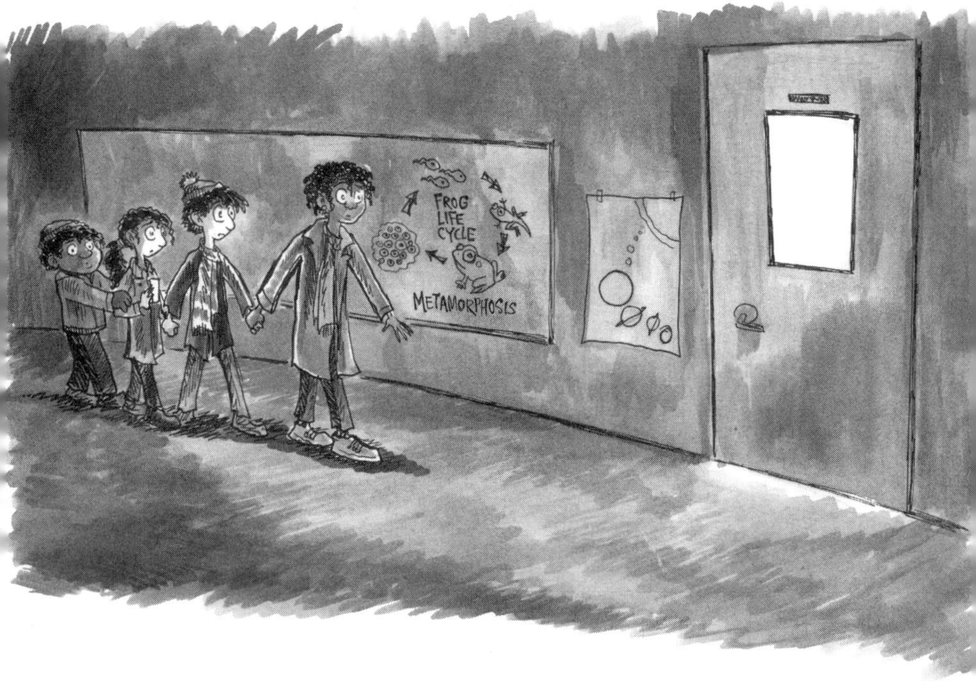
FROG
LIFE
CYCLE
METAMORPHOSIS

They froze.

"It's the science lab!" said Ms. Padilla, almost cheerfully. "The power's back!"

"Then why are all the other lights still off?" Levi asked.

Ms. Padilla peered through the lab door's window. "I don't see anyone," she said. She took the door handle and gingerly turned it. The door creaked open. "Wait here for just a moment," she said to the students. She poked her head into the room. "Hello?" She slowly stepped through the door.

Levi squeezed Twila's hand. "Stay here a sec." He followed Ms. Padilla into the classroom. He looked around. "Empty."

And then the door
slammed shut.

Chapter 19

"LEVI!" screamed Twila. She shoved the light into Jordan's hands and threw herself against the classroom door. She jerked the handle with all her strength, but it wouldn't turn. "Locked!"

The light from the window flickered, and the science lab went dark.

"No!" She kicked at the door again and again. No answer from the other side.

They both tackled the closed door together, rattling the handle and pounding the heavy wood.

"This just keeps getting worse!" moaned Jordan. He slid to the ground and curled into a ball like a distressed pill bug.

Twila knelt and shook him. "Don't do that! You'll attract the snowmen!" She paused. "Maybe we should call for Kat and Donte and Mr. Chuck again. Maybe they can help us get the door open."

"Wait," said Jordan. His head was pressing against the cold floor. "What's that?"

"What?"

"That sound . . . Like something scratching."

They held their breath.

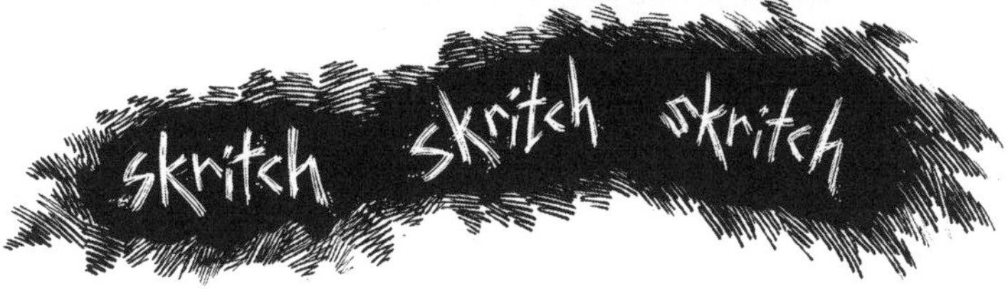
skritch skritch skritch

"It's coming from the exit door," whispered Jordan.

Twila took a hesitant step toward the fire door across the hall. "Hello?"

The scratching stopped.

"Twi-loonigan?" asked a raspy voice from the other side.

"Willow?" Twila rushed to the door and reached for the handle. "How are you out there, Willow? Ms. Padilla opened the door. There was nothing but a wall of snow!" The door popped open.

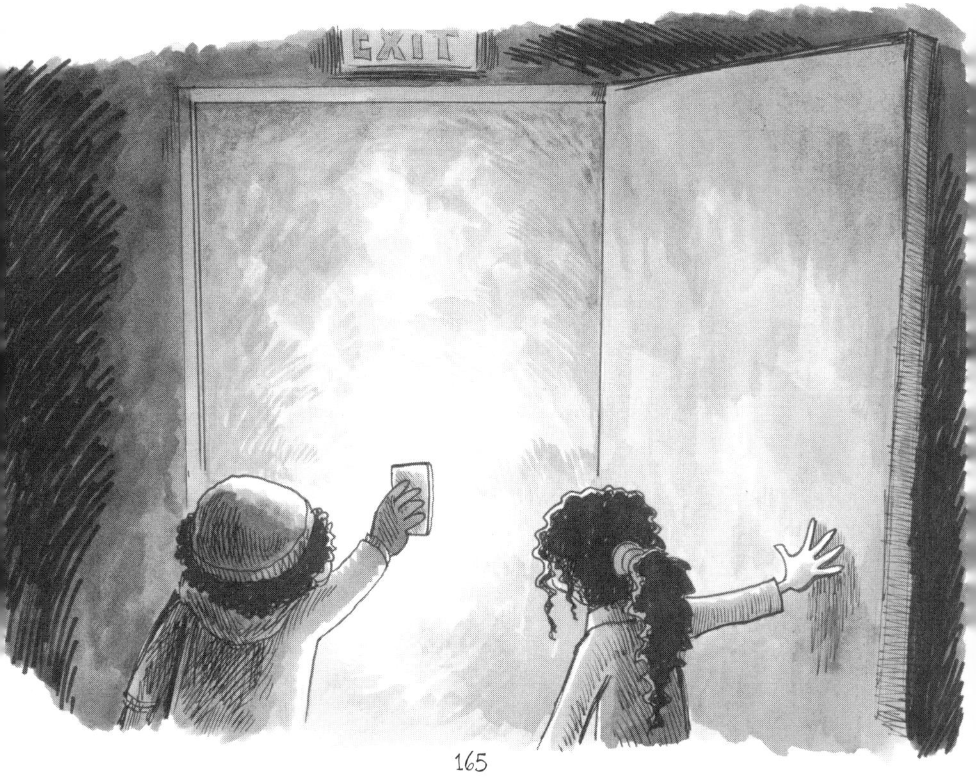
EXIT

The phone's light glinted off the snow wall.

"Nothing!" Jordan said. "A ghost?"

"Down here, goofooligans!" said the voice. Jordan shined the light down to knee level. There was a hole in the snow. Two fluorescent green orbs gleamed out from it.

Jordan gasped. "It's . . . an alien demon ghost?"

"It's just Willow!" said Twila.

Willow's scraggly head poked out from the hole. "Quickly, kiddies. You must come with Willow if you want to live." Her eyes flashed as they scanned the dark halls. "Where are Levi and Kat-hooligan?"

"We lost them! Levi and Ms. Padilla are locked in the science lab!"

"Then we must help them," said Willow. She started out of the hole, then froze. Her spines went rigid. Her lip curled.

Twila took her phone back from Jordan and shined it in the direction Willow was staring.

"Oh, maaaan! Not them again!"

"More that way!" Jordan whispered, pointing in the opposite direction. "They're closing in!"

Willow's eyes blinked in the dark like malfunctioning satellites. "Then we must go. Now. Back to Margalo, for what we feared is happening."

"You mean the wildlife clinic?" Twila asked. "But the school is buried! We're trapped!"

"No. Levi and Kat-hooligan are trapped, but not Twila and . . ." She stared at Jordan.

"Oh, that's Jordan," said Twila. "My buddy. It's okay, Jordan. Willow is a friend. I'll explain later."

"Good," said Willow. "Now follow Willow. Quickly, before the snow bogeys reach us." She pulled back into the hole in the snow and was gone.

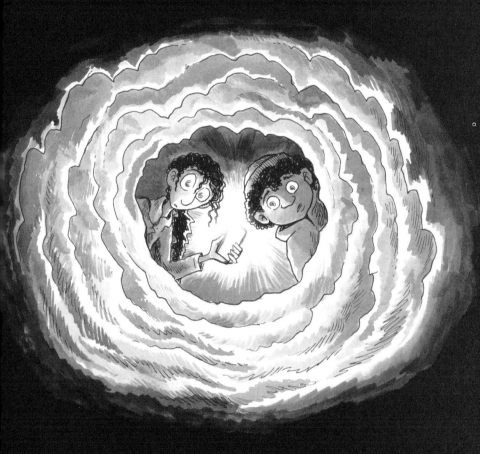

Twila knelt and shined the light into the hole.
"It's a tunnel!"
Twila and Jordan exchanged looks.
"Guess we're in for a tight squeeze."

Chapter 20

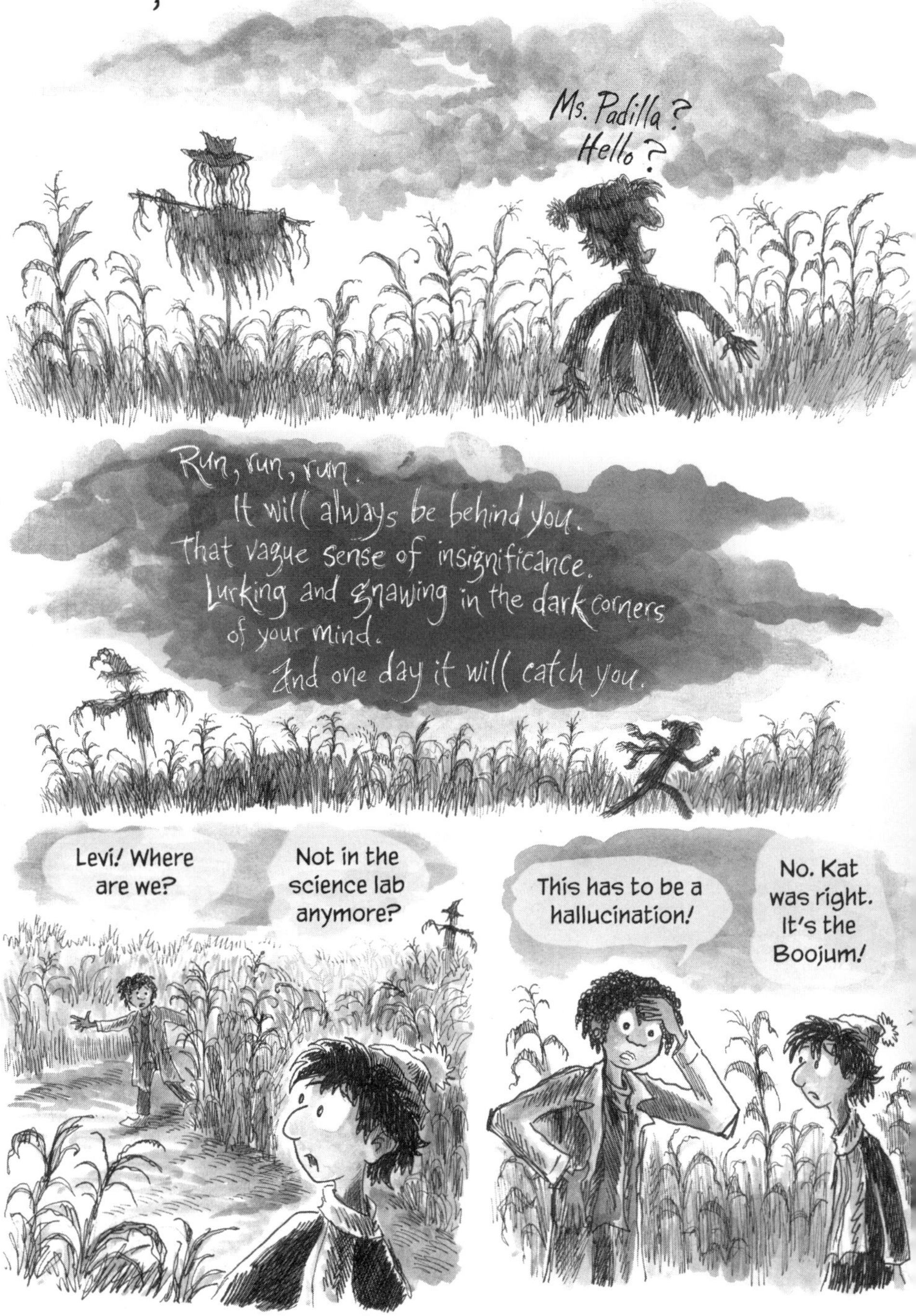
Ms. Padilla? Hello?
Run, run, run. It will always be behind you. That vague sense of insignificance. Lurking and gnawing in the dark corners of your mind. And one day it will catch you.
Leví! Where are we?
Not in the science lab anymore?
This has to be a hallucination!
No. Kat was right. It's the Boojum!

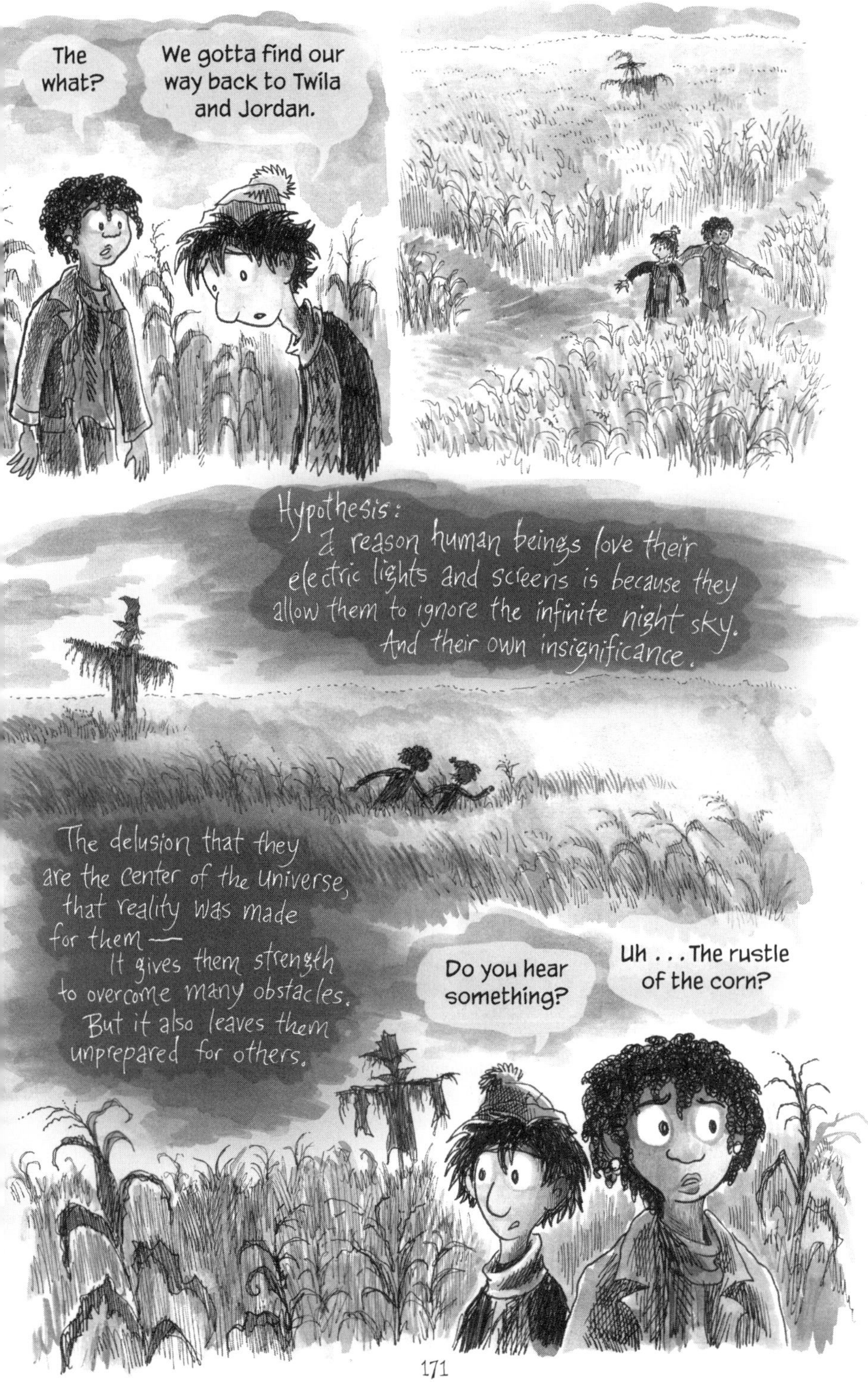
The what?
We gotta find our way back to Twila and Jordan.
Hypothesis:
A reason human beings love their electric lights and screens is because they allow them to ignore the infinite night sky.
And their own insignificance.
The delusion that they are the center of the universe, that reality was made for them—
It gives them strength to overcome many obstacles.
But it also leaves them unprepared for others.
Do you hear something?
Uh . . . The rustle of the corn?

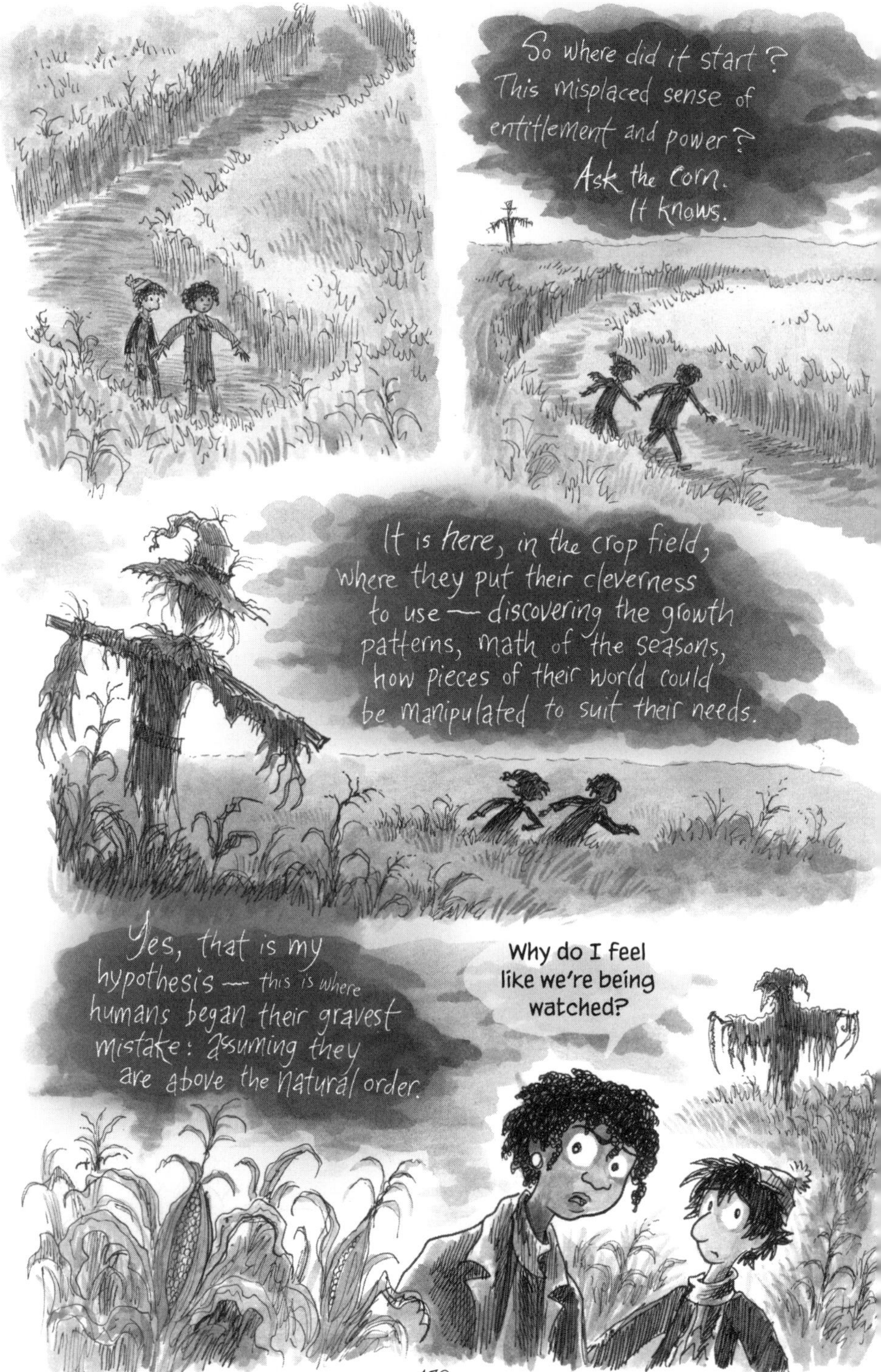
So where did it start? This misplaced sense of entitlement and power?
Ask the corn. It knows.
It is here, in the crop field, where they put their cleverness to use—discovering the growth patterns, math of the seasons, how pieces of their world could be manipulated to suit their needs.
Yes, that is my hypothesis — this is where humans began their gravest mistake: assuming they are above the natural order.
Why do I feel like we're being watched?

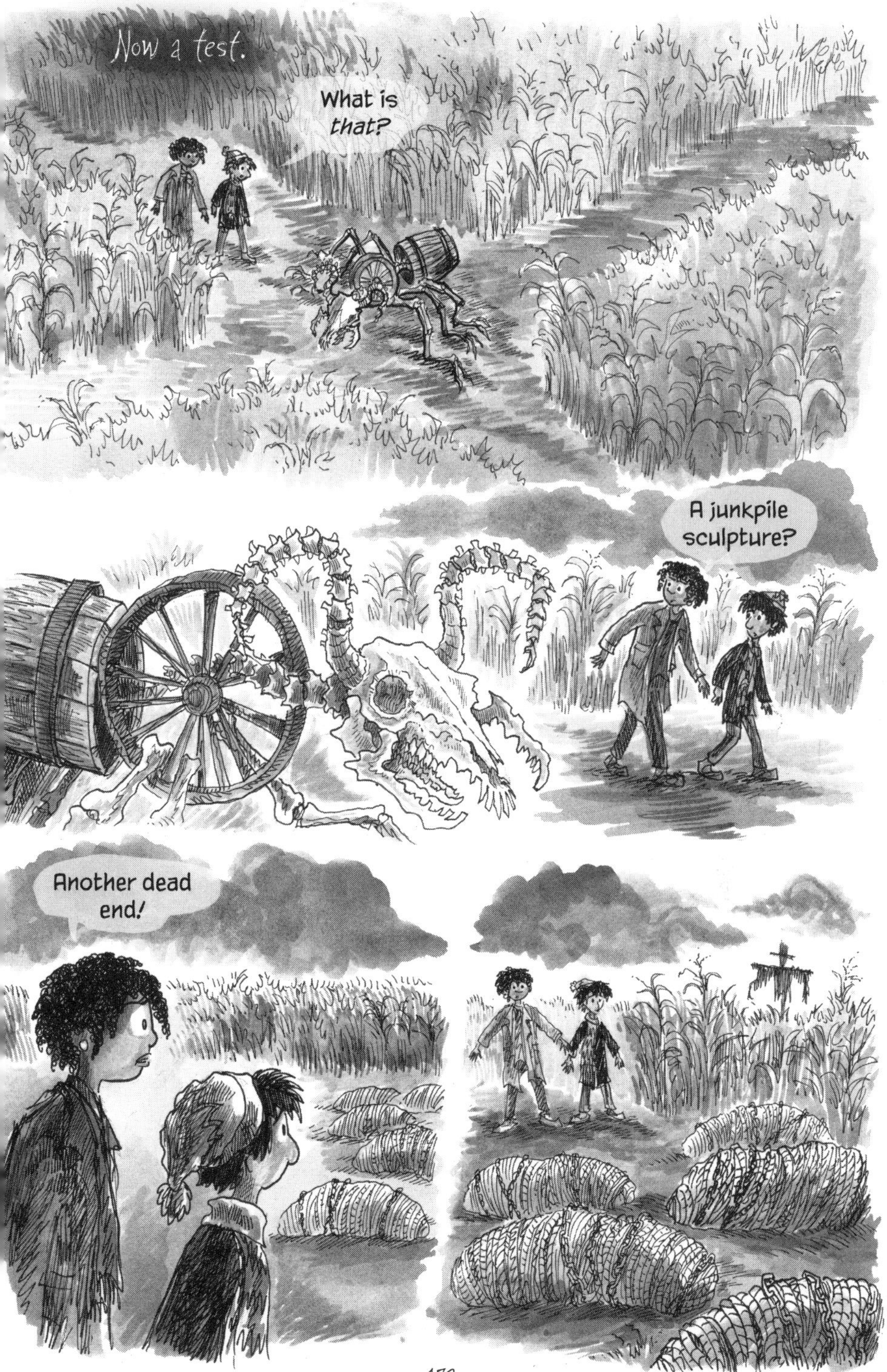
Now a test.
What is *that?*
A junkpile sculpture?
Another dead end!

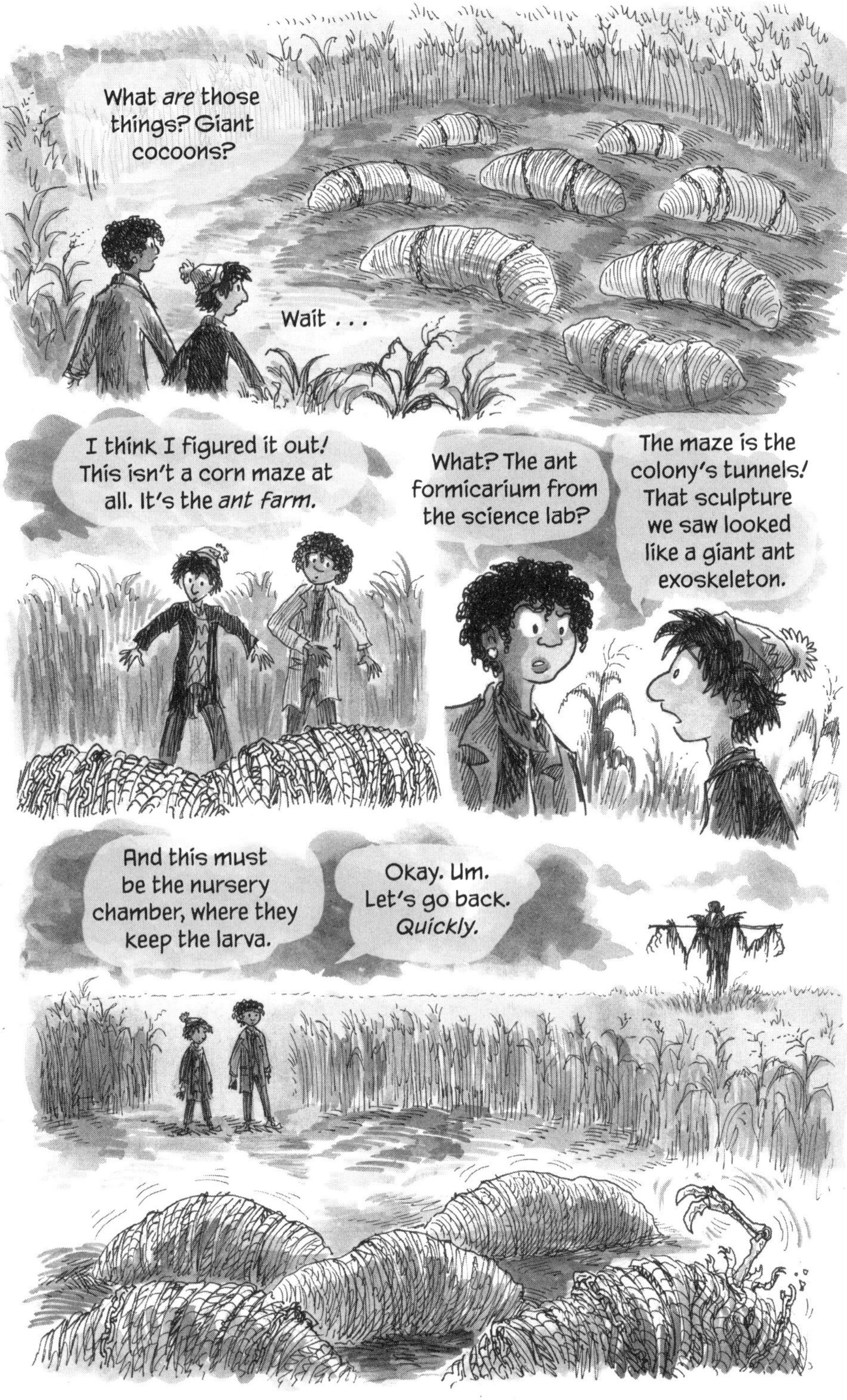
What *are* those things? Giant cocoons?
Wait . . .
I think I figured it out! This isn't a corn maze at all. It's the *ant farm.*
What? The ant formicarium from the science lab?
The maze is the colony's tunnels! That sculpture we saw looked like a giant ant exoskeleton.
And this must be the nursery chamber, where they keep the larva.
Okay. Um. Let's go back. *Quickly.*

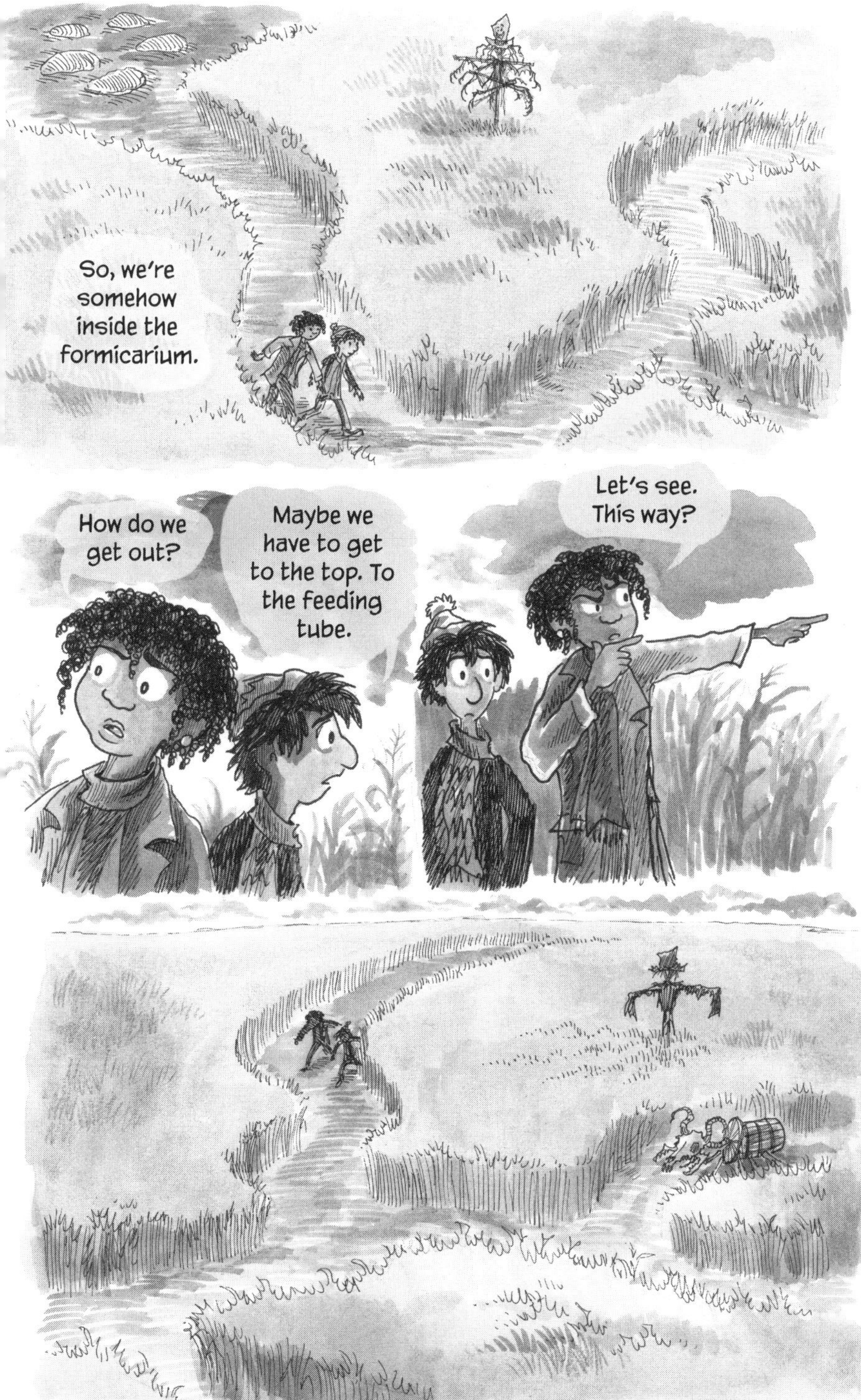
So, we're somehow inside the formicarium.
How do we get out?
Maybe we have to get to the top. To the feeding tube.
Let's see. This way?

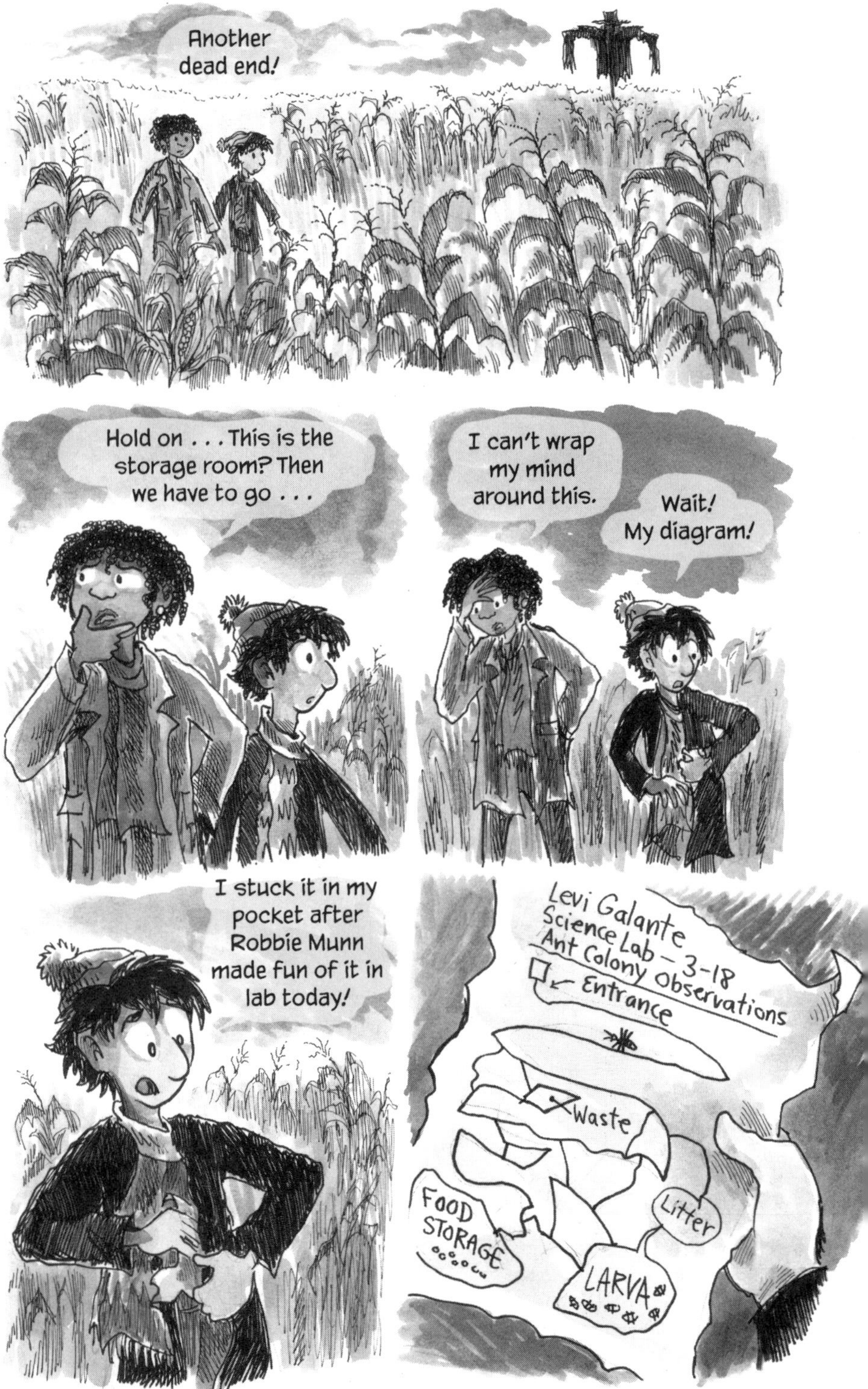

Another dead end!
Hold on . . . This is the storage room? Then we have to go . . .
I can't wrap my mind around this.
Wait! My diagram!
I stuck it in my pocket after Robbie Munn made fun of it in lab today!
Levi Galante
Science Lab – 3-18
Ant Colony Observations
Entrance
Waste
FOOD STORAGE
Litter
LARVA

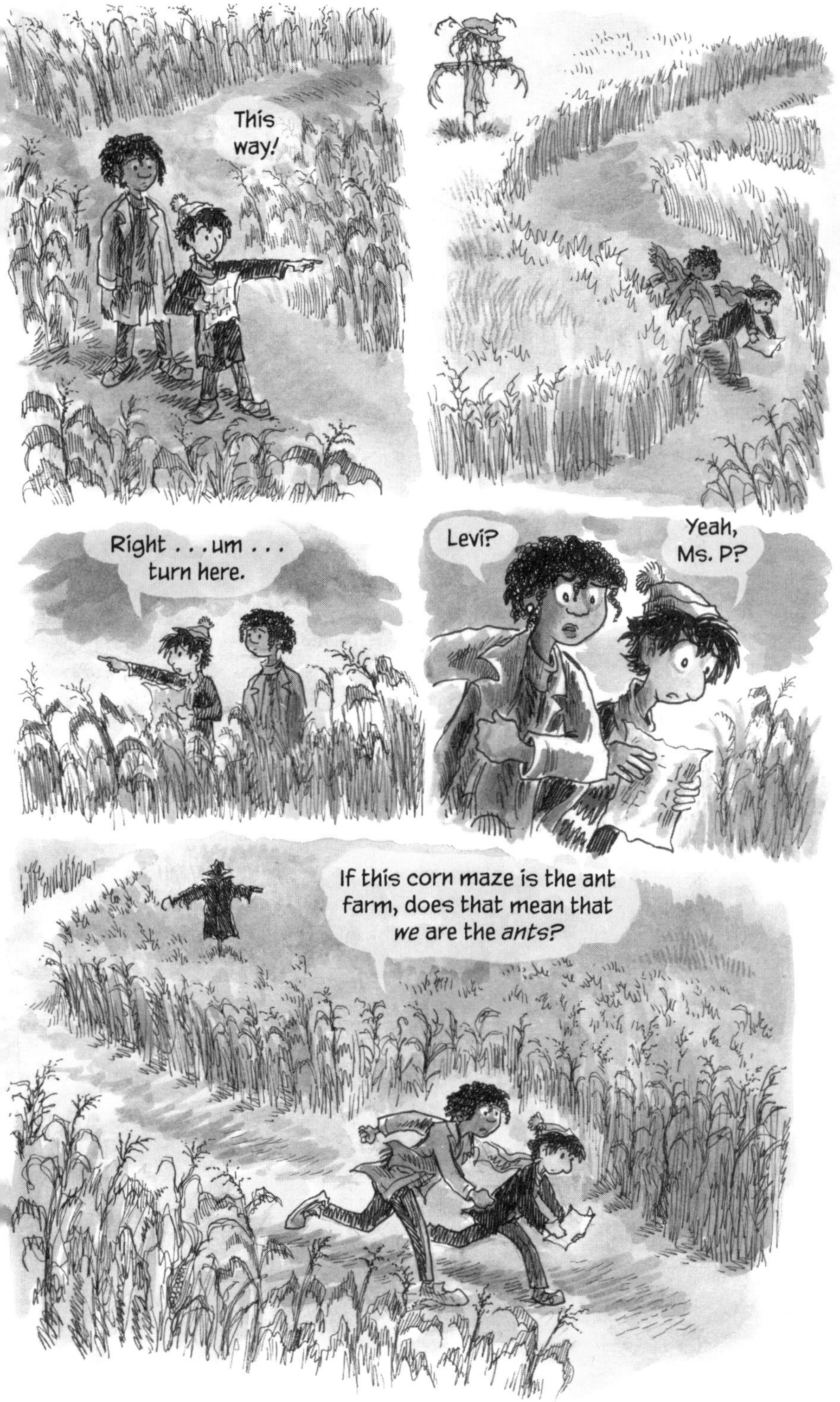
This way!
Right . . . um . . . turn here.
Levi?
Yeah, Ms. P?
If this corn maze is the ant farm, does that mean that *we* are the *ants*?

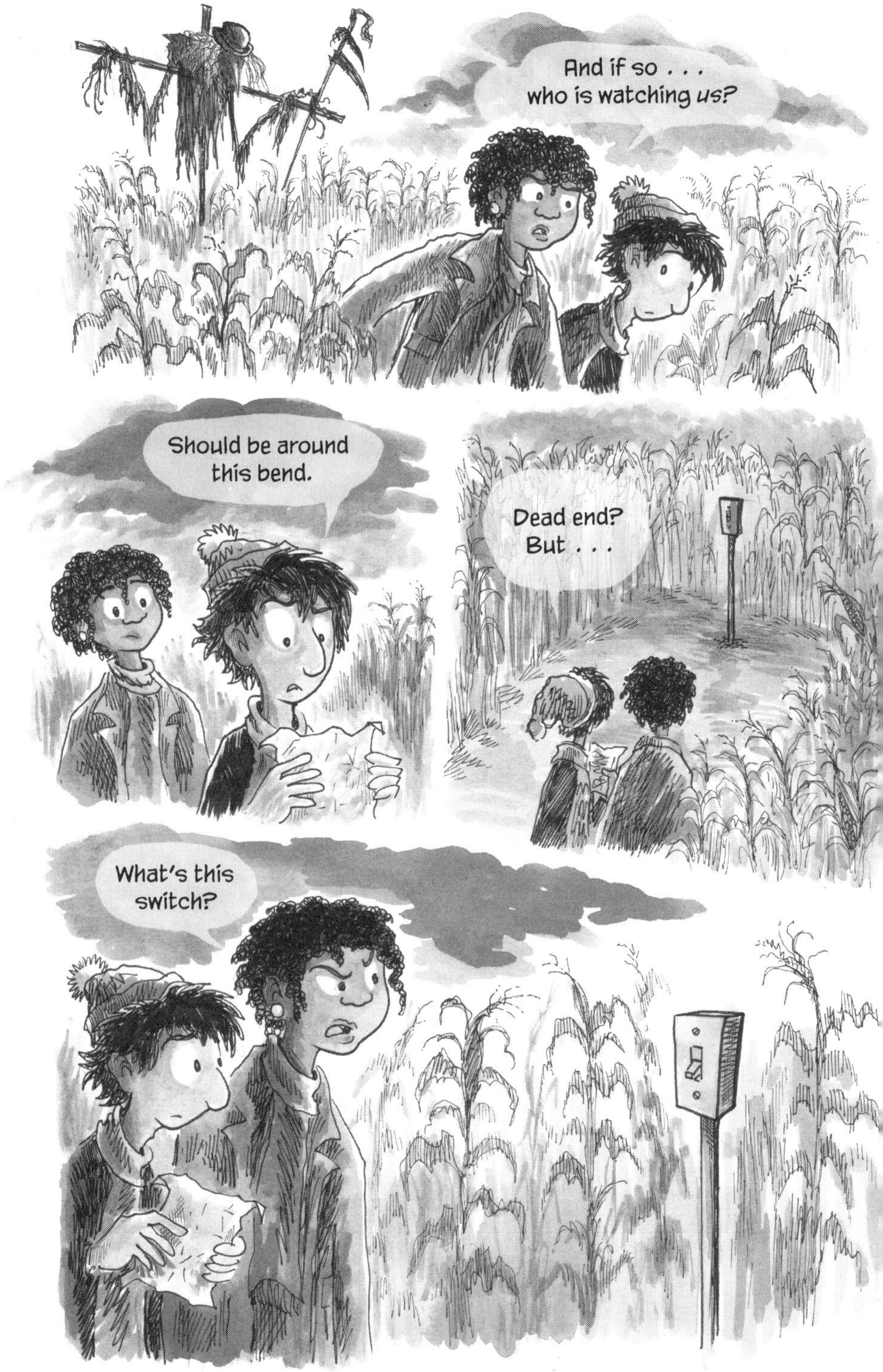
And if so . . . who is watching *us*?
Should be around this bend.
Dead end? But . . .
What's this switch?

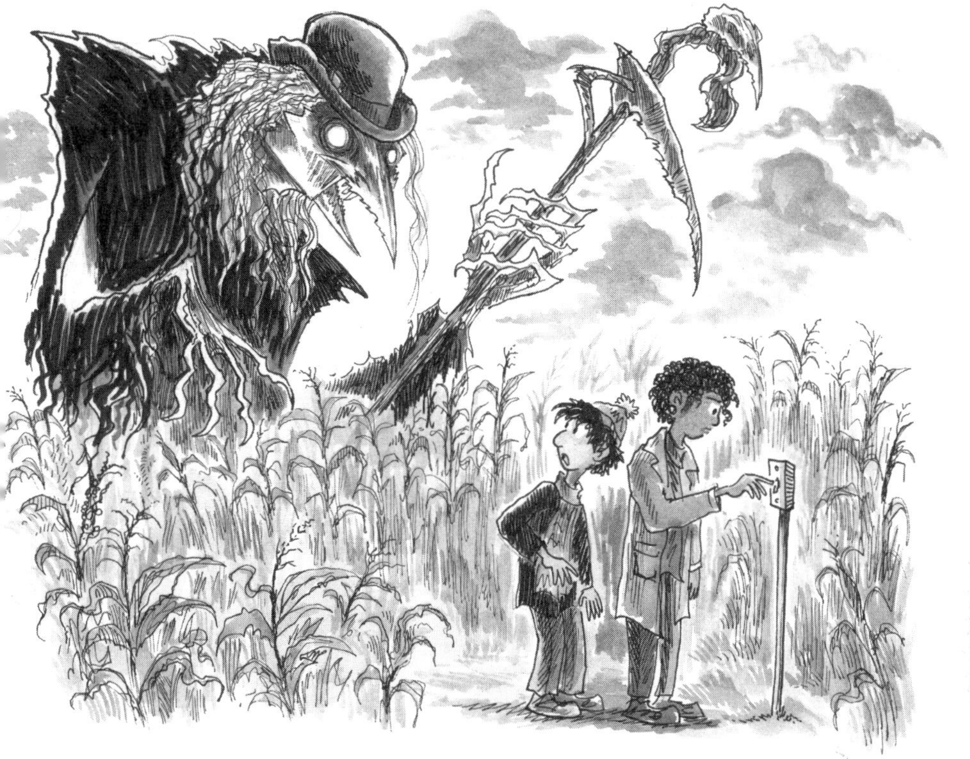

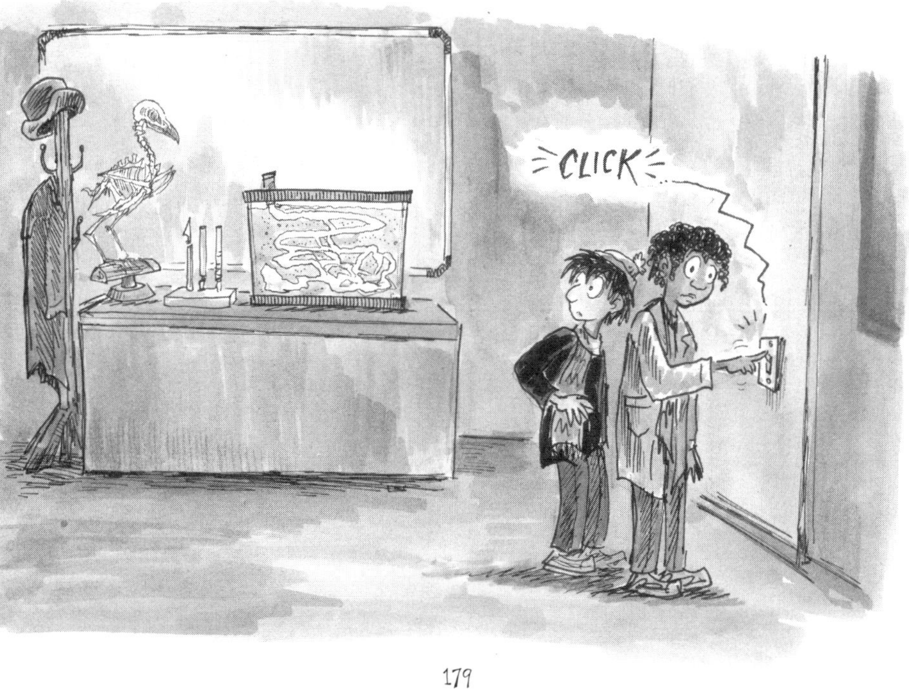
CLICK

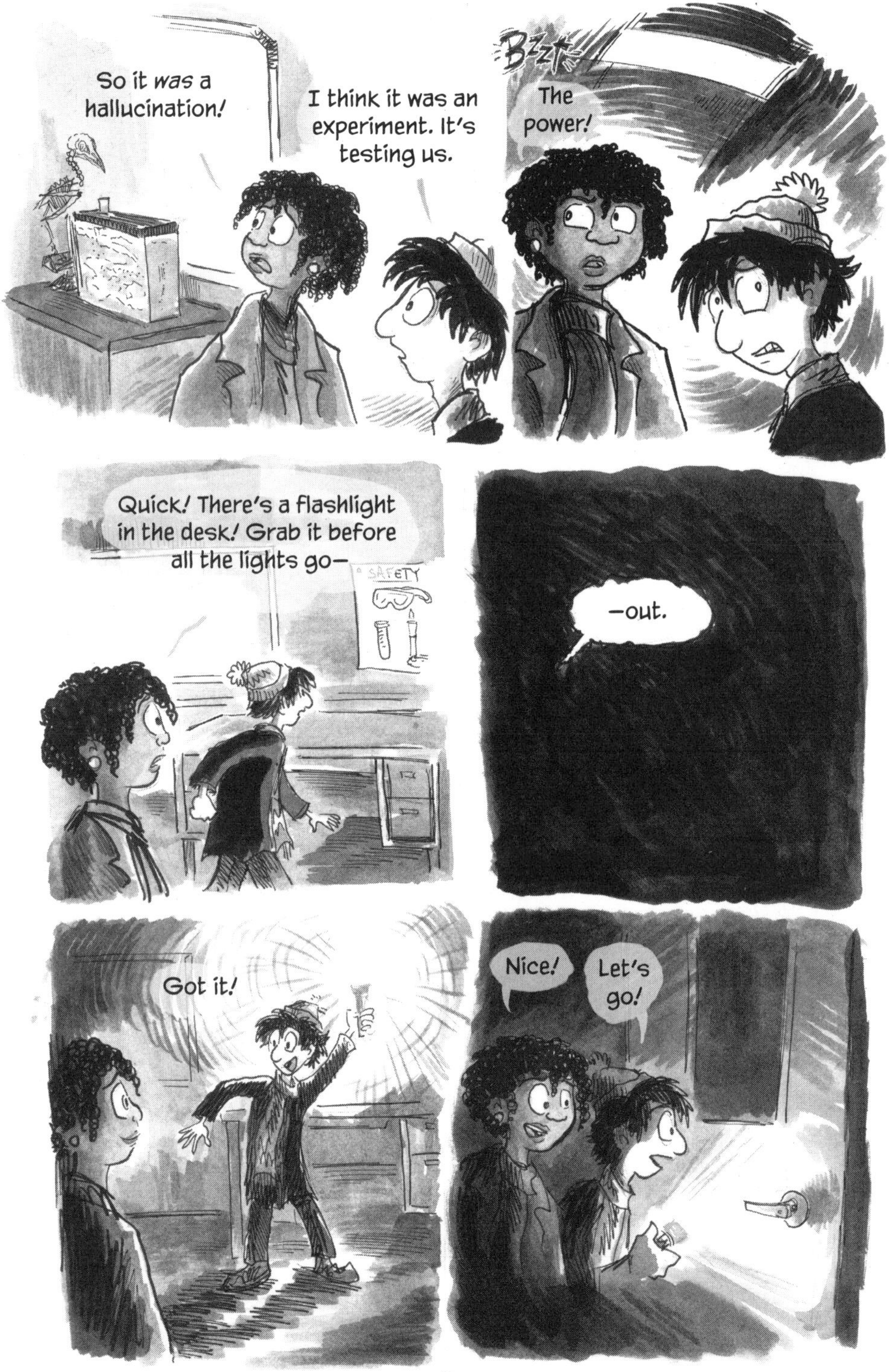
So it *was* a hallucination!
I think it was an experiment. It's testing us.
Bzzt
The power!
Quick! There's a flashlight in the desk! Grab it before all the lights go—
SAFETY
—out.
Got it!
Nice!
Let's go!

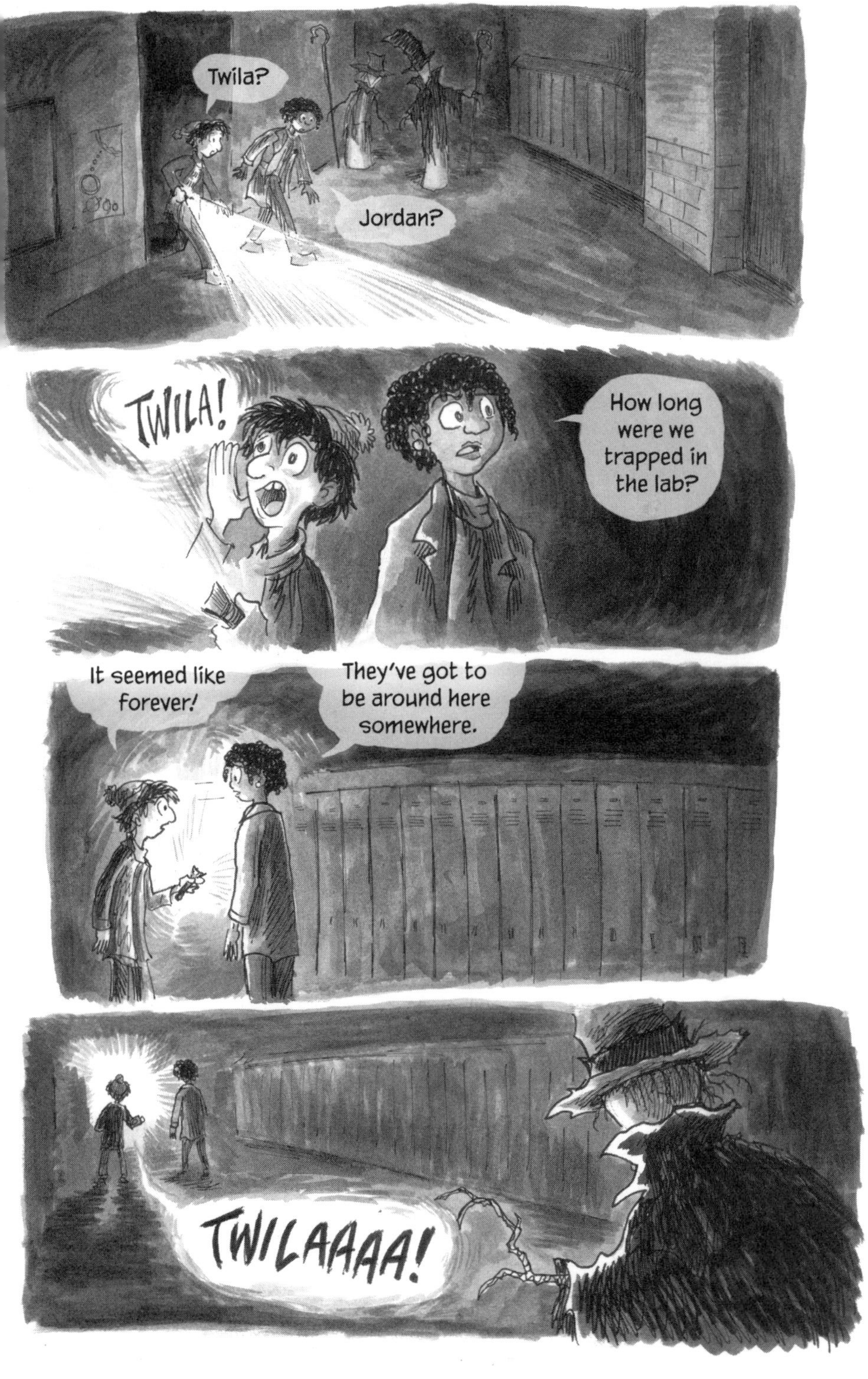

Twila?
Jordan?
TWILA!
How long were we trapped in the lab?
It seemed like forever!
They've got to be around here somewhere.
TWILAAAA!

Chapter 21

"Hurry, goofooligans! No time to doodle-dawdle!"

"We're trying!" called Twila. "It's hard! We're not used to crawling on all fours!" She glanced back. "You good, Jordan?"

"Think so," heaved Jordan. "Hope it's not too much farther."

Several minutes passed. Twila shined her phone's light ahead, hoping against hope to see the glow of the outside world.

Nothing. The tunnel stretched on, twisting and turning, but showing no signs of ending.

"Hustle your haunches!" called Willow from somewhere ahead. "It is still a long way to Margalo's!"

"Wait . . . but first we get to the surface, right?"

"No surface! There is too much snow and wind, and the Boojum might spot us!"

"You mean this tunnel goes all the way to the wildlife clinic?"

Jordan groaned. "The wildlife clinic is, like, two miles away!"

"Naw, it's only about a quarter mile," said Twila. But this was of little comfort. It was still a very long way to crawl, especially through a cold, dark tunnel.

They scooted on. If the storm still raged above, it was lost in the muffled world of the tunnel.

"Look!" shouted Jordan abruptly.

Twila twisted around and flashed her light at Jordan's discovery.

"What's a fire hydrant doing down here?"

"Because we're out on the street. The whole town is buried."

"What if the tunnel collapses?" Jordan asked.

"Don't think about it," said Twila. "Willow? Did you dig all the way from Margalo's to the school by yourself?"

"Do not be a noodle-noob! Willow can dig, but never this far, this fast," snapped Willow. "Dunwich helped me. Dunwich can dig through snow and ice, faster than any."

"Who's Dunwich?"

"Dunwich is just ahead, widening the tunnel and shoveling debris so you can move faster."

Twila's spine prickled. "Is . . . Dunwich like you, Willow?"

"Do not be silly," said Willow. "Dunwich is nothing like Willow."

Something was blocking the path ahead. A big, lightless shape that filled the whole tunnel. Twila froze. Jordan bumped into her.

"What is it?" asked Jordan.

Twila pointed her light at the shape. "I have absolutely no idea."

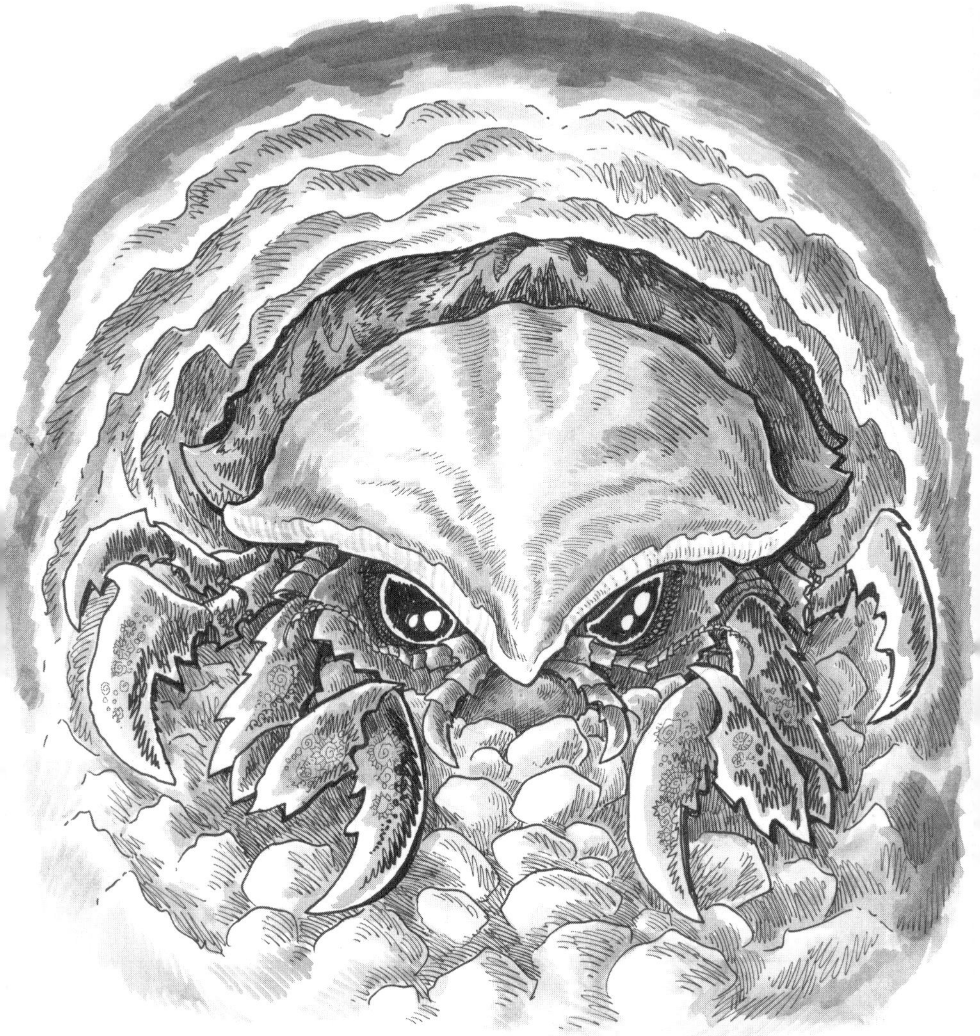

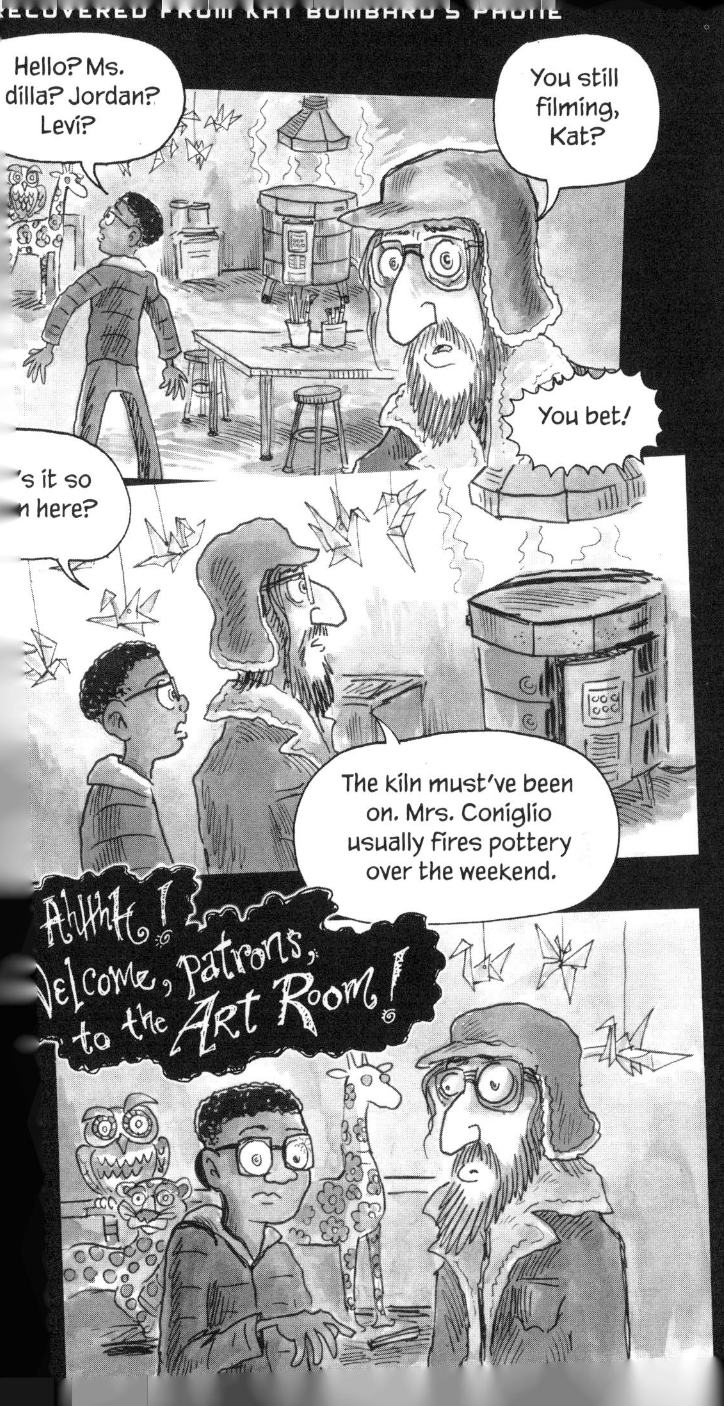
ECOVERED FROM KAT BOMBARD'S PHONE
Hello? Ms. dilla? Jordan? Levi?
You still filming, Kat?
You bet!
's it so n here?
The kiln must've been on. Mrs. Coniglio usually fires pottery over the weekend.
Ahhhh! elcome, patrons, to the Art Room!

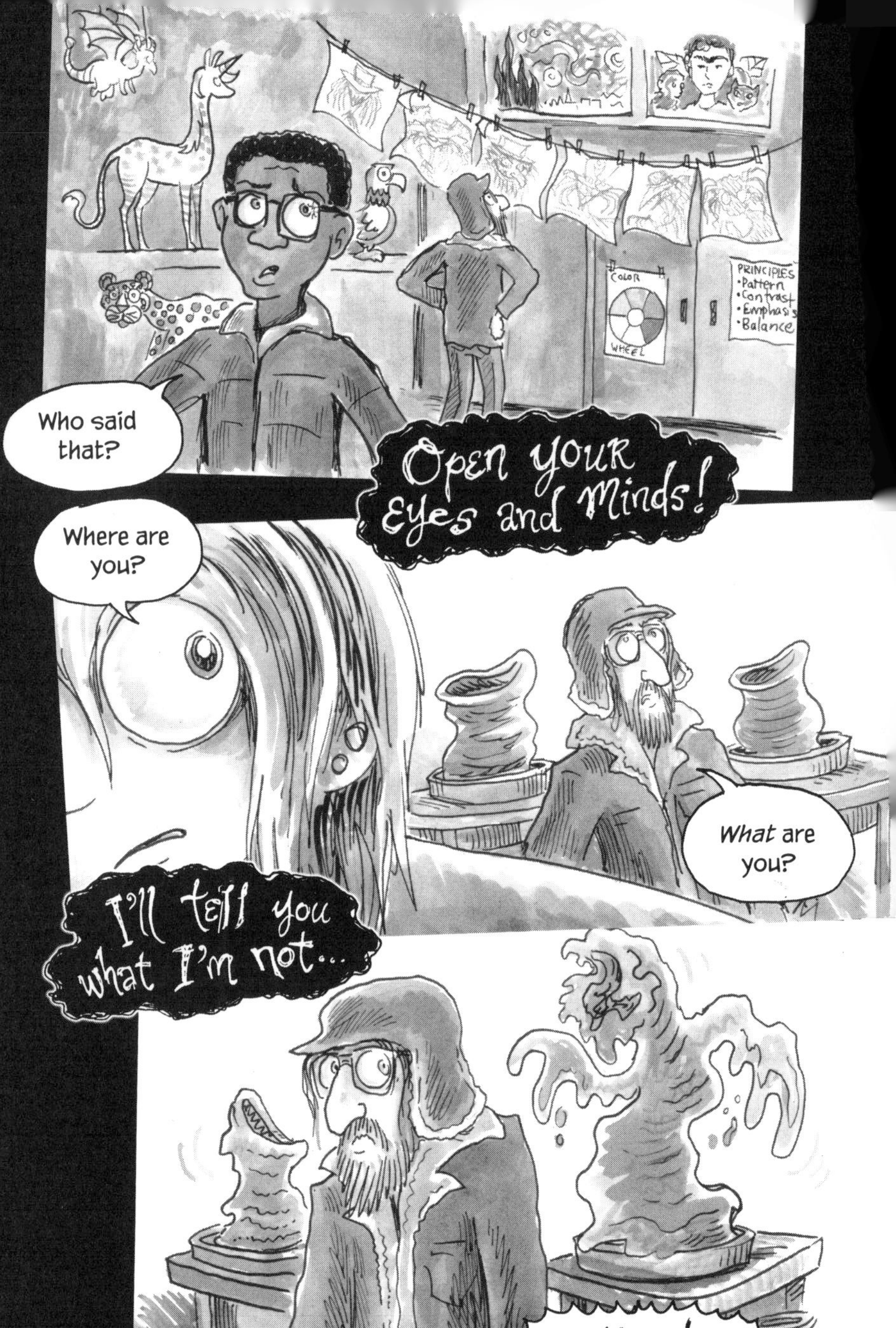
PRINCIPLES
•Pattern
•Contrast
•Emphasis
•Balance
COLOR
WHEEL
Who said that?
Open your Eyes and Minds!
Where are you?
What are you?
I'll tell you what I'm not...
Look out, Mr. CHUCK!

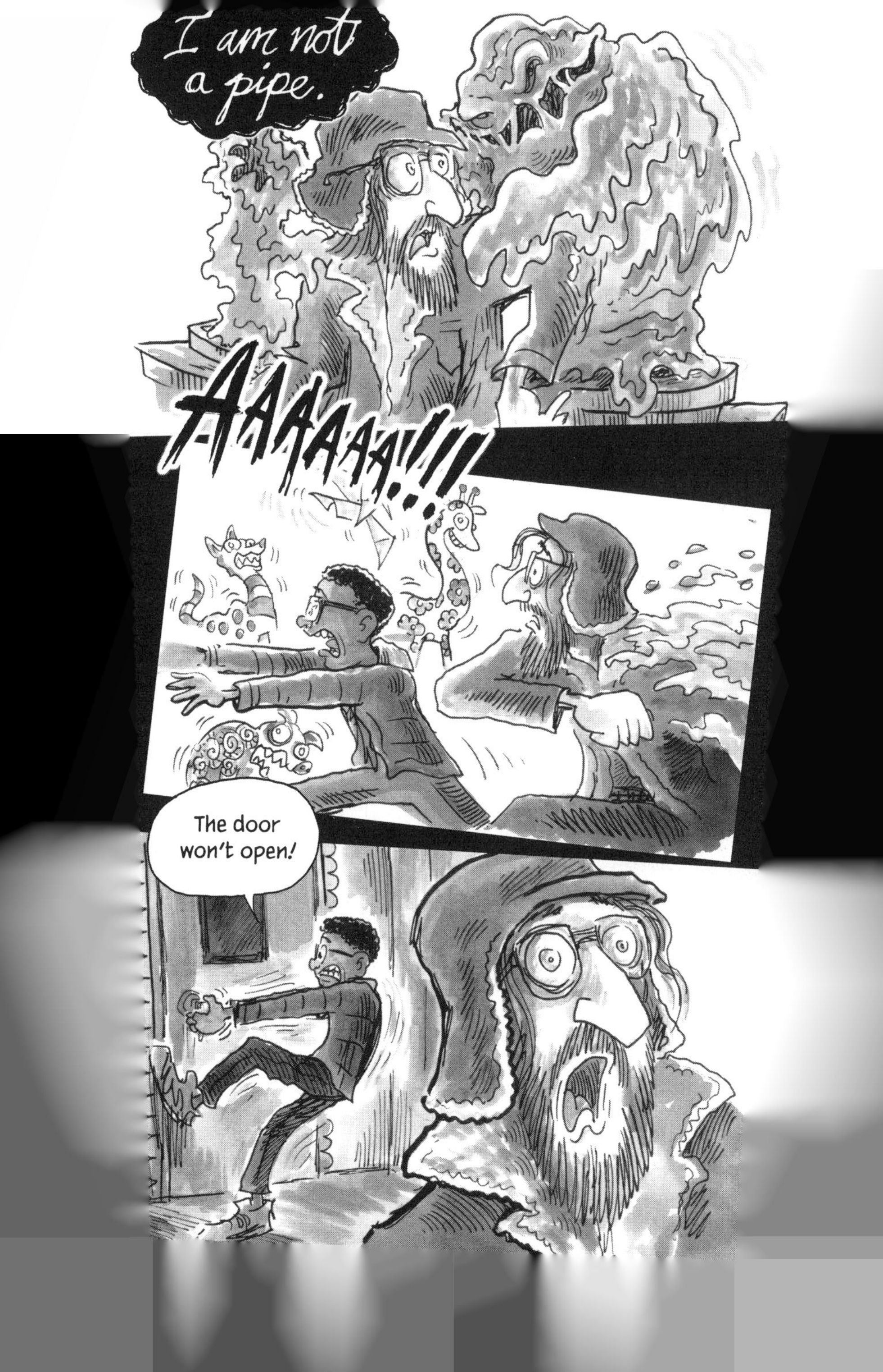
I am not a pipe.
AAAAAA!!!!
The door won't open!

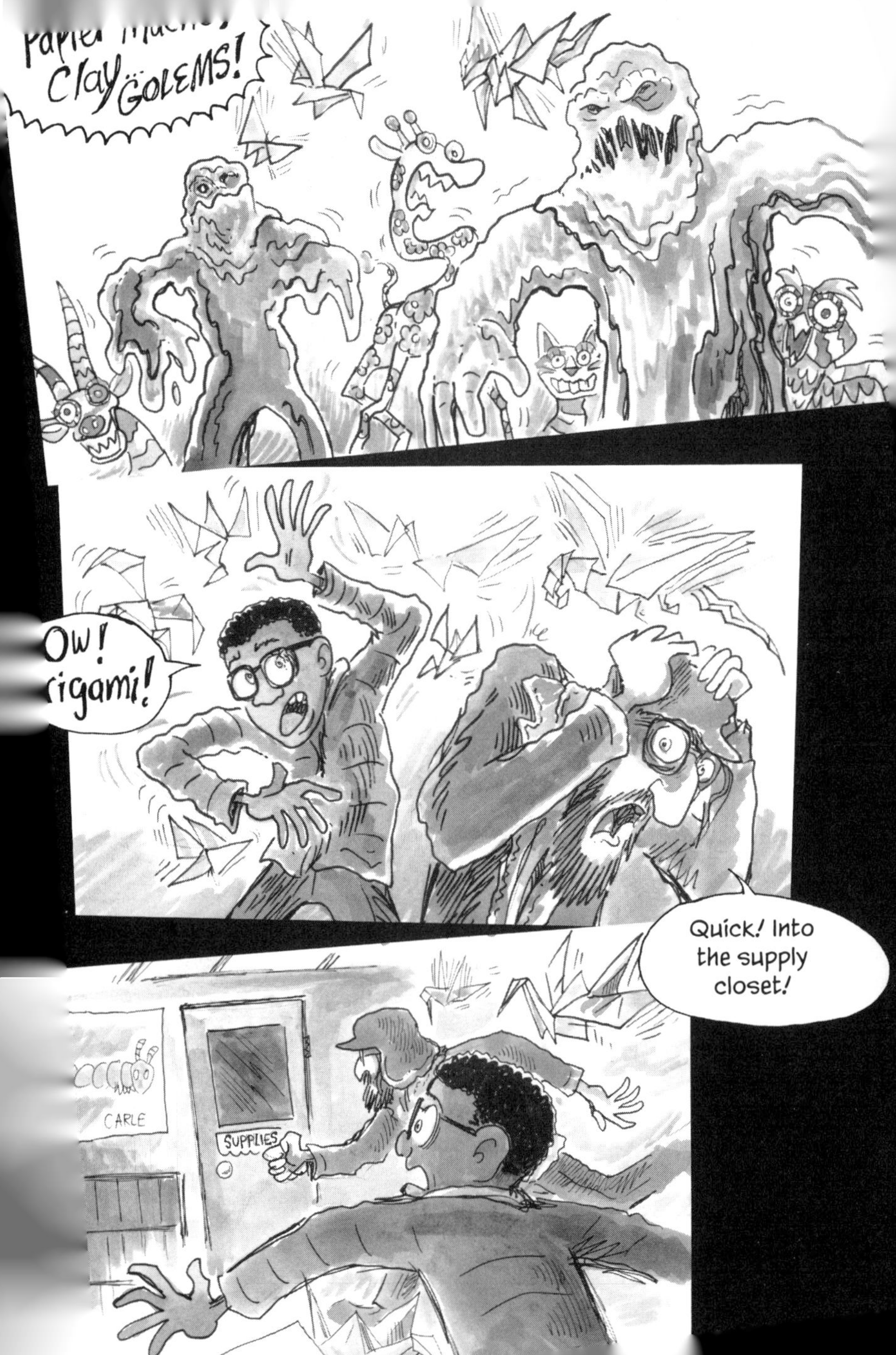

Clay GOLEMS!
Ow!
CARLE
SUPPLIES
Quick! Into the supply closet!

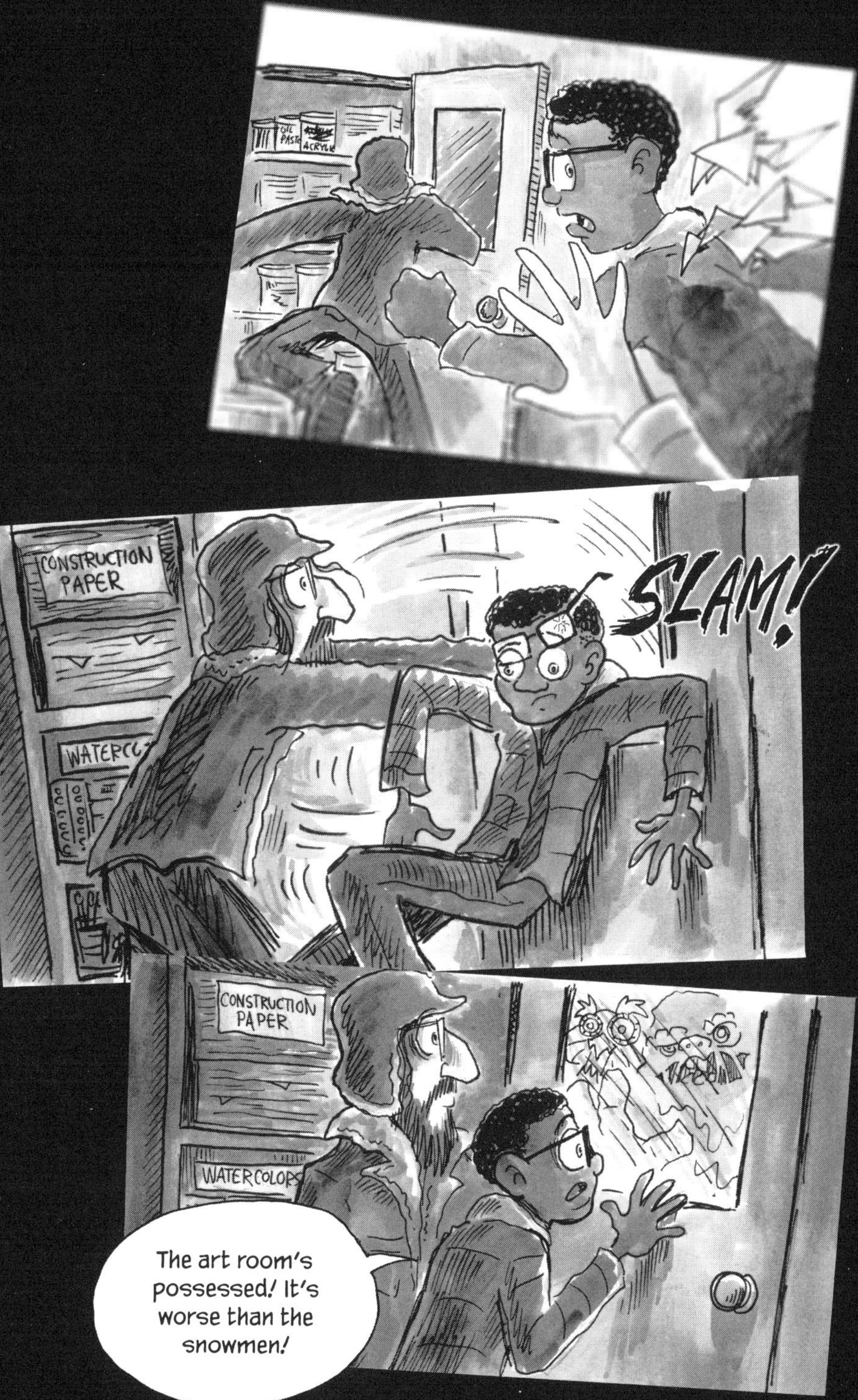
OIL PASTEL
ACRYLIC
CONSTRUCTION PAPER
WATERCO
SLAM!
CONSTRUCTION PAPER
WATERCOLORS
The art room's possessed! It's worse than the snowmen!

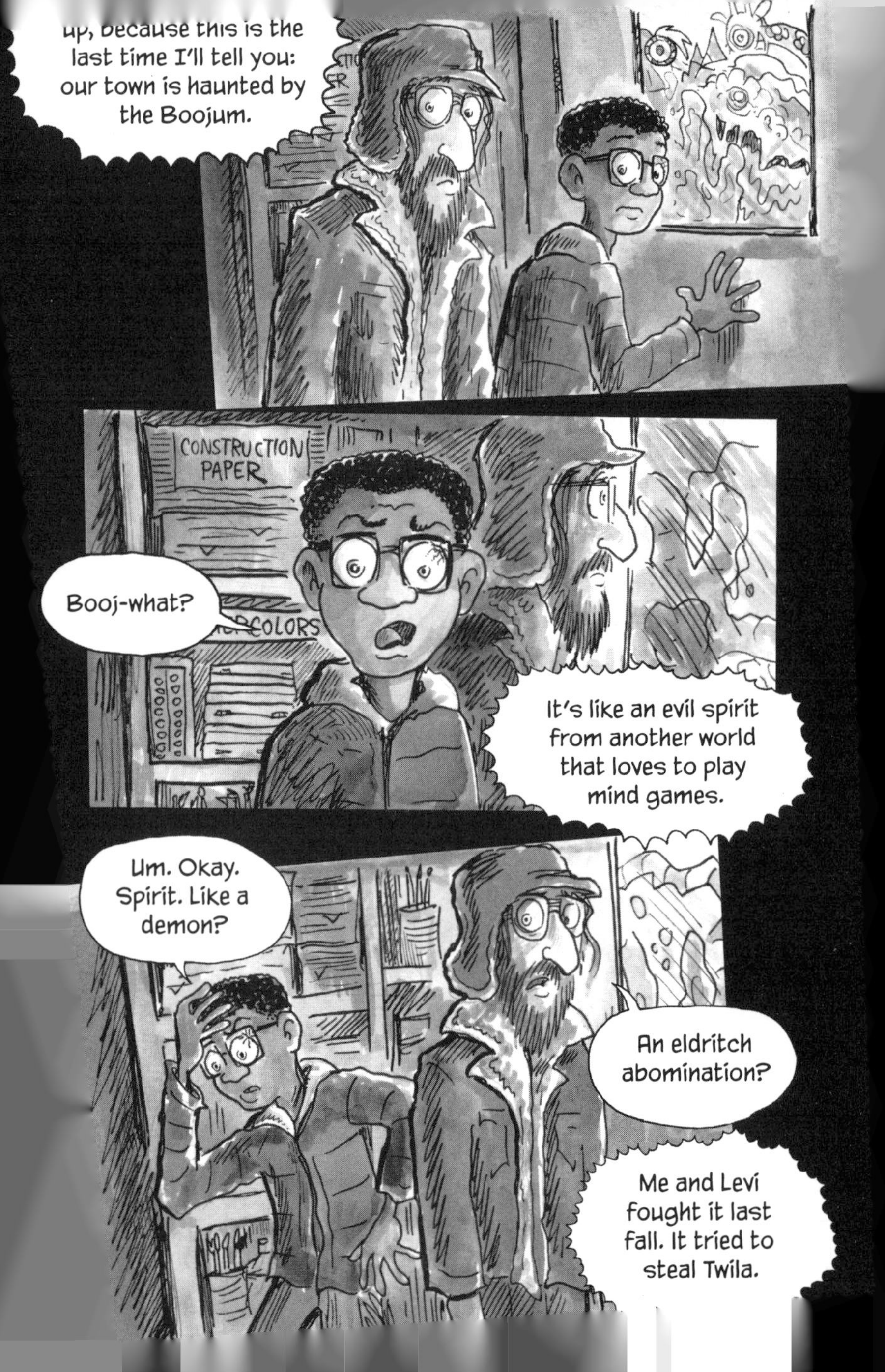
up, because this is the last time I'll tell you: our town is haunted by the Boojum.
CONSTRUCTION PAPER
Booj-what?
It's like an evil spirit from another world that loves to play mind games.
Um. Okay. Spirit. Like a demon?
An eldritch abomination?
Me and Levi fought it last fall. It tried to steal Twila.

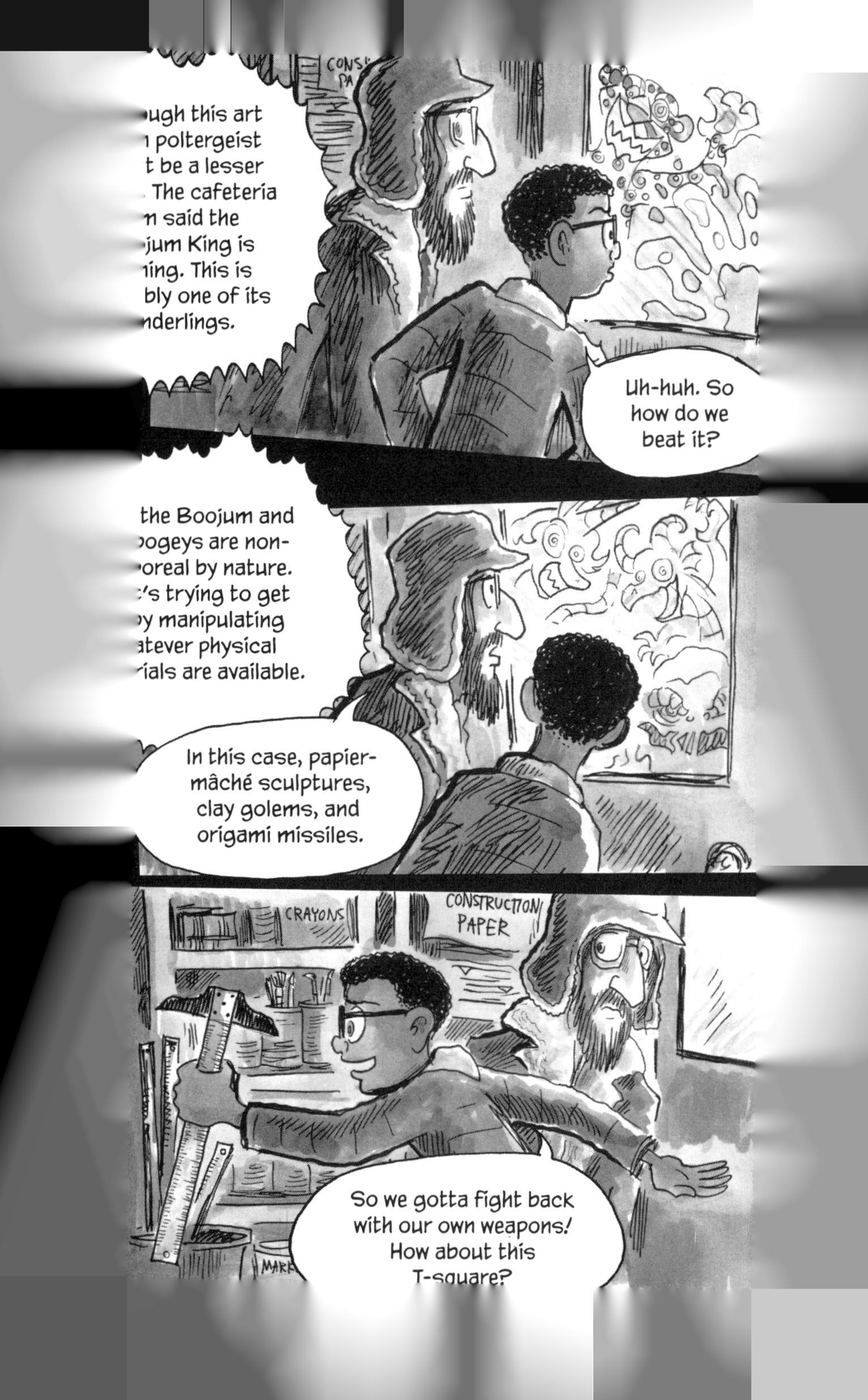
ugh this art
n poltergeist
t be a lesser
. The cafeteria
n said the
jum King is
ing. This is
bly one of its
nderlings.
Uh-huh. So how do we beat it?
the Boojum and
ogeys are non-
oreal by nature.
's trying to get
y manipulating
atever physical
ials are available.
In this case, papier-mâché sculptures, clay golems, and origami missiles.
CRAYONS
CONSTRUCTION PAPER
So we gotta fight back with our own weapons! How about this T-square?

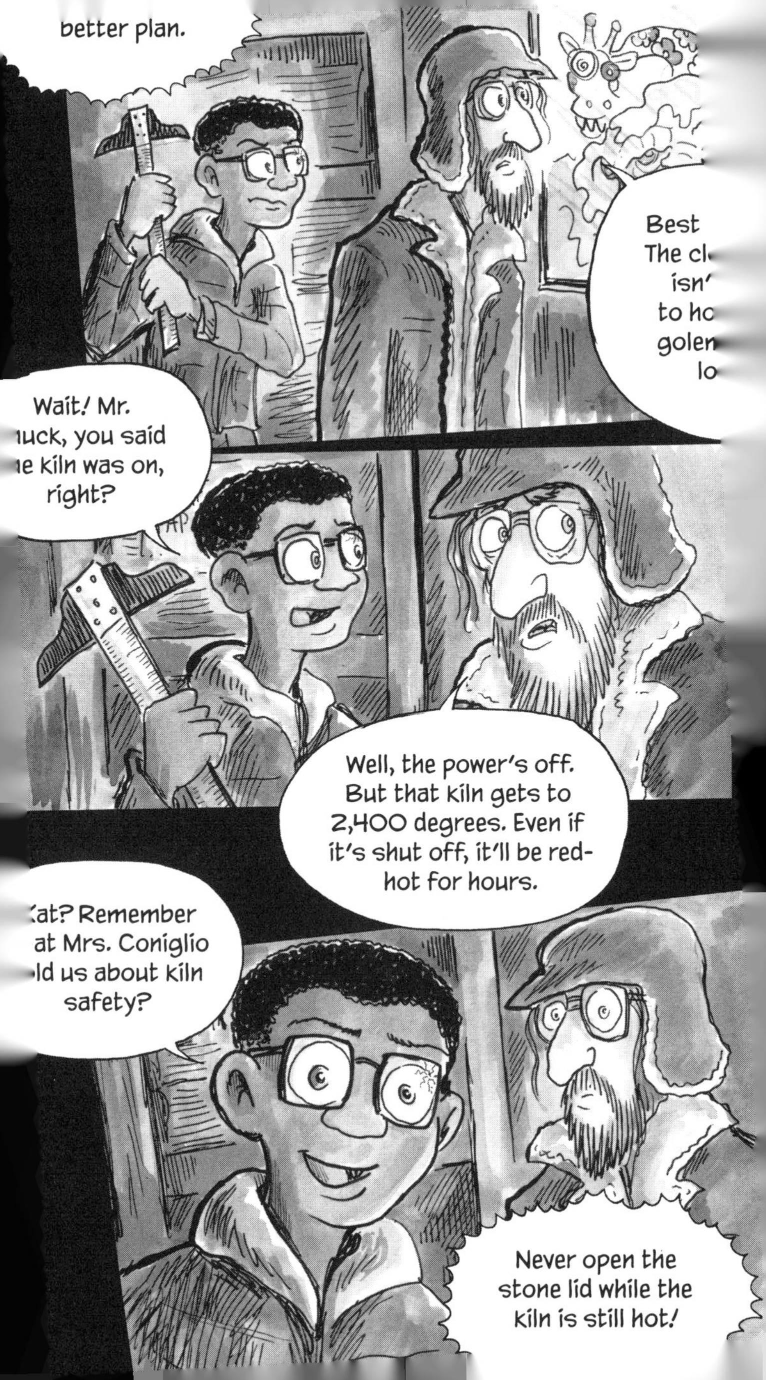

better plan.
Best
The cl
isn'
to ho
golem
lo
Wait! Mr.
uck, you said
e kiln was on,
right?
Well, the power's off. But that kiln gets to 2,400 degrees. Even if it's shut off, it'll be red-hot for hours.
at? Remember
at Mrs. Coniglio
ld us about kiln
safety?
Never open the stone lid while the kiln is still hot!

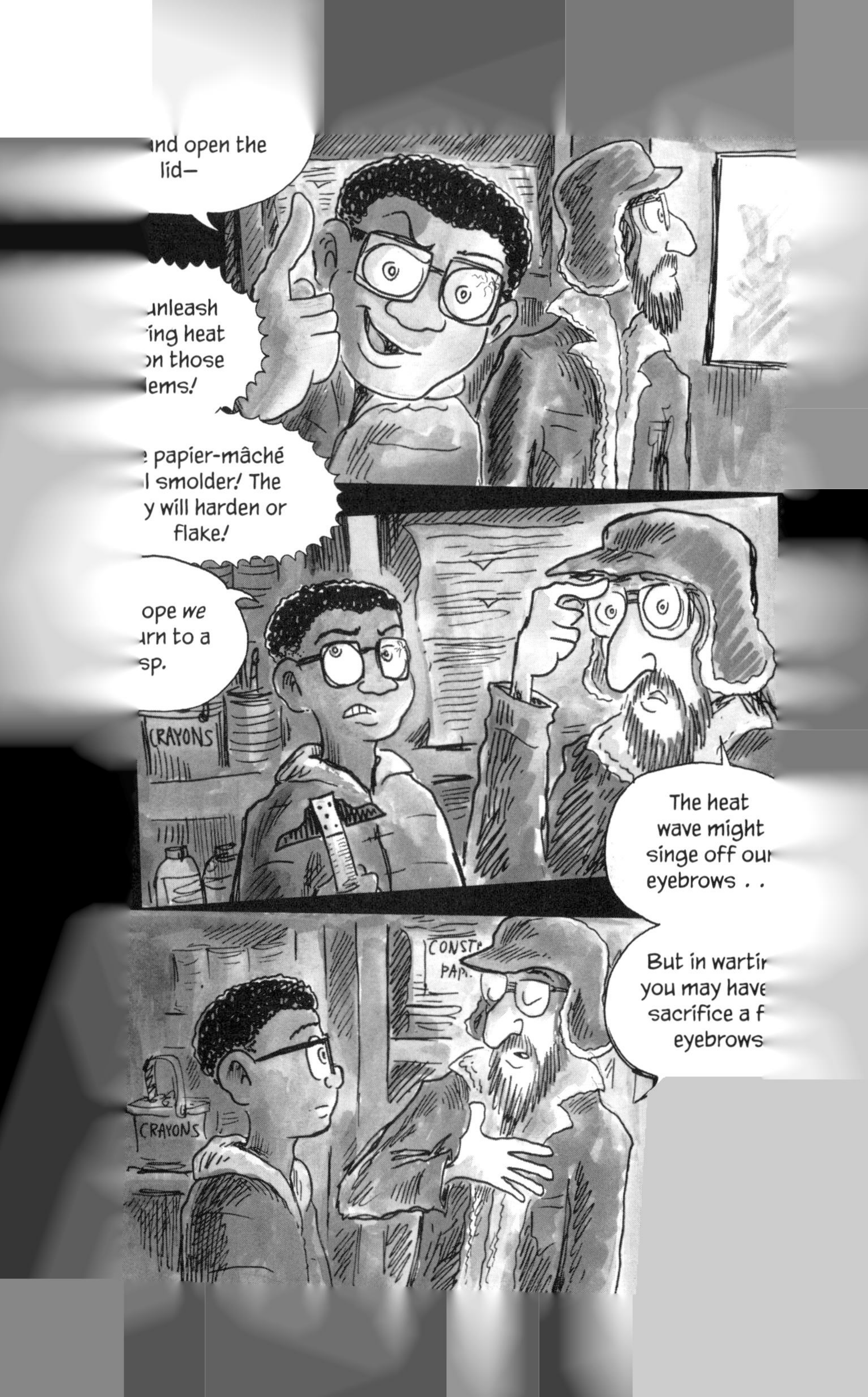

ınd open the lid—
ınleash ring heat on those lems!
e papier-mâché l smolder! The y will harden or flake!
ope we urn to a sp.
CRAYONS
The heat wave might singe off our eyebrows . .
CONST PAP
But in wartir you may have sacrifice a f eyebrows
CRAYONS

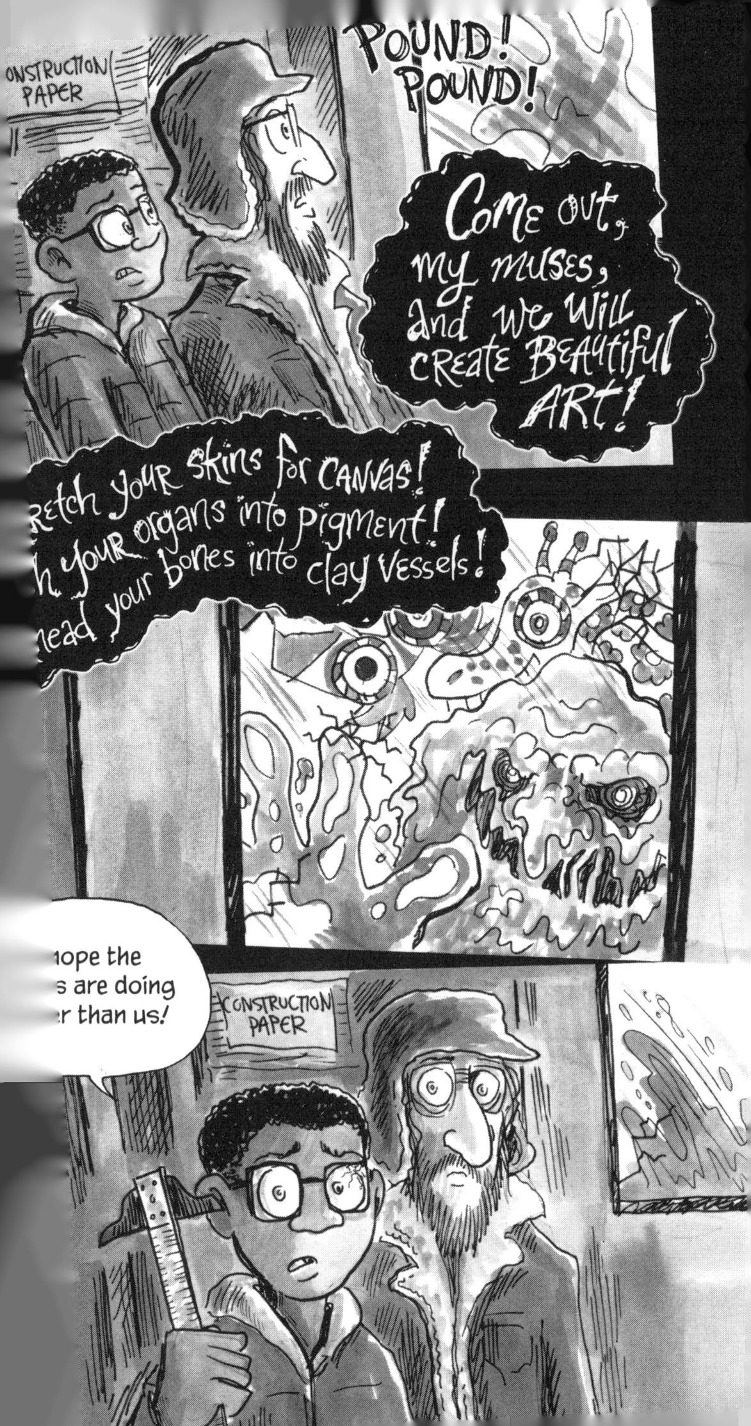
CONSTRUCTION PAPER
POUND! POUND!
COME OUT, MY MUSES, AND WE WILL CREATE BEAUTIFUL ART!
retch your skins for canvas!
h your organs into pigment!
nead your bones into clay vessels!
ope the
s are doing
r than us!
CONSTRUCTION PAPER

Chapter 23

"Um . . . hi, er, Dunwich," said Twila.

"Whoaaaa!" said Jordan.

The monstrosity shuffled segmented appendages and clicked enthusiastically.

"No, Dunwich!" snapped Willow. "This is no time for nicey-nicies! Move! We need to get through!"

The creature clicked again, turned, and scurried down the tunnel, its numerous limbs scratching and carving the icy walls.

Twila heaved a sigh of relief.

"Was that a giant isopod?" Jordan asked.

"Margalo will explain," said Willow. "Hurry!"

"You weren't scared of that thing?" Twila asked Jordan as they continued down the tunnel.

"Uh, no," said Jordan. "It was cool!"

"Erm. Right." Twila flashed her light ahead. Willow was again out of sight. "Hey, Jordan? Why do kids at school call you Bug-Man? It's because you play with bugs, right?"

"Guess so," said Jordan. "I love looking for weird bugs—praying mantises, cicadas, huge toe-biter water bugs. So Donte's friend Robbie Munn started calling me Bug-Man."

"Does that bug—I mean, *bother* you? It's not really a nice name."

"Maybe it was meant to hurt my feelings," said Jordan. "But I actually kinda like it."

They climbed over a ridge in the tunnel that may or may not have been a street curb.

"You're lucky," said Jordan abruptly. "You have a nice big brother."

Twila snorted. "Levi's not always nice. He can be a jerk sometimes. He doesn't like any of my friends, and he throws a fit whenever there's too much change. He's also overprotective—-which is funny, sorta, because he's not very tough."

"At least he likes you. Donte is embarrassed by me," said Jordan. "Like, one time I was late to school because it rained, and all the worms were up on the sidewalk. They were just squirming there, and they'd soon get dried out by the sun or squashed by kids. So I went around and moved them all back into the soil. But Donte got mad at me. He said I cared more about creepy-crawlies than having real friends."

"Ow," said Twila.

"Yeah," said Jordan. "But I guess he's right. I am pretty weird."

"Sometimes weird isn't bad," said Twila after a moment.

She stopped suddenly. Jordan bumped into her again. "What?" he said.

She held up the light. The tunnel had ended. In front of them was a solid wooden wall with a rectangle in the middle.

Twila squinted at the rectangle. "Is that a—"

The pet door popped open.

"Lolly-gaggy goofooligans!" yipped Willow. "Come in already!"

Twila looked back at Jordan. "We're here."

Chapter 24

"TWILA! Please answer me! TWILAAAA!"

"Levi," Ms. Padilla said slowly, "do you know anything about what's happening?"

He was silent for a moment. "Maybe," he said at last.

"Then I think you'd better tell me."

Another pause. "Something happened to me last fall. Actually, it happened to Twila. Something really weird."

They turned a corner, and Ms. Padilla's light flashed off two snowmen partway down the hall. "Back this way," she said, ushering Levi down an adjacent hall. "Go on."

"So, one morning I woke up, and Twila wasn't there anymore. Her room was empty. No bed. No stuff. No sign of her anywhere."

"She ran away?" interrupted Ms. Padilla.

"No. I found out later she'd been stolen away in the night."

"I never heard about any of this!"

"I know. No one knows except me and Twila and Kat. And Willow, but, uh, never mind."

"Your mom never found out?"

"No. She didn't find out because she didn't remember Twila. Neither did my big sister Regina. And everyone at school. It was like Twila had never existed."

"But what about records? Photos?"

"Those were all gone or changed. I even started to wonder if I'd gone crazy and was remembering a sister who'd never really existed. But then I talked to Kat, and Kat remembered Twila. And Kat knew something weird was happening in town. You know how Kat's always talking about aliens and cryptids? Most of that is just fantasy, but this time she'd started to notice something that wasn't just a joke. We called it the Boojum."

"What's a Boojum?"

"It's the thing that took Twila. It's like . . . I still don't know. It's hard to describe. It's almost like just a bad presence in town, and sometimes, when it gets hungry or angry or just bored, it takes a child away, and it's like that child never even existed."

"But Twila came back," said Ms. Padilla.

"Kat and I found her, with some outside help. And after we found her, all the memories came back, too."

Another pause. Their shoes squeaked along the empty hall.

"I know it sounds crazy," said Levi, "but I think what's happening now is similar. I think it's the Boojum again. Except this time it wants to take a whole lot of kids. Maybe the whole school."

"How would that even be possible?" Ms. Padilla asked. "I can barely believe the world would forget a single child, let alone a few hundred."

"I don't know," said Levi. "But that's what I think. The Boojum sees Cowslip Grove as a farm, and the kids are the harvest."

"That's an awful thought," said Ms. Padilla.

"What about the cornfield we saw in the science lab?" asked Levi. "It's testing us. It wants to see how far it can push our minds and emotions. That's what the Boojum does. It plays mind games. Breaks us mentally, until we don't fight back."

"Games," muttered Ms. Padilla. "This Boojum seems to have a twisted sense of humor."

They were silent again. They could see their breath streaming past the beam of Ms. Padilla's flashlight.

"It's getting colder," said Ms. Padilla. She cupped a hand to her mouth. "Twila! Jordan! Kat! Donte! Mr. Chuck! Hello? Anyone?"

A door down the hall lit up.

"Oh no," said Ms. Padilla. "The science lab again?"

"No," said Levi. "It's the gym."

They crept to the gym door and peered through the window.

"It looks empty," said Ms. Padilla. "But why is the light on?"

"Kat and Twila and the rest could be inside," said Levi. "Or it could be another trap."

"Could be," said Ms. Padilla. "What do you think we should do?"

"I think we don't have much of a choice."

They opened the door and stepped into the glow of the gym.

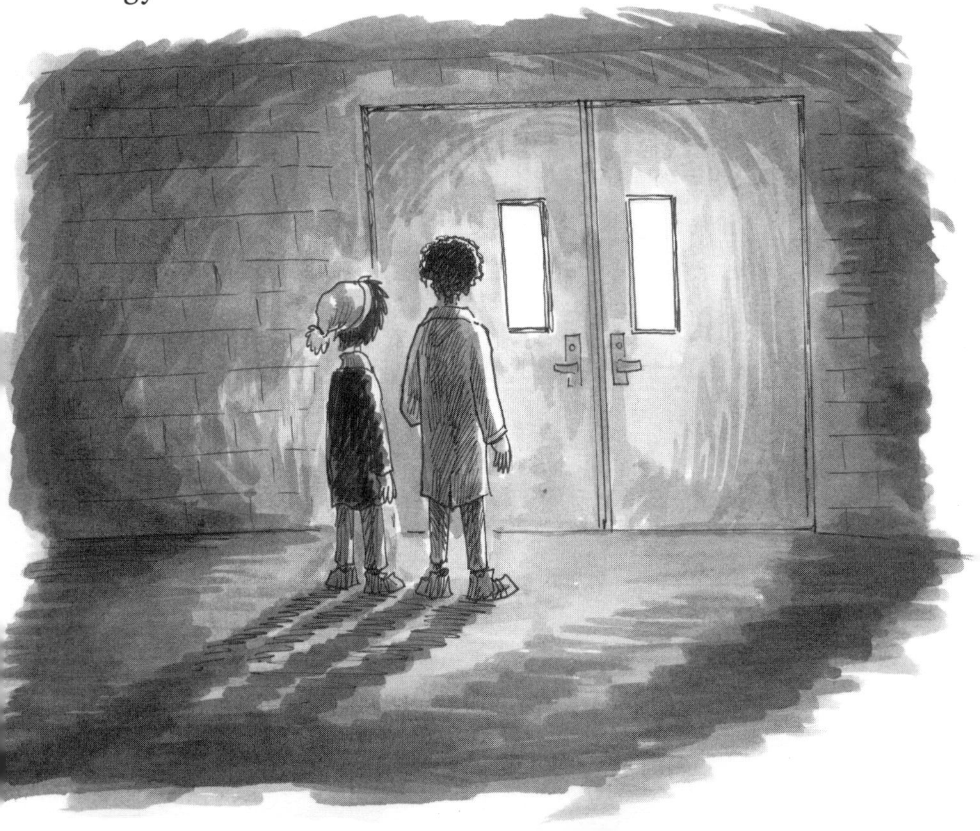

Chapter 25

"Margaloooo," called Willow as Twila and Jordan followed her into the wildlife clinic's candlelit living quarters. "Willow is back with the kiddies."

The old floorboards creaked under their feet. The roof and walls moaned as the storm raged outside. Dunwich scuttled past them and curled up in a corner like a dog with an exoskeleton in place of fur.

Margalo sat slumped in an armchair, mouth open, glasses askew, and an empty coffee mug dangling from her limp hand.

Willow snagged Margalo's stocking between her fangs and tugged. Margalo didn't move. "Margalo! Wake up! It is no time for slugabedding!"

Twila's eyes widened. "Is . . . she—?"

"No!" said Jordan. "Look! She's breathing."

Willow stopped tugging and examined her unconscious caretaker. "A sleeping spell," Willow announced. "Margalo has gone into hibernation. Probably everyone in town, too. It does not want anyone to interfere with what is happening at your school."

Jordan grabbed Margalo's shoulder and shook. "Come on, Margalo! Wake up! We need some good magic right now!"

Margalo's head lolled to one side.

"It is no use," said Willow. "Sleeping spells are very stubborn. She will not wake until the storm is over."

"Then why are *we* still awake?" asked Twila.

Willow shrugged her spines. "You are a part of the harvest. At least you were supposed to be." She turned and started back toward the door. "You should be safe here, away from the school."

"But where are you going?"

"Back through the tunnel, to look for Levi and Kathooligan and any other survivors. If Margalo cannot help, it is all up to Little Willow."

"We can't let you go back there alone!" said Twila.

"No offense," said Jordan, "but you look kinda scrawny. I don't think you could take those killer snowmen by yourself."

Willow sniffed indignantly. "The whole point of Dunwich's tunnel was to rescue you, silly half-size dibbuns! Let Willow worry about the others!"

"They're *our* family and friends!" argued Twila. "We wouldn't have followed you if we'd known you were just going to ditch us here!"

"Right!" said Jordan. "I thought we were going to Margalo's so we could get some magic to fight those creepy snowmen!"

"Magic?" Willow snorted. "For the last time: Margalo is *not* magic! Neither is Willow!"

"But what about *him*?" said Jordan, pointing to Dunwich's curled form in the corner.

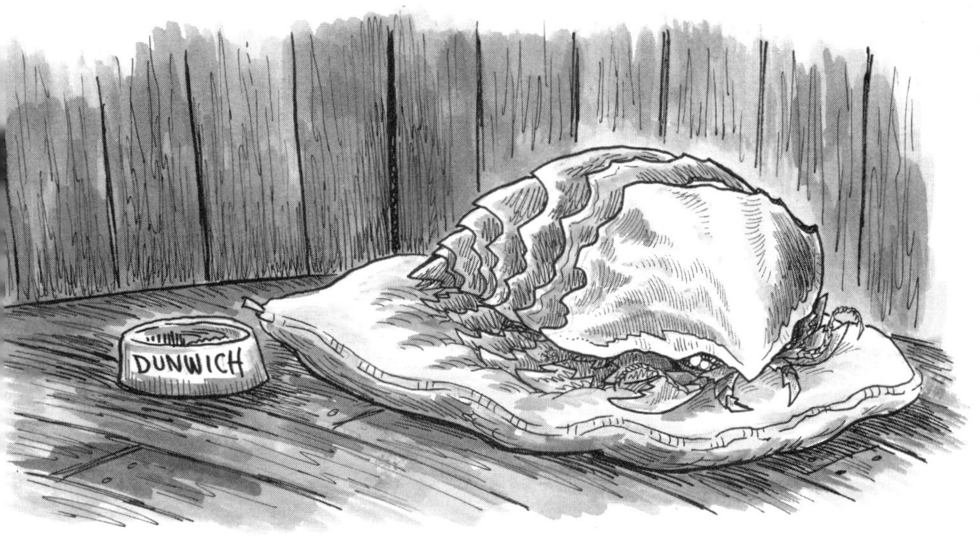
DUNWICH

"Dunwich is not magic, either."

"Then what is he?"

"Oh," said Willow, and when she spoke again her usually raspy, stilted speech became a passable imitation of Margalo. "Dunwich is a colossal glacier isopod. Margalo says they were once common in the Antarctic pack ice, digging tunnels in the ice floes. Secretive creatures."

"I *knew* he was some sort of isopod!" said Jordan.

"Yes. But Margalo says Dunwich is one of the last of his kind. The pack ice is melting."

Both Twila and Jordan were staring wide-eyed at the giant isopod, their dire predicament forgotten for a moment.

"Margalo has collected some very, very strange creatures," said Willow slowly.

"Stranger than Dunwich?" asked Jordan. "Stranger than *you?*"

"Rude!" snapped Willow. "But yes, stranger than Dunwich and Willow. There are creatures in this house that no one knows about. Not even Levi."

Twila chewed her lip. "Where does Margalo keep them?"

"The cellar," Willow said.

Twila and Jordan exchanged looks. "Can we meet them?"

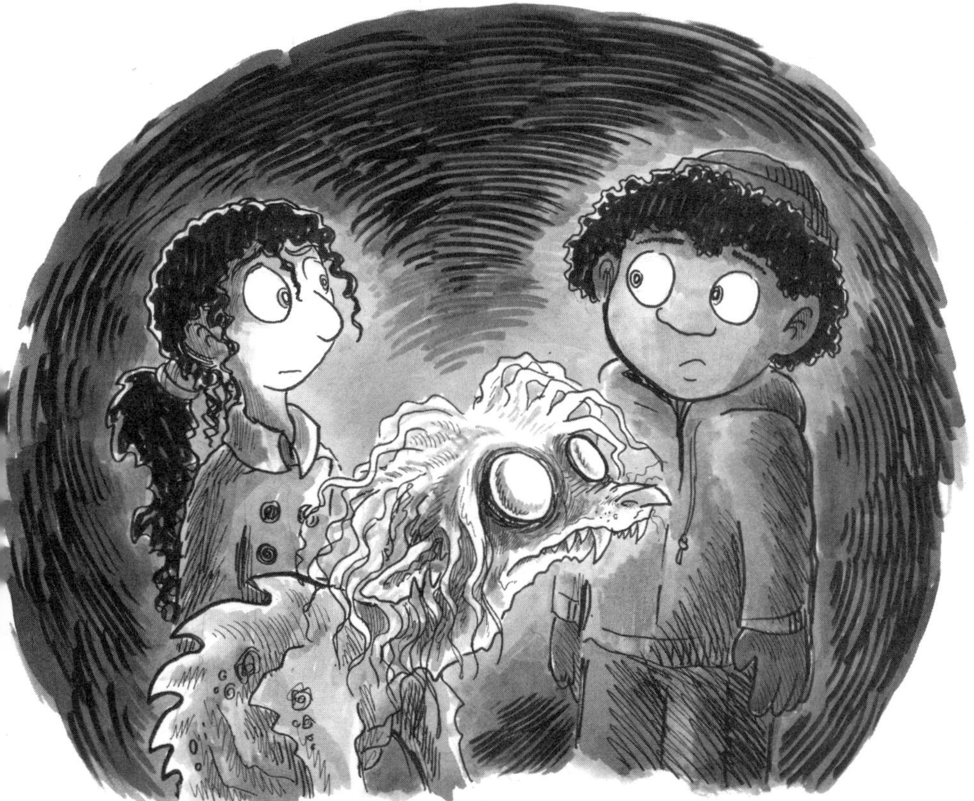

FOOTAGE RECOVERED FROM KAT BOMBARD'S PHONE

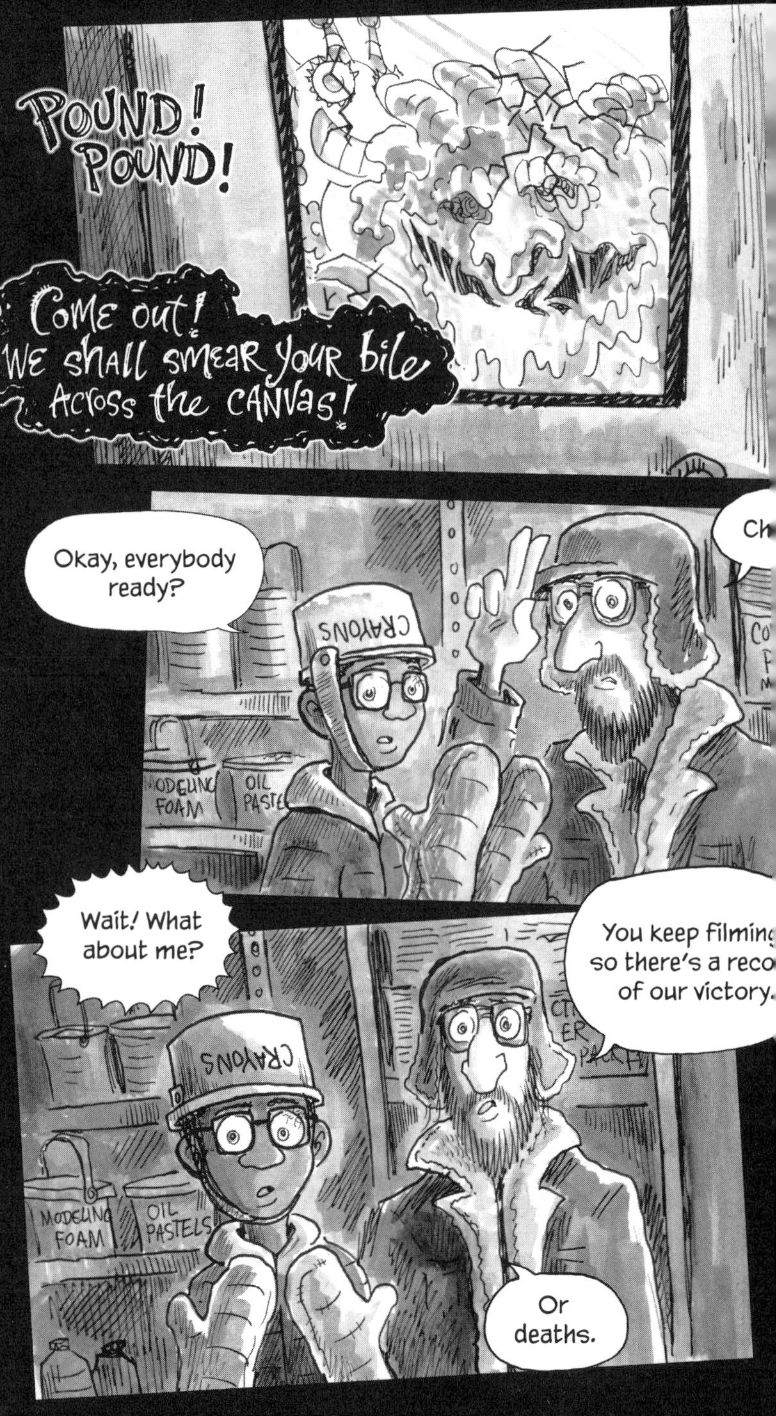
POUND! POUND!
Come out! We shall smear your bile across the canvas!
Okay, everybody ready?
Ch
CRAYONS
MODELING FOAM
OIL PASTELS
Wait! What about me?
You keep filmin
so there's a reco
of our victory.
CRAYONS
MODELING FOAM
OIL PASTELS
Or deaths.

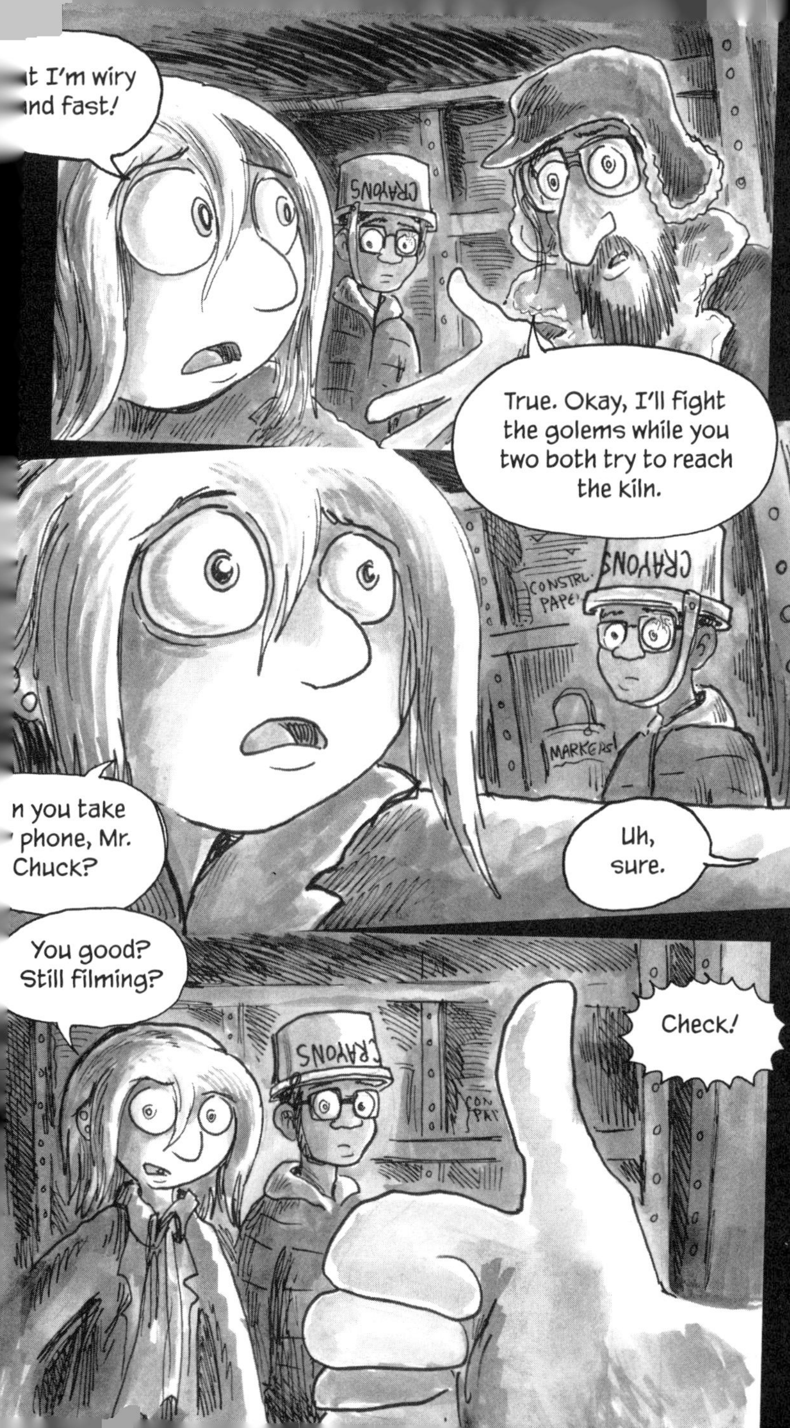
t I'm wiry
nd fast!
True. Okay, I'll fight the golems while you two both try to reach the kiln.
CRAYONS
CONSTRU. PAPE
MARKERS
n you take
phone, Mr. Chuck?
Uh, sure.
You good? Still filming?
CRAYONS
Check!

They'll get us as soon as we open the closet door!
CONSTRU PAPER
We need a distraction!
Relinquish your bodies and become one with Artistic Expression!
Perhaps we shall mold your molecules into a coil-pot!
Perhaps we shall use

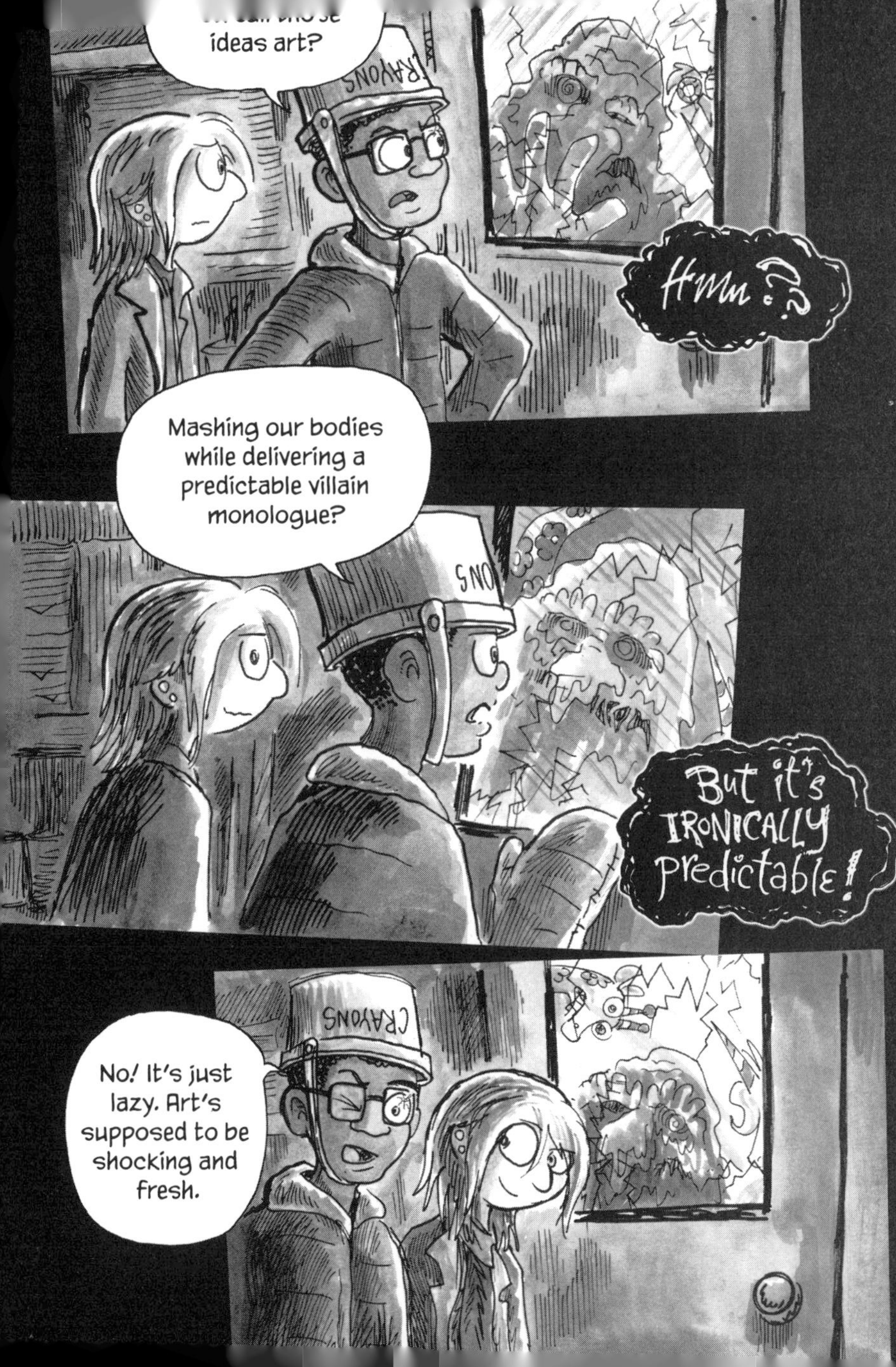

ideas art?
CRAYONS
Hmm?
Mashing our bodies while delivering a predictable villain monologue?
But it's IRONICALLY predictable!
No! It's just lazy. Art's supposed to be shocking and fresh.

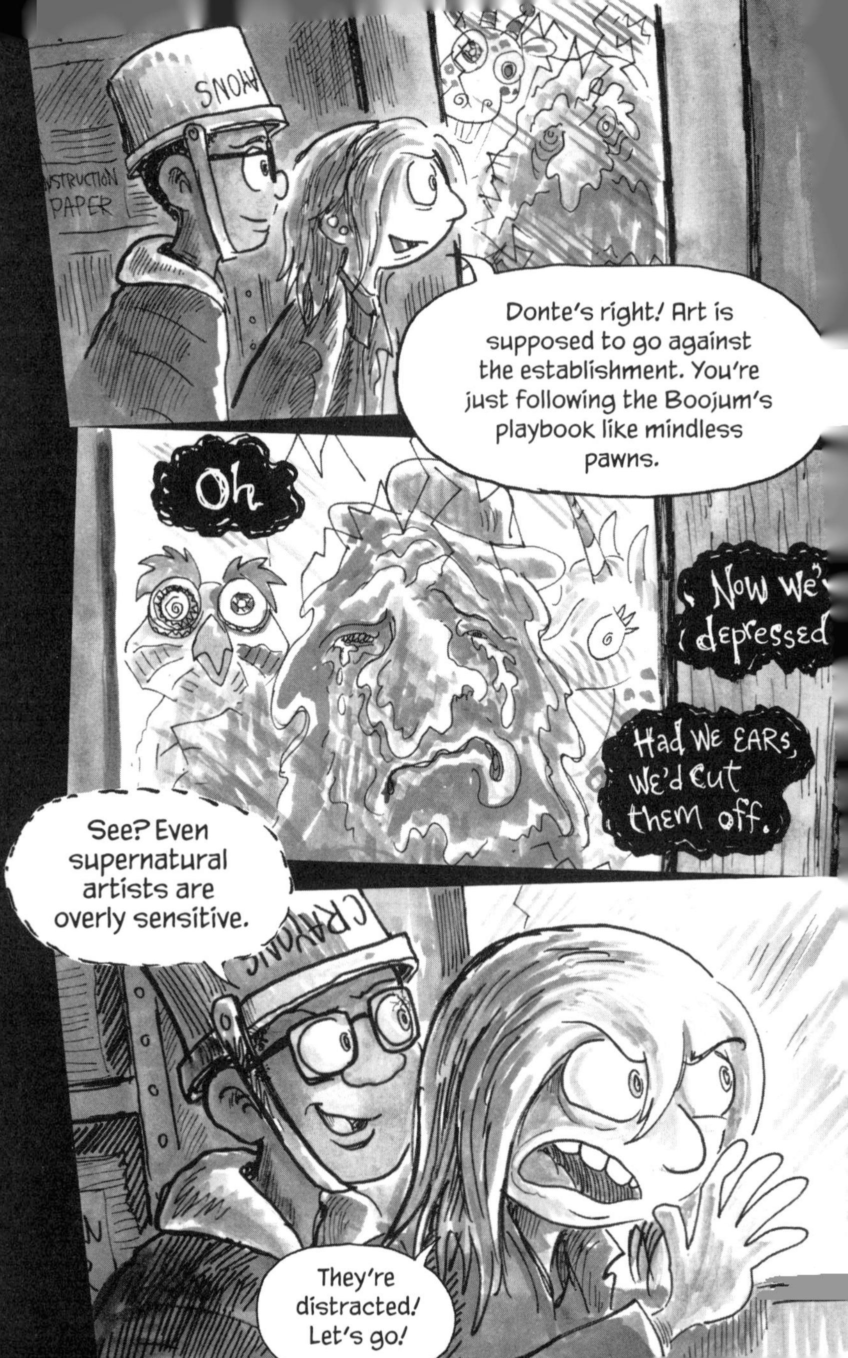
SNOW
INSTRUCTION PAPER
Donte's right! Art is supposed to go against the establishment. You're just following the Boojum's playbook like mindless pawns.
Oh
Now we're depressed
Had we EARS, we'd cut them off.
See? Even supernatural artists are overly sensitive.
CRAYONS
They're distracted! Let's go!

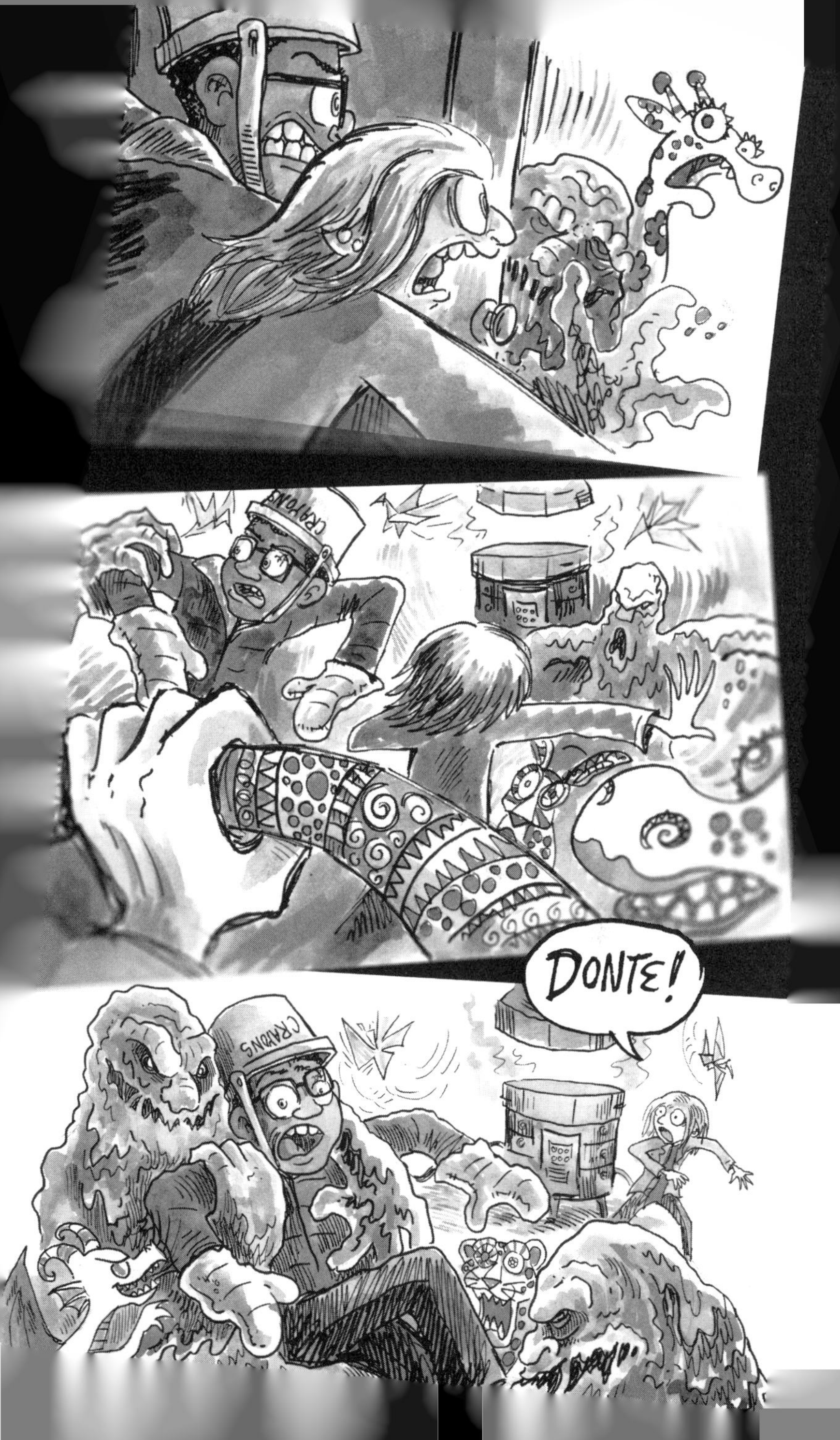
CRAYONS
DONTE!
CRAYONS

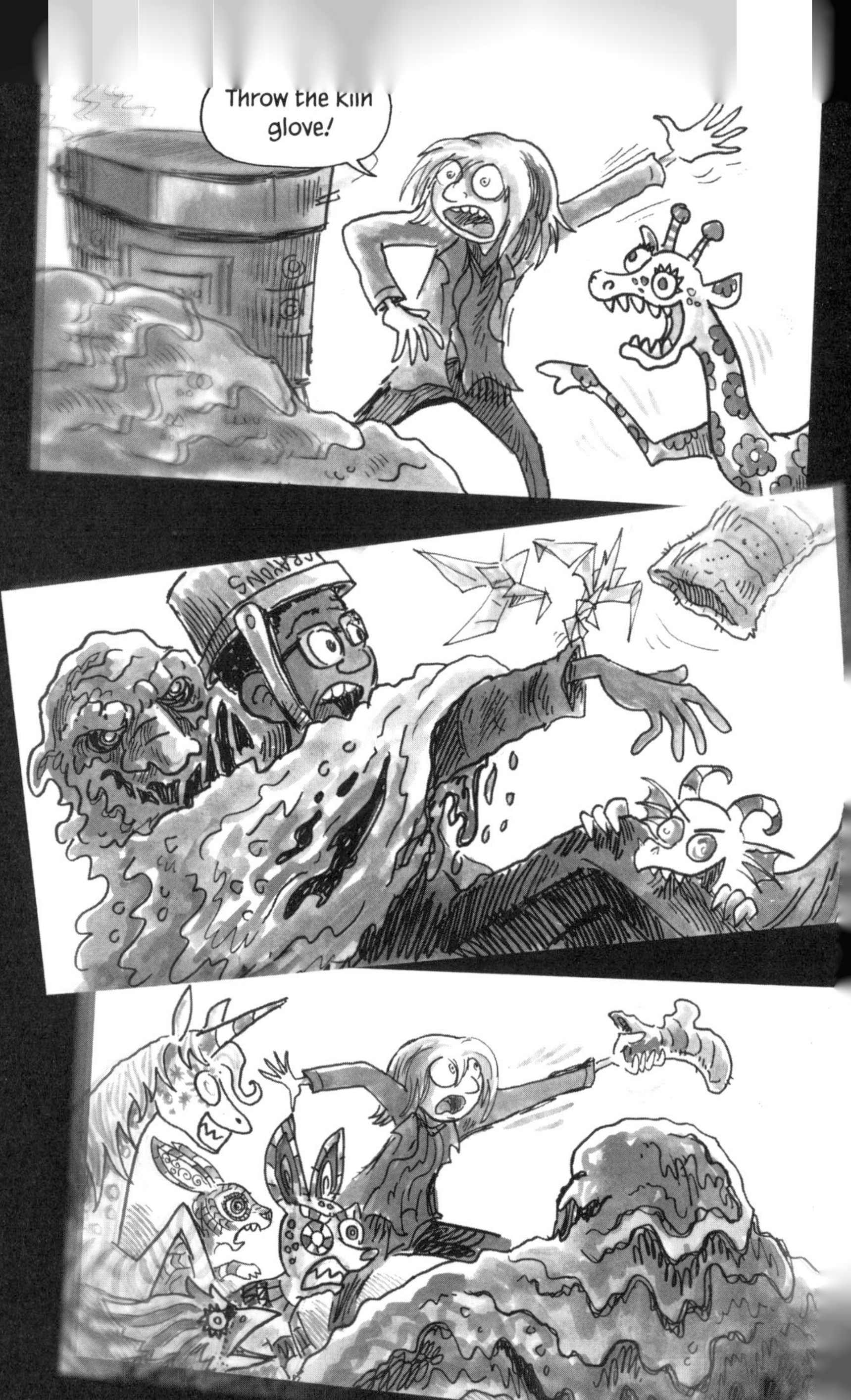
Throw the kiln glove!
CRAYONS

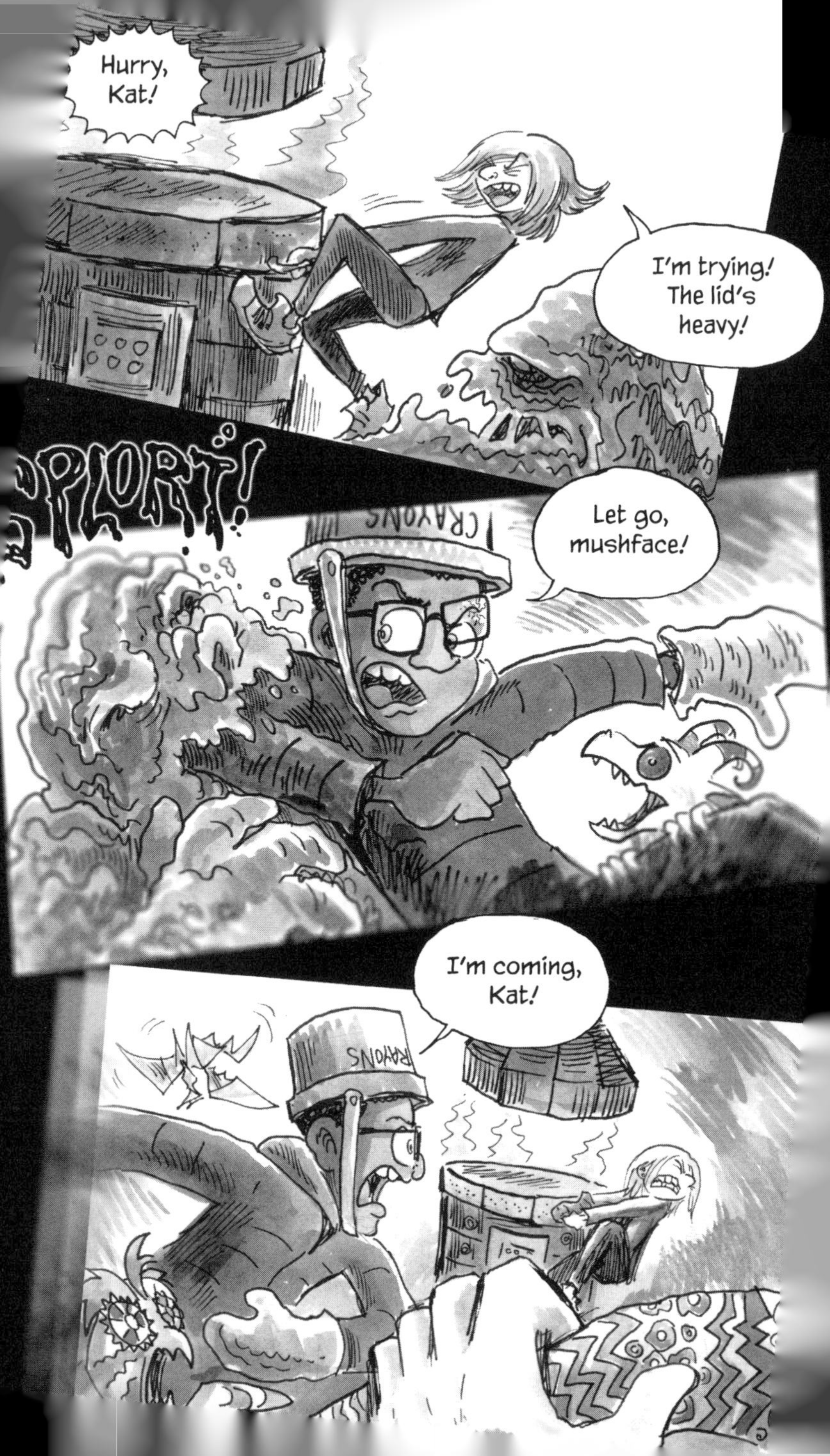
Hurry, Kat!
I'm trying! The lid's heavy!
PLORT!
Let go, mushface!
I'm coming, Kat!

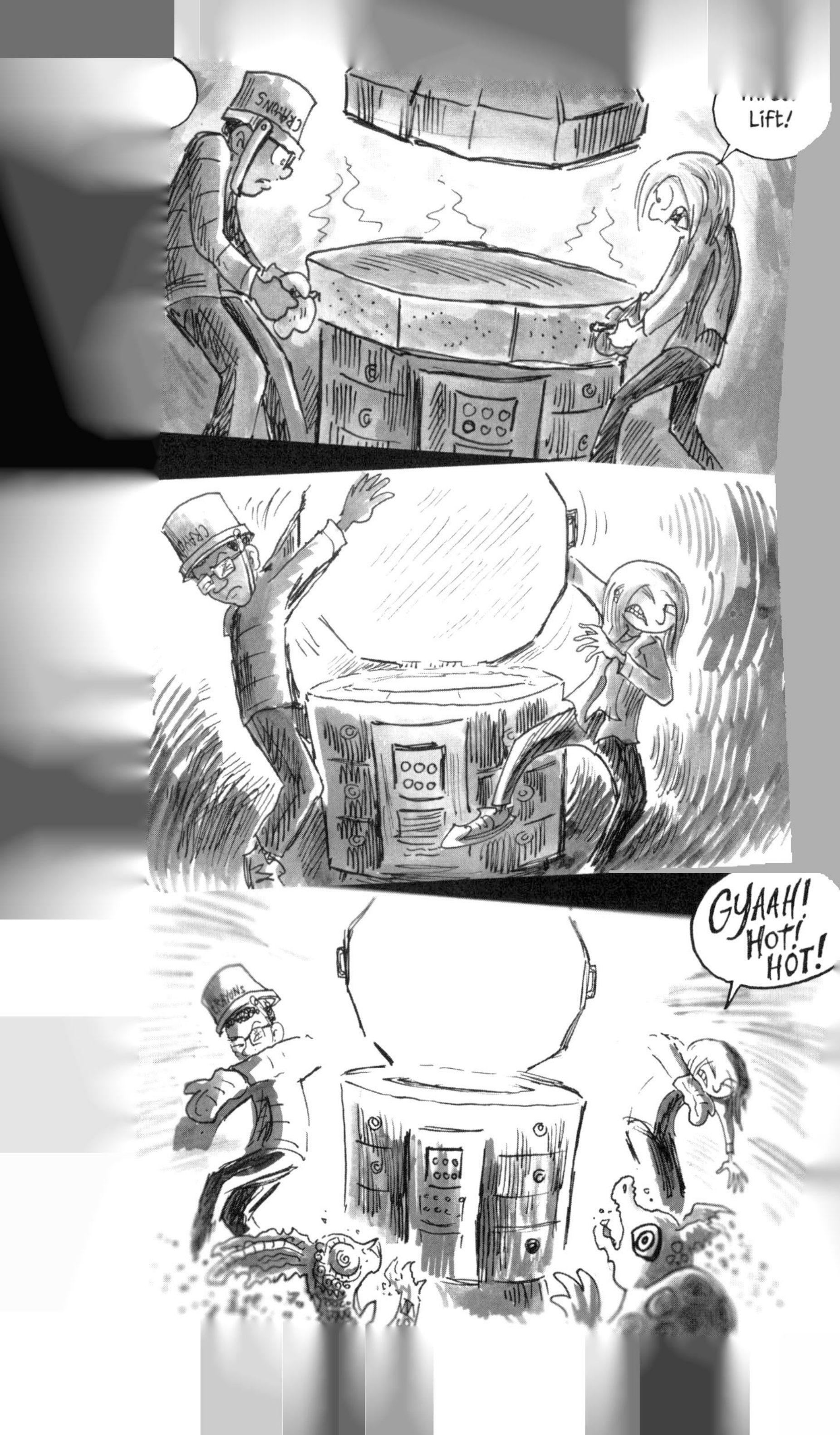
Lift!
GYAAH! HOT! HOT!

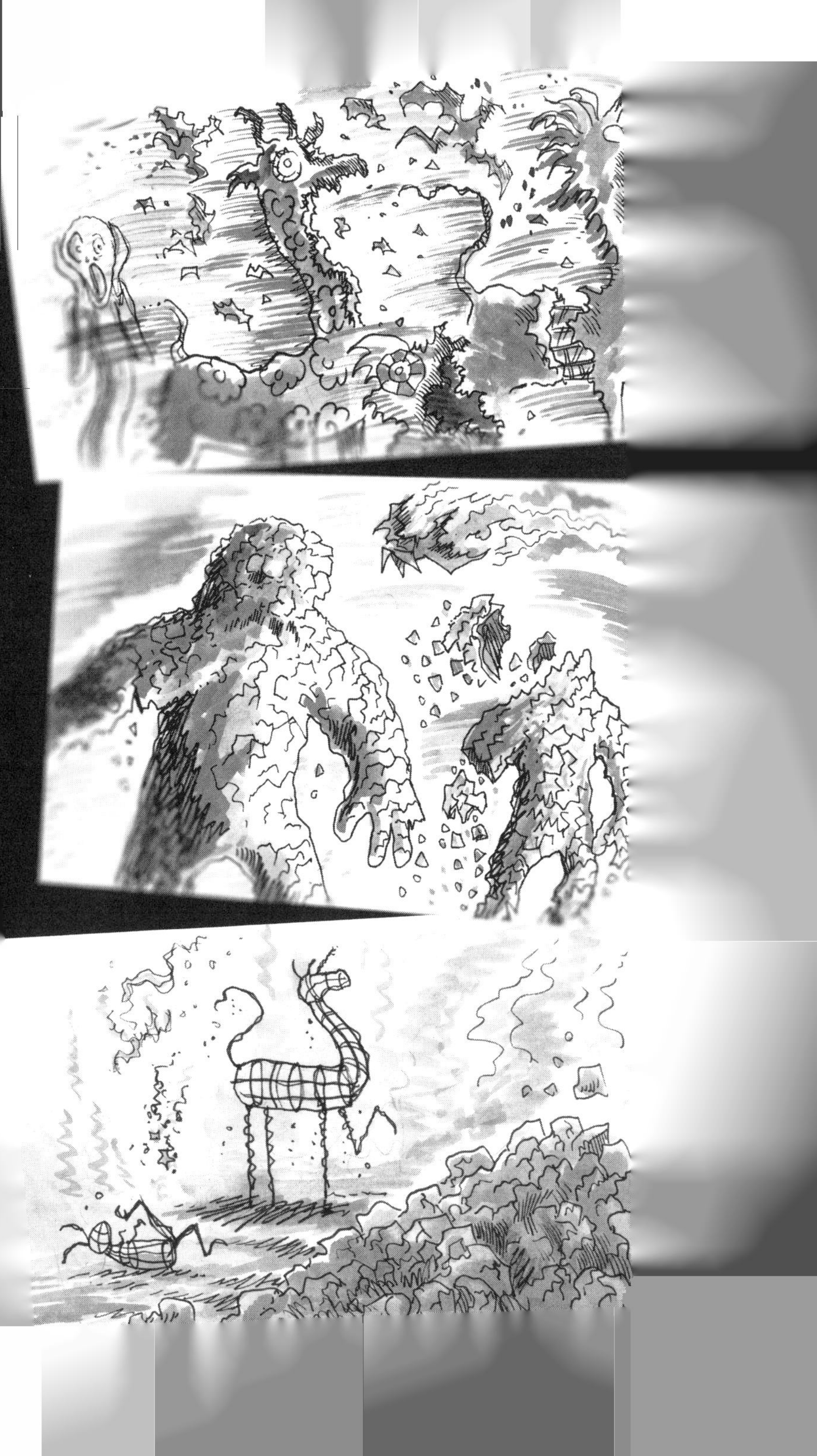

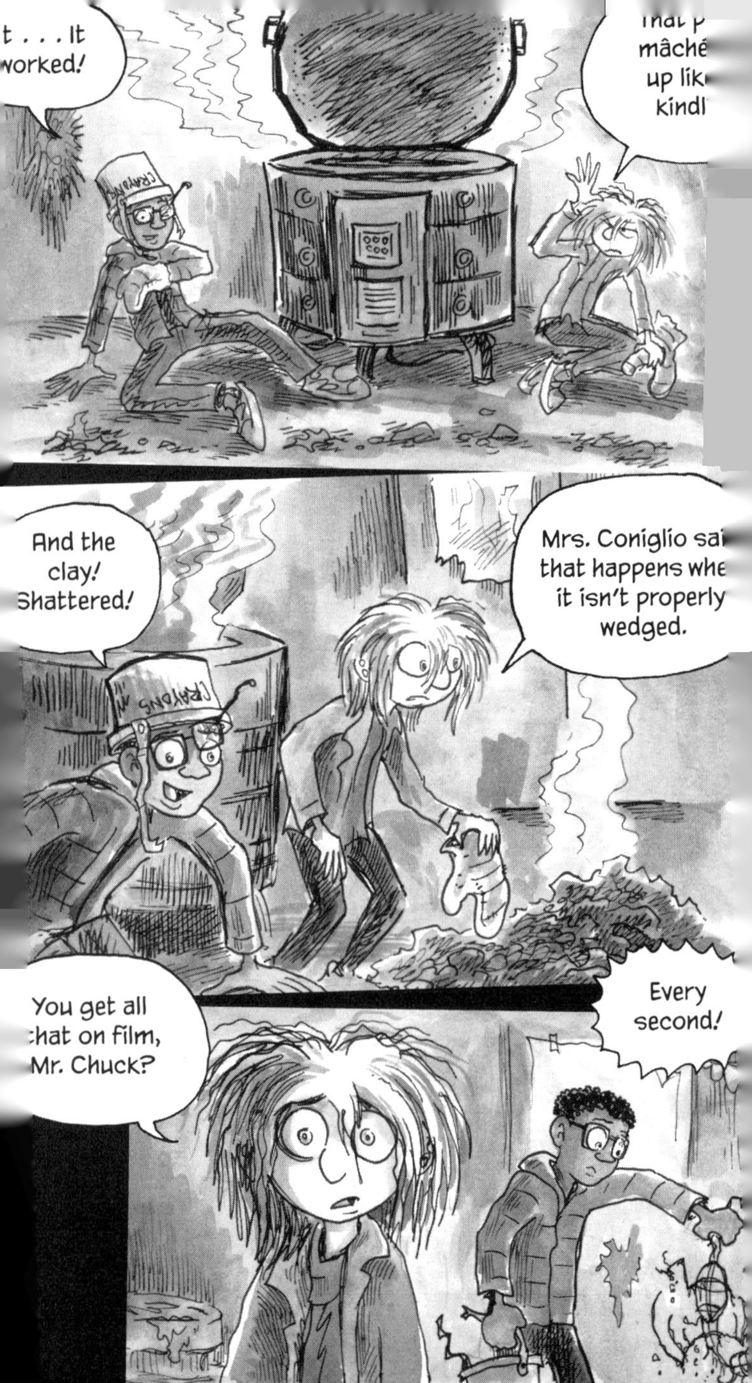
t . . . It
worked!
mâché
up lik
kindl
And the clay! Shattered!
Mrs. Coniglio sai
that happens whe
it isn't properly
wedged.
You get all
that on film,
Mr. Chuck?
Every second!

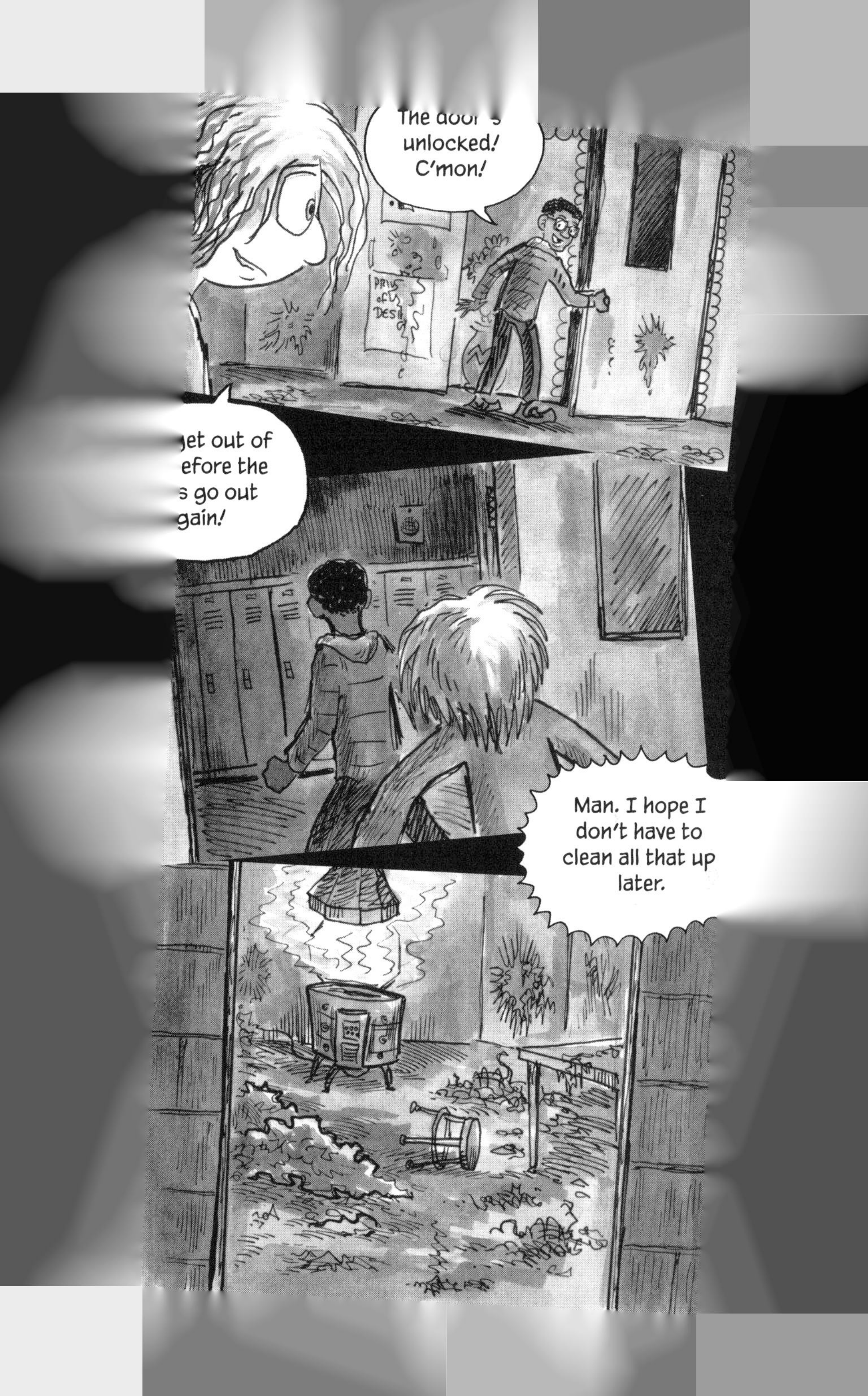

The door unlocked! C'mon!
out of the go out
Man. I hope I don't have to clean all that up later.

Chapter 27

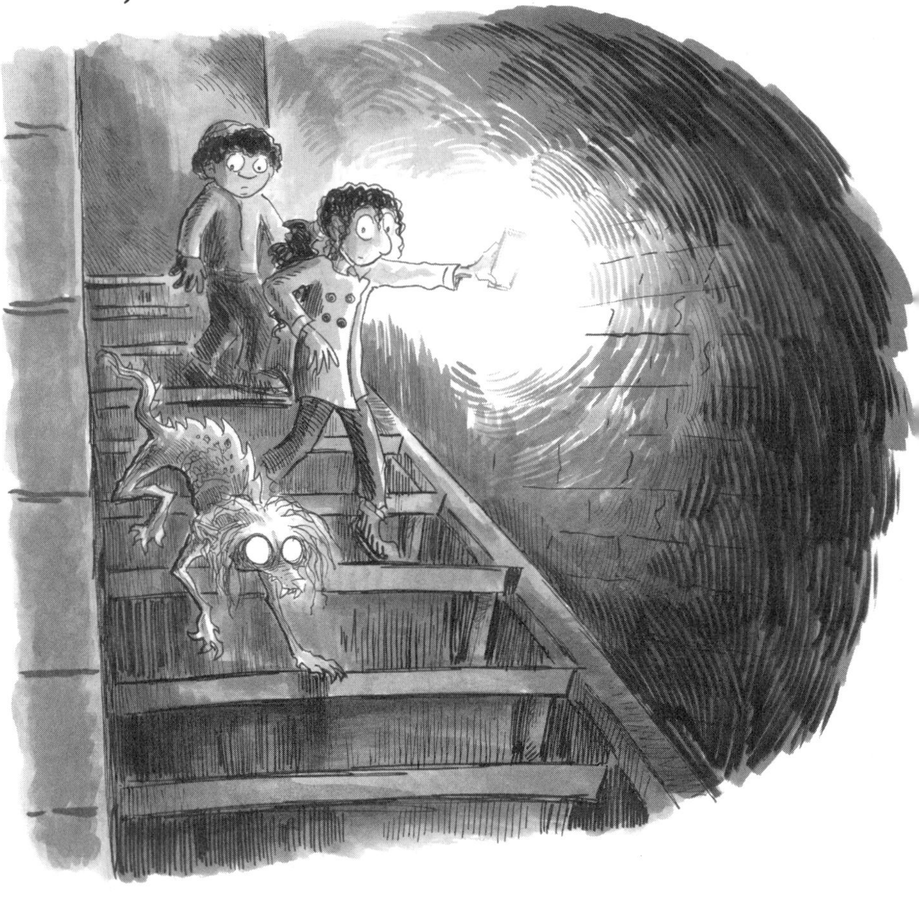

"Remember, keep your hands to yourself . . . if you wish to keep your little fingies."

They started down the creaky steps. Willow led the way—if not for her fluorescent eyes, she would have been hardly more than a shadow in the dim light.

"Hold your lantern high, Twila," ordered Willow. "But be careful—some of Margalo's tenants hate the light."

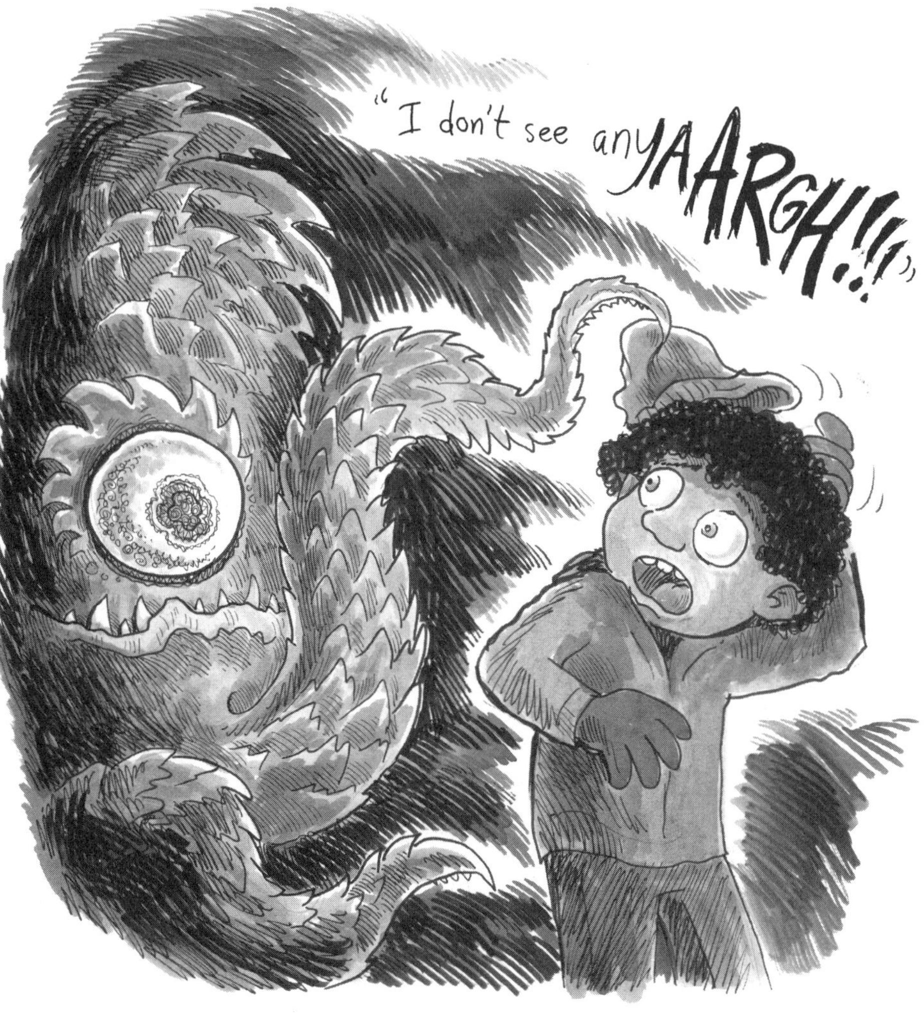
"I don't see anyYAARGH!!!"

"Pratchett! Keep your sneaky tentacles to yourself!" Willow scolded.

Jordan and Twila stared with bugged eyes and slack jaws.

"Mottled cuttlegorg," said Willow, her voice again mimicking Margalo's speech patterns. "Native to the Underglades, before they were drained to make room for housing tracts and golf courses. Do not worry. He is very gentle. He just wanted your hat."

Twila raised her phone, filling the entire cellar with pale light.

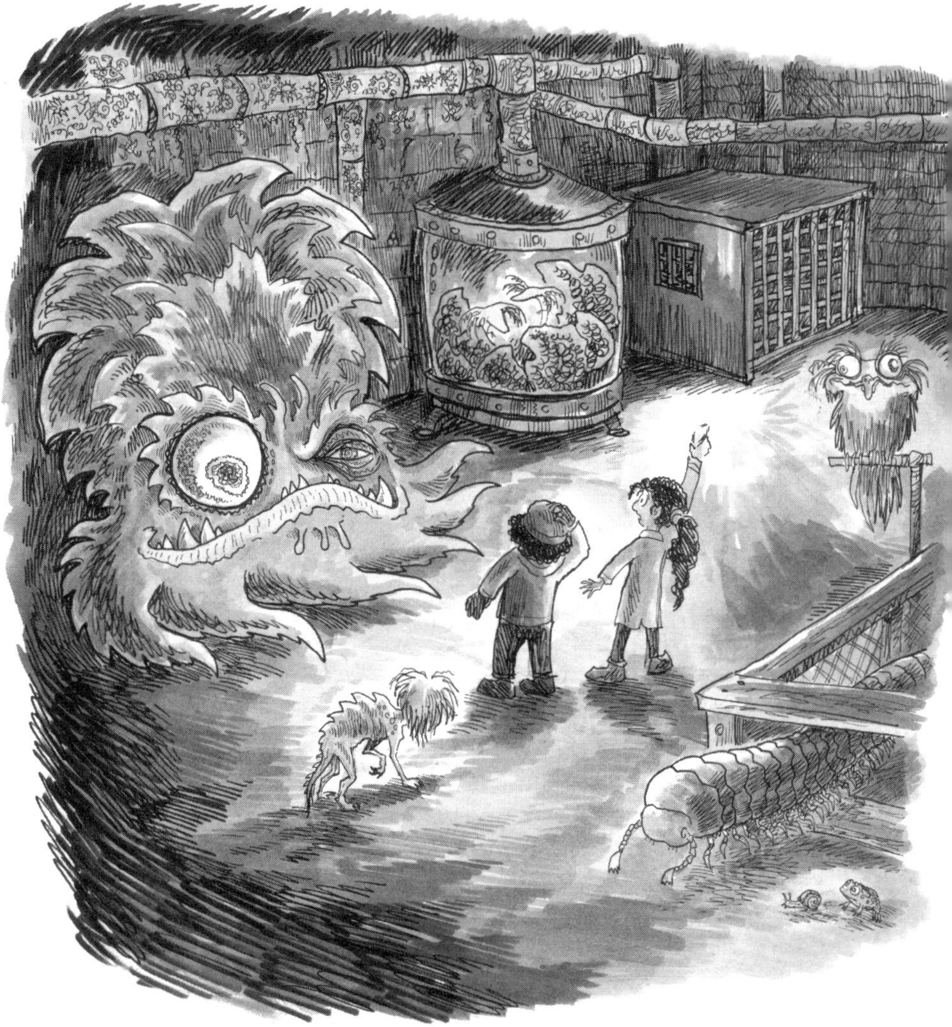

"Where did they come from?" she asked, her voice full of awe.

"From all the lost corners," Willow said. "All the castaways that have no place in today's squeaky-bright world."

"Cooool!" said Jordan. "A giant millipede!"

"Her name is Atwood. From the deepest, dampest rainforest . . . now a cattle field, says Margalo. Twila! Careful!" She pulled Twila back from a dark terrarium. "Telepathy olms."

"Are they dangerous?"

"Not physically—but beware! They will read your mind and reveal your most embarrassing secrets."

"Don't have a Cow, Man!"

cackled a shrill voice behind them.

"That is very rude, Harlan," Willow scolded.

"Is that a Muppet?" Jordan laughed.

"No, a giant potoo. A real bigmouth."

"How *YOU* doin'?

Did I do THAAAAAAT?

No SOUP FOR YOU!

WUZUUUUUP!"

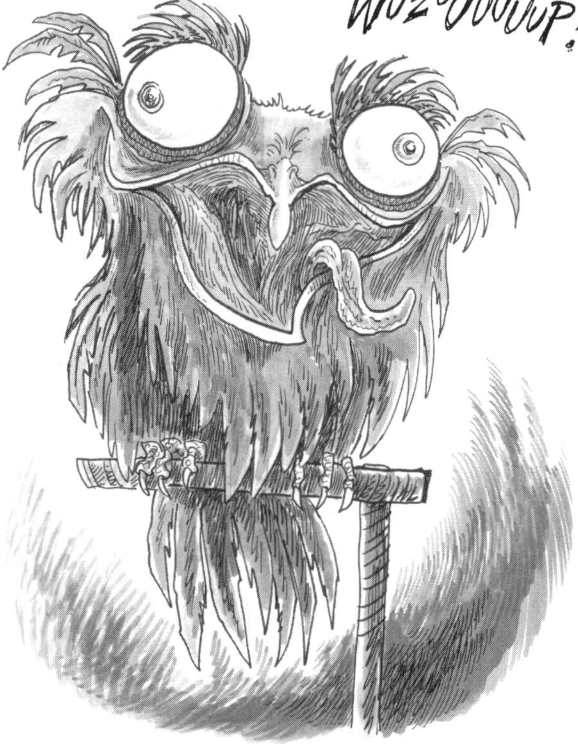

"Harlan likes repeating dated sitcom catchphrases," sighed Willow. "It is very annoying."

"How did Margalo get them all to Cowslip Grove?" asked Twila.

Willow shrugged her spines. "Margalo belongs to a very secret club. That is all you need to know."

Jordan reached toward Atwood and stroked her exoskeleton. Willow started to remind him to keep his hands away, but fell silent when she saw the look of wonder on his face.

Twila stopped admiring the creatures and crossed her arms. "Okay, Willow. Cool critters. But what about the Boojum?"

"What about it?"

"C'mon! Margalo has a cellar full of monsters, and you try to pretend it doesn't have anything to do with the freaky stuff at the school?"

"It does not. These 'monsters' are just my roommates. Misfits. They have nothing to do with the Boojum and the attack on the school."

Jordan stopped petting Atwood. "What's the Boojum?"

"It's a bad thing that's haunting our town," said Twila. "And it makes people disappear. But the scariest part is that the kids it takes don't just disappear. They cease to exist. No one remembers them."

"Wait, so everyone at the school is just going to disappear?" asked Jordan.

A pause. The house above creaked, and the wind outside howled.

"Well," said Twila at last, "cool cellar, but back to business. There's nothing left for me to do but crawl back through the tunnel and try to find Levi by myself."

"Twila, do not be a dunder-melon," Willow hissed.
"Levi would want you here where you are safe."

"I don't care," said Twila. "Last year Levi was there for
me when no one else was. So was Kat." She started back
toward the stairs.

"I'm coming too!" said Jordan. "He drives me nuts, but
I can't let Donte be snowman food."

"Wait! Willow commands you to stay!" Ignoring her,
the two third-graders continued toward the cellar stairs.
"Please!" heaved Willow. "This is bad! Margalo is under a
sleeping spell, we have no magic—"

"But we have an army of cool cellar monsters who
might be able to help," Jordan said. "Fight monsters with
monsters!"

"We can't send Margalo's patients out into the storm!" Willow sputtered. "And they would be useless in a fight! Pratchett is a big softy, Harlan is all stale punchlines, the telepathy olms are just gossips! They would be no use against the Boojum and its trickery!"

And then there was a scratching noise from the farthest, darkest corner of the cellar. Twila and Jordan turned toward the one remaining cage.

"What's back there?" asked Twila.

Willow's spines bristled. "Willow stays far away from that cage. That cage is the home of a very bad monster. Margalo calls her Charlotte."

"I want to see her," said Jordan.

Willow winced. "Not a good idea."

"Why not?" asked Twila. "You said all these creatures are harmless, right? None of them would be good in a fight against the Boojum, right? So where's the harm?"

Willow stared at Twila. Twila stared back.

"Fine," said Willow at last. "But stay behind Willow, and no sudden movements."

They tiptoed to the far corner of the cellar.

"Charlotte?" Willow whispered. "You have visitors."

A long, hairy limb poked through the wire mesh.

"Hello, Charlotte. Please be nice."

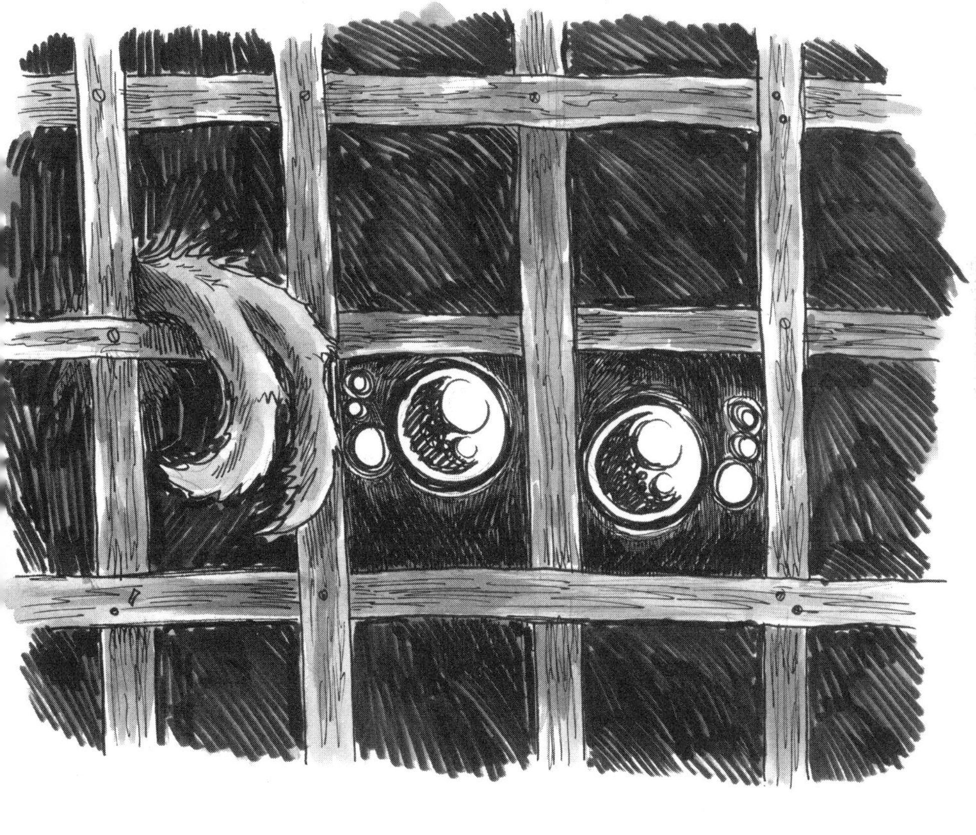

Chapter 28

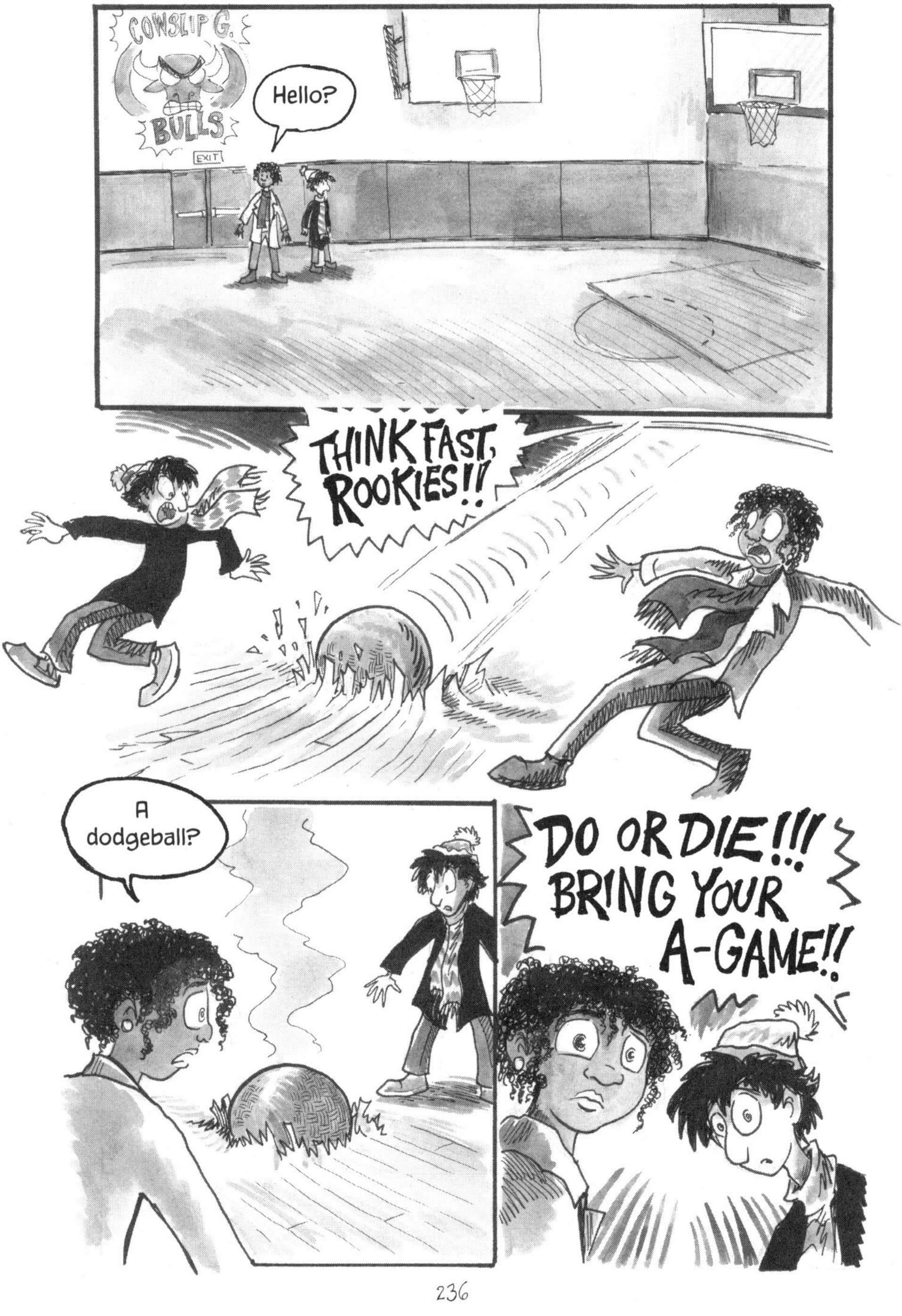
COWSLIP G.
BULLS
EXIT
Hello?
THINK FAST, ROOKIES!!
A dodgeball?
DO OR DIE!!!
BRING YOUR A-GAME!!

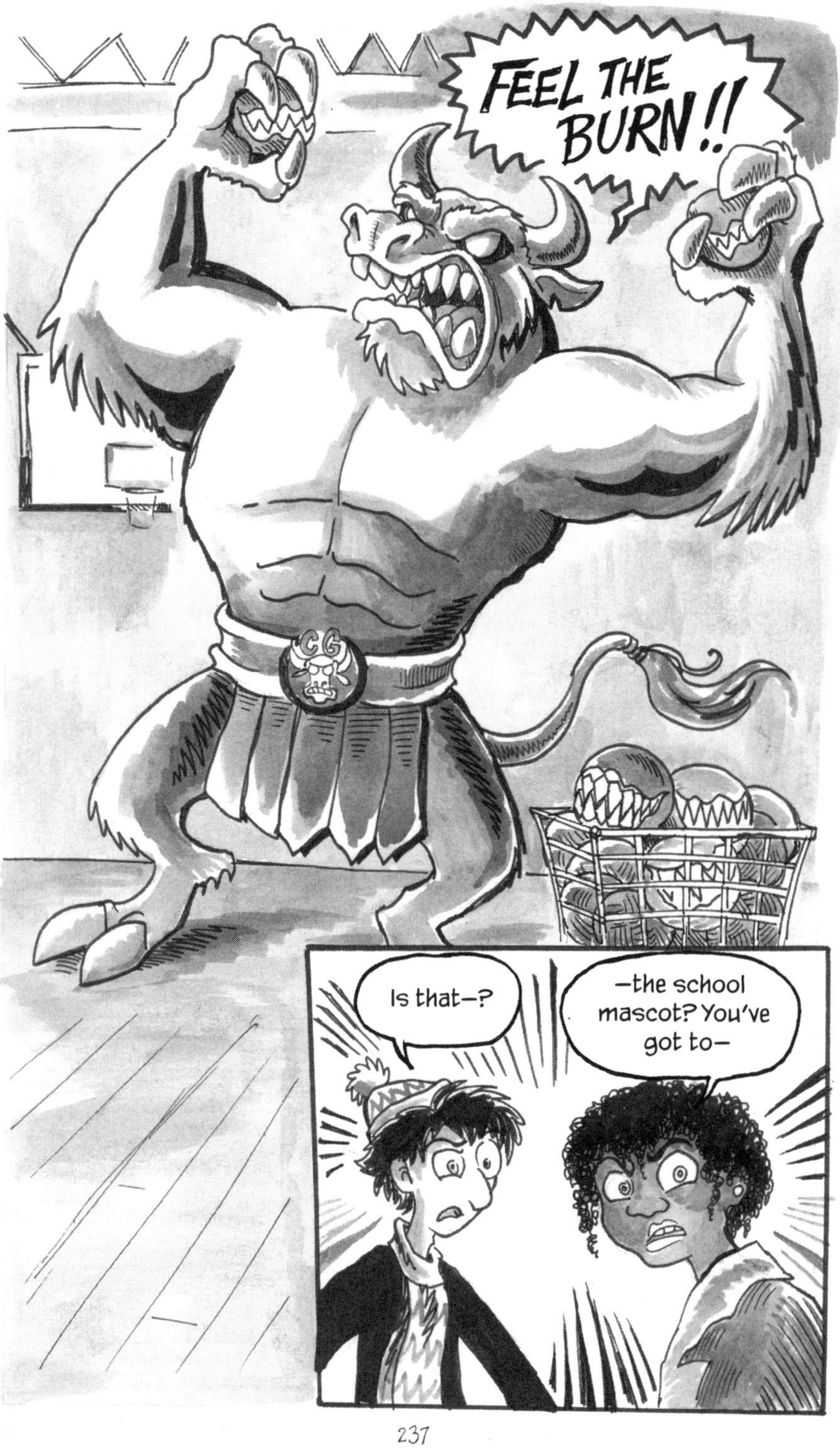
FEEL THE BURN!!
Is that–?
–the school mascot? You've got to–

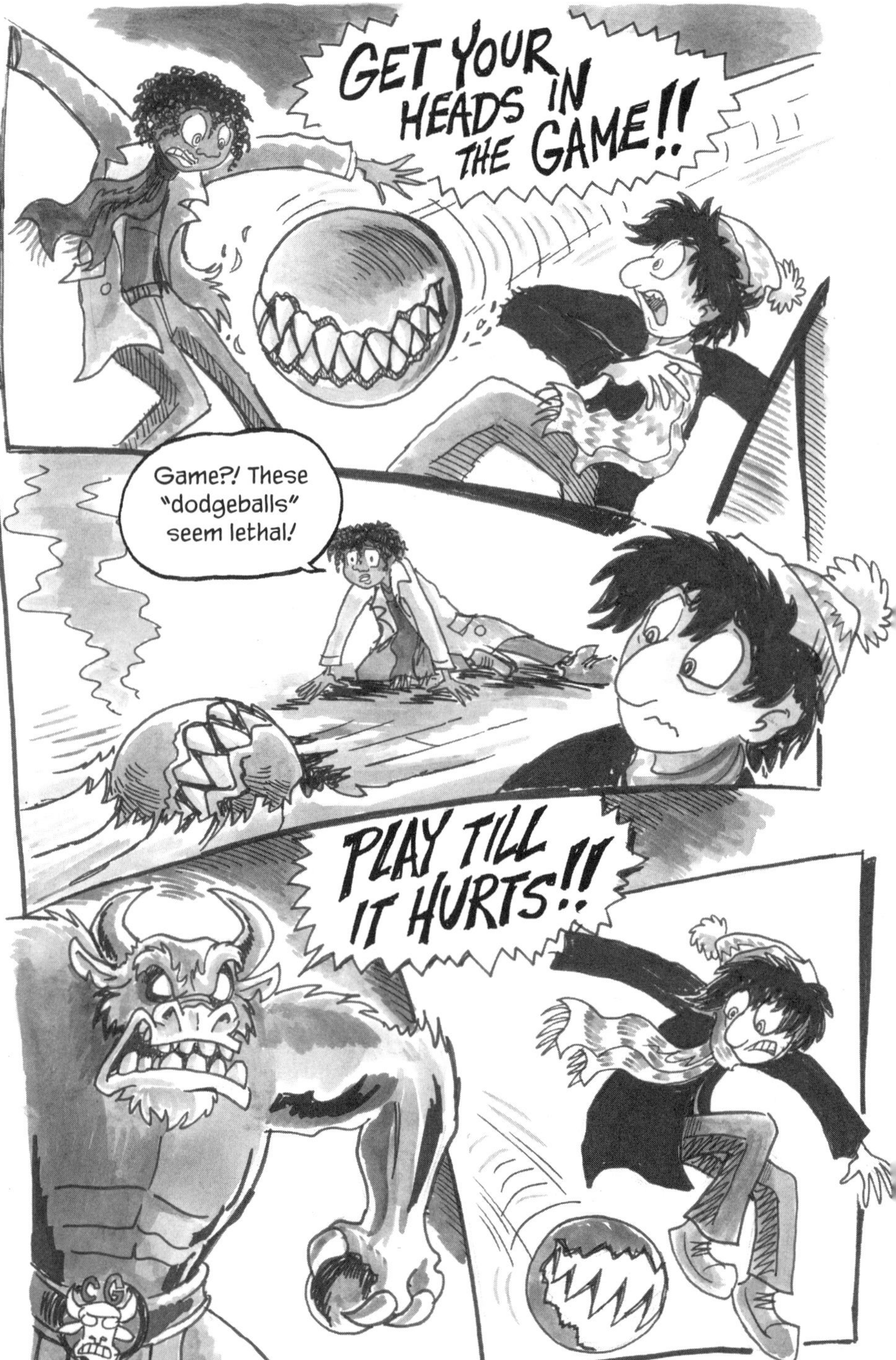
GET YOUR HEADS IN THE GAME!!
Game?! These "dodgeballs" seem lethal!
PLAY TILL IT HURTS!!

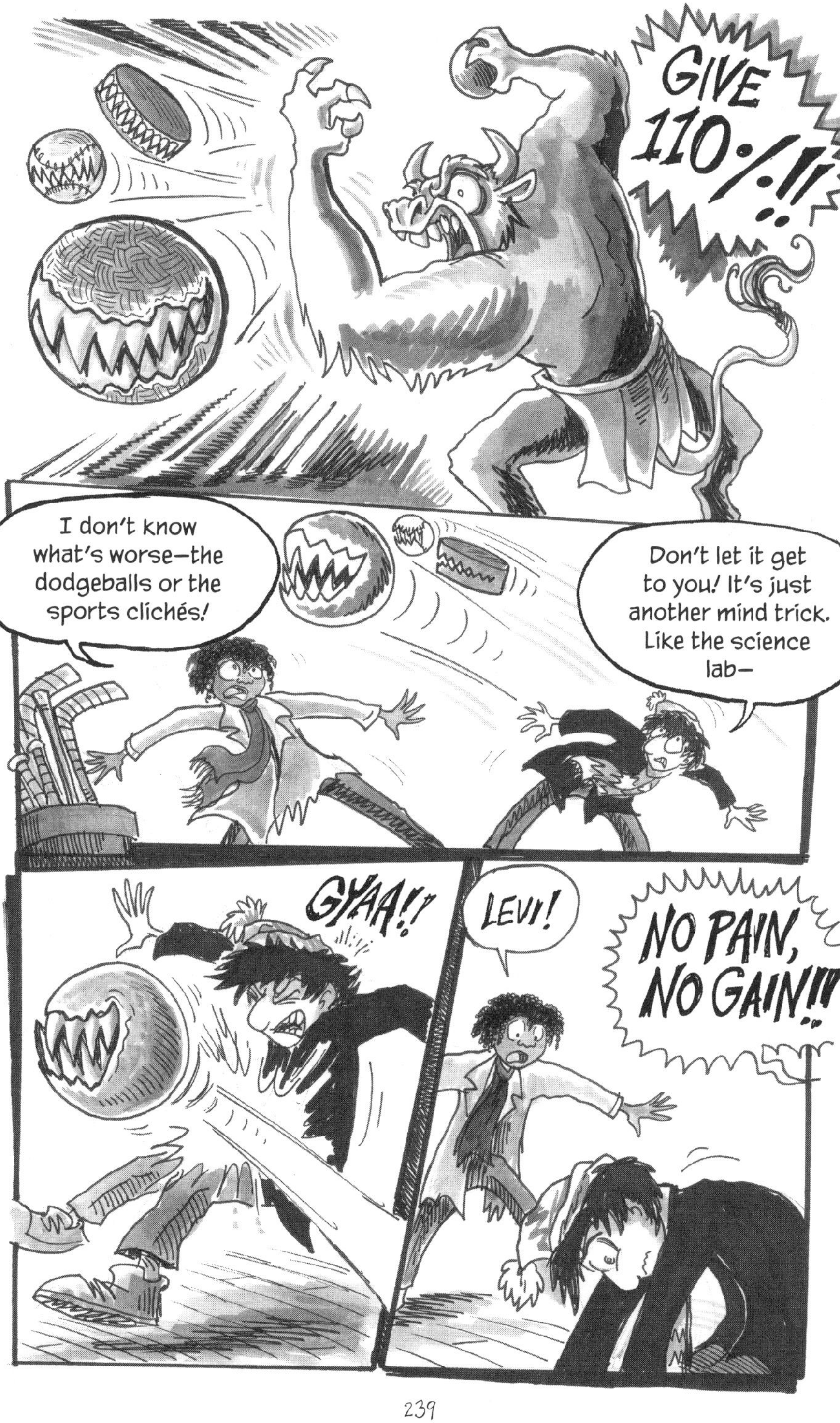
GIVE 110%!!!
I don't know what's worse—the dodgeballs or the sports clichés!
Don't let it get to you! It's just another mind trick. Like the science lab—
GYAA!!
LEVI!
NO PAIN, NO GAIN!!!

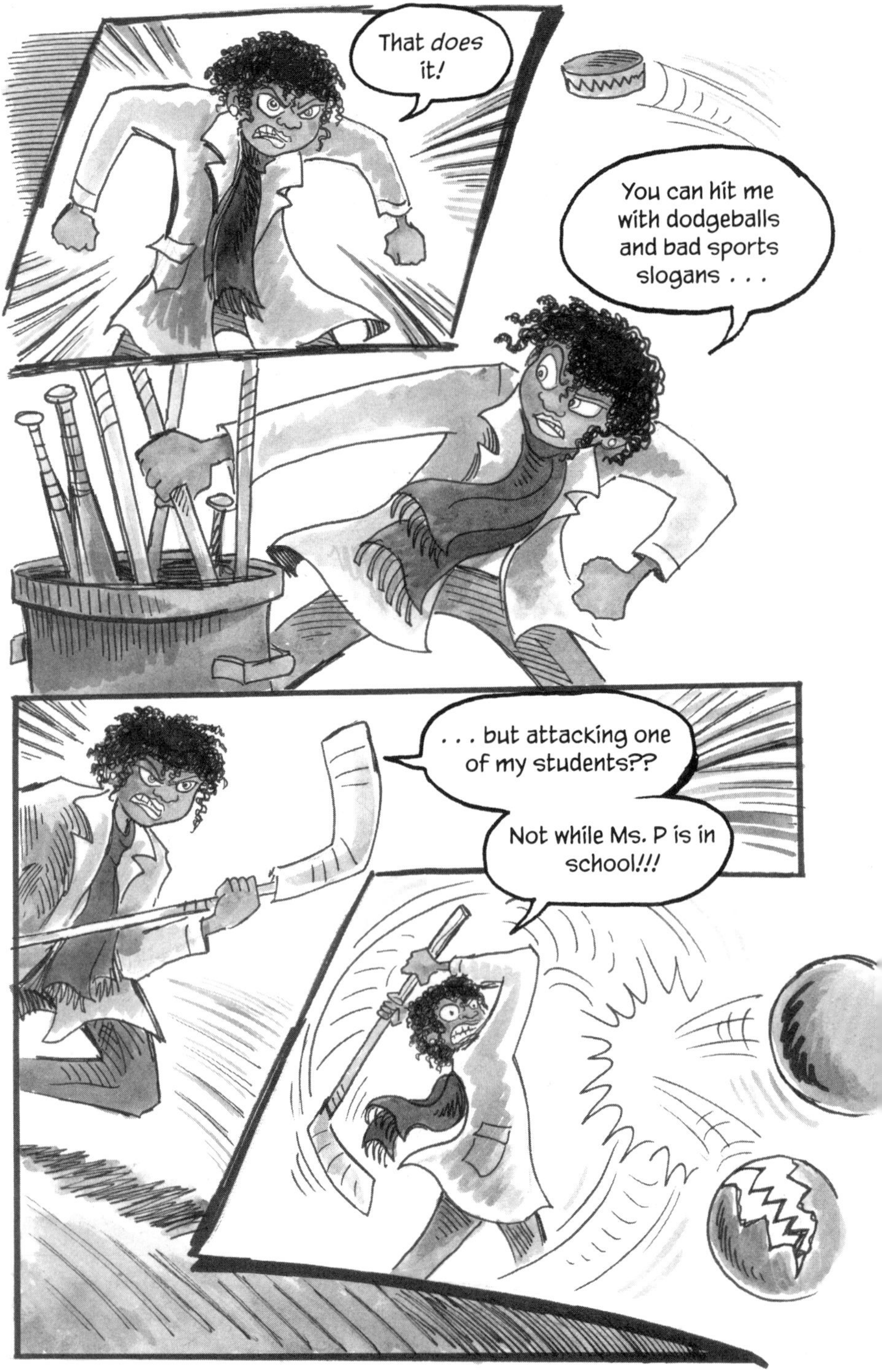
That *does* it!
You can hit me with dodgeballs and bad sports slogans . . .
. . . but attacking one of my students??
Not while Ms. P is in school!!!

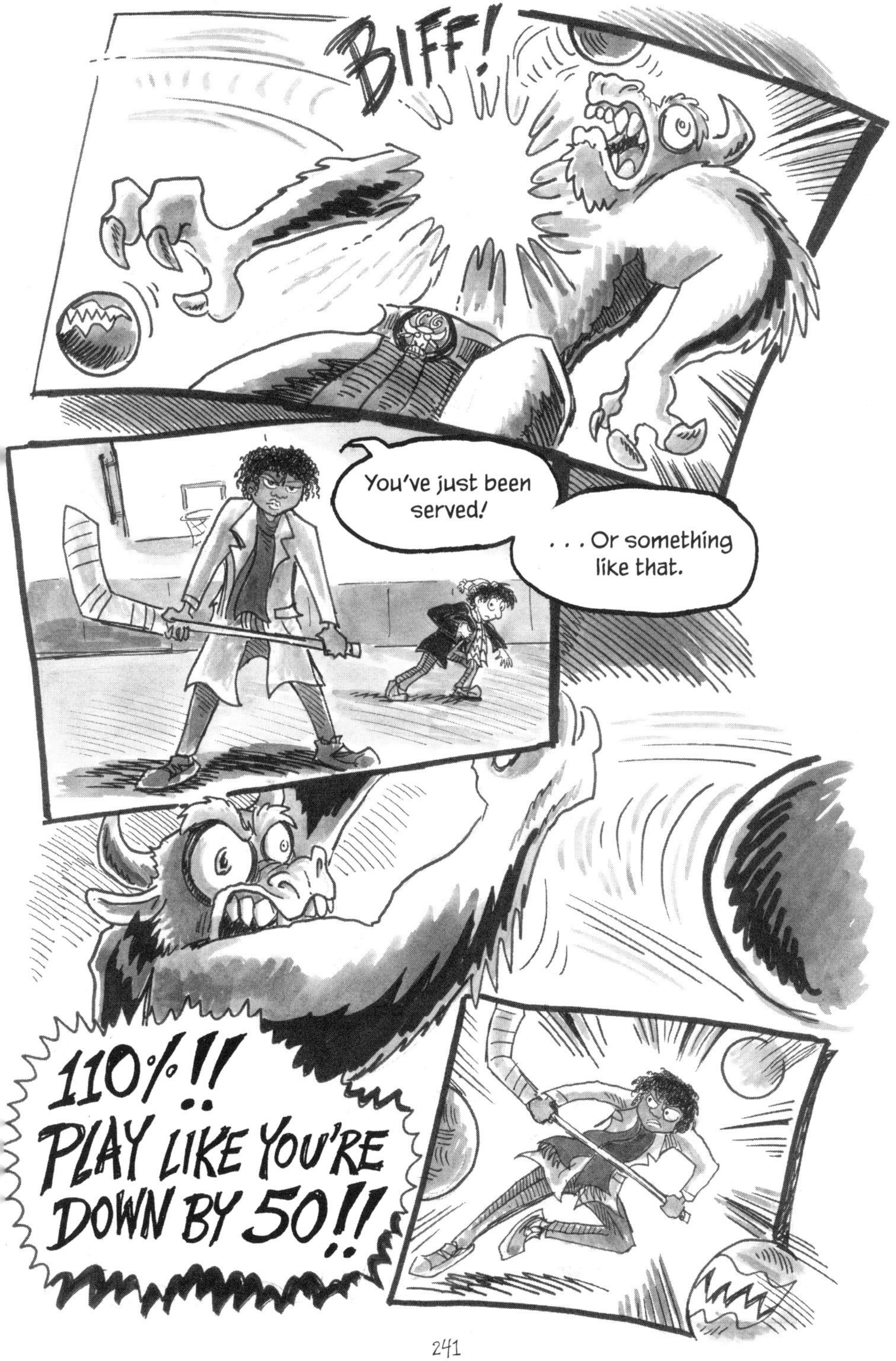
BIFF!
You've just been served!
. . . Or something like that.
110%!!
PLAY LIKE YOU'RE DOWN BY 50!!

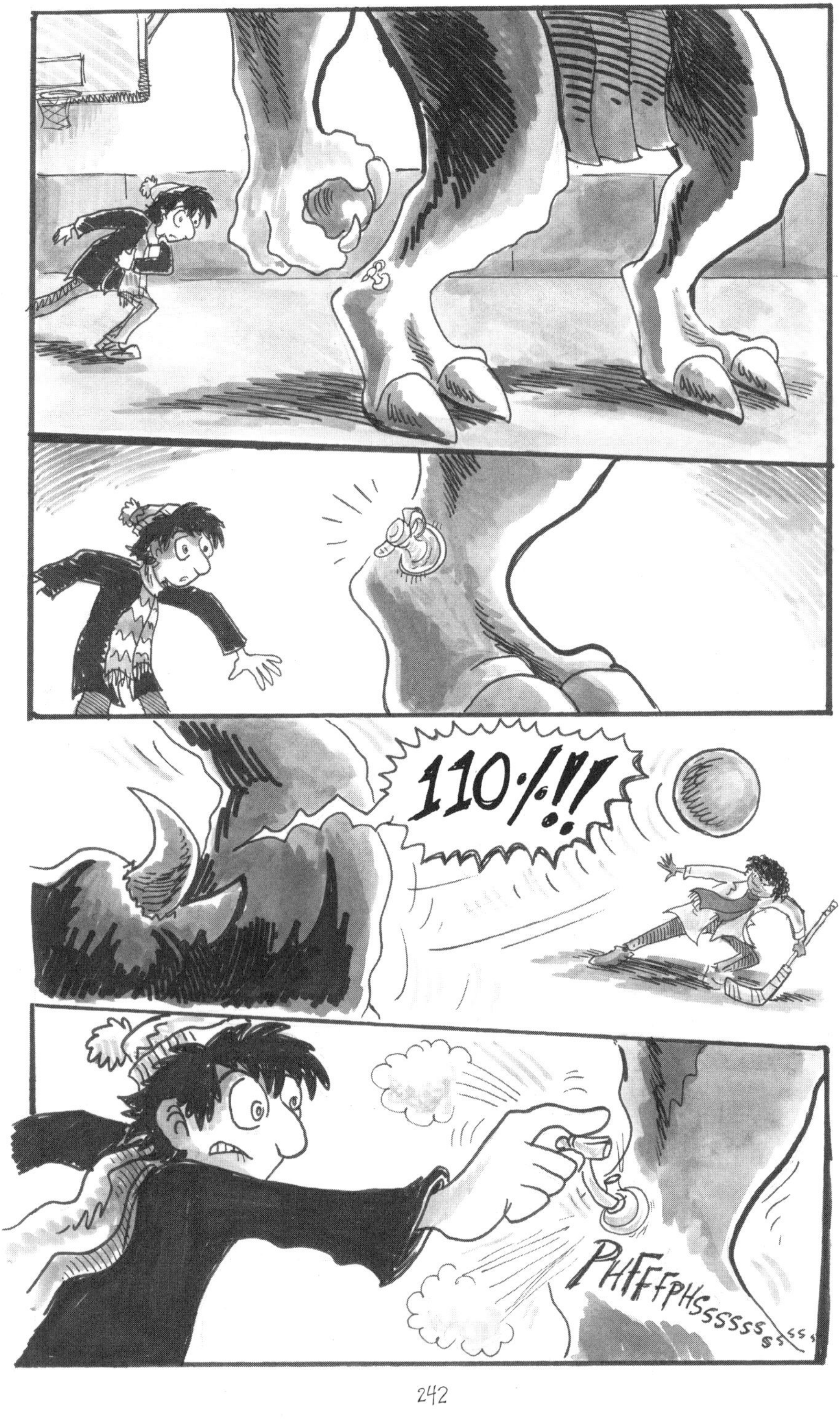
110%!!
PHFFFPHSSSSSSSSSSS

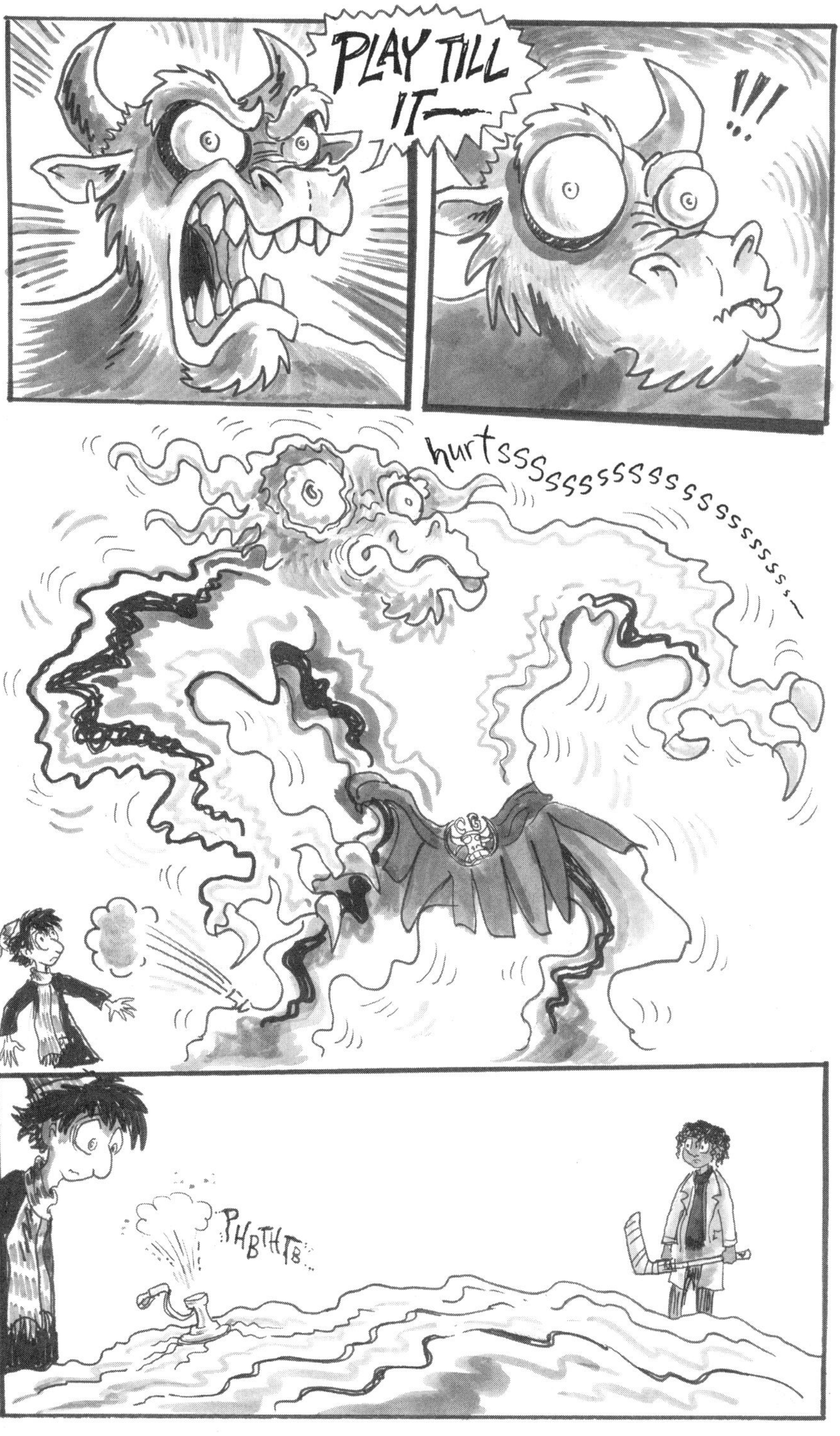
PLAY TILL IT—
!!!
hurtsssssssssssssssssssssss—
PHBTHTB...

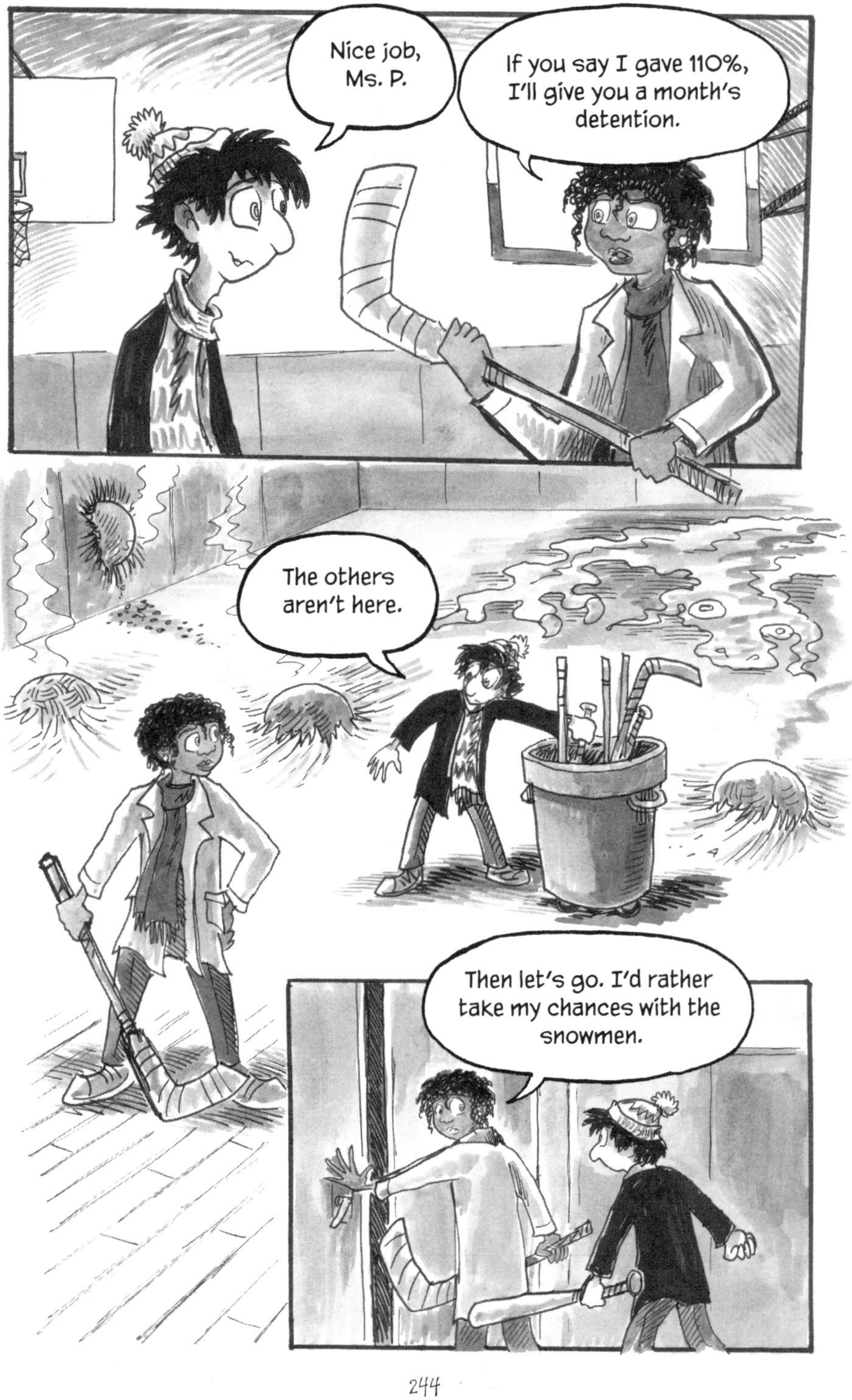
Nice job, Ms. P.
If you say I gave 110%, I'll give you a month's detention.
The others aren't here.
Then let's go. I'd rather take my chances with the snowmen.

Chapter 29

"But we need to do something! I'm not going to just sit here and wait out the storm while the Boojum takes my brother, my teachers, and all my friends!"

"Yes, but sending Charlotte into the tunnel and setting her loose in the school is not a good idea."

"But look at her eyes!" Twila persisted. "*All* of her eyes! She's like *you,* Willow! She'll be able to see the Boojum's tricks for what they really are!"

"Maybe," Willow said. "But Charlotte is *not* like Willow. She is unpredictable. Especially now, since she is . . . erm, expecting."

"You mean she's pregnant?" asked Jordan.

"In a sense. See the sacs along her back?" Willow said. "But that is not the point. We do not know if Charlotte will attack the Boojum and its tricks. She might instead attack *us.*"

Twila shrugged. "Guess that's a risk we'll have to take."

"No. Willow forbids this rotten plan."

"Miss Willow," said Twila slowly. Her voice was calm, but her big brown eyes were suddenly fiercer than Willow's green searchlights. "Why do you think the Boojum keeps targeting our town?"

Willow shrugged her spines. "Margalo thinks it is because Cowslip Grove seems like such a safe place. It is so soft, ordered, predictable. It is the perfect prey."

"Right," said Twila. "Then we need to toss a wild card into the mix and throw the Boojum off its game."

"But Charlotte . . ." Willow started.

Twila's eyes narrowed. "Unless you have any better ideas."

"What about the thing in the red room?" said Jordan abruptly.

Twila and Willow looked at him.

"When we were here with Levi," explained Jordan, "there was a room upstairs. It was glowing red. And I saw something inside. It looked like a big egg."

Willow opened her mouth to object, but Twila and Jordan were already running back up the cellar stairs. They raced past the upstairs cages, past the sleeping vulture, past the snoozing snake, to the closed door of the incubation room.

"Wait!" shouted Willow as she scrambled after them. But it was too late—Jordan threw the door open, and the entire house filled with heat and crimson light.

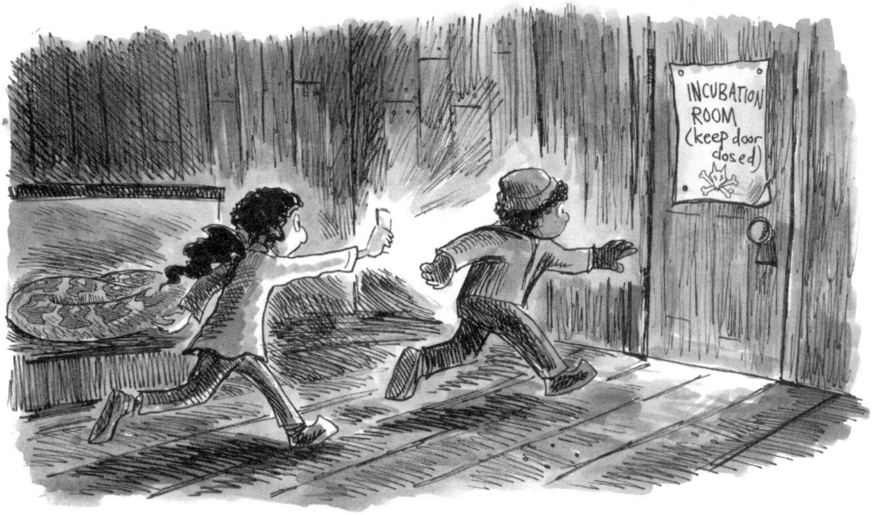
INCUBATION ROOM (keep door closed)

Upchuck the vulture perked up and beat her wings. Willow cringed and shielded her sensitive eyes.

"Whoaaaa," said Jordan and Twila together.

Willow sighed and shook her head. "Third-graders. You are worse than snow bogeys."

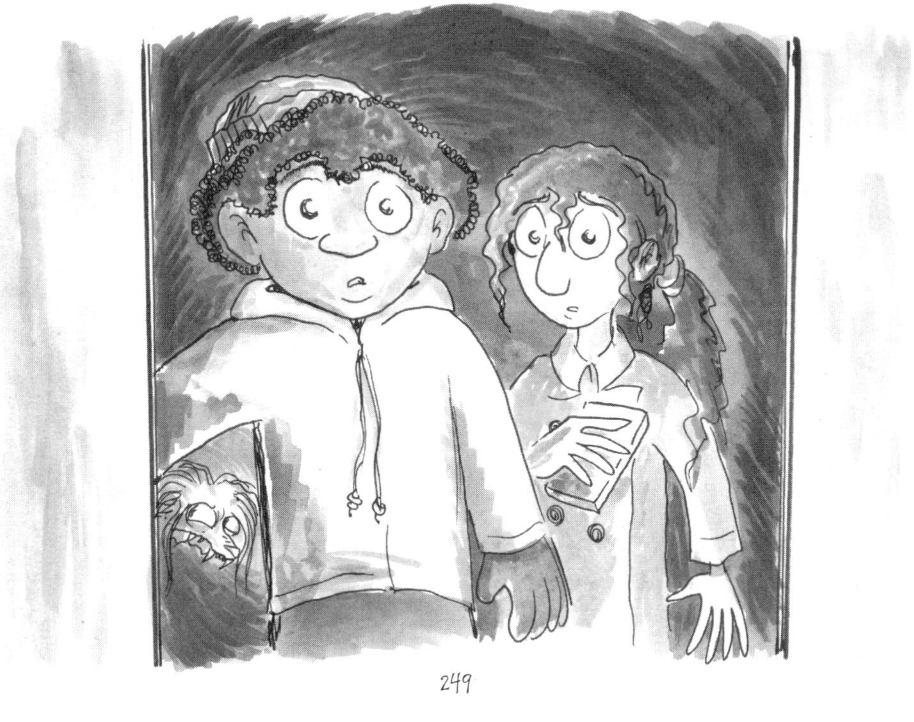

Kat? I think your phone's about to die.
Keep filming, Mr. Chuck!
Jordan! Can you hear me?
Do you think he's okay?
I'm surprised you're so worried about Jordan. All you ever do is complain about him.
What? No! C'mon, he knows I'm joking. Deep down, I really . . .

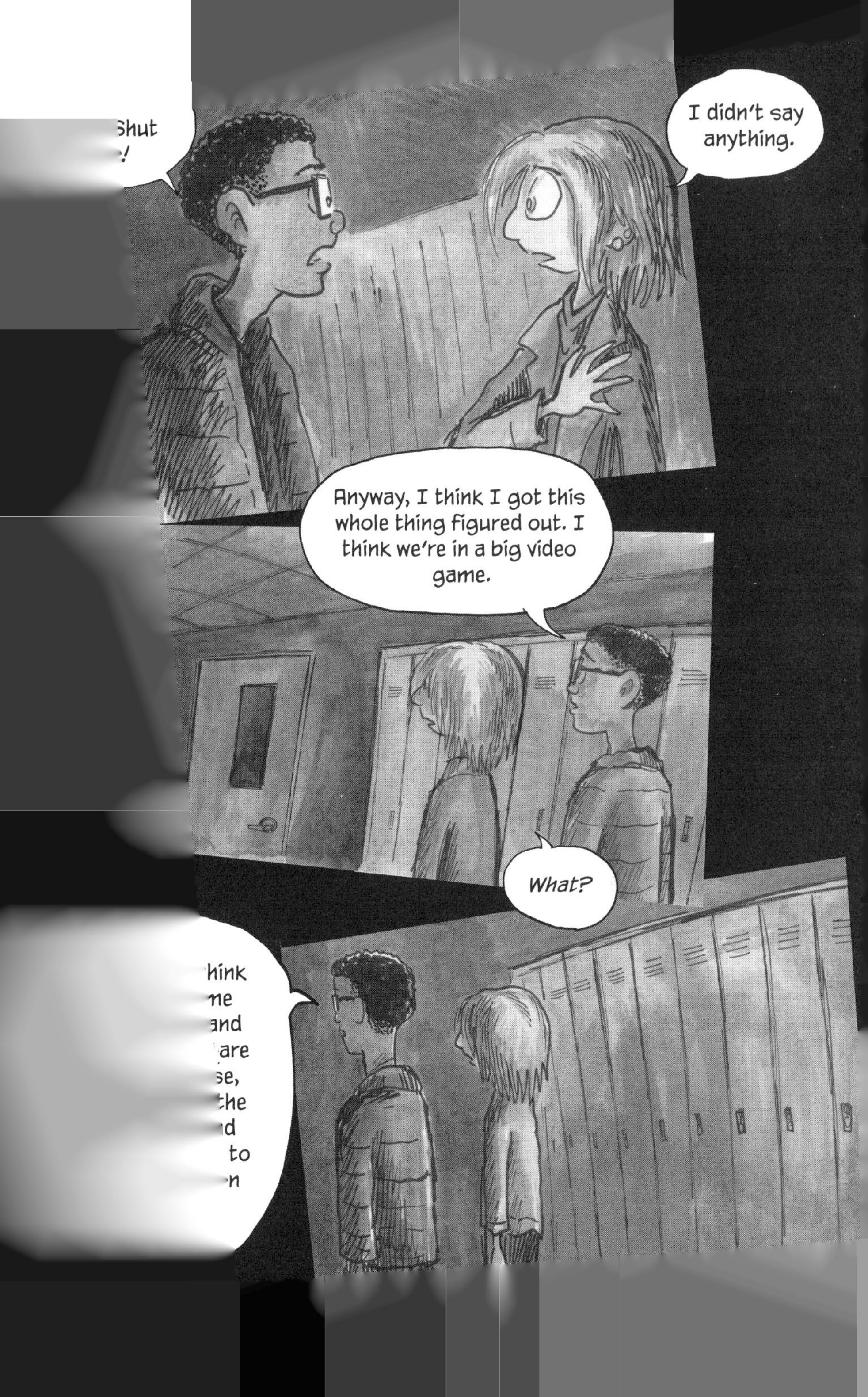

I didn't say anything.
Anyway, I think I got this whole thing figured out. I think we're in a big video game.
What?

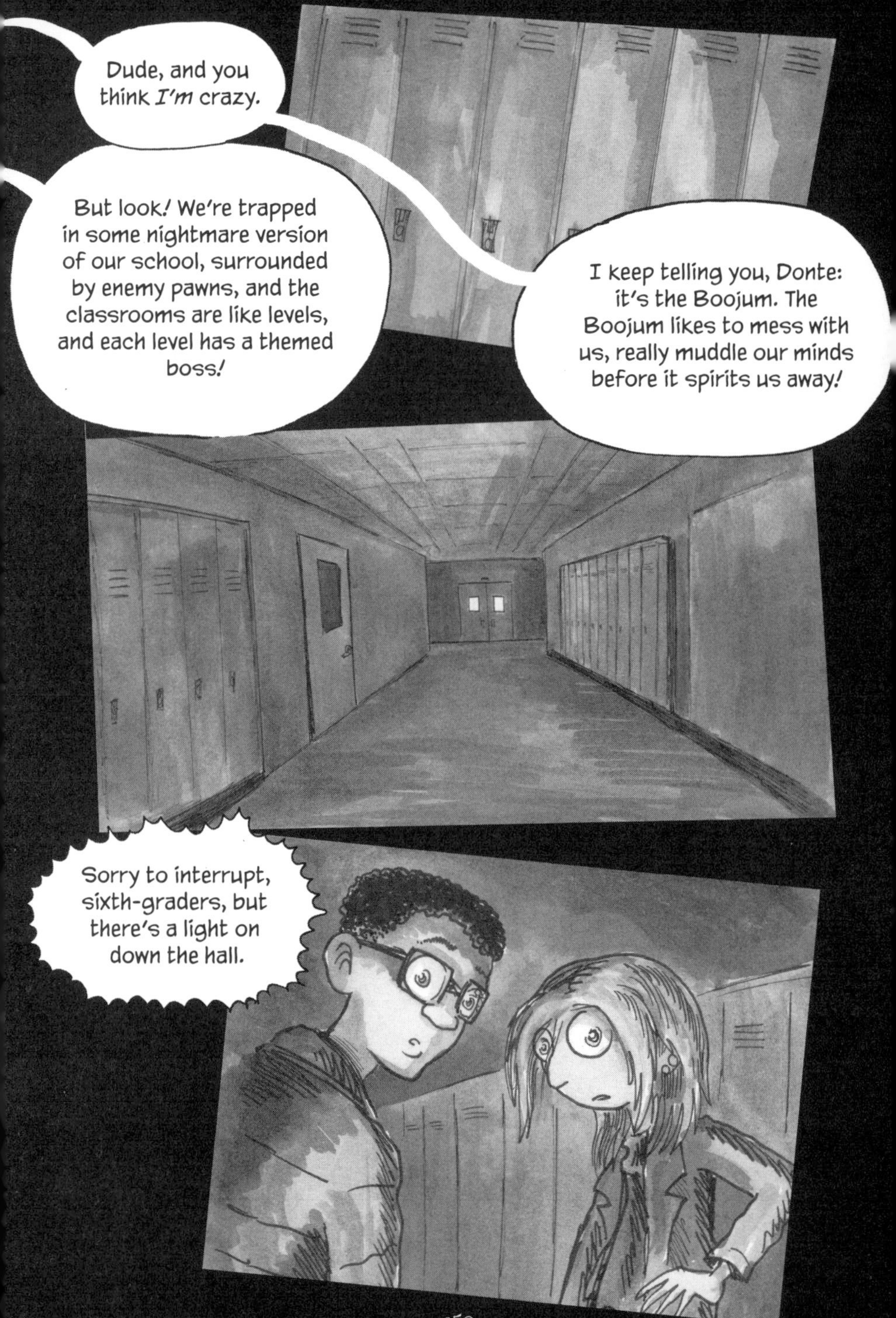
Dude, and you think *I'm* crazy.
But look! We're trapped in some nightmare version of our school, surrounded by enemy pawns, and the classrooms are like levels, and each level has a themed boss!
I keep telling you, Donte: it's the Boojum. The Boojum likes to mess with us, really muddle our minds before it spirits us away!
Sorry to interrupt, sixth-graders, but there's a light on down the hall.

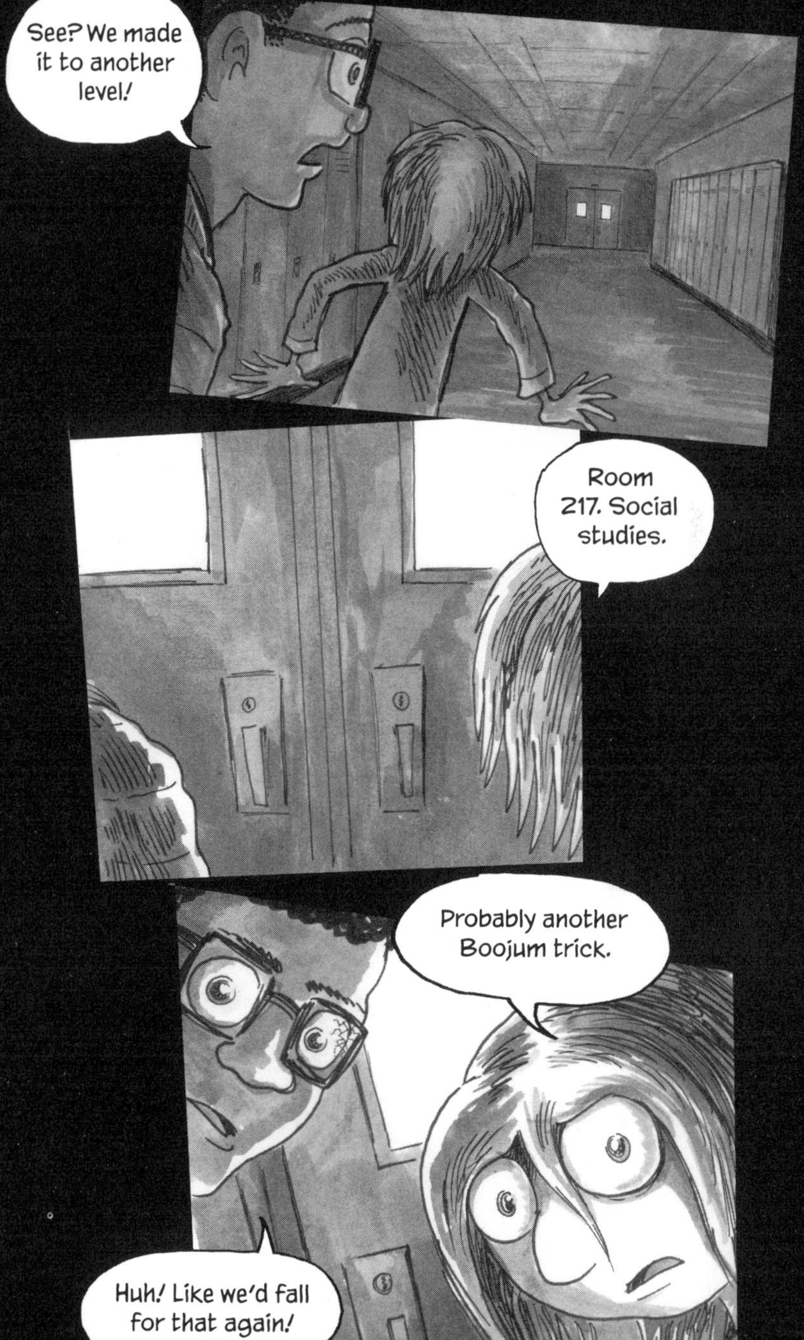
See? We made it to another level!
Room 217. Social studies.
Probably another Boojum trick.
Huh! Like we'd fall for that again!

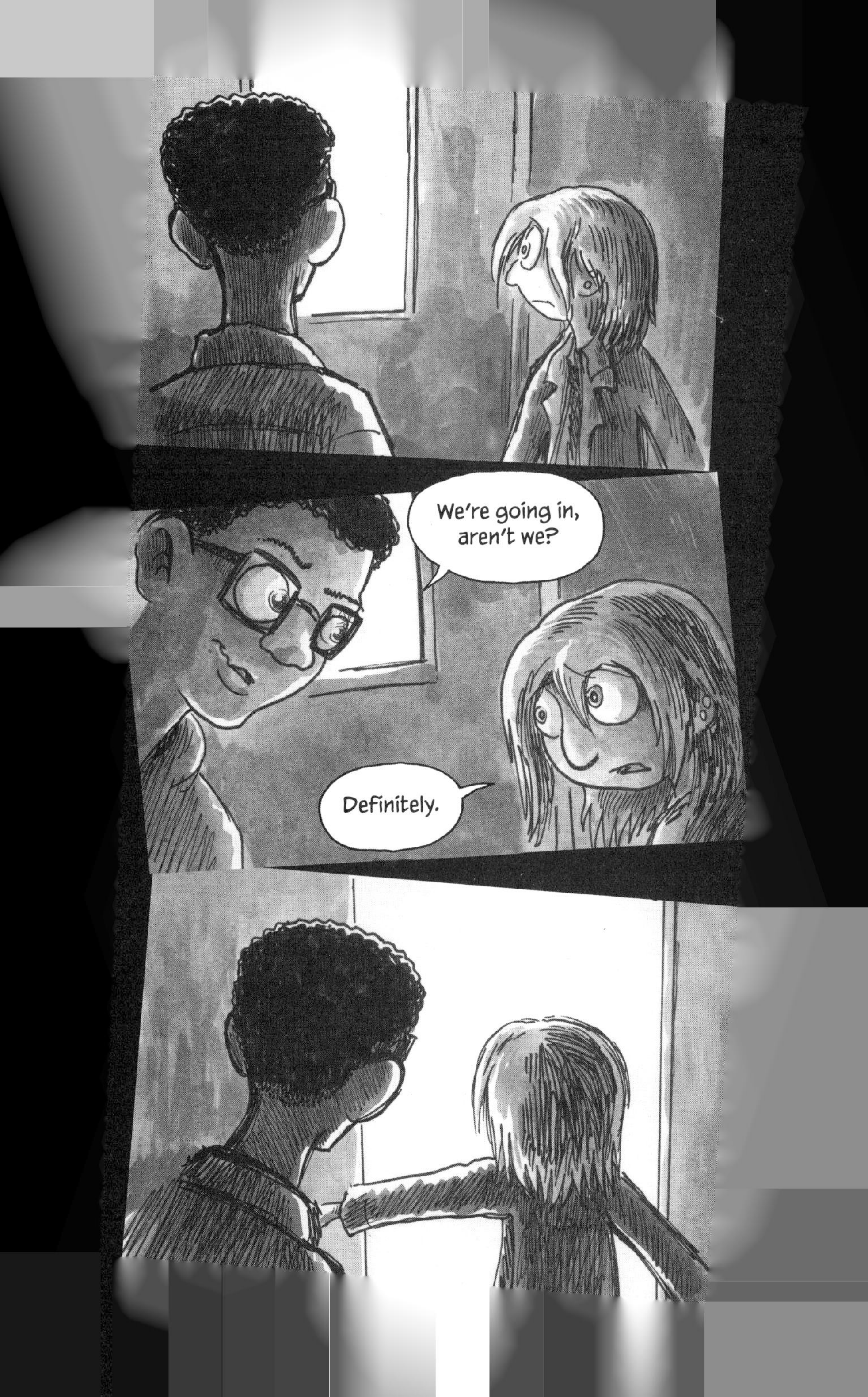
We're going in,
aren't we?
Definitely.

Chapter 31

"TWIIILAAA!" called Levi. "KAAAAAT!"

"Watch out," said Ms. Padilla. "Snow goons down there." She directed Levi down a clear hall. "I think I'm getting the hang of this."

"You were great in the gym," said Levi. "I didn't know teachers were so good at dodgeball."

Ms. Padilla snorted. "I wasn't always a teacher. I used to be very active, back when I was a kid. Used to go running and climbing through the woods every day. I wanted to be a scientist when I grew up: explore rainforests, document all the undiscovered wildlife."

"That makes sense," said Levi. "Since you teach science."

"My family moved here when I was very young," continued Ms. Padilla, "and, I don't know, I guess I always felt out of place with the other kids. So I didn't really have any friends. Except my twin brother, Ajay. He was my best friend. We used to take my dad's video recorder and go into the woods and try to make nature documentaries."

"Cool," said Levi. "Like me and Twila."

"Except Ajay wasn't real," said Ms. Padilla. She was silent for a while, and Levi wondered if he'd misheard her.

"Ajay was just an imaginary friend," she said at last. "Well, an imaginary brother." She forced a chuckle. "I was a weird kid, I guess. And one day, when I was around nine or ten, I just stopped believing in him." Another pause. "No, not exactly. I thought he'd disappeared."

A chill ran down Levi's spine.

"I must've had a mental breakdown or something, because I was convinced that someone—or *something*—had come during the night and stolen my brother. My *imaginary* brother, I mean."

"Why do you think your brother was imaginary?" asked Levi.

Ms. Padilla gave an empty laugh. "Of course he was imaginary! My parents didn't know him—they said they only had one kid. Me."

"But did they *used* to know him? I mean, before he disappeared?"

"I thought they did," said Ms. Padilla. "But . . . I guess I imagined that, too. I imagined it all. The birthday parties, the family nights, the nature films we made in the woods."

"Nobody else remembered him?" asked Levi.

"No. Trust me, I asked everyone in school, kids and teachers. No one knew him. Well, one kid said he remembered him—a weird kid no one liked. I think his name was Rafe. But I'm sure he was just messing with me."

They turned another corner and carefully sidestepped a lone snowman.

"Anyway, I was pretty hysterical for a month or two. I missed school. My parents took me to see lots of doctors. I couldn't sleep."

"What happened next?" asked Levi.

"Nothing. I finally realized Ajay had been imaginary all along. I just outgrew him."

"What about the tapes? The nature documentaries you made?"

"Oh, I still had copies of them," said Ms. Padilla. "And I watched them all. It was just me, alone in the woods with a camera, filming birds and frogs."

Silence. Their shoes squeaked through the empty hall.

"I don't know why I told you all that," said Ms. Padilla. "I guess it sort of reminded me of that story you told me about you and Twila."

"Do you believe that story?"

She sighed. "I don't know what to believe anymore."

A classroom door lit up down the hall.

Ms. Padilla swept the light across the room number. “Room 217,” she said. “Social studies.”

Levi turned away from the door and cupped his hands to his mouth. “TWILAAAAA! KAT! JORDAN! DONTE! CAN YOU HEAR ME?”

They waited. The storm outside howled.

“Ready?” said Ms. Padilla.

Levi took a deep breath. “Let’s do it.”

Ms. Padilla opened the door, and they stepped inside.

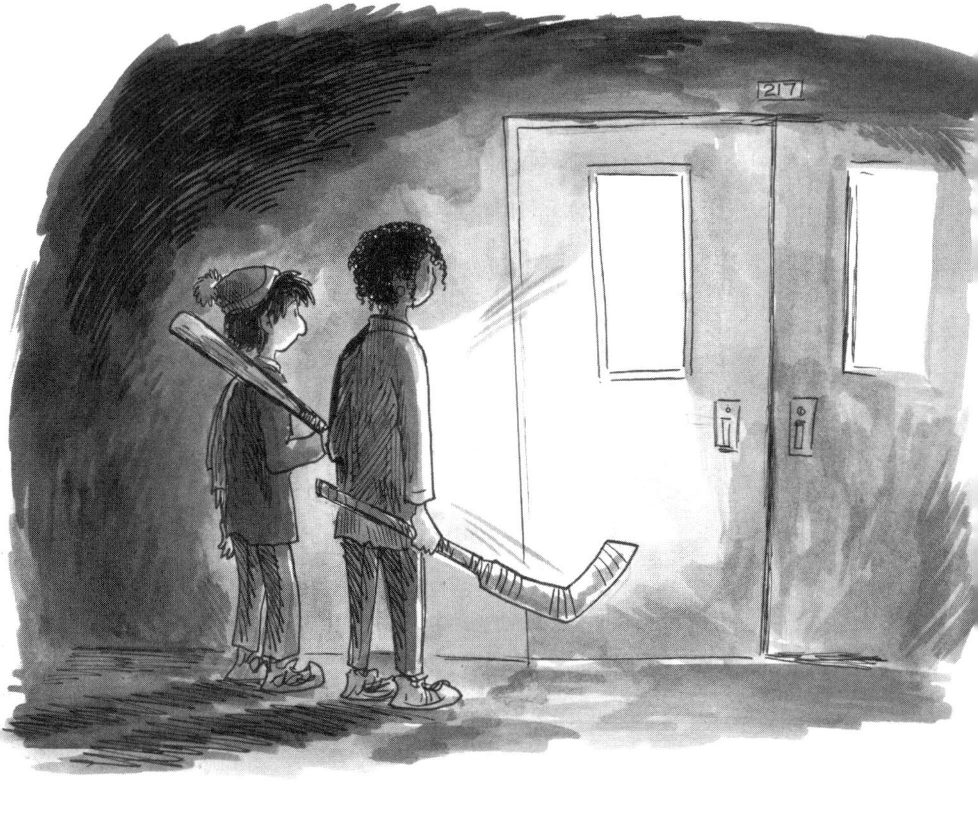
217

Chapter 32

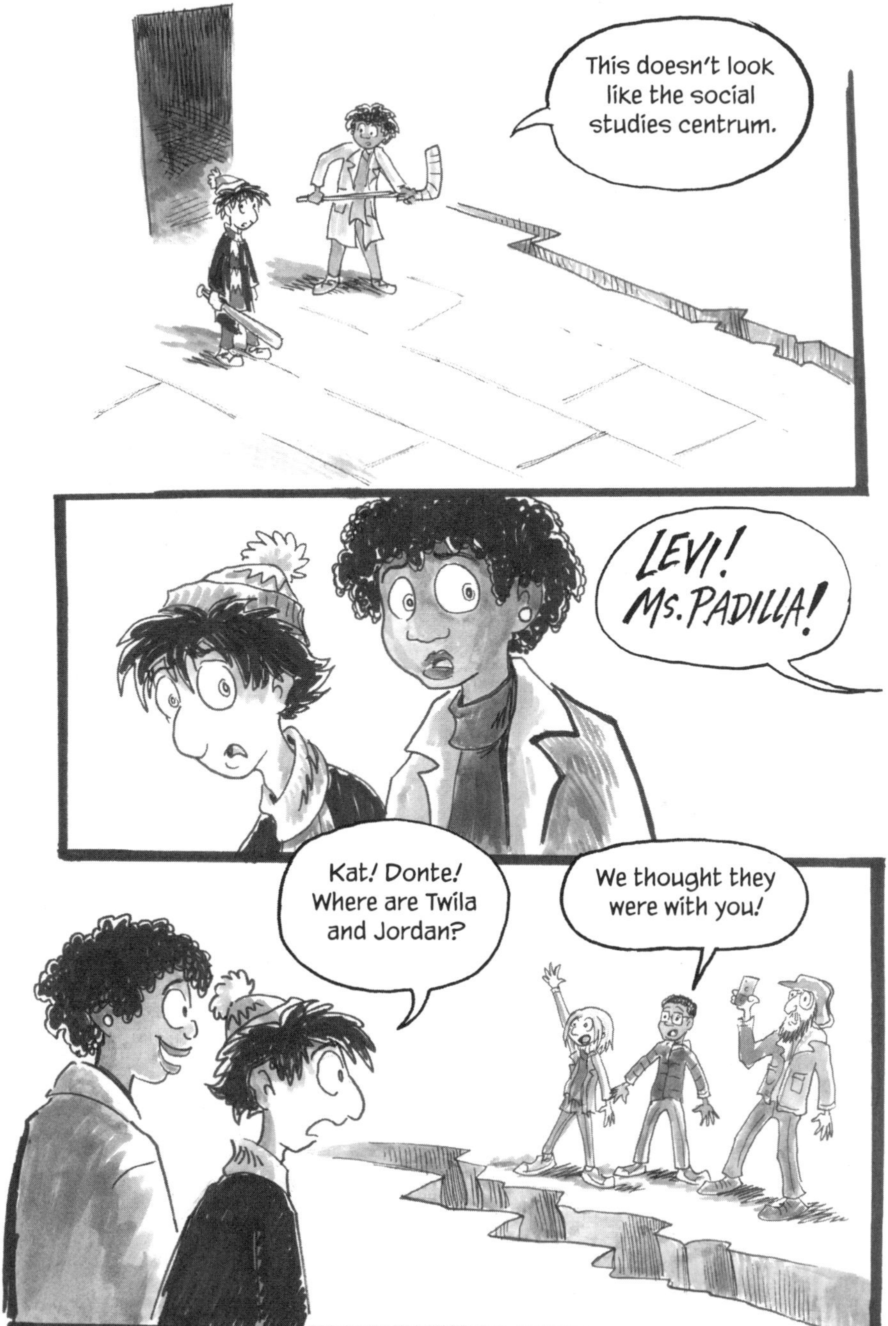
This doesn't look like the social studies centrum.
LEVI! Ms. PADILLA!
Kat! Donte! Where are Twila and Jordan?
We thought they were with you!

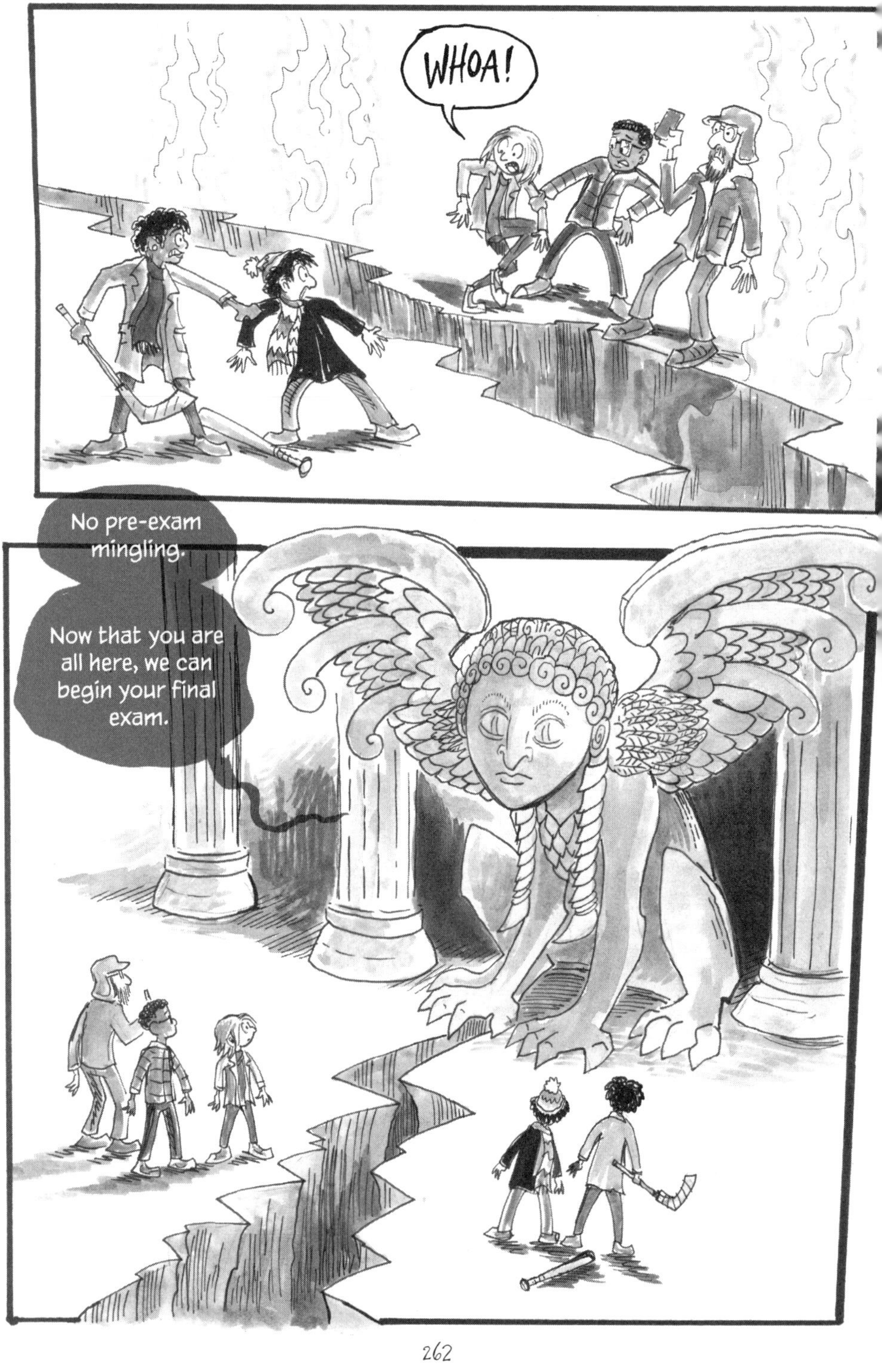
WHOA!
No pre-exam mingling.
Now that you are all here, we can begin your final exam.

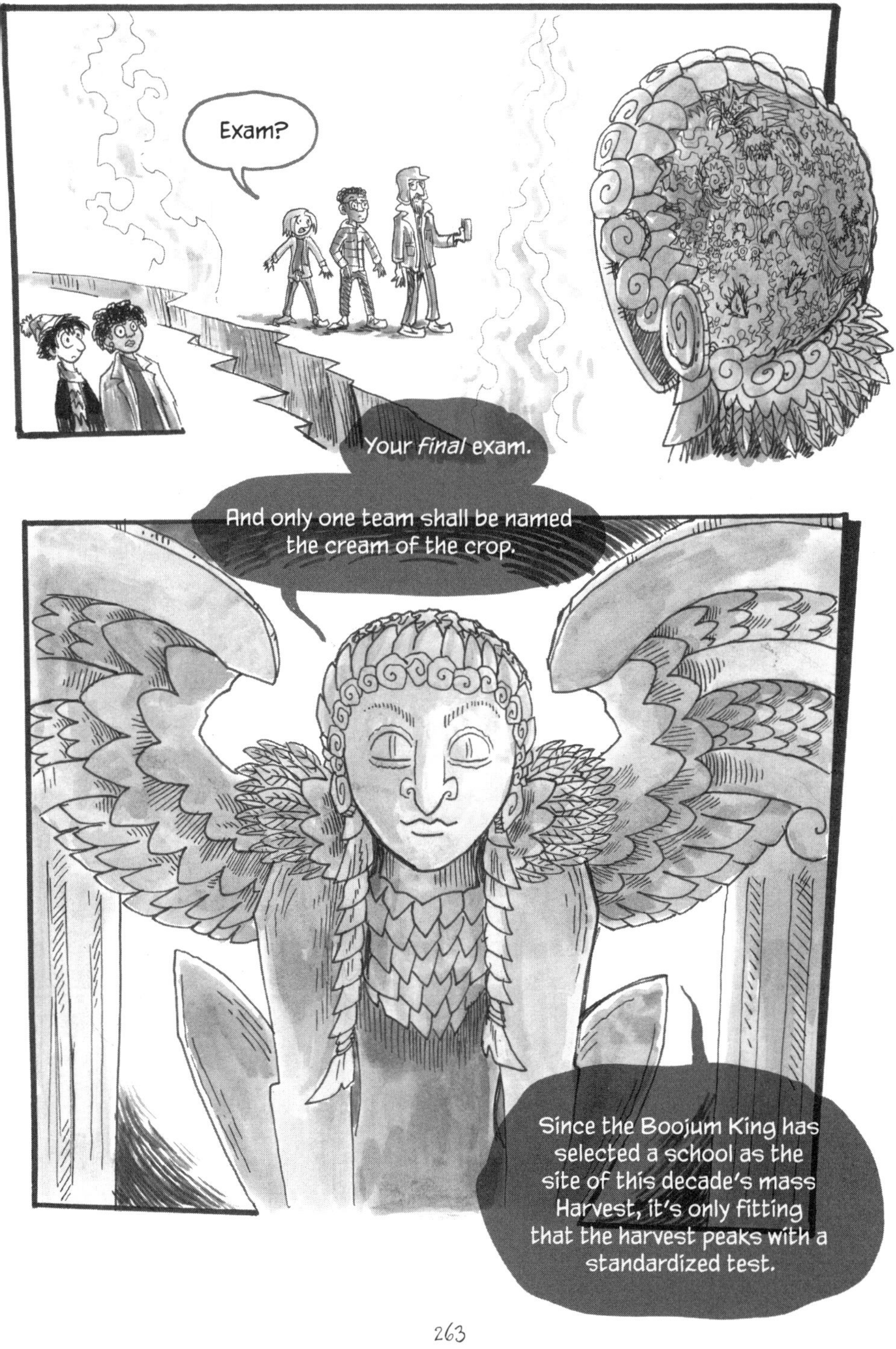
Exam?
Your *final* exam.
And only one team shall be named the cream of the crop.
Since the Boojum King has selected a school as the site of this decade's mass Harvest, it's only fitting that the harvest peaks with a standardized test.

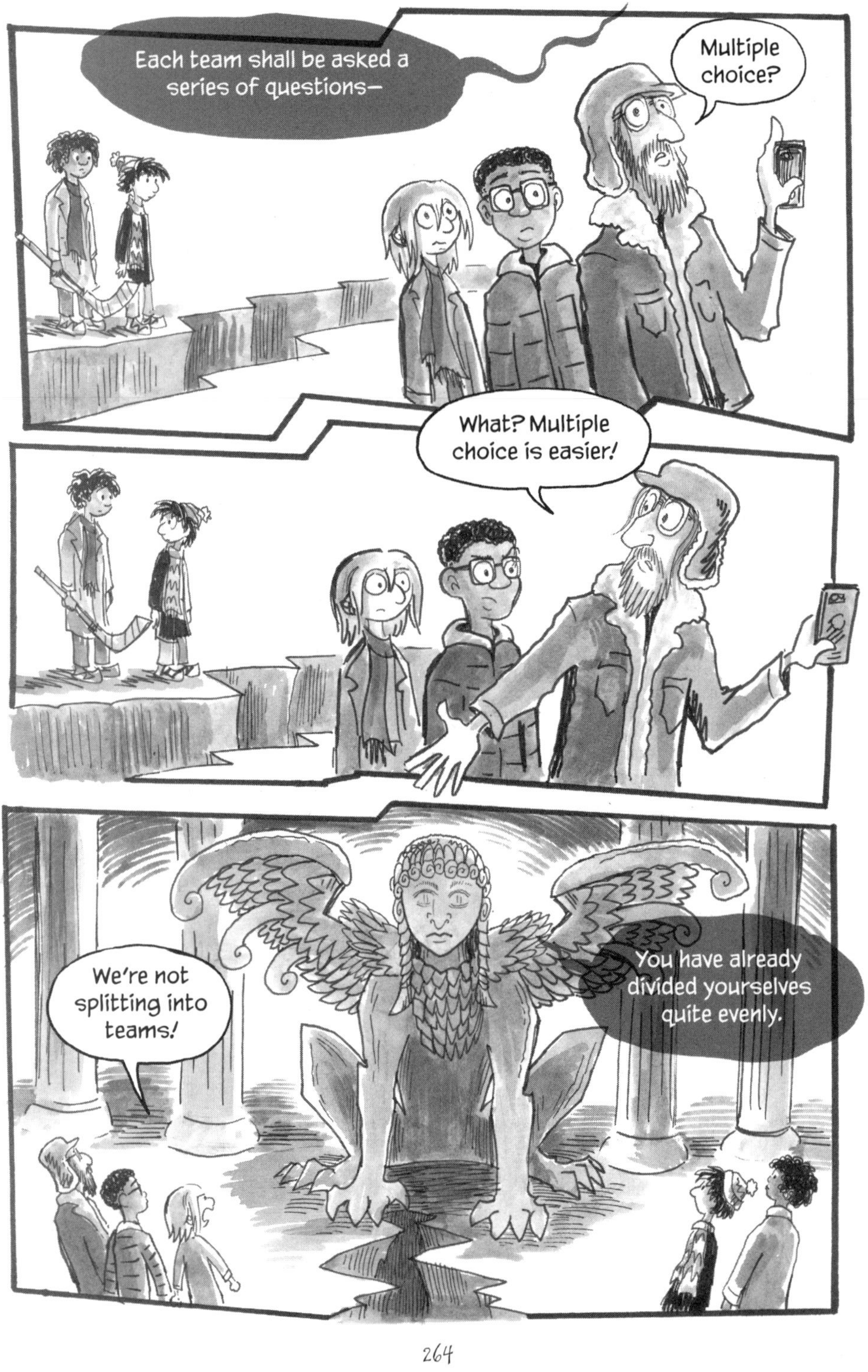
Each team shall be asked a series of questions—
Multiple choice?
What? Multiple choice is easier!
We're not splitting into teams!
You have already divided yourselves quite evenly.

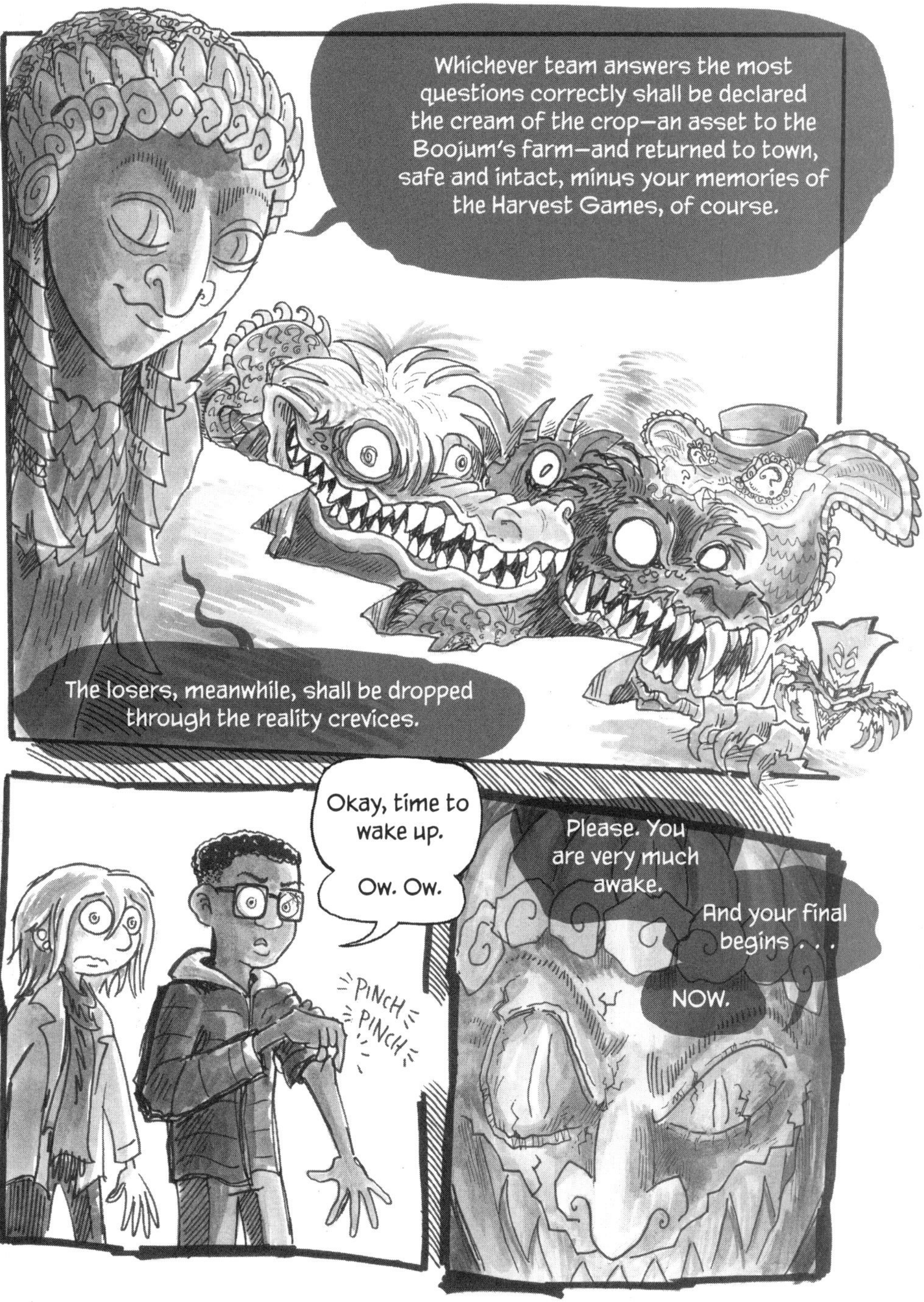
Whichever team answers the most questions correctly shall be declared the cream of the crop—an asset to the Boojum's farm—and returned to town, safe and intact, minus your memories of the Harvest Games, of course.
The losers, meanwhile, shall be dropped through the reality crevices.
Okay, time to wake up.
Ow. Ow.
PINCH PINCH
Please. You are very much awake.
And your final begins . . .
NOW.

Chapter 33

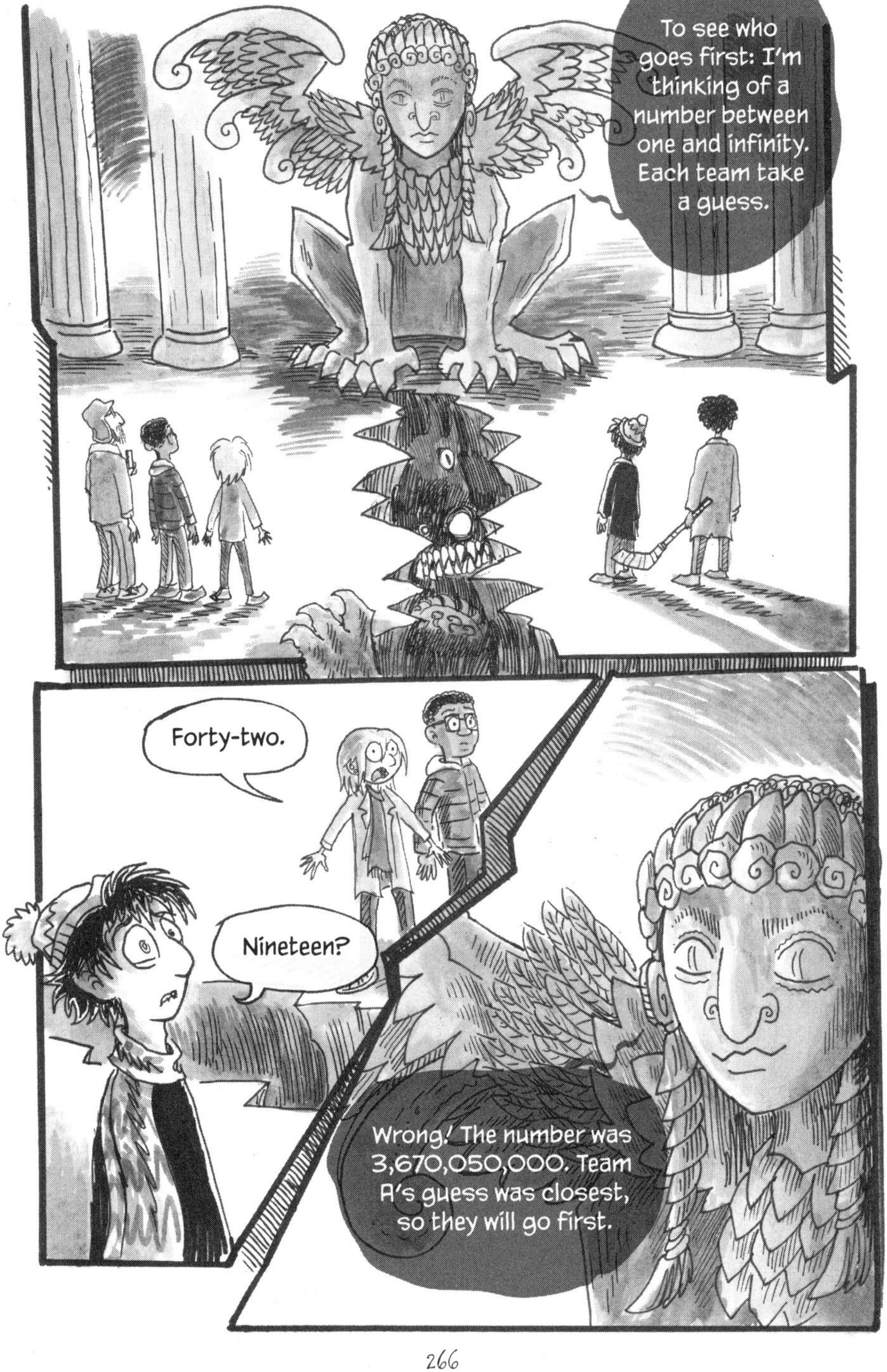
To see who goes first: I'm thinking of a number between one and infinity. Each team take a guess.
Forty-two.
Nineteen?
Wrong! The number was 3,670,050,000. Team A's guess was closest, so they will go first.

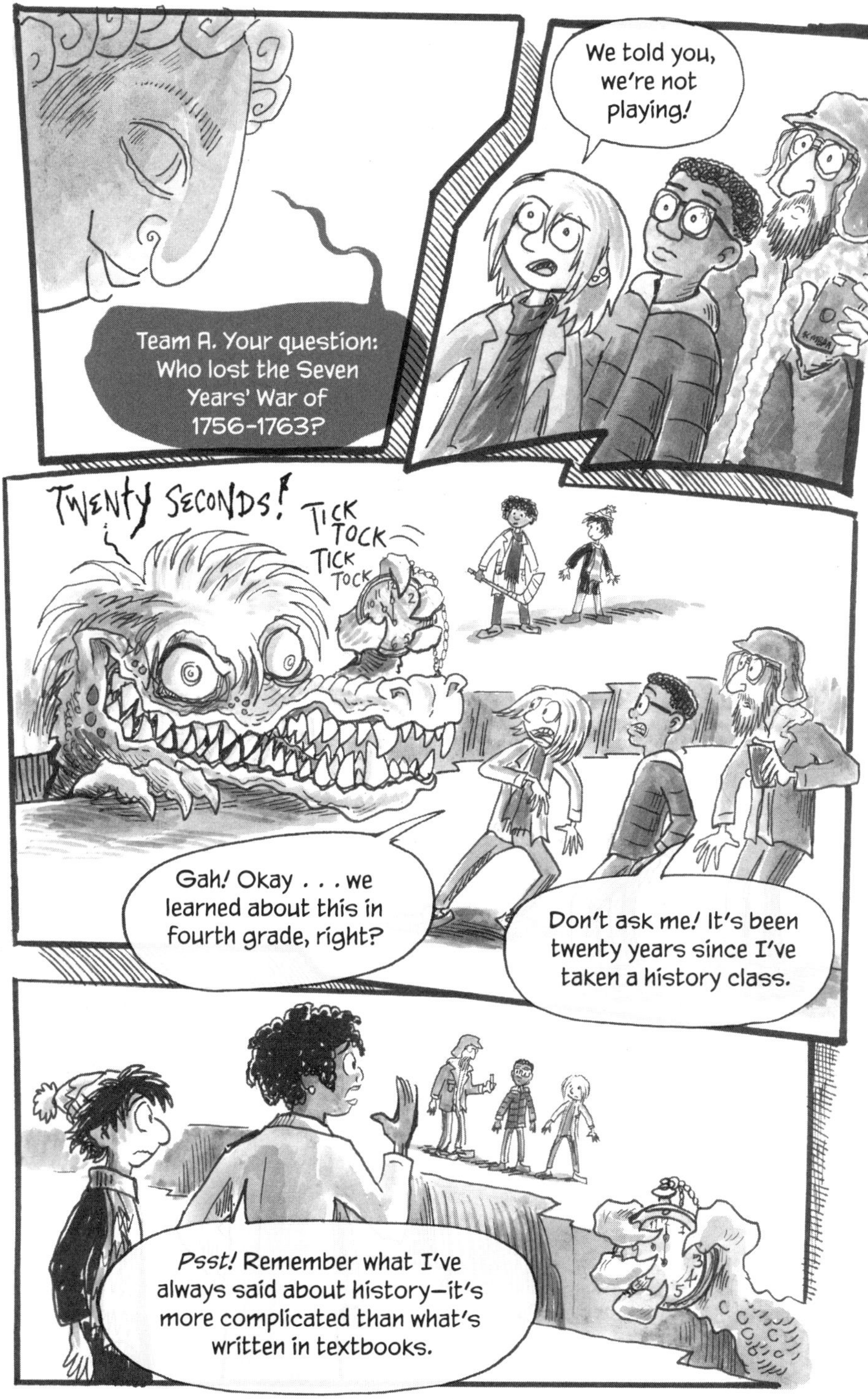
Team A. Your question: Who lost the Seven Years' War of 1756–1763?
We told you, we're not playing!
TWENTY SECONDS!
TICK TOCK TICK TOCK
Gah! Okay . . . we learned about this in fourth grade, right?
Don't ask me! It's been twenty years since I've taken a history class.
Psst! Remember what I've always said about history—it's more complicated than what's written in textbooks.

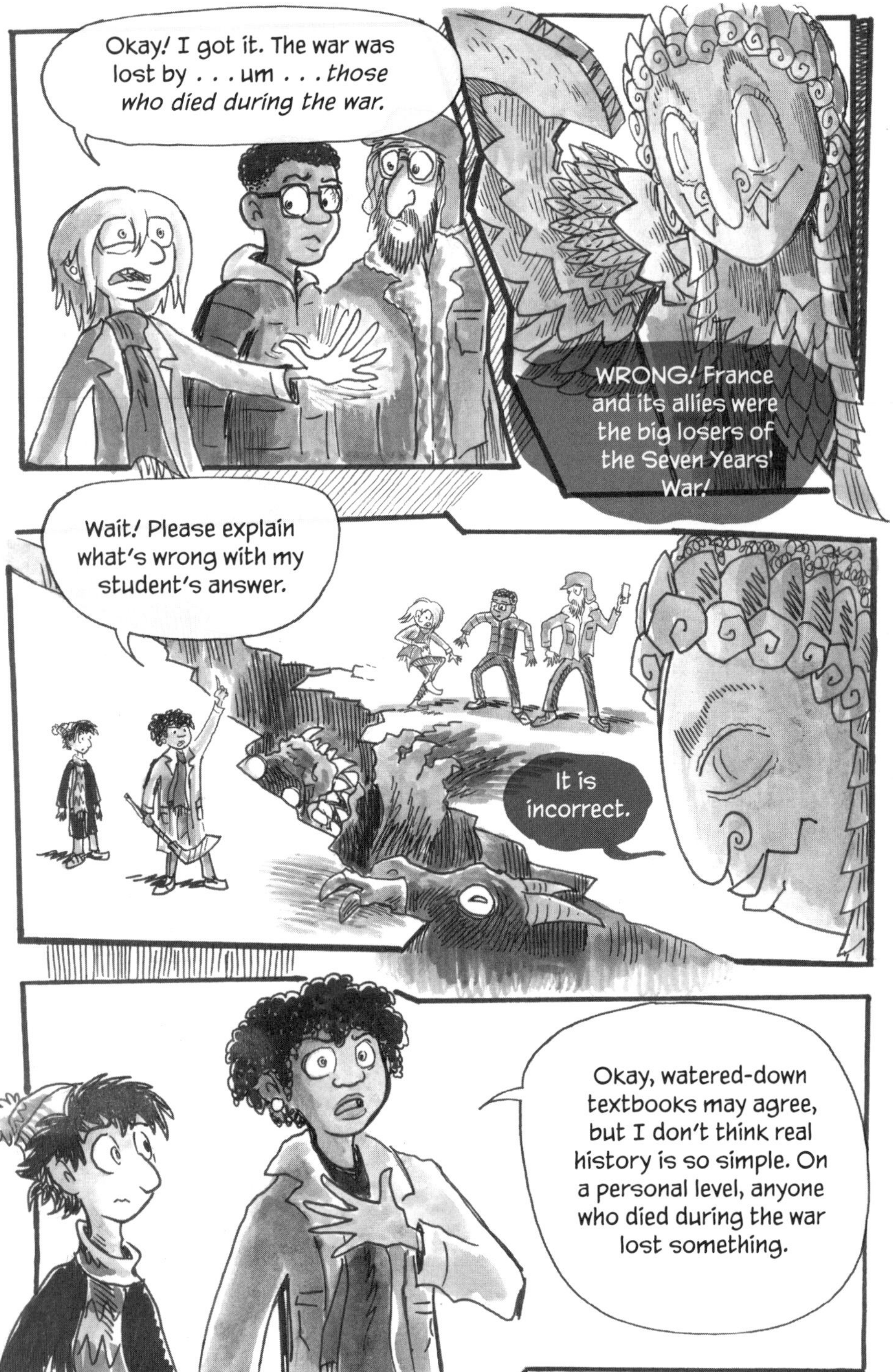
Okay! I got it. The war was lost by . . . um . . . *those who died during the war.*
WRONG! France and its allies were the big losers of the Seven Years' War!
Wait! Please explain what's wrong with my student's answer.
It is incorrect.
Okay, watered-down textbooks may agree, but I don't think real history is so simple. On a personal level, anyone who died during the war lost something.

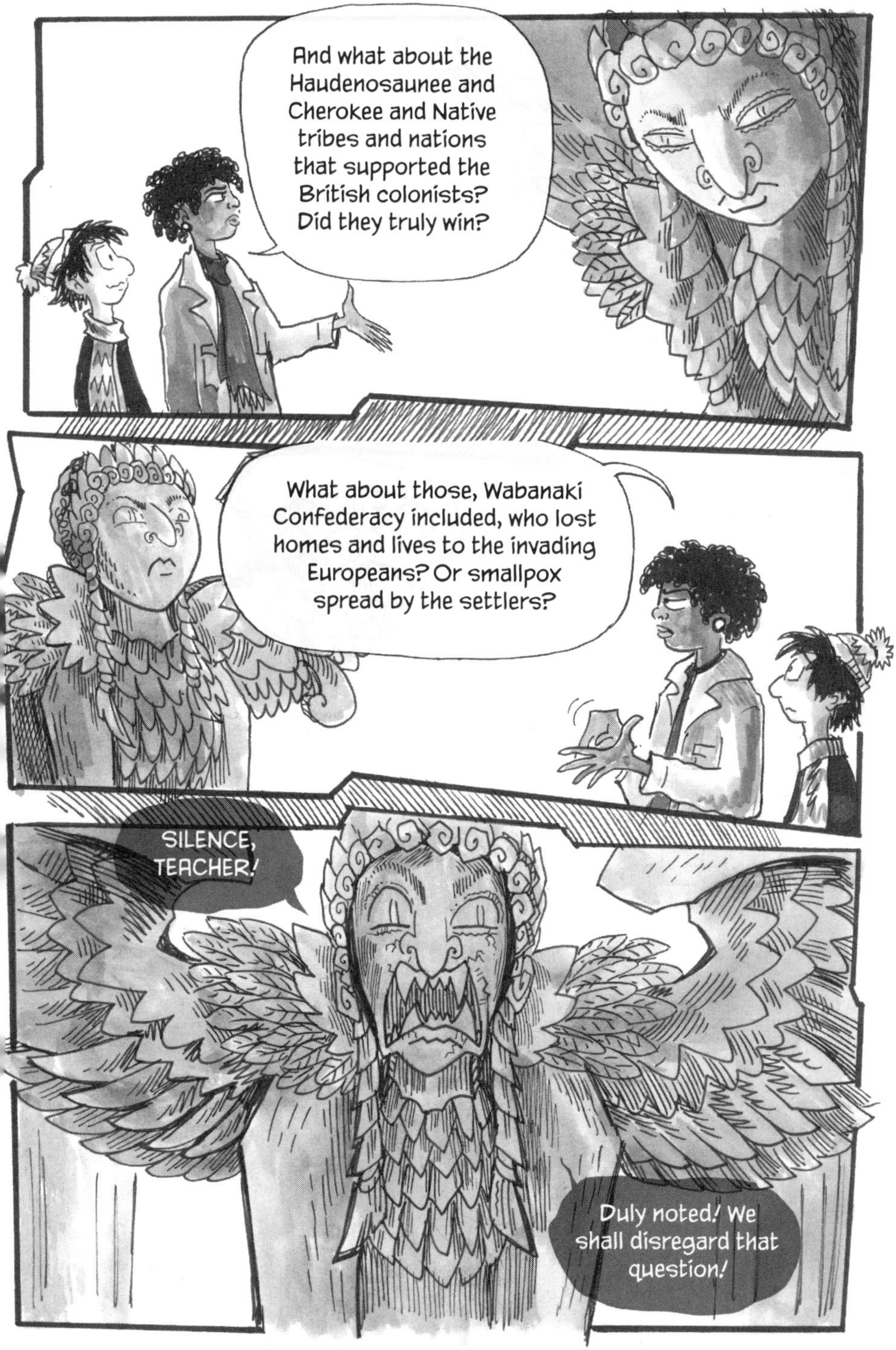
And what about the Haudenosaunee and Cherokee and Native tribes and nations that supported the British colonists? Did they truly win?
What about those, Wabanaki Confederacy included, who lost homes and lives to the invading Europeans? Or smallpox spread by the settlers?
SILENCE, TEACHER!
Duly noted! We shall disregard that question!

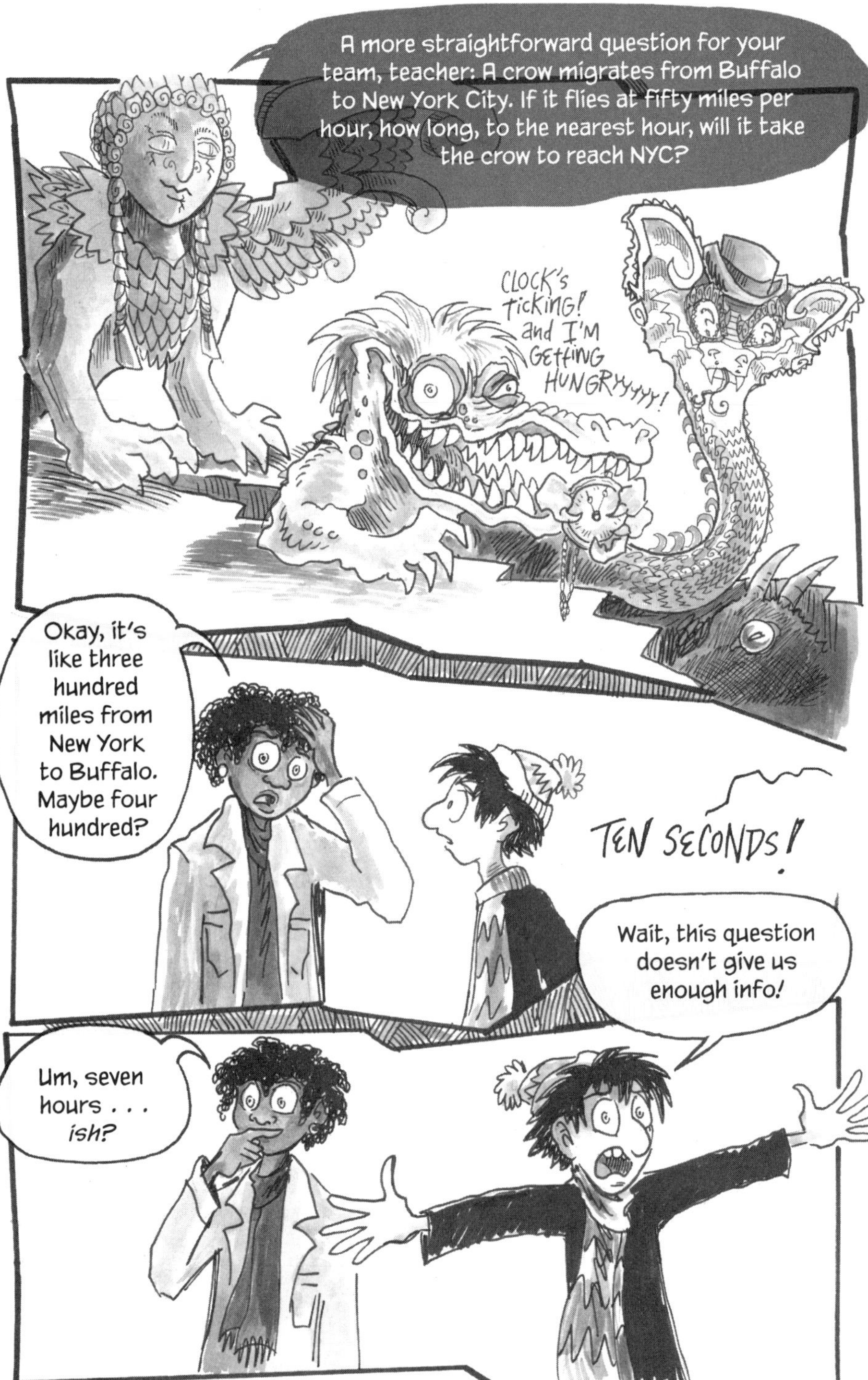
A more straightforward question for your team, teacher: A crow migrates from Buffalo to New York City. If it flies at fifty miles per hour, how long, to the nearest hour, will it take the crow to reach NYC?
CLOCK's TiCKING! and I'M GETTING HUNGRYYYYYY!
Okay, it's like three hundred miles from New York to Buffalo. Maybe four hundred?
TEN SECONDS!
Wait, this question doesn't give us enough info!
Um, seven hours . . . *ish?*

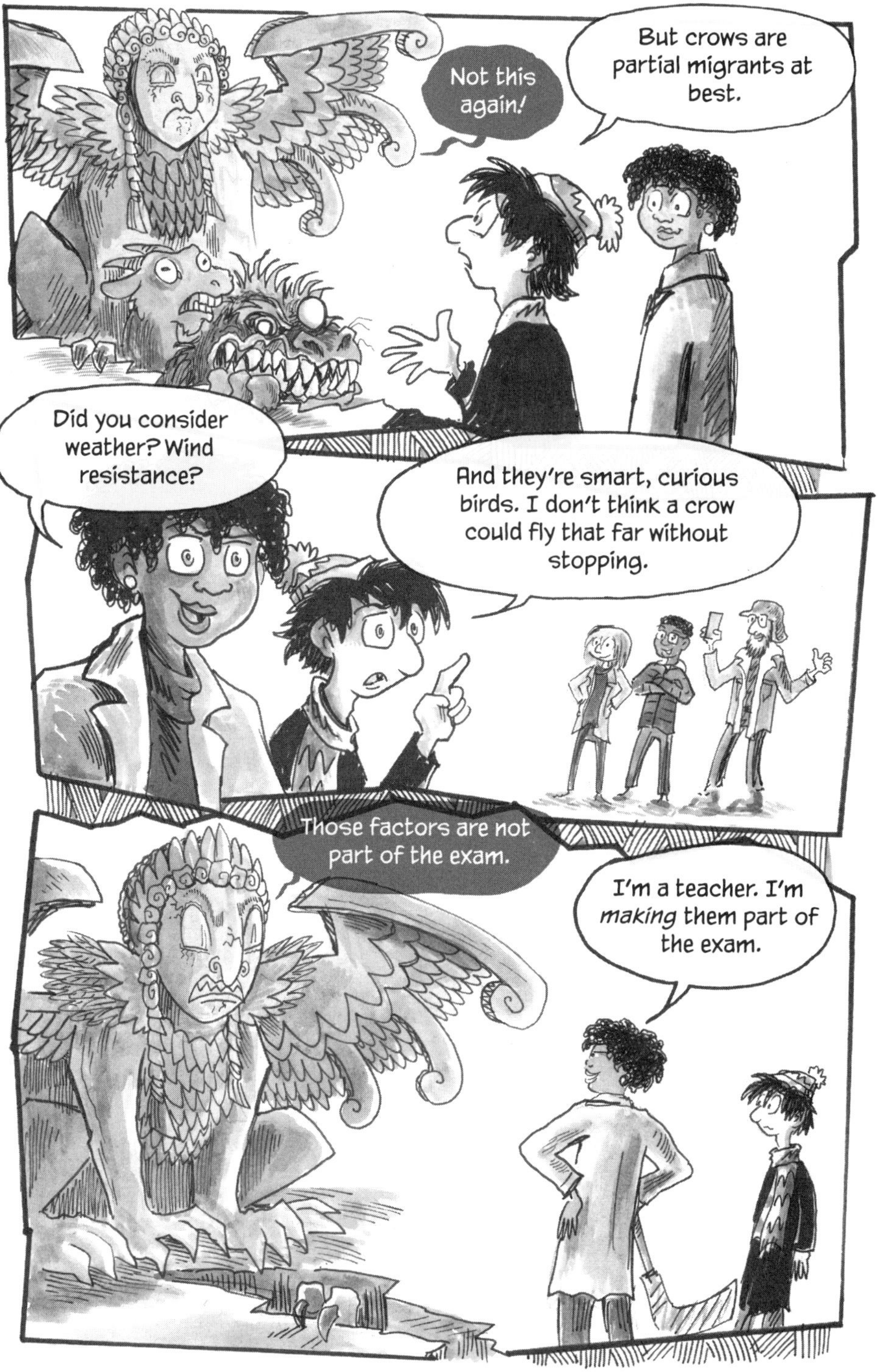

Not this again!
But crows are partial migrants at best.
Did you consider weather? Wind resistance?
And they're smart, curious birds. I don't think a crow could fly that far without stopping.
Those factors are not part of the exam.
I'm a teacher. I'm *making* them part of the exam.

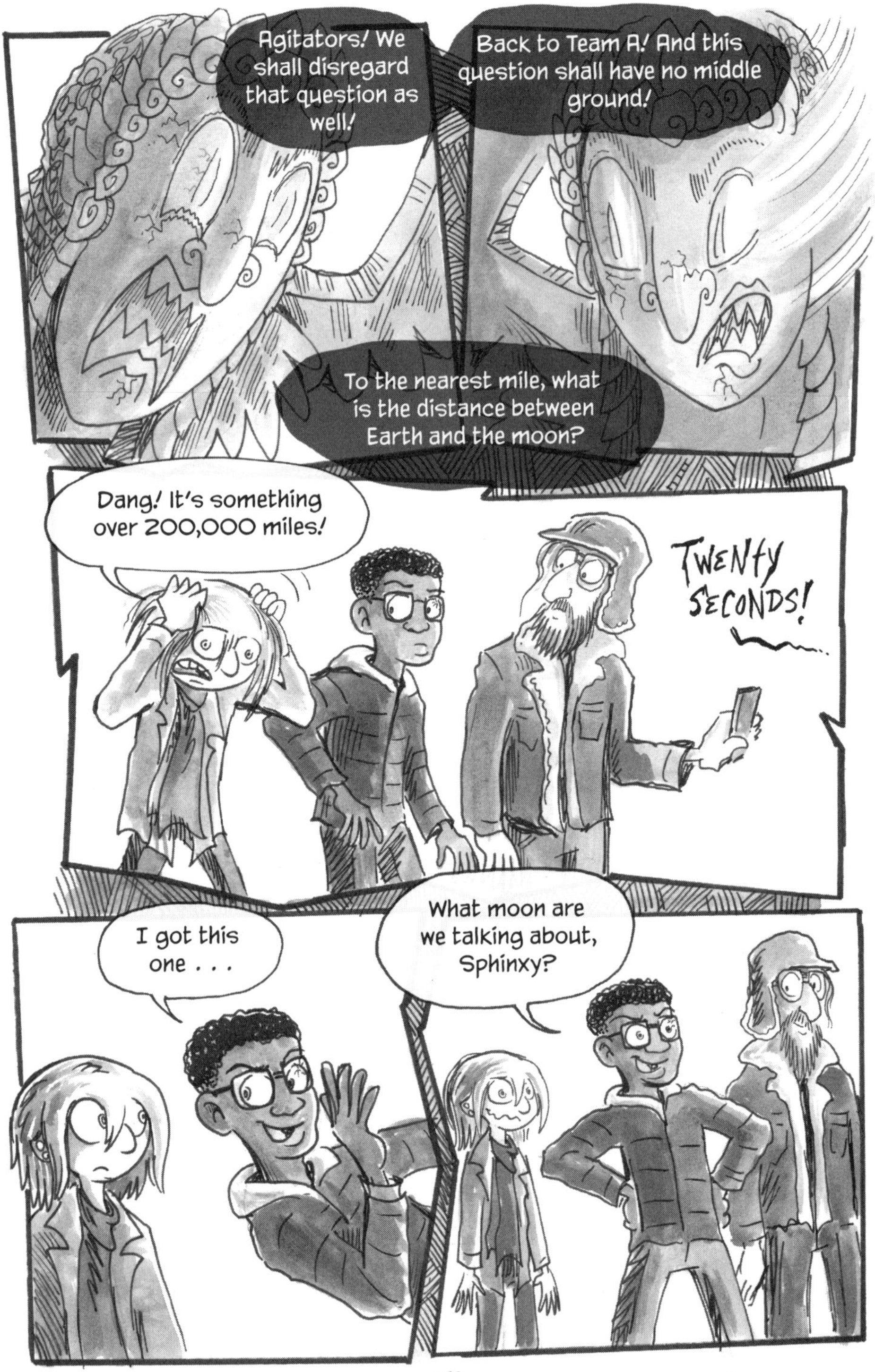

Agitators! We shall disregard that question as well!
Back to Team A! And this question shall have no middle ground!
To the nearest mile, what is the distance between Earth and the moon?
Dang! It's something over 200,000 miles!
TWENTY SECONDS!
I got this one . . .
What moon are we talking about, Sphinxy?

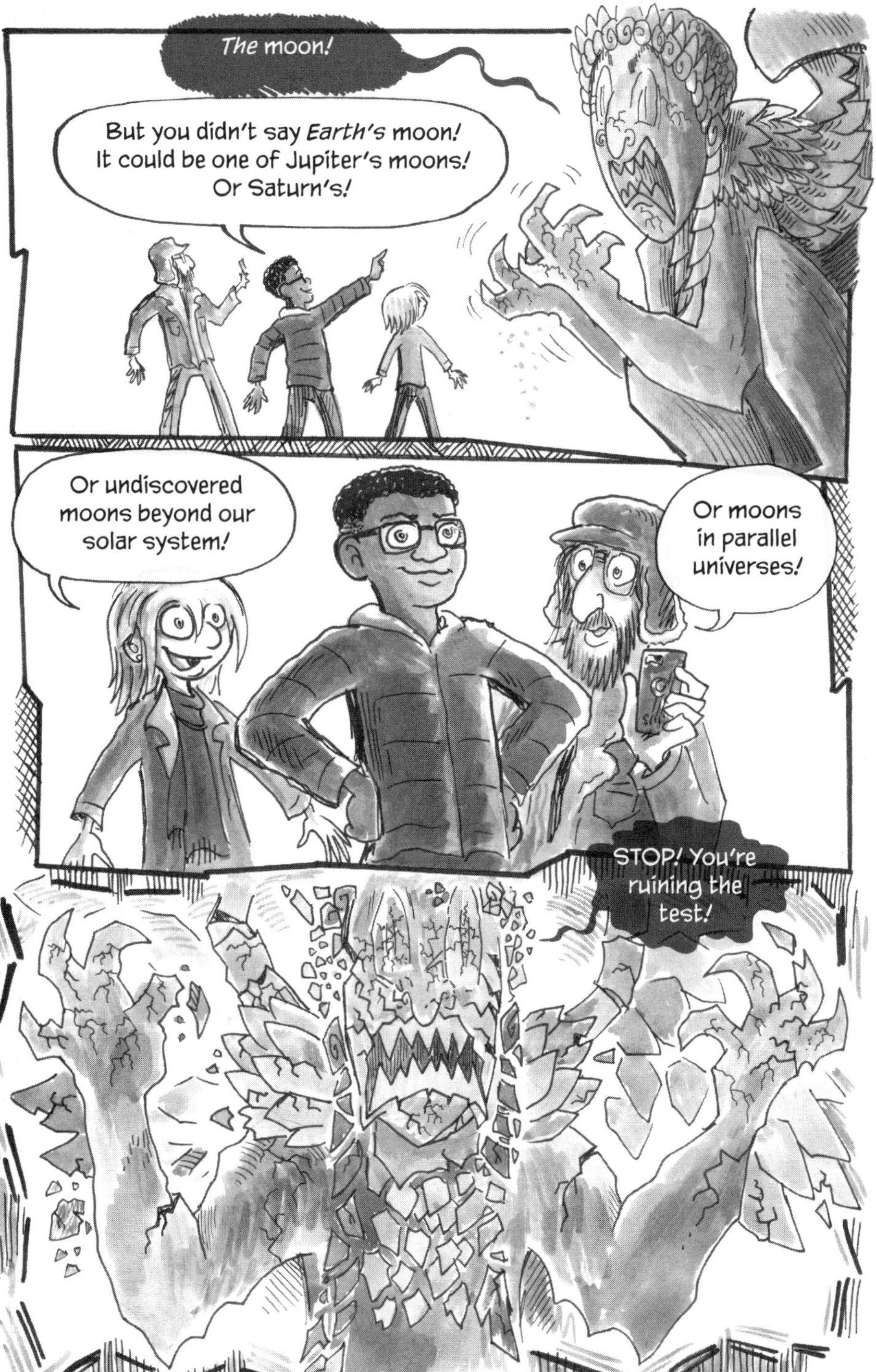
The moon!
But you didn't say *Earth's* moon! It could be one of Jupiter's moons! Or Saturn's!
Or undiscovered moons beyond our solar system!
Or moons in parallel universes!
STOP! You're ruining the test!

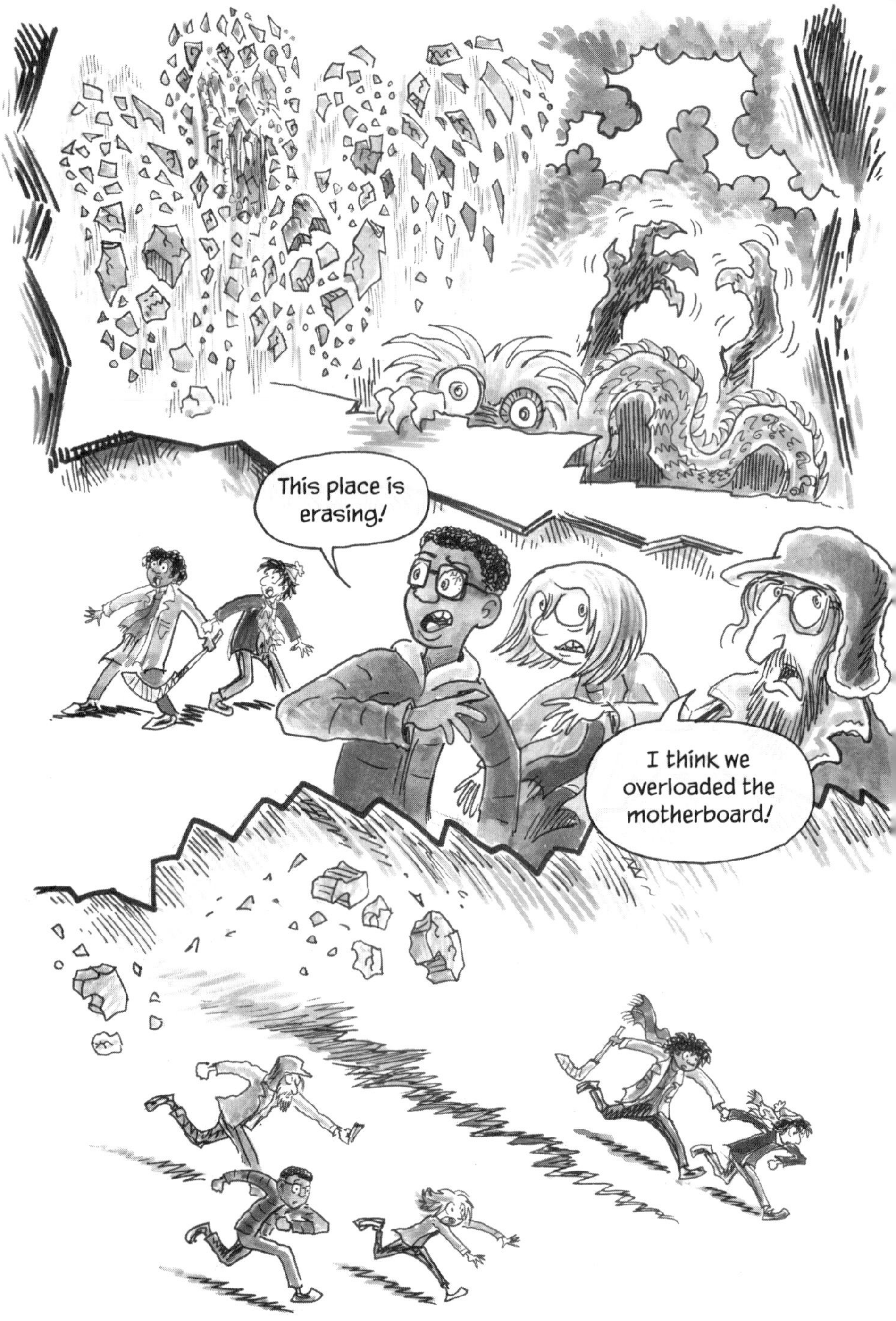
This place is erasing!
I think we overloaded the motherboard!

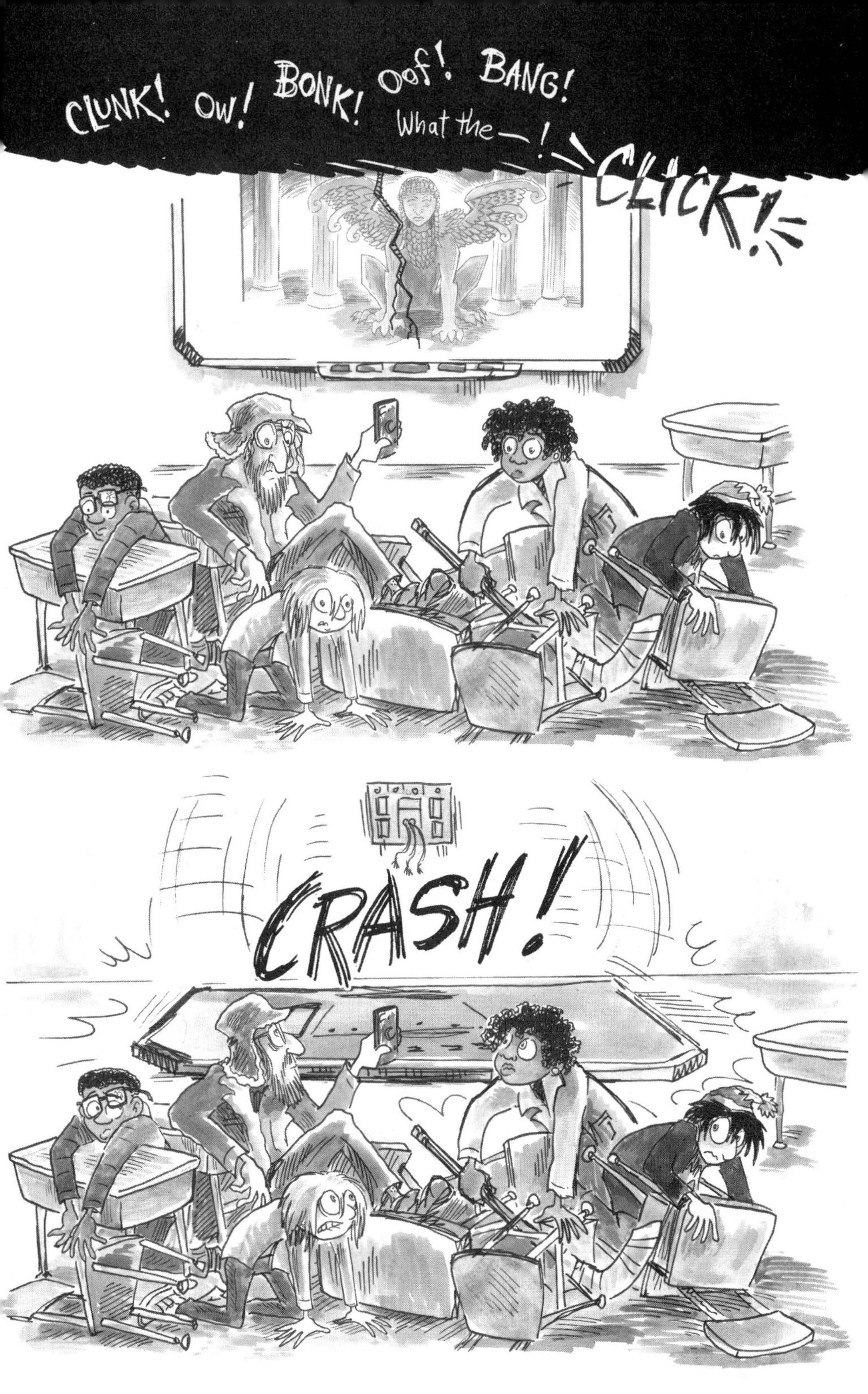
CLUNK! Ow! BONK! Oof! BANG!
What the—!
CLICK!
CRASH!

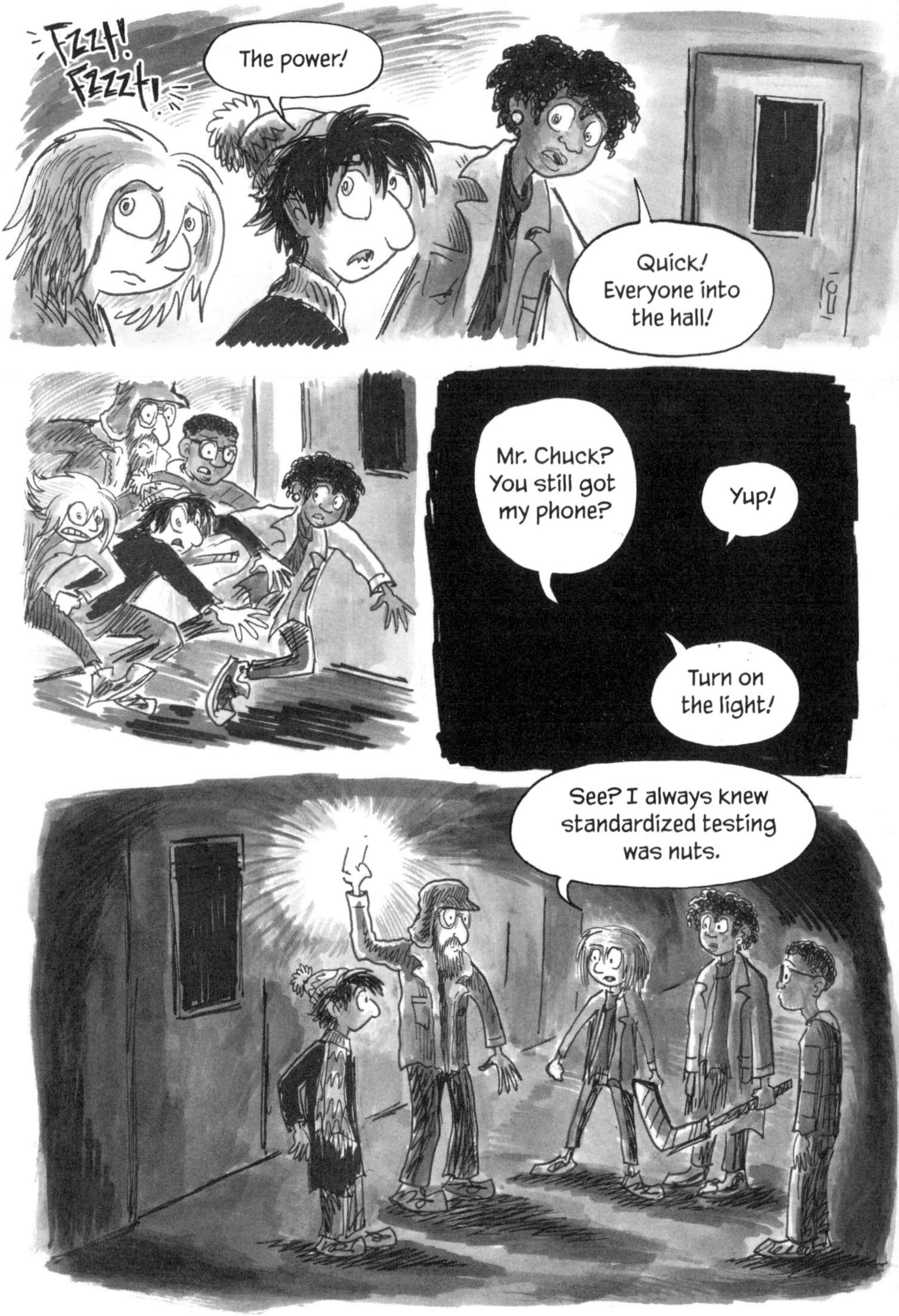
FZZT! FZZZT!
The power!
Quick! Everyone into the hall!
Mr. Chuck? You still got my phone?
Yup!
Turn on the light!
See? I always knew standardized testing was nuts.

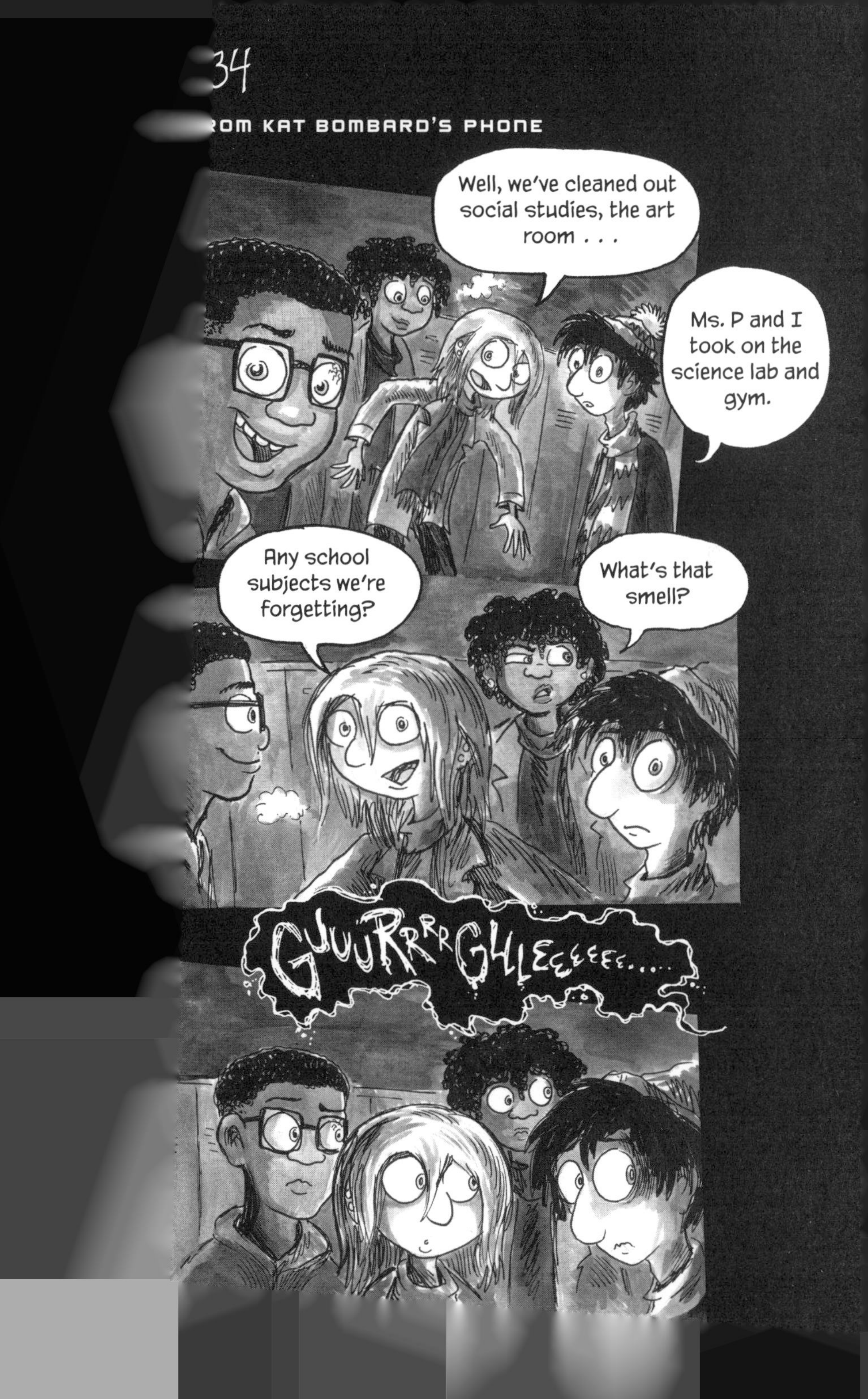
Well, we've cleaned out social studies, the art room . . .
Ms. P and I took on the science lab and gym.
Any school subjects we're forgetting?
What's that smell?
GUUURRRRGHLEEEEEE. . . . .

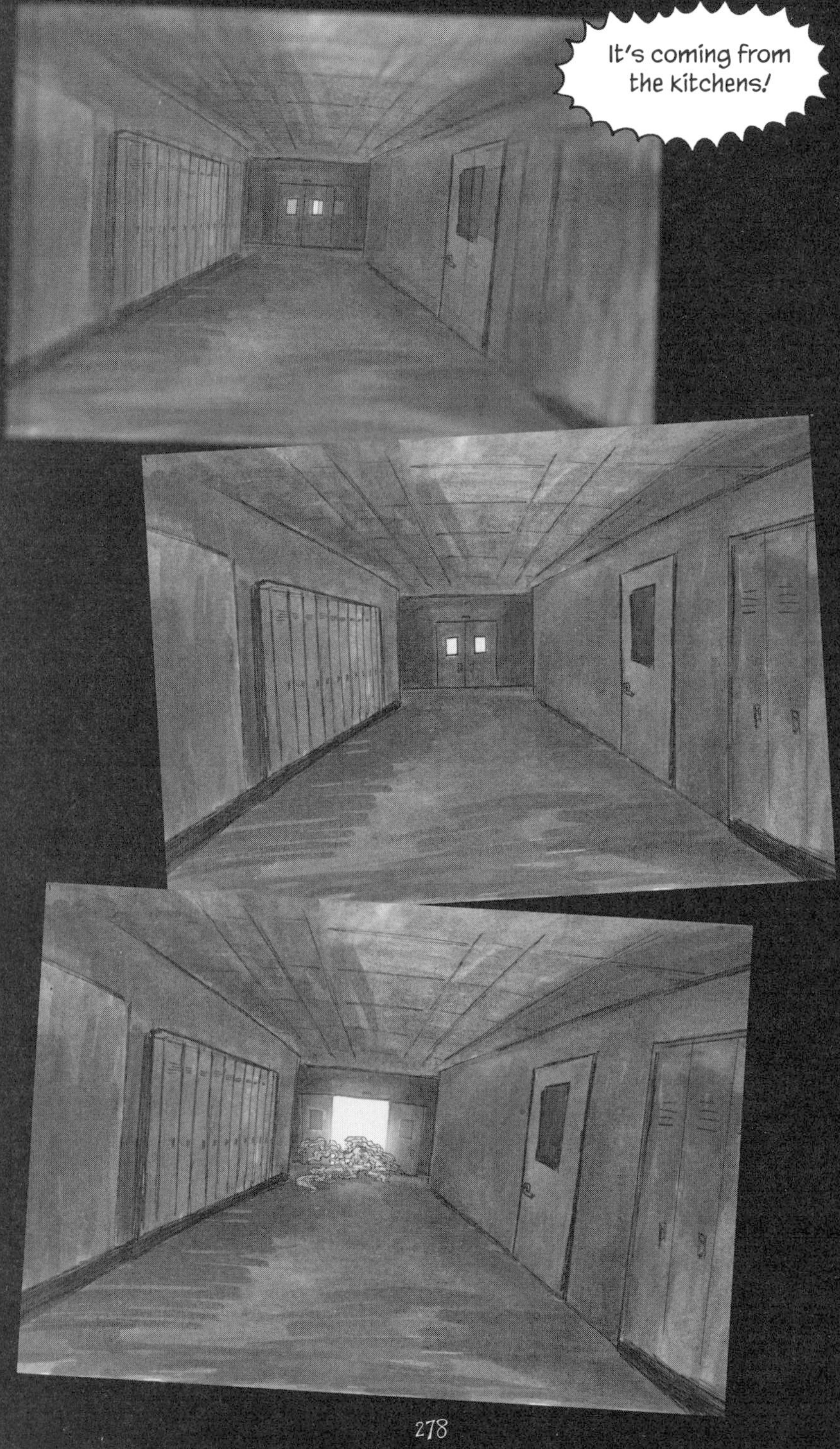
It's coming from
the kitchens!

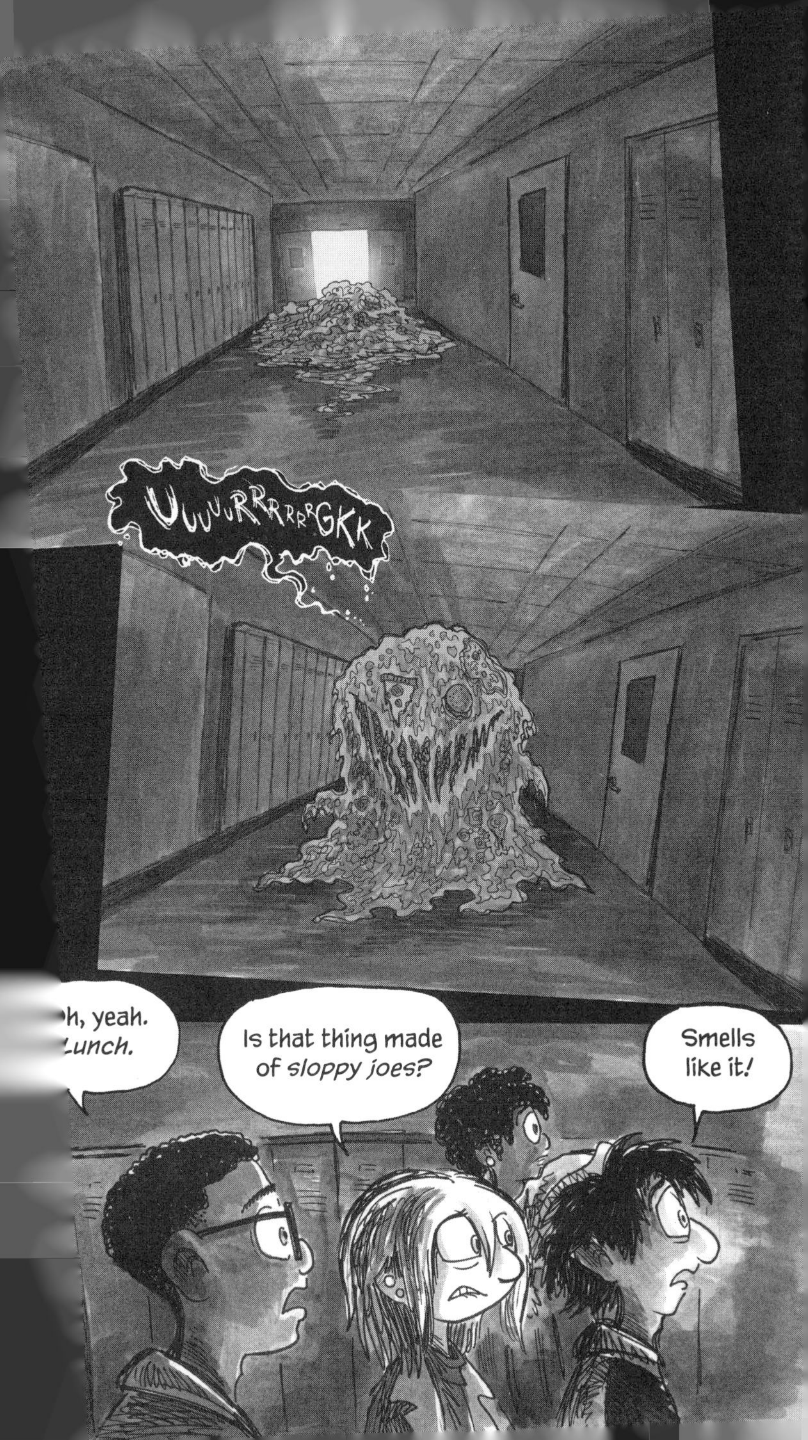
UUUURRRRRRGKK
h, yeah. Lunch.
Is that thing made of *sloppy joes?*
Smells like it!

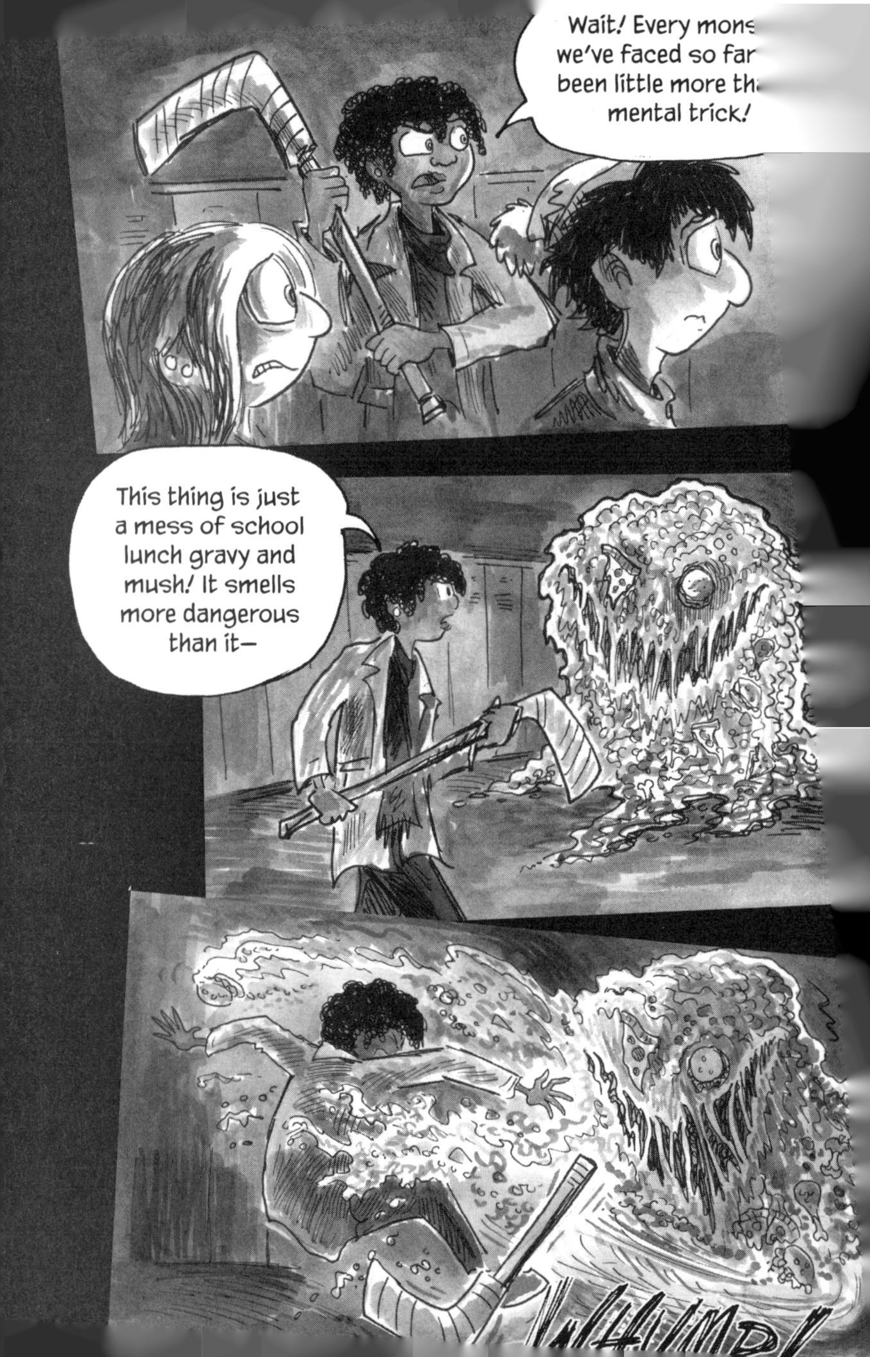
Wait! Every mons we've faced so far been little more th mental trick!
This thing is just a mess of school lunch gravy and mush! It smells more dangerous than it—
WHUMP!

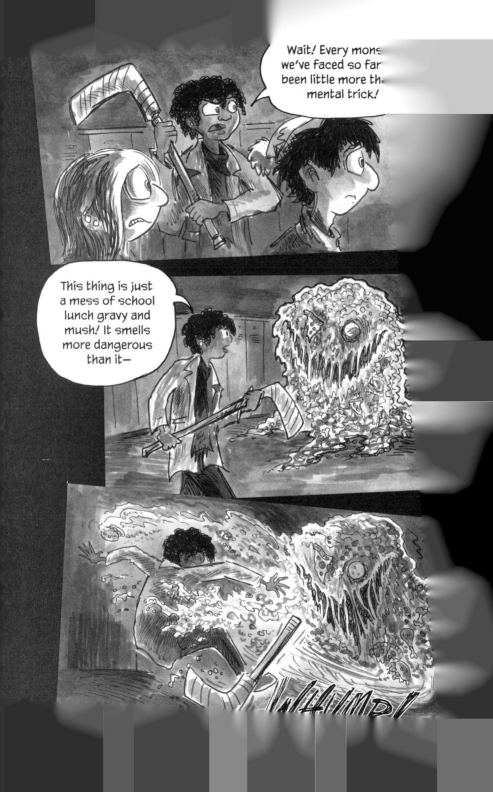

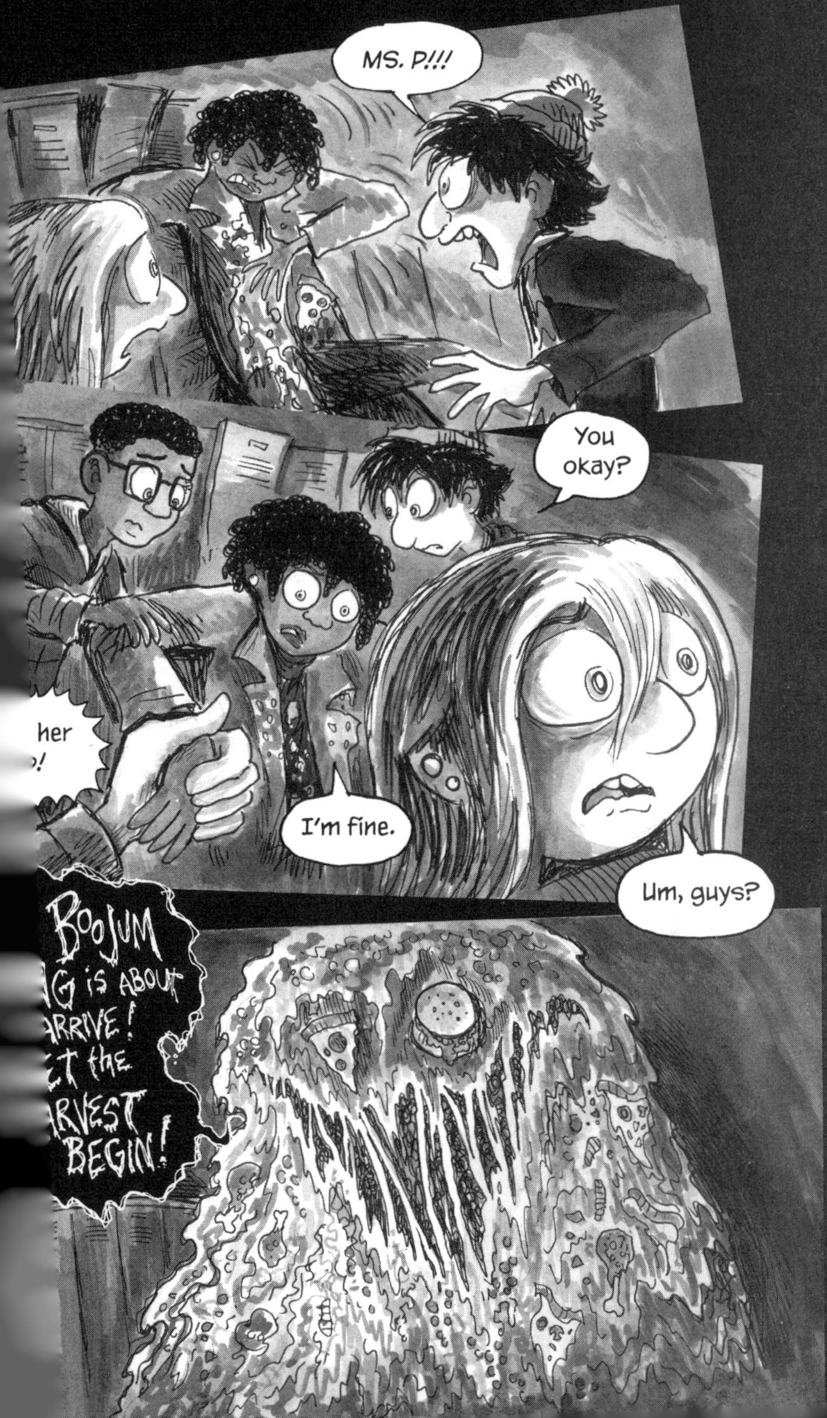
MS. P!!!
You okay?
her
I'm fine.
Um, guys?
BOOJUM
G IS ABOUT
ARRIVE!
T THE
ARVEST
BEGIN!

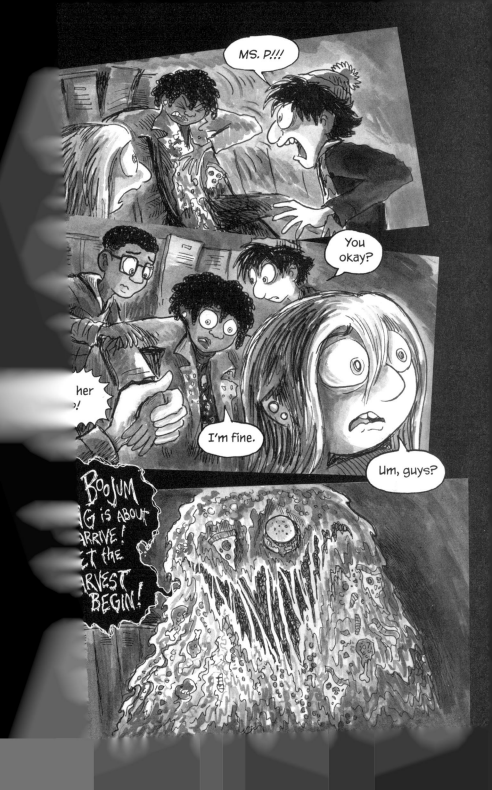

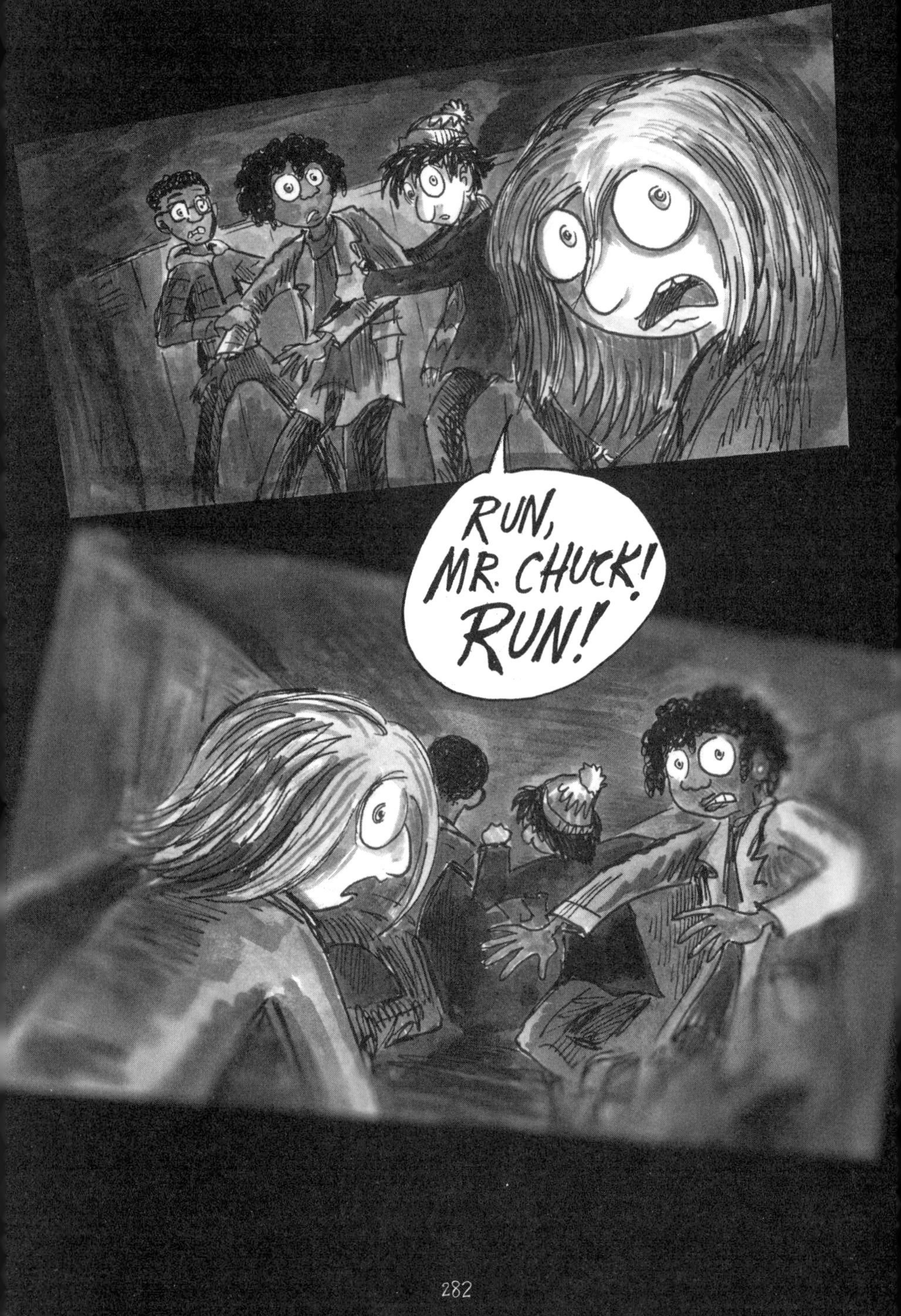
RUN, MR. CHUCK! RUN!

OTAGE FROM SCHOOL SECURITY CAMERA, 200 HALL
TTERY OPERATED)

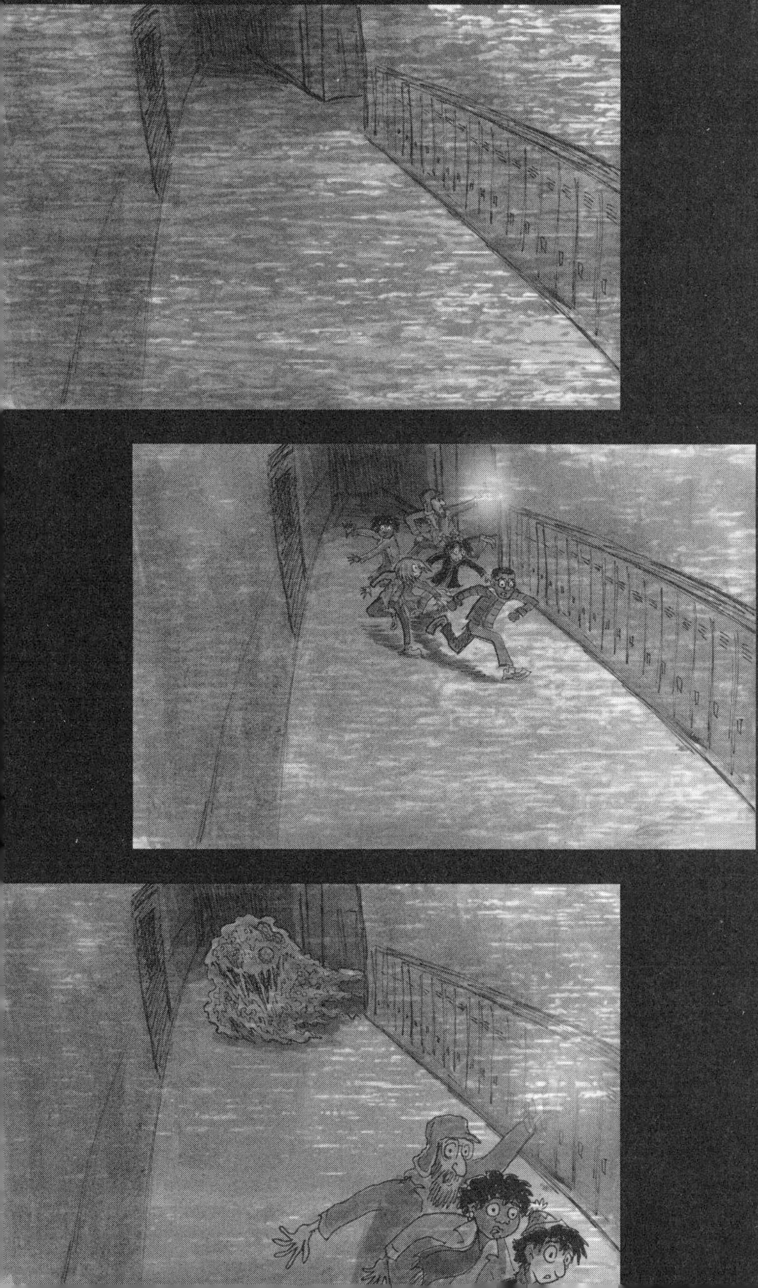

FOOTAGE FROM SCHOOL SECURITY CAMERAS, CAFETER
HALL (BATTERY OPERATED)

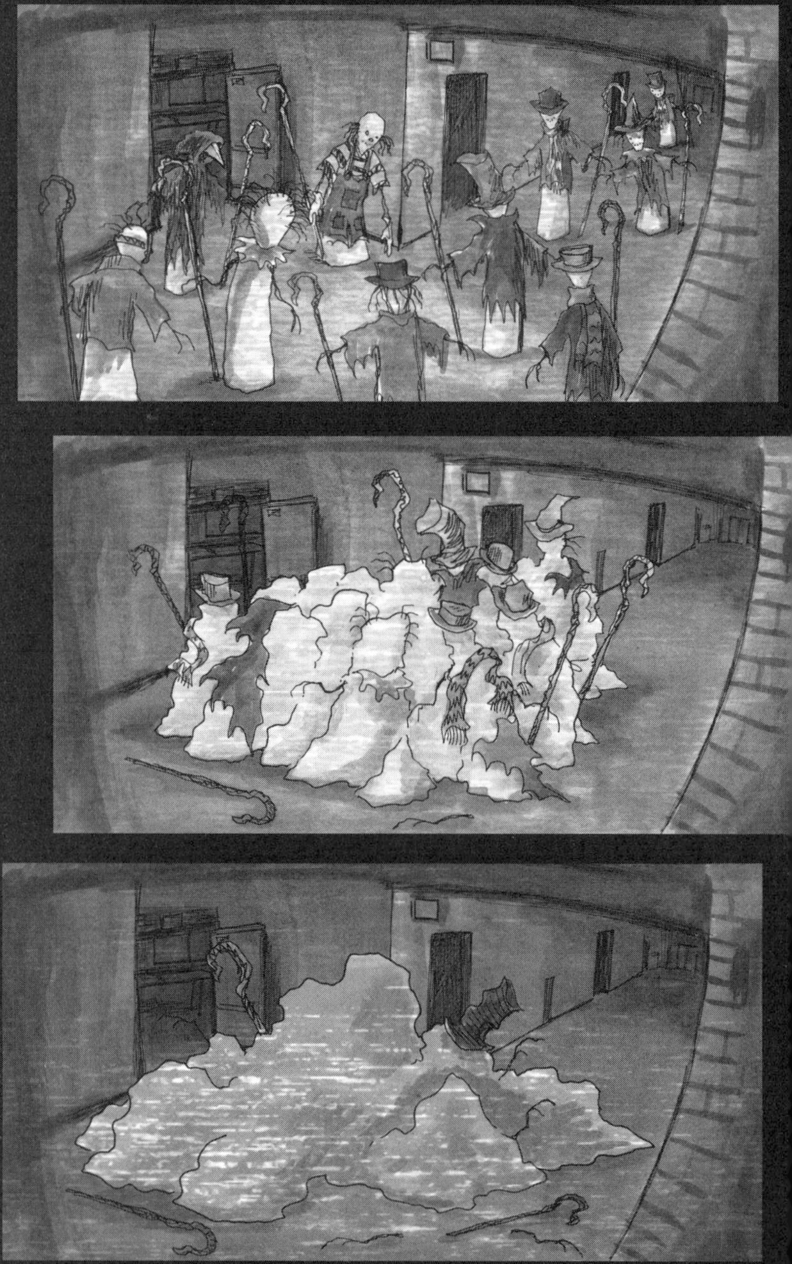

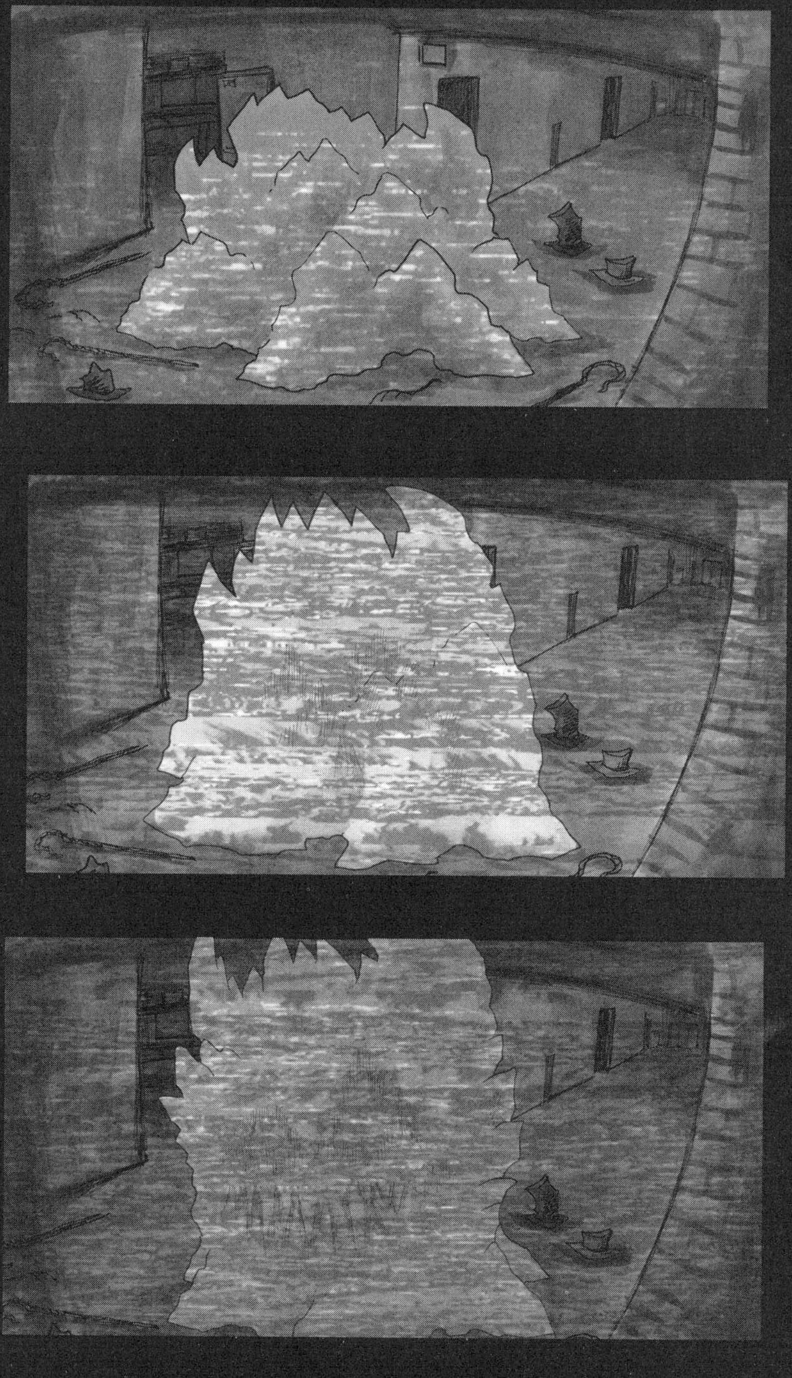

Chapter 35

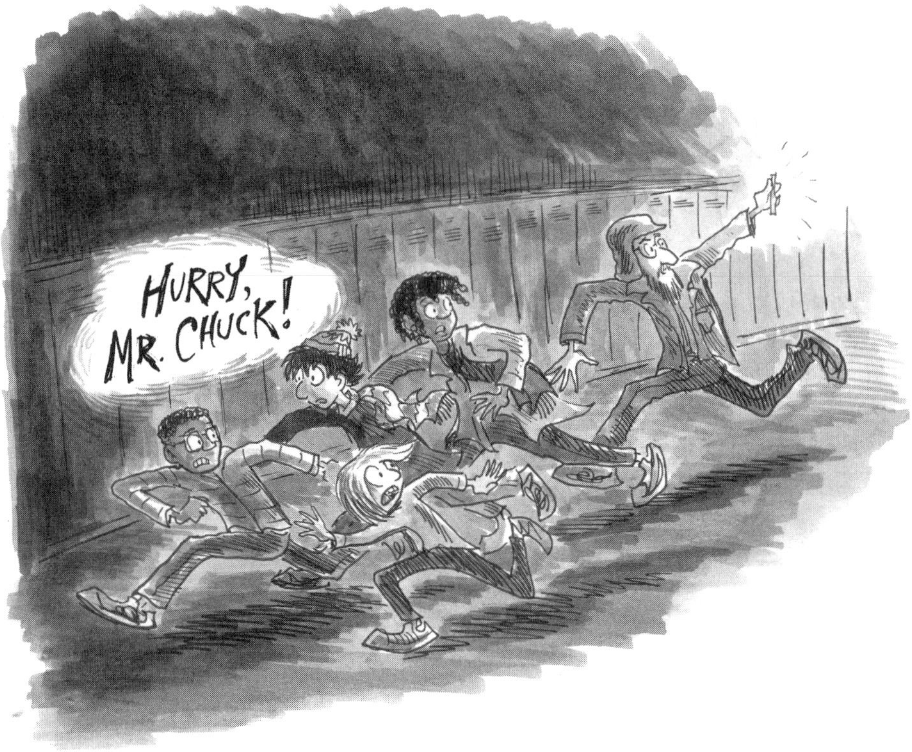
HURRY, MR. CHUCK!

"I'm coming!" called Mr. Chuck. He was still filming over his shoulder as the lunch-food monster bubbled and lurched down the hall.

They whipped around a corner, dashed through a centrum, and regrouped in the 100 hall.

"We lost it," said Ms. Padilla.

"It'll find us!" Kat panted. "We gotta get out of the school!"

"I'm not leaving without Jordan!" said Donte.

"And Twila!" added Levi. "We're trapped in here, anyway. We tried the fire door." He pointed to the exit down the hall. "The school's buried. Exits sealed in snow."

"The school's big," said Donte. "We can outrun that gross blob."

"Keep running until the snow melts?" exclaimed Kat. "It's just a matter of time before that thing finds us and corners us!"

"Then we need a plan," said Ms. Padilla.

"Well, it's a big, soggy slop pile," said Mr. Chuck. "Maybe if we had some bread, we could soak it all up."

"Where are we going to get a huge piece of bread?" asked Donte.

Mr. Chuck shrugged. "Hadn't thought that part through."

"Wait, do you guys hear that?" asked Levi.

"What, the blob?" said Donte.

"No, it's—"

"Hello?" called a muffled voice from down the hall.

"Jordan!" Donte gasped. He ran toward the sound of the voice. The others followed.

Mr. Chuck swung the light left and right.

"Here!" said Jordan.

The light turned toward the open fire door and the wall of snow behind it.

"Down here!" said Jordan. He tumbled out from the tunnel.

"Jordan!" Donte pulled his brother upright and squeezed him close.

Levi pushed past them. "Where's Twila?"

"Chill, Brother-Man!" said Twila's voice. Her front half popped out of the hole. "Hi!"

Levi reached to help her, but she pulled back. "Careful!" Something roughly the size of a bowling ball was cradled in her arms.

"What's that?" asked Kat.

"Explain later!" heaved Twila.

"Where did that tunnel come from?" asked Ms. Padilla.

"Willow dug it, with some help," said Twila. "She doubled back to check on—"

Something small and spiny shot from the tunnel.

"Stay back!" said Ms. Padilla, pushing her students behind her.

"It's a rodent of unusual size!" Mr. Chuck yelped.

"Willow is not a rodent, you big-nosed scruff-muffin ape!"

"And it talks!" said Mr. Chuck.

"It's okay," said Kat. "She's a friend!"

Ms. Padilla blinked. "I can't tell if I should be relieved or alarmed that this doesn't really surprise me."

"Stupid, stupid goofooligans!" hissed Willow. "Charlotte is coming!"

"Who's Charlotte?" Kat asked.

"Not now! We must get away from the tunnel!" Willow started skittering down the hall, her claws clacking along the floor. "Hurry! Run! R—" She froze. Her spines bristled. She bared her fangs.

The lunch monster turned the corner.

"This way!" cried Ms. Padilla, ushering her students down the south end of the 100 hall.

"It's a dead end!" Donte shouted.

"Not if we cut through the testing centrum!" said Ms. Padilla.

"Come on!" said Levi, pulling Twila's arm.

"Careful!" She tightened her grip around the thing in her arms. "This thing's heavy!"

Donte threw himself against the centrum door. "It's locked! Mr. Chuck, you got the keys?"

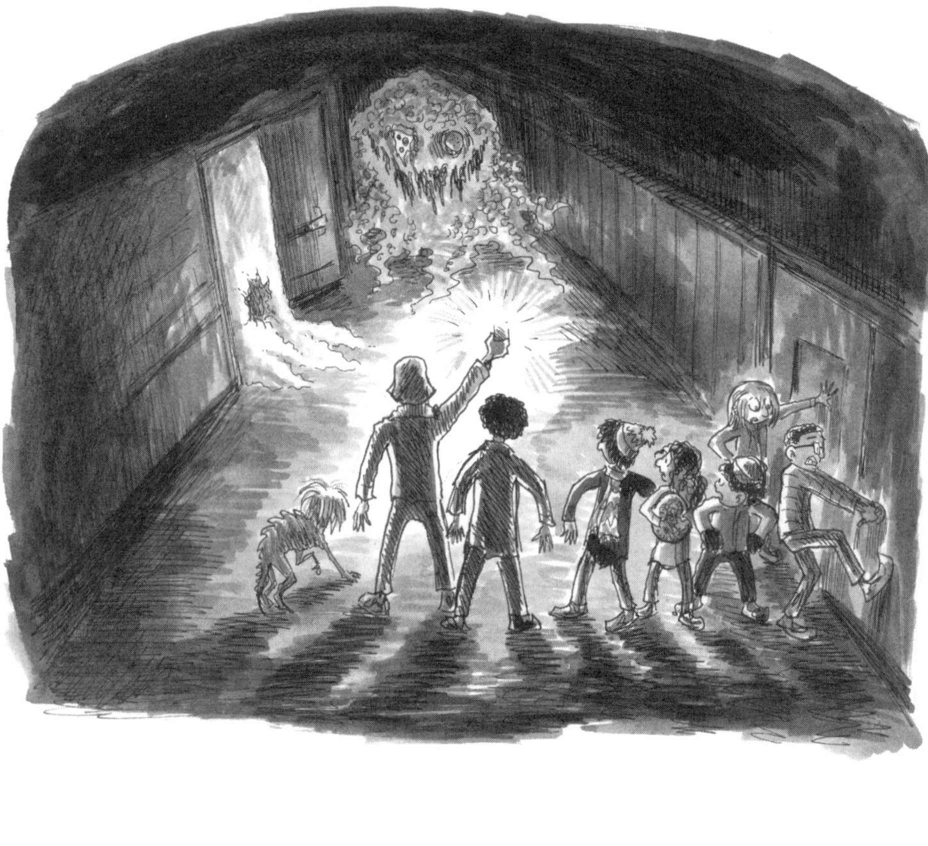

"Oh, uh." Mr. Chuck checked his belt.

Kat looked over her shoulder. "Hurry, Mr. Chuck! It's coming!"

"I think the keys are in my office," Mr. Chuck said.

The survivors turned and stared in horror at the approaching lunch-food monster.

Donte and Jordan held hands. Levi put an arm around Twila's shoulder. Mr. Chuck raised Kat's camera over his head. Willow arched her spiny back and snarled.

And then, halfway between the survivors and the blob,
a long, hairy limb reached out from the snow tunnel and
probed the floor.

The blob stopped. It quivered.

Another limb emerged. And another. And another.

"Charlotte is here," said Willow flatly.

Another limb. Another. And then all of Charlotte
emerged from the tunnel.

Chapter 36

FOOTAGE FROM KAT BOMBARD'S PHONE

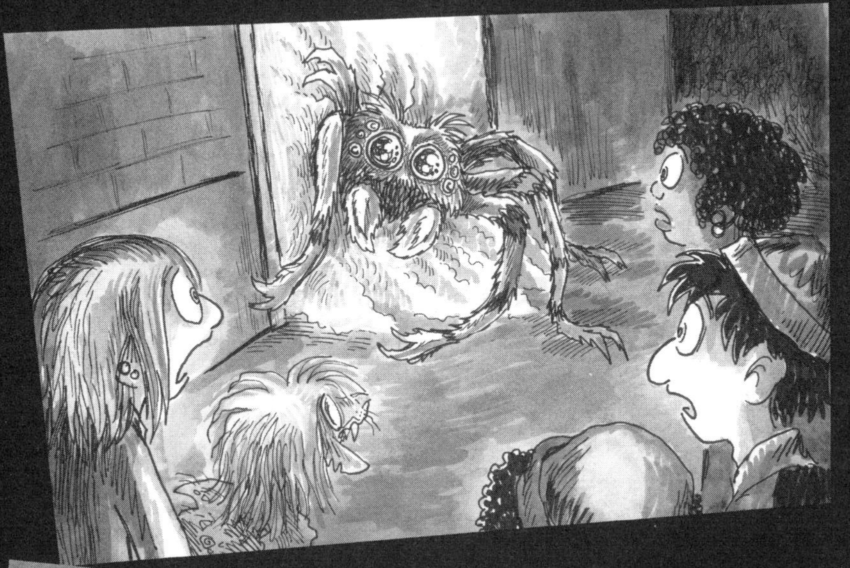

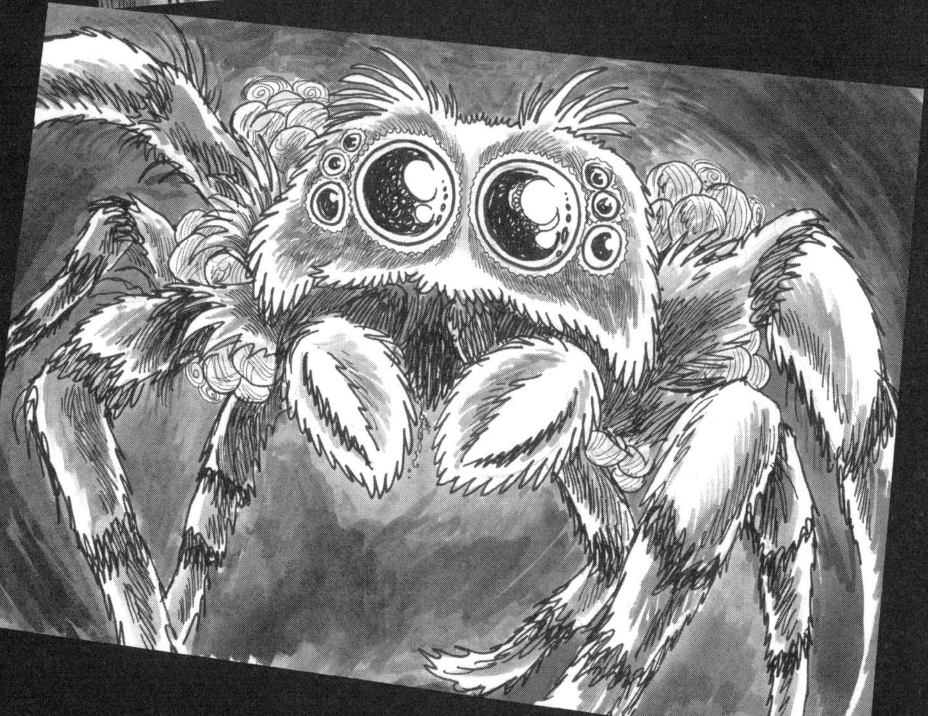

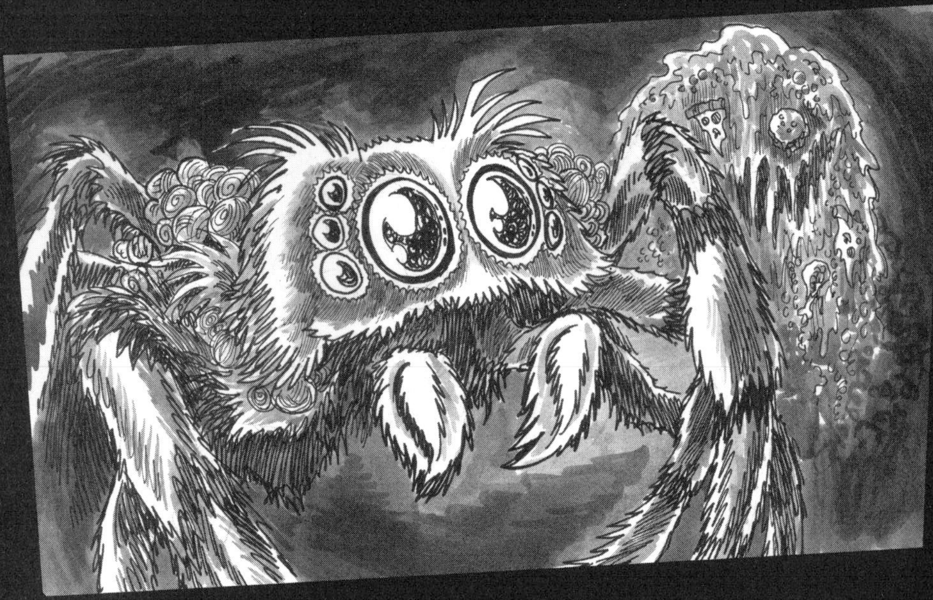

FOOTAGE FROM SCHOOL SECURITY CAMERA (BATTERY OPERATED)

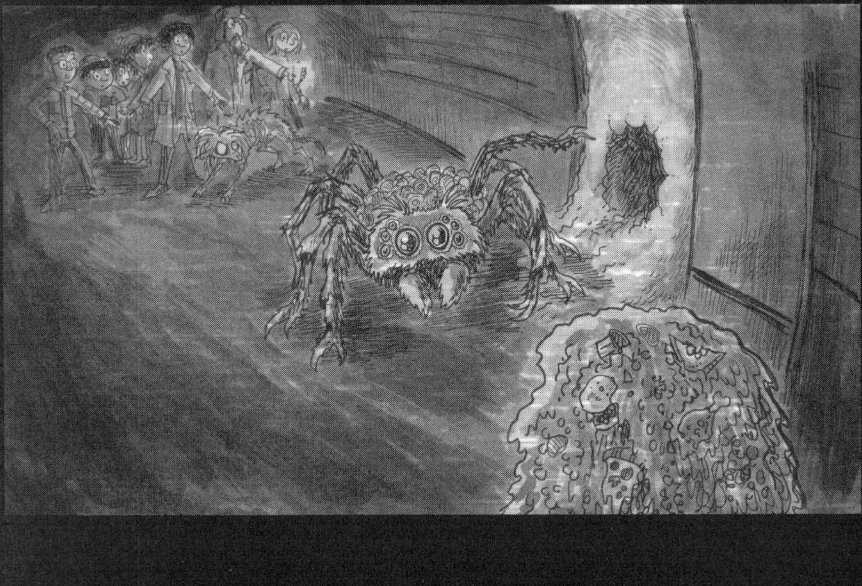

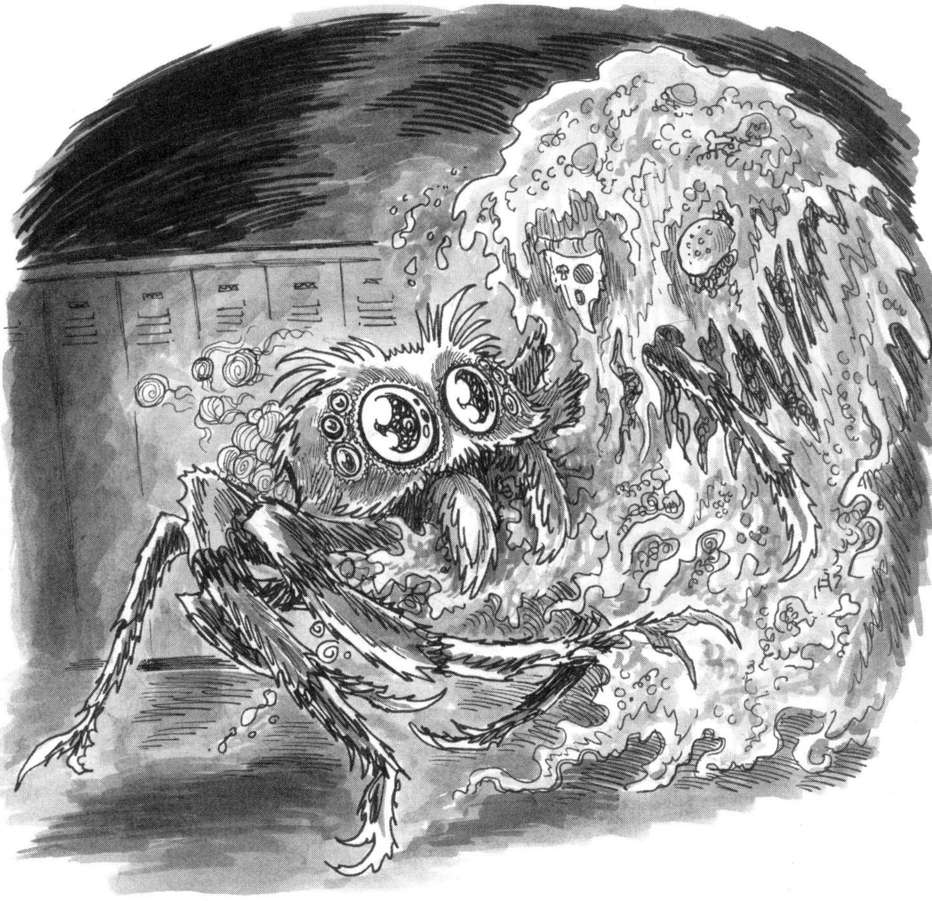

Five students, a teacher, and a custodian stood paralyzed as the monsters collided.

Charlotte's eight limbs flailed, her mandibles clacked, and she tore into the lunch monster. The lunch monster lurched and spasmed as it struggled to regain the advantage.

"Go, Charlotte!" said a small voice. It was Twila.

Jordan joined her: "Go, Charlotte! Monster fight! Monster fight!"

"You got this, Charlotte girl!" said Mr. Chuck, holding Kat's phone high as he filmed the battle.

The lunch monster was rebounding. It snagged two of Charlotte's limbs and snapped them into unnatural angles. Charlotte mewled and spit a stream of green fluid at her opponent. The blob jolted and shuddered as the fluid sizzled and left a steaming gap in its body.

"C'mon, Charlotte! Defense!" chattered Kat.

"Whup that giant sloppy joe!" cheered Donte.

"Eat it for breakfast!" shouted Levi.

"Mop the floor with that overgrown pile of empty ~~ies~~!" screamed Ms. Padilla, her teacher voice

Charlotte spewed another stream of corrosive saliva, and a victory cheer rang from the onlookers. But the blob suddenly lurched upright, seized all eight of Charlotte's limbs, and slammed her body against the lockers. The lockers buckled and something—part of her exoskeleton, perhaps—gave a sickening crunch.

The onlookers winced.

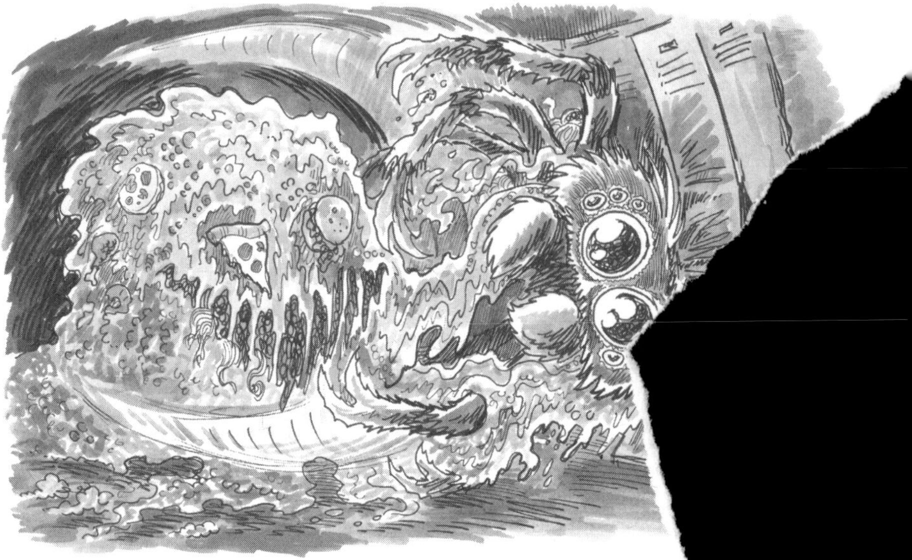

“Leave her alone, you tub of grease!” scream

Suddenly Donte broke away from the onlook
charged forward. “Come on! We can’t just stand
gawking while that spider fights our battles!”

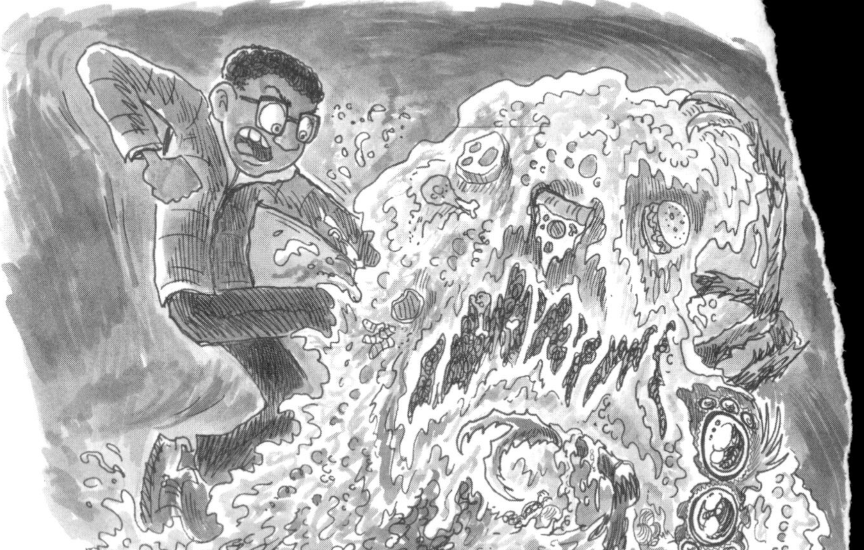

The others joined him. They climbed onto the oozing mass—kicking, punching, scooping.

"Let go of that spider!" bellowed Jordan.

"Surrender, blob!" roared Kat. "I eat scum like you for lunch! Literally!"

But the fight had turned. The lunch monster gushed over Charlotte, smothering her struggling body. Her limbs twisted, shivered, and went limp.

"No!" screamed Jordan. He pounded his fists into the blob. He tried to pull free, only to find his arms stuck to the elbows. "It's got me!"

Donte and Kat jerked him free.

"Fall back!" cried Ms. Padilla, pulling her students away from the blob.

Willow tugged on Levi's pant leg. "We must flee!"

"We can't!" said Levi. "It's a dead end!"

Charlotte was gone now—the blob had engulfed her battered body. The monster turned slowly and started sliding toward the trapped survivors.

They took a collective step back.

Willow flashed her fangs. "Then we go down fighting!"

The blob burbled laughter and started to rise up over the onlookers like a great processed-food tsunami.

The survivors braced for the attack.

The attack never came.

The lunch monster stopped. It spasmed. It jerked. It bubbled and boiled and blistered.

Something burst from the blob—something small and dark that skittered around its quivering body.

Another eruption. And another, and soon dozens—maybe *hundreds*—of tiny, fist-size, eight-limbed creatures were bursting from the blob, swarming over it, spitting acid and tearing apart its body with clacking mandibles.

Levi turned to Willow. "Those things on Charlotte's back, the little round things covered in webbing, were those—"

"Egg sacs," said Willow. "Charlotte was expecting."

They watched in horror and amazement as the mini-Charlottes swarmed over the lunch monster's remains. Within a minute the feeding frenzy was over, and as if following an unheard cue, the tiny nightmare army dispersed, scuttling off down the halls, up the walls, across the ceiling, disappearing into the shadows.

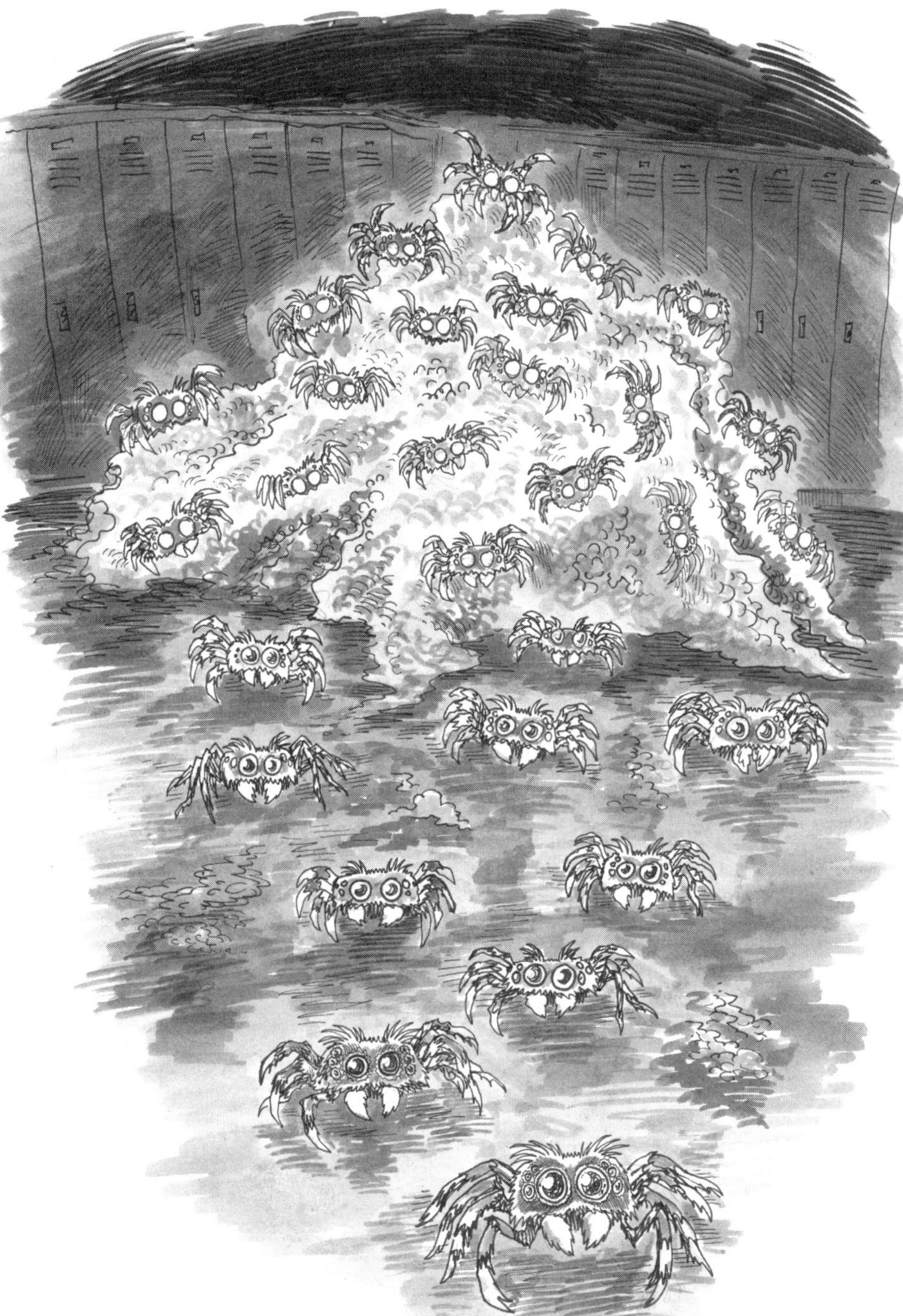

Mr. Chuck jumped aside as one scurried over his foot and disappeared under the centrum door. "Well, on the bright side, we may not need to worry about mice this spring," he said with a shrug.

The survivors exchanged shocked, exhausted, disgusted looks.

"What are you slackadillies waiting for?" snapped Willow.

Ms. Padilla shook herself. "Come on!" she said to the others. They followed her back down the hall, skirting around the steaming remains of the monster carnage, and back to the school's main corridor. "Enough is enough!" said Ms. Padilla. "We're busting out of this place, even if I have to dig through a mile of snow with my bare hands!"

There was a crackle, and they froze in their tracks as a voice came over the intercom. The voice was no longer cheery. It sounded hollow—the rasp of winter wind.

"Please report to the cafeteria. The Boojum King has arrived. It is time for the Harvest."

They looked at one another.

"We don't fall for it, right?" said Levi.

"But we're still trapped in the school," said Kat.

"We could try escaping through Willow's tunnel," suggested Twila.

"There's no way we can all fit through that little tunnel," said Mr. Chuck.

"And we can't just abandon all the people in the cafeteria!" said Donte.

Ms. Padilla clenched her fists. "I'll go. You kids stay here with Mr. Chuck."

"No!" said Kat. "Horror Movie Survival 101: No Splitting Up!"

Ms. Padilla thought for a moment. "Then stay behind me. We'll go slowly, size up the situation."

Chapter 37

Twila stopped abruptly and adjusted her grip. "I . . . I thought I felt something move . . . inside it. And it's getting hot. Almost too hot to hold."

Levi waved his hand over the round thing. "Wow! I can feel the heat coming off it! What is it, anyway?"

"I don't think even Margalo knows," said Twila. "I just got—I don't know—a feeling about it. Like it's calling to me."

They continued toward the cafeteria. The sound of the children singing grew louder.

"You still filming, Mr. Chuck?" Kat asked.

"Filming to the bitter end," said Mr. Chuck. "We'd better at least win a posthumous Oscar for all this."

Jordan tucked his hands into his armpits. "Does it feel like it's getting colder?"

"Yeah!" agreed Donte. "And what happened to all the snowmen?"

Ms. Padilla stopped suddenly. The others peered around her.

"You just *had* to ask about the snowmen," said Kat.

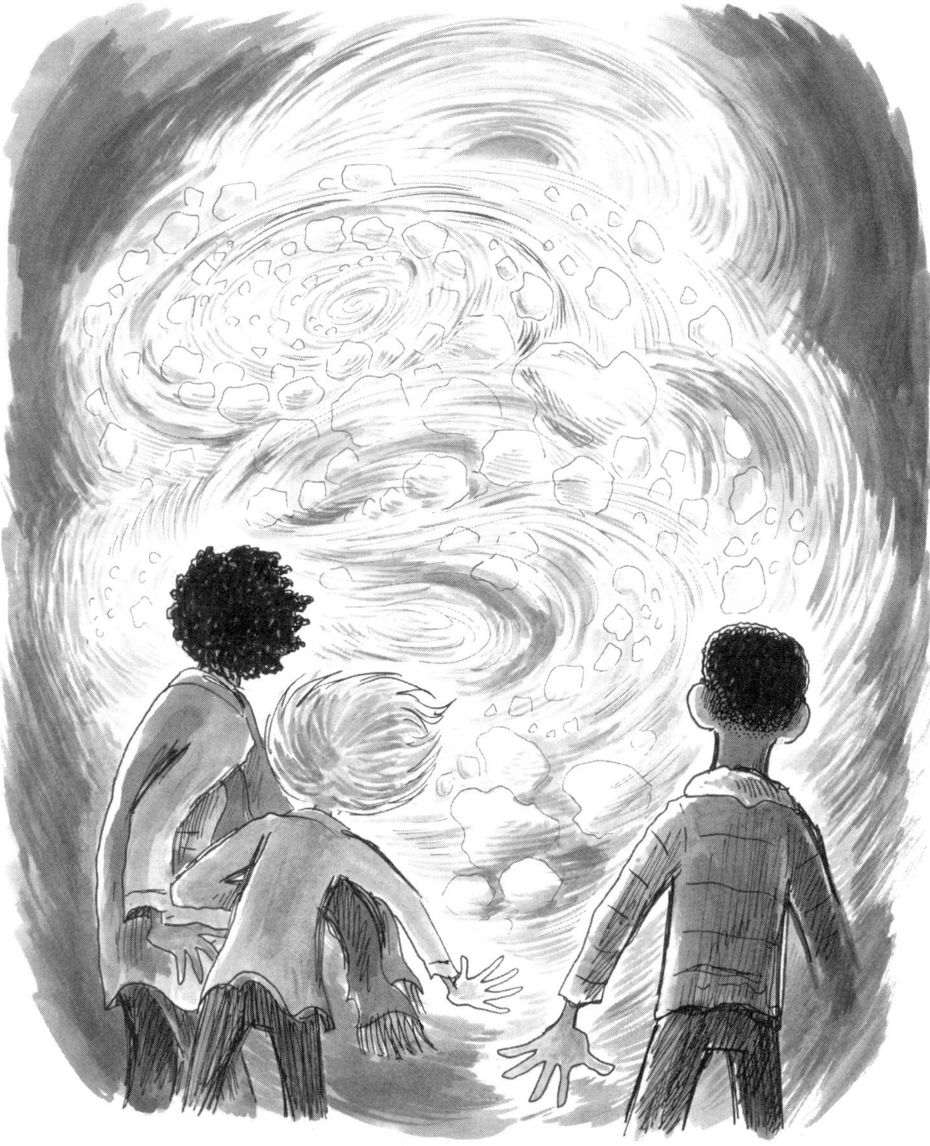

Ahead was a great mass of crushed snow and ice—the combined bodies of the snowmen. It churned and roiled like a collapsing glacier, reconfiguring the snowmen's bodies into something huge and terrible.

The thing rose up to the ceiling. Tiles crunched. Plaster crumbled.

The loose ice and snow within its maw spiraled faster and faster—a raging white vortex. The hall filled with an icy blast.

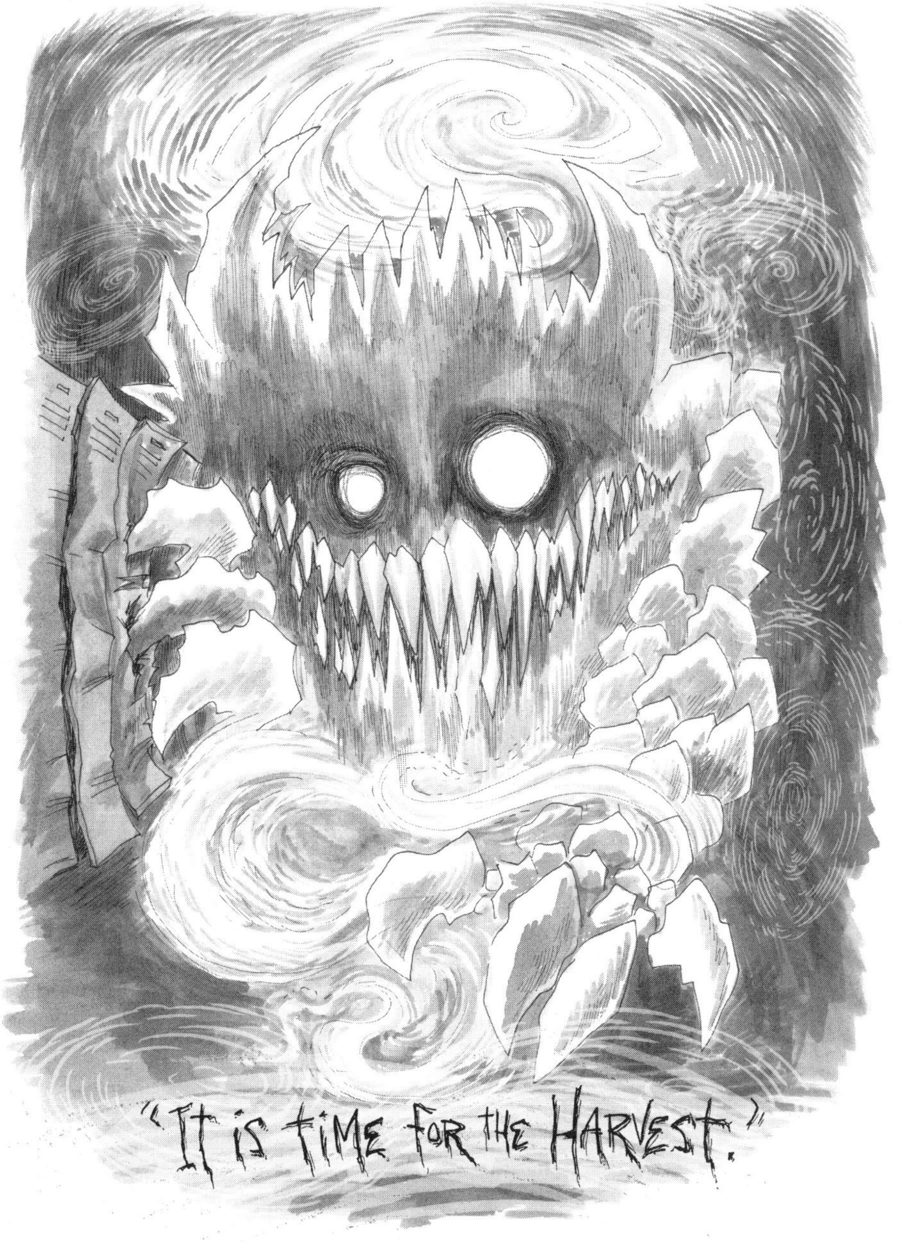
"It is time for the Harvest."

FOOTAGE FROM KAT BOMBARD'S PHONE

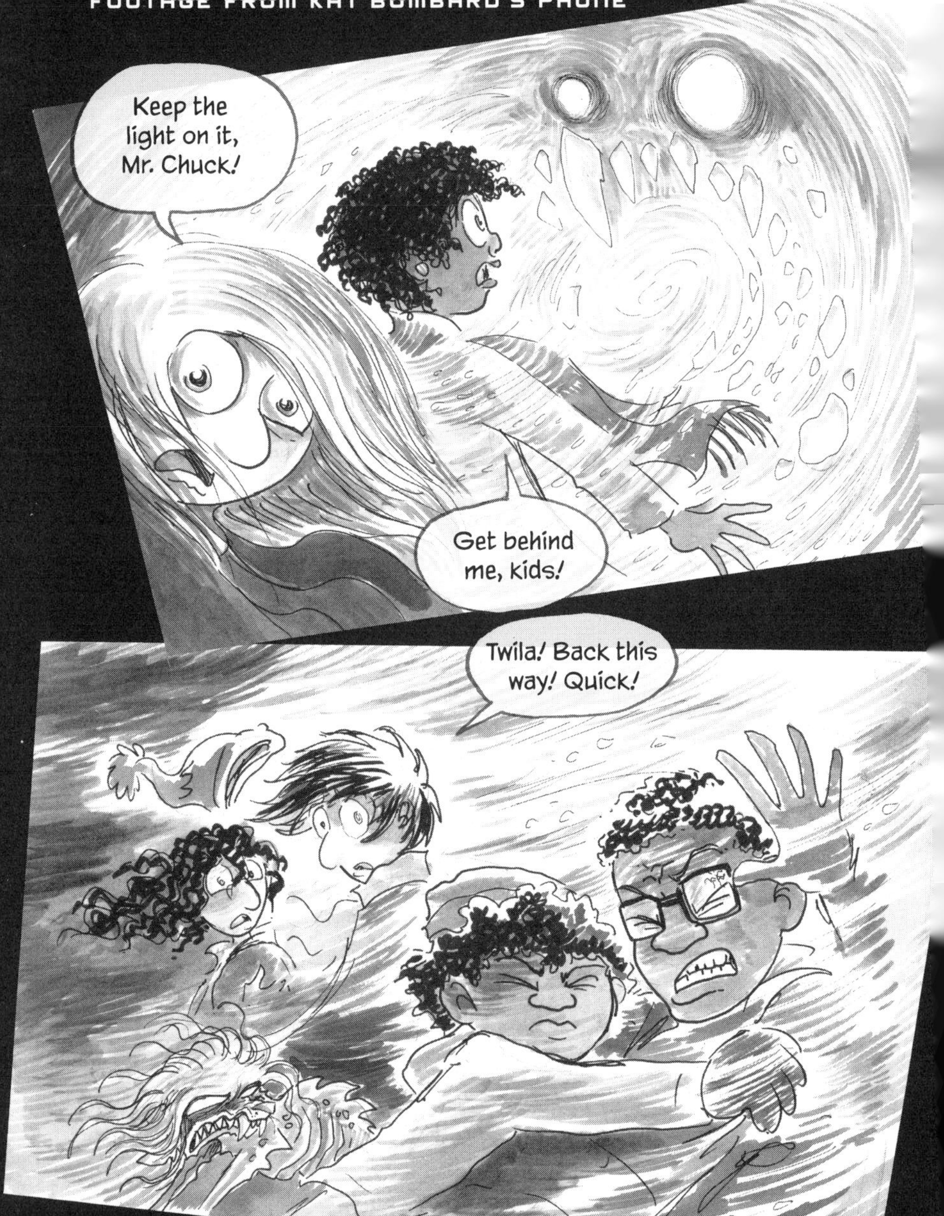
Keep the light on it, Mr. Chuck!
Get behind me, kids!
Twila! Back this way! Quick!

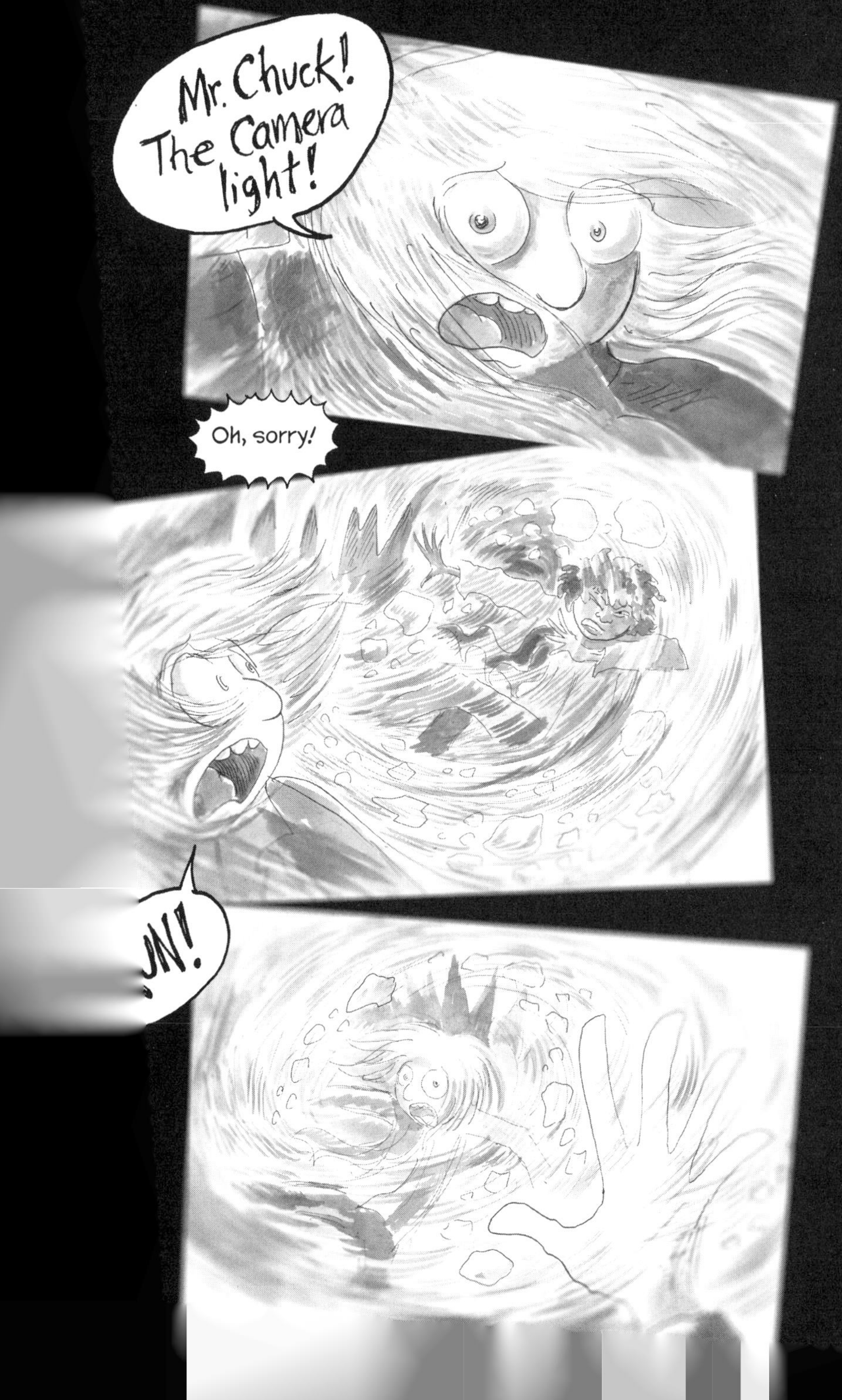
Mr. Chuck! The Camera light!
Oh, sorry!

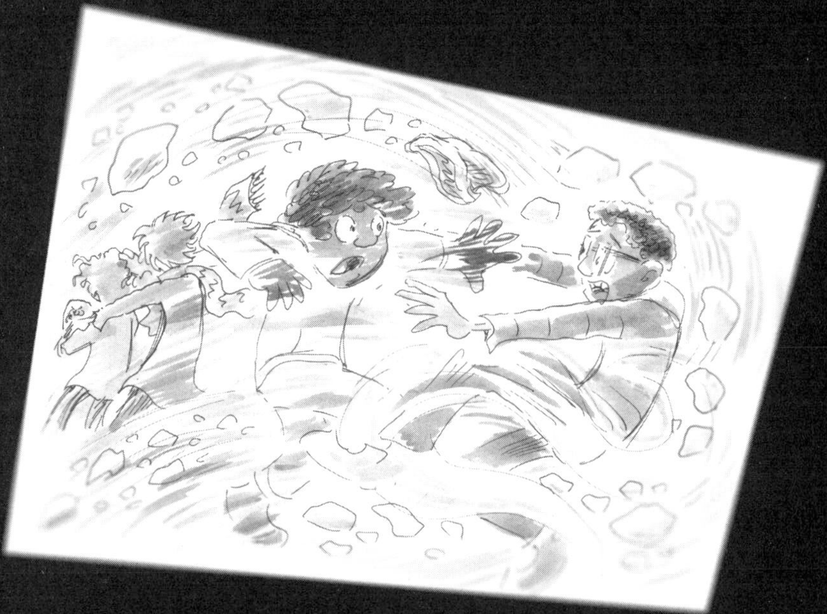

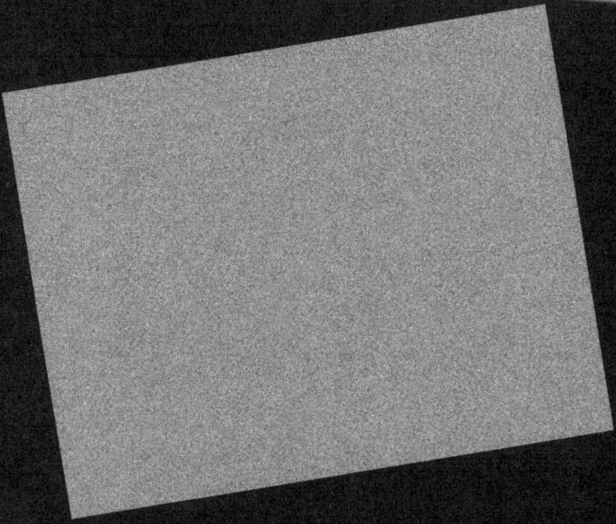

ARCHIVIST'S NOTE: It was at this point that Katherine Bombard's phone footage abruptly ended. It is assumed that the battery died. What follows is a rendition based on eyewitness accounts and speculation. Please draw your own conclusions.

Chapter 39

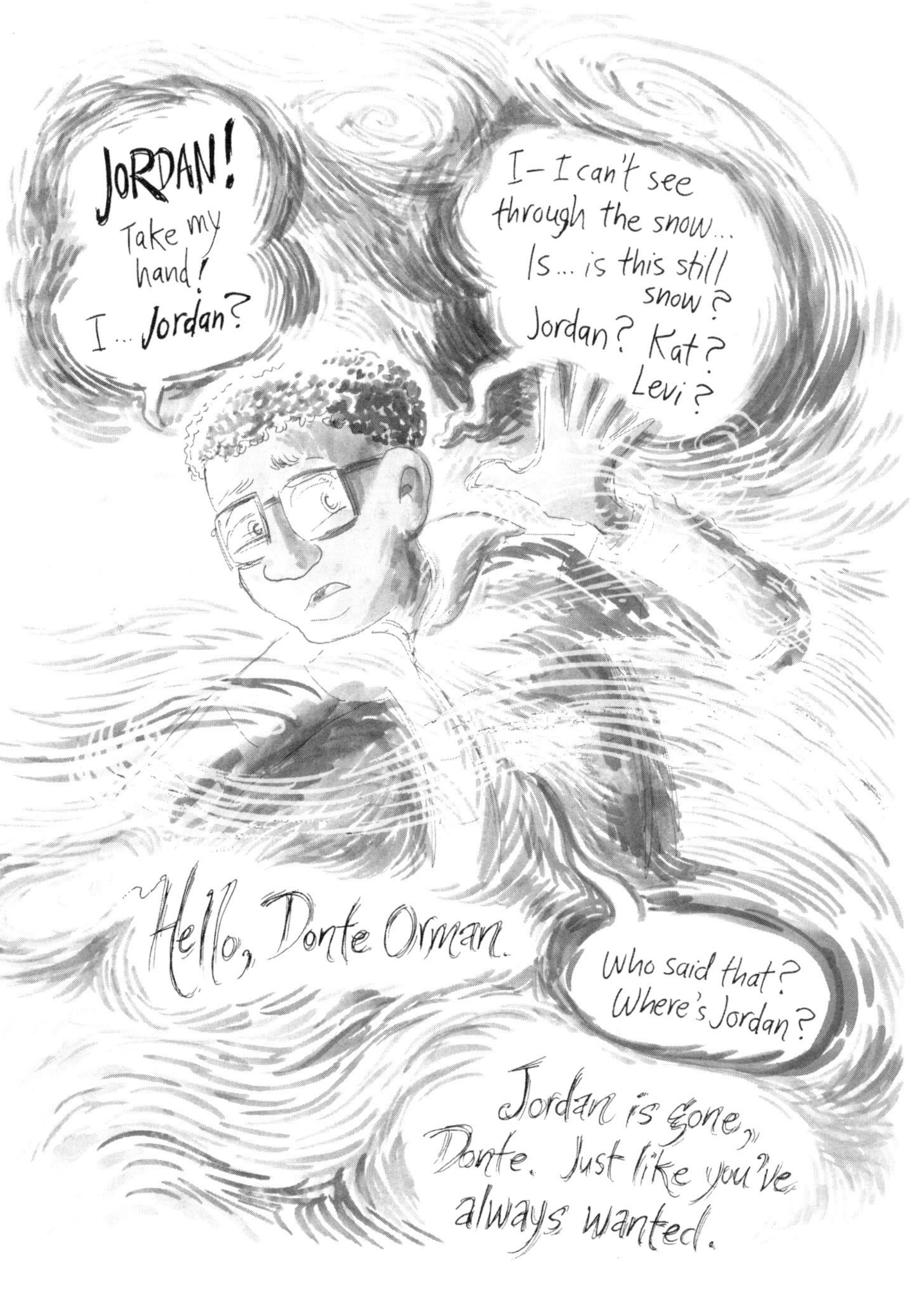
JORDAN! Take my hand! I... Jordan?
I– I can't see through the snow... Is... is this still snow? Jordan? Kat? Levi?
Hello, Donte Orman.
Who said that? Where's Jordan?
Jordan is gone, Donte. Just like you've always wanted.

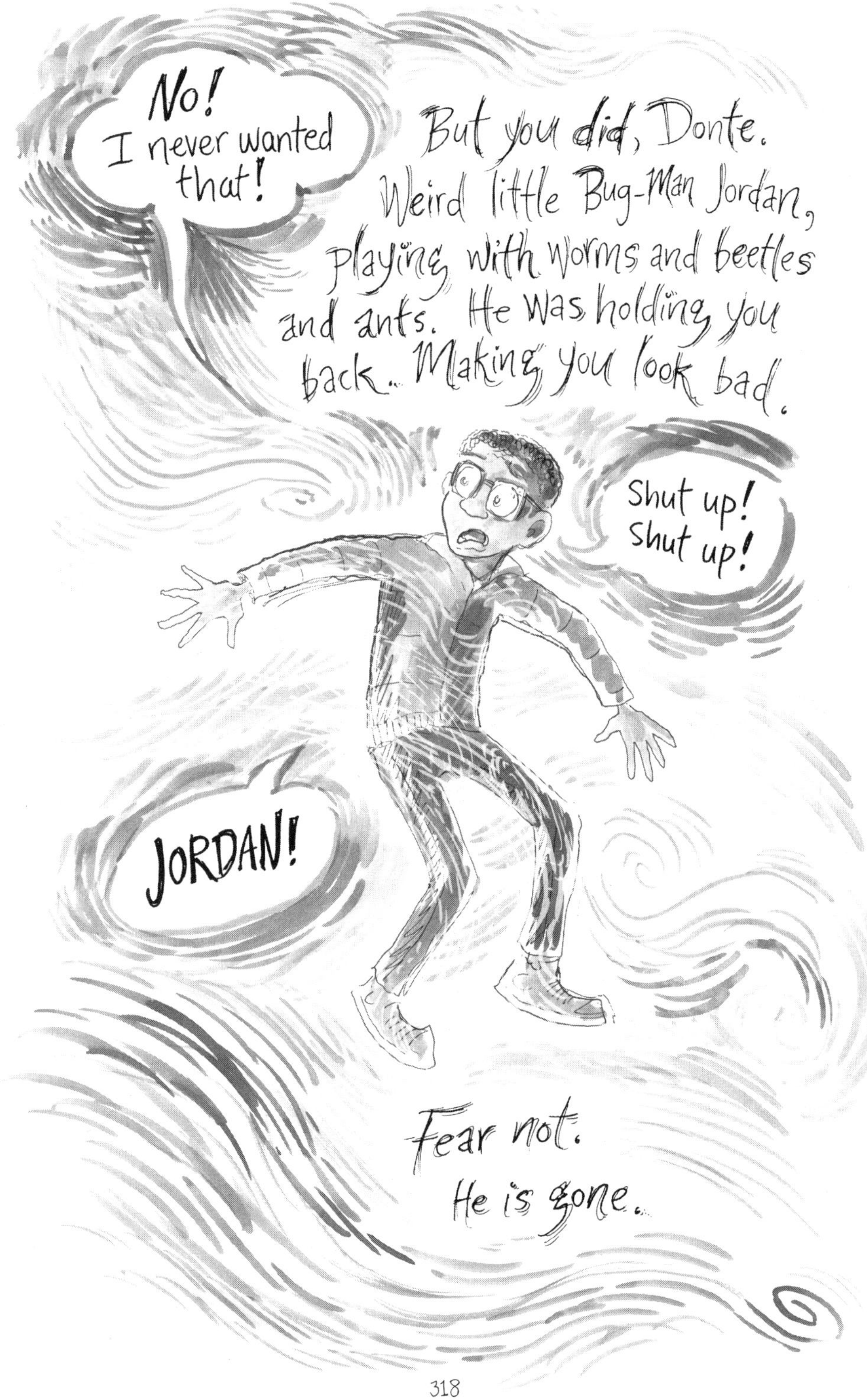
No! I never wanted that!
But you did, Donte. Weird little Bug-Man Jordan, playing with worms and beetles and ants. He was holding you back... Making you look bad.
Shut up! Shut up!
JORDAN!
Fear not. He is gone...

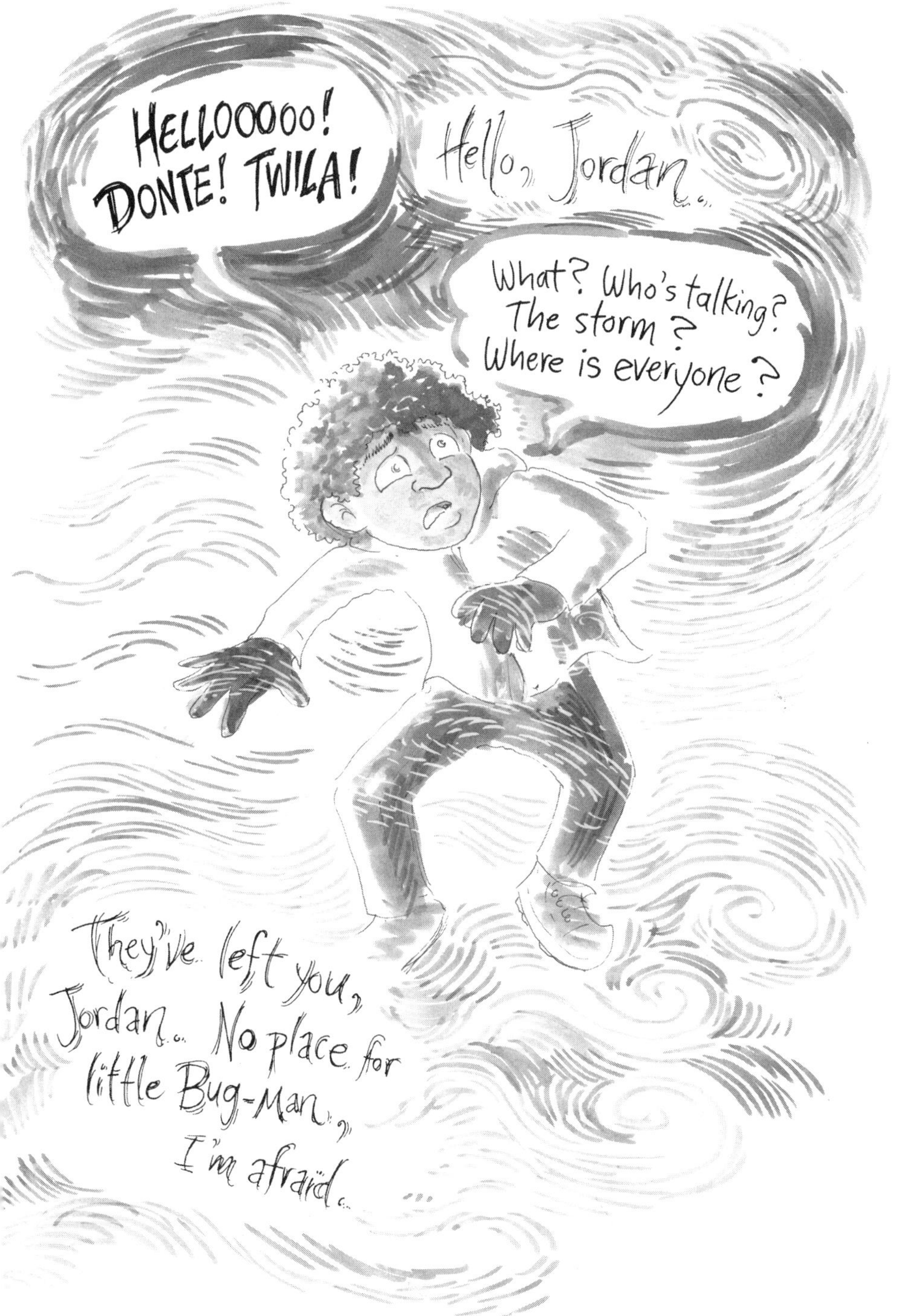
HELLOOOOO! DONTE! TWILA!
Hello, Jordan...
What? Who's talking? The storm? Where is everyone?
They've left you, Jordan... No place for little Bug-Man, I'm afraid...

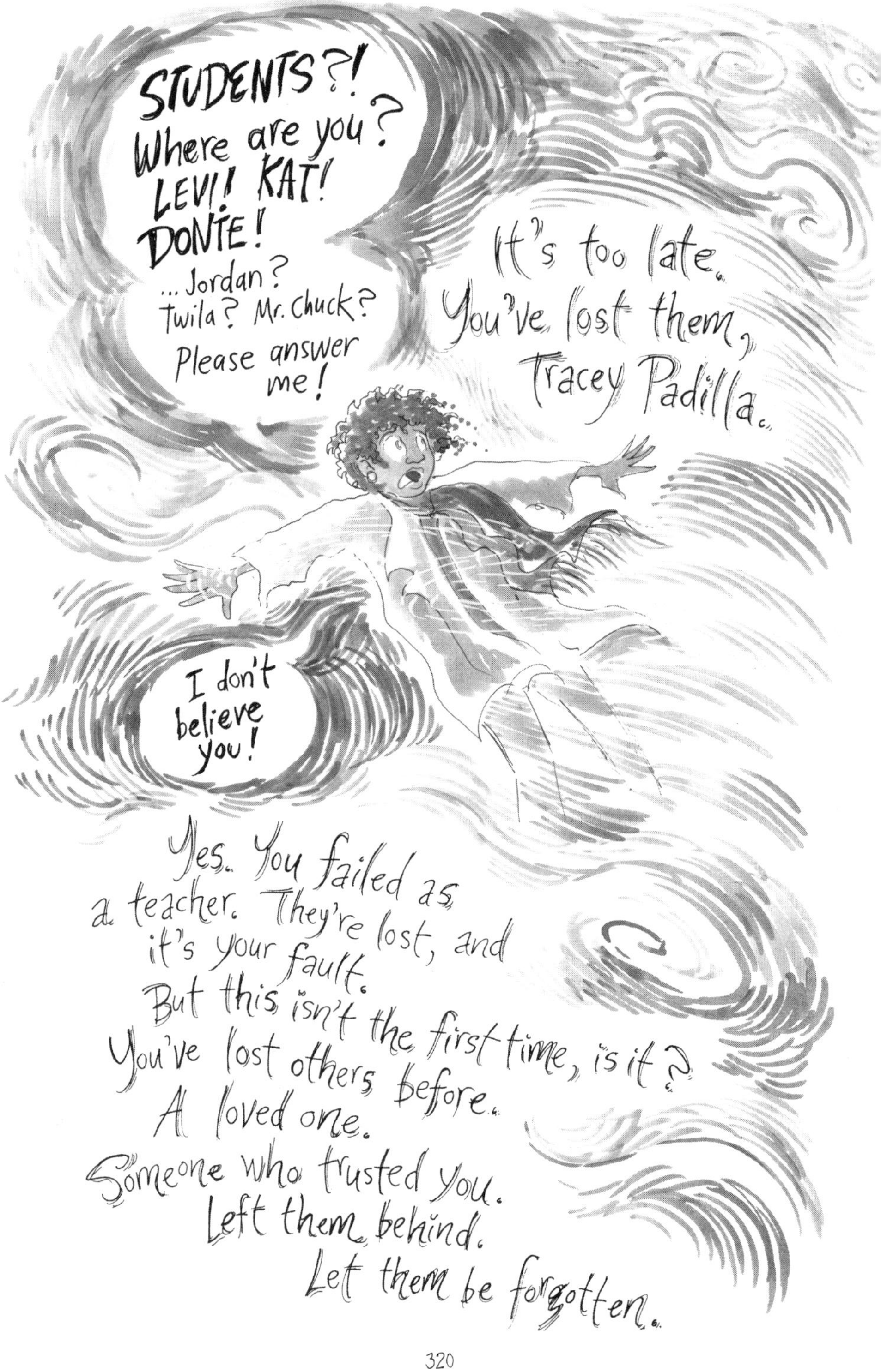
STUDENTS?! Where are you? LEVI! KAT! DONTE! ...Jordan? Twila? Mr. Chuck? Please answer me!
It's too late. You've lost them, Tracey Padilla.
I don't believe you!
Yes. You failed as a teacher. They're lost, and it's your fault. But this isn't the first time, is it? You've lost others before. A loved one. Someone who trusted you. Left them behind. Let them be forgotten.

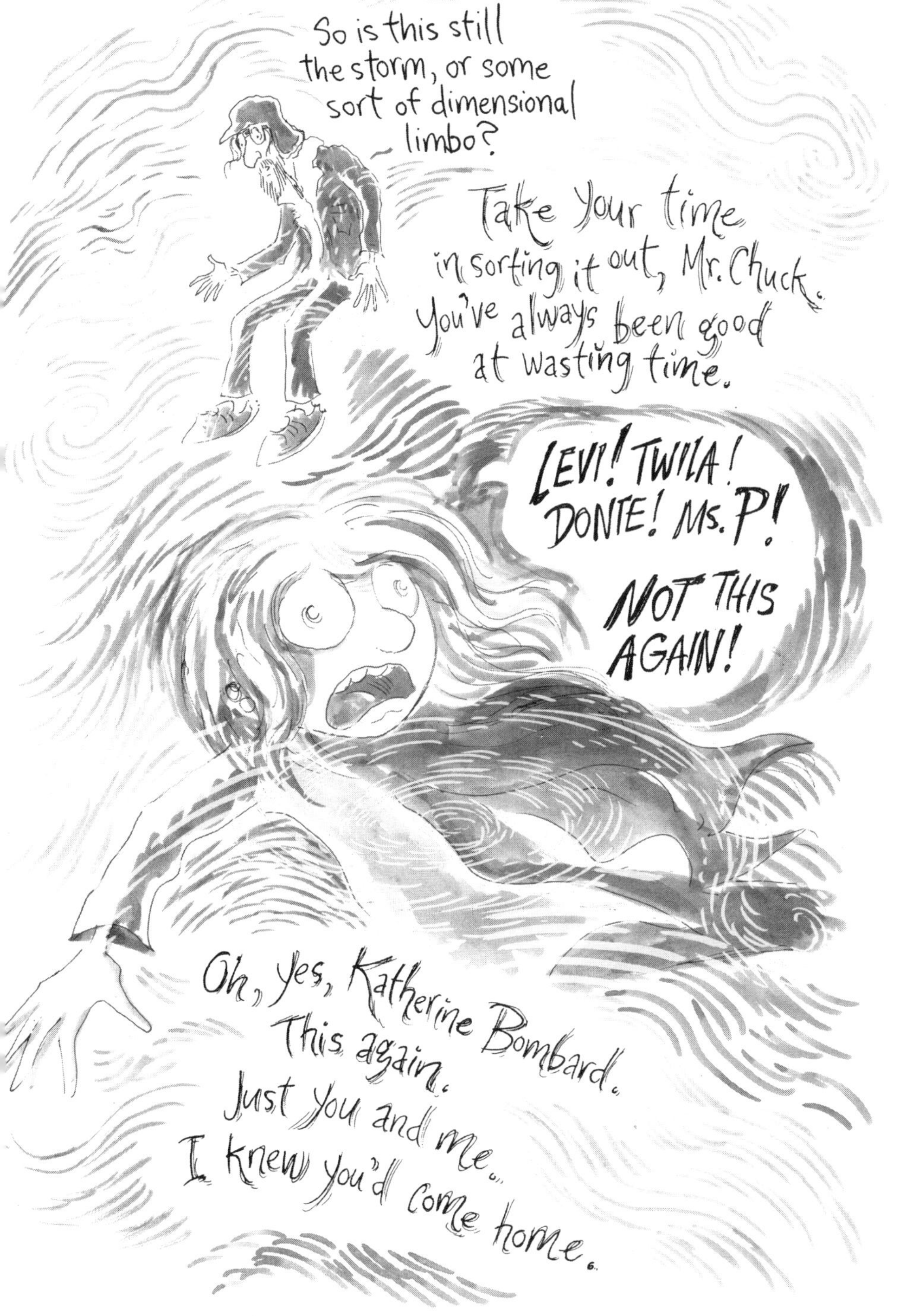
So is this still the storm, or some sort of dimensional limbo?
Take your time in sorting it out, Mr. Chuck. You've always been good at wasting time.
LEVI! TWILA! DONTE! MS. P!
NOT THIS AGAIN!
Oh, yes, Katherine Bombard. This again. Just you and me. I knew you'd come home.

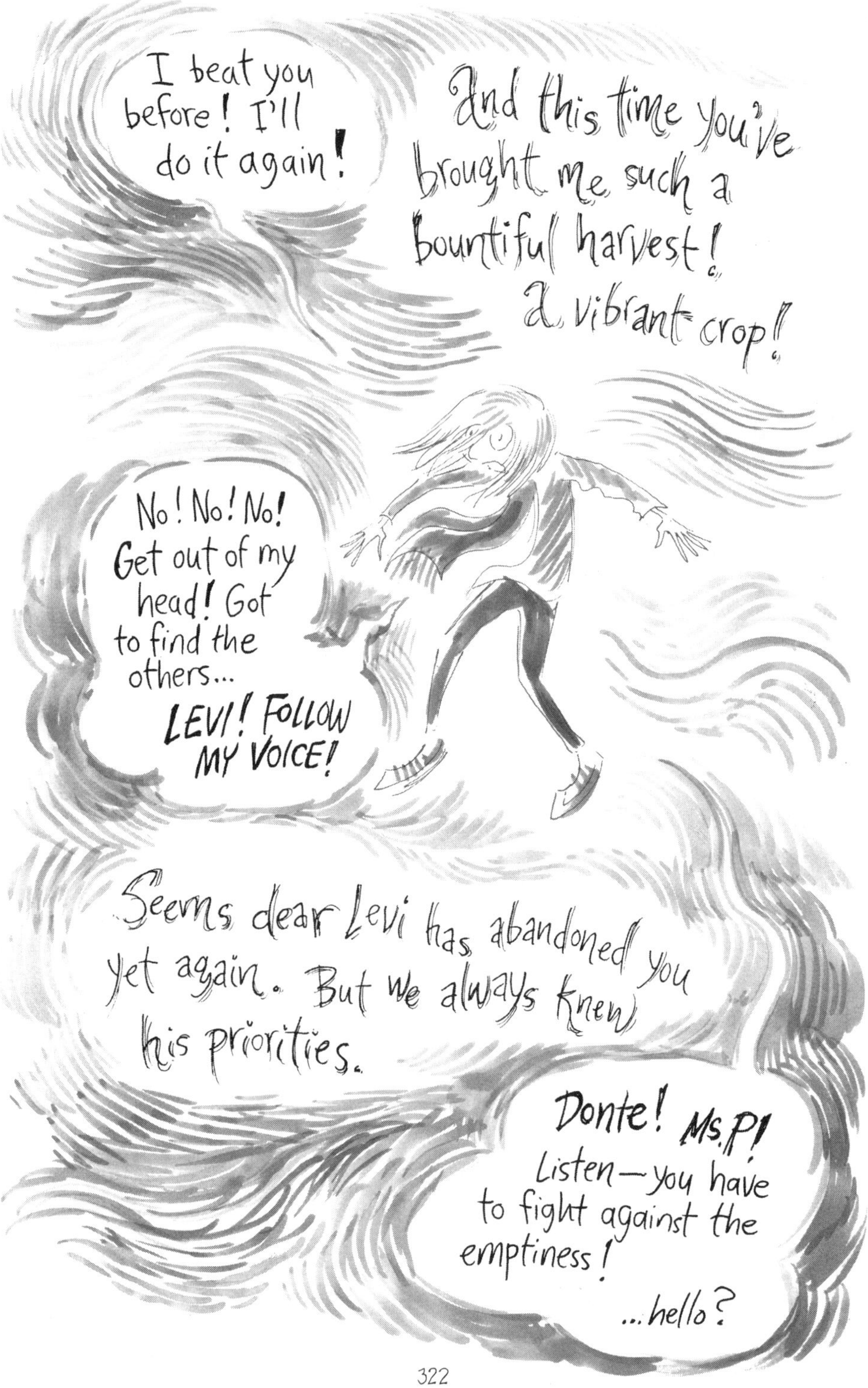
I beat you before! I'll do it again!
And this time you've brought me such a bountiful harvest! A vibrant crop!
No! No! No! Get out of my head! Got to find the others... LEVI! FOLLOW MY VOICE!
Seems dear Levi has abandoned you yet again. But we always knew his priorities.
Donte! Ms. P! Listen—you have to fight against the emptiness! ...hello?

Chapter 40

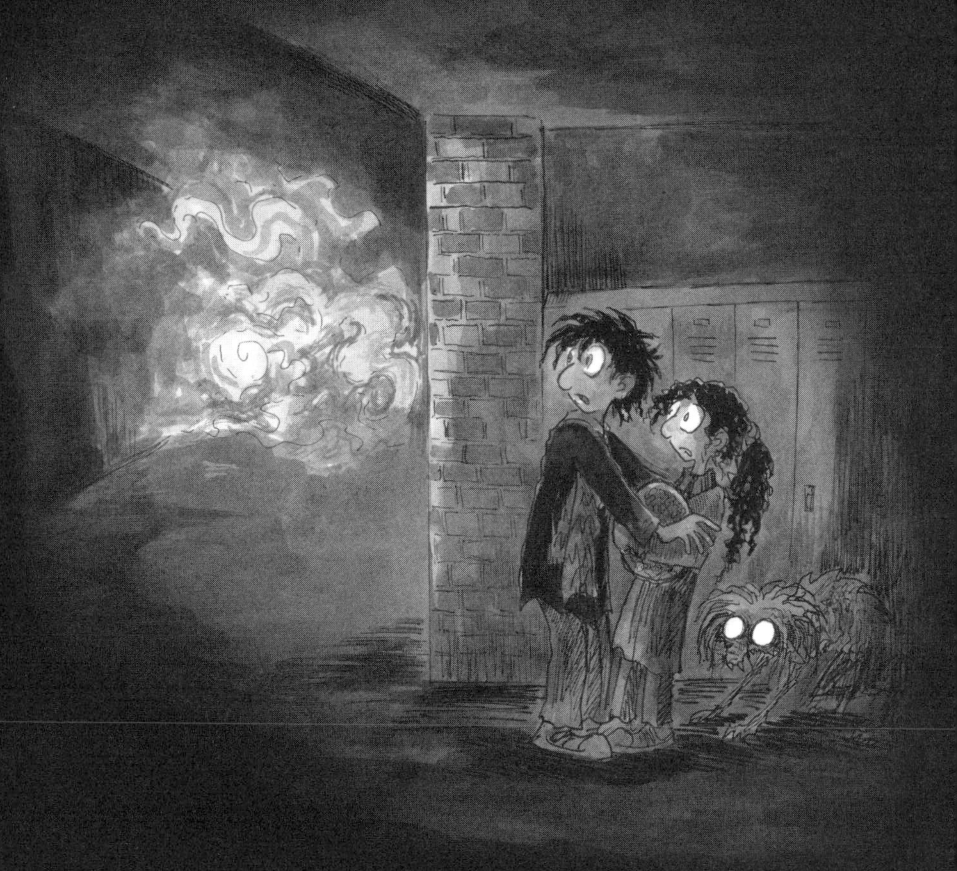

Levi pulled Twila around the corner. The icy maelstrom raged down the main corridor, howling as it searched for the remaining victims.

"Where are the others?" whispered Twila.

"Don't know," Levi whispered back. "I think it . . ."

Down a nearby hall, the howling rose to a shriek. Lockers slammed and glass shattered. Levi and Twila huddled together.

"I'll go back for them," Levi whispered when the howling had moved to a distant part of the school.

"You—" began Twila, but her voice became a gasp as something brushed past her leg in the dark. Two green fluorescent lights blinked up at them.

"Hush! It is just me."

"Willow!" Levi said. "The others—"

"The ice storm—the Boojum King—it swallowed them," said Willow.

Levi gripped Twila's shoulder. "Go with Willow back to the tunnel. Crawl out of the school, back to Margalo's, and stay there." He took a deep, rattling breath. "I'm not leaving without the others. Not this time."

"You will be helpless against the ice and emptiness," said Willow. "It will swallow you too!"

A pause. The phantom storm's howls echoed down a distant hall.

"Just go back to the tunnel," said Levi. "Quick. Before the storm finds us."

Another howl. The school trembled.

"Hurry!" Levi reached to push Twila along, but pulled his hand back when he felt the heat from the ovoid stone she was carrying.

"It's waking up. See?" Twila shifted the thing in her arms, revealing a glowing crack along its surface. "It's my body heat, I think. Margalo tried to hatch it with heat lamps, but I think it really needed . . . I don't know. *Life*."

The howling drew closer.

The crack widened. Orange light flickered across their faces.

Twila continued: "You know how you're always talking about the natural world and ecosesmics?"

"Ecosystems," said Levi absently.

"Right," said Twila. "How the world has a way of balancing out?"

The howling was very near. Lockers rattled.

The orange streak spread down the length of the ovoid. Heat filled the hall.

"I think this is what it was meant for," said Twila.

"We do not have time!" hissed Willow. "The storm will have us!"

"Trust me," said Twila. She hugged the ovoid closer, her eyes squeezed shut, wincing and watering from the heat.

There was a blast of cold air from the opposite end of the hall. Something great and powerful and furious thundered toward them. Icy claws screeched across lockers.

"It has found us!" moaned Willow.

"Trust me!" Twila said.

Levi shut his eyes and put both hands on the ovoid.

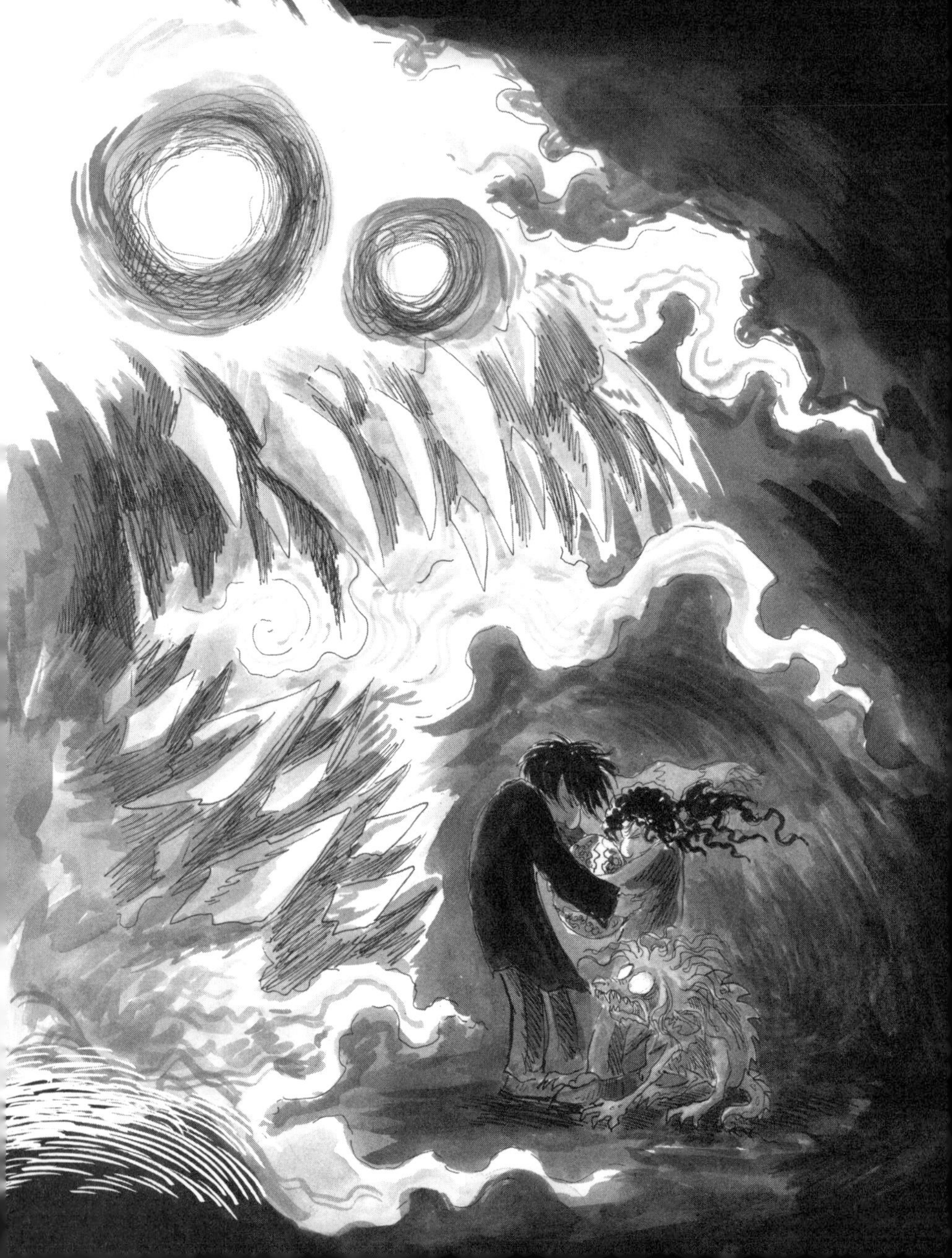

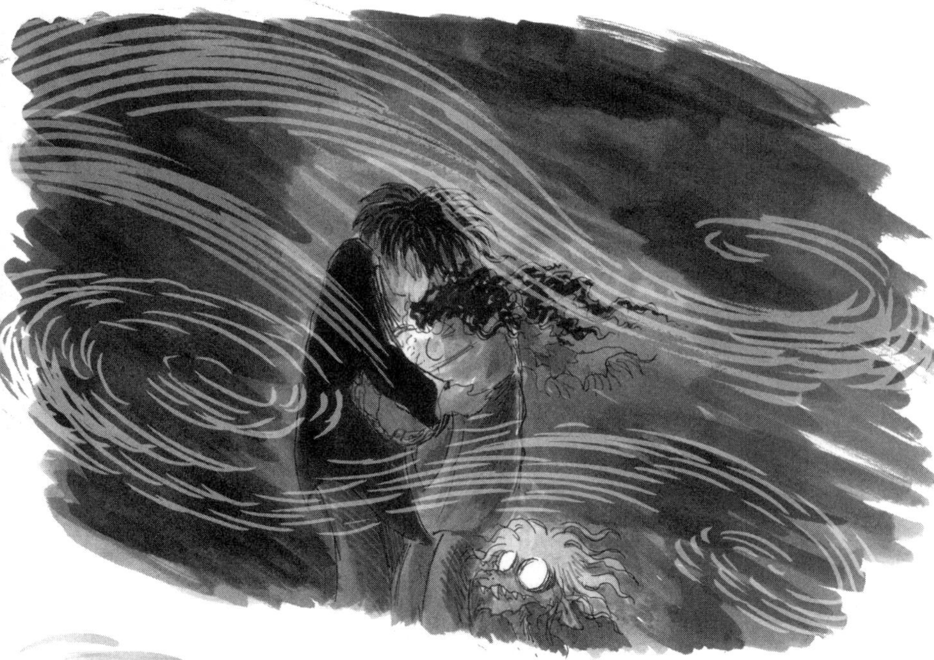

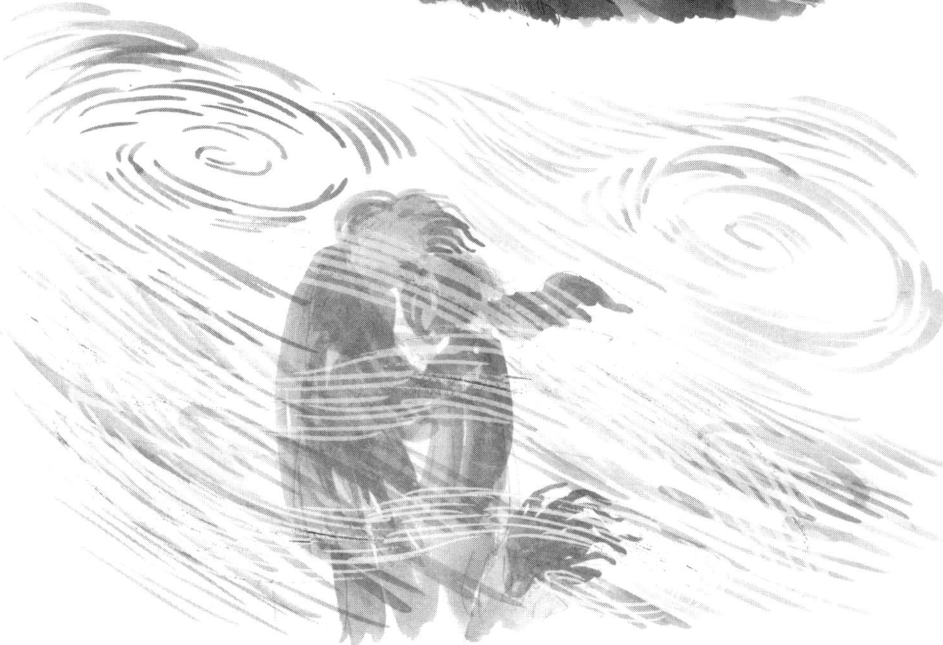

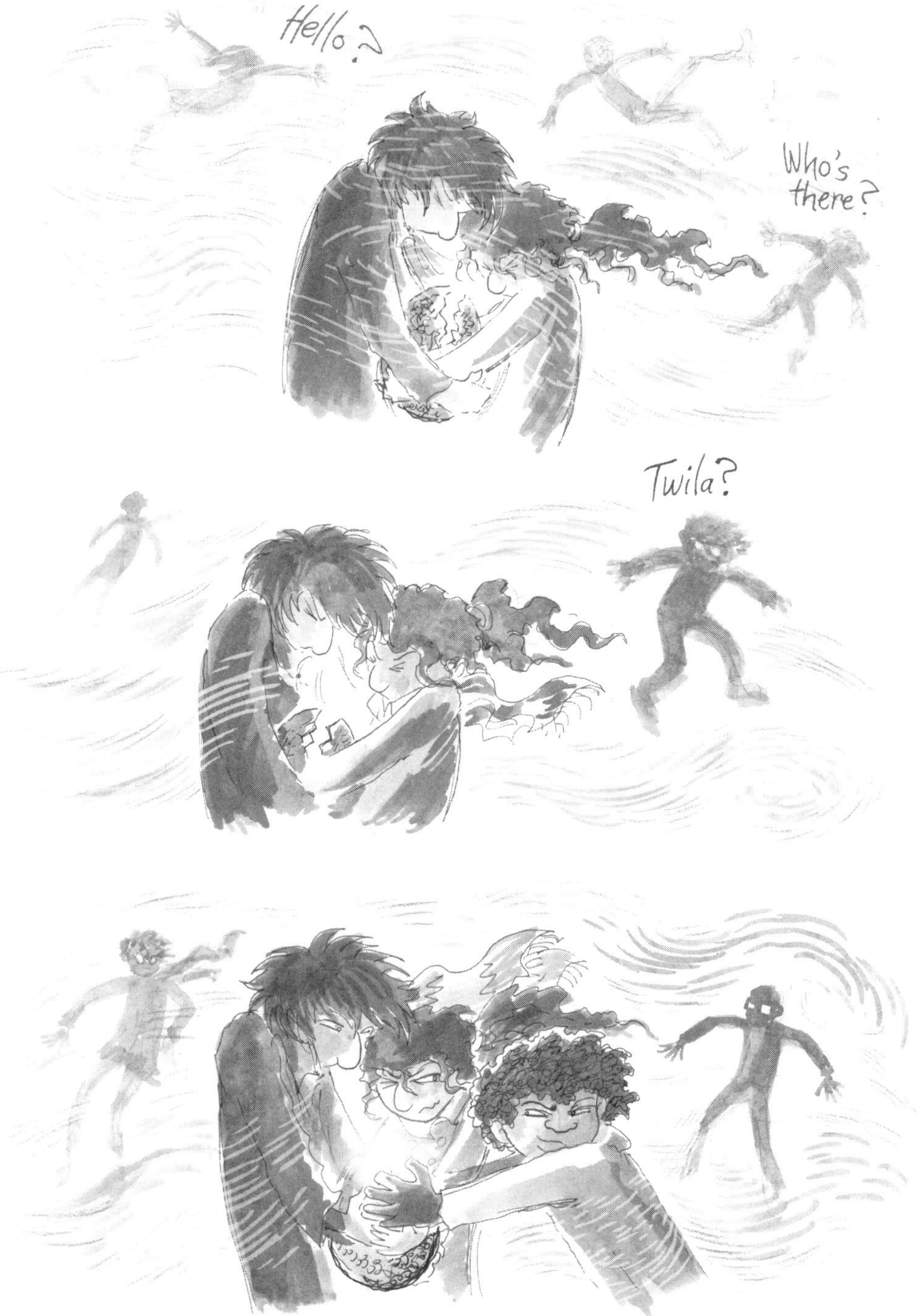
Hello?
Who's there?
Twila?

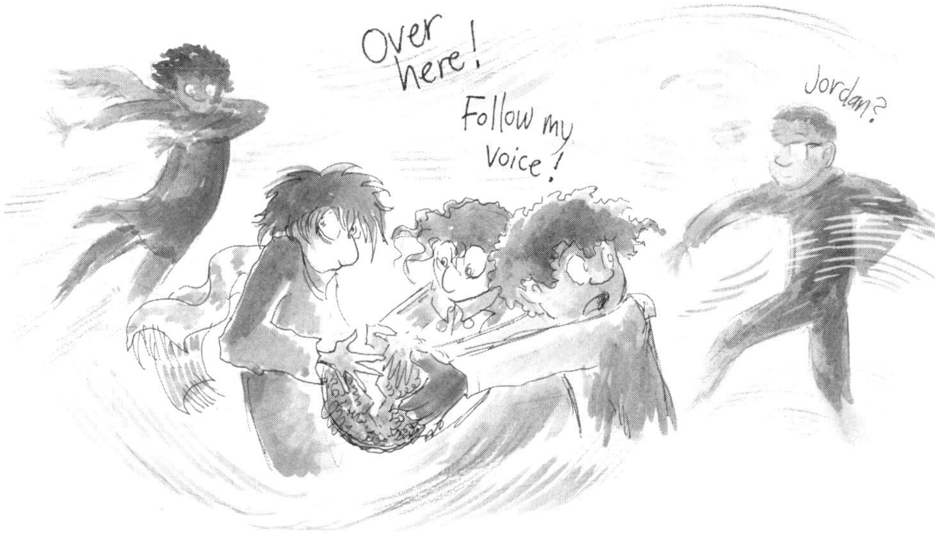
Over here!
Follow my voice!
Jordan?

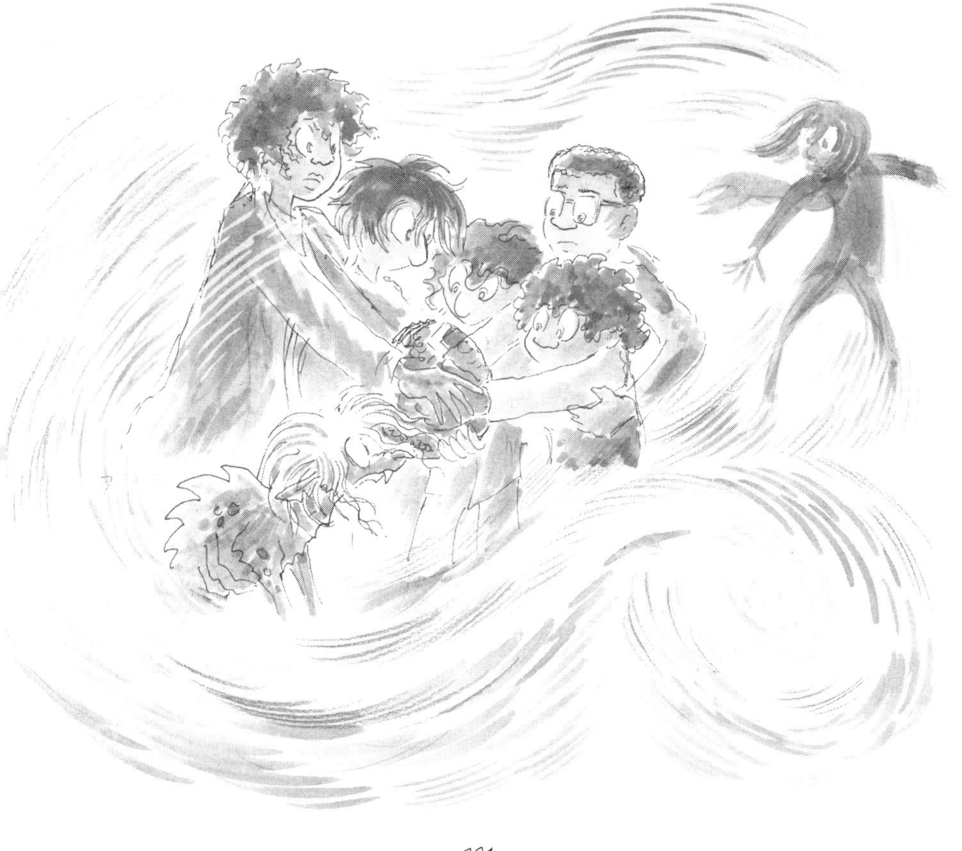

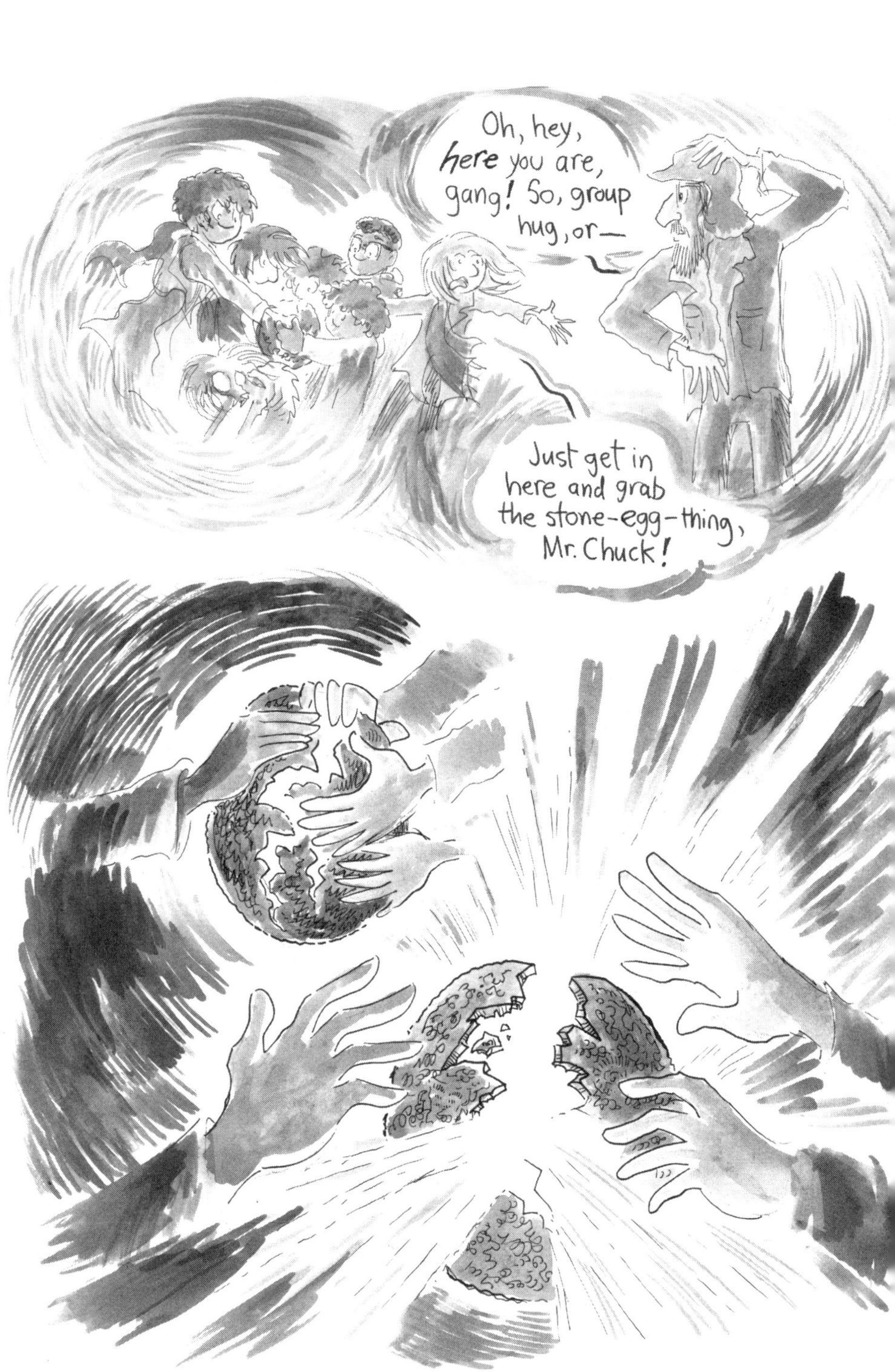
Oh, hey, here you are, gang! So, group hug, or—
Just get in here and grab the stone-egg-thing, Mr. Chuck!

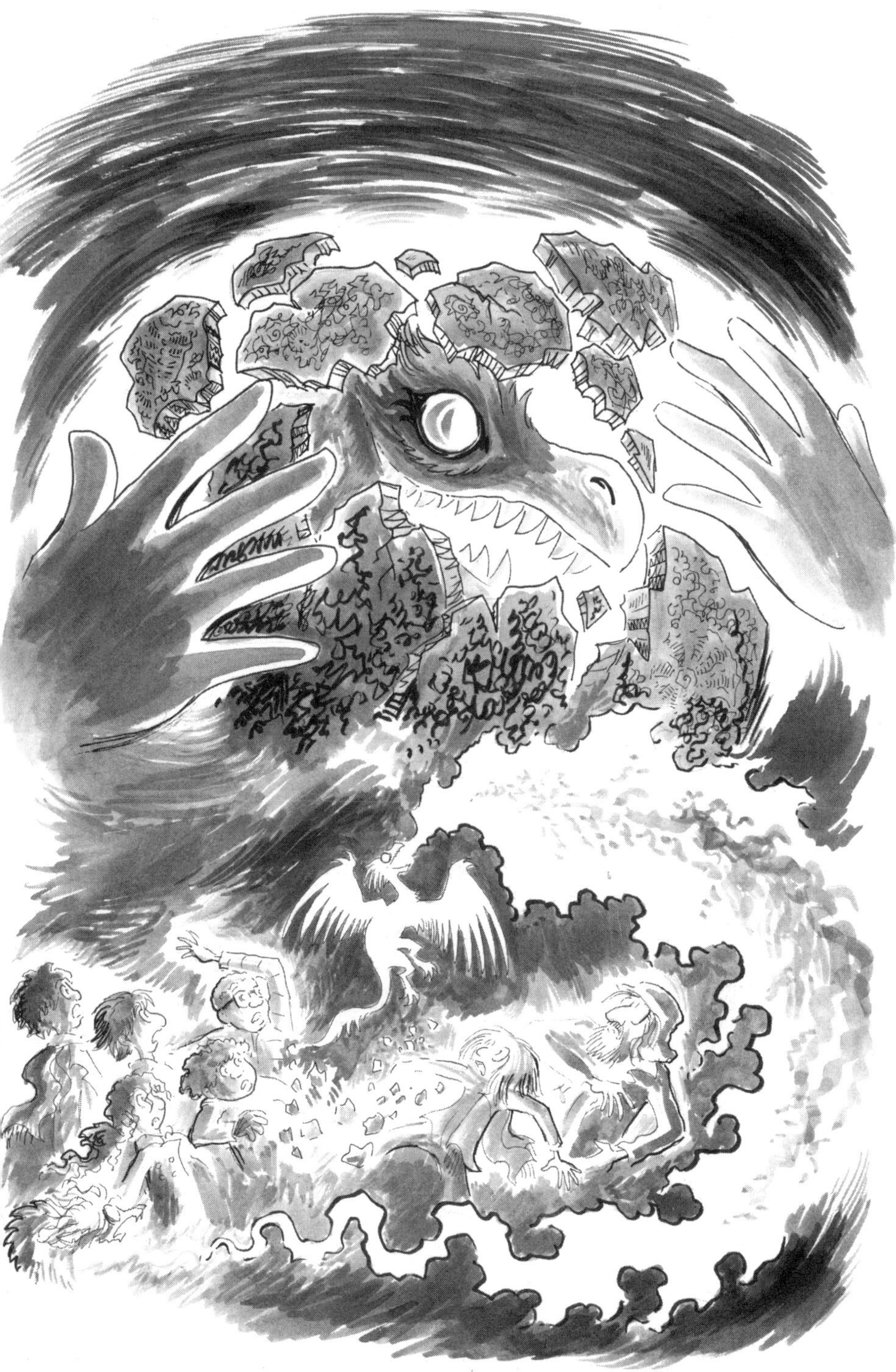

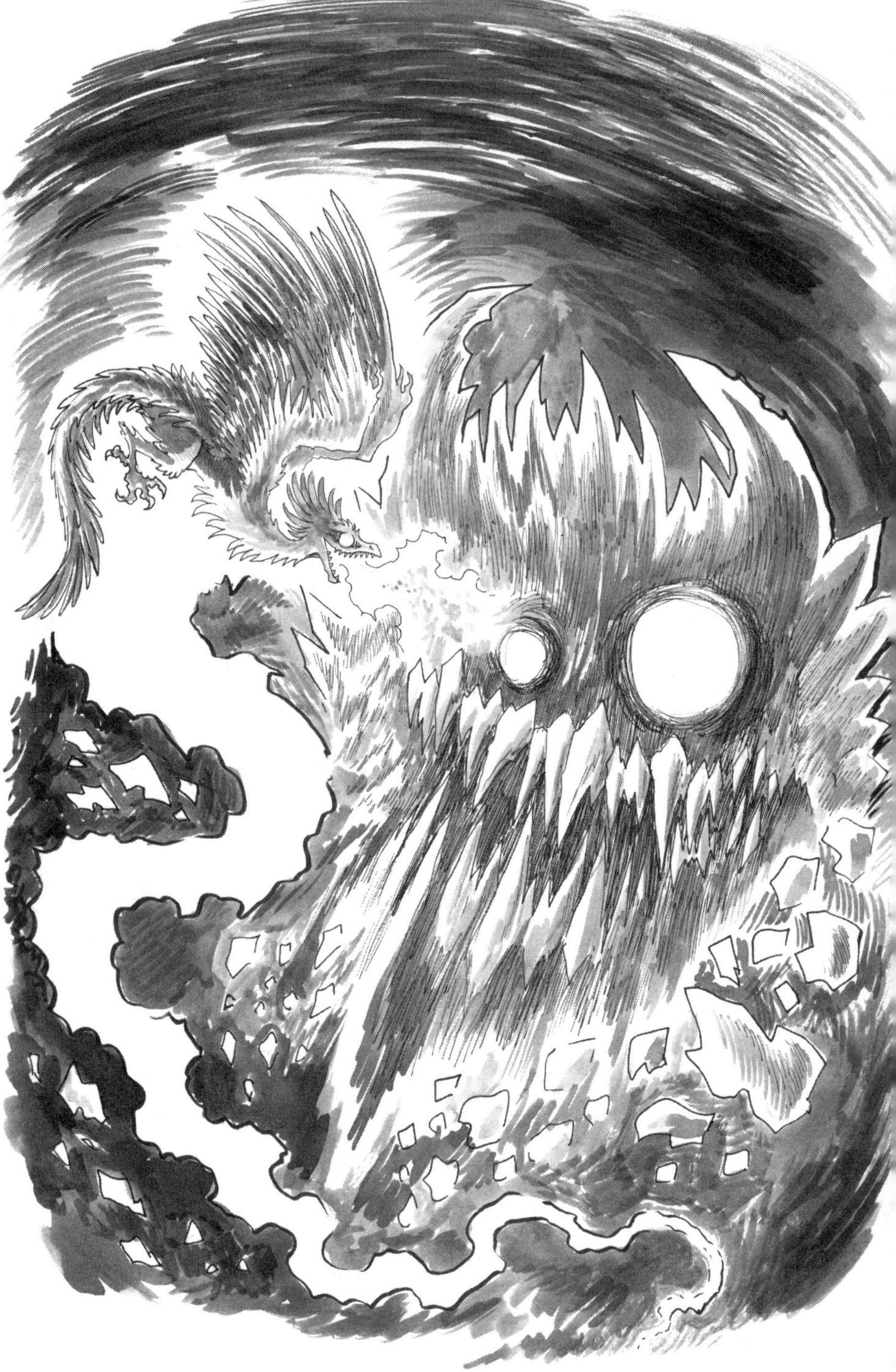

DEO RECOVERED FROM SCHOOL SECURITY CAME
BATTERY OPERATED)

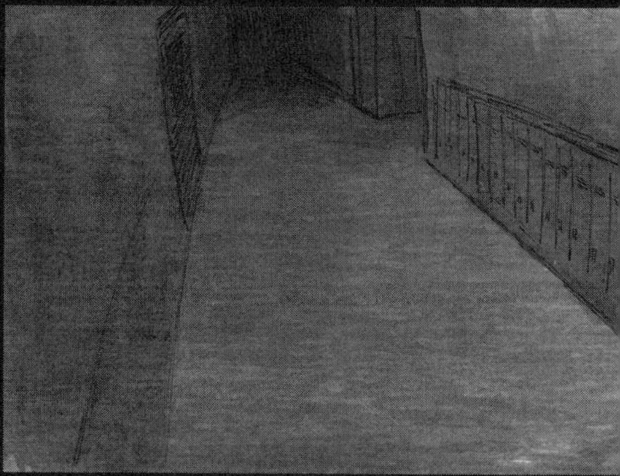

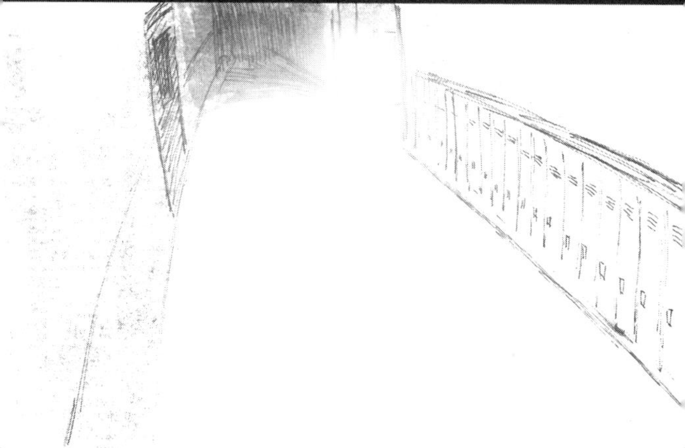

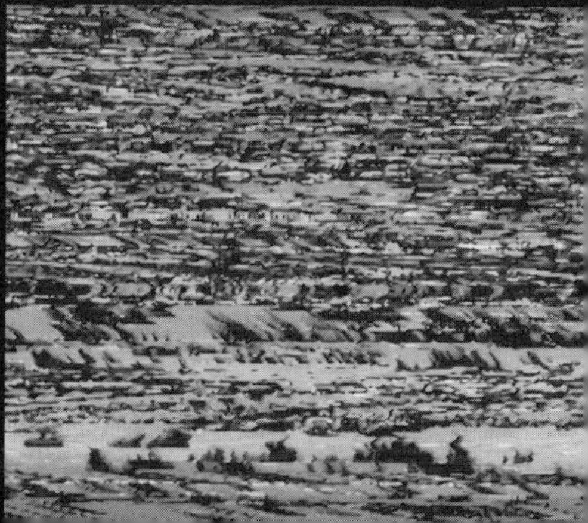

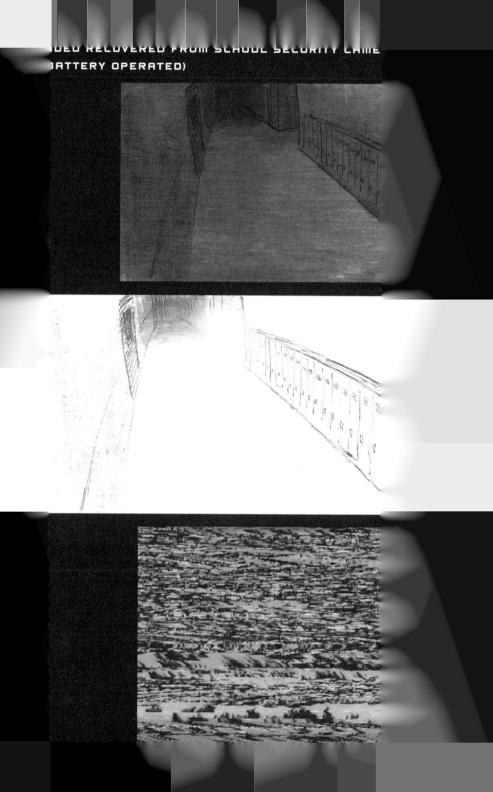

HOOL EXTERIOR PHOTOS (ANONYMOUS MOTION
PTURE CAMERA)

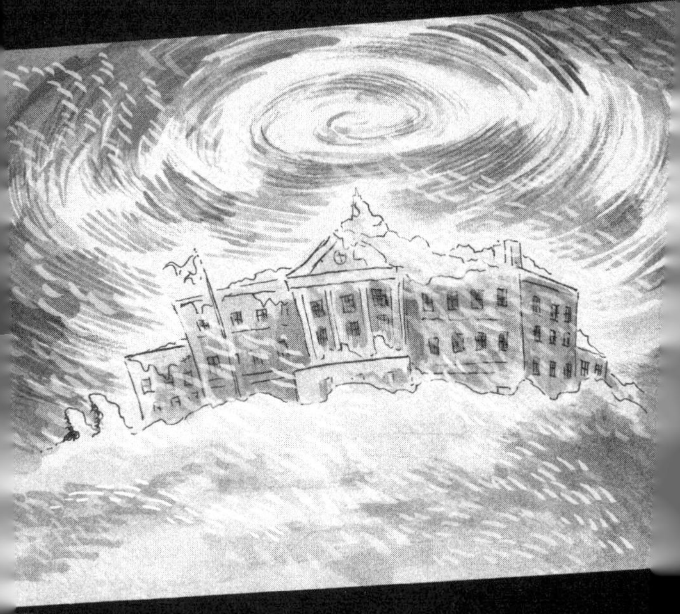

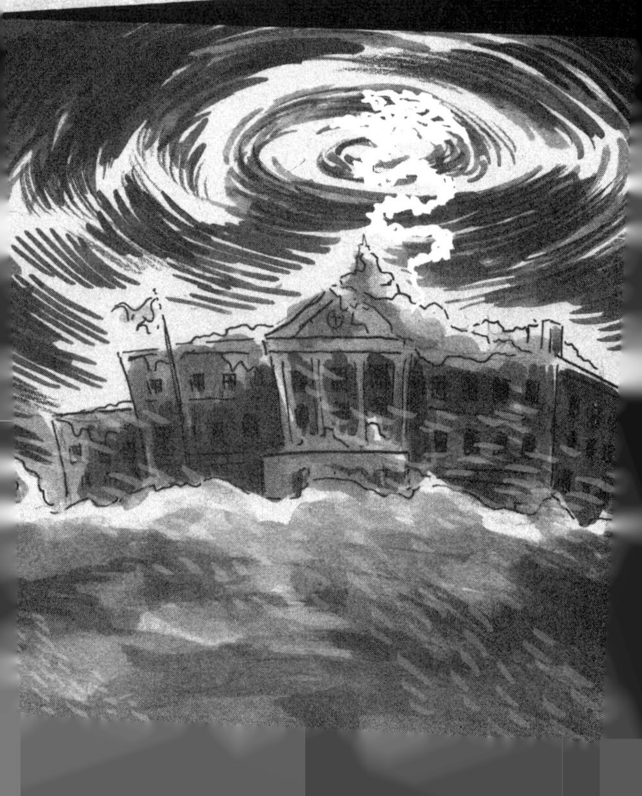

Chapter 41

Margalo's Journal of Strange Creatures Entry #42

There are many strange creatures still hiding in the forgotten corners of the world . . . Spittlers and cuttlegorgs, heckbenders and bogglemyres and gigundopods.

But one legend that has always eluded me is the dragon.

Just what is a dragon? Though an unproven genus, cultures around the world seem to agree on several features: serpentine bodies, wings, claws/talons, scales/feathers.

But many creatures, both past and present, meet this feature checklist: Archaeopteryx from the late Jurassic, pteranodons from the Cretaceous, terror birds from the Cenozoic Era, living harpy eagles, gliding lizards . . . Even animals from your own neighborhood: the crest and claws of the pileated woodpecker or serpentine neck and scaly legs of the mallard duck may seem dragon-like.

But here's the bit that separates the dragons of myth from the dragons of reality: Dragons, according to countless stories, can breathe fire.

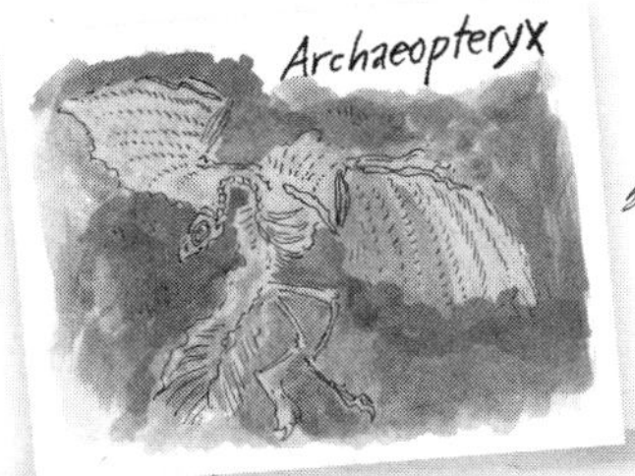
Archaeopteryx

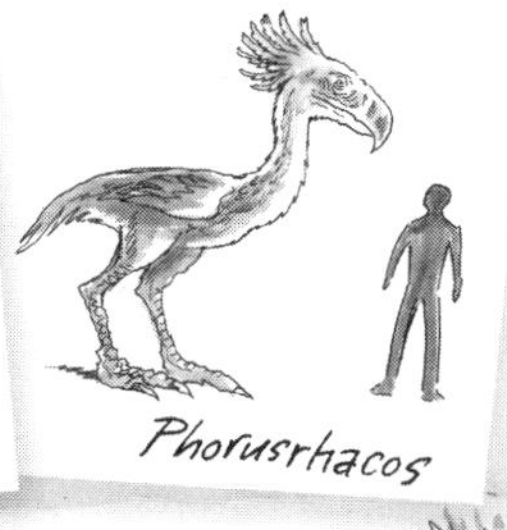
Phorusrhacos

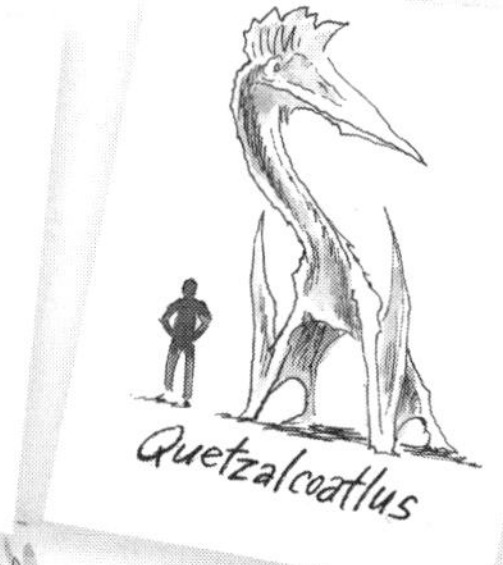
Quetzalcoatlus

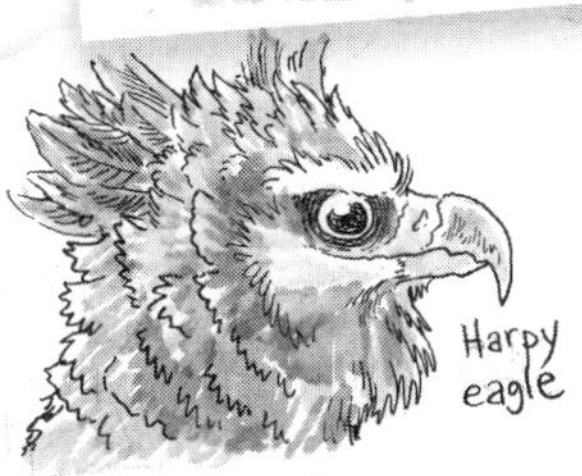
Harpy eagle

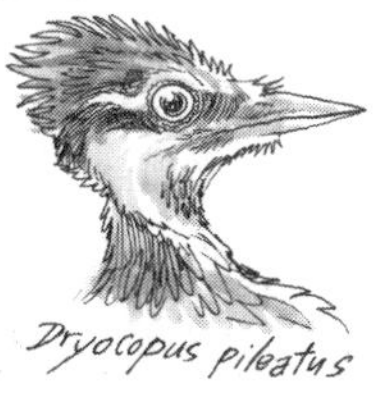
Dryocopus pileatus

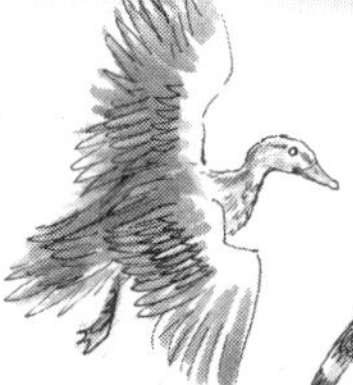

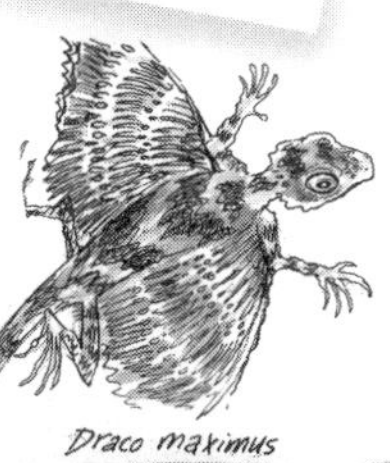
Draco maximus

Now, many known species are able to produce chemical reactions that give off dazzling light (bioluminescence): deep sea fish and invertebrates, fireflies, glowworms . . .

But nothing close to the fire-breathing dragons of ancient lore.

As a scientist, I have no reason to believe such a feat is possible. It's far more logical to assume that fire-breathing dragon tales have been embellished over time.

But still.

I wonder about that petrified egg left to me by Aunt Olga and Uncle Emmet. How it seems to give off its own heat, even when the incubation lights are out.

I wonder.

And I worry.

Me with
Aunt Olga and Uncle Emmet

Oct. 12

Chapter 42

Willow was the first to wake. She struggled upright, shivered miserably, and crept to the nearest body. She nipped and tugged at its coat. "Wake, you lazy slubbermuffin!"

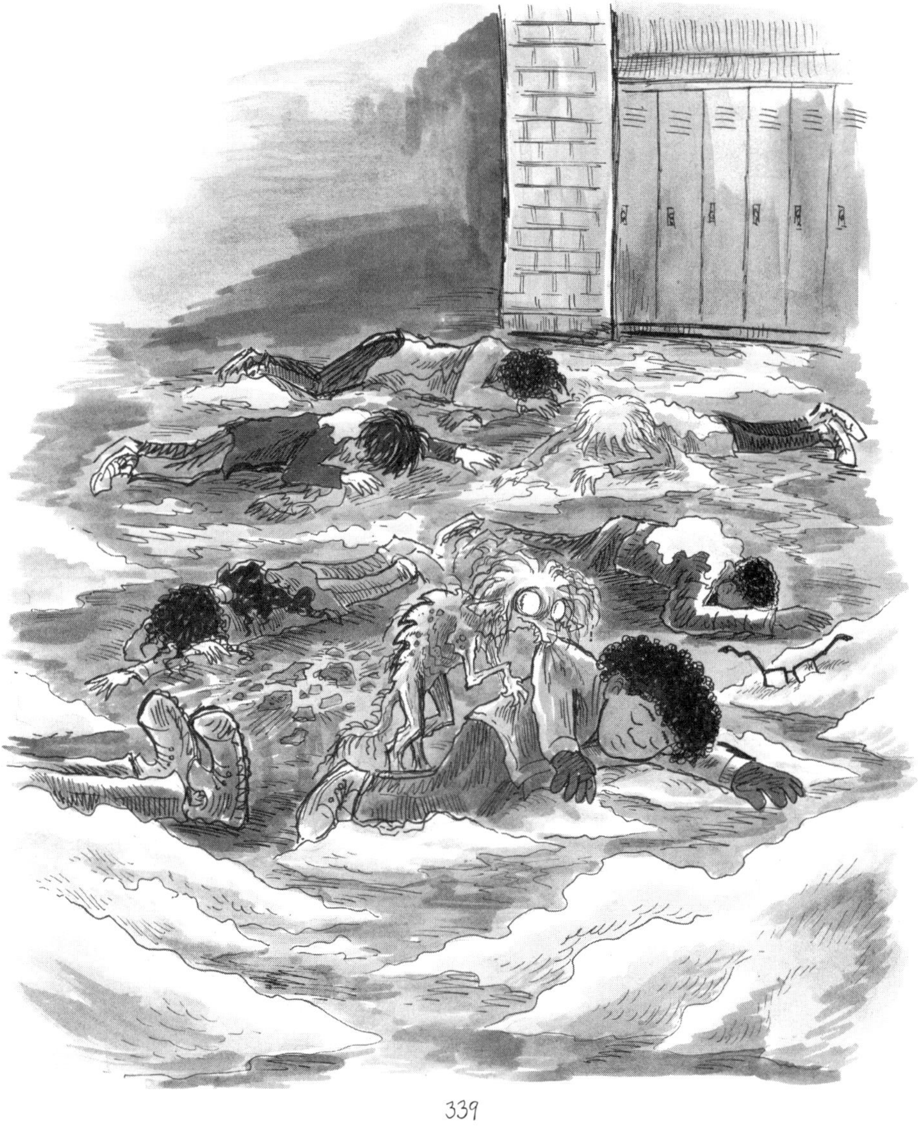

Jordan's eyes fluttered open. He patted his soaking clothes. "Uh-oh. Did I have an accident?" Then the memories came flooding back, and he sat bolt upright.

"Guys!" he said. He crawled across the slushy hall floor until he reached Twila's unconscious body. "Twila! Please be okay!"

Twila groaned, curled into a tight ball, and shivered.

Willow was now tugging at Levi's pant leg. "Sleep later, you goofooligans!"

"Has anyone seen my glasses?" mumbled Donte.

Jordan scanned the hall until he saw something gleaming in a slush puddle. He scooped them up, wiped the melted snow from the lenses, and rushed to Donte. "You, uh, probably need a new pair."

Donte put the glasses on, blinked, and hugged Jordan close.

"Ow! You're squishing me!" said Jordan, but he didn't fight back.

The others were now awake and wiping cold slush from their clothes.

"Is everyone all right?" asked Ms. Padilla. Her finger traced through the air, bouncing from head to head, taking attendance.

"Hey!" cried Kat. "The power's back!"

The others stared dumbfoundedly at the warmly lit halls.

"Huh! Seems the backup generator finally kicked in," said Mr. Chuck.

Donte brushed sludge from his pants. "What's all this?"

"Snow monster guts," said Jordan.

"What's left of the Boojum King," said Kat.

Willow was sniffing at a pile of smoking stone fragments near Twila. Levi knelt and prodded the remains. "That round thing you got from Margalo's," he said. "What was that?"

"Some sort of alien grenade?" asked Donte.

Twila shook her head. "I think . . ." She stopped and looked up. The others followed her gaze.

There was a gaping hole in the school's ceiling. The tile and wire surrounding the hole were blackened, as if a nuclear warhead had blasted through the roof.

"Whoa," said Ms. Padilla. She pointed up at the exposed sky. "At least the storm is over." The sky was still dark, but the clouds seemed calm and pale enough to suggest that dawn was on the horizon.

Mr. Chuck whistled softly. "Mr. Huff is going to have conniptions when he sees that hole." He looked around at the assorted debris. "Guess we know how I'll be spending my spring break."

Twila was still staring at the hole in the roof. "Did *anyone* see what came out of Margalo's stone?"

"It was an explosion!" said Donte.

"I saw a wave of white fire," said Ms. Padilla.

"There was something else," said Kat. She stopped suddenly and looked about frantically. "My phone! Mr. Chuck, where's my phone?"

Mr. Chuck glanced down at his empty hands. "Er, I must've dropped it."

Kat fell to her knees and started digging through the melted snow. "We gotta find it! We had it all recorded!"

"Not the fireball," said Mr. Chuck. "The battery died just before the grand finale."

Kat moaned and continued her search. "But we got everything else! The snow goons, the art creatures, the test monsters, the big ice Boojum-thing! C'mon! Help me find it!"

"Wait!" Ms. Padilla said. She cocked her head.

Muffled whimpers and groans drifted down the hall.

"The others in the cafeteria!"

They started down the hall, toward the lunchroom.

"Hold on!" said Jordan. "Where's Willow?"

"That little spiky lizard-fox?" asked Mr. Chuck.

Donte shrugged. "What kind of dog was that anyway?"

"Funny. It almost seemed like it could *talk*."

They scanned the hall. Willow was nowhere in sight.

Levi patted Jordan's shoulder. "She does that a lot. Don't take it personally."

They reached the cafeteria and surveyed the scene. Children were sprawled across the floor, groaning and rubbing their eyes.

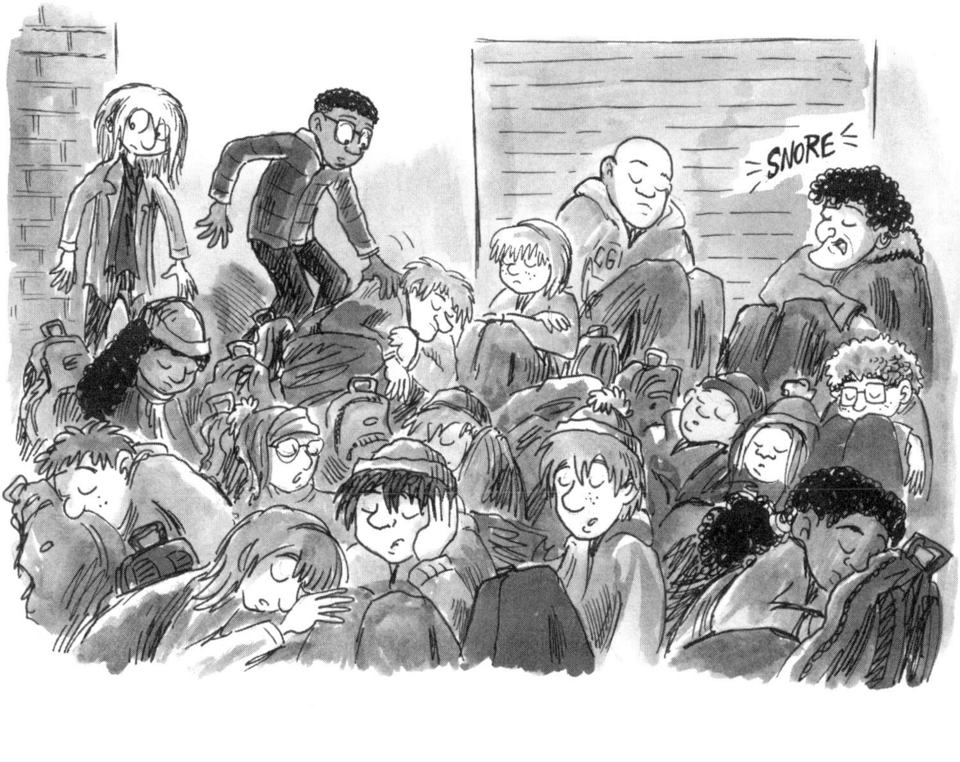
SNORE
CGI

Donte knelt and shook Robbie Munn.

"No, Mom, please. I don't wanna go to school today," mumbled Robbie.

Donte turned to Kat. "I think they're gonna be fine."

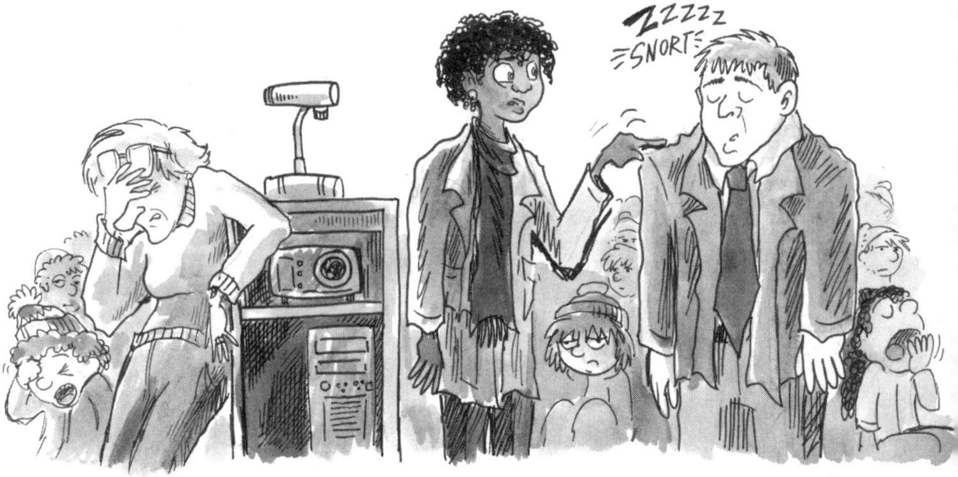
ZZZZZ
SNORT

"Oh dear!" said Mrs. Pine. She sat up and yawned. "I must've nodded off during the movie. How embarrassing!"

"Um, Mr. Huff?" said Ms. Padilla.

Mr. Huff snored.

"Mr. Huff, wake up." She gave him a nudge.

Mr. Huff's eyes fluttered open. He looked around blearily, wiped drool from his chin, and cleared his throat. "Oh, uh, hello, Tracey. What's happened?"

Ms. Padilla took a deep breath. "I don't know where to begin."

KRAZY KAT PICTURES PRESENTS:

The LOST CORNERS of COWSLIP GROVE

DIRECTED BY
Donte Orman

CRYPTID/WILDLIFE CONSULTANT... Levi Galante
ARTHROPOD EXPERTISE ... Jordan 'Prof. Bug-Man' Orman

FEATURING... Twila Galante
Mr. Charles Chuck

ACADEMIC ADVISOR ... Ms. Padilla
SPECIAL THANKS TO MARGALO'S
HOME FOR UNLOVED CREATURES

KAT PICTURES P

DIRECTED BY
Donte Orman

CRYPTID/WILDLIFE CONSULTANT
ARTHROPOD EXPERTISE ... Jordan   Orman

FEATURING... Twila Galante
Mr. Charles Chuck

ACADEMIC ADVISOR ... Ms. Padilla
SPECIAL THANKS TO MARGALO'S
HOME FOR UNLOVED CREA

Can't we add the credits in post, Donte?

I prefer linear filming. Helps me visualize.

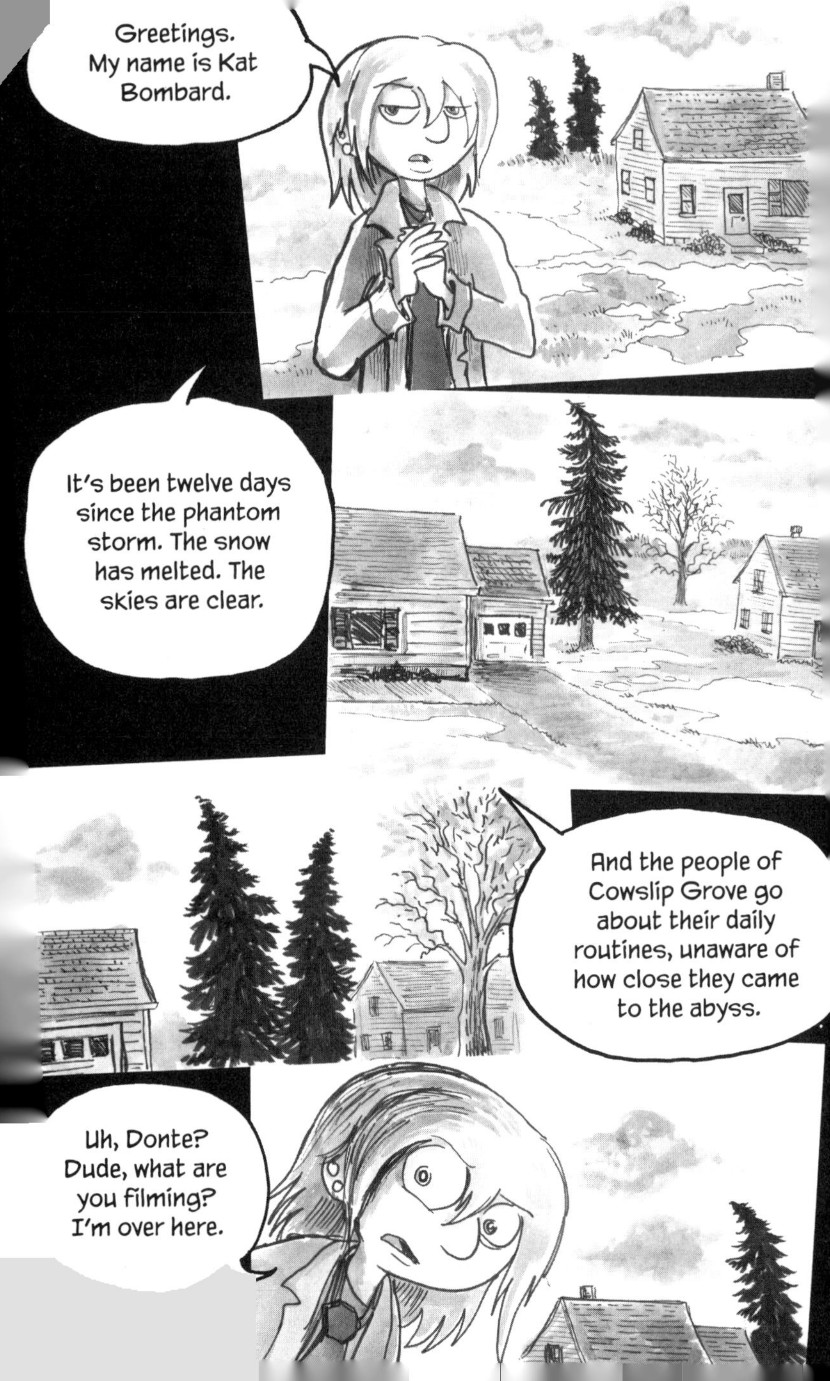
Greetings. My name is Kat Bombard.
It's been twelve days since the phantom storm. The snow has melted. The skies are clear.
And the people of Cowslip Grove go about their daily routines, unaware of how close they came to the abyss.
Uh, Donte? Dude, what are you filming? I'm over here.

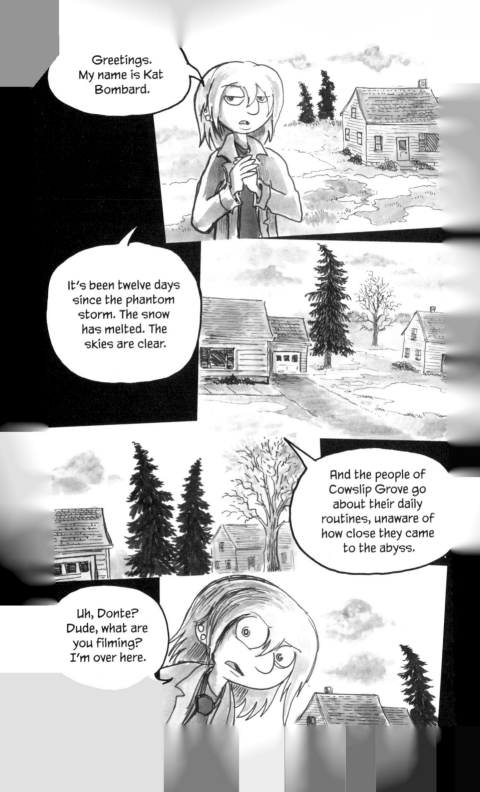

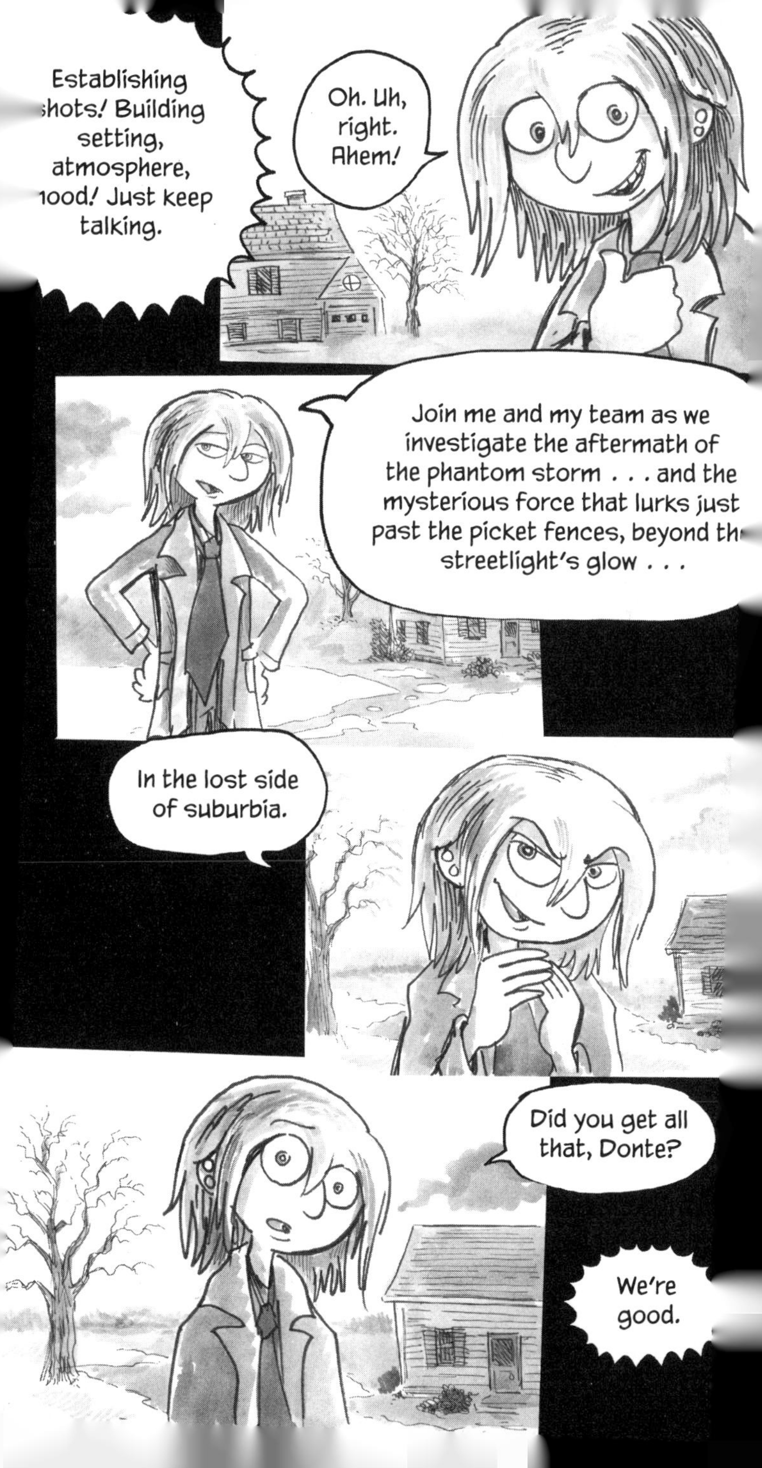
Establishing shots! Building setting, atmosphere, mood! Just keep talking.
Oh. Uh, right. Ahem!
Join me and my team as we investigate the aftermath of the phantom storm . . . and the mysterious force that lurks just past the picket fences, beyond the streetlight's glow . . .
In the lost side of suburbia.
Did you get all that, Donte?
We're good.

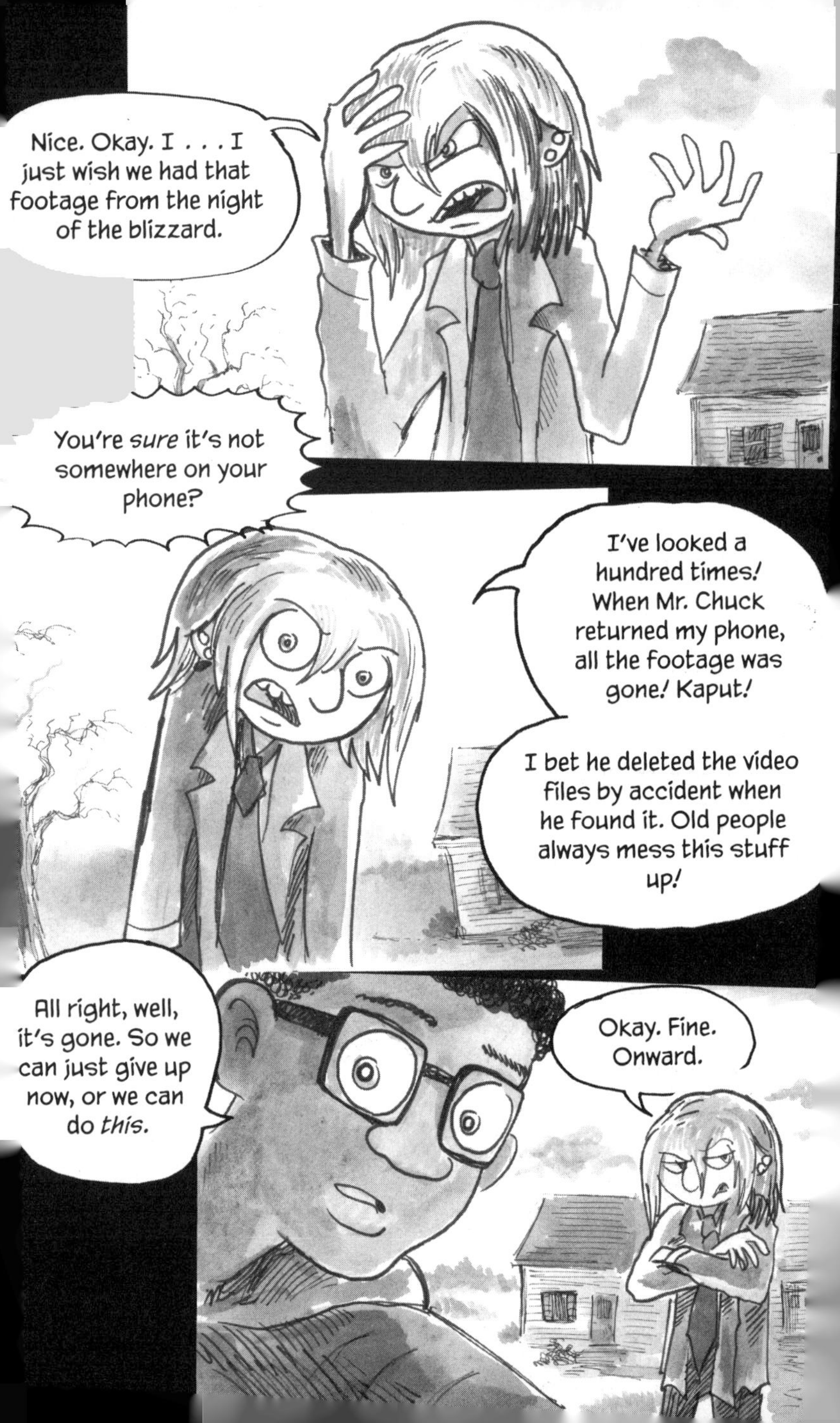

Nice. Okay. I . . . I just wish we had that footage from the night of the blizzard.
You're *sure* it's not somewhere on your phone?
I've looked a hundred times! When Mr. Chuck returned my phone, all the footage was gone! Kaput!
I bet he deleted the video files by accident when he found it. Old people always mess this stuff up!
All right, well, it's gone. So we can just give up now, or we can do *this*.
Okay. Fine. Onward.

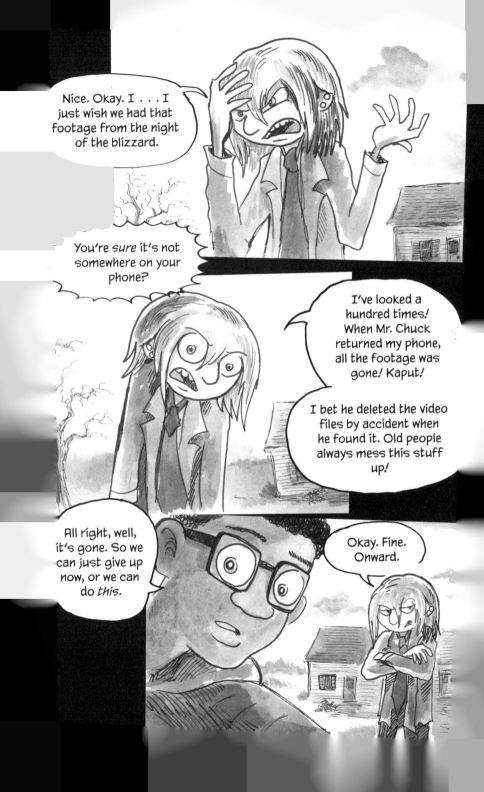

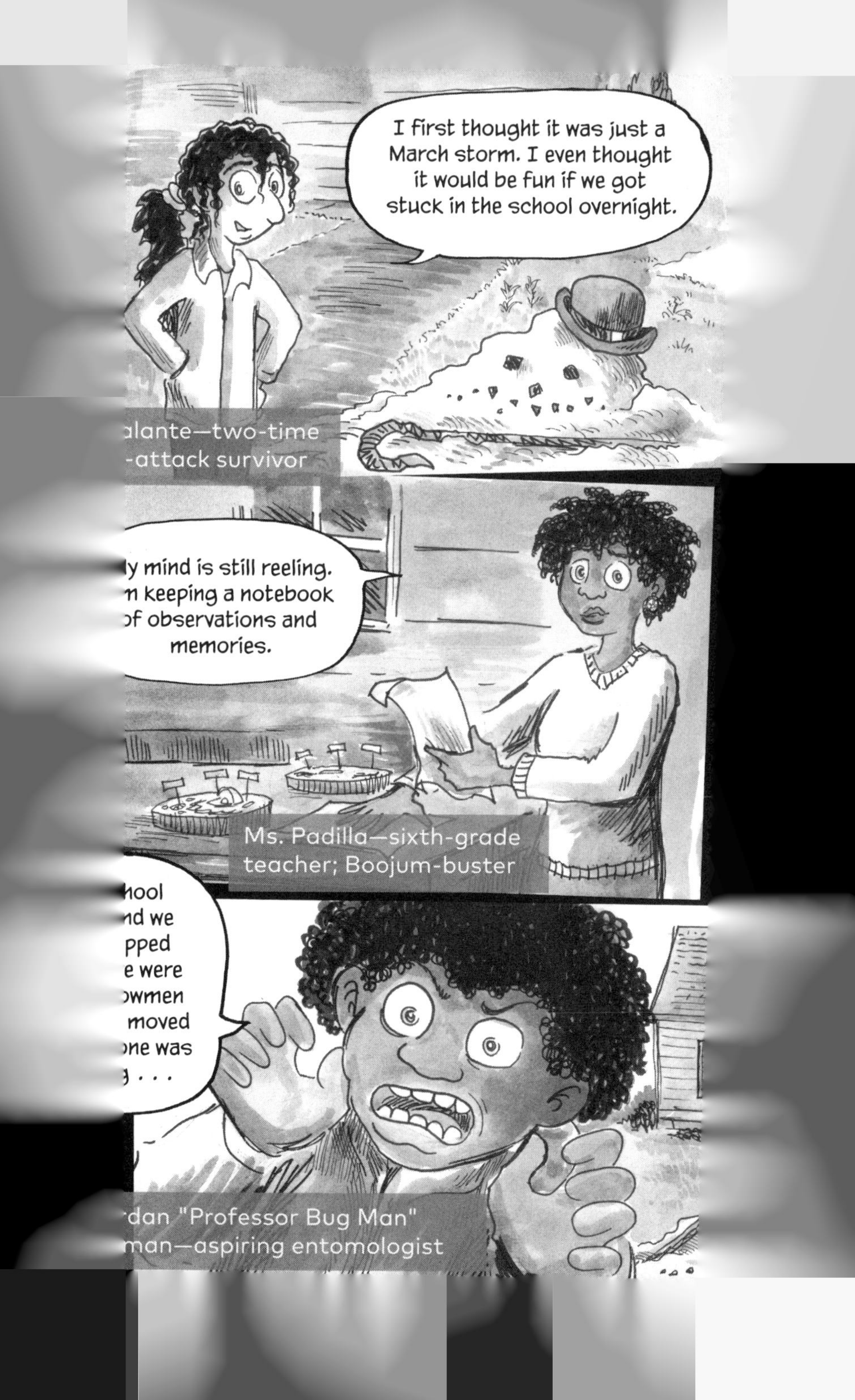
I first thought it was just a March storm. I even thought it would be fun if we got stuck in the school overnight.
alante—two-time
-attack survivor
ly mind is still reeling.
n keeping a notebook
of observations and
memories.
Ms. Padilla—sixth-grade teacher; Boojum-buster
hool
nd we
pped
e were
owmen
moved
one was
rdan "Professor Bug Man"
man—aspiring entomologist

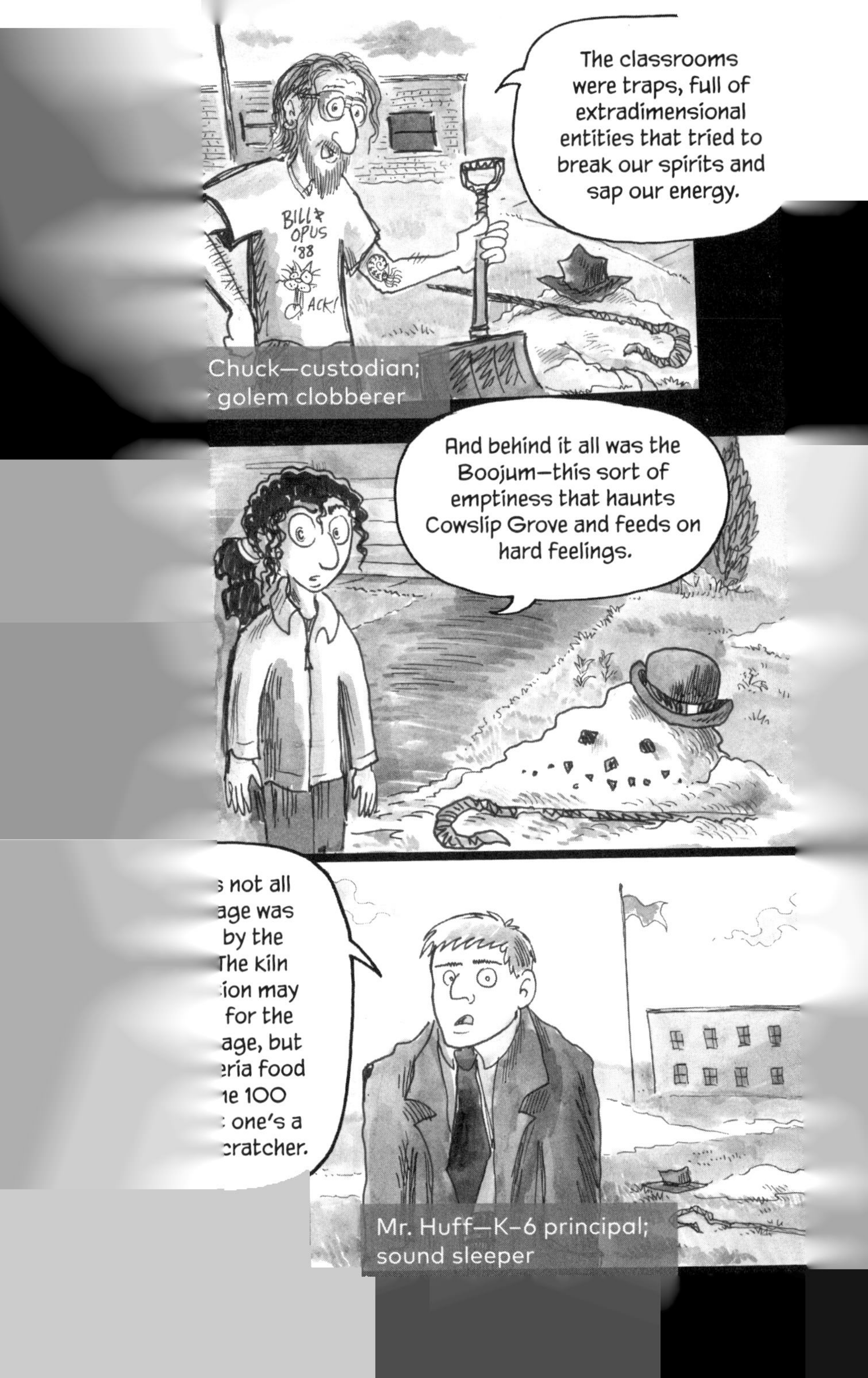

The classrooms were traps, full of extradimensional entities that tried to break our spirits and sap our energy.
BILL & OPUS '88 ACK!
Chuck—custodian; golem clobberer
And behind it all was the Boojum—this sort of emptiness that haunts Cowslip Grove and feeds on hard feelings.
not all age was by the The kiln ion may for the age, but eria food ne 100 one's a cratcher.
Mr. Huff—K–6 principal; sound sleeper

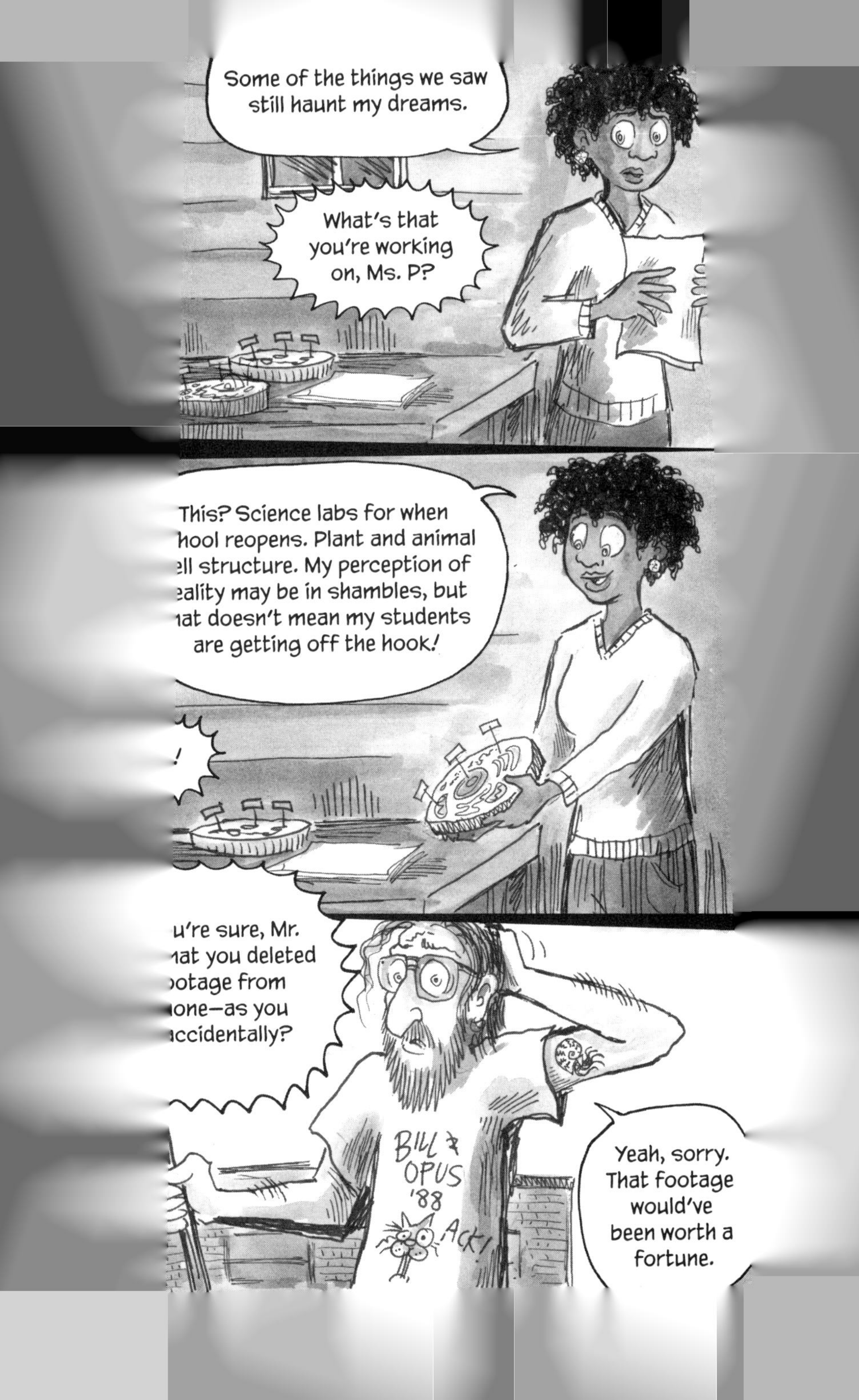
Some of the things we saw still haunt my dreams.
What's that you're working on, Ms. P?
This? Science labs for when hool reopens. Plant and animal ell structure. My perception of eality may be in shambles, but at doesn't mean my students are getting off the hook!
!
u're sure, Mr. at you deleted ootage from one—as you ccidentally?
BILL & OPUS '88
ACK!
Yeah, sorry. That footage would've been worth a fortune.

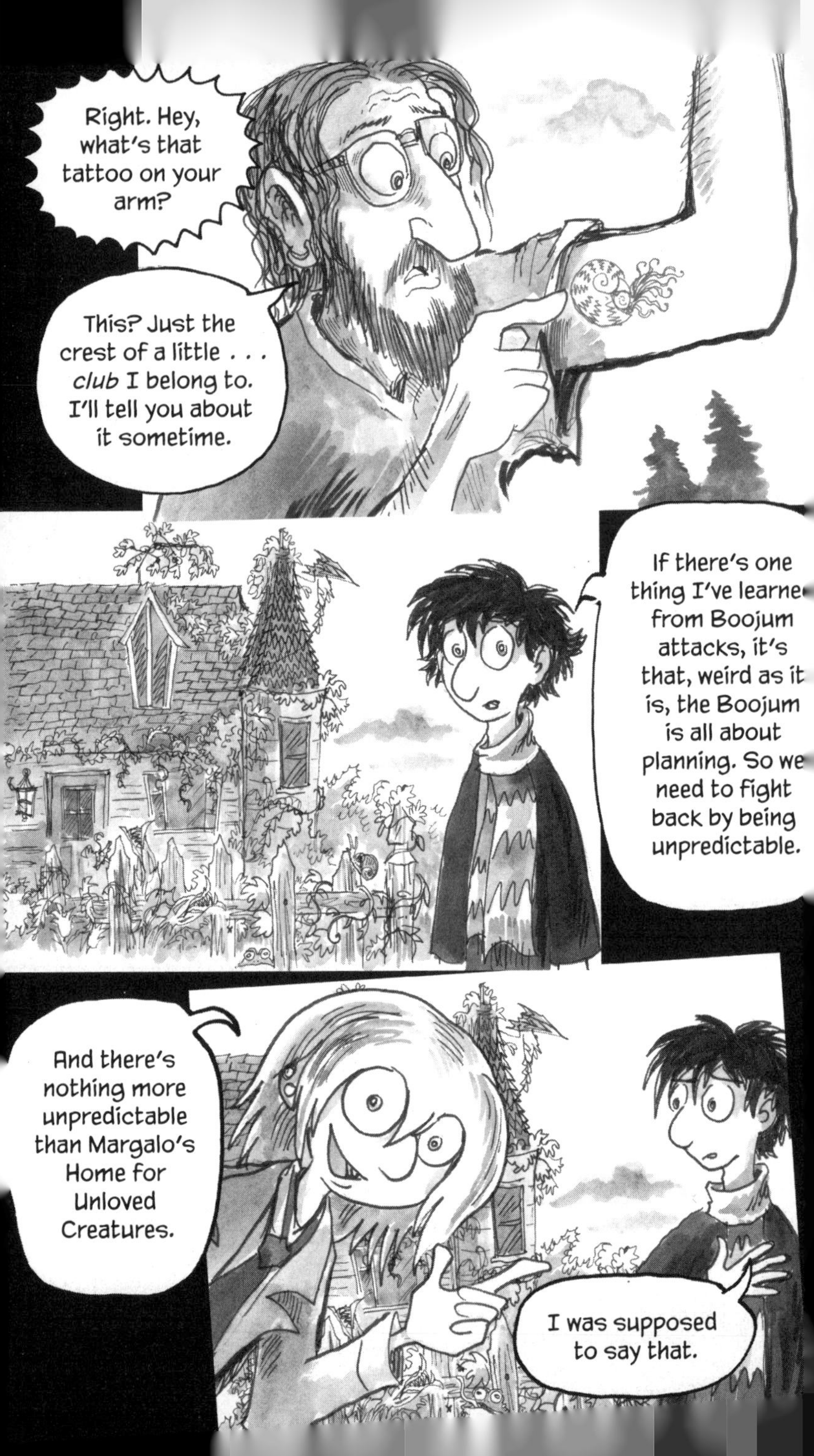

Right. Hey, what's that tattoo on your arm?
This? Just the crest of a little . . . *club* I belong to. I'll tell you about it sometime.
If there's one thing I've learne from Boojum attacks, it's that, weird as it is, the Boojum is all about planning. So we need to fight back by being unpredictable.
And there's nothing more unpredictable than Margalo's Home for Unloved Creatures.
I was supposed to say that.

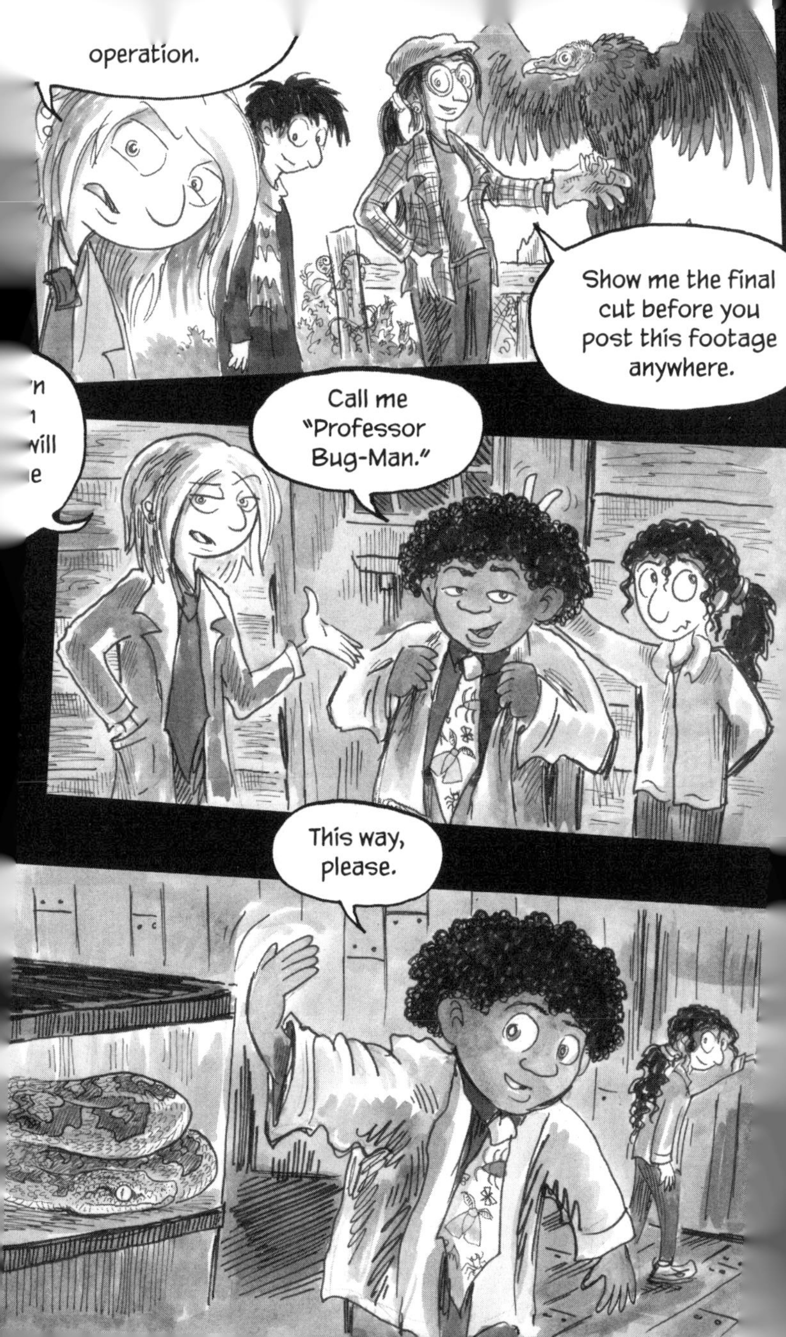
operation.
Show me the final cut before you post this footage anywhere.
Call me "Professor Bug-Man."
This way, please.

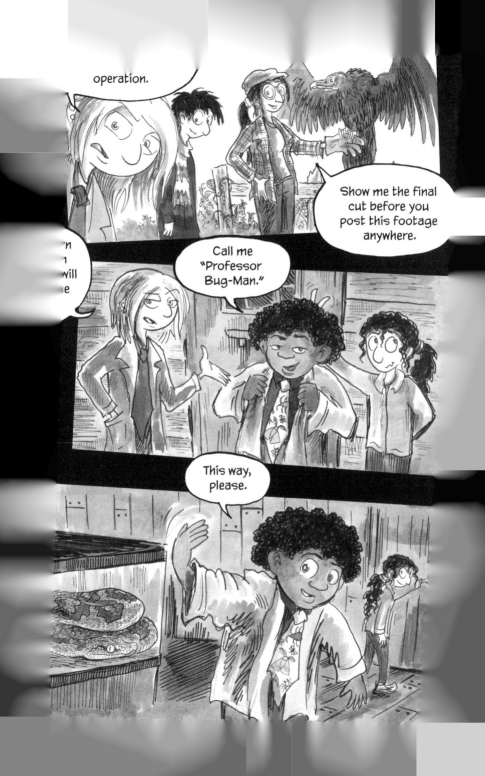

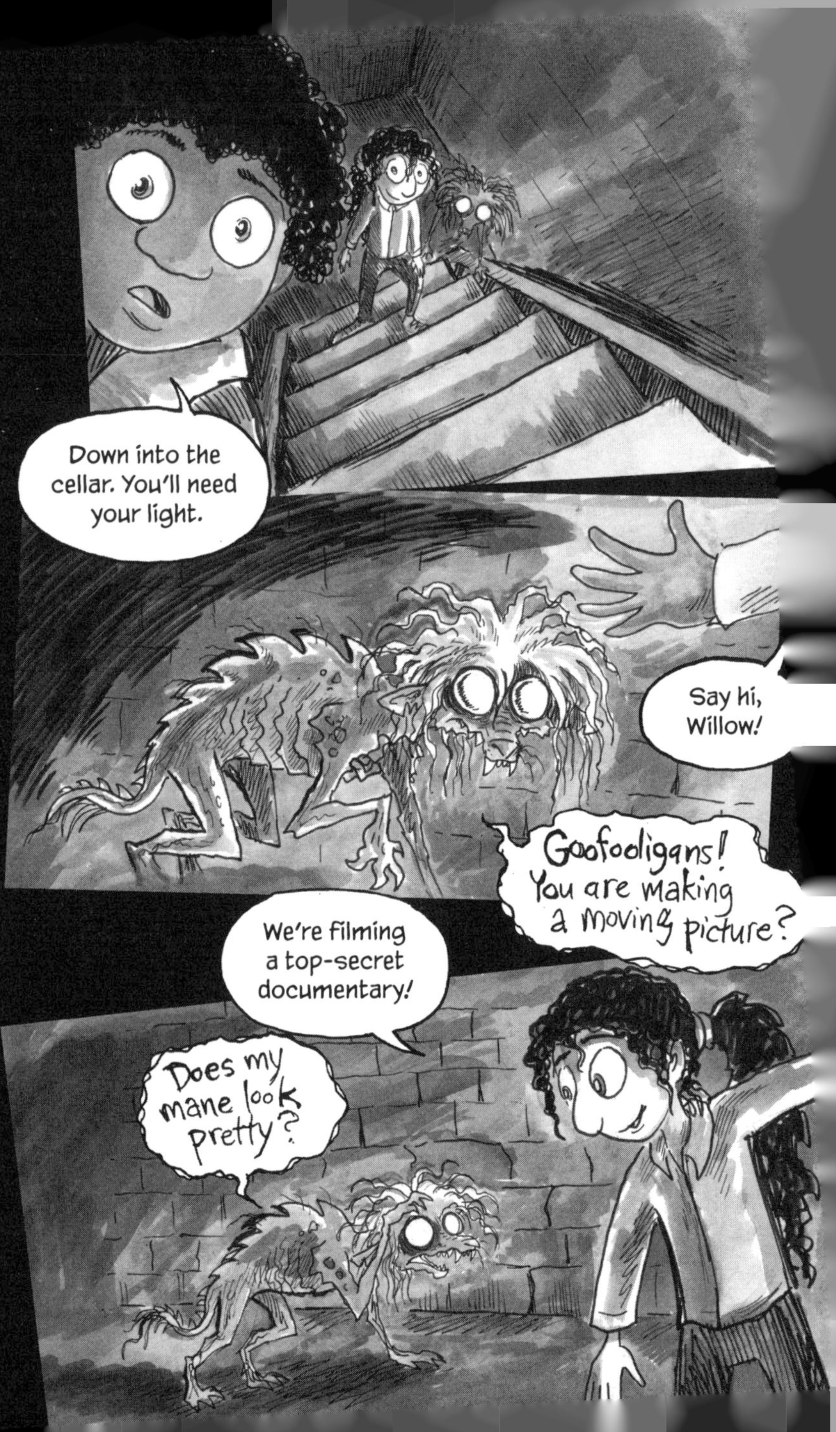
Down into the cellar. You'll need your light.
Say hi, Willow!
Goofooligans! You are making a moving picture?
We're filming a top-secret documentary!
Does my mane look pretty?

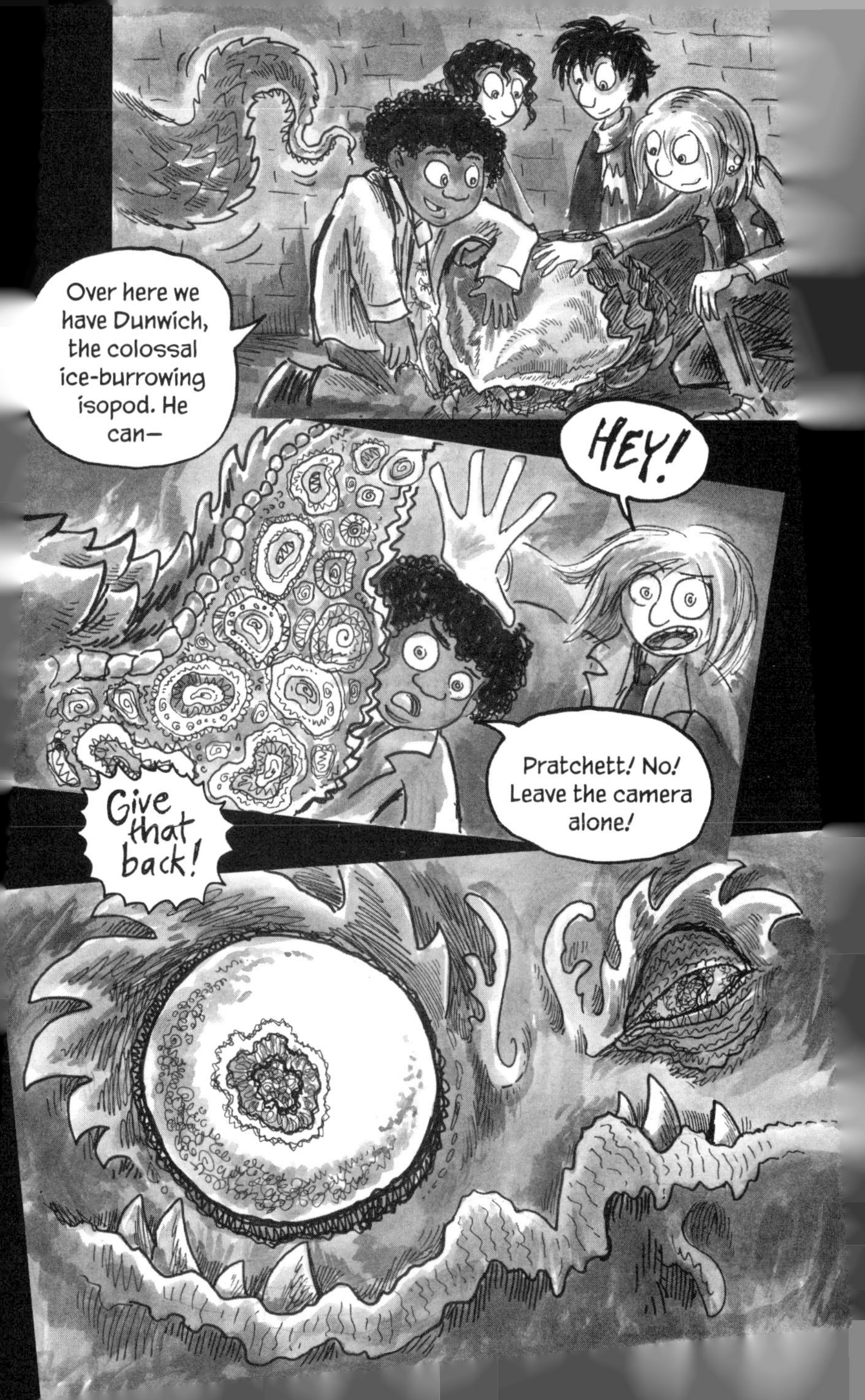
Over here we have Dunwich, the colossal ice-burrowing isopod. He can—
HEY!
Pratchett! No! Leave the camera alone!
Give that back!

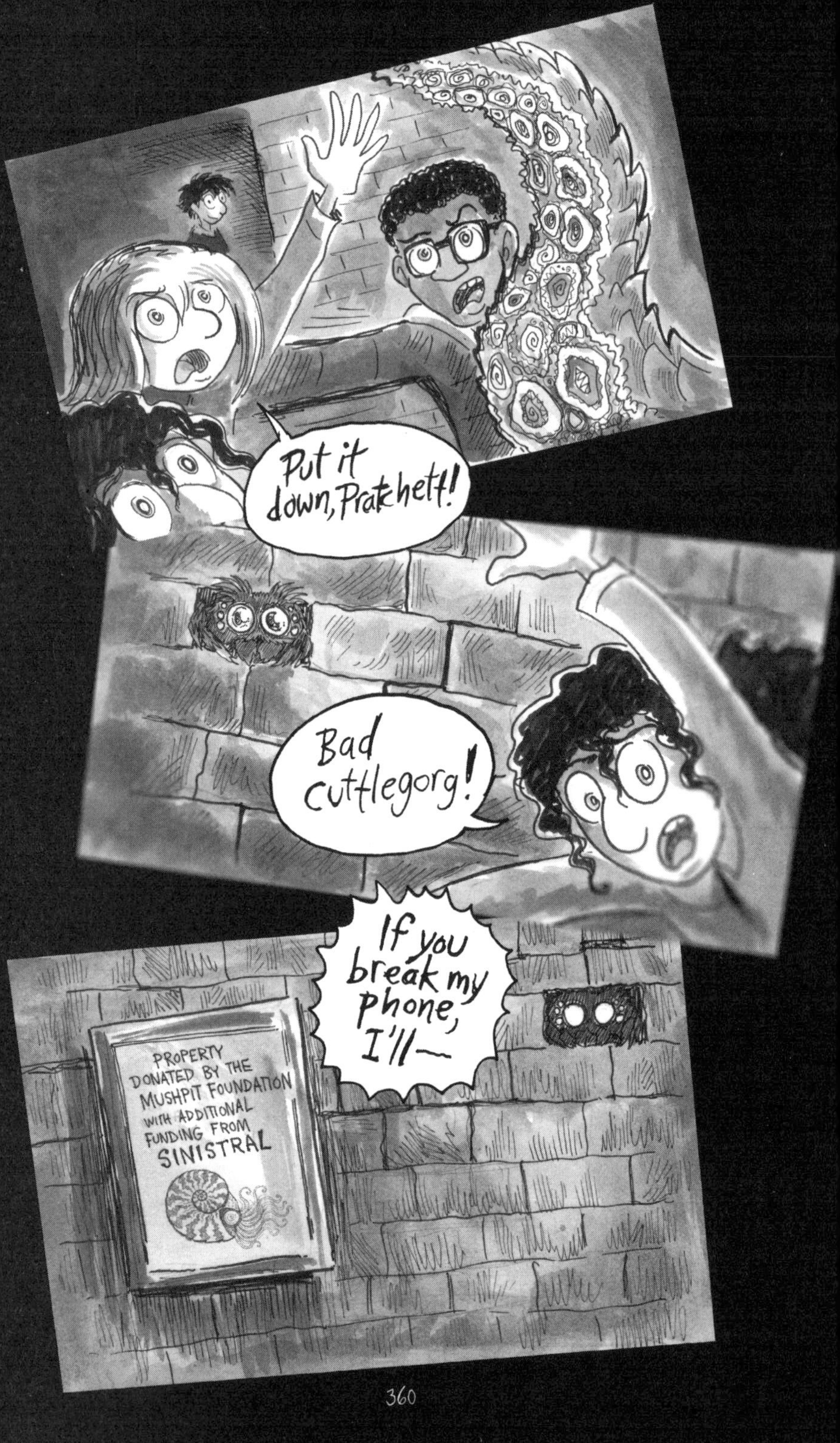
Put it down, Prakhett!
Bad cuttlegorg!
If you break my phone, I'll—
PROPERTY DONATED BY THE MUSHPIT FOUNDATION WITH ADDITIONAL FUNDING FROM SINISTRAL

This concludes our report of the Phantom Storm—
the events that transpired in Cowslip Grove
between March 16 and 18.

Like us here at SINISTRAL, you will likely have
lingering questions, and we feel the time for a final
reckoning is fast approaching. The mysterious
entity—or, as the child witnesses have described it,
the emptiness—known as the Boojum still haunts
Cowslip Grove. It will undoubtedly be back to stir
fears, sift through dreams, and spirit children
away in the cold of night while the town sleeps
soundly, as blind as the ants in a formicarium.

But the time of reckoning is not here yet. Now is
time to recoup. Recharge. And explore.

For perhaps exploration and discovery are the very
things that keep the Boojum at bay. Boojums, it
seems, thrive on the order and predictability you
might find in a quiet suburban town. Or school.

But throw in some outside thinkers, some dreamers, plus a few unpredictable wild things, and suddenly the Boojum's hold seems a lot less stable.

We have hope that these children, plus others like them, will continue to learn, grow, explore, and embrace things that are strange and different. Their minds will open and blossom with their world . . . and a calculating thing like the Boojum will never stand a chance.

Thank you for your careful consideration, and we look forward to your insight.

—SINISTRAL
Report filed by Agent M and Agent C

Acknowledgments

REPORT SUPERVISED BY DIRECTOR
Amy Cloud

SIDE-MISSIONS SUPERVISED BY DIRECTOR
Gabriella Abbate

ARRANGED BY VISUAL OPERATIVE
Celeste Knudsen

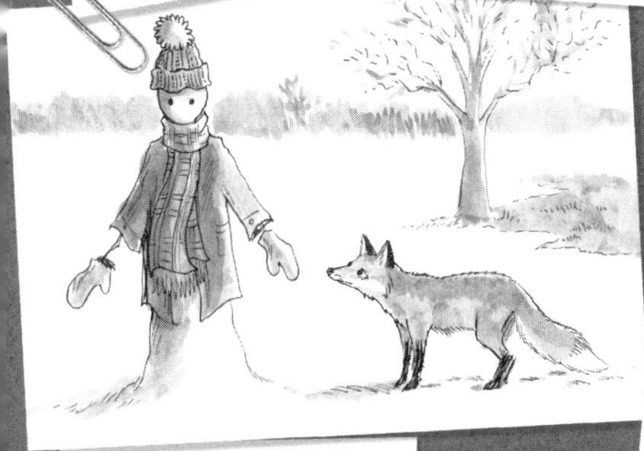

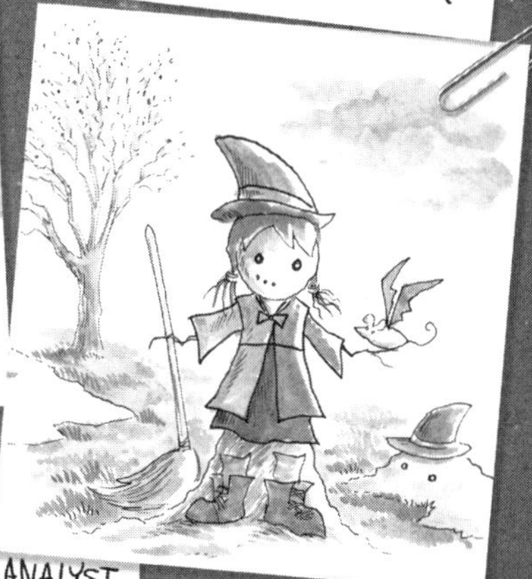

SECURITY FOOTAGE OBTAINED BY SECRET AGENT
Dan Lazar

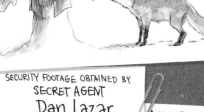

AND INTELLIGENCE ANALYST
Torie Doherty-Munro

ADDITIONAL EVIDENCE CORROBORATION BY:
Sammy Ruth Brown
Zoe Del Mar

ARCHIVED BY:
Helen Seachrist
Emily Andrukaitis

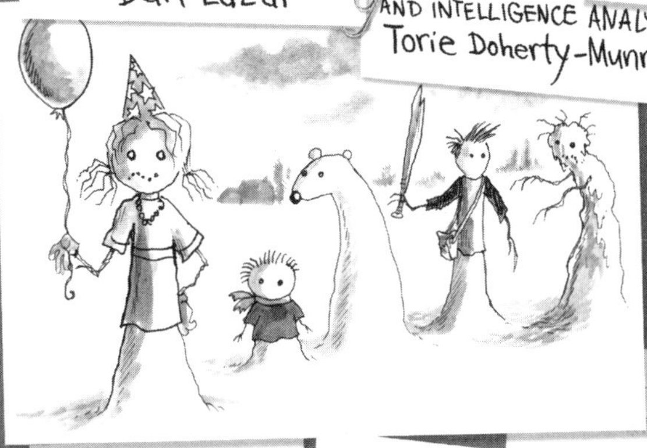

WARNING:
At all costs, keep this report from falling into the clutches of Super-spy **J. Kinney** and **Dr. J. Brallier**.

PEDESTRIAN EYEWITNESSES:
"Patti & Rick"

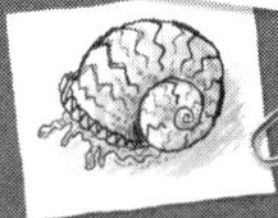

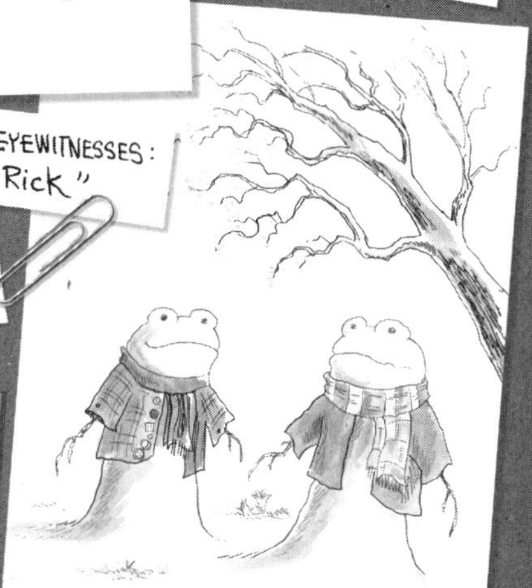

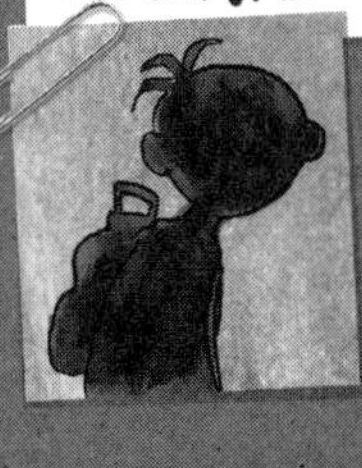

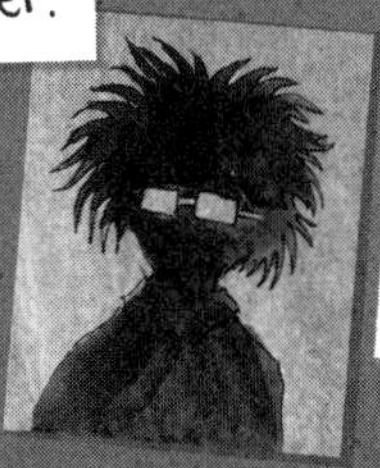

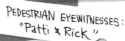

Kory Merritt is the author of the acclaimed *No Place for Monsters*. He is a former public school art teacher who has also worked as an illustrator for the online game franchise Poptropica and its spin-off book series.

Praise for *No Place for Monsters*

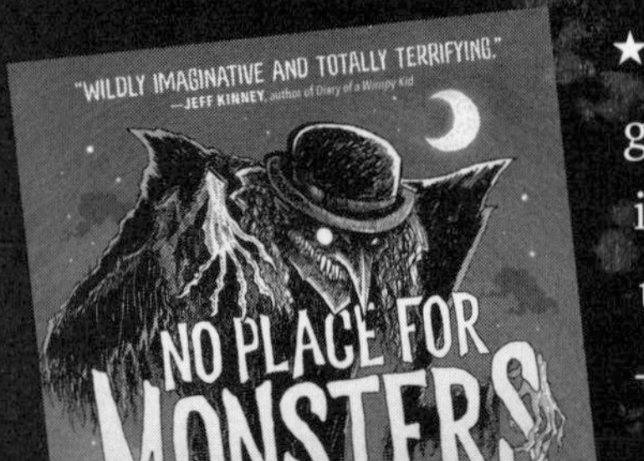
"WILDLY IMAGINATIVE AND TOTALLY TERRIFYING."
—JEFF KINNEY, author of Diary of a Wimpy Kid
NO PLACE FOR MONSTERS
KORY MERRITT

★ "This is one hell of a middle-grade read, the kind that will spark imaginations as it is read late at night under the covers with a flashlight."
—*Kirkus Reviews,* starred review

★ "Weird, wild, and warmhearted, this is a real page-turner for the spooky season."
—*Publishers Weekly,* starred review